NINE OF SWORDS

Morpheus Media, LLC

Fort Worth, TX

www.MorpheusMediaLLC.com

MORPHEUS MEDIA, LLC

For the people (and dog) who made this all possible – Mom, Dad, Grammy, and Major Tom.

Mom,

Thank you for being such a great example of how to persevere and succeed. Thank you for all the work and sacrifices you've made so that my dreams could come true. You are, and forever will be, my hero.

Dad,

Thank you for always being the president of my fan club and my number one cheerleader. Your undying support and positive attitude have been integral in my pursuit of writing. Without your support and words of encouragement, I don't think I would've ever finished writing this behemoth of a book.

Grammy,

I want to thank you for putting up with all my late-night phone calls and my constant nagging. I know it was annoying when I called every hour on the hour to ask if you'd read the most recent chapter I wrote. But know that your feedback and encouragement was invaluable. Without you, this book would be very different. I love you a bushel and a peck.

Major Tom,

Thanks for always being my companion. You're a good boy – the BEST boy.

CONTENTS

PROLOGUE

He stalked through the halls like a cat who knew its way to the saucer, easily finding the door he was looking for.

Moriah paused before it and drew in a deep breath, the sort that stretches your lungs and rattles your ribs. He wrapped his knuckles against the door, careful not to be too loud.

The door opened.

There, standing almost toe to toe with Moriah was Prince Felix, whose eyes were red-stained. His expression was bleak.

Upon seeing who his visitor was, the prince opened the door further and nodded for Moriah to enter. "I didn't think you'd get here so quickly," Felix muttered as he closed the door and resumed his seat at the side of the bed.

Moriah stood just behind Felix's chair, staring over the prince's shoulder towards the shrouded figure lying still upon the mattress. He replied quietly, "I wanted to get here as soon as I could."

"Thank you," whispered Felix.

A pale, long-fingered hand fell softly over the prince's shoulder and gave a gentle squeeze. Moriah's voice was like a deep purr as he asked, "How long had she been sick?"

Felix reached out his hand and set it over the bedding. He traced the woven field of the shroud that covered the princess. He choked back a sob, desperate to keep his composure. "Months," he answered thickly. "Many, many months."

"And the child?"

Felix's summer-blue eyes welled with fresh tears. They stung as they slipped down his cheeks. "Alive and well."

"Did she live to see the child?" Moriah inquired.

Felix smiled wistfully. "She did. She got to hold him, too. She even sang to him."

The corners of Moriah's mouth quirked into something akin to a weak smile. "I'm glad." His hand slipped away from Felix's shoulder as he approached the princess's bedside carefully. He reached out and set his hand upon the softness of her shroud. "She doesn't have to suffer any more. She deserved peace."

Felix stood and crossed the room. "You want to see him, I imagine." His voice was hollow.

Drawing away from the still figure beneath his touch, Moriah straightened to his full height. His tall and lithe body, garbed all in black, stood in marked contrast to the whiteness of the princess's room. Green eyes glanced down one last time to the body of the woman he'd known so well. Moriah didn't look away for some time. When he did, he stayed quiet. Finally, he nodded.

Both men left the room and headed into the long corridors of the castle. They hadn't walked far before Felix stopped before a door. He announced, "This is the nursery."

Moriah sidled up beside the prince. "It will be alright," he assured. "You've your children still. You're not alone"

Felix turned toward Moriah, eyes wide and almost pleading. He stammered, "I…don't know what I should be doing. I don't know what I should do for the children…for all of us."

"Stay away from the capital as long as you can," advised the man in black. "You *and* the children."

"I don't want to go back there anyway," the prince admitted sheepishly.

Felix and Moriah entered the nursery quietly. Both men found their way to the cradle that stood pressed against the far wall. There, etched into the wood over the sleeping child's head, were a crown and the letters 'FDF.' Moriah ghosted his fingertips over the lettering, following each line precisely.

Looking back to Felix, Moriah quirked a brow and asked, "FDF?"

"The boy's initials," explained the prince.

"Yes." Moriah snorted. "I expected as much. Well, what've you named him?"

"Fynneas. Fynneas Draekon Fog," Felix elucidated. Warmth found its way to the prince's eyes as he smiled down at his sleeping son. "It's a name I think he'll grow into. For now, we all just call him Fynn."

At the sound of his father's voice, the baby turned over and opened his eyes. Burning red irises glowed through the darkness of the nursery for a moment before the color receded from the child's eyes like waves from the shore, leaving no more color than a pale shade of grey. His eyes were ghostly then, shining like twin moons as he stared up at the men. Chubby, little arms the color of snow reached toward them imploringly.

Felix scooped the boy into his arms and held him tightly to his chest. The sounds of the little prince's garbled giggles echoed like thunder, breaking the morbid silence of the castle.

"He's a happy boy," cooed Felix as he rocked from foot to foot. "Would you like to hold him?"

Moriah took the swaddled infant from Felix's hold and, much like the prince, settled the child close to his chest. He whispered to the baby in a rumbling voice, "You're quite small, you know?"

Fynn's hand reached up and pulled on Moriah's black hair. The tiny prince beamed as his cheeks flushed with humor. His icy eyes were gleaming with mischief.

The man in black shook his head. A pleased smirk quirked his lips. "You think you're funny, do you?"

There was a moment when Felix felt warmed by the sight of Moriah coddling Fynn. But the moment was fleeting, soon replaced by the ever-present melancholy that had befallen the royal. Felix bowed his head; black hair tumbled in front of his eyes. He kept his voice low as he said, "Strange things have been happening here, Moriah. *Very* strange things."

Moriah held tighter to the child he cradled. He stared down into the boy's spectral eyes. "What sort of things?" he asked slowly.

"I...well...things go missing...accidents happen. I hear voices in the middle of the night," the prince explained. "I hear voices coming from the nursery." He drew in a shaky breath. "I hear the voices in here, but when I open the door... no one's here. It's just the baby."

The grey eyes staring up at Moriah continued to twinkle in the dimness.

"Are you scared of the boy?" the man in black asked evenly.

Felix shook his head. "No. He's my *son*. I'll do everything I can to protect him."

"One day, Felix, he'll need to go out on his own. But until that time, keep him close."

There was a long stretch of silence wherein Felix fidgeted uneasily. Finally, he asked, "Is something bad going to happen?"

"Yes," Moriah replied as he set the baby down into the crib. "But not for a while. Not until he's older. Then, I suspect, a great many bad things will happen."

"Will you be there to help him?" Felix's voice sounded broken.

Moriah loomed over the crib like a shadowed sentinel, watching the child curl into his blankets and fall back asleep with ease. "I'll do the best I can to keep him safe... to help him along. I promise."

Felix came to stand at the other man's side. They were silent, both watching the now-sleeping baby. The prince whispered, "What do you think of him?"

Moriah reached into the crib. His hand hovered just over the child's chest. He marveled as Fynn, quite deep into his sleep, reached out. Tiny fingers curled around Moriah's little finger and held tightly. The man couldn't help the smile that twisted his lips. "I think your son will either be the shining light to guide the kingdom...or he will become Death and be our destruction. Only time will tell."

1

HOMECOMING

"It was an accident," Fynn quickly explained. He glanced down to the shattered glass that littered the floor. He cringed when he heard the crunch of a shard breaking beneath his booted heel. "I didn't mean to," he offered sheepishly.

Novian took his grandson's hand and turned it over, grimacing at the sight of the jagged cut that tore over the boy's palm. "What did you break this time?"

"A vase."

"Think nothing of it," the old man insisted. "Does it hurt?"

Fynn shook his head.

"Ah," smiled the lord as he looked down at the prince, "that's the excitement. You're far too wound up to feel it. But, trust me, it'll hurt in a while. When you're all settled down in your carriage and off on your way, you'll start to notice it more, I'm sure."

Fynn shrugged as he idly watched his grandfather prod at his wounded palm. He ventured nervously, "You're not mad?"

"Not at all."

The boy's mood lightened immeasurably at that and he allowed the first smile of the morning to curl his lips. Since he'd woken, he hadn't quite had the presence of mind to smile about anything. He'd thrown his things together best he could, frantically almost, as he bounced around his room. He scarcely had registered that he'd bumped into one of his grandfather's prized vases until he heard the smashing of the glass over the stone floor.

Novian released Fynn's hand gently and rose back to his full height. He tilted his head curiously and asked, "Nervous?"

Fynn chewed on his bottom lip as he toed at the broken shards absently. The feeling of something tightening in his chest, cutting off his air and choking him, was becoming more and more bothersome. "I...well," he

1

stammered. "Yes." He turned large, grey eyes up toward his grandfather's tired face. He hesitantly asked, "What if they don't like me?"

"What's not to like?" joked Novian as he reached out and pat the boy's cheek heartily. "You're a royal, *same as them*. More than that, Fynny, you're a kind lad. Brave, too. If a little clumsy sometimes."

"You've been to the capital," Fynn said. "What're they like?"

"They're the worst sort of people," snorted Novian. A hardly contained scowl tugged at his features. "But, they're your *family*, so you'll just have to learn to live with them. It's only for a while."

"Do I have to go?" Fynn shifted his weight from foot to foot. "Can't I stay here?"

One large, wrinkled hand reached out and combed through Fynn's mess of black hair. Novian's voice was soft as he replied, "When the king calls for you, Fynneas, you must *always* answer." He smoothed his hand over the boy's unruly tresses one last time and then continued, "Now, let's not keep your father and sister waiting."

It was true that Felix and Fiona had been waiting for Fynn, though not for terribly long as they'd only just stepped into the chilly embrace of the snowy morning some minutes ago when Novian and Fynn joined them. The carriages were loaded with their things already. Tired servants were traipsing back from the drive to the castle.

Fiona, upon spotting Fynn, brightened. "Morning," she cooed as she stole across the white path to her little brother's side. "Overslept?"

Fynn smirked. "No…well, not this time. I was getting all my things ready and I got…distracted."

"Distracted?"

Wordlessly, Fynn held out his still-bleeding palm for his sister to see. He rolled his eyes when she snatched his hand and pulled him closer. He huffed. "It's *fine*, Fi. Just a scratch."

"It is most certainly not *just a scratch*," Fiona all but hissed. "Now stop whining or I'll feed you to Biel. Bad little boys are his favorite snack, you know."

"Don't be stupid," scoffed Fynn. "Biel's just a story people tell children to get them to behave better."

"Clearly it didn't work on you," Fiona muttered.

The boy peeked back over his shoulder, pleading for his grandfather to rescue him from Fiona's medical ministrations. Rather unfortunately for Fynn, Novian offered little more than an amused chuckle before saying,

2

"She's right, Fynny. It's a nasty looking cut. You should try and be more careful."

Felix, looking as though he hadn't slept in days, sidled up beside his father-in-law and watched as his daughter fussed over his son. "She coddles him too much."

"You're no better," Novian insisted.

"You're one to talk," Felix countered.

The old man ran a withered hand over his face as if trying to brush away his own weariness. "You're not wrong there. The lad just has a way about him. I can't help but coddle the boy."

"I know." Felix sighed. "But it'll do him no good. Once he's off to Morancy, there won't be anyone around to watch him. He's going to be on his own."

"Fynneas will never be on his own. Not really," whispered Novian. He watched Fiona wrap Fynn's hand with a silk handkerchief that she'd pulled from one of the bags.

"Thank you," started Felix as he fixed his attention upon the old lord, "for everything you've done for us. I don't think I could've gone back to the capital after Celestine died. I don't know what I would've done if you hadn't let us stay here."

Novian shook his head. "Think nothing of it. They're my grandchildren and you're their father. I'd never turn any of you away. Besides, you and I both know it was safer for *all* of you to remain here rather than go back to Batsbeckon."

Felix nodded. When he spoke again, there was a sadness that touched his words. "He looks so much like his mother. It's almost eerie at times."

"I take comfort in it," Novian asserted. "When I look at him, I see her there. It makes missing her hurt just a little less."

"It will *always* hurt," Felix muttered grimly.

Novian's hand clapped over the younger man's shoulder and held steadfastly. "But what is life, my boy, if not pain? It's the pain, Felix, that reminds us we're alive."

Fynn whirled around to look back at the men, his grey eyes sparkling like ice in the sunlight. It was as if a thousand rainbows were caught in the pale depths of his irises. Felix and Novian both watched him with smiles that reached beyond the twist of their lips. They were the sort of smiles that touched their eyes and warmed them to the bone. In that moment, it truly did seem as though Celestine was staring back at them. Fynn had the same pale complexion and light eyes, the same small nose and thin, pink lips, and the same angular cuts to his face. The only thing that kept the men from believing they'd seen a ghost was the black hair that stood out against the white tableau, the messy mane that stuck out wildly in all directions as the wind pressed by.

"Are we leaving soon?" asked the boy, curious as to why both men were staring at him so intently. They did that sometimes, he knew. They would just stare at him almost wistfully. And no matter how odd Fynn found it, he never said a word about it.

"Yes, yes, we're leaving now," Felix nodded.

Fynn was the last to climb into the carriage. He lingered for a moment until he felt the familiar brush of a hand through his hair and smiled. He looked up at his grandfather. "You'll miss me?" the tiny prince asked.

"More than you can ever know, Fynny," Novian assured. "But I take comfort in knowing you'll do great things this year."

"You can't *possibly* know that," argued Fynn with a smirk.

The old man chuckled. "Of course, I do! You were born for nothing less."

Only moments later the carriages were off, lazily touring through the grounds of Godsreach towards the gates. The lone figure of Novian stood against the summer snow, arm outstretched as he waved his farewell. Fynn stared through the hazy pane of the carriage window and watched as the white-stone towers of the castle dwindled and shrank as the carriage rolled further away. He barely suppressed the sinking feeling that overtook his stomach when the gates closed behind them, severing his ties to the castle he'd called home all his life. With great hesitancy, Fynn looked away and settled into the plush seat of the interior, shifting ever so slightly toward the comfort of his sister. As the carriage rocked over the stony road, Fynn let his eyes flutter shut and allowed sleep to claim him with hardly more than a muttered protest.

When next he woke, the prince stretched out his arms and gave a great yawn. Spying his sister frowning, Fynn quirked a brow and asked, "What is it? Why're you looking as though I've grown a second head?"

"The wrapping over your hand's fallen off," Fiona commented dully.

"So?"

She pointed. "Look there."

Raising his palm up for a better view, Fynn smiled upon seeing the gash healed. There was little trace left of the wound that had looked so fiercely jagged only a day earlier. He turned his hand over and stretched his fingers experimentally, noting, "Doesn't hurt at all."

Fiona shook her head. "Strange."

Felix, sitting opposite the children, shrugged his shoulders carelessly. He took his son's hand into his and assessed the afflicted palm. He shook his head as he said, "It always amazes me how fast you heal up. It's only been a day and yet, look at your hand. Nothing there at all. I don't think it'll even leave a scar."

"Like I said," mumbled Fiona, "*strange*."

"Strange?" chuckled Felix. "Most certainly. But I'd wager it's also advantageous. Especially with you heading off to Morancy soon."

"Are you expecting me to get hurt there?" Fynn inquired incredulously.

"Almost certainly," Felix replied. "There are plenty of dangers awaiting you on the island. But I'm sure you'll do well to listen to your instructors and keep out of trouble."

"Fynneas?" Fiona snorted and cast a sidelong look to her brother. "You expect *Fynny* to stay out of trouble? I'll believe it when I see it."

Fynn grumbled, "I'm not *that* bad."

"You're a terror," laughed Fiona, combing her hand through his hair fondly. "But you're *our* terror."

"She's right, you know," Felix added. "We love you all the more for it."

Easy conversation flowed between the three. The journey from the northern peninsula down to the eastern coast was a long one. The snowy north gave way to the middle country where trees lined the road and there seemed to be an endless sea of green on either side of the way. Towns were sprinkled here and there amongst the vast tangle of trees and roll of hills.

By daybreak on their thirteenth day of travel, Felix found himself weighed down by the eventuality of his homecoming. Fynn dozed lightly at Fiona's side. Felix couldn't help but watch the subtle rise and fall of the boy's chest before leaning back into the plush softness of his seat.

"They really are rather terrible," sighed Felix.

"If they're that *awful*, why did we have to come?" Fiona asked, exasperated by far-too long traveling in the cramped space. "Seems like a complete waste of effort, really."

Felix shrugged. "They're family."

"Yes, by blood, I suppose they're family. But we never come down to see them. Honestly, I don't recall what most of them even *look* like," she muttered.

"Your uncle thought it would be nice for us to all get together before the boys head off at the end of the summer. And when the king comes calling for you, you respectfully answer…no matter how asinine the call may be." Felix picked at the linen threads of his shirt, plucking at a frayed piece thoroughly until there was a slight tear. He frowned. "I know this isn't how you wanted to spend your summer," he said, his voice rather even in spite of his own mounting anxieties. "But let's do our best to make it as painless a visit as possible, yes?"

Fiona looked into her father's tired eyes. His brows were knit together, his thin lips drawn into an uncharacteristic scowl. His normally well-maintained hair was, much as his daughter's, messed beyond all repair; his normally clean-shaven face bore the black sprinklings of a fledgling beard. "Have you slept much?" Fiona asked knowingly.

Felix shook his head and leaned further back into the softness.

"You ought to close your eyes while you can."

Thin lips parted into a half-hearted smirk. Felix lazily laughed, "You worry too much, Fi."

The princess rolled her eyes. "Now you sound like Fynn."

"He's *right* you know."

Fiona glanced down to the ruffled, black hair nestled at her side. "Sleeping as always," she noted with a wry look in her eyes. "Do you want me to wake him?"

"No, no, let him sleep." Felix grinned. "He's a growing boy; he's bound to be tired from the journey here."

The princess smiled. "You're too easy on him, you know."

"Funny you should say that," Felix cheekily retorted.

Not more than an hour after the sun had found its way high into the blue sky of summer, Fynn woke with a weary stir. He blinked the bleariness from the edges of his vision and sat up straight, rolling the soreness from his shoulders. "Morning," he greeted sluggishly.

"Not hardly. It's afternoon," Felix informed. "Sleep well?"

Fynn nodded. "Are we there yet?"

The sound of barely contained annoyance colored Felix's reply. "Yes. Just about."

Fynn smiled. He turned to his sister and beamed. "We're here! Aren't you excited?" Any trace of trepidation about the journey to the capital had clearly fallen away and been usurped by boyish expectation. "You *must* be!"

Fiona quirked a black brow skeptically. "I don't think excited is the word I'd use."

"Well, you should stop being such a grouch," joked Fynn. "It's exciting, I think. We don't get to come around to the capital often ... or *ever*. Well, *I've* never been, at least."

"I've only been once and, as I recall, it wasn't much to go on about," assured Fiona. She reached out and gently ran her thumb over Fynn's cheek. "Quite dull really. Just a bunch of prissy women in prissy gowns and self-important men going on about self-righteous things."

"Is it that bad?" the boy asked curiously. "It can't be!"

Fiona offered him a smile, ever amazed by Fynn's readiness for new experiences and adventures. Twelve years on and he still had such a bright-eyed enthusiasm about almost everything around him. "It's not...*nightmarish*, I suppose," concluded Fiona. "Tolerable...*maybe*."

Fynn snorted. "That's not really a rousing endorsement, Fi."

She brushed her spindly fingers through his thick hair, combing out some of the knots and brushing it back. Unlike her own, Fynn's hair was rather straight. Making him look presentable was an infinitely more manageable task than doing the same for herself. "I suppose it won't be all too terrible, no. We'll have each other, of course. We may even have a little fun."

Fynn nudged her with his bony shoulder playfully. "You're not exactly painting a rosy picture. I'm sure we'll find something to do!"

Fiona shook her head as she laughed. "I'm sure we will."

The carriage proceeded onward, nearing the castle more so with every moment. Felix offered his children a weakened smile before leaning further back into his seat and looking out the window. He watched as they toddled over familiar, cobble-stoned streets and went by familiar shops; there were familiar people pecking about familiar market stands down towards the capital square and there were familiar banners hanging from shop windows and corner posts. Felix sighed. Everything was just so terribly familiar even after being away for so long.

Their carriage carried on, rolling over uneven streets and twisting up the road towards Batsbeckon castle, which sat at the very top of the only hill in the capital like some all-seeing force forever looming just out of reach of the common city kneeling at its feet. Once they were beset by the shadow of the castle, Felix tensed. The carriage lulled to a halt and their door was opened. Steeling himself quietly, Felix slipped from the carriage into the afternoon warmth. He reached out his hand and helped Fiona step down.

Even after she had settled herself next to him, Felix kept a tight hold on her slender hand. Both cast an amused glance back toward the carriage as Fynn leapt out with all of his normal, graceless exuberance.

The three of them stood there, side by side, looking toward the castle as a woman appeared amidst parting doors. She was a slight figure dressed all in blue with her black curls tied back by means of a blue ribbon. She had a pleasant face, quite reminiscent of Felix's own, but with daintier features. Though unfortunately, she did have the same frightfully thick brows. A family trait supposed the children as they studied her. Her eyes were a pale sort of blue that lacked warmth and her mouth was so tightly drawn into a fine line that she appeared as though she scarcely had lips at all.

"She's rather severe looking," whispered Fynn.

Fiona nudged his ribs with her elbow. "Quiet."

The woman came bustling toward them, stopping just an arm's length away. She regarded the three of them with her wintery stare. "You're late," she pronounced in a terse, yet still sickeningly prim, twitter.

"Lovely to see you too, Gem," mumbled Felix as he gave his older sister a polite nod in greeting.

"Yes, well," she continued as she waved her arm forward in a grand beck, "come along. Everyone's here already, you see. We had expected you earlier. This *morning* perhaps." She led them into the castle. "Mother's waiting in the dining hall. She wants everyone to join her for a light afternoon meal. Lemon cakes, I think she requested."

"I love lemon cakes!" Fynn grinned. His loudly rumbling stomach punctuated his proclamation effortlessly.

Gemma quirked a hearty brow as she observed the child coolly. "Yes, wonderful," she chirped sourly.

Fiona caught Fynn by the wrist, hauling him nearer to her. She leaned down close to his ear, never missing a step, keeping pace just on Gemma's heels, and hissed, "*Try* to behave. Please, at least *try.*"

"I'll see what I can do," countered Fynn in an astoundingly accurate imitation of Gemma's own uniquely pinched chirrup of a voice.

Fynn shrugged from his sister's hold and cast her a fleeting glance once more before returning his attention to the myriad of paintings hanging from the walls. There were knights atop horses and kings on thrones. There were grand fields spangled with hunters and landscapes of foreign ancestries. There were images of holy figures and there were portraits of people who seemed rather plain in comparison. As his pale gaze roved from painting to

8

painting, it astounded Fynn that each intricately fashioned work was confined in an even more intricately fashioned frame. Many of them were brazen golds with painstakingly worked etchings to accentuate the subject held therein.

The foursome entered into the dining hall wherein a somber tension filled the room. The king sat at the head of the table, back straight and shoulders set. The rigidity of his posture seemed uncomfortable and nearly defensive. His deep blue eyes shifted to the woman at his side. There was a glint held there in the depths of his stare, the sort of sheen that would come off the sharp of a dagger. The queen to King Lachlan's left, Ursalyn, sat mutely. Her posture was a mirror of the king's, painfully stilted and tense. The thin set of her lips drew the beauty from her features, as did the purple shade that bloomed over her high-set cheek. The queen mother, Elsinora, sat to the king's right. The old woman's withering gaze did not falter as it lingered unyieldingly over Ursalyn.

The only other occupants of the table were two children, one with red hair, the other a blonde boy. The red-haired prince, Hollyn, was the younger of the king's two children. The blonde, James, was the only child of Princess Gemma, and a rather meek looking boy. Both seemed absolutely resolute in their endeavor to ignore the palpable unease crashing like waves all around them.

Gemma cleared her throat; the sound echoed through the dining hall. Lachlan looked up, a spark of recognition igniting over his austere features. Instantly, he perked up and leapt to his feet with a broad gesture of welcome, calling out, "You've arrived!"

Felix recoiled, but only slightly. Never before had he seen his brother so elated at his presence. It was, truthfully, unsettling. He continued to watch nervously, never taking a step past Gemma, as Lachlan came strutting towards them. Gemma stepped aside without a parting word and took her seat beside Elsinora, letting her own frigid stare linger on Ursalyn for only a moment before brushing nonexistent lint from the shoulders of her gown and daintily lifting her goblet to her lipless mouth.

Lachlan clapped his hand over Felix's shoulder forcefully. Though whether it was intentionally overdone or not, Felix was not sure. They looked at one another for some time as if studying the other for any faults. There were plenty.

The king stood just inches taller than his younger brother, but he was a significantly more imposing man. His curly, black hair was slicked back.

Thick, black brows arched dramatically on either side of a nearly straight, freckle-dotted nose. His face was long and squared and his chin was scarred from a childhood accident. His shoulders were broad, his chest was wide, and his arms were muscled. His hands were surprisingly calloused for a king.

"You look well," Lachlan observed.

In an instant, the king had disregarded his brother, who seemed quite content at that, and turned his scrutiny toward the children. Fiona stood just a step behind Felix. At sixteen, she was quite tall, standing just a touch shy of her father's shoulders. Her hair, the inherited curly mess that it was, was hastily drawn back with a white ribbon. Save for the barely contained chaos of her hair, she was a beauty. Her eyes were like summer skies, a warm and supple blue. Her face was round, but not pudgy. Her nose was small, but not disproportionally so. Altogether, she looked a great deal like her father.

With supreme grace, the sort that had clearly been doled out inequitably between she and Fynn, Fiona curtsied.

Lachlan nodded and then, in much the same manner he had disregarded Felix, he cast his assessing stare from Fiona and looked down at Fynn.

Fynn was a slight boy, quite small for his age. His hair was not the customarily unruly mane that the Fog family sported. Rather, it was thick and straight, combed back nicely but still, somehow, looked slightly askew. The prince's features were sharper than his sister's, his cheekbones higher and nose pointier. What took Lachlan aback were the boy's eyes. They seemed to be almost like ice, reflecting all the colors around. But, despite their chilly color, they appeared all the while gentle and warm. They held within them all the incongruity of glaciers thriving in the sweltering summer.

On cue, Fynn bowed his head respectfully.

"My children," introduced Felix when he had decided that Lachlan had surveyed the two long enough. "You've met Fiona before, but she's grown since." Felix gestured toward his son. "And this is my boy, Fynneas."

Lachlan hadn't looked away from the peculiar child before him. True, he hadn't been there when his nephew was born, nor had he ever taken the time to go see his brother's children over all these years. There was a time, some years ago, when Felix and Fiona had come to the capital for one of the queen mother's grand, and by his account unnecessary, birthday celebrations. But that was so long ago, and Fiona had, as Felix said, grown a great deal since then. The king scoured his mind for another occasion he had spent with his younger brother. The only instance he recalled was Felix's wedding. Lachlan set aside the nauseating feeling that sparked in him at the very thought of that particular occasion.

"It's a pleasure," the king said thoughtlessly, still lost in his own recollections of times far flung from the present. As if sensing their unease at his distraction, he hastened to continue. "Yes, right. Well, Mother's been waiting for you to arrive before we enjoy our afternoon lemon cakes. So, go on." He waved his hand theatrically toward the dining table.

Thankfully, as they all settled, the palpable tension between Elsinora and Ursalyn had dissipated for the most part. The strain seemed to dissolve the moment the queen mother took note of her newly arrived grandchildren.

Fiona and Fynn sat side by side, both awkward in the uncomfortable silence.

"My, how you've grown, my dear," crooned Elsinora.

Fiona forced a smiled.

"How old are you now, child?"

"Sixteen," Fiona replied.

The servants delivered their lemon cakes and fill their goblets with wine. Gingerly cutting her cake, Ursalyn commented, "Sixteen already? Doesn't seem like too long ago when you were here, visiting with Felix. I remember how you and Ciaran went toddling off to play in the gardens."

Fiona's smile-muscles were straining. "Where *is* Ciaran?"

"Off with some of his friends from Morancy," Lachlan interjected. "Popular boy, really."

Again, Fiona forced herself to appear convincingly interested in the exchange. "Yes, I remember hearing about how well-liked Ciaran is at the academy."

"He should be back this evening. I'm sure he'd love to catch up with you, darling. It's been too long," Ursalyn continued. There was a stinging indifference to her voice.

"That would be nice," the princess agreed.

"And you, child? Off to Morancy this year, so you must be twelve already?" Elsinora asked Fynn.

He nodded.

"A bit small, aren't you?"

The boy bristled at that but retained a friendly expression. "Father says I'll grow soon."

"Yes," Elsinora said, "let's hope you do."

11

As Fynn settled in his chair, choosing to not be irritated by his grandmother's acute observation, he heard muffled snickering. He spied the red-haired boy next to him smirking.

Prince Hollyn leveled a dangerous stare upon Fynn. Though his eyes looked positively predatory, his expression affected an amiable mask. His smirk quirked into some imitation of a genuine smile. He offered his hand to Fynn in greeting. "Prince Hollyn."

Fynn took the offered hand. "Prince Fynneas."

Hollyn's eyes were a tempestuous color, as if the darkest blue and steeliest grey were intermingling like the eye of a storm within his irises. "Better hope your father's right and you grow sometime soon, runt."

Fynn stole his hand back as if he'd been burned. He sneered. "Oh please, spare me the intimidation tactics."

"Brash thing, aren't you?" laughed Hollyn darkly.

Fynn shrugged. "No. Just not easily scared off."

"We'll see," purred Hollyn as he returned to munching on his cakes.

Fynn stabbed his fork into the crumbling mass of yellow pastry before him. "So, you're off to Morancy this year too?"

Hollyn didn't bother to turn to face Fynn but regarded him coolly from his periphery, silently mortified by the other prince's lack of social tact. "All the grace of a three-legged, blind donkey, I see."

There was another snort of laughter barely muffled by a hand hovering over curled lips. Fynn looked up to find the blonde boy across from him stifling a silly grin. He eyed him curiously, snapping, "Think he's funny, do you?"

"Most of the time," agreed James, without so much as looking back at Fynn.

Before Fynn could bite out a quip truly worthy of a laugh, Fiona elbowed him in the ribs again, harder than last time. He leaned back in his chair, poking his cake with the prongs of his fork. Then, the all too familiar hiss of his sister flitted by.

"I asked you to *behave*. We haven't even been here an hour and you've decided to pick a fight?"

Fynn turned to her, petulantly explaining, "*I* didn't do anything." His voice was hardly more than a whisper. "I swear. It's *them*. They're teaming up on me."

"Yes, well the *them* in question happen to be in a bit better standing than you at the moment, so try to get along," she chided. Her focus fell upon the maimed lemon cake on Fynn's plate. "And do stop stabbing at your cake like some sort of continental barbarian, won't you?"

The remainder of their afternoon munching went by fairly gently with only mumbled arguments breaking out here and there. Lachlan, for his part, remained positively indifferent for the majority of the conversation, only chiming in with something close to a semblance of interest when Felix brought up the work he'd done a few years back with the maritime merchants he'd met during his travels. However, that particular topic of conversation shriveled and died after one withering look from Gemma.

Felix pulled away from the table first, careful to bow his head in his brother's direction respectfully before offering the excuse of being weary from their travels and aiding in his, and his children's, escape from the assembled royal household. As the three retired from the dining hall and headed towards their assigned rooms, Felix ran his hand through his hair and shuddered. "Dreadful." He groaned. "But it's over."

"Until supper," Fiona added ruefully, wrinkling her nose at the very idea of suffering through another dismally unpleasant meal with those who, by her measure, seemed to be a handful of some of the sourest people she'd ever come across. Yes, they were certainly as awful as she remembered them.

"Morancy's a big place, right?" asked Fynn.

Felix hadn't expected that question. "I suppose so. Why?"

"I won't have to see Hollyn all the time, then, right?"

Felix's hand fell upon Fynn's shoulder comfortingly.

The boy knew all at once that he wouldn't like the answer.

"He's your year mate, Fynn. You'll probably be seeing quite a lot of him."

Fynn shrugged his father's hand from its perch and stomped along.

"Try to get along with him, won't you?"

The boy whirled around to face his father, a nasty look on his face. "Why should I?"

"Because, *as your father*, I'm asking you to," Felix insisted, desperately trying to restrain his own frustrations.

"He didn't seem like he cared to be my friend much, so why should I?"

Felix was utterly exhausted and Fynn's snappish attitude wasn't helping him quell the headache that had been insinuating itself into his temples since early morning. He closed his eyes and breathed in deep, choosing to let Fynn stew in his own temper for a moment longer before continuing. "It would just be best for all of us if you didn't fight with Hollyn, alright?"

"It's not fair," huffed the younger prince.

Felix knelt before his son and ruffled the boy's hair. He looked into those familiar, grey eyes and couldn't help but smile a sad smile. "I know it isn't."

"Liar," grumbled Fynn.

Felix shook his head. "Trust me. I know it's unfair. I do." He sighed. "But there are just things that you have to accept about life."

"Like what?"

"Like your place."

Fynn looked puzzled. "What do you mean?"

"We're all born into our roles, Fynneas. It's time that you just accept yours." Felix reached his hand out and ran his thumb over the curvature of Fynn's cheek. "You're my son, my *only* boy. You're afforded a great deal as a result. Your cousin James, for instance, didn't inherit the same royal title as the rest of you simply because of who his father is."

"I don't understand," Fynn admitted.

"Aunt Gem, none of her children will ever have the title of prince or princess. But you and your sister, you do. That's your place."

"Why?" Fynn asked. "Why isn't James a prince like Hollyn and I? His mother is a princess."

Felix nodded. "The titles are passed down through the male heirs. By virtue of being born to a princess instead of a prince, James didn't inherit that title. So, you see, he has to acknowledge his place in the family, just as you do."

"So, what's my place, then?" queried Fynn.

"Your cousin Ciaran is next in line for the throne and after him it's Hollyn. Should something happen and the crown needed a place to rest after Hollyn, it would be bestowed upon me. Then, after me, you would succeed to the throne."

"So, I'm fourth in line. I *knew* that," argued Fynn. "What does that have to do with my being friends with Hollyn?"

"The likelihood that you will ever wear the crown is quite slim," explained Felix. "So, you see, your role as prince is not to ready yourself your entire life to sit on the throne and rule, but to fight in the name of the king and his lands. Understand? One day, when Ciaran is king, you and Hollyn will be heading up his military. So, it would be best if you two could maybe find some common ground. Your lives are rather intertwined, really. Best to make the most of the lot you're given, Fynneas." He smiled. "At least try?"

"I'll try," promised Fynn solemnly.

Felix drew his son into an embrace, firmly holding the boy against him for a moment.

"I didn't mean to upset you," whispered Fynn.

Felix rubbed circles gently across the small of his son's back. "You didn't. This is all a bit much. I understand."

"I'll try and behave," offered Fynn.

Fiona laughed at that. "Fynn, the day you manage to behave yourself is the day all my hair falls out."

Fynn whipped around in his father's arms and looked up to his sister who stood just a few feet away with her arms crossed over her chest, a cheeky grin in place. "I didn't say I would *succeed*, Fi. I said I would *try*."

"Try hard, for *all* our sakes," she muttered.

The three parted then and while Felix and Fynn headed toward their rooms, Fiona couldn't bring herself to lie down and do nothing. The princess didn't know where she was headed off to or what she intended to do when she arrived at her mystery destination, but she was happy to be stretching her legs.

With the sort of poise most would attribute to a woman of more years and experience, Fiona glided down the winding stairs and into the breezeway of the castle. She spied the gardens and was immediately enchanted by the sheer amount of greenery. She stepped into the courtyard and headed toward the rose bushes. The roses were an exceptional red and looked so picturesque that, for the briefest of moments, Fiona thought they couldn't be real. But as her fingertips ghosted over the satiny petals, she was assured of their authenticity.

"Do you like them?" asked the queen mother as she appeared from the other side of the bushes, one of the roses having been freshly plucked and placed behind her ear.

"They're beautiful," Fiona said.

Elsinora plucked another rose from the bush and held it between her thumb and index finger, aloft for Fiona to see. The two admired the pristine flower. The old woman reached forward and, obligingly, Fiona bent her head down and allowed her grandmother to situate the rose behind her ear.

"There now." The elderly royal smiled. "Right where it belongs. It looks lovely on you, dear child."

Fiona flushed at her grandmother's words. It was the first time she'd heard the old woman sound entirely genuine. "Thank you."

The queen mother waved her hand, beckoning Fiona forward. "Come with me, child. Let us have a walk through the gardens."

For some time, they walked in companionable silence. The elder of the two took the opportunity to steal glances toward her granddaughter, curiously observing that Fiona seemed to be the mirror image of Felix. Likewise, Fiona took the time to ponder why on earth her grandmother and the queen didn't get along. If their display that afternoon was anything to go by, Fiona supposed there was a long-standing dislike between the two women.

"How have you been?" inquired Elsinora.

Fiona hadn't been paying too much attention to where they had wandered off to, but when she was startled from her thoughts and brought back to reality, she found that they were deep into the gardens within the courtyard. There were hedges that reached higher than she stood and rose bushes here and there. There was a small pond with gently wrinkling water that swayed the lily pads on the surface. Little frogs hopped this way and that.

"I've been well, thank you," Fiona replied as she knelt down beside the pond, running her hand along its banks before her long fingers breached the water's surface. Ripples emanated from her touch. She watched her reflection in the water dance before her as the little waves stretched from her fingers outward.

"And your brother?"

Fiona didn't look back towards the old woman, but she smiled fondly nonetheless at the mention of her little brother. "He can be difficult sometimes. But I don't know a kinder soul."

"That's good to hear," commented Elsinora. She stood, unmoving, watching Fiona lazily run her hand through the water. "I was afraid my comment about his size might have upset him."

"It did." No one could say Fiona wasn't blunt, but she wasn't unkind in her matter-of-fact response. It was simply the truth and nothing more. She continued, "Don't worry about it though. You're not the first one to mention it to him. He's a tough boy. He'll be just fine."

"I hope so," admitted Elsinora with a long sigh. "I worry for the children, all of them, when they go off to Morancy. It's so hard to be young and away from home like that. I think it wears on them."

"My father didn't seem too fond of it," agreed Fiona as she stood and turned to face her grandmother. "But he said it was necessary and that he enjoyed the later years."

"Yes, Felix was the obstinate one when it came time to send them off. The poor dear, he tried to bargain with your grandfather to not go. But, once he got to his third year, he seemed to really enjoy it. I think it was the sailing that changed his mind, you know. Once they let him in the water and onto the ships, he was beside himself. The boy has always loved the sea." A wistful longing overcame Elsinora and she seemed, in that moment, to be so much older than she was. "Does Fynneas like the water?"

"I don't really know. He hasn't had much chance to see water, really. Everything up north is snowy and frozen," answered Fiona. "I know most everyone in the family ends up in the Armada Division. And I know Fynn would never want to disappoint our father. But…I don't think he'll follow in Father's footsteps this time. He doesn't strike me as the type to want to be on a ship for days or weeks at a time." She laughed. "He has far too much energy to be confined to a ship for so long."

Their conversation was disturbed by the sound of leaves rustling just behind them. Both women looked back and spied a rather tall man in all black stepping out from behind one of the large hedges. He had black hair slicked back, far neater than any of the Fogs could ever hope to manage, and slim, black eyebrows that arched stylishly. His nose was thin and pointed; his lips were a pale shade of pink. Fiona had never seen skin so white, save for that of her own brother. But here this man stood, impossibly pale in the summer sun. Yet, it was his eyes that were the most interesting of his features. Framed by fiercely thick, black lashes were eyes as green as the garden. They were a deep green, a rather abnormal looking color. The man's expression was mostly devoid of emotion, unless one was considering boredom an emotion. It took him only a moment to spy Elsinora. It seemed that the instant he caught sight of her, some of the heaviness lifted from him and some light sparked there in the eerie greenness of his eyes.

"Moriah," called Elsinora as the man came nearer.

She reached her hand out to him and he gently took it in his gloved one. He leaned down and pressed a tender kiss to her hand.

When Moriah released Elsinora and drew back to his full height, he spoke. "I didn't mean to interrupt. My apologies." His voice was dark and impossibly low, so much so that it came out as if a rumble of thunder. Only a moment later, his eyes fell upon Fiona and he curiously surveyed her from head to toe, never uttering a word. Once his inspection was completed, the bored look returned to his features, and his eyes dulled again.

17

Fiona, for all that she knew better, couldn't help but feel as though her mere existence had left this strange man unimpressed.

"My granddaughter, Princess Fiona," introduced the queen mother.

Moriah nodded curtly in Fiona's direction.

"And he," Elsinora gestured towards the increasingly irritated looking man, "is Moriah Mordray, Lord Commander of the Night Corps. He's been instructing at Morancy."

Refusing to allow Moriah's foul mood to infect her, not with having been so uplifted by the charm of the gardens, Fiona reached out her hand in much the same fashion Elsinora had. She waited expectantly for only a moment before he repeated the process of taking the smaller hand into his own with all the force of a feather and placing a kiss to the pale flesh. Though, whereas he had looked at Elsinora with recognizable affections, the emerald gaze, instead, levelled upon Fiona with barely concealed annoyance.

"A pleasure." There was no feeling in his voice, just that ever-present dullness Fiona was beginning to equate with him.

Elsinora caught the look in the man's eyes and swatted him playfully on the back. "Play nice, Moriah," she chided as if he were a child.

He drew away from Fiona and smirked, looking to Elsinora as he jested, "If I must."

"I insist." Elsinora laughed.

Fiona couldn't help but be stunned by the strange interaction taking place before her. The old woman, who was nothing short of acerbic during their lemon cake interaction and sweetly interested during their conversation in the garden, was now skirting dangerously close to flirting with a man young enough to be her son. And he, for the few minutes Fiona had been in his presence, was in a similar humor.

Moriah entirely disregarded Fiona's presence as he turned back to the queen mother, a twinkle in his cat-like eyes. "May I escort you back, Your Grace?" he inquired almost charmingly.

Wordlessly, the old woman offered her arm to Moriah and he took it, lacing their arms together and keeping her close to his side. As they took off back the way Elsinora and Fiona had come, the old woman called in a singsong voice, "Hurry along, child! I think I could do with some more cakes. Do join me."

A scowl firmly set upon her face, Fiona trudged back into the castle in the queen mother's wake.

All the while, as Fiona had meandered through the gardens in the company of their grandmother, Fynn had made his way to his room for the summer. Tiredly, he pushed open the door and crossed over to the bed. Fully intending to fling himself down onto the mattress and soft bedding, Fynn stopped suddenly when he saw a piece of sealed parchment set beside his pillow. The red seal bore the embossed symbol of a nine-pointed star. Scrawled in black ink at the corner of the parchment was 'FDF.' Carefully, Fynn took the missive and pried open the seal. It read:

To one Prince Fynneas Fog,

I hope this letter finds you well. I've a present for you. A gift for my prince before he goes to Morancy. You'll know it when you see it.

Should you need me, you need only call my name.

2

THE LETTER IN THE FLAME

Fynn and Fiona, accompanied by Sir Jaeryn of the King's Guard, had spent days perusing the shops in the capital, stopping at each one and having a look around. Occasionally, they would find one that particularly caught their interest and there they would stay for the afternoon. Their first jaunt into the city didn't yield any findings of note and left the siblings to spend the evening in Fiona's room, lamenting the boredom that had taken hold of their lives. Fynn, that night, feeling especially despondent and wishing to go back home, had lazed about counting the cracks in the stones of the ceiling—a new past-time of his that he resorted to when all else failed. With strange nightmares plaguing him since their arrival at Batsbeckon, the prince found that idly counting cracks helped stave off the wariness now associated with sleep.

The sixth day proceeded much the same as the first and left the two siblings once more with little to show for their efforts. The seventh day, however, they happened across a bookshop situated at the far end of a long street that they had only, by chance, found when they made a wrong turn the street previous, losing their accompanying guard in the process—at least for the time being.

Fynn, never having seen the use of bookshops, felt himself oddly attracted to the run-down storefront. It was as though there was something reaching out to him, scraping just by before pulling at him bodily, urging him to enter. Distantly, he thought back to the odd little note he'd found upon his bed the first day they'd come to the capital.

Fiona pressed into the shop with widened eyes as she took in the sight of books as far as she could see. The books lined dilapidated looking shelves that were covered in a thick blanket of dust. The princess plucked a book from its place; a place, she assumed, it had been sitting, untouched, for ages. Brushing the dust away, she saw the title emblazoned in red standing out against the black leather of the cover. She traced her fingers along the words, following each dip and curve curiously.

Fynn popped up at her side. Peering around her, he saw the book in her clutches. He quirked a brow. "*The Mortanomicon?*"

Startled, Fiona stumbled to the side, the book still in her hands. She sighed. "Don't just come out of nowhere like that."

Fynn disregarded his sister's surprise and remained studying the title of the book. "Have you heard of it before?" He wasn't quite sure what it was, but something about that book lured him closer, had hold of him in a way he wasn't certain he could explain. It was as though he could hear the book breathing beneath Fiona's touch.

"Of what?"

The boy pointed at the book Fiona cleaved to. "That. This *Mortanomicon* book?" It was such a strange title, he noted. It wasn't a word he knew, or one he believed to even be Estherian in origin. It seemed impossibly other-worldly in its allure.

"Oh." Fiona smiled as she looked down at the found treasure in her arms and shook her head. "No." She brushed more dust from its leather binding. "No, I've never heard of it." There was a light in her eyes that was unmistakably the embers of burgeoning curiosity. "I think I'll get it, though—look through it tonight."

Fynn shrugged, breaking the spell that had mesmerized him only moments ago. "I'll go find the shop keeper then, I suppose. Maybe I'll have a look around, too."

Fiona gave a curt nod. "Yes. Thank you. I'll wait here. And, Fynn… don't *break* anything."

"You can't *break* books," grumbled the prince as he went off in search of the shop's proprietor.

He wandered down the aisles of tomes, not really caring what sort of works lined the shelves. Much like his father, Fynn did not possess a proclivity toward the written word. Yet, despite his own disinterest, he would never begrudge his sister for finding literature so fascinating. It was, he supposed, one of the few things that truly excited Fiona. He smiled at the thought of her, thinking of the longing way she looked at the book.

"Hello?" he called out, still not having found the shopkeeper. "Is anyone here?"

Fynn heard something clatter to the ground; more books he supposed. Following the sound, he happened upon a small, little man hunched over a stack of fallen books and parchments. Skeletal looking hands began to rake them back into order. Fynn, at once, fell to his knees and began assisting the man.

"Sorry," the prince began as he gathered up a heap of scrolls in his scrawny arms, "did I startle you?"

As if just realizing Fynn had joined him in his scramble to gather his things, the man looked up. He was old, his gristly skin reminiscent of the leather binding many of the tomes that lined the shelves of the shop. His eyes were a watery blue and his hair a smoky grey that twisted every which way in the most unkempt manner Fynn had ever seen. His nose was quite beaklike, crooked and hooked, protruding out over thin lips. He shook his head.

"Oh, no, no, just clumsy, you see!" His voice sounded tired but familiar.

The two stood. Fynn held the heap of scrolls carefully, ever mindful of his sister's earlier warning.

The old man, frail looking as he was, held a stack of seven books in his quaking arms. He nodded to the side. "This way, if you will, child."

Obligingly, Fynn followed the man through the shop towards the back where he saw a small writing desk situated; parchment was stretched out across its face and there was a quill poised in an inkwell. Just to the side there was a small table whereupon the old man set his books.

Wiping the sweat from his wrinkled brow, the man then pointed a claw-like finger toward the chair that waited before the writing desk. "You can place those just there, if you will, child," he instructed.

Fynn nodded and gently set down the scrolls. Curiously, he peeked at the parchment laid out upon the desk and found that nothing yet had been written there, save for what looked to be initials scrawled in one corner. He couldn't quite make out the letters. Fynn looked back to the man and asked, "Are you the shopkeeper here?"

The old man nodded.

"Great!" Fynn beamed happily, icy eyes aglow. "My sister would like to purchase one of your books. She's waiting towards the front."

The old man offered Fynn a kindly smile. "Of course."

As the two proceeded toward the front to collect Fiona and her book, the old man said, "My name is Barnaby, Barnaby Lot. I've been keeping this shop since I came back to the capital. I don't get many customers. People don't tend to come in here, I find."

There was a very eccentric way in which the old man was speaking that set Fynn's nerves on end.

"You see, my father owned this book shop. Loved books, he did! He left it to me when he died, and I've been running it ever since." Barnaby reached a spindly hand up to flatten the wrinkles from the collar of his shirt. "What brings you and your sister into my shop?" He smiled easily.

"We've been out exploring the city," replied Fynn evenly as he fought back the twitchy feeling arising in his stomach. "We try and go down different roads each day so we can see as much as we can while we're here."

"Not from the capital, then?"

The boy shook his head. "No. We're only here for the summer."

"How are you liking it?"

Fynn shrugged. "I prefer the north lands. I find the people there much friendlier overall."

"Well." The old man laughed chillingly. "I hope I haven't put you off."

The boy shook his head nervously. "No, no! You've been perfectly kind, really."

Barnaby smiled another odd little smile, a knowing sort. He watched Fynn for a moment and then seemed to notice his eyes for the first time. He stopped; the sudden halt in the old man's step caught Fynn's attention and he, too, halted.

Fynn turned back to regard the old bookkeeper and arched a brow. "Is everything alright?"

Barnaby reached out a hand and took Fynn by the chin; his spider-leg like fingers curled around the boy's jaw and crept along his cheek.

Fynn didn't move, but his eyes went wide.

"You never told me your name, child."

"Fynn. Fynneas Fog…*Prince* Fynneas Fog," Fynn replied hastily. "I didn't intend to be rude. It slipped my mind, I suppose. My apologies."

A crooked grin etched across the man's face, revealing yellow teeth that seemed close to rotting completely. "It is an honor, my prince." Suddenly, he released the boy's face, and his hand went combing through thick, black hair, brushing a few strands from the prince's eyes. Barnaby's toothy grin broadened. "Like I said, I don't get many visitors to my shop. And here, Gods be blessed! Here stands the *prince*, and in my shop no less!"

Fynn nodded dumbly.

"Ah yes!" The old man clapped his hands together. "Let's be off then to get your sister that book, eh? Right then, let's go."

Fynn watched as Barnaby stole along by him and continued toward the front of the shop where Fiona most likely still waited. He followed almost reluctantly. They came upon her then and, much as Fynn had suspected, she remained rooted to the spot he had last seen her, the black book still nestled in her arms comfortably.

Seeing the pair arrive, Fiona perked up.

Her eyes, Fynn noted, were still alight with barely contained excitement.

Barnaby bowed in greeting. "Princess, your brother tells me you've found a book to your liking?"

Fiona nodded.

"Might I see?"

She handed the book to the man slowly, her eyes never straying far from her treasure.

Barnaby's gaze fell upon the book and, much the way Fiona had done, he reached out a finger and traced the letters of the title. "This is the book you wish to purchase?"

Once again, Fynn thought he could almost hear the book breathing, alive beneath the strange shopkeeper's touch. He stared at Barnaby's fingers as they swept over the red on the cover. It was then that he thought he heard what sounded like a heartbeat emanating from within the pages of *The Mortanomicon*. The twitchy feeling in Fynn's stomach became almost painful at the thought.

Again, Fiona nodded.

"Most interesting," Barnaby mumbled.

"Is something the matter?" Fiona inquired.

Barnaby shook his head. "Not at all." His voice seemed tired again. "If this is the book you wish to have, it is yours." He handed the book back to Fiona. "Consider it a gift, princess. I would be most humbled if you took it."

Fynn carefully watched the man as he interacted with Fiona. The look of apprehension that flitted across her features did not go unnoticed and he resolved, instantly, to ask her about it later. He wondered if maybe she felt the same odd, sickly feeling he did the longer they stayed in the shop. Fiona held onto the book tightly, but her attention shifted to focus solely on the very strange man before her.

Barnaby bowed again. As he straightened, he asked, "Is there anything else I might assist you with?"

Both Fynn and Fiona shook their heads.

The prince chirped, "Thank you, Barnaby, for your gift. That was very kind of you." He looked back at Fiona and reached out his hand for her. She took it wordlessly. "We ought to be heading back to the castle; it's getting late." Fynn hoped his voice didn't sound as jumpy to Barnaby as it did to him.

"Of course." Barnaby smiled, watching as the siblings made to leave the shop. "It's not *safe* out in the city for you two."

"Safe?" repeated Fiona with a hint of displeasure. "What do you mean?"

"Only that the city is fraught with commoners who may not see eye to eye with the Crown sometimes," Barnaby replied innocently. "We wouldn't want you two caught in the middle of anything...*unpleasant*."

"No...no, we wouldn't," the princess tersely replied. "Thank you again for the book."

It was midafternoon and the sun was shining unforgivingly bright this day, no clouds to obscure its golden tendrils or lessen its heat. Sir Jaeryn Beckett was leaning against a stone wall lazily and fiddling with the King's Guard pendant he wore around his neck, tired after hurrying along to find the royal siblings. Though his resolute gaze had never left the bookshop, he looked bored, nevertheless. Seeing his charges emerge from the shop, he drew himself to his full height and greeted them. He was a tall man with curly blonde hair that all the women in court envied and all the men scoffed at. His eyes were a deep ebony color, made all the darker looking as they sat beneath thick, black eyebrows. Jaeryn was certainly a most handsome man, hard to miss amongst a crowd. As such, Fiona was quick to spy him coming toward them.

"Jaeryn," she greeted. Her eyes kept darting back in the direction of the shop. She combed her hand through her hair a few times. "Jaeryn, have you ever been to that bookshop just there?"

The knight shook his head. "No, princess. Though, I can't say I frequent shops such as this. Books were never to my liking. Much too quiet a pursuit for me, really."

"Is there a family called Lot that lives in the city?" asked Fynn.

"Lot?" Jaeryn repeated.

Fynn nodded.

"Seems it could be a rather everyday surname amongst commoners. Why? Has this *Lot* done something?"

Fynn shook his head, though he did cast a fleeting glance back to the bookshop where he could have sworn he saw Barnaby peeking out through the drawn drapes. He turned back to the knight. "Sir Jaeryn, could you do me a favor?"

"Of course," assured the knight confidently. "Anything."

"The shopkeeper, he said that his father had run the bookshop before he did. I don't know his father's name, he didn't say. But the shopkeeper is called Barnaby Lot. Could you look into him and his shop for me?"

"Anything in particular you want me to find out?"

"No," replied Fynn. He looked back to the shop. He no longer saw Barnaby Lot spying through the curtains out at them. "No, Sir Jaeryn. Any information you come across would be welcome. There's just something *odd* about the man. Something most curious."

The remainder of the afternoon was spent out in the gardens. Fiona was curled up on a bench that leaned against one of the many rose bushes, the sun warming her as the hours wore on. A tray of lemon cakes, a newly discovered favorite of Fiona's thanks to her grandmother, sat half-ignored just at her side. Fynn was not far from her. Upon their return to the castle, Fynn had asked his father to join them that afternoon before supper. Felix had readily agreed, thankful for an escape from Gemma's incessant nagging. Father and son stood in the grass of the garden's, encircled by walls of hedges and, in a way, cut off from all the to-dos of royal life. All decorum disregarded, the two had cast off their formal clothes and garbed themselves in plain shirts and trousers. They looked, for all the world, nothing more than a commoner and his boy.

Both Felix and Fynn held aloft wooden, practice swords.

Sweat beaded at Felix's brow. "Right." He laughed as he brushed the sweat from his face. "Again then!"

Fynn went charging forward, brandishing his sword like a barbarian swinging a club. He flailed wildly at Felix who, with very little effort at all, parried the attack and, with nothing more than a well-placed flick of the wrist, disarmed the boy. Felix couldn't help but laugh as Fynn, watching his sword clatter to the ground, scowled. The expression just didn't look right on the child, which made the whole scene all the more humorous.

The elder of the princes leaned down and retrieved the sword, handing it back to his son with an amiable grin. "Well, there was certainly some *power* behind that one."

Fynn pouted. "Clearly not enough."

Felix tousled Fynn's sweat-slicked hair. "Power isn't everything, Fynny. You've got to *think* too."

Fynn pulled away from his father, sword in hand, and readied himself for another round. "What does *thinking* have to do with it?" he huffed.

"Going into any fight mindlessly is how you get killed," chided Felix. "Think, Fynn. Think about all the factors at play in a fight."

"What do you mean?"

"Think about your opponent. I'm much bigger than you, right? So, chances are you aren't going to outmuscle me." Felix combed a hand through his hair. "Think about your surroundings. We're on an even field, so you won't be able to take the high ground." He bent his knees and leaned forward. "Think about your weapon and mine. We're both using swords. So, close range combat. You won't be able to get to me from afar."

With that last word, Felix lunged forward. Fynn had taken notice of the way his father had been bending low, the way his weight had shifted forward, the way his sword's point had tilted ever so slightly downward. He'd been ready and was quick to sidestep his father's sudden foray. As Fynn dodged the swing of Felix's wooden blade, he struck out with his own and only narrowly missed his father's shoulder. Fynn was surprised by how quickly the man recovered from the near miss. Felix's own sword appeared as if out of nowhere and slammed into Fynn's.

Once again, Fynn was disarmed.

This time, instead of pouting at the result, Fynn stood confused. His grey gaze was fixed on the sword lying in the grass. "How'd you do that?"

"Power and thinking are important in a fight, but so is form." Felix clapped his hand onto Fynn's shoulder and grinned widely. "But that was much better, Fynny, my boy! So much better."

Finally, Fynn looked up at his father. "But you still won."

"But you were using your head this time, weren't you?" Felix studied Fynn as the boy took in his words. "You knew I was going to lunge at you. You knew and you took steps to avoid the strike. That was very good. See, using your head sometimes pays off, doesn't it?"

Fynn looked back at the sword in the grass. "I was thinking this time just like you said. But you were thinking too. You *knew*." Fynn smiled weakly. "You knew what I would do, and you were ready for it." He shook his head. "No, not ready, I suppose. You planned on it. You planned on me sidestepping you … that was your intention all along."

"Yes."

"You were thinking three steps ahead."

Felix retrieved the sword and again handed it to Fynn. "You always have to be thinking three steps ahead, Fynny."

"*Three* steps ahead? I'm lucky when I can manage a step at a time," scoffed Fynn.

Felix's voice took on a lower timbre as a sudden severity darkened his words. "It's a dangerous world we live in. If you get caught unawares, you never know what could happen."

Fynn held the sword in his hands. He didn't make himself ready for another round. Rather, he held the sword there before him and studied the weapon. Transfixed by the knots in the wood here and there and the splinters that littered the sharp of the false blade, the prince was silent for some time. When he did find his voice again, it was quiet and tentative. "What do you mean?"

Felix straightened. "There will come a time, Fynneas, when you will have to make decisions. Sometimes those decisions will regard you or your family and sometimes they will be decisions that will impact the kingdom. It's not going to be easy, not at all. Sometimes, to do the right thing, you have to make a decision you don't want to." He inhaled deeply, taking the moment to feel his lungs expand as air filled his chest. "When that time comes, Fynneas, I may not be here to help you. I *hope* I am. I *pray* I am here to guide you as long as I can. But there will inevitably be a time when you will be on your own. That will be a dangerous time for you, my boy. I cannot keep you from the world forever. I have as long as I could. But hopefully, I can keep it from you a little longer … keep it away until you're ready. Or at least as ready as you can ever really be."

"What's out there that's so dangerous?"

"People."

Fynn traced one hand over the sword, feeling the wood beneath his fingertips. It was hard and sturdy. Yet now and again, he felt the familiar pinch of splintered wood spear his flesh. There was an underlying flimsiness to the sword that seemed, in a way, wrong. "People?"

"People have secrets, Fynny. And secrets can be very dangerous."

Fynn looked up at his father. "Do *you* have secrets?"

Felix shook his head. "None from you."

Staring into his father's blue eyes, Fynn couldn't help but feel that those words weren't true. He was certain that his father wasn't keeping anything from him with any sort of malicious intent, but the unwavering feeling that there were most certainly things Felix wasn't telling him made Fynn bristle.

Felix left Fynn there in the garden as he took his leave. He called to the boy as he headed toward the castle, "We'll practice again tomorrow, yes?"

"Alright," Fynn agreed, still clutching the wooden sword. Tension had claimed his muscles and, as much as he wanted to smile at his father's promise of another afternoon spent together, he couldn't quite bring himself to feel so at ease.

"Get ready for supper soon or your gran will have your head," warned Felix as he disappeared from the gardens entirely.

Fynn carelessly threw the sword to the ground before flopping down beside his sister.

Fiona looked up from the book. "How did training go?"

"Fine." He popped a lemon cake into his mouth, gnashing at it like a hungry cow. "How's your book?"

She closed it suddenly. "Fine."

He eyed her suspiciously for a moment but chose not to press the matter. "We should get ready for supper. I'm a right mess." Fynn laughed, gesturing to the dirt and sweat on his shirt and trousers. "Gran will have a fit if she sees me in such a state."

Fiona stood and offered Fynn her hand. "Let's get inside. You'll need a bath before supper." She grinned. "Or you'll be right, Gran will have an absolute fit at the very sight of you. Not to mention the stench."

As they made their way into the castle, the sun began to dip beyond the horizon and the summer blue of the sky faded into a deep plum shade. The clouds began to gather in heavy droves, clambering about each other and clinging to one another as the unmistakable bellow of thunder split the silence and flashes of lightning jolted through the coming darkness.

Fiona had gone to her room, book still in hand, while Fynn left to take a bath in the chamber close to his own quarters. He settled into the tub, the water near scalding hot. His muscles eased as the water ebbed around him and the scented oils that had been poured into the bath wafted into his nose. He leaned against the cold metal of the tub and closed his eyes.

Water splashed in steady beats against the small, stained-glass windowpanes that lined the chamber.

"It's raining," Fynn commented to himself dully as he sank further into the water.

"Yes."

His eyes shot open at the sound of someone speaking to him. He looked around the room and saw no one. The door was still tightly shut, just as he had left it. His chest rose and fell unsteadily as he tried to calm his breathing.

"Is anyone there?" he called.

Silence sounded and nothing more.

The once relaxing waters no longer soothed him and instead became cool and uncomfortable. Fynn rose and stepped from the tub, dripping water all along the stone beneath his feet as he padded through the room. He dried quickly and tossed the cloth aside. There was a frightful chill permeating the bathing chamber, one that he was sure had not been there before. Dressing hurriedly, Fynn retreated from the room and jogged down the corridor toward his quarters.

He hadn't seen Fiona coming down the hall. It wasn't until he was pulling himself off the ground that he even realized he'd run right into her. "Sorry," he grumbled as he righted himself.

"What's got you off in a hurry?"

Pushing the damp hair from his face, Fynn looked away. He chewed his lower lip for a moment before squeaking, "I thought I heard a voice."

"Here?" Fiona asked worriedly.

Fynn nodded. "I thought they wouldn't follow me here. I thought—I don't know," he stammered self-consciously, "that things would be *different* here."

"Is it the same voice you've heard before?"

"I can't tell," admitted the prince.

Disconcerted by her brother's sudden sheepish demeanor, the princess forced herself to remain calmly resolute. "Why don't you head into your room and take a moment. Maybe lie down? You've got some time before supper. Why don't we both just finish getting ready and we can talk more later?"

"You look ready to me," replied Fynn.

"I want to put on something nice." Fiona blushed.

Fynn snorted in a most undignified manner. "The city is ruining you, big sister."

She playfully shoved him. "Be that as it may, *baby* brother, I want to try and fit in. Aunt Gemma is a real nuisance, you know? That woman always finds something about my appearance to complain about. Just for once, I'd like her to keep her mouth shut!" Fiona bristled for only a moment before demurely smoothing out the non-existent wrinkles on the shoulders of her dress. "So, I intend to look *presentable,* as she would call it, this evening."

"Do what you must." Fynn shrugged.

"I intend to," she assured darkly as she took her leave from a moderately less distraught Fynn and headed back to her own room.

Fynn was the first of he and Fiona to arrive in the dining hall for supper, opening the doorway from the antechamber to reveal that only Hollyn, James, and Elsinora had already arrived and taken their seats. Fynn situated himself in one of the vacant chairs opposite Hollyn and James, who sat side by side with their heads bowed together as they whispered on about something or other.

Elsinora warmly asked, "How has your day been, child?"

"Just fine," Fynn replied simply. He was oddly at ease around the old woman. "What have you been doing all day, Gran?"

"I spent my day doing nothing in particular," she explained. "Just up in my tower."

The very thought of sitting up in a tower all day made Fynn's skin crawl, but he choked back the urge to sneer and, instead, chirped, "Did you enjoy your day?"

"I did," the queen mother assured. "I most certainly did." She looked about for a moment and then asked, "Where's your sister?"

"I suppose she's still getting ready," Fynn offered.

Elsinora snorted in a manner reminiscent of Fynn's rather un-aristocratic mannerism and instantly he knew where he must have picked up that particular quirk.

"Foolish girl," the old woman chided under her breath.

"I think she just wants Aunt Gemma to like her," started Fynn, unsure of Elsinora's thoughts on the matter. "She says it doesn't bother her that all the women in the capital are *that way*, but I think it does…at least a bit."

"Well, of course it does," Elsinora tersely insisted. "But my Gemma, that girl, she's wound tighter than twine! Honestly, Fiona shouldn't give a damn what Gemma thinks."

Fynn's eyes went wide and his jaw tightened. He hadn't expected that. "I…um…well…I think she just wants us all to…well…get along."

As if having been summoned the moment her name rolled sourly off Elsinora's lips, Gemma bustled into the dining hall. Her features looked pinched by irritation. Her brows were settled into a furrowed bunch. She sat beside her mother, glaring viciously at the empty place Ursalyn normally occupied.

"Something the matter, dear?" asked Elsinora in a sickeningly sweet voice.

"That woman—"

Elsinora interrupted bitingly, "The *queen*." She patted Gemma on the shoulder with a condescending lightness in much the way one would placate a child.

"The *queen*—"

"The queen *what?*" Ursalyn asked as she sauntered into the room with all the serpentine grace of a snake slithering through tall grass. As she sat, she arched a brow and let her focus linger entirely upon Gemma. The other woman had fallen deathly silent. "Gem, dear, weren't you just saying something? About *me*, I believe?"

Gemma gnashed her teeth like a wild dog but remained silent.

A vicious twinkle lit up Ursalyn's eyes as she smirked. "I must have been mistaken then."

Fynn noticed that James and Hollyn had ceased their hushed conversation and, much like him, were ensnared in silent rapture as the three women interacted. The uncomfortable tension between the trio was palpable and Fynn couldn't help but fidget under the oppressive feeling of the situation. Relief flooded through his small frame when he noticed his father and uncle join the rest of them in the dining hall. However, the relief was rather short lived when he observed the strained look masking Lachlan's handsome features and the evident annoyance discoloring Felix's expression.

"Great," mumbled Fynn as he took an interest in picking at the fabric of his sleeve. He knew, in that moment, that supper would not be pleasant, by any means.

Felix sat down beside his son and discreetly nudged his shoulder, gaining his attention. "Where's your sister?" he asked in a hushed tone.

"Late, it would seem." Fynn frowned.

"What's keeping her?"

Fynn shrugged. "Don't know."

Just as the family settled into a simmering silence, the doors to the dining room burst open with a loud bang. All eyes at the table snapped up and looked to the doorway, each of them expecting to see Fiona come rushing through the doors. To their mutual surprise, it was Jaeryn who bound into the dining hall with a wild look about him. He gasped, catching his breath, and then announced, "Your Graces! Sires, there's a fire in the city."

"A fire?" Lachlan repeated as he leapt from his seat in a rush. "Where?"

"The middle quarter!"

Lachlan lurched from the table and ran up to Jaeryn. "Have you dispatched your men to contain the fire?"

32

The knight nodded in the affirmative. "Everyone's left to do what they can, sire."

"Take me," insisted the king as he flew through the doors and sprinted out of the castle.

While Elsinora and Gemma remained seated rather stiffly in their places, the rest of the family followed suit and sprang from their chairs and clambered to the doorway. Hollyn took off on his father's heels with James close at his side.

Felix, before making his way out of the castle, told Fynn, "Stay here."

Fynn watched as Felix went after his brother and nephews. Curiously, Jaeryn remained there at Fynn's side in the wake of everyone's hasty departure. His dark eyes fell upon the prince and he pulled from his sleeve a piece of parchment sealed with red wax.

"Prince Fynneas," the knight spoke quietly.

Fynn looked at Jaeryn and the outstretched hand that held the parchment. He took it. "What's this?"

"It flew out of the fire."

The boy scrutinized the parchment. It was partially burned in the corner, but other than that, it seemed unscathed. "Where is the fire *exactly?*"

"I had gone back to the bookshop," explained the knight, "and when I arrived it just burst into flames. I've never seen so much fire in all my life… and so *quickly*. Everything…*everything* was just on fire." His focus never wavered. He looked Fynn steadfastly in the eyes. "That parchment leapt out of the fire and fell at my feet. Most *unnatural*, really. Very *strange*."

Jaeryn then took his leave in a flash, dashing off to rejoin Lachlan.

Fynn watched him go and then looked back to the parchment in his hand. "Strange indeed," he muttered as he spied writing in the burnt corner. He could just barely make out the initials 'FDF' amongst the golden splotches of charred parchment. A sickening tremor slid down his spine at the sight of those letters. He gulped back his misgivings.

Carefully, he unsealed the parchment and read its contents:

> *I'm glad you've found your present. Give it a look.*
> *You're sure to have questions.*

3

FALL APART

"**I**s there something you're not telling me?"

Fiona, seated upon the windowsill beside her brother, balked at Fynn's blunt accusation. She shook her head sharply. "No."

"You're sure?"

"Why're you asking?"

Fynn looked away and shrugged, suddenly finding the cracks in the stone walls far more interesting than the conversation at hand. Rather non-committally, he answered, "The other day, when you were reading *the book*, you acted weird when I asked you about it. What could you have read in it that you don't want me to know?"

"Nothing. You're being silly."

"Am I?"

"Yes," snapped Fiona. "I'm going down to the library."

Fynn piped, "I'll go with you."

Fiona reached out to the boy sitting next to her and slowly ran her hand through his tangled hair, fondly smiling as she whispered, "No. It's late, Fynny. Get some sleep."

"Will you be in the library tomorrow as well?"

"I suspect I will be."

"Can I come then?"

Fiona's hand fell from the boy's head and traced down his shoulder. "Tomorrow should be a lovely day. You should play outside, run around, have a spar with Father. The summer won't last forever."

Fynn forced down the suspicion bubbling up inside. "Will you join me outside when you've finished *whatever* you're doing?"

"Sure," Fiona obliged with a smile. She placed a kiss to Fynn's forehead.

They remained where they sat for a moment, both staring out the window down to the city. Where most would find the silent bleakness of the night disconcerting, Fynn found it enchanting. There was something haunt-ingly beautiful about the city at night. He marveled at the way the roads appeared almost black as pitch and stretched out in meandering patterns and twisted and turned like the spindly legs of some great spider spreading out from the castle.

"Try and get some sleep tonight, won't you?" the prince meekly asked as he stood from the sill and yawned. "You need to sleep too, you know."

"I won't be long tonight, I promise." Fiona offered her brother a parting smile.

The library was on the ground floor of the castle, encased behind two large, wooden doors. Fiona stepped in and stared, wide-eyed, at the sight. The room was far larger than she had anticipated. It stretched for what seemed like an eternity; a seemingly endless sea of books was splayed out before her. The books were neatly arranged on dark, wooden shelves that reached from the stone floor up and almost all the way to the ceiling. Here and there between shelves there were sconces fixed to the wall, casting just enough light to see further on into the expanse of tomes. Portraits of peo-ple Fiona didn't recognize also decorated the space, each hung in ornate, golden frames.

As she walked by, Fiona ran her hand over the spines of countless works, feeling the leather under her touch. It was evident by the dust congealing on many of the collected tomes that they hadn't been read in ages. What a waste, she thought. She halted, seeming to be at an impasse of how to pro-ceed. There had to be something here in the library that would help explain the strange old man, his mysterious bookshop, and maybe even the fire.

"But, where to look?" Fiona whispered to herself as she cast a nervous glance around the room. "There must be thousands of books in here."

"What're you doing up so late?"

Fiona cringed. She'd been discovered. She didn't bother to turn around. She recognized the haughty tone of voice. "Just doing some midnight read-ing. That's all."

"You shouldn't go skulking around the castle," the young man half-heart-edly scolded.

"I was not *skulking.*"

"Could have fooled me, the way you kept out of sight and stayed quiet all the way here."

"So, you *followed* me?" Fiona accused.

"I was curious," he replied. "Wanted to know what had you *skulking* around the castle at such an hour."

"Well, you have your answer. You can go now."

The young man stepped in front of Fiona, eyeing her like a cat that'd cornered a mouse. Ciaran wasn't much older than Fiona, but he stood a full head taller than her. His dark red hair was slicked back neatly; familiar thick, black eyebrows were finely arched. His eyes were blue, like his father's, but there was a light there that sparked in their depths that was so profoundly dissimilar to the king's. Ciaran was broad of shoulder and chest, most likely attributed to all the time he spent at sea and hunting when he wasn't at Morancy training. He cut a fine figure; it wasn't at all hard to see what all the ladies of Estheria saw in the young prince. Fiona, however, found his lopsided grin and jovial air appallingly arrogant.

"I don't think so," he said.

Fiona pushed past him. "Fine. Do whatever you want."

He watched as she continued down the row of books, desperately in search of something. "If you're going to just stand there, could you at least make yourself useful?"

Ciaran quirked a brow. "What're you looking for?"

"Where would books on the families of Estheria be?"

Ciaran trotted after Fiona and soon found himself in step beside his cousin, peering over her shoulder to read the spines of the books more easily. "Which families? Nobles? Royal?"

"I don't know," Fiona admitted as she pressed on, relentless in her search. "Have you heard of a family called Lot? They owned a bookshop *supposedly*. And what do you know of Moriah Mordray?"

Ciaran stopped abruptly. "*Moriah*? Why do you ask?"

The princess followed suit and stopped, looking over her shoulder and admiring the surprised look on Ciaran's face. She smirked. "So, you know him?"

Ciaran nodded.

"How well?"

The prince shrugged. "I don't know, pretty well I suppose." He schooled his features. "He's friends with my mother. They've known each other since they were children. He's a friend of Gran's, too. She's quite fond of him." He snorted in a manner reminiscent of Fynn. "I think that may be the *only* thing she and Mother have in common."

36

"I saw him," Fiona said. "The day my family and I arrived, he was in the garden with Gran and I."

"So?"

"*So*, is he here often?"

Ciaran looked away from her as if he was searching for a suitable answer. "Yes and no. He was around a lot more a few years ago. He only comes by now and again, as of late. The last two years he's been teaching at Morancy, so he's been even more scarce."

"What does he teach at Morancy?"

The annoying, lopsided grin returned to Ciaran's handsome features, making him look, if possible, even more arrogant. "Aren't you just full of questions tonight."

"What? Is it some sort of secret or something?"

Ciaran laughed. "No, not at all. It's just curious, really, that you'd have so many questions about *him*."

Fiona ignored Ciaran and the cheeky twinkle in his eyes. "Do you or do you *not* know where I can find books about the families in Estheria?"

"I don't. I suggest you ask Gran in the morning. Of all of us, she spends the most time in the library. I'd wager she's read most of the books in here."

"That's impossible," insisted Fiona. "That would take someone ages!"

"Well," Ciaran pointed out smugly, "she *is* rather old."

He yawned then. It was, quite possibly, the most dramatic yawn Fiona had ever witnessed. Ciaran looked like a bored lion disinterested with the world around him. His flippant nature, she decided just then, certainly made him less attractive. Absently, she wondered why none of the women around her cousin seemed to notice this about him. Or was it that they just didn't care? She watched, annoyed, as he leaned back against one of the bookshelves and crossed his arms over his chest.

"If you're so exhausted, Ciaran, just go to bed. I don't *need* you here," Fiona insisted.

"And leave you alone in the castle at night? Certainly not, Fiona." He chuckled tiredly. "I would be remiss—yes, *absolutely remiss*—in my role as crown prince if I left you. It's not right, you know, to leave a girl alone at night. You never know who could be *skulking* about the castle."

"The only one *skulking* about the castle, per your assessment, is *me*! And I think I can handle myself, thank you."

"Regardless," the young man argued, "I'd feel better if I stayed."

Fiona grudgingly huffed. "Do whatever you please."

Ciaran remained lounging against the bookcase, lazily watching as Fiona prowled the rows of shelves in search of answers. Lost in thought as he admired the books, Ciaran hadn't noticed Fiona slip away. He drew himself upright and leaned forward, peering down one of the rows of books.

"Fiona," he called.

There came no answer.

The night was deathly silent. He strained to hear any sound he could— her breathing, footsteps, the jostling of paper.

"Fiona," Ciaran called again. His blue eyes darted about in a desperate search to detect any sort of motion. "Fiona, where've you gone?"

"Ciaran," the familiar, melodic voice of the princess chided, "stop yelling. It's the middle of the night and I'm *trying* to read."

The prince rounded the corner to find Fiona seated amongst a pile of books. Noticing the titles all had to do with the family trees of the noble houses of the kingdom, he arched a brow curiously. "I don't think you'll find what you're looking for in any of those."

Fiona continued to furiously turn the pages of one of the books she held. Without looking up, she grumbled, "And why is that?"

"You said you were looking for information on this mysterious *Lot* family?" When Fiona nodded, the prince continued coolly, "That's *not* a noble house. There won't be anything about them in those books you've got there."

Fiona shook her head. "You don't get it, do you?"

Ciaran, with remarkable grace, sat down on the floor beside her. He peeked over her shoulder and scanned the page she was reading. There wasn't much there about the family tree itself, but more so about the founding of the house in the first-years of the kingdom. "Get what?"

With a sigh, Fiona pushed the book into Ciaran's hands. "Look." She thrust her index finger upon the page with astounding force. "It's not just about the family—who married who and so on. Each book relates the founding of the house, how they obtained their noble status. So," she continued, a sly grin curling her lips all the while, "it mentions, of course, the vassals of each of the noble houses. The Lots, even if they aren't nobles themselves, may have sworn fealty to one of the noble families. If that's the case, then we know where to start looking."

"Alright." Ciaran handed the book back to Fiona. For a moment he remained quiet, looking over the assorted family names emblazoned upon each of the tomes. "Right." He clapped his hands together. "Why don't we divide and conquer, yes?" He reached out and selected three books from the pile beside Fiona. "These three houses," he gestured towards the three books in his grasp with a curt little nod, "are noble houses in the west. I'll start with these." He dropped them at his side and then looked back to his cousin, pleased by the shocked look on her face. He shrugged carelessly; a smirk graced his features. "If I'm here, I might as well help. Don't look so surprised." He studied the remaining assortment of books. "Right." He pulled another four books from the pile and pushed them toward Fiona. "These four and the one you're holding are the houses in the south. Start with these."

For the next two hours, the cousins remained in companionable silence; both of them were hunched over their respective books, eyes furiously looking for any traces of the mysterious Lots. There were moments where one of them thought they might have found something. In those moments, there was a quick "ah-ha" that was almost instantly followed by a muttered "never mind."

Ciaran's back began to ache. His eyes were growing heavy, far too heavy for him to keep them open. He set his book aside and leaned forward, his forehead settling atop his folded forearms. He felt the muscles in his shoulders relax and the sinews loosen as if he were melting. He sighed and, before he had time to realize it, he'd fallen asleep.

Fiona, poking her head out from the folds of her book, could hardly stifle the laughter when she saw Ciaran in a heap with drool gathering over his chin like an over-tired child. Deciding to let him sleep, she returned her attention to her book and pressed on.

By the time morning came and the fresh tendrils of golden light slipped in through the stained-glass windows, casting rainbows in every direction, Fiona could hardly hold herself up. Books upon books were piled all around her and scrolls of all sorts were strewn in every direction, though careful placed so as to avoid the drool-dampened ground around Ciaran who remained sleeping quite soundly. The princess' back ached terribly as she had spent the entire night tensely hunched while reading. She sat up straight and let her head lull downward for a moment, feeling how her muscles stretched and pulled almost painfully. She stood, noting the headache that was mounting in her temples with a nasty scowl. Fiona looked to her cousin, envious of how he slept as easily as a toddler.

"Ciaran," she called.

He didn't stir.

Fiona leaned down and shoved his shoulder. "Ciaran, it's morning. Get up."

He groaned and shifted away from her.

Again, she shoved his shoulder. This time she did so with more strength than was probably necessary. "Get up."

Nearly jumping through his skin, Ciaran scrambled to keep his balance and then shot to his feet. He yawned that same dramatic, lion-like yawn from the night before, and then flashed her a lopsided smile. "Good morning, Fiona." His weary stare swept over the mountains of books and the heaps of scrolls before finally returning to his cousin. She looked terrible, he observed. There were dark circles hanging beneath her eyes and her hair, which at the best of times was just shy of being considered a mess, was far unrulier than he had ever seen. "Did you sleep at all?"

Fiona shook her head.

"Did you at least find anything useful?"

Again, she shook her head.

"Nothing at all?"

"No," she growled. "Nothing at all."

"Where did you hear this name again?"

As the two proceeded out of the library, Fiona mentioned, "There was this strange old man…Lot—Barnaby Lot—who had this bookshop Fynn and I went to a few days ago. There was something very odd about him."

"Where was this bookshop?"

Fiona sighed. "The middle quarter. It caught fire along with some other shops that night…burned down entirely."

Ciaran perked up, "Have you gone back?"

"No," replied Fiona hesitantly. "Why would I? It burned down. Don't you listen?"

The prince grinned from ear to ear. "Let's go have a look around! We can go this afternoon."

The two turned the corner and continued down the corridor toward the dining hall.

"Why?" asked Fiona.

"Maybe there's something there."

"You're just looking for a bit of trouble," mumbled the princess.

Ciaran shook his head defiantly, but the brilliant smile he flashed undercut the insistent gesture. "Me? Never, Fiona. Just curious is all."

"I don't think it matters," mused the princess. "I don't think your father or *mine*, for that matter, will let us go running down to the middle quarter. It's been mad down there ever since the fire. People are having a fit. It wouldn't be safe."

Ciaran playfully nudged Fiona with his shoulder, laughing, "Well, of course they won't let us go traipsing around down there! They would be mad to let us, really. That's why we aren't going to tell them."

"And how, pray tell, are we supposed to just slip out of the castle undetected?"

There was a challenging look in Fiona's eyes that sent a cold chill over Ciaran for just a second, as if she was all at once daring him to defy the rules and yet pleading for him to come up with a brilliant idea to do just that.

"A distraction of course," he replied easily.

One thick, black brow arched dramatically. "A distraction?" Fiona repeated, unimpressed. "That's what they teach you at Morancy? How *clever*." She snorted.

"Have you a better idea?"

A heavy silence fell upon them as Fiona looked away, steadying her focus on the corridor laid out before them. She pouted like a child. "No."

Ciaran slung his arm around his cousin's shoulders as they entered into the dining hall, laughing warmly. "Then we go with my plan. No complaints."

As Fiona and Ciaran entered, Ciaran's laughter garnered the attention of everyone already at the table. That attention turned to barely contained astonishment at the sight of the two newcomers seemingly sharing an amiable joke between them, Ciaran alight with laughter and Fiona looking at ease with the situation. They took their seats and the attention of almost everyone at the table resettled onto the conversation that had been momentarily interrupted, their heads all turning to face Lachlan and Felix who, once again this morning, had their horns locked like two bucks in the field, arguing heatedly about something of consequence.

Ciaran and Fiona, sharing a mutual disinterest in whatever matter it was their fathers were currently arguing over, both dawned visages of profound boredom and proceeded to lightly spear at the food gathered on their plates.

Hollyn was seated at his brother's side. He looked up at Ciaran, but the elder paid him no mind. Annoyed, Hollyn leaned closer to his brother and conspiratorially whispered, "What was all that about?"

"All what?" was the dull response Ciaran offered as he punctured another grape with his fork.

"You and Fiona."

The elder prince smiled and turned to his brother, ruffling the younger's red hair happily. "We were just laughing about something I said earlier. It's called *getting along* with your family, Hollyn. Do try it sometime, won't you?"

Hollyn pulled away from his brother's touch, as if he'd been burned. "Liar."

Ciaran shoved Hollyn gently and returned to mindlessly stabbing at his food. "Whatever you say, Hollyn."

Neither Ursalyn nor Elsinora made an appearance for breakfast that morning, a fact that did not go unnoticed by those in attendance. Though everyone was mutually interested in the two women's whereabouts, no one dared mention their absence for fear of inciting some sort of knee-jerk from Gemma who, thankfully for the time being, was remaining silent and complacent as her brothers continued their relentless arguing.

For his part, Fynn remained quietly speculative as to his sister's appearance that morning with Ciaran, but he was not so taken aback by it as Hollyn had clearly been. The boy's pale eyes glanced up from his plate only to notice Hollyn looking straight back at him. Fynn didn't flinch away from the unintentionally begotten staring contest, but instead steeled himself and impertinently glared back.

Fiona shouldered her brother softly, but he didn't bother to break focus and look at her. She grumbled, leaned down, and whispered, "What are you doing?"

"He keeps looking at me," replied Fynn, still refusing to wholly acknowledge at his sister.

"Looking at you isn't a crime," she admonished. "You're acting like a child."

"He started it," insisted Fynn.

Fiona huffed and drew away from him. She noticed Ciaran across from her, looking about as bored and irritated as she felt.

"If you'll all excuse me," she proclaimed, suddenly shooting to her feet. No one even looked her way, save for Ciaran who quirked a brow. "I'll be retiring to my chambers now," she continued, bowing her head ever so slightly before hurriedly taking her leave.

Ciaran wasn't far behind, excusing himself to go to his own chambers for a nap. Much as they had when Fiona had departed, no one paid any attention to the prince stealing away from the gathering. Pushing through the doors of the dining hall into the antechamber, Ciaran nearly ran into his mother. He stepped back, righting himself, as he greeted her. "Good morning." He smiled one of his rare, genuine smiles at her.

Ursalyn seemed to have not noticed him immediately for she had side-stepped the near collision with absentminded grace and rounded toward the antechamber door when she finally looked up at her son at the sound of his pleasant voice. "You're leaving breakfast already?"

"I'm tired." Ciaran shrugged as he combed a hand through his hair. "Didn't sleep well last night," he continued by way of an explanation. "I'm going to go lie down for a bit."

Ursalyn didn't say a word but remained quietly studying the young man before her.

Ciaran did the same. His mother's red hair was pulled back messily. The whites of her eyes were tinged pinkish and there were dark circles that looked almost like bruises beneath her eyes. Where she would normally be adorned in some fine silken dress with borderline garish embellishments, presently she wore a plain dressing gown of pale blue and nothing more.

"You're going to breakfast dressed like that?" asked the prince.

The queen looked down at herself and staggered back at the sight of her state. She snapped her head back up and looked at Ciaran, eyes wide. "Is your grandmother there already?"

Ciaran shook his head. "No. I haven't seen her all morning." He continued in a lower voice, "Aunt Gem is inside though. You may want to go get dressed...*properly*. Take breakfast in your quarters, maybe?"

Ursalyn nodded numbly. Her son reached out his hand and took hers gently, pulling her toward him.

When she stood toe to toe with him, Ciaran whispered, "Why don't I help you back to your room?"

Without a second thought, Ciaran adjusted his course and, his mother's hand in his, proceeded toward the queen's chambers silently. He pushed open the doors and watched wordlessly as Ursalyn walked by him and sat atop her bed. The prince closed the doors and whirled around on his heel. He stood, fixedly standing at the forefront of the chambers while Ursalyn remained silent, sitting with a straight back atop her bed, dignified and regal as one could be whilst burning tears trickled down her face.

"What happened?" Ciaran asked softly.

Ursalyn wiped the tears from her eyes, looking away from him all the while. "Nothing to worry over."

"Nothing to worry over?" repeated the prince as he strode across the room and knelt before the queen. "You come to breakfast late and dressed in nothing more than your nightgown looking like you haven't slept in days and tell me that's nothing to worry over?"

Ursalyn's voice was devoid of warmth and emotion, gusting over Ciaran like a frigid wind. "It's none of your concern."

He clapped his hands over hers and argued, "I beg to differ, Mother." He rose to his full height, towering over her. "What happened?"

She shook her head.

Frustration mounted as Ciaran bit, "*Tell me* what happened."

Ursalyn moved in a blur. She stood before Ciaran. She pushed him backward and he stumbled for a moment. "*Who* are *you* to command an explanation from *me*?"

As she went to strike at him, Ciaran caught her by her slim wrist, wrenching her forward. Defiantly, she pulled back, but his hold was too strong, and she was forced to remain where she was. "I'm your *son*."

A smirk appeared on Ursalyn's face, one that was far too familiar for comfort. Instinctively, Ciaran tensed for a moment before taking another step closer to his mother, her wrist still firmly trapped in his grasp.

She responded in the like, stepping nearer with a vicious glint in her eyes before hissing, "I'm your *queen* and I *demand* that you let go."

Ciaran's grip didn't loosen. "Right now, you're only my *mother*," he contended before releasing her arm. "Now, please, tell me what's happened."

"Your brother wouldn't step so far out of line," Ursalyn rebuked. She held her wrist against her chest; her other hand trailed over the barely bruised flesh. "He would never treat me so horridly."

Ciaran huffed, rolling his eyes. "Of course not. Not your *precious* Hollyn."

This time, he didn't see it coming and couldn't react in time. Ursalyn's hand struck out with such force that Ciaran's head snapped to the side when her palm came crashing upon his cheek like lightning splitting the earth.

"How dare you. How *dare* you!" screamed the queen.

Ciaran felt his skin prickle and burn; he inhaled a sharp breath and tried to suppress the anger that was seizing every fiber of his person and taking hold slowly, tightly coiling in his muscles. "You hit me."

"Well spotted," the queen drawled with a roll of the eyes. "I should hit you again and knock the insolence right out of you."

Ciaran straightened. "What have I done? What have I *ever* done to so anger you, Mother?" The prince's voice was almost pleadingly desperate. "What have I done to make you *hate* me?"

Ursalyn reached out, her movements almost painfully slow this time, and took her son's chin into her talon-like grasp, pulling him forward. Her eyes roved over him, inspecting every fault they fell upon and assessing the overall damage of his existence. "You're a vain, foolish, little boy. That's what you are, you know? You're a little boy who oversteps his place and demands answers from those above him."

Ciaran jerked out of her clutches. He snapped, "I'm not a little boy, Mother. I am the prince – the *crown* prince – and I will be *king* one day, you know. You are *my inferior*, Mother. You would do best to remember that."

"And what a fine king you'll be, won't you? One who has to protest so much that he is the rightful ruler need not rule at all, if you ask me."

"It isn't up to you, is it?" he whispered, eyes narrowing. "No. No, it's not up to you if I rule or not." He stepped away from her but was snatched by the arm and hauled back. Ciaran watched with an amused air, knowing full well at any moment he could break out of her hold. "I'll be king, no matter what you think of me. You can go on hating me; it doesn't really matter."

"You're vicious, you know," Ursalyn surmised dully.

Ciaran shrugged. "Like mother, like son, eh?"

With that, Ciaran left. He swept from Ursalyn's presence and left the queen standing alone in her chambers, trapped in the oppressive silence of her isolation as the door closed with a bang at the prince's heels.

A soft knock sounded at a door far removed from the queen's apartments. Fiona looked up from the book she'd been skimming. She sighed. "I don't believe I gave you permission to come in."

There, in the doorway, Ciaran stood with a petulant expression. His voice lacked its usual humor. "I didn't think you'd mind if I came in. You were expecting me, after all."

"You've got a distraction thought up and ready, then?"

He nodded as he stepped into the room, casting a quick glance around and inspecting the chambers. "The servants seem to be doing a good job keeping your chambers tidy," he commented as he took a seat in the vanity's chair.

Fiona gently set her book down. "No." The grace with which she pulled herself from the bed and came to stand just a few steps from Ciaran was quite astounding.

The action was made even more astonishing when, Ciaran thought back, one remembered that she was related to the maladroit, black-haired prince.

She said simply, "I cleaned everything myself."

Ciaran leaned back in his seat, studying Fiona with an astute stare as she made her way to the windowsill where she stopped and looked away from him, her attention somewhere far from their conversation and the castle entirely.

"Why?" he asked curiously.

It was funny, she thought, that the capital could be as silent as the depths of the sea at night, but almost deafening when day broke. It was quite nearly mid-day and even from her perch in the tower, she could see the unmistakable blurs of people rushing about far below them. There were so many colors that shone in the golden sunlight of the summer that she hadn't seen during the twilight hours. She smiled weakly. The princess set her palm against the thick pane of glass. It was warm to the touch. The colors below in the capital, those that presently bespangled her view, were lovely and interesting. But still, she found herself preferring the view from the night before, when everything was sleepy and quiet.

"I'm perfectly capable of cleaning my own room," Fiona answered distractedly.

"I don't think you understand how this *princess* thing works." Ciaran laughed as he jumped from his seat. "You don't *have* to be cleaning, you know! That's what the servants are here for."

Fiona traced her hand along the glass of the pane. It was smooth beneath her touch. Her eyes followed along, trailing in the invisible wake of her roaming hand. "Being a princess doesn't mean people need to clean for me and pick up after me. There's no reason I can't do it myself." Her voice was like a dirge. "I think you confuse your station," she added coolly. "You act entitled to the servitude of others but don't give a thought to the responsibility inherit to your position." She looked back at Ciaran who, she noted, looked annoyed by her musings. "Simply put, cousin, you *want*, but you don't understand what you need to *give*."

Ciaran clapped his hands over his hips. A haughty look of irritation marred his easy-going features. "And *what* is it I'm supposed to be *giving*?"

Fiona shook her head and sighed. She pulled herself from the windowsill and headed for the door. "Never mind. Are you coming?"

"You didn't answer my question," argued Ciaran.

The look in Fiona's eyes was pitying and pained, and her voice sounded deadened and flat. "I don't have to."

She left without another glance back.

It wasn't long before Ciaran decided to peel himself from his place and trot after Fiona, quickly catching up to her and falling into stride at her side. "I'm sorry," he offered.

"For what?" She didn't spare him a glance.

Nervously, the young man ran his hand through his hair. "I shouldn't have tried to pick a fight with you." He laughed an empty laugh. "If you want to clean up your chambers yourself, by all means."

"The entire point of the conversation was lost on you," mumbled the princess under her breath. A few moments passed in an uncomfortable silence, a heavy sort of silence that weighed on both young royals. Fiona relented and looked up at Ciaran, barking, "Do you want to know something?"

"Enlighten me."

"Fynneas catches on quicker than you. Do you know that? He's only twelve and he gets more than you do! You...you just go on doing whatever you want and expect that everyone's going to give you a pat on the back and tell you how brilliant you are." She looked away from Ciaran and averted her gaze to her feet, watching as she stepped over cracks and dips in the stones below. "It's sad really. You *are* going to be king one day. You should think about that more, you know?"

"You're the second person to mention my impending *king*dom." Ciaran scowled.

"Have you thought about it?"

"About what?"

There was no more malice or irritation welling up inside Fiona. Rather, she felt dulled to everything and tired—terribly, terribly tired. "Being king."

"I've thought about it every day since I can remember," Ciaran admitted softly.

"And?"

The numbing effect this conversation usually took on him began to crop up, rearing its emotionally disfiguring head and lancing him through the chest, spearing at his lungs so fiercely he scarcely believed he could go on breathing for another moment. Yet, despite the suffocating feeling of his lungs being impaled and filling up, choking him until he could barely remember what air was, Ciaran's face remained utterly impassive. His eyes, for only a moment, lost all their familiar sparkle and seemed achingly hollow. But it was only for an instant and soon, within the blink of an eye and barely perceptible if you didn't know what to look for, the boyish glint returned.

"To be honest," he started off with a weak smirk, "I don't really *want* to be king."

"It doesn't matter."

"I know."

"So, you should stop bemoaning your position and start thinking about it." The woeful dullness that had stained Fiona's voice was gone and replaced by a crisp assuredness when she spoke. "You haven't a choice in the matter. Why not think about what kind of king you want to be? What do you want to do when you have the crown?"

"I suppose I should give it more thought," relented the prince.

Fiona smiled, feeling the palpability of tension rising within every moment they lingered on this matter, she chose to change course. "So, what's this distraction you've planned?"

"Well—"

Ciaran was interrupted when Sir Jaeryn came bounding from the stairwell. Both he and Fiona stopped the moment they saw the familiar, blonde-haired knight.

He took his place before them with a bow of the head. "Prince Ciaran, Princess Fiona," he greeted dutifully.

"Jaeryn," acknowledged Ciaran.

The knight straightened, his attention at once settling on Fiona. He quirked a brow and quickly spared the prince a glance before refocusing on the princess.

She smiled, wordlessly answering his unasked question. Noting that the knight still looked unsure as to if he should proceed, Fiona prompted, "Go on. If it has to do with what I think it does, Ciaran knows."

"I've spent the last few days looking into this mysterious *Lot* fellow you and your brother asked about." There was a distinctly jittery quality to Jaeryn's voice. "There are no records of any *Lots* in the capital. As you're probably already aware, Lot is not a noble house. I looked into the records for the capital; anyone who owns a shop—well, a proper shop and not a street cart or something—they're on record. The young prince mentioned that this *Lot* man said his father had passed the bookshop along to him. If that *was* the case, there would definitely be records of it." Jaeryn shook his head, a thoughtful look in his warm eyes. "But there are no records of it.

You see, Your Graces, the strange thing is, there's no record of any Lots owning any shops in the middle quarter of the capital…or *any* part of the capital for the matter. What's more, there are no records of any bookshop being there at all."

Fiona frowned. "But we *know* it was there. You and I both saw it."

The knight nodded agreeably. "I know, princess. So, I looked into it some more. But that's where everything seems to get stranger. There are no records of *any* shop ever being there."

"Well, it didn't just come out of nowhere," argued Ciaran.

"No, sire. But I don't have any other explanations for you…either of you. There are *no* records of a bookshop and there are no mentions *anywhere* of any *Lots* in the city," summarized the knight confidently. "I found it odd myself," he admitted. "So, I looked everywhere I could think for any records or ledgers, but I found *nothing*."

"Curious," mumbled Fiona thoughtfully.

Ciaran poised to interject a snide remark when a loud thundering rocketed through the castle walls. All three stood straighter at the sound, looking desperately for the cause. Fiona's eyes widened in horror when she saw, through the small, angular windows lining the corridor, the blackest smoke she'd ever seen, billowing around the glass, licking at it hungrily as the heat seeped through the panes. Instinctively, she backed away until her shoulders collided against Ciaran. In an instant, embers began crackling from the smoke. The glass broke, falling dangerously to the floor around them.

At once, Jaeryn leapt into action and took hold of Ciaran and Fiona, pulling them along the hall and leading them to the stairwell. He pushed Ciaran, who held tightly to Fiona, toward the stairs. "Go! You have to get out of the castle."

The prince nodded crisply as he proceeded to descend the stairs. He was nearly knocked over when Fiona wriggled from his hold, violently thrashing away from his arms.

She yelled, "I have to get to Fynn! We can't just leave him."

Ciaran snatched hold of Fiona's wrist and hauled her down the stairs. "Jaeryn! Jaeryn make sure Fynn, Hollyn, and James make it out of the castle! I've got the princess."

The knight bolted down the corridor. He ran, undeterred by the shaking in his legs. He saw thick clouds of smoke gathering. Hopeful that the castle may remain standing—at least during his madcap search for the young princes—Jaeryn hurried along.

The first room he came to was James's. Jaeryn burst through the door and allowed a relieved grin to spread across his face when he spied both James and Hollyn huddled together in the corner, terror streaking their expressions.

Hollyn's eyes went alight at the sight of the knight and he sprung to his feet in an instant and rushed to him. Jaeryn settled his hand upon the boy's shoulder firmly, holding him close at his side. His attention shifted to James, who remained curled in the corner, trembling.

"My lord," beckoned Jaeryn as calmly as he could. "We have to go."

James shook his head and screwed his eyes closed tightly.

"We don't have time, my lord. Please," encouraged the knight.

Hollyn frowned and stole from the knight's side, taking hold of James's arm almost painfully. He hauled the other boy to his feet. "Let's go," urged the prince.

The boys made their way to Jaeryn's side and looked up at the man expectantly. The knight peered around the threshold and looked into the corridor in either direction, noting the left was beginning to fill with smoke.

"Take my hand," Jaeryn commanded.

Hollyn latched onto the proffered hand without protest.

Jaeryn asserted, "We have to find Prince Fynneas. Hopefully he's in his room."

The trio took off down the hall, the heat biting at their heels. Some of the tower wall fell in upon itself, letting the heat from the fires below reach in like warm, golden claws hungry to rake against all they could touch. The smoke persisted and crawled into the partially exposed corridors. It was harsh and thick, and it was all too soon before the trio were coughing and hissing, eyes reddening.

James fell to the ground, clutching his chest and hacking nastily. Hollyn whirled around and kneeled over his cousin, his arms outstretched in an awaiting embrace. James fell against him in a heap.

Hollyn closed his arms around James tightly and held him close. "James, we have to keep going."

James shook his head. His shoulders shook with every pained gulp of air he pulled in.

Hollyn felt warm tears dampening the collar of his shirt.

"I'm scared," James whispered.

Hollyn's hold tightened. "I know." Slowly, he admitted, "I am too." He stood, taking James with him so they came to stand toe to toe. "But we have to keep going."

James nodded weakly, huddling himself against Hollyn like a crutch.

They proceeded to keep on down the long hall. Hollyn grew increasingly concerned by the rattling sound of James's breathing. The young prince pulled his shirt from his slender person and bundled it, handing it to James. "Cover your nose and mouth with this. It may help to keep the smoke out."

The younger of the two did as he was told, quietly asking, "What about you?"

"Don't worry about me."

The smoke was thickening in the corridor, oppressive in its darkness. Jaeryn, though his eyes were bleary and stinging, could see the silhouettes of the boys amongst the darkness. He took hold of them once more, careful to keep them close by.

"Fynn's room is still a long way off. We won't make it there," Hollyn pointed out. There was no sharpness to his voice, but more a pragmatic sensibility born from the ever-present threat of James collapsing from smoke inhalation.

Jaeryn's eyes darted around, frantic in their search for a way out. "There's a stairwell not far down the hall." He coughed deeply. "If you go down, you'll make it to the throne room in no time at all if you keep going and don't stop."

"You're not coming with us?" asked Hollyn.

"You go. Take James with you. Finding your way out of the castle after you get to the throne room should be easy." Jaeryn coughed again. "I'll go and find Prince Fynneas."

The knight watched from the hall as the two boys descended into the darkness down the curling stairs. He remained there, unflinching in his commitment, until he could no longer see their forms amidst the smoke. Once they had disappeared into the shadows completely, Jaeryn spun on his heel deftly and proceeded on towards Fynn's room.

Without the two boys slowing him down, he made it to the entrance of the private chambers quickly and with little difficulty. He charged through the door, horrified to find that the room was nearly filled with smoke. Screaming into the inky darkness of the smoke-filled chambers, he called, "Prince Fynneas! Are you here?"

"Jaeryn!" a small, disembodied voice called. "Jaeryn, help!"

The knight waded into the waves of smoke without a second thought. "Keep talking, sire! Where are you?"

"Here!" Fynn squeaked. "Here! Jaeryn, help!"

The boy's voice was panicked, as though he were on the cusp of shedding tears.

Jaeryn found Fynn near the corner of his chambers, the wardrobe having fallen onto his right leg. He was pinned to the ground. The knight was alarmed by the nearly vacant look in the child's eyes. Jaeryn knelt beside Fynn, taking the prince's head into his lap and brushing the black hair from his face.

"Prince Fynneas?" Jaeryn kept his voice gentle. "I'm here."

"Jaeryn," croaked the boy as he coughed. Silvery streams of tears rolled down his cheeks. He bit down on his bottom lip, trying valiantly to stop himself from crying. "My leg hurts," he whimpered pitifully.

Indeed, the boy's leg looked a sight. Through the darkness, Jaeryn could make out the tell-tale scarlet of blood. Red stained the boy's trousers just above his knee, peeking out from the heavy wood of the wardrobe.

"Shit," muttered Jaeryn. He brushed his hand soothingly through Fynn's hair. "Shit. This isn't good." He looked down to see that Fynn's un-seeing eyes were now closed and his breathing had slowed. Seized by fear, Jaeryn shook the boy's shoulders. "Fynneas! Fynneas, you have to wake up."

The boy's eyelashes fluttered before he blinked his eyes open. Expecting to see the familiar grey eyes looking up at him, the knight was startled by the flicker of red that tinged the prince's irises for a moment. Jaeryn's breath hitched in his chest at the sight.

"I'm tired," the boy whispered groggily. He blinked his eyes, unseeing.

Jaeryn let out a shaky breath of relief when the paleness of Fynn's eyes returned to their rightful place, the red gone as quickly as it had seemed to appear. The knight leaned over the child more, curling around him like a shield. He continued to run his hand through the black hair. "I know, but we have to go." He gave the boy another shake when he saw Fynn's eyes drifting closed again. "I'm going to get the wardrobe off you, alright? Then we're going to get out of here and it'll all be fine."

Fynn nodded weakly.

Jaeryn gently set the boy's head onto the stone floor and stood. He eyed the wardrobe as if it were an enemy in and of itself, pinning the young prince down to the ground, trapping him in the mounting catastrophe all around them. Jaeryn knelt, taking hold of the wardrobe tightly, and levered it off of Fynn's leg. His knees wavered under the weight, but the knight continued and leaned the wardrobe back against the wall. He was breathing heavily, a task made difficult by the smoke all around him. When Jaeryn looked back down at the prone prince, his eyes nearly fell from his skull. There was much more blood than he originally thought. The boy's leg was mangled from where the wood had smashed into it. A deep gash, down to the very bone, marred the pale flesh exposed by the torn trousers. Jaeryn fought back the nausea encroaching at the sight.

"That's *really* not good," groused the knight. "Prince Fynneas, are you still with me?"

"Yes," Fynn replied, his voice barely audible above the crackling of embers and swirling of smoke.

"Alright, we're going to go now. Ready?"

Jaeryn reached down and pulled the prince into his arms. He settled Fynn against his chest, holding him tightly. His mind was steadied by the feel of the gentle breath brushing against his throat. Conversely, his stomach lurched and knotted at the feel of warm, thick blood spilling over his arm. Steeling himself, Jaeryn tore from the chambers and staggered down the hall. Another thunderous clap was heard. The castle seemed as though it trembled. Peeking over his shoulder, the knight was horrified to see flames scratching at the walls and bursting embers blinking all around.

A last roar sounded and shook the castle, throwing Jaeryn to the ground. Fynn fell from his arms and rolled away from the knight as he collided with the ground. Jaeryn's head smashed painfully into the stone, carving the flesh from his skull. Blood flowed freely from the wound, pooling about the motionless man.

Fynn, through his fuzzy vision, could see Jaeryn's still body just a few feet from him. He tried to push himself up, but his body was numb. His arms felt like strings attached to nothing. His leg throbbed dully, nothing more than an ache steadily growing from his knee. His head felt like a boulder, immovable and resolute in its position there upon the floor. Fynn blinked back the tears brimming in his eyes.

"Jaeryn," he whispered hoarsely.

The fire bristled.

Fynn felt its heat warming his back like a flickering blanket laid over him. Embers snapped in and out of focus as he remained staring into the encroaching darkness. The prince's eyes closed and, this time, he hadn't the energy or desire to force them back open. Instead, he fell into the darkness willingly. He could still hear the sound of fire crackling.

The prince felt something wrap around him suddenly. It was something warm and soft. He nestled his cheek against it, reveling in being relieved of the feeling of stone scratching his face. He smelt smoke, but also earth and spice. It was a pleasant scent. Fynn's eyes fluttered, but they didn't open. He could feel someone holding him. He felt the rise and fall of a strong chest against him; but he didn't feel the metal plating of armor Jaeryn had worn. Instead, he felt more softness. He heard a deep voice speaking to him, but he couldn't make out the words. Instead of trying to understand, Fynn contented himself with being lulled by the lowness of the voice, the melodic purr of the words. He smiled at the sound of a heart steadily thudding beneath his cheek.

And then everything was quiet and still.

4

LITTLE LION

Warm softness brushed against his forehead. Lips. Fynn opened his eyes and saw a woman with white hair leaning over him. Her eyes were gentle and there was something peculiarly familiar about them.

She leaned back, rose to her full height, and watched with a smile as Fynn awoke and sat up in bed. She ran her hand through his hair gently. "How are you feeling?"

Fynn recalled the pain he'd felt when the wardrobe fell on his leg. He was sure the bone had been broken. He remembered how his head hurt, how his eyes stung, how his throat felt raw. He recollected the numbness when Jaeryn had dropped him to the ground. The heat from the fire lingered for a moment as if it were still nipping at him, but it was gone just as quickly. He examined his hands. There wasn't a mark on him—no soot, no ash, no cuts or burns. He reached down to the blanket and drew it away from his lower body, revealing his legs perfectly intact. The whiteness of his shins mingled with the whiteness of the blankets and sheets.

The prince looked back to the woman at his bedside. "Did it really happen? The fire, I mean."

Solemnly, she nodded.

"How come," he whispered, looking back at his leg, "there isn't a mark on me? I was sure...I was sure my leg was broken."

The woman kneeled. A long-fingered hand reached out and ran the length of Fynn's leg from hip to ankle, her touch as firm as a ghost's. Her smile faded and her eyes seemed sad, but her voice remained even as she spoke, "You'll see."

Fynn narrowed his eyes at the cryptic response but chose to not continue with that line of questions. Redirecting, he inquired, "Is everyone alright?"

The woman's fingers traced little circles over Fynn's ankle. She absently replied, "No."

The prince's stomach knotted, and he felt as though he might be sick. "Are Fiona and my father alright? They're not hurt...right?"

"They're fine," she answered.

"Are they here? Can I see them?"

The woman stood once more and peered down at the boy through long, white lashes. He looked so small amongst the thick, white blankets. "No one else is here, Fynn."

"Where *is* here, exactly?"

"Smart boy," clucked the woman. She offered her hand to him. "Come with me, won't you?"

The prince eyed her for a moment, suspicion abounding. His curiosity warred for dominance. Hesitantly, he took her hand in his. She pulled him from the bed. Fynn stood at her side, hardly coming up further than her elbows. She seemed quite tall for a woman; at least, taller than any woman he'd ever met. It was only then, once he was standing, that he peered around the room. It seemed strangely white. The stone walls and floor were white; thick, white rugs lined the room, white blankets covered the bed, and there was a white door at the far end. Fynn looked down to see he, himself, was dressed in all white. He quirked a brow curiously.

"Who are you?" the prince asked.

"I didn't expect you to recognize me. You were so little then. But, alas, it hurts all the same that you don't know." She sighed.

"We've met?"

Once they were through the door she stopped and turned to face him. She knelt on bended knee. She cupped the boy's cheek in her hand; her thumb brushed along the angles of his face softly. "Don't I look familiar?"

Fynn studied the woman's features intently, searching her face for some semblance of recognition. Then he saw it in the shape of her eyes, the incline of her nose, the arch of her brows, the curve of her cheeks. "Mother?"

She pressed a kiss to Fynn's forehead as she had done before.

"I've missed you," she whispered. Her long fingers raked through his hair as she pulled him close to her. "You've grown so much."

Fynn relaxed against her, feeling all the tension and unease flee from his body as lightness overcame him. She held him gently, but he felt secure there in her arms, nevertheless. He nestled into her shoulder. Hot tears sprang into his eyes. "How can you be here?"

"I need to show you something," she answered softly.

They pulled apart, each reluctant to do so. She took the boy's hand in hers and began leading him down what seemed to be an endless, white hallway. They stopped before a red door. There was a weightiness around them all of a sudden, an oppressive pressure that clawed at Fynn relentlessly. He shifted from foot to foot.

"Look in there," the woman instructed.

Fynn pushed the door open, revealing a small chamber inside. Unlike everything else he had seen so far; it was not white. The stone walls were warm, earthy tones. There were torches alight here and there; their warm glow leaked over the room. He stepped into the small chamber. There were two bodies beneath white shrouds laid out on the ground. Fynn glanced back at his mother questioningly. She nodded.

The boy reached down and pulled the shroud from one of the bodies. He gasped. "Aunt Gemma?" He knelt at her side and shook her by the shoulders. "Aunt Gem? Wake up. Wake up!" Tears were streaking down his cheeks as he continued to frantically shake the woman. He didn't feel the pang of loss he would have had it been his father or sister, but to see anyone lying there motionless like that was just too much for him. Hysteria overtook Fynn as he began trembling uncontrollably. Gemma was there at his feet, motionless. The left side of her face looked like a candle that had begun melting to the wick, the skin sickly red and peeling from her face.

The boy doubled over and retched painfully. He screwed his eyes shut. "Wake up, please," he pleaded as he beat his small fists against the ground.

His eyes snapped open at once as he remembered the second body in the room. Shakily he climbed back to his feet and stalked over to it. Apprehension arrested him presently, but he knew he had to look and see who was there, resting beneath the shroud. He pulled the covering aside, revealing his grandmother. She was not disfigured by the fire as Gemma had been. Rather, she looked as though she were simply sleeping. There was a restful look about her features and ease there in her form that spoke of a woman who hadn't suffered before death. Nevertheless, Fynn fell to his knees. He reached out to her; his fingertips traced the lines of her jaw and then down her neck. She felt very cold.

"Gran?" His voice came out as barely more than a whisper. "Gran… wake up, won't you?"

The stillness was palpable.

"I'm sorry," Fynn lamented. He laid his head down upon her chest. She didn't stir. He felt no heartbeat. "I'm so sorry."

His mother's hand fell over his back and traveled in light circles between his shoulder blades. "She didn't suffer, Fynneas," assured the woman to the nearly inconsolable boy. "The smoke killed her, not the flames."

Fynn found little comfort in those words. He continued to shake, clutching to his grandmother desperately. "Where are we?" he asked again, his words warbling.

He felt a tug at his shoulder and was urged back to his feet. His mother's hand sought his once more and she led him from the room. The red door closed behind them and seemed to fade into white like everything else. They continued along down the hall until they came upon another door. This door was black—the blackest black Fynn had ever seen.

The prince asked, "What's through here?"

The woman's hold on her son's hand tightened. "*You* are."

Utterly baffled by her explanation, Fynn pushed open the door. It was a room quite similar to the last—stone walls and a stone floor. There were torches burning brightly, casting great sheets of yellow and red over the room. A bed was set in the corner. It was small. A chair was at the bedside, currently occupied by a man Fynn didn't recognize. The boy stepped into the room and crept up to the bed, curious as to who was there. He recoiled with fright when he saw that he was looking down at himself.

Fynn jumped back and turned toward his mother. "What is this? I don't understand. How can I be here and there?"

His mother was at his side within a moment. But she wasn't looking at him. Her attention was fixed on the prince in the bed. Fynn looked back; a sinking feeling swelled in the pit of his stomach. There he was lying in bed, unconscious. There was a wet rag resting on his forehead. His features shone with sweat in the firelight. There were bruises on his cheeks, his shoulders. His arms were stretched at his sides, uncovered by the thick blankets hefted upon him. There were scratches and scrapes over his knuckles, his wrists were bruised nastily; there were burns on his palms that looked as though they had been tended to with a salve. Fynn's gaze traveled downward until he saw what he was looking for. Where his right leg would be resting beneath the blankets, he saw red speckles.

"That's really me, isn't it?" Fynn cast a curious look at his mother who nodded wordlessly. "Am I dead?"

She shook her head. "No."

Fynn looked away from the sickly version of himself in the bed and steadied his gaze upon the man at his bedside. He had expected his father to be there, but this man was too tall to be Felix. Fynn studied him. The man sat with his back perfectly straight, which looked to be rather uncomfortable given the wooden nature of the chair he occupied. He wore all black, from his boots to his high-collared shirt. The green embroidery at the collar of his leather jerkin was the only color he sported. His black hair was slicked back neatly. His eyes were what really caught Fynn's attention. The man's eyes were a vibrant, catlike green.

"Do you know him?" asked Fynn, still staring at the man in the chair.

"Moriah."

"Moriah? Fiona told me she met a man named Moriah at the castle," Fynn commented. "She said he's friends with Gran."

The woman nodded. "He *was*."

Fynn looked away from Moriah and back to his mother. "Why do you suppose he's here?"

"He was the one who pulled you out of the fire."

The boy lowered his head solemnly. "Why isn't my father here?"

"I'd wager he's busy in the wake of all that has happened."

Fynn stole his mother's hand into his. He held onto her with all his strength, as if she was going to slip away. "Will I die then?"

"No."

"How can you be sure?" he rasped. Fynn leaned his forehead into his mother's side, shoulders slumping. He began to cry. "I'm going to die!"

"I *promise* you."

Fynn looked up.

She wasn't facing him, wasn't even looking at him in her periphery. Her attention remained resolutely fixed to the wounded boy in the bed. "It's going to hurt when you wake up."

"Bad?"

She nodded. "Very bad."

"Can you make it go away?"

She shook her head. "Pain is how you know you're alive."

Fynn's shoulders hung weakly, defeated. "When can I go back?"

His mother reached out and tapped the bed with her hand sharply. "Sit."

Fynn jumped up on the bed and settled himself before looking up at his mother again. Her eyes were sad looking, but her expression remained blank and unreadable.

"Close your eyes," she instructed.

He did as he was told and sat there, expectantly. There was a long span of time where they remained that way, comfortable in the silence.

Then, she pressed a kiss to his forehead one last time and whispered, "Open your eyes."

When Fynn's eyes blinked open, he found himself lying on his back, buried beneath multiple blankets. All at once his body was assaulted by violent lances of pain darting up from his leg and a sharp throb in his temples. He winced and tried to curl away from the pain, only to find his whole body weaker than he could ever imagine. There was no way he could even conceive of moving so much as an inch.

Moriah stood from his chair and leaned over the bed. He plucked the damp cloth from Fynn's forehead and tossed it aside. He smoothed the wet locks from the boy's face. "How are you feeling?"

Fynn wanted to tell the man that, that was possibly the most asinine question he had ever been asked, but he didn't have the strength. His head felt heavy and his vision was blurry. He could hardly make out the green of Moriah's eyes. "Cold."

Moriah gave a curt nod before securing the blankets tightly around Fynn's body. He pulled them up to the boy's chin, tucking his previously exposed arms under as well. "I'll be right back."

Fynn could only nod silently in acquiescence as he watched Moriah slip from the room. Alone, the boy let himself relax into the warm embrace of the blankets, eager to ignore the unrelenting stabs of pain. He tried to breathe deeply and slowly; he focused on the rise and fall of his own slight chest. Time seemed to pass at a crawl and what had been assured to be 'right back' was, in fact, taking an eternity. Or so it felt to the boy suffering in the bed.

By the time Fynn thought he would give into the madness induced by the pain and silence, Felix burst into the room and bound over to his son's bedside. He collapsed on his knees. His hands gently ran over Fynn's face, brushing the hair away from his eyes.

He grinned stupidly, eyes welling with tears. "You're awake!" Felix gasped, as if not quite believing it. "You're finally awake."

"Finally?" rasped Fynn.

Felix continued brushing his hand through his son's sweaty hair. The other hand busied itself by smoothing nonexistent wrinkles from the blankets covering the child. "Yes, yes, you've been in bed for days." He shook his head and stammered, "We didn't know...if you would...would ever wake up."

Apparently, what had felt like only minutes in the white place with his mother was, in fact, days there in the realm of reality. The very thought struck Fynn as odd. His brow furrowed as he contemplated the possibility of time being warped in such a way.

"Is something wrong?" asked Felix, noting his son's expression. "Are you in pain? Feeling ill?"

"Hurts," mumbled Fynn quickly. His mind was still far off and he didn't feel much like talking. But he couldn't dismiss his father, in the state that he was—it would be cruel. He sighed. "Cold."

Felix nodded dutifully. "Moriah said as much. I'll have him gather some more blankets for you. We'll do our best to keep you snug." Tears fell from his blue eyes and streaked down his cheeks. "I'm glad you're awake...here with us."

Fynn blinked rapidly, trying to will the blurriness from his vision. He regarded his father and suddenly an epiphany dawned. The man looked truly haggard. Fynn frowned. He had never seen his father look so worn and tired. Dark circles bruised beneath Felix's eyes and his hair was an absolute mess—more so than usual. Fynn did his best to smile. "Me too."

The days proceeded on with little entertainment to be had for the prince who found himself confined to his bed. He saw his sister now and then in the mornings and just before he went to bed for the night. His father would pop in when he could. The king, so Fynn had been told, had ordered Felix to remain at his side since the incident at the castle. There was much to do, relayed Fiona during one of her visits. Everyone seemed to be in a frenzy, fraught with unspoken panic and looking more and more ragged as time went on. Fiona had been the one to tell him of Gemma and Elsinora's deaths; her tone had been melancholy but not exactly overcome by emotion, simply factual and saddened. Jaeryn, he had been told, also perished in the fire. Fynn saw little of anyone else and found himself bored senseless, maddened by the silence and tedium of bed rest.

On the fifth day of Fynn's sick-room imprisonment, a young boy swung the door open and stood there, in the threshold, observing the prince curiously. He was the same age as the royal laid up in bed, but of a slightly taller build. His hair was a bright red, shorn close at the sides and curling atop his head in elegant twists. His eyes were a stunning blue that arrested Fynn's attention immediately.

"Hello," greeted Fynn curiously. "Morning. Or, is it not morning anymore? Hard to tell, really."

"It is." The boy came inside, closing the door behind him gently. He sat in the chair that Moriah had once occupied. "Good morning, Prince Fynneas." He reached out and offered his hand to the young royal, casually smiling. "I'm Godryk. It's nice to meet you finally."

"Finally?" asked Fynn as he clasped the boy's hand in his own.

Godryk nodded. "Yes. You've been here for a while, but everyone said you were too tired to have any visitors...other than your father and sister, I mean."

"Oh," sighed the prince, settling back against the assortment of pillows that lined his headboard like the ornate embellishments of a leisurely throne.

"Your father and the king have gone back to the capital to see to the repairs of the castle," explained Godryk. He made himself comfortable in the wooden chair. "They should be back in a few days."

For a moment, Fynn was confused by the statement given so matter-of-factly, but he recalled distantly, on his first morning of being wake, that Fiona had mentioned they had left the capital. For the life of him, as he searched his memories, he couldn't recall where she said they had relocated to. Fynn laughed darkly. "I don't mean to sound daft, but...where are we?"

Godryk straightened up. He cocked his head to the side like a dog listening to a command. He remained silent for a moment before chirping, "Oh! You probably don't remember, what with all the tonics and concoctions they've been pouring down your throat. You're here at my family's castle, Claw Keep near Lion's Bay." He smiled warmly. "We're honored to have you here!" he added hastily. "Are you feeling alright this morning?"

Fynn took the time to take stock of himself. He raised his hands, inspecting his knuckles and noting that the once torn flesh seemed to be perfectly fine now. Flipping his hands over, he surveyed his palms and saw that the burns were healed. Lastly, he reached down and pulled the blankets from his lower half and inspected his leg. He saw linens wrapped tightly about his right leg just under his knee, but he didn't feel any pain. He arched a brow at the odd sensation of feeling absolutely fine, given the ordeal he'd been dragged through. "Great, actually." Fynn smiled.

Godryk's attention was riveted to the exposed leg. He had heard everyone talking about how ghastly an injury Fynn had sustained and had listened with rapt trepidation as they discussed the likelihood of the young royal being unable to attend Morancy at the end of the summer. But, as he looked on at the linen clad leg before him, he didn't see what all the fuss had been about. "Doesn't look bad," he commented.

Fynn shrugged. "Looks fine, really." He turned to face Godryk; a toothy grin spread across his features. "Do you think you can help me get out of bed?"

The red-haired boy looked shocked. He went astoundingly still. "I… don't think that would be a good idea."

Fynn pouted. "Why ever not? I feel fine. My leg doesn't hurt, *really*!"

Godryk sighed. "Well, everyone keeps talking about how you won't be able to go to Morancy with your leg as it is and all."

"You're acting as if I'm a cripple," whined the prince. He fell back against his pillows again, nestling in their fluffiness as he crossed his arms over his chest petulantly. "Everyone's acting as if I'm a toddler!"

Godryk laughed. "I'm sure they're not." He eyed the bandaged leg once more. "It really doesn't hurt?"

Fynn shook his head. "Not at all."

The prince sat up straight and reached down to his leg, carefully peeling away the bandages. Godryk jumped to his feet, mouth agape. "You shouldn't do that!"

Fynn smiled a lopsided smile as he continued peeling the linens away. "It's *my* leg, you know." Layer by layer he stripped the bandages from his spindly leg until he revealed the pale, white flesh beneath. All that remained of the nasty gash that had cut down to the bone was a pink scar that stretched from his knee and twisted across his shin like a jagged crescent moon.

"Looks alright to me," Fynn assessed as he traced along the scar with his index finger. "Tingles a bit but doesn't hurt."

Godryk's eyes had gone wide at the sight of the scar. "Whoa."

Fynn laughed at the look on the other's face. "So, will you help me up?"

"Where do you want to go?"

Fynn shrugged. "What's there to do around here?"

"Your cousins have been out in the gardens these last few days. The weather's been nice, so it's been a comfortable place to relax."

The prince felt all the excitement flutter out of him as he thought of Hollyn and James. He deflated. "I should probably see them at some point," Fynn muttered. "How are they? I haven't heard much about anyone…other than Gran and Aunt Gem, you know."

"James was sick for a few days. He just got out of bed three days ago. But, honestly, he still looks awful," replied Godryk. He continued, his tone souring, "Hollyn...*Prince* Hollyn, he's well...Hollyn."

"Not your favorite, then?" snorted Fynn.

"It's not that—"

Fynn interrupted Godryk with the good-natured assurance, "He's not mine either."

The prince pushed himself up and swung his good leg over the edge of the bed; he gently moved the right one in its wake.

Godryk reached out his hand. "Let me help you, if you insist on getting out of bed."

Fynn took Godryk's hand firmly with a laugh. "I insist!"

Gently, Godryk helped ease Fynn to his feet. The prince leaned on the young lord as he tested out his leg's tolerance. He started with just touching his toes to the ground. Feeling no pain at that, he settled more and more weight onto his right foot until he was able to stand fully upright and unassisted. Fynn beamed eagerly. "Looks like I'm good as new."

Godryk marveled at the prince before him, stunned that the boy was able to stand up and bear weight on a leg said to have been broken and mangled beyond reasonable repair. "Remarkable," he awed softly.

Fynn walked around in a small circle experimentally. Feeling as though nothing had ever happened, he proceeded to bounce in place, smiling all the while. "Well, shouldn't be a problem, then!" He spun around on his heel with all the recklessness he usually exhibited and went bounding toward the door. He glanced over his shoulder at the still-stunned Godryk. "Coming?"

Godryk nodded dumbly and followed Fynn into the corridor. "Head down the hall and take a left," instructed the young lord. He took a few large steps to fall into pace with the prince.

"So, where is this Claw Keep?"

"Hmm?"

"In relation to the capital, I mean," added the prince thoughtfully. "North? South?"

"South," provided Godryk. "It's not far at all. Day's ride at the most."

"Do you go the capital often?"

Godryk shook his head. "My father doesn't like me to wander too far from the castle. Honestly, it's astounding that the man's going to let me go to Morancy at summer's end."

Fynn grinned. "So, you'll be a first-year too?"

Godryk nodded. He eyed Fynn nervously. "Do you think with what's happened and all that they'll still let you go?"

"I don't see why not. I'm fine," insisted the prince. He gestured down to his leg. "Look, I'm walking and everything. Not even a limp!"

"Yes, but that scar looked pretty nasty."

"Plenty of knights have scars," argued Fynn.

Godryk huffed. "You're no knight. You're a *prince*."

Fynn rolled his eyes. "Yes, yes. Tell me something I don't already know."

They went down the winding stairs and into another short corridor before arriving in a breezeway. It was a warm day with no clouds in the sky. The air was fresh and crisp. It was quiet and serene for a moment, but it wasn't long before Fynn heard the distant voices of Hollyn and James. He stopped in the breezeway, cocked his head to the side, and listened to the sound of their voices carried on the gentle winds. Fynn sighed deeply before adjusting his course in pursuit of his cousins.

He found the two sitting in the grasses of the courtyard, contentedly munching on thick loaves of buttered bread.

James was the first to see Fynn appear from around one of the perfectly manicured bushes. He eyed him curiously, his blue stare immediately drifted down to Fynn's leg. Hollyn quickly followed suit, eyeing Fynn inquisitively as the other prince and his companion came to stand before them.

"Surprised to see you up," drawled Hollyn as he resumed snacking. He fell back down upon the grass, apparently not feeling the need to remain upright and congenial during the conversation. "Thought they were going to hack that leg of yours off."

James smirked, but his eyes remained humorless. "Guess you'll be keeping the leg," he muttered. "Does it hurt?"

Fynn shook his head. "No."

"You're a weird one, you know?" puffed James. "Only person I know who could get their leg smashed to bits like that and be up and walking about so quickly. Just weird. *Freakish*, really."

Godryk sidled up beside Fynn, offering a form of silent support for the prince who remained wordless for the time being.

Fynn's expression darkened as he stared at Hollyn and James. "How have you two been?" he asked.

James tossed his bread roughly. His eyes were ablaze as he ground out, "Oh, just lovely, thanks." He stalked off without another word.

Hollyn remained reclined on his back. He tossed his bread casually, a languidness to his actions. He didn't bother to look at Fynn. "Fine way to start, Fynneas."

"What's that supposed to mean?"

"Aunt Gem died in the fire," reminded the red-haired prince. "You could maybe show some compassion."

"Oh." Fynn rolled his eyes haughtily. "That's rich, coming from you of all people."

Hollyn rolled up onto his feet and stood. He eyed Fynn with the interest a lazy cat would show a mouse it was considering chasing. "I'm not the one that drove James off, now am I?"

Fynn bit down on his bottom lip, hard, trying to repress any acidic remark that may trip from his tongue.

"Thought not." Hollyn took a few steps until he was standing toe to toe with his cousin. His eyes were sharp, fierce. "Try to stay out of everyone's way."

The red-haired prince made to step past the other, purposefully knocking his shoulder into Fynn's. Hollyn's tactical retreat was abruptly halted, however, when Fynn caught hold of his arm and hauled him back.

"I'm getting really tired of this." Fynn shoved Hollyn. "I don't know what your problem is…why you hate me *so* much. But I've had enough."

Hollyn straightened, making a show of scraping away imagined grime from where Fynn had touched him. "That was stupid of you."

"Oh?" mocked Fynn dangerously. He took a step closer to the other boy.

"Quite," purred Hollyn. "I'm not really in the mood for you right now, so why don't you limp along and go play somewhere else?"

"I'll go wherever I please," Fynn snapped. "You're not the one in charge here, Hollyn."

A careless smirk appeared on Hollyn's face. "Not *yet*, at least." He pushed Fynn back roughly. "Remember that."

Fynn stumbled for a moment before catching himself. "You've no right." He grimaced darkly.

Hollyn squared his shoulders, arrogantly looking down at the hunched Fynn before him. "I've *every* right." He shoved Fynn again and watched as the other fell back onto the grass. "Stay down, Fynneas. It'll be much easier for all of us if you do."

If there was ever a chance that Fynn would stay down, it was completely destroyed by Hollyn's jeer. The black-haired prince was quick to his feet and struck out, his fist like a bolt of lightning streaking between them, colliding painfully with Hollyn's jaw and sending him falling in a heap onto the grass. Fynn loomed over him, panting heavily.

Hollyn reached to cup his afflicted jaw with one hand, eyes shimmering with unshed tears as he narrowed them like a feral cat ready to pounce. "Bastard!" he howled. He struggled back to his feet. "Damned bastard punched me," he muttered, absentmindedly stroking the bruising flesh beneath his touch. "Bad move, Fynneas."

Godryk could only stand in bewildered horror as Hollyn and Fynn exchanged blows, knocking each other down and springing up again. It wasn't too long before they were clawing at one another, rolling over each other on the grass, pinning one another down and smashing knuckles into the other. Blood spilled out of Hollyn's nose like some grotesque red river, bubbling over his lips as he yelled. Fynn's left eye was bruised and a nasty cut streaked over the bridge of his nose. The two boys snatched and clawed and raked and yowled as they went toppling over each other through the grass. Their clothes, once pristine, were coated with dirt and grass stains, some speckling of blood splashed here and there. The whole scene spread out before Godryk was appalling.

Hollyn was astride Fynn. He balled his fists in the others shirt, heaving him upward before forcibly slamming him down into the ground. The air was knocked from Fynn's lungs and he gasped in surprise, choking for a moment. He curled his hands around Hollyn's wrists, prying his cousin from his person and knocking him to the side jerkily. Hollyn was relentless in his attack, unfortunately, and was quick to pin Fynn down again. He forced his weight down on the smaller prince, his left palm pressed firmly into Fynn's chest while his right hand knotted into a fist and went smacking into Fynn's face.

"You just don't get it!" yelled Hollyn as he struck his cousin again. "You think you're being so damn *nice* coming out here, don't you? You don't even care. You didn't even know Aunt Gem and Gran! You just show up and think it's all about you." He struck Fynn again, oblivious to the gurgled sounds of Fynn's breath mingling with the blood pooling in his mouth from his split lip. "My *home* was destroyed. My *home*! You have no idea what it's like. No idea!"

Godryk finally managed to bring himself to move. He caught hold of Hollyn's arm before he could strike again. He threw all his weight into the red-haired prince, knocking him off Fynn. Godryk and Hollyn tumbled to the ground together in a heap of tangled limbs.

The prince thrashed violently and spat out, "How dare you!"

The young lord restrained Hollyn with all his might. He was unable to keep the prince from regaining his balance and leaping back up to his feet; but he was effective in extinguishing Hollyn's momentum. Godryk cast a cursory glance at Fynn, who remained prostrate in the grass, lip bleeding profusely at this point. "That's enough," insisted the young lord. "You've made your point."

Hollyn looked away from Godryk and back at Fynn. He wrinkled his nose and spat on the fallen prince before stalking off, muttering under his breath about what a disgrace Fynn was to the family.

Godryk watched the red-haired prince take his leave before kneeling beside Fynn. "He really knocked the life out of you," he commented wearily. "How're you doing down there?"

Fynn touched his fingertips to his lip and felt the warm blood pooling. "Damn," he grumbled as he rolled onto his side. He worked to push himself up to his hands and knees. His vision was blurry and distorted. Everything seemed to be melting around him. "What's his problem?"

Godryk took hold of Fynn's arm and helped pull him upright. He offered the prince a sad smile. "Everyone's been really touchy since...well, you know."

Long after the sun fell below the horizon and darkness descended upon the castle, when the final whispered conversations behind the stone walls faded, Fynn wasn't able to sleep. He sat perched upon one of the battlements of Claw Keep, looking out at the bay off in the distance. He watched the moon flicker against the water; the reflection of the stars spangled the calm surface by the port. There were ships harbored, rocking gently over small waves. The hour was abnormally cold for a summer night this far south, but the young prince found himself too enthralled with the sights to bother to go in search of something warmer to wear. The silence and scenery, he mused, were preferable to lying in bed, staring at the ceiling in some desperate attempt to fall asleep. Absentmindedly, he rubbed at his eye where a nasty, purple bruise had blossomed.

"Not tired?"

Fynn glanced over his shoulder and saw Moriah standing just behind him looking bored. The prince looked away and back to the ships. "Can't sleep." He heard shuffling behind him but didn't care enough to look back. He laughed when he felt Moriah drop his heavy cloak over his shoulders. "Thanks," Fynn mumbled as he wound the thick material around him, co-cooning himself in the warmth of the garment.

Moriah took a seat beside Fynn, swinging his legs over the edge of the battlements with feline grace. They sat there, sides nearly touching. Moriah looked out at the bay and seemed equally interested in the subtle swaying of the ships. "It's cold. You shouldn't be out here."

"I don't mind the cold, really."

"Godryk told me what happened."

Fynn snorted. "I bet he did."

Moriah arched a brow at the boy's derisive tone but didn't look away from the water. "He's a good boy, Godryk. You should take that into consideration."

Fynn ran his hand through his hair. He sighed resignedly. "I know. I didn't mean to sound…well, I don't know. I just—"

"I know," interrupted Moriah. "It's been a long day."

"You could say that." Fynn scowled.

Finally, Moriah turned to look at the boy at his side. The prince seemed quite tired, expectedly so. The bruise tracing around his eye and grazing his cheekbone was nasty, but it would heal. Moriah reached out and took the boy's chin in his grasp, turning his face so they saw eye to eye. He smirked. "First real fight?"

Fynn didn't try and break away from Moriah but staring into the man's unnatural green eyes was becoming unnerving. He diverted his attention after a moment, glancing down at the stone beneath their dangling legs. "Yes."

"May I offer you some advice?"

Fynn remained silent.

"If you're going to get into a fight with someone, you need to be willing to end the fight." Moriah's voice lowered to a thoughtful whisper. "You have to make every action count. If you're going to strike, do it with enough force so your opponent won't be able to get back up. If they get back up, they're just going to be even madder than they were before you hit them." He smirked. "Trust me." His hand fell from Fynn's face gently.

The prince regarded the man swathed all in black for some time. When he spoke, his voice was shy, but the curiosity glinting in Fynn's icy eyes was hard to miss. "Fi says you know Aunt Ursalyn, that you two are friends?"

Moriah remained quiet, looking out, once more, at the water in the distance.

"How did you meet her?" Fynn persisted.

Those unsettling green eyes swept over the harbor, inspecting every wave that rolled into shore, seemingly absorbed by the reflection of the moon on the water's surface. "I was friends with your father and uncle—sorry, the *king*—as a boy. We went to Morancy together—all of us, Ursalyn too. She was two years below me. I'd seen her around before that too, when we'd come to the mainland for something or other, she was at court, you see, positioned to be queen even as a child, I suppose."

"And Gran? You knew her well too, didn't you?"

Moriah nodded.

"You're from the province, then? In Erza?"

Again, Moriah nodded.

"But you came up to the capital a lot?"

"My father was close to your grandfather. All of us children were together, back then, as a result. It was as though half my life was spent at Batsbeckon." There was a momentary flicker of sadness in Moriah's deep voice, but it was soon replaced with detached indifference as he continued, "But things change, life gets in the way, and we were all born into certain roles—as I'm sure you're aware."

Fynn nodded. "My father says my role is to raise the banners for Ciaran when we're older, to lead armies and all that if the time ever comes for another war."

Moriah smiled sadly as he threw his arm around Fynn's slight shoulders. "You, Fynneas, were born for that and so much more."

"More?" Fynn asked. Moriah's embrace wasn't the sort of emotionally clinging gesture that Felix's was; instead, Moriah's touch acted as an anchor. Where Fynn had felt adrift before the other's arrival, Moriah's arm curled over his shoulders brought him back and he felt stable. Said arm tightened for only a moment as if all too aware of Fynn's thoughts on the matter.

"Can I ask you something else?" the boy softly questioned.

"Yes."

Fynn couldn't bring himself to look at Moriah, thinking himself silly for what he was about to ask. He felt the warmth of a blush creep into his cheeks. "Do you believe in life after death?"

Moriah's body tensed against Fynn's, as if every muscle in the man's long form had gone rigid all at once. He inhaled sharply, almost as if pained. "Why do you ask?"

"I…before I woke up…I had a dream. Only, it wasn't a dream, really…. I don't think. I saw my mother. She's been dead for my whole life. But I saw her, and she spoke to me. She showed me Aunt Gem and Gran. They were in a room and covered by shrouds. Dead from the fire. Then she showed me into another room, and I saw...*you*." Fynn took in a shaking breath, the memory quite vivid in the forefront of his mind. "I saw you sitting at my bedside watching over me. I saw myself just lying there." Tears warmed the corners of his eyes. "It didn't feel like a dream. It felt so *real*."

Moriah's arm snaked away from Fynn's shoulders; his hand reached up and brushed the tears from the boy's face. "Don't cry over it."

Fynn huffed indignantly, swiping at his face, and wiping away the remaining tears. "I think I saw something. I don't know what it was or, rather, *where*. But I think I was really with her, or she was with *me*. I just don't think it was a dream." He turned expectantly toward Moriah, his pale eyes pleading with the other to believe him. "I'm not mad! I'm not. It's just, well...I don't know. *Please*, at least say something!"

The man in black shook his head solemnly. "I think you should get to bed." Moriah swung his legs back over the battlements and stood, waiting. He held out his hand to the boy. "I'll walk you back."

"You think I'm mad," mumbled the prince as he took the proffered hand and was eased down. He hadn't noticed how tall Moriah was until they were standing side by side. Next to this man, Fynn felt utterly weak and insignificant. He pouted. "You probably think I'm just some loon, utterly mad just like Hollyn and James think."

Moriah's hand clapped over Fynn's shoulder as he began to guide the boy along, gently urging him forward. "I don't."

"Then why won't you look at me?"

They stopped. Moriah dragged Fynn back and turned him around until they stood facing each other, their features dimly illuminated in the light of the full moon. Fynn had to crane his neck to see into Moriah's eyes. He was readying a snappish exclamation when he faltered, seeing the darkness encroaching upon the man's expression. The bored look he had seen gracing Moriah's visage before was gone and replaced by one of regret thinly veiled by latent anger.

"How was she? Your mother, I mean, from your dream."

The boy blinked dumbly as if not having heard the question properly before stammering, "Fine...fine. She seemed...*alive* in a way."

The corner of Moriah's lip quirked upward for a moment before falling back into a neutral line. "That's good."

"Did you know her too?"

"A long time ago."

"What was she like?" Fynn asked, poorly contained eagerness bubbling up into his voice.

"You," Moriah whispered. He forced himself to look away from the boy and proceed forward. He reached back and snagged hold of Fynn's arm, pulling the prince along effortlessly.

They continued in silence, winding their way through halls and doors and up the stairs until they rounded a corner, and both jerked backward, narrowly avoiding Fiona.

The princess looked startled, hopping back and dropping the candle she had been using for light in the darkened corridors. "Oh! I didn't see you there." As she collected herself and calmed down, she took note of Fynn standing just behind a once-again-bored looking Moriah. "Fynneas! What're you doing out of bed?"

The boy shrugged. "I couldn't sleep."

Fiona pursed her lips. "That's your excuse for wandering around the castle in the middle of the night?"

Fynn nodded sheepishly.

Fiona looked from Fynn up to Moriah who, presently, found inspecting his nails far more engaging than Fiona's scolding of her brother. "Moriah," she greeted tersely with a curt nod. "You've brought him back for bed, I should think?"

"Princess Fiona," the man in black spoke coolly. "We didn't mean to disturb you."

"Not at all," she mumbled.

"Yes, I was just escorting the prince back to his room. It's late, you see, I didn't want him walking back alone." He took a cursory look about them for effect before adding, "Is there a reason *you're* out of bed at such an hour?"

She narrowed her eyes. "I don't think it's within your bounds to ask such a thing."

Moriah smirked, amusement lighting up his eyes eerily. "Far be it from me, princess, to overstep my place." He gave her an unnecessarily withdrawn bow before turning on his heel and taking leave of the royal siblings.

Fynn watched Moriah's retreating back with interest before turning back to look at his sister. "What *are* you doing out of bed, Fi?"

Fiona shoved her brother back playfully, her nose wrinkling. "Don't you go asking questions too!"

The boy threw his hands up in mock surrender, assuring her, "No, no questions! I was just curious, is all."

5

THE HUNT

"What were you thinking?"

Fynn squirmed in his chair, unable to meet his father's gaze. "I don't know." He bit down on his bottom lip.

"You don't know?" Felix repeated.

Fynn shook his head.

Felix sighed. Every muscle in his body ached and a nasty three-day-old headache was still hammering away at his temples. He pinched the bridge of his nose. "Fynneas, I don't understand. We talked about this." He gestured wildly about the room. "We talked about this, *us*, before we ever got to Batsbeckon. We—you, your sister, and I—have to stay together. Stay strong." He shook his head and closed his eyes. "I know this summer hasn't been the best. I understand that a lot has happened, Fynn. But I need you to pull it together."

"I will," whispered the boy weakly.

Felix suddenly smiled broadly. He slapped his large hand over the boy's shoulder. "Alright, enough of this pouting, then. You agree to behave and we'll have no more talk of this unfortunate little incident with you and Hollyn. Alright?"

The child nodded wordlessly.

Felix pawed through Fynn's hair gently. He tilted the boy's head to the side with an urging twist of the wrist and admired the purple bruise marbling the white flesh around Fynn's eye. He sighed. "Looks like Hollyn got the best of you."

Fynn shrugged. He muttered, "*This* time."

Felix rolled his eyes and laughed. "Right. Save the fighting for Morancy, boy. No more of that while we're here. Agreed?"

"Agreed." Fynn pouted.

Felix stood. He took Fynn's hand in his and pulled the boy to his feet. "Let's say we have a day together?"

For the first time since the two had sequestered themselves off from the rest of the castle's residents for a little fatherly chat, Fynn looked up and beamed happily. "I'd like that."

"I had planned to go out for a hunt with Warwyk today. Are you amenable to that plan? I'm sure I could convince the old codger to bring Godryk along. What do you say?"

Fynn's smile broadened.

"I'll take that as a yes." Felix laughed and ruffled his son's already unkempt hair. He watched, amused, as Fynn went bounding toward the door. He shook his head. "Honestly, I can't believe you're up and about so soon after such an injury. I didn't think you'd be making it to Morancy this year." He gestured at the boy who stood waiting at the door. "But look at you, jumping around like nothing ever happened. Amazing."

Fynn shrugged. "Honestly, it doesn't hurt at all."

Felix pulled open the door and ushered his son into the hall. "Child, you'll never cease to amaze me." He pushed Fynn forward some more and shook his head. "Go on and get dressed. I'll meet you in the courtyard in an hour."

By the time the hour waned and came to an end, the sun was stationed firmly in the sky; the warmth of the late morning was nearly oppressive. Felix was hunched over a short, stone wall that lined the breezeway around the courtyard, dully admiring the gardens. He quirked a brow when Moriah settled next to him. He grinned dumbly as his old friend lingered silently. The prince greeted, "Good morning to you too." Felix chuckled and gently nudged Moriah with his shoulder. "You look tired. Up late, were you?"

Moriah turned his bright, green eyes in Felix's direction. His expression was void of anything resembling emotion, but his eyes shone with amusement, nevertheless. A crooked smirk appeared on his countenance. "I've never been one for mornings," he groused.

Felix straightened to his full height, standing just hardly higher than Moriah's shoulder. He snickered. "Yes. I'm aware." He playfully cuffed Moriah's shoulder and laughed even more when Moriah shrank away as if he'd been burned. "To what do I owe the pleasure of your company at this most *ungodly* hour?"

"Haven't slept."

"At all?" Felix marveled.

Moriah shook his head.

"You think maybe you should go lie down?" Felix lightly inquired, noticing the dark circles coloring Moriah's pale features just below his eyes. "You do look a mess."

"Can't sleep," Moriah grumbled. He inhaled sharply. "Have you got everything sorted out back at the capital?"

Felix snorted. He recognized a change in conversation when he heard one. "Lachlan stayed and sent me back here for the time being. They've already started reconstructing the part of the castle that was damaged. Anything that was important is being relocated to other towers and all that." He returned to leaning against the little wall casually. "They're getting ready for Mother's funeral, and Gem's. There'll be a procession through the capital and all that pomp. I think that's what Lachlan's working on but, honestly, I don't know. He doesn't tell me much. Word of the funerals has been sent to the older houses and some to the lower nobility." Felix laughed mirthlessly. "Houses from the province will be in attendance, as well. It's going to be chaos in the city in a few days."

"How have you been?" Had anyone else asked, their tone may have been laced with a certain degree of concern. But that wasn't the case with Moriah. His voice was nearly cold as he asked after the other.

"As well as can be expected."

"The boy seems to have recovered quickly," commented Moriah. His attention was wholly focused on admiring the garden. He didn't spare Felix even a quick glance.

"He's supposed to be coming down here any moment. We're off for a hunt with the Redmaynes this morning. Care to join, Moriah?"

"I'll stay here."

Felix shrugged and pushed back off the wall. Righting himself almost lazily, he smirked. "Right, of course. Do try and stay out of trouble."

Finally, Moriah turned his attention to Felix. He arched a fine, black brow and grinned a catlike grin. He purred, "Now, where's the fun in that?"

Moriah turned to take his leave when he stopped and watched Fynn round the corner. The boy came springing toward he and Felix, an ear-to-ear smile splitting his face.

Fynn skittered to a halt just before the man in black. "Moriah!" he chirped cheerfully.

Moriah looked from Fynn to Felix. "Is he always this cheerful in the mornings?"

"I usually can't get him up before midday," Felix replied.

The man in black glanced back to Fynn. The boy stood resolutely before him, a curious look in his eyes as he watched the two men converse. "And what, young prince, has you so excited this morning?" asked the lord commander.

"We're off for a hunt with Godryk and his father," explained Fynn, excitement dripping from every word.

"Oh?" prodded Moriah.

Fynn nodded happily. "Yes! We're off soon, aren't we, Father?"

"Yes, in just a moment I suspect," answered Felix. "Moriah, it's unfortunate that you couldn't join us this morning."

Fynn was quick to launch into pleading at the mention of Moriah joining. "Moriah, you should come! Won't you, *please?*"

A scowl wormed its way across Moriah's lips as he soured. He regarded the boy before him, far more energetic than he'd been last they had spoken. The despondency was gone and replaced by hardly contained enthusiasm and lightness. Moriah began, "I—"

Felix interrupted and sarcastically jeered, "Fynneas, if this is you angling for special treatment at Morancy, you will be hard pressed to convince Moriah. He isn't known to show favoritism for *anyone.*"

Moriah swiveled and stood beside Fynn. His hand fell over the boy's head. His unnerving eyes settled on Felix. "I would *love* to go, Prince Fynneas."

Felix stood, mouth agape. "Oh, so you like him more than *me*, do you?" Mock offense ghosted into his voice. "I see how it is."

"The boy's just so cheerful, Felix, honestly I can't be expected to say no to him," insisted the man in black. He looked down at Fynn and winked. "Can I?"

The elder prince huffed and admitted, "I find it's nearly impossible."

Presently, both Moriah and Fynn cocked their heads to the side, spying two red-haired lords rounding the opposite side of the breezeway and headed their way. Seeing their reactions, Felix turned and regarded the newest additions to the hunting party.

Godryk trotted toward them at a quicker pace than his father. He gave a respectful bow to Felix and grinned pleasantly. "Good morning, Prince Felix." He then turned his attention to Fynn, the boy snuggly settled at Moriah's side. Godryk's blue gaze wandered from Fynn to the mysterious man next to him, curious as to their relation. He was certain the man in black was

76

not a brother of Felix's, but he seemed comfortable enough around both princes. "Prince Fynneas," Godryk greeted cheerily.

Felix, seeing the curiosity in the child's demeanor, waved his hand at Moriah and introduced, "Godryk, this is Lord Commander Moriah Mordray. He's a friend of mine and one of the instructors - if you want to call him that - at Morancy. He'll be joining us today."

Godryk offered a curt nod and a smile. "A pleasure to meet you, my lord."

Moriah, his expression once more that of sheer boredom, nodded in kind. "And you, young lord."

Warwyk was amongst them not long after the introductions were concluded. He was a slender man, taller than Felix but not quite reaching Moriah's height. His dark, red curls were slicked back, revealing a high forehead speckled by light freckles. His eyes were the same summer blue as his son's, though they looked far more tired and worn. Thin lips sat in a firm line just below the curling tip of his long, sharp nose. "Good morning," he greeted heartily.

"Warwyk," welcomed Felix. "I was just introducing Godryk to Moriah. He'll be joining us this morning for our little venture. I hope that's alright with you."

It was clear to Warwyk that Felix's words asked for no argument. He eyed Moriah, arresting anything acerbic he might say by chewing on the inside of his mouth and pursing his lips. Not trusting himself to say anything nice to the green-eyed noble, he turned his full attention toward Felix and forcibly smiled. "Of course."

The party of five made their way from the courtyard to the stables where their horses awaited. The three adults were to the front of their small procession; Felix strategically stood between Moriah and Warwyk. The boys, some steps behind them, walked shoulder to shoulder.

Fynn leaned closer to Godryk and whispered, "What was all that with your father and Moriah?"

Godryk studied the three men walking ahead of them. He wasn't oblivious to the way his father occasionally eyed Moriah with poorly veiled distrust and resentment. "No idea."

Fynn had looked away from Godryk to continue watching the tense interactions between the three men when he nearly pitched headfirst into the ground. Godryk, in a moment of quick thinking, had seen Fynn lose his footing and had snagged him by the back of his jerkin and pulled back. The result was not as anticipated and both boys fell in an awkward heap to the ground, Fynn flat on his stomach and Godryk half sitting atop him, dazedly looking around for whatever had tripped them. He spied a little fox sneaking off around the wooden column of one of the stalls. Godryk could have sworn he saw the fox smirk in his direction before scurrying away.

Their clattering to the ground had apparently been louder than they had imagined. Both boys looked up to see the equally concerned and amused faces of the three men staring back at them.

Warwyk pinched the bridge of his nose in exasperation and sighed. "What happened?" he asked.

Godryk rolled off from atop Fynn, offering the other boy his hand before hauling the prince to his feet.

Fynn brushed the dirt from his person before reaching out and brushing some dust and hay from Godryk's shoulder. "I fell," the prince began, "and Godryk tried to catch me. Then we *both* fell." He looked away from Warwyk and back to Godryk. "Are you alright?"

The younger Redmayne nodded. "You?"

A careless grin appeared on Fynn's face. "It's going to take more than that to slow me down."

Godryk chuckled. "I've noticed."

"Tripped over your own feet?" asked Felix, bemused.

"No," insisted Fynn indignantly, "something tangled up my feet. I swear, I'm not *that* clumsy."

"Thought I saw a fox," added Godryk.

"Dug!" cheered Felix as he swept his eyes about the stables, intently searching for something. He knelt down and held out his hands. "Dug?"

"Dug?" asked Fynn.

Moriah rolled his eyes and stepped up behind Felix, casually resting his hands on the prince's shoulders and leaning over him. He called, "Skullduggery, come out this instant."

Fynn and the Redmaynes looked perplexed at the two, neither of which seemed to be paying them any attention. Felix had taken to gently clapping his outstretched hands and cooing while Moriah muttered under his breath.

"Skullduggery?" repeated Godryk, looking at Fynn for answers.

The prince simply stared back, equally as confused. "I have no idea."

The boys watched as a small fox poked its head out from behind a bale of hay stacked in the corner. A sly smile wrapped around its tiny, black muzzle. Its yellow eyes shone mischievously as it looked from Felix over to Fynn and Godryk. Felix, catching sight of the fox, brightened even more and jumped to his feet, tossing Moriah off balance. As Moriah stumbled back, Felix bound over to the little creature, arms still outstretched. Fynn watched, dumbfounded, as the fox leapt into Felix's arms and snuggled up against the man's chest comfortably.

Warwyk was the first to recover from the shock of such an odd scene. He cleared his throat and asked curiously, "Care to explain, Prince Felix, what's going on here?"

Felix turned to face them; a triumphant smile was painted across his features. He glanced down at the creature nestled in his arms and then back to the confused onlookers. He nodded at the fox. "This is Skullduggery. Dug for short."

"You've taken to keeping a fox?" Lord Redmayne pressed.

Dug peeked out from over Felix's arms and spied the lord with narrowed eyes before looking up to the man who held him protectively. He returned to nuzzling his nose into the crook of Felix's arms.

Felix laughed, "No, he's not mine. He's Moriah's."

"Of course," muttered Warwyk.

"Bratty little thing." Moriah eyed the furry bundle curled in his friend's arms. "You've had your fun," admonished the lord commander. He held out his arms. "Come along, Skullduggery."

Fynn watched as the fox jumped up from Felix's embrace and into Moriah's. The little, black muzzle nestled into the crook of Moriah's neck gently. A small, hardly perceptible smile appeared on Moriah's face as he admired the fox. Dug wormed his way out of Moriah's hold and clambered up atop the man's shoulder before gracefully slinking down and curling into the hood of the lord's cloak.

Fynn was amazed. He marveled, "How'd you train him to do that?"

Moriah reached back and scratched at the fox's head lightly. "I didn't," he assured casually. "He just does his own thing. There's no telling Skullduggery what to do, really."

"Bratty fox," agreed Felix. He crept up behind Moriah and took to gently stroking the creature's ears. "Always finding trouble."

"Do you expect to take him on the hunt?" huffed Warwyk indignantly. "The hounds won't like that one bit."

Felix appeared at Moriah's side still beaming. He offered Warwyk a conciliatory nod of understanding before adding, "Dug isn't a normal fox, I assure you, Lord Redmayne. Really, he'll be fine. I suspect he'll stay in Moriah's hood the whole time, odd little thing that he is."

"That's most *irregular*," commented Warwyk heatedly. "Honestly, who's ever heard of keeping a fox as a pet?"

"He's not really a *pet*," insisted Moriah. His eyes narrowed and darkened. "I wouldn't *debase* him with such a term."

"*Friend*, I think, is more appropriate," asserted Felix.

Warwyk nodded as he drawled, "Right. Well, if we're all here then, might we head off?" He forced himself to smile when Felix nodded his head happily, eyes alight with anticipation. Lord Redmayne held a hand aloft and waved, beckoning the stable boy over with an exasperated motion. "Morgan!" he called.

Fynn turned at the sound of rustling and watched as a nervous looking young man came rushing toward them. His hair was a shade of red reminiscent of Warwyk's, though decidedly less tidy. Unkempt, red curls fell around a square-jawed face and twisted at the touch of thin shoulders. His eyes were a deep brown set beneath spectacularly thick, red eyebrows. Freckles muddled his sun-tanned complexion and a smattering of dirt swept over the bridge of his nose. He stopped just before his lord and bowed his head, averting his gaze and seeming to intensely study the hay-littered floor beneath his booted feet. "M'lord?"

"Ready five horses and do make it quick," ordered Warwyk.

Morgan never looked up, just scooted away nervously and began assembling saddles and reins before pulling open stalls and readying the horses for the morning's hunt. Fynn thought it curious that the young man, every so often, would chance a glance toward Godryk and then immediately look away, as though his eyes burned at the very sight of the boy.

The young prince leaned close to his friend and nudged him with his elbow. Once the younger Redmayne's attention was solely his, Fynn whispered, "What's wrong with your stable boy? Seems a bit skittish."

Godryk laughed sweetly and replied in a hushed tone, "Don't worry about him. That's just Morgan. He's nice enough, really."

Fynn turned his focus back toward the young man readying a black horse. He watched intently as Morgan situated the saddle and began buckling the straps, occasionally stroking his calloused hand over the steed's thick neck.

"I don't know; he seems a little off," mumbled Fynn.

"Trust me," Godryk insisted, "he's always been that way. He's just a nervous sort."

Warwyk inched his way closer to Felix until he stood just to the prince's side. He hadn't looked away from Morgan for some time. "I apologize, I

80

thought Morgan would have had the horses readied by the time we got here." He shook his head. "I don't know what I'm going to do with the boy."

"It's no trouble, really," assured Felix. He clapped his hand over Warwyk's tense shoulder. He felt the man go absolutely rigid beneath his palm. "I'm in no rush to get on with things. The quicker we finish the hunt this morning, the sooner I have to be back to Lachlan and his court." Felix rolled his eyes and offered up an exaggerated sigh of annoyance. "Honestly, I wouldn't mind if we got lost in the woods for a few days."

It wasn't too long before Morgan readied the horses and offered up the reins to his lord and the rest of the party. Fynn hadn't any trouble settling onto his horse but noted that Godryk, despite being the more poised between them, struggled into the saddle with all the grace of a newborn chick learning to fly. The way his legs flailed about before his foot found its purchase in the stirrup made Fynn want to cringe, but the prince schooled his features and continued to smile encouragingly. Once Godryk had made himself comfortable and straightened up on his mount, the other four had already settled in and were chattering amongst themselves.

Warwyk directed his horse to Felix's side and the two sat, leaning toward one another, deep in conversation; their eyes were fixed in the direction of the wood beyond the castle walls. Moriah's steed faced opposite Fynn's, allowing the man to observe the young prince without having to crane his neck to the side. His eyes narrowed when he noted how truly scrawny Fynn looked when sitting up that high upon an animal so wide and muscled. The boy's small hands clutched at the leather reins, but Moriah honestly doubted that the child had any control over the creature.

"Is everything alright?" asked Fynn sheepishly, having noticed Moriah's scrutiny. He turned his grey eyes up towards the lord commander shyly.

Moriah smirked, but said nothing. Green eyes trailed once more from Fynn's booted toes up to his thick, black tresses in appraisal before nodding. "Ready?"

The prince beamed, grinning a toothy grin from ear to ear. "Definitely!"

"Morgan," Warwyk called from the front of the party. They'd made their way from the stables out into the open, nearly ready to make their leave for the wood. "Morgan, I think it would be best if you came along with us."

"M'lord?"

Warwyk soured. "Don't just stand there, boy. Ready your horse and come along. Quickly now!"

Morgan dashed back into the stables without so much as a second thought. His horse, thankfully, was already saddled from earlier that morning.

He was quick to jump into the saddle and join the hunting party. He spared a parting glance for Fynn before his dark eyes chanced another peek at Godryk. Hastily, he looked back down, once more finding the ground immensely interesting. "Ready, m'lord."

The six-man hunting party departed the castle grounds, making leave of its comforts for the morning and headed into the wood that was just an hour east of Claw Keep - the Lion's Wood. Their hounds were barking at the hoofed heals of the procession. The day had only grown warmer as the morning wore on.

Warwyk monopolized Felix's time, forcing the prince into conversations that he most evidently couldn't find to be any less entertaining. Lord Redmayne had his stare fixed upon the ever-approaching wood while Felix, lost to the throes of sheer boredom, hazarded fleeting glances over his shoulder towards Moriah. For his part, the man in black seemed content to ignore everyone in the company and ride apart from the others. He lingered there behind Redmayne and Felix but in front of the boys and Morgan. Every so often, Fynn could spy Dug popping his tiny head out of Moriah's hood and looking around before settling back into the folds of the fabric.

"Do you think we'll manage to down anything?" asked Godryk sunnily.

Fynn combed his hand through his hair, feeling the sticky residue of sweat beginning to mat his locks. He laughed. "I hope so! I'm not up this early for nothing."

"Not a morning person?"

Fynn shook his head and huffed. "Not at all. You?"

Godryk looked up towards the clouds, watching the white puffs creep across the sky at a lazy pace. "I love the mornings. They're quiet." He reached his arm out and pointed skyward. "See that one there?"

"Which one?"

Godryk waved his hand more. "That one there! It looks like a rabbit, doesn't it?"

Fynn squinted, peering through the bright rays of light assaulting his eyes. "Looks like a *cloud.*"

"Well, yes," chuckled Godryk. "But look closer. Look, there are two points that look like ears and a curvy bit that could be its tail at the bottom."

"If you say so," muttered Fynn. "It's nice, all this. Quiet like you said."

"While it lasts," Godryk agreed.

"While it lasts." Fynn sighed. "I want to enjoy the woods and country before we go back to Batsbeckon. I want to have some fun and just be happy for a while."

"When do you go back?"

"Father said in a few days. They're not waiting for all the repairs to be done, just cleaning things up enough that we can go back," Fynn explained. "Can't say I'm looking forward to it."

The horses plodded their way into the wood. It was a dense wood populated by trees that reached higher than one could have imagined. As his horse trotted by, Fynn admired the sheer size of the trees. He almost felt rather insignificant next to them; the sheer breadth of their stature was intimidating. He cooed as he took in the sights. The sunlight hardly penetrated the thick tangle of branches weaving their way overhead, leaving the six-some in the eeriness of the wild. Shadows stretched all around and cool breezes wafted over them as they proceeded further into the depths of the wood. A thick silence fell upon the party as they kept alert, each of them straining to see any signs of movement. Even the hounds were quiet; their noses twitched every few seconds.

The silence became wicked; a malevolent sort of discomfort befell them after nearly two hours of having found not a single living creature. Warwyk's already tense shoulders seemed to have gone completely stony; the muscles in his jaw clenched and unclenched as he scanned his surroundings in a desperate attempt to will a deer or fox into happening across their path. Felix tiredly raked his hands through his tangled hair to keep it from falling into his eyes, though his efforts were yielding little success. Moriah, still separate from Redmayne and Felix, was sitting unnaturally straight in his saddle. His eyes seemed keen, constantly darting in every direction at the most minute of sounds, but his expression remained impassive.

"Godryk," Fynn called in a whisper.

The young lord turned in Fynn's direction, cocking his head to the side questioningly.

Fynn whined, "This is boring."

Godryk nodded his agreement. "The *most* boring."

"What say you to going off and having a look around?"

Godryk furrowed his brow. "I don't know. I don't think we're supposed to go off from the others."

Fynn's horse came shoulder to shoulder with Godryk's. The prince leaned closer; his voice lowered. "They won't notice. Look at them. They're not paying any attention to us."

Godryk chewed on his lower lip. "I don't think my father, or *yours* for that matter, will like it if we go off on our own."

Fynn quirked a brow. "Where's your sense of adventure?"

"It's tempered and restrained," mumbled Godryk, "as yours should be."

"We'll be quick," promised Fynn pleadingly. "Come on, Godryk, there's got to be more to this wood than just trees and us sitting around."

"Fine," relented Godryk hesitantly. "But...like you said, let's be quick about it. We'll have a look around...just a *quick* look, not too far...and then be right back."

Fynn smiled and sharply nodded his head. "Agreed."

Morgan watched curiously as the two young boys conversed in hushed tones before slipping from their mounts to the damp ground beneath silently. They gathered up their reins and tied them around one of the slenderer of the trees before finally realizing they were being watched.

Fynn, having felt the prickling of someone's steady gaze upon his back, turned to see Morgan staring back at him. The prince sauntered up to Morgan and his mount. He looked up at the stable boy with a wry smile. "Morgan, right?"

The young man nodded.

"Could you do me a favor?"

Morgan's stomach clenched at the playful sound of Fynn's voice, knotting uneasily as the boy continued to smile up at him innocently. He chanced a look toward Warwyk and noted his lord still carrying on a muttered discussion with Felix, gesticulating wildly to punctuate his mounting annoyance with the fruitless hunting trip. The stable boy looked back to the prince who waited expectantly. "Yes?" chanced Morgan.

Fynn tilted his head toward Godryk and explained, "Godryk and I are going to go have a look around. We'll be right back. Honest. Can you keep an eye on the horses and our fathers? Maybe give us a signal or something if they look like they've noticed we're gone?"

"A signal?"

"Yes." Fynn mused, "I don't know, you could make a bird sound or something. Just, whatever you do, do it loud enough for us to hear. Alright?"

Morgan bit down on his lower lip; his eyes looked pensive. He fidgeted in his saddle before agreeing. "Be quick?"

"Of course," Fynn promised. He turned around on his heel in a fluid motion and bounded off, looping his arm around Godryk's and stealing into the woods away from the party.

Fynn honestly didn't think they'd gone too far, but when he looked back in the direction they'd come from, he didn't recognize anything. The same unnerving silence of the woods was all around them, though it was no longer pervaded by the hushed tones of muttered boredom emanating from the three agitated men of the hunting party. It seemed, the further they went, the darker the Lion's Wood became. The dirt under their feet was damp and gave way beneath their weight as they carried on.

Godryk huddled up against Fynn, once again gnashing his teeth over his bottom lip as his eyes grew fearful. "We should go back."

Fynn jerked away from Godryk. He knelt down; his palms ghosted over the underbrush while his eyes scanned his surroundings carefully. "We've only just started looking around."

"Prince Fynneas—"

Fynn interrupted with an irritated growl, insisting, "Stop calling me that. Just *Fynn*, alright?"

Godryk crouched down at the prince's side, still looking frightful. "*Fynn*, I think we should go back. We've gone off pretty far; I'm sure they've noticed by now."

Willfully ignoring the way the other boy was nervously wringing his hands together, Fynn asserted, "If they had noticed, Morgan would have given us a signal. I'm sure we're fine. It's really quiet here. If Morgan had called for us, we would've heard him."

Godryk shook his head. "It's *too* quiet."

"What do you mean?"

"That's exactly what I mean," bit Godryk. "It's just too quiet. It's creepy."

Fynn finally took the time to regard the boy at his side. He settled his hand over Godryk's, effectively halting the boy's nervous pawing. "It's fine."

"You don't know that!" Godryk pulled his hands free of the prince's calming gesture.

"Trust me." Fynn grinned lopsidedly.

"Alright." Godryk rolled his eyes. "I trust you."

A twig snapped not too far from them. The sound of the slight action seemed near thunderous in the vacuum of silence that was the wood. Both boys jerked their heads up, frantically searching the vicinity for whatever had made the noise.

"Did you hear that?" whispered Fynn.

"What do you think it was?"

Fynn slowly climbed back to his full height, meager as it was. "Did you bring anything with you? A knife or something?"

"No. I didn't think we were going to *kill anything* alone," replied Godryk.

Fynn soured. "Nor did I."

Another twig snapped with equally boisterous results; the sound reverberated through the wood. They heard rustling in the underbrush and the gentle breathing of something lurking not far in the distance. Fynn narrowed his eyes, forcing himself to see through the dark myriad of shadows cast by the entangled branches of the monstrous trees. He caught sight of a sloping figure lumbering not more than twenty feet or so from where they stood. He saw, in the scarce light afforded by the wilds, golden eyes flashing in their direction.

Fynn took a step back, took hold of Godryk's wrist, and tugged him along. "I saw something," he whispered breathily.

"What was it?"

"I don't know," Fynn admitted, still retreating slowly with Godryk in tow.

They took yet another step back as more twigs snapped beneath the weight of the unknown creature stalking them. The sound of breathing grew louder and more insistent, lancing through them with every exhalation. Godryk stepped back, but as his foot made contact with the dirt, the ground beneath gave way and he went tumbling backward with a high-pitched yelp. Fynn's hold on his wrist was wrenched away as he twisted awkwardly before his back slammed into the ground, knocking the breath right out of his lungs. Godryk gasped painfully as he tumbled backward over himself and down a steep decline, the trees looking as though they were leaping and bounding and twisting all around him.

Fynn watched, wide-eyed, as Godryk fell down a hill he hadn't noticed before. It felt as though his heart stopped when he saw Godryk's body come to a decided halt at the bottom, limply curled around the brush and twigs and stones. The fleeting image of Jaeryn sprawled motionlessly on the castle floor, embers bursting in and out of sight, flickered across Fynn's mind.

"Godryk?" Fynn yelled in a panic.

There was no answer.

"Godryk!" he cried louder.

The very distinct roar of a bear sounded with all the loud aplomb characteristic of a beast from a children's tale. If the twigs breaking had sounded like thunder, the sound of the bear wailing was tantamount to the splitting of the earth. Fynn cast a quick glance in the direction of the roar before hurling himself down the hill. His feet caught themselves awkwardly on the slope and soon he found himself tumbling head over heels down toward Godryk. He rolled painfully to a halt just a few feet from the young lord. Painstakingly, Fynn forced himself to his hands and knees. He felt the familiar sensation of blood, hot and sticky, running down from his hairline and tracing over the curve of his cheek. His vision was muddled from the long tumble and his stomach churned, making him ill. Fynn's breath quickened and became shallow and every muscle in his body seemed to coil painfully.

He crawled over to Godryk. One scraped and bloodied hand reached out and brushed the red hair from the boy's eyes, revealing a face that looked as though it were sleeping.

"Godryk," Fynn said, his voice weighty with unshed tears. "Godryk, we have to go." He shook the other boy, watching breathlessly as Godryk's eyelashes began to flutter. "Godryk, you have to get up."

Blue eyes were finally revealed beneath bronzy lashes. They focused on the prince crouching over him. "My head hurts," Godryk offered weakly.

"You probably hit it when you fell," suggested the prince.

Fynn pulled Godryk into his arms. He forced himself up on quaking legs; Godryk leaned on him heavily. Pale eyes looked upward to where they had been standing before Godryk fell. There was nothing there.

"I heard something," Fynn began. "I'm sure it was a bear."

Godryk nearly choked as he repeated, "A *bear*?"

Fynn looked grim. "I'm sure of it."

"Fynn, what're we going to do?"

Biting back his fear, Fynn placed his hand over Godryk's chest. "We're going to stay quiet, so it doesn't hear us." He felt Godryk's heart pounding away in his chest with such force that Fynn half suspected it would come bursting from his flesh and into his palm.

Both boys fought back their fearful whimpers as they methodically began heading back in the direction they had come—or at least, believing they were headed in said direction. They moved slowly, silently, so as not to rouse the attention of the lurking beast. Occasionally, one boy would look to the other for some silent reassurance, being granted it by means of a careful nod and steely gaze. They staggered onward - Godryk's arm draped over Fynn's shoulders and Fynn's arm laced around Godryk's waist - for some time without hearing any more rumblings from the bear.

"Do you think it's gone?" Godryk asked tentatively.

"I'm not sure."

A flash of red fur darted from the brush and wound around Fynn's ankles, nipping at his boots. The boy looked down and, relief washing over him, cooed, "Skullduggery."

The fox seemed to grin at the sound of its name while weaving between Fynn and Godryk's feet as they ambled along soundlessly.

"If Dug is here, do you think we're close?" inquired Godryk hopefully.

"We must be," Fynn asserted.

The red fur of Skullduggery's tail bristled, and he bared his teeth, small as they were. His long, black ears flattened against his head as his eyes went wide.

The uncomfortably quick pace of Fynn's heartbeat began drumming along even faster. His chest felt tight and his head was swimming. He looked off in the direction Dug was hissing only to be met with a pair of yellow eyes shining through the shadows like pale stars winking in the black of night.

"Godryk, we need to run," the prince insisted, not able to look away from the eyes in the darkness.

"Wha…" gasped Godryk, his voice leaving him when he, too, spied the fierce eyes pinning Fynn.

A deafening roar spilled from the tooth-lined jaws of the bear as it bellowed; silvery saliva slickened the points of its teeth, thick tendrils of drool dripped from its jowls like stalactites from a cave. The very sound shook the boys to their cores. Cold chills raced down their spines and their legs felt as though they were made of lead. They stood there, wide-eyed and stricken dumb by terror, until the furtive hissing of Skullduggery turned into cackling barks.

Fynn seized Godryk by the arm and pulled him along as he took off running. He didn't know if he was going in the right direction. He didn't care. Another vicious rumble burst from the throat of the beast. Something heavy collided with the trees. The boys tore through the wood, rushing through underbrush and frantically jumping over fallen trees. They careened around a group of trees only to find themselves once more plummeting down a steep decline. The twigs and stones struck their faces and arms, scraping their palms and tearing the fabric of their shirts and trousers. When at last they came to a stop, they were strewn amongst the leaves and dirt.

Godryk sat upright immediately, nervously looking back to where he believed the bear to be. "Fynn?"

The prince grumbled as he forced himself up, quickly assessing his person for any injuries. Finding none too worrisome, he outstretched his hand. Godryk took hold and the prince hauled the boy to his feet. Again, they were off running.

"Fynn! Fynneas!" Felix's voice echoed through the trees. "Fynneas! Godryk!"

"I hear them," Godryk panted as he continued to race along at the prince's side.

"Me too," Fynn wheezed.

"Fynneas! Godryk!" Felix's voice sounded again.

"Father!" Fynn yelled out, helpless desperation coloring his voice as he screamed. "Father! We're here!"

Neither boy could tell from which direction Felix's voice had originated. But the sound of the bear's paws pummeling the ground was well-defined and certainly coming from just behind them, drawing ever nearer. Numbness overcame them both as they recognized they would be unable to outrun the great beast.

Godryk fell to his knees; tears welled in his eyes and trickled freely down his face. He bit down on his lower lip hard enough to draw blood. Fynn stepped in front of him, a shield between he and the oncoming bear.

"What're you doing?" Godryk asked hopelessly.

"Run," ordered Fynn.

Godryk shook his head. "You're mad! I'm not leaving you here."

"No use in us both dying. Run!"

"No," Godryk shot back defiantly.

"It's my fault we're here! Let me do something to make up for it. Run! You have to while you still have the chance," pleaded Fynn.

Godryk mustered all the will he had and stood up. His blue eyes bore into Fynn's grey stare. His lips set themselves in a thin, straight line. He shook his head. "I...I won't leave you."

"You're mad!"

Godryk nodded. "Absolutely."

Skullduggery appeared at their feet again, thankfully still intact. Fynn opened his arms to the creature as he'd seen his father do in the stables and marveled as the fox leapt into them. The young prince held the fox close to his chest, feeling the warmth of Dug's fur brush against his neck and chin.

"Are they close?" whispered Fynn. His tears dampened the fox's fur. "Please…let them be close by."

The fox chattered against Fynn's neck, nuzzling his nose into the fabric of the boy's collar.

The bear roared again, the viciousness of its cries intensifying.

The sound of hooves beating against the earth and howling hounds soon became all-consuming, echoing through the silence. Fynn perked up. He beheld three horses rushing towards them, seven floppy-eared dogs not far behind. He saw his father ahead of the other two, eyes full of worry. The brown horse the royal rode slowed and circled around the boys.

"Fynneas," Felix exhaled carefully, the fear straining his voice. "You're alright?"

Fynn nodded, rushing to his father's horse. He stopped beside the steed, resting his head against his father's leg. A hand came down to sit atop his head, fingers knotting in the black hair gently.

Warwyk's tawny colored horse was the next to come stomping toward the boys, similarly circling them. Though, Lord Redmayne didn't bother to ask after his son. Instead, he remained stiffly upright in his saddle and looking off in the distance, searching for the still-stalking predator. "It's close," he said, his voice even and devoid of anything resembling an emotion.

Felix looked away from Fynn and off in the direction Warwyk was staring. "I heard it too. It's definitely nearby." Felix drew his bow and strung an arrow, readying himself to aim and fire at a moment's notice.

Warwyk prepared likewise.

Moriah's black horse was the last of the three to emerge. When the man in black came into sight, Skullduggery wriggled free of Fynn's hold and traced circles around the black horse's hooves. Moriah's eyes surveyed the boys, not missing the nasty cuts and bruises littering their faces and arms. He turned away. "Felix?"

"How big do you think it is?" asked Felix.

"Not the biggest we've ever encountered," Moriah haughtily assured. He led his horse to saunter up next to Felix's. "I'm sure, with the three of us, we'll make quick work of the beast."

"Arrogant, aren't you?" sneered Warwyk.

"Confident in my abilities, naturally," drawled Moriah as he strung an arrow on his bow. "You should try it some time, *my lord*."

Fynn, despite the situation he presently found himself in, had to fight back laughing at Moriah's cool indifference and sarcastic comments.

That, in and of itself, was difficult enough without having to factor in the red-faced outrage distorting Warwyk's expression. Fynn looked over to Godryk, thinking the sight of his friend cowering in place would sober him and quell the smirk that threatened to rear itself on his face. Sure enough, Godryk looked as though he were about to collapse under the sheer weight of his terror as he shuddered in his father's presence. Instinctively, Fynn recoiled backward and felt his shoulder brush against the hip of Felix's horse.

Felix drew back his arrow, his arms raising and shoulders squaring, when he spied the lugubriously approaching beast; its black hackles bristled as it took in the sight of the party, three arrows trained upon it. The great beast raised itself to its full height upon stout back legs and bared large, yellowed, dagger-like fangs; its jowls curled back as it bellowed mightily. Its bright eyes fixed upon them, large paws raised, and clawed toes flexed.

Fynn's chest constricted; he could scarcely breathe. He stumbled backward, away from the horses and their riders, and tripped into Godryk who caught hold of him before he could wheel around too far and pitch face first into the dirt.

Felix let loose his arrow. The snap of the bowstring caught Fynn's attention. The young prince watched as the arrow sailed through the air like lightning and buried itself deep into the bear's chest. Two more arrows burst forth, each hitting the mark. One nestled into the bear's shoulder, the other plunged into the beast's throat.

The quaking cry of the creature as it was struck seemed incongruous with its vicious demeanor. Its eyes went wide as the pain settled in. Not allowing the creature a moment's rest, Moriah sent another arrow winding through the air. It landed just beside his first, puncturing yet another portion of the animal's throat. The bear gasped for breath; blood began to churn in its mouth. It collapsed forward limply.

Fynn watched, morbidly transfixed by the scene before him. The bear twitched in the dirt, shoulders trembling. Its breath was labored and frantic as it drowned in its own blood. Where once fear had held Fynn still, now a more poignant emotion took its place. He couldn't look away from the tragedy that was the creature's slow and, most likely, rather agonizing demise. He watched as the broad chest of the beast heaved once more before stilling with finality.

"Is it dead?" Fynn whispered. He looked up in time to see Moriah's eyes catch his. Fynn looked away, ashamed.

Moriah gracefully dismounted and approached the fallen animal. He knelt at its side and reached out. His palm smoothed over the thick, black fur. He brushed his hand across the bear's head. His green gaze lingered over the creature's face, staring into its unseeing eyes. Moriah frowned. "It's done," he said. He slowly stood. The man in black didn't look back at any of his companions. Rather, he remained resolutely staring into the bear's eyes. Skullduggery came up to Moriah's ankles, sitting himself down and leaning his small head against his master's leg.

Felix jumped from his saddle and approached the scene. He cast a concerned look toward Moriah, who remained deathly silent. Looking away, the prince knelt down before the beast. He took hold of one of the arrows and dislodged it from the furry neck, then proceeded to repeat the process with the remaining three arrows. Red rivulets trailed through the black fur and spilled onto the damp soil. Felix stood; his hands were bloodied. "We should go back to the castle now," he spoke in a shaky voice.

Warwyk looked away from the deathly scene and fixed his focus on the boys. "Come along," he instructed. It was evident, by the tightness of his lips and the way he seemed unable to look either boy in the eyes, that he was working diligently to fight back his urge to scream at them. "Morgan is waiting with your horses."

Godryk nodded numbly and followed as his father began leading the way. Fynn watched the Redmaynes head back to where Morgan awaited them. He watched their fleeting backs, Warwyk's tensing more and more with every passing moment and Godryk's slumping further and further as he retreated into himself. Fynn sighed. He turned away and watched as Moriah mounted his horse, never bothering to look at him, and followed in Warwyk's wake.

Felix had stolen away from the bear's lifeless carcass and bunched his horse's reins in his hand, leading the animal along. He clapped his free hand over Fynn's shoulder and urged him forward. They remained a far way behind the others. "Care to explain?" prompted Felix.

Fynn hung his head. "It's my fault."

"I figured as much," Felix joked humorlessly.

"I just...got bored. Nothing was happening and I was tired of sitting around waiting for something to come up...so...so I convinced Godryk to come exploring with me," Fynn tried to explain, but even he didn't want to hear his excuse for what had happened. "We could have died."

Felix nodded. "Very likely so."

"It would have been my fault."

"Yes."

Fynn's shoulders fell even further; his whole body deflated under the reality of the situation. "It would have been all my fault," he repeated dully.

"Yes. It would have. And, as a result of your carelessness, a poor creature had to die senselessly." Felix's voice had an unnatural coldness to it as he spoke. "The bear was doing nothing more than acting on instinct. Had you and Godryk not gone traipsing through the wood alone, it–more than likely–would never have happened into your path and could have lived another day. And yet, your actions led it to its death."

"But we were out hunting," Fynn began lamely. "We came out here to kill something *anyway*."

Felix shook his head. "A stag, a boar…maybe a fox if Moriah would've been alright with it. But not a bear."

"I don't understand," admitted Fynn.

"In a war, people are going to die. You know that. Your soldiers are fighting the soldiers of your enemies. There will be casualties. You have to accept that as a given reality. But when there are innocents killed, that's harder to accept because, most of the time, it can be avoided. Carelessness, Fynneas, is what leads to innocents being killed. Think of it like that. Do you understand what I'm saying?"

"The bear was innocent. We weren't here for it and if it weren't for me, it would still be alive." Heaviness settled in the boy's chest. "I'm sorry," Fynn whispered.

"Sorry doesn't change what happened."

The son looked up to his father curiously. "I don't understand. I really *am* sorry, though."

"You're not a child anymore, Fynneas. You *need to understand* that your actions have consequences. You *need to understand* that your position, your title, lends you a great deal of power and influence. You *need to understand* that you have to be careful with such power."

"What do you mean?"

Felix took a long, deep breath. "Today it was a bear that died needlessly because of your actions. But tomorrow, it may be your friends who die. When you're older, it may be your soldiers who die because you made a bad decision. You have to use your head. *Think*."

"Oh," muttered Fynn.

"We talked about this," continued Felix. "We talked about this no later than this morning. We can't keep doing this. You can't keep acting like a child, Fynneas. You have to pull yourself together. I won't be with you at Morancy, Fynny. You're going to have to learn to make the right decisions by yourself and, truthfully, I'm worried you won't be able to."

Fynn sulkily argued, "I will. I promise."

"*Show* me, then. Please, show me that you can think."

They continued on in silence until they arrived where Morgan waited for them. Warwyk motioned for Godryk to climb up upon his mount and the boy did so. Fynn did likewise. The party proceeded through the wood back toward Claw Keep. Warwyk led them, carefully ignoring his son and willfully remaining silent, not so much as looking at Felix. The prince was close behind Warwyk and, in much the same manner, seemed unyielding in his decision to remain quiet. Moriah continued to look disinterested in those around him. Skullduggery was once again curled into the man's hood, his small head poking out and resting on Moriah's shoulder.

Morgan rode between Godryk and Fynn. "What happened, little Lord?" he asked genuinely.

Godryk pouted. "Father's real mad."

"We got into a spot of trouble," Fynn added. Inwardly, he cringed at his own drastic understatement.

"Oh." Morgan looked away from them and settled his attention on Warwyk's back in the distance. "Lord Redmayne does seem…upset."

"He's *more* than upset," whined Godryk pitifully. "He'll kill me."

The hunting party, empty handed and looking more than agitated, made their way through the castle gates. As they dismounted and gathered in hushed conversation, save for Moriah who remained silent, in the stables, Morgan dutifully began stripping the horses of their saddles and bridles. Once he closed the gate of the final stall, head hanging and nervous eyes shifting around, Morgan shuffled toward Warwyk. "Will there be anything else, m'lord?"

"Yes."

Morgan nodded expectantly.

Warwyk's hand shot out and seized the stable boy by the chin, forcing him to look into the lord's burning eyes. His voice was dangerously low. "You were supposed to be *watching* them."

"M'lord, you're right," the stable boy agreed weakly. "I'm sorry. I beg your forgiveness, m'lord."

Lord Redmayne shook his head, eyes narrowing. "You needn't beg."

"M'lord?"

"You'll have my forgiveness once you've earned it." He released his hold on the younger man's chin and shoved him back forcibly. He eyed Morgan like a predator would its cornered prey. "Fetch the whip."

"M'lord?"

"I don't believe I stuttered," snapped Warwyk.

"Yes, m-m-m'lord," stammered Morgan as he scurried away through the stables to fetch the whip in question. Returning, head still hanging low, he proffered the whip to his lord obediently. "M'lord."

"I require a rope as well."

Once more, Warwyk watched maliciously as Morgan hurried off and fetched him a rope before returning, bowing his head again.

"M'lord," Morgan said warily.

Warwyk snatched up the rope from the stable boy's hands. "Hold out your hands, boy." Morgan did as was commanded. He held out his hands; they were shaking terribly. Lord Redmayne wound the rope around the young man's wrists, pulling the twine painfully tight against the flesh beneath until the friction burned with every tug. Once his hands were bound, Morgan could do little more than watch with frantic understanding as Warwyk hefted the remaining rope up and looped it over one of the lower hanging rafters in the stables. He pulled hard, wrenching Morgan's hands up and above his head. Warwyk eyed him impassively as he proceeded to tie the dangling rope to one of the stable's columns.

Fynn looked on with mounting dread as Morgan stood there in the middle of the stables, arms drawn over his head, small trails of blood seeping from his hewed wrists. "Father," he whimpered. He backed into Felix's front. The older prince encircled him with one arm. "What's Lord Redmayne going to do?"

"There are consequences for your actions, Fynneas. The bear's death was one. This is another," Felix replied coolly.

Warwyk had come over to where the rest of the party was huddled together. He eyed Godryk for a moment before pressing the whip into the boy's hands. He nodded toward Morgan. "Ten lashes should do it."

Godryk's blue eyes looked startled and began to swell with tears. "I...I don't—"

He was interrupted by the forceful jerk of his body as Warwyk's iron hold took purchase upon his slender arm and dragged him forward. He pushed Godryk toward Morgan, waving his hand at the stable boy's back.

"*Fifteen*," barked Warwyk.

The boy was quaking uncontrollably. Godryk shook his head, pleading-ly. "Father...no, I—"

Warwyk raised his hand in a halting gesture. "*Twenty* and let's be done with this nonsense."

Godryk did his best to tighten his grasp on the whip as he raised it just above his head. He swung his arm and cringed as the leather slapped against Morgan's back. "One," he whispered. His chest heaved violently with the force of his hastened breathing.

"Harder," Warwyk commanded.

Godryk bit down on his lip with such unbidden urgency that he drew blood yet again. He didn't seem to notice. He screwed his eyes shut as he raised his arm. He swung again. This time, the crack of the whip seemed to echo through the stables. Morgan yelped as the leather licked his back, tearing away the thin fabric of his shirt and grazing against his now exposed skin. "Two."

6

THE INCIDENT AT THE FUNERAL

Flynn struggled to keep down the feeling of betrayal that wormed its way through him. He sat with a painfully stiff back, shoulders squared, eyes trained forward. He recalled the words scrawled over the parchment he'd found in his room at Claw Keep three days prior, the parchment that had sat atop *The Mortanomicon*.

Do try and keep track of the book I've given you, instead of leaving it to burn with the castle. There are those who would do terrible things with the information found inside. That said, prince, it would behoove you to give the book a look yourself. Don't trust that your sister has told you everything.

A scowl tugged at the boy's lips as he tried to keep his mind from reeling downward into a dark pit from which he doubted he'd be able to pull himself free. A sidelong glance cast toward Fiona did little to set Fynn at ease. Rather, it spurred the churning in his stomach onward with renewed vigor. He thought he might be sick.

Before him there were two caskets. Each was draped in a black banner graced by the image of a red bat, wings spread and wearing a golden crown. The caskets sat side by side upon the altar in the temple. Torches, with golden flames that burned consistently and dully, lined the altar and the stairs that led down to those gathered in the solemn embrace of the holy structure. There, bearing witness to those caskets that lay before them all, were men, women, and children from all the great noble houses and many from lower nobility. At the front, seated in perfect silence, were the Fogs. Solemnity had befallen each of them and so they sat, never looking at one another, with their eyes trained forward, unwavering in their intensity as they all seemed to study, with a sort of morbid fascination, the fine embossments that decorated the caskets of the queen mother and Princess Gemma.

Lachlan sat with a perfectly straight back and squared shoulders, his gold crown in stark contrast to the black of his hair. The beginnings of a beard speckled his cheeks and chin. All in black, he looked quite the morbid figure sitting there beside the queen, swathed in his cloak despite the intense heat of the morning. To his side sat his brother who, much unlike Lachlan's dulled expression, bore the unmistakable visage of a man biting back indignation and annoyance; a conversation with his brother preceding the morning's events had left a sour taste in his mouth. Felix's hands, resting upon his black-garbed thighs, balled into fists with knuckles whiter than snow. His shoulders were squared proudly but were rigid and strained. To the king's left sat the queen with her red hair drawn back and mostly hidden beneath a sheer veil. Similarly to Felix, Ursalyn seemed to be a mass of rage roiling beneath the surface. Her long nails clawed against the fabric of her dress, impatiently raking as she waited in silence.

The children of the royal house seemed no less uneasy than their parents; the tension that simmered beneath their pallid flesh made each of the five seem like serpents coiled and waiting to strike.

Ciaran sat like a perfect replication of his uncle, clenching and unclenching his fists against his thighs and gnashing his teeth reflexively, blue eyes narrowed and trained toward the altar. Occasional furtive glances toward the queen only darkened his expression further. His brother at his side was the image of their mother, composed and outwardly cold, but his fingers clawed at the thick fabric of his black trousers, nails snagging against threads.

Sitting at Hollyn's other side was James. With his blonde hair and softer features, he seemed a contrast to the rest of his family. The melancholy of the occasion poured off him in waves. His eyes were fixed to the altar. There shone no underlying anger or frustration, but a bitter sadness that had, in recent days, taken ahold of him more firmly.

Fiona was beside James, preferring to sit nowhere near her brother this morning. She reached out and gently placed her hand over James's but didn't look at the boy or say a word. A veil obscured her features, but it was clear by the unnaturally still manner in which she sat that she was doing everything she could to not burst out screaming.

To Ciaran's other side sat Fynn. His black hair was slicked back, his pale eyes, no longer obscured by tousled tresses hanging in front of his face, seemed more intense in their ghostliness than usual. Quick glances toward his sister sparked an ember of indignation in him, though his expression remained impassive. His hands were motionless upon his lap. It was the measured, purposeful, deep breaths he drew that betrayed his anger and frustration.

All around them, from the rafters of the temple, hung banners from all of the houses gathered. Respectfully, the colors that normally adorned those banners were muted in tone and the fields upon which their sigils sprawled were black, reflective of the mourning that pervaded the realm.

Finally looking away from the caskets after what seemed to be ages, Fynn caught sight of the familiar red lion that denoted the Redmaynes and swept his gaze over those in attendance, searching for Godryk. It wasn't long until he spotted his friend huddled in the middle of a large group of Redmaynes, their distinctive, red hair being hard to overlook. Like everyone in the temple waiting for the funeral to officially commence, Godryk was dressed in black. Fynn thought it odd; the color certainly didn't suit the young boy at all. Yet, there he sat in black from head to toe as he nervously chewed on his lower lip and twiddled his thumbs in in his lap.

Footsteps sounded. Though it hardly seemed possible, the temple became even more overbearingly silent. Fynn turned his attention to the man who walked at an impossibly slow pace up the aisle at the center of the temple. He held a candle in his grasp. It wasn't lit. Unlike those gathered, he wore white. A long cloak trailed behind him as he continued toward the altar. At last, he reached the steps and ascended to stand before them. Once he seemed resolute in his position, carefully equidistant between both caskets, he looked out to the sea of aristocratic faces that stared up at him and he gestured, still holding the candle, for them to rise. They did. As if one body, the whole of those gathered stood like a wave rising from the surface and ready to crash upon the shore. But they did not crash. Instead, they lingered there in silence, unified by a collective feeling of unease and restlessness.

It was only then, when standing amidst the tides of nobility, that Fynn heard the faint sounds of screaming from beyond the temple walls, the sounds of muffled yells and hoof-falls over stone, of shattering glass and scraping steel. Odd, he thought, that he hadn't noticed before. Even odder was that no one paid attention to the chaos that seemed to be underway just outside. Or was it that they hadn't noticed? Strange, as now that he listened for it, Fynn heard the raging like thunder clapping through a silent valley. Everything seeming to shudder in the wake of the vast loudness. But still, not a head gathered cocked toward the sound to listen.

The man in white lowered his hands and cradled the unlit candle to his chest. Still, everyone remained standing. He smiled at them with a weak and worn sort of smile that divulged, to those who truly looked, his somberness. He was an old man with sagging, leather-like flesh that looked as though it were melting from a face that was once handsome. His eyes were a watery blue peeking out beneath sunken, wiry, white brows. His hair, a dusty color, was neatly combed back and kempt. He was an austere man and the graveness of the occasion that called for him to perform his duties seemed to only intensify his natural severity. He held the candle from him, aloft.

All eyes followed the motion with interest.

Lachlan pulled away from his family and moved to stand at the foot of the altar. He did not ascend the stairs to stand before the man in white but knelt, his black cloak folding about his frame like a heavy shadow. Felix went to stand beside his brother. He stood, towering over the kneeling king; his blue eyes roved from the altar, whereupon the caskets of his mother and sister rested, to settle on his brother's back. As if somehow feeling Felix's gaze upon him, Lachlan shifted nearly imperceptibly. Felix drew in a long, shuddering breath and then he knelt, his head bowed.

"Your Graces, my lords, my ladies," began the man in white, never looking down to the royal brothers kneeling at the foot of the altar, "we've gathered here, on this day, to mourn the deaths of the queen mother, Elsinora Fog, born to the House of Astor, and Princess Gemma Bowary, born to the House of Fog. Their lives were tragically taken by fires that destroyed part of Batsbeckon, fires the likes of which we've never seen before and, I do sincerely hope, never see again. Yet, as the House of Fog was born from flames, it is befitting that our beloved queen mother and princess would return to the waiting arms of The Mother by way of fire."

Two young men, hardly older than Ciaran, appeared upon the altar similarly dressed as the old man. Each held in their hands a bowl filled to the brim with oil. They stood on either side of the old man. The man in white turned to the left and spoke into the boy's ear. The young man handed the elder the bowl and, in exchange, the man gave to him the candle.

The man in white then stood before Elsinora's casket and began to pour the oil over it saying, "With this oil, I anoint thee as our eternal queen mother, to be made a patroness of our noble faith, an eternal servant to The Mother. In Her name you will be known as the Watcher of Our Children, for your dedication to the children of Estheria."

Fynn watched, enraptured, as the oil cascaded over the casket, dampening the banner. He didn't notice when the old man had taken the bowl of oil from the younger to his right and came to stand before Gemma's casket.

The man in white proceeded to repeat the process, letting the oil slowly flow from the mouth of the bowl down to the casket below. "With this oil, I anoint thee as our eternal princess, to be made a patroness of our noble faith, an eternal servant to The Mother. In Her name you will be known as the Heralder of Youth, having died far too young and ever beautiful."

Once more the man in white stood at the center of the altar, the unlit candle held in his wrinkled hands. His eyes drifted over the crowd until they rested upon James and he gave a nod. Fynn looked to the side and observed as his cousin proceeded toward Lachlan and Felix, a torch in his small hands.

Everyone watched as James stood between his uncles, torch held aloft toward the altar. There was a confident look in his eyes; gone was the despondent gloom that had kept a steady hold over him and, in its place, was a defiant sureness.

Again, the man in white nodded. "Young lord, you stand before us the bearer of the torch that will return our queen mother and princess to the arms of The Mother. Such honor is normally bestowed upon our sitting king, but the exception has been made for you, child. Do you accept the duty bestowed upon you by he, our noble king?"

James replied evenly, "I do."

One of the King's Guard proceeded forward and lit the torch James held before withdrawing into obscurity once more. James clasped it firmly, watching the dancing of the golden flame.

The man in white nodded again. "Then, please oblige. Send our queen mother and princess back to The Mother."

James ascended the steps and stood upon the altar. He proceeded first to Elsinora's casket and touched the torch upon the banner. His eyes went wide when the black banner erupted in flames; the red of the bat seemed to leap from the fabric and into the fires, scarlet abounding in the swirl of gold, and soon the casket was aflame and embers were borne forth, flickering as they swept into the stale air of the temple and extinguished once they fell lifelessly to the ground. James repeated the rite and stood, equally amazed the second time, as the same thing happened when the flame touched the banner over Gemma's casket. Soon, James stood between two pillars of fire that shot up from where the caskets rested upon the altar toward the stained-glass ceiling of the temple. Remarkably, the flames caused no damage to the holy building; though, Fynn supposed, this was not the first time a funeral was held there and this was, more than likely, a well-practiced rite by this point in history.

As the fires began to dwindle and black smoke began its slow crawl into the air, the man in white started to descend the stairs of the altar whilst the two young men who had assisted disappeared behind a door that led from the altar to an antechamber. Once the man in white reached the foot of the stairs, he stood between Lachlan and Felix and beckoned them to rise. They did and stood before the old man, neither looking at the other.

The man in white smiled at Lachlan, one sun-spotted hand draped over the king's shoulder. "You've been a good son," he whispered before stealing along by the brothers and down the aisle.

Lachlan proceeded behind the man in white, with Felix just behind him. Obediently, Ursalyn followed and so, too, did the children. Once the Fogs had begun their walk toward the temple's entrance, the nobles started to file into the aisle, one from each house holding aloft their black banners.

Casting a glance behind him, Fynn noticed the Mordray banner emblazoned with its fierce sigil - a coiled, golden snake. Curiously, the boy searched the throng of lords and ladies assembled in the banner's wake and found Moriah to be notably absent. Fynn pouted.

The large, double doors that served as the entryway to the temple swung open. Blisteringly hot tendrils of sunlight swept into the temple, making the gold of the statues that lined the interior shimmer and glow. The man in white led the procession into the morning light, squinting as he began to make the descent down the long and winding stairs that led from the temple's doors to the city that lay in its shadow. Still, he cradled the unlit candle to his chest.

Lachlan was not far behind the old man, his black cloak dragging along the steps as he continued wordlessly. Ursalyn and Felix, shoulder to shoulder, dutifully followed their king.

Ciaran had raised the Fog banner and held it proudly as he marched behind his mother. With its wings triumphantly spread and golden crown adorning its head, the ancestral bat seemed nearly otherworldly. The crimson of the stitched bat leapt against the black of the banner's field and seemed almost alive.

Hollyn and James followed behind Ciaran. Their heads were bowed together, their hushed murmurings drowned out against a sea of noise that erupted from the masses gathered at the bottom of the stairway.

The sounds Fynn heard earlier, those of metal clattering and yelling, steel smashing and glass breaking, sprung like waves, ready to wash away the mournful quietness.

Fiona and Fynn were left, the last of the royal house, to march along behind their cousins.

Fynn scowled. "You should've told me my name was in the book."

Fiona didn't bother to look down at him. "This isn't the time."

"Isn't the time?" The prince spat disdainfully. "You've known all along and didn't *deign* it the time to tell me. So, tell me, when's the time going to be?"

She shoved him roughly. "Stop it. Not now."

He shoved her back. "Yes *now*. You've been avoiding talking to me about that *damn book* since I first asked you about it."

"Because you've been in a mood." Fiona huffed.

"Oh, I wonder why?" Fynn sneered. "A *mood* she says." He laughed dully. "*Me*, in a *mood*."

"Yes. A *mood*, Fynneas." Her tone was biting and asked for no further argument.

Fynn was disinclined to take the hint. "You should've told me my name was in that creepy book."

"I was trying to keep you out of it."

"Why?"

The princess sighed. "To *protect* you, you *idiot*. Who knows why your name is in it! It can't be anything good. You said it yourself, it's a *creepy* book."

Fynn looked away from his sister and scowled. "I'm not a little kid anymore, Fi. I don't need you to protect me from everything."

"Hush," she insisted, reaching down to take her brother's hand in hers.

He jerked his hand away and snapped, "I don't need you! I don't need you to treat me like an infant. I don't *need* you all to treat me like I'm made of glass, like I'm weak!"

Fiona snatched at Fynn's jerkin and hauled him closer; leaning down to his ear, she hissed, "You're making a scene. Stop it."

The boy wrenched himself from his sister's hold and stumbled back, nearly tripping down the stairs but for Fiona's hand clutching him by the upper arm and righting him.

She quirked a brow. "So, you *really* don't need me?"

Fynn narrowed his eyes, the greyness of his irises looking icier than they'd ever been. "No."

Fiona shrugged. "Fine. Next time I'll let you fall."

"Whatever," Fynn grumbled as he allowed Fiona to walk ahead of him.

Presently walking a great deal apart from the rest of his family, Fynn clearly saw the hoard that had assembled at the base of the temple's stairs. Where he would have anticipated the masses to be crying their lamentations at the death of the queen mother and Princess Gemma, he instead spied what was clearly an angry mob. The people looked filthy. Dirt was smudged across their faces; their clothing was stained and tattered. They pushed and shoved; some swung their fists wildly about. They all shouted and howled viciously as the nobility of Estheria drew ever nearer. Their fervor seemed to intensify when they saw Lachlan and his crown of gold.

Fynn tensed when several commoners lunged forward, yellowed finger-nails clawing and snatching at the air, trying to get to the king. But the King's Guard and their bronze shields kept them at bay. The boy bit down on his lower lip, eyes wide as he watched the peasants of the capital launch them-selves into the shields. They were waves crashing against the shore wildly, as if whipped into a frenzy by some unseen tempest.

The king stepped onto the main street of the city with his brother and wife close behind him. They all seemed to easily ignore the ferocity of the surrounding crowd. Ciaran then stepped into the street, his banner still aloft and swaying gently in the morning breeze. With no difficulty at all, he ig-nored the mob, his head held high and expression undaunted.

Hollyn and James, however, stared at the rabid hoards with intensity, derision evident in their eyes as they continued on down the street toward Batsbeckon. Fiona, Fynn noted, seemed unsure of the situation. Her steps faltered and her shoulders were curled inward as she tried to withdraw from the maddening pack.

As Fynn stepped onto the street, the heaviness of the crowd's presence descended upon him. He was all too aware of their vengeful hands darting out like lightning snapping through the clouds, intent on tearing him apart if just one of them got hold.

Something glinting overhead caught Fynn's eye. He forced himself to look from the distorted faces of the commoners to the long line of rooftops that traveled parallel to the main road. He saw it then. There stood a masked figure holding a bow and strung arrow. The sunlight was reflecting off the arrowhead, drawing the attention of many of the lords and ladies just be-hind Fynn. They all stopped and looked up, terrifying realization dawning within each and every one of them as they watched the figure raise his bow and arrow and level it toward the road. With pale eyes having gone wider than he thought possible, Fynn followed the line of fire until his gaze settled on the three figures far off in front of him—Lachlan, Ursalyn, and Felix. He let loose a breath he hadn't realized he was holding before sprinting forward, his body lurching under the abruptness of his motions. He jerked and twisted around his sister and cousins as he barreled toward his father.

Nothing around him felt real anymore. It was as if it were all falling away into obscurity, blurring as he rushed forward. Despite the archer being perched high up atop the roof, Fynn still heard the vibration of the bowstring as the arrow was let loose. Time seemed to slow until nothing was moving, nothing but the arrow that shot down toward Felix.

Fynn watched in absolute horror as the arrow sailed cleanly through the air, nearly blending in with the pale morning sky. It plunged downward and found its purchase in Felix's throat.

Before anyone could react, Prince Felix clasped a hand to his throat with desperation as pain lanced through him and blood–thick, red pools of blood–oozed from the wound and down his front, seeping onto the cobblestones beneath his feet; it ran like a thin, scarlet river through the cracks and divots of the roadway. His knees buckled as he gasped for air. He fell to the ground, hardly moving at all.

Booming, terrified screams exploded. The sounds of horses wailing and shields clattering against bodies were monstrously loud. Lachlan was yelling, hauling Ursalyn backward and away from Felix's unmoving body. The King's Guard was doing their best to keep back the crowd of commoners who were now riled to the point of eruption; peasants threw themselves and lunged forward, scraping their cracked nails against the gold-plated armor of the guards with malicious intent alight in their eyes. They yelled and screamed and called for blood, for equal lamentation for their dead lost in the first fire that had ignited in the middle quarter.

Lords pulled their ladies back from the searching claws of the enraged peoples. Knights drew their swords from their scabbards and stepped up to defend the nobility.

All the while, the high-born children valiantly tried to be brave in the face of the madness that was unleashed.

More arrows began to rain down from the rooftops. Fynn made it to his father's side. He was the only one, as Lachlan and Ursalyn had rushed toward their sons and dragged them far back, closer to the guards who held their glinting swords aloft, shields raised.

Fynn placed his hands atop his father's chest, feeling the nearly imperceptible rise and fall with each strained breath the elder prince took. The boy trembled. He bit back his cries so forcefully that he drew blood from his lower lip. Stinging tears gushed from his pale eyes and rolled down his cheeks. He shook Felix by the shoulders and pled, "Please, you've got to get up!"

Felix's hand fell limply from his throat, his red-stained palm a terrifying reminder of the blood loss. The arrow remained there, protruding from his white neck. Ghastly red trails slipped from the corners of his mouth as he choked on his own breath. His eyes fluttered open, straining to focus on the boy crouched over him. He blinked, desperate to rid himself of the blurriness.

Fynn remained there, hunched over his father's crumpled form, shaking him with all the strength in his body, willing him to be all right.

Felix reached up to his son's face, tracing the curve of the boy's cheek with his bloodied fingertips, leaving a faint trail of red behind. He brushed his forefinger over a scar that cut through Fynn's black eyebrow. Felix smiled. "I don't...think...I'll heal up...quite...like you do." His voice was weak and rattled with effort. Blood bubbled in his mouth.

Fynn placed his hand carefully over the wound, stemming the blood flow only marginally. It wasn't long before he felt the familiar, sickly stickiness of blood filling his palm, oozing between his fingers. He grinned painfully down at his father. "You'll be okay," Fynn croaked. Tears slipped from his chin and fell into the gruesome well of redness that covered Felix's entire front.

Felix's hand combed through Fynn's hair softly. "No."

The boy shook his head feverishly. More tears streaked down his face. "Don't say that!"

"Fynn," the man implored tiredly.

The child ceased his hysterics and forced himself to look into his father's ever-dulling blue eyes.

"You've got to be...strong."

"Not yet! Not yet, Father. *You're* still here. I don't need to be strong because *you're* still here!"

Felix's bloody thumb stroked the boy's cheek, brushing the tears away. "I won't be for long."

Fynn's hold upon his father tightened. "I won't let you go!"

"You don't have a choice." Felix coughed; flecks of red bespangled his now too-pale lips.

"No! Please, no. *Please*...don't leave me."

"I'm proud of you." Felix's eyes closed; his chest stopped moving.

Fynn shook his father again. He shook him by the shoulders, horrified by the limpness of the form beneath his grasp. Felix's head lolled lifelessly to the side. "No!" Fynn's hand balled into a fist. He beat his father's chest. "No! *Damn* it! No...you can't! You can't leave me." He shook uncontrollably. "Please don't go." His voice was so quiet, so meek. "You can't leave me yet. I'm not ready."

Arrows were striking through the sky like feathered lightning bolts, imbedding in men, women, and children as they staggered through the streets. It seemed the arrows didn't discriminate between high and low born. Fynn, still kneeling at his father's side, watched as peasant and noble alike howled in pain, arrows protruding from their flesh. There was so much blood—so much red everywhere.

Fynn's hands shook as he stood on quivering legs. He looked around and, for the first time, truly beheld the magnitude of the madness that had seized the city. There were overturned carts and destroyed carriages. Horses were running wild through the streets, shrieking as they darted through the maelstrom. There were children lying lifelessly on the ground beside their mothers or fathers, their siblings left defenseless as they shouted and wailed. Lords had drawn their swords alongside their knights and were swinging wildly at the commoners who rushed them. Ladies were being ushered through the road toward the castle with their children clinging to their dresses or safely nestled in their arms. Peasants had drawn swords and knives and sickles and were gracelessly hacking away at the shields of the guards and the knights. The slashing sound of metal clattering against metal was overwhelming, nearly obscuring the pained howls of those the arrows impaled.

Where once time seemed to stand still, now it sped by unnaturally. Fynn could hardly decipher what was happening anymore; everything was a blur, a wicked whirl of colors and sounds. He searched the throngs of bodies, desperate to find Fiona. He didn't see her. With one last look at his father lying at his feet, Fynn forced himself to peel away from Felix. He dove into the chaos.

"Fi!" Fynn cried. His voice was scarcely heard amidst the riot. "Fiona!"

Fynn was knocked to the side by a large man who hadn't seen him. The man continued on stumbling forward as Fynn fell to the ground. The prince forced himself up on his hands and knees but was knocked onto his back by another man storming into him and kicking into his side. Prostrate on the ground, Fynn gasped for breath. His side hurt, his palms were cut from the fall, and his trousers were ripped at the knees where he had scraped against the cobblestones. He quickly noticed that no one was aware he was on the ground or, if they were, didn't care in the least about trampling him. Clumsily, Fynn clambered to his feet and stumbled forward again. More and more people knocked into him, pushing him in every direction. Fynn faltered, his ankle twisted awkwardly. He fell to the ground once more, wincing as his already damaged palms scraped painfully against the road again.

"Fiona!" he called. Tears swam down his cheeks. "Fiona! Fi!"

He'd only just managed to get up when he was shoved to the ground again. His chin smacked against the stone. Fynn looked down to see red droplets spill from his chin, coloring the grey stone of the road. "*Damn* it," he muttered as his hand reached to the split flesh, wiping away the blood. "Damn it *all*."

Fynn drew himself up again and staggered forward with all the strength he had left. Arrows continued to rain down upon them, swords still smashed into swords, shields still beat against the meaty flesh of their adversaries. All the yelling, and whining of steel, and stampede of hooves against stone melded together into a foul cacophony that overwhelmed the city. Fynn continued to call for Fiona, but his voice was lost amongst the destruction. Colors, people he supposed, swirled by, slamming into him, pushing him carelessly, shoving him this way and that. He did his best to stay upright, but eventually found himself upon the ground once more.

The prince felt his strength, what little he had possessed, leaving him. Every sinew in his body seemed as though it would snap asunder. His muscles felt raw. His back ached. His knees were bloodied. His palms were torn painfully. And he couldn't keep himself from crying. Fynn shook uncontrollably. He choked back the bile that threatened to jump from his sore throat and managed to, once again, stand on thin, quaking legs. He knew where the castle was, relative to where he was standing. But, as he gazed through the swell of bodies all around, it seemed impossible to get to Batsbeckon.

Regardless, he forced himself onward toward the castle. As he staggered and pushed through rabid commoners and enraged knights, he saw a flash of red streak by before disappearing. "Godryk?" he whispered breathlessly as he began to chase down the red. "Godryk!"

But, as Fynn wormed his way through the crowd, he found that the red was not Godryk, but a young girl about his age. She was dressed in fine black silks. Her red hair was drawn back in a long braid. It didn't matter that he didn't know who she was. It didn't matter at all. When she turned to him with bright, blue eyes welling with tears, blood smeared across her alabaster face, errant strands of scarlet tangling in front of her eyes, Fynn didn't hesitate to reach out for her hand and pull her towards him. He was surprised when she didn't cling to him fearfully, but instead her hold on his hand was strong, resolute, determined.

She looked around for a moment, peering through the gaps in the crowd, and then jerked Fynn's arm awkwardly. Having spied what could be their refuge, a shop that seemed quiet and abandoned, the girl began running forward through a break in the chaos, dragging the prince along with her. The two weaved and dodged and ducked through the rioting crowd.

Finding their escape into the sanctity of the shop proved more difficult than initially expected. The girl was heaved to the side by a bear-like man with meaty hands. She fell hard to the ground, pulling Fynn down with her.

The girl was up before Fynn and snatched his jerkin into her scraped hands and forced him to his feet. Dazedly, Fynn regarded her before she threw all her weight into him and sent them both careening toward the edge of the road.

Once more they both found themselves upon the ground. This time they looked up with grateful eyes as they were huddled before the shop door. Quicker than Fynn thought possible, the red-haired girl was up again, swinging open the door and waving her hand, beckoning the young prince to follow. As the boy crossed the threshold, she slammed the door shut behind him.

"Are you alright?" she asked.

He hadn't thought about how bad he probably looked until he peered down and saw how filthy he was. His jerkin was ripped, revealing the grey shirt beneath. His sleeves were torn, muddied, and covered with blood. His chin was still bleeding. The blood trickled down his neck. His face was an array of purples and blacks from the bruises born from repeatedly being hit and thrown to the ground. He raised his hands, scowling when he saw the many cuts that littered his fingers and palms.

He nodded. "I'm fine." He turned his attention to the girl and his scowl intensified. "Did they hurt you?"

She shrugged. "I'll be all right." She raised her hand and wiped the blood from her nose. "Just a few bumps and cuts."

Fynn assessed the girl before him. Her dress was torn and stained from the incident. There were bruises and bumps and scrapes aplenty all about her exposed, freckled flesh. Her right shin was, by virtue of her destroyed dress, exposed and, Fynn noted disdainfully, badly cut.

He gestured toward her leg. "May I?" he asked carefully.

She nodded, confusion in her eyes.

Fynn tore his grey shirt and knelt before her. Gently, he wrapped the material over the wound and tied it just firmly enough. "Should stop the bleeding," he offered meekly as he stood.

She smiled at him. Her eyes were an odd shade of blue, darker than most Fynn had seen, but still very warm and inviting.

"Thank you." She held out her hand to him. "I'm Lux Astor."

He took her hand in his. "Fynneas Fog."

Her smile faded as sadness dawned in her blue eyes. "I'm sorry about your family."

Fynn combed his hand through his filthy hair and looked away from her. He couldn't stand the look in her eyes. His chest felt heavy. "Thank you."

Lux, undeterred by Fynn turning away from her, circled him until they once again stood toe to toe. She looked down at his chest and torso. Though the leather jerkin was black, the sickening sheen of blood was still apparent. It covered most the boy's front. "Are you sure you're okay?"

Fynn whispered, "It's not *my* blood."

Lux took a step back. "Oh," she gasped. "I'm sorry."

The prince was about to say something but stopped when the door began to shake. Both children turned around and watched, horrified, as the door rattled beneath the weight of repeated blows.

Lux said softly, "I locked the door soon as you came in." She took his hand in hers. "They won't be able to break it down, right?"

Despite the fear roiling in his chest, Fynn's hold on Lux's hand tightened. He shook his head. "I don't think so." His words were hollow. "We'll be fine."

They watched nervously as the door quaked beneath the unseen force slamming against it from the other side. The wood looked as though it would give way and splinter at any moment. The rusty hinges rattled and creaked.

Lux stood firmly; Fynn shuffled closer to her.

Her voice was low. "Did anyone see us come in here?"

Fynn shook his head. "No. No, I don't think so. They were all too busy ripping each other's throats out."

"Someone must have seen," Lux insisted. "They're coming to get us."

The prince shook his head. "I won't let them get you."

Lux rolled her eyes. "That's all very well and gallant of you, but do you have a plan in mind?"

110

The boy faltered. "No…not exactly."

The door trembled again. The hinges bent from the wall. Another smack into the door and it gave way, swinging open. The sunlight spilled into the shop, exposing the two children clinging to one another. There in the doorway stood a figure, robed in black. The man's chubby face was smeared with dirt and soot; his eyes were an angry brown. In an instant, he reached out and grabbed Fynn, hauling the boy forward, almost lifting him clear off the ground. The prince struggled against the man's grasp, clawing at the hand that held him.

Fynn kicked out his legs and writhed beneath the intruder's hold. "Let me go! Let me go, I *command* it!" He shrieked when the grip near his throat tightened, inching him forward.

"Oh," chuckled the man, "you *command* it, do you?" He tightened his hold on the prince, holding him flush against the wall. At the sound of Fynn's startled yelp, the man smiled a yellow-toothed grin and mocked, "Go on, *command* me again, little shit!"

Lux struck out at the aggressor. She swung her fist at the man; thin knuckles twisted into the side of the assailant's head. Her eyes widened when she realized he didn't even flinch. Rather, he slowly turned in her direction, head cocking to the side as he observed her wordlessly. She took a step back when the man tossed Fynn aside as if he weighed no more than a pebble. She shuddered when she saw the heaviness with which Fynn struck the ground and crumpled. Lux took another step back, raising her arms defensively. She narrowed her eyes and growled. "Leave us alone! We haven't done anything to you!"

Fynn forced himself up in time to throw himself at the man. He lunged forward with all the strength he had left. He collided with the man's back and succeeded in forcing him off course and away from Lux. In turn, he tumbled back to the ground. Fynn's already shredded palms tore further as they skidded across the splintering wood of the floorboards. He winced when a particularly sharp piece of the boards dug under his skin.

Ignoring the fiery pain in his hand, the prince leapt back to his feet and stood in front of Lux. "What do you want with us?" Fynn demanded in the most even voice he could muster.

Lux gasped when the man's fist collided with the side of Fynn's head, sending the boy careening back to the ground. She was unable to move, too arrested by fear. Blood flowed freely from a fresh wound just along Fynn's hairline.

Blue eyes snapped back to the assailant when he drew nearer. Lux found herself backing up until she ran into the wall and had nowhere left to retreat. She shook her head, stray curls tumbling over her welling eyes. "Get away! Get *away* from me!"

The man reached out a gloved hand and wiped the tears from the girl's cheek. His leather clad thumb brushed over her lips and then ran through her hair, tangling in the mess that once was her braid. His hand wandered from her red hair, down her cheek, and then along her soft jawline; it traveled languidly down her slender, white throat before long fingers wrapped around her neck. Lux choked as her head was thrown backward into the wall. The hand encircling her throat tightened until she could scarcely breathe. She struggled and kicked, pushing her hands against the man's chest with all her strength as she gasped and writhed.

Fynn was back on his feet at the sound of Lux's gurgled cries. His vision was blurred. He felt blood dripping down from his matted hair. The boy shook his head, trying to clear his vision. When at last he found he could see again, he gasped at the sight of the man choking Lux, holding her to the wall as she clawed and scratched at him frantically. Fynn leapt forward, clinging to the man's back as he wrapped his slender arms around the assailant's throat, constricting with all the strength he had left.

Having not expected Fynn to be up so soon, the man was caught unaware and reeled back at the shock of the boy choking him. He let go of Lux; she clattered to the ground in a gasping mass, both hands flying to her throat as she sought deep breaths. Meanwhile, Fynn had not released his hold on their attacker. The man's hands clamped over Fynn's arms and pried the boy from his neck, tossing him headlong over his broad shoulders and into the wall. Fynn was now no more than a tangle of limbs awkwardly sprawled at Lux's side.

"What do you want?" asked Lux as she scooted away from the once-again approaching assailant.

"*Want?* What do I *want?*" the attacker repeated incredulously, eyeing the children. "Everything I'm owed! You do nothing! You're just born with titles and money. Meanwhile, I work 'til my fingers can't bleed no more and what do I have? Tell me!"

"Leave her alone," Fynn demanded. He forced himself up again. "It's not our fault!"

"The sins of the father, little boy, the sins of the father. The middle quarter goes and burns down and what do you and your king do? Nothing. You preach and moan, but you do nothing at all to help us. Then you have the gall—that's right, the *Gods be damned gall*—to throw a funeral because some *damned* old woman and her sodding bitch daughter died? Like we should care." Spit spluttered from the man's lips as he raged. "It's *madness* out there! Just look. I don't think they'll be missing you little pretties for a while, eh?"

By this time, Fynn hardly had the energy left to stand, let alone fight off anyone. Every breath was labored, and he felt like his thoughts were swimming in his head. His vision was blurring again, and blackness encroached on his periphery. He swayed uneasily where he stood. Nevertheless, he made an effort to drag himself in front of Lux. He stared from behind the tangled, black locks that hung in front of his unfocussed eyes. There was a viciousness in those grey depths that only occasionally reared and, for just a moment, there was a flicker of red through his irises.

"Get away from her," Fynn ordered. His voice was lower, steadier.

The man halted his foray toward the prince.

Fynn marveled, thinking he had truly intimidated the blood-lusting rioter. That was, until he saw the reason for the man's sudden halt. At the sight of Moriah, swathed in black, green eyes almost aglow, Fynn couldn't help the hysterical sob of relief that nearly choked him.

"Leave the children be," the lord commander ordered.

Fynn felt like his heart was beating so fast it would rip his chest apart, but he couldn't stave off the smile that burst onto his features. He didn't know how the man had found him; truthfully, he didn't care. Fynn gathered Lux into his arms and pulled her to her feet. The pair slowly began retreating toward Moriah, nervously looking back to their former attacker.

Moriah's green gaze wandered over the man appraisingly, assessing the shabby clothing, dirt-stained face, and wild look in his eyes. The lord commander stepped forward, urging Fynn and Lux behind him. He looked over his shoulder to the boy prince and whispered, "Stay where I can see you."

Fynn nodded.

Looking back at the rioter, Moriah's voice once more found its usual note of bored disinterest as he ordered, "Leave now and I won't kill you where you stand."

"You?" The man snorted, a wry look upon his face. "I weigh two of you. What do you think you'll be accomplishing here?"

"So that's a no to leaving, is it? Shame. I was in a particularly magnanimous mood, but you've gone and spoiled it," purred Moriah. His features darkened as his eyes narrowed. "Last chance."

"C'mon then. Let's see what you can do, pretty boy! Have at it," goaded the rioter.

With languid grace, Moriah raised his hand aloft. With the flick of his finger, fire erupted and blazed across the room, scorching the man. The wretched sound of agonized wailing echoed through the small shop thunderously until it faded to nothing more than a deathly whine. The blackened body, charred to the bone, crumbled to the ground into ashes. Embers swept into the air, winking for a moment before dying out into nothing.

"How did," Fynn stammered, "what even…how…that was *fire*! Where'd it come from?"

Lux's eyes had gone wide as saucers. "He's gone," she whispered disbelievingly.

Fynn could do little more than nod.

"How?" she queried.

"Don't know," Fynn answered, the shock of the situation still stealing away his breath away.

"Moriah!"

All attention in the shop turned to the doorway to behold another man, the newest arrival to the odd gathering in the abandoned, and now slightly burned, building. Fynn and Lux both retreated away from the doorway, each casting furtive glances back to the simmering pile of ash that lay heaped upon the ground.

"Do you know who *he* is too?" Lux asked quietly.

Fynn shook his head. "Your guess is as good as mine."

Moriah sighed and ran his hand through his hair, shaking his head. "Noel, what're you doing here?"

Noel, as Moriah had called the newly arrived man, was tall and slender of build. He had a handsome face with soft features. His tousled hair was a light brown, his eyes the most spectacular shade of blue. He smiled a crooked, boyish smile, as he laughed. "Well, I *followed* you."

"Why, pray tell, did you do such a thing?" asked Moriah.

"I thought you'd need my help, of course!" chirped Noel as he sauntered up to Moriah's side brightly. His sharp eyes then fell upon the ashen pile. "Seems you may have already handled it. Whatever *it* was?"

"*It* wasn't important," assured Moriah tiredly.

Glancing around the room, Noel found Fynn and Lux. Quirking a brow, he smirked. "*It* clearly involved a certain prince."

"Well," drawled Moriah, "as you can see, *it's* been taken care of."

114

"What was *it*, might I ask?"

"An angry commoner." Moriah huffed. "One who seemed to think he could take out his troubles on two innocent children. *Petty*, really."

"*Misguided*, possibly," Noel offered affably.

"You've too gentle a heart," chided the lord commander.

Noel smiled warmly. "And you've too stern a heart, big brother. We balance each other out, I suppose."

With all immediate danger apparently nullified, Fynn edged closer to the lord commander. He nudged Moriah with his shoulder, drawing the older man's attention. The prince looked up into the green eyes he had found himself missing and stated rather plainly, "You flicked fire out of your hand."

Moriah stood there. "Yes. That's one way to describe what happened."

Fynn arched a black brow. "You...don't seem very surprised."

Moriah smirked. "Why should I be?" He looked down at the prince and laughed at the boy's absolutely bewildered expression. He added, "It was *only* fire."

Fynn balked. "*Only?*"

"Lightning would've been a bit much, I think," Noel added, bored.

"*Lightning?*" repeated Fynn.

Moriah nodded. "Not as easy to control. Thing's could've gotten... messy. Fire was easier."

"Wise choice," agreed Noel.

Fynn chuckled numbly. "Right."

Moriah took the time to survey the prince. He noted the blood and dirt and frowned. "You look worse for wear."

It was then that the enormity of the day's events truly fell upon Fynn's shoulders. Whatever ease he had felt upon Moriah's arrival slipped away like sand from between his fingers. "Someone...an angry commoner I think... killed my father. Shot him from up on the rooftops." Fynn tried, he really tried, to keep the tears at bay. But, alas, they broke free of his emotional restraints and raced down his cheeks. He didn't want to look at Moriah, but the man caught the boy's chin in his hand and forced Fynn to stare him in the eyes. "I'm sorry. I shouldn't be crying like this," croaked the prince.

Moriah shook his head. "Don't apologizing for being sad." He knelt before Fynn. His hands draped over the boy's shoulders. Moriah held Fynn firmly. "Don't *ever* be ashamed of mourning the loss of someone you love."

"*Loved*," corrected Fynn. "He's dead."

"Do you no longer care for him?"

"Of course…*yes*…I do," stammered the boy.

Moriah softly pat the child on the cheek. "Then it is *love*, not *loved*."

"You're right."

The lord commander reached out and ran his fingers through the boy's hair. It was becoming a habit. "You'll find I usually am." Moriah smirked.

The prince tilted his head toward the doorway where the slightly obscured pounding of steel and fists could still be heard. "Moriah?" Fynn ventured.

"Hmm?"

"They hate us, don't they?"

"Don't worry about them right now. They're upset. They've suffered losses in the fire and the way Lachlan…the *king*, handled it…well, it's no excuse for what they've done. Hatred is a terrible thing. It does things to people, twists their minds. You saw for yourselves." Moriah's voice softened. "Be better than that. Be better than them. Don't let hatred cloud your judgement."

Fynn nodded docilely, not entirely convinced that the commoners wouldn't try and tear him limb from limb the moment they saw him. Absently, the prince said, "But I don't think I *hate* anyone."

"You will," Moriah assured.

7

THE FAREWELL FEAST

The King's Guard stood like statues, straight backed, hands draped over their sheathed swords at their hips. Their eyes watched. They watched everything. Four days had passed since the rioting and chaos that followed the royal funeral. Four days of repairing the broken doors and walls of the shops that lined Temple Road, corralling the horses that had panicked and gone racing off, repairing the damage done to the road itself, mopping the blood from the street, removing the bodies. Four days of eliminating any trace of the unrest that still permeated every inch of the capital city. So, the King's Guard kept watching, all its members quite aware of the hateful looks they received from passersby. They didn't care. It wasn't their job to care. Their job was to watch and observe, to put an end to another riot before it had a chance to begin. So, they stood there on the edges of the roads, spread amongst the four quarters of the city. Those nearest Batsbeckon weren't nearly as on edge as though who were positioned in the lower and bottom quarters. The festering viciousness and callous disregard for hundreds of years of tradition were stifling. Those guards standing watch were far quicker to draw their swords, for they received far more than nasty looks and hateful whispers. In just four days, three knights of the guard had been attacked by rabid rogues. Only one died, the other two merely sustained flesh wounds that would heal in time. Nevertheless, the guards were on edge, tetchy at even the faintest sound.

In the middle quarter, two guards stood side by side. Their eyes swept over the streets and observed, bored, the people who came and went. They'd grown used to the looks of derision they received from the middle quarter's residents. It didn't really bother them. There in the middle quarter, things may not be as overtly chaotic as the lower and bottom, but there were physical reminders that spoke of the reason for the commoners' anger.

Where the guards stood in the middle quarter, the burn marks and fire-licks from where the city had gone aflame earlier in the summer were still visible. The king hadn't deigned to repair the quarter yet; explaining, by way of messenger, to the residents that there were far more pressing matters to attend to, coin that needed to be spent on more urgent issues that the Crown believed more deserving of their attention. As such, middle quarter residents had gone on with their lives in a section of the city that seemed to now permanently smell of smoke and ash. They did their best, with what little they had, to repair their shops and homes. They swept away the ashes and replaced what they could of the destroyed wood, but the stones were still darkened by the fire's touch and the tapestries and rugs that decorated the shops and homes there were frayed by embers or reeked of sickly smoke.

It was a hot day.

All the days recently seemed to be unnaturally warm.

Noel sighed. There was no escaping the heat. He continued along down the hall towards the prince's chambers. He knocked. It was silent. He knocked again. Still, there was nothing. He pushed the door open, not caring that the boy hadn't invited him in. He stood just a few paces beyond the threshold, staring at the small figure of the prince curled up on the windowsill, staring out at the sweltering city. In that moment, Fynn looked fragile.

"Prince Fynneas?"

Fynn didn't even look in Noel's direction.

"Sire, your sister says you haven't left your room since…*that* day."

Fynn shrugged, still not bothering to even look at the man who now stood, fidgeting, in the middle of the room.

"Can we talk?"

Fynn looked at him then and Noel was stunned by the vacant expression in the boy's eyes, the hollowness of his features. The whites of his eyes were reddened, his skin puffy and swollen looking, fresh tear stains streaked his cheeks. Noel was next to him in an instant. He enveloped the child in his arms and pulled him to his chest, resting his chin atop Fynn's head as the boy quaked beneath him. It wasn't long before the barely contained sobs turned into full-on hysterics. Noel let the prince tire himself out, all the while tracing small circles over his back. Finally, Fynn went limp in Noel's arms, nestling his forehead against the man's shoulder.

The prince's voice was small. "You're Moriah's brother?"

The man combed his fingers through the boy's black hair. He smiled. "I am."

"You two are kind of strange, you know," Fynn commented.

Caught off guard by that assessment, Noel couldn't help but chuckle. "You're not the first person to say something like that. I'm sure you won't be the last."

Fynn pulled out of the man's arms. He rubbed his eyes, desperate to remove all traces of his earlier breakdown. "You don't seem very much like him."

Noel shrugged. "No. I don't suppose we're very similar." He smiled warmly. "What would the fun be in that if we were exactly the same, eh?"

For a moment, there was a spark in Fynn's eyes. But it faded far too quickly for Noel's liking. Another silvery tear slipped from icy eyes, but Noel was quick to brush it away.

"I'm sorry," Fynn whispered.

Noel cocked his head to the side curiously.

The movement reminded Fynn of a confused dog.

"For what?" Noel inquired.

Again, Fynn scraped furiously at his face. He was unable to bite back the whimper that escaped his throat as he looked away, hiding the tears that kept coming. They wouldn't stop. "I shouldn't be *crying* like this."

Noel caught the boy's chin in his grasp. It was an action Fynn was all too familiar with, a shared habit between Felix and Moriah.

Fynn pouted, but Noel was undeterred and managed to get the boy to look at him. His thumb traced over the prince's chin gently. "I would be far more concerned if you *weren't* crying." His other hand reached out to the boy and wiped away another offending tear. "You're allowed to cry. No one thinks any less of you for it."

Fynn couldn't break free from Noel's grasp, but he managed to avert his eyes. "Moriah wouldn't cry."

Noel snorted, rolling his eyes. "*Please* don't tell me you're trying to emulate *him* of all people"

Fynn looked back to Noel quickly, eyes narrowing. "Why not? He was friends with my father. *Good* friends! And from what I've seen, he's really *strong* and *brave* and *smart.*"

Noel smiled. It didn't reach his eyes. "You're not wrong there." He shrugged his shoulders again. "But he's not, *what I would call*, good with dealing with things."

Puzzled, Fynn asked, "What do you mean?"

"He's never been a crier. I don't think I ever remember him actually crying over anything, now that I think about it." Noel looked away from Fynn and toward the window, searching for something that wasn't there—something that would never be there. "No. I can't recall a time Moriah has cried over anything…or *anyone.*" His eyes darkened as he continued his fruitless search, somberness overcoming him. It was the sort of somberness he had been working hard to ward off in the days following Felix's death—his murder. All of a sudden, he felt weighty and saddened and a particularly vicious, most rancid sort of melancholy was tangling itself in his chest. Noel felt as though he could scarcely breathe. He added thoughtfully, "It's not that he doesn't care." He looked back at the confused face of the boy prince and tried, truly tried, to smile genuinely. But he failed. His smile faltered and his eyes remained dark, tempestuous. "Have you seen him since that day?" Noel asked.

Fynn shook his head.

"You should." Noel drew himself up to his full height and offered his hand to the prince. "Come with me."

Fynn didn't want to go. He was perfectly happy festering in his own little pit of misery and despair. He didn't want to have to bother with everyone else because he really didn't care. He scowled, feeling callous about his own thoughts. His stomach dropped when he realized he hadn't bothered to even speak to his sister after that day. Reluctantly, Fynn took Noel's hand and allowed himself to be led from his room and through what seemed to be an endless number of halls until he stood before a door. He waited quietly at Noel's side as the man wrapped his knuckles against the wood.

There was silence.

Noel knocked again.

Still, there was nothing.

Noel huffed and rolled his eyes before glancing down at Fynn. "You know, you two are *very much* alike. It's annoying really."

Something about that statement, the comparison, made Fynn smile. He followed Noel as the man pushed open the door and marched into the room. Fynn stayed behind him, not wanting to incur any ire from Moriah that may be stirred by coming into his room unannounced and entirely uninvited. He peeked around Noel and scanned the dark chambers before his eyes settled on the long, lean form of Moriah curled up under a mountain of blankets upon his bed.

"Go away, Noel," Moriah grumbled as he burrowed further beneath the warmth of the thick, wool coverings.

Noel looked back at Fynn and smirked. *"Siblings."* He winked. "Am I right?"

Fynn nodded dumbly. He was aware how difficult it was to deal with a sibling who was in no mood to talk to you. Many a time, he was on the receiving end of such treatment from Fiona. But Fiona was usually quick to come around and welcome him back into her confidence with open arms. Moriah didn't strike Fynn as the type to behave in such a way.

The boy watched with rapt interest as Noel jumped up onto Moriah's bed like a faithful dog searching out his master's side. His movements were languorous, reminding the prince a great deal of Moriah himself.

Noel shook his brother by his shoulder. "Really, get up," the younger Mordray implored.

Moriah rolled away from his brother's touch. "No."

Biting his cheek, Noel shoved his brother hard. Moriah tumbled off the bed in a heap while Noel remained kneeling on the mattress, watching his brother topple over the edge with mild interest. "Well, you're up now, aren't you?" Noel laughed pleasantly.

Moriah sat up, brushing his hair out of his face. His green eyes were as sharp as ever. It wasn't long before they found Fynn and seemed to soften. He quirked a brow, nodded toward Noel, and asked, "He dragged you here?"

Fynn nodded sheepishly.

Moriah groused, "Pain in the ass, isn't he?"

The prince smiled. There was something very reassuring about the familiar, dull tone of Moriah's deep voice. Fynn watched as the lord commander pulled himself to his feet before forcefully throwing his fallen blankets at Noel.

"Want to come for a walk?" the now mostly awake Moriah asked with a weak smile.

Fynn's eyes lit up for the first time in days.

Moriah took the prince by the shoulder, pushed him out the door, and left Noel alone without another thought. The two didn't speak at all until they were in the gardens, the sunlight bearing down on them.

Fynn was inwardly awed at how Moriah managed to always be swathed in head-to-toe black garb and never seem to sweat in the sweltering summer. Moriah continued guiding Fynn along through the expanse of green until they were sitting side by side beneath a large tree; the thick branches tangled overhead provided a comfortable shade for the pair.

Moriah was settled against the trunk, his head leaned back, eyes closed. His voice was low and, as ever, sounded entirely too disinterested with the conversation. "How have you been?"

"Fine." Fynn shrugged. He looked away. Nothing in particular had caught his attention. He fidgeted some, trying to create space between himself and the somnolent man. He thought about peeking to the side and seeing if Moriah had given any indication that he was going to say anything, but the very thought of looking at the man right now bothered Fynn. He could feel the familiar sting of tears welling in his eyes. He bit down on his lip and furrowed his brow. The prince shook his head, wiping the unshed tears from his eyes.

Moriah shoved him gently, but with enough force to knock Fynn off balance for just a moment. As the boy righted himself, he finally looked back at Moriah, stunned to see those catlike eyes staring back at him, one fine brow raised curiously.

"You don't look fine," Moriah said. There wasn't outright concern evident in his tone, but the momentary spark of energy in his voice was new. "Your eyes are red. You've been crying." He cocked his head to the side. "Still are."

Fynn's cheeks reddened as he furiously pawed at his eyes, desperate to eliminate any trace of tears. He snapped, "I am not!"

Moriah's lips curled into a smirk. "Oh?" Moriah drawled. "Really, now?"

Fynn squared his shoulders and turned toward Moriah fully. "Yes." His small voice was harsher than it had ever been. "I'm *not* crying!"

Moriah noted, "Pity."

Fynn was caught by that sentiment. He hadn't expected Moriah to retort so concisely. The prince chewed on his lower lip and looked away again, once more struck with the irrational feeling that if he looked at Moriah for too long, he may spontaneously burst into flames. His voice was no more than a whisper when he asked, "Why do you say that?"

"Crying might help. Or at least, that's what I've been told."

"Noel says you don't *ever* cry."

There was a pause in the conversation before Moriah answered evenly, "I suppose he's probably right."

"Why don't you?" Fynn wiped at his eyes again, annoyed to find the lingering presence of his salty tears dampening his palm. "Cry, I mean."

Indolently, Moriah reached up and combed his hand through his black hair. He looked away, staring at something far off or maybe staring at nothing at all. "I just have never seen the point, I suppose."

"Oh." Fynn's shoulders fell ever so slightly.

"Have you been sleeping at all?" Moriah was still staring off at nothing. "I find sleeping helps. Your mind just…sorts things out, I believe, when you're sleeping. It helps you come to terms with things…calms you down."

Fynn shook his head. "I can't. I've tried."

"Why not?"

Fynn pulled his knees to his chest, encircling them with his lanky arms. His forehead rested upon those drawn-up knees tiredly. He curled in on himself. "I've been having nightmares."

"About what happened?"

The prince shook his head. "No."

Curiosity now piqued, Moriah pulled himself from his thoughtless reverie and looked at the boy at his side. Fynn's lean shoulders were quaking as he forced himself to swallow down more sobs. Unsure of what compelled him to do so, Moriah settled his hand over the boy's back and began tracing along the lines of his shoulders gently. "What are your nightmares about?" he asked carefully.

"It's a very dark place. I can't see anything," Fynn began reluctantly. His hold on his legs intensified. "It's cold there." The feeling of Moriah's long fingers tracing small figures over his back was comforting. It was an anchor, keeping him secured and safe as dark waters poured over him. It had been that way for days; the incessant feeling that black waves were going to wash him away, carry him far off to somewhere he knew he didn't want to be. Locking himself in his room hadn't helped. The waters managed to find him there. But now, sitting next to Moriah, knowing he was watching him, the prince felt settled, at ease. "I can hear people, but they're far away. I can't tell what they're saying. I don't think it's important." He unfurled his arms from around his legs and sat up straighter. He sighed, disappointed as Moriah's hand left its perch on his upper back. "There's someone there with me. I know there is. I know there's someone there, but I can't see them." He looked up at Moriah, unshed tears still swimming in the depths of his wintery eyes. "Then that someone's gone and I'm alone. I'm all alone and it's dark," Fynn whispered helplessly.

Moriah's longer fingers raked through Fynn's messy hair. He marveled as boy's eyes fluttered shut. Moriah vowed, "I won't leave you alone in the dark."

Ghostly, grey eyes opened in a flash and were staring Moriah down. Fynn's voice was measured, eerily calm. "You promise?"

"I promise."

"Moriah?"

"Hmm?"

Fynn's voice was weary. The exhaustion that had accumulated over the last few days was crashing down upon him. "*That* day when I was running toward my father, I could see him with everyone else. I could see them all standing together, and I was running toward them. But then my father was alone. There was so much going on and everyone was in a panic, but he was *alone.*"

Those pale eyes that only moments ago shone with absolute despair now looked at Moriah with a breed of shrewdness he wouldn't have attributed to Fynn. But there, staring back at him, were two grey eyes hardened and perceptive, frosty to their very core.

Fynn's voice was flat as he asked, "What happened to the old man who led the funeral?" He furrowed his brows. "He was leading them, leading my father and Uncle Lachlan. But all of a sudden, he was just *gone.*"

"I don't know."

Fynn shook his head disbelievingly. "You're lying."

"No." Moriah's voice was firm. "I promise you, I'm not. I don't know what happened to him. I didn't see. I wasn't there when it all happened."

"Can you find out?"

Moriah smirked. "I'll look into it."

Fynn's features contorted and Moriah felt himself relieved when the uncharacteristic coldness was gone from the boy's features and was replaced by the far more familiar liveliness as the prince grinned wryly.

"Moriah?"

"Hmm?"

"Are you going to tell me how you conjured up fire out of nowhere? I feel that *may* be worth discussing," pressed Fynn.

Moriah couldn't help but laugh as he rolled his eyes. "Oh, I forgot you saw that."

"No, you didn't."

Moriah relented, "You're right. I was just hoping *you* wouldn't remember."

Fynn shoved Moriah playfully. It was the first time since his father's death that he didn't feel that terrible weightiness in his chest. He felt much more himself and he couldn't help but smile broadly. "How could I forget *that?*" His eyes were shining. "It's not every day you see something like that! It was like *magic* or something."

"Yes, *or something,*" Moriah muttered. His hand draped over Fynn's shoulder and settled the boy back down until he was, once again, calmly leaning against the tree. He could still feel the excitement and energy shaking through the boy's shoulders, but it was preferable to the despondency they were contending with earlier. "There are a great many things in the world that would surprise you. You're young yet, you'll see it all in time. I'm sure," said Moriah.

"That's very cryptic," mumbled Fynn.

"It is, isn't it?" jested Moriah.

"Does that mean you're not going to tell me?"

"Fynneas." Moriah's tone was sobered, all amusement washed away. "When it's time, I'll tell you everything. But right now, you have other things to focus on."

Fynn pouted. "Like what?"

Moriah watched Fynn unwittingly snuggle closer into his side. It was almost comical the way Fynn was seeking out the comfort of being nearer to him while simultaneously crossing his arms and petulantly whining about wanting to know more. "You'll be leaving for Morancy in a few days. I would think you'd be concerned about that. Or at least, maybe excited?"

"What do you teach there?" asked Fynn.

"Mostly close quarter combat," explained the lord commander. "And... other things."

"Other things?" queried Fynn.

"Yes, *other* things. Don't worry over it right now."

Fynn sighed. "I *am* excited...really," he protested weakly. "I just thought that my father would be there to see me off, you know?"

"I know." Moriah's hold on the boy tightened. "I know exactly what you mean."

"I miss him already," admitted Fynn quietly.

"I doubt you'll ever *stop* missing him."

A strange sharpness darkened Fynn's voice as he said, "I need to know what happened, who took him from me."

"Why?"

Fynn's left hand curled into a fist in his lap. "I want them to pay for what they've done."

"Revenge isn't always the answer. Actually, I've found it very *rarely* is," Moriah whispered. "Don't let it take over, Fynneas."

"It's not," Fynn assured him. "It's just...I *need* to know what happened, who did it."

"Alright." Moriah nodded.

The conversation abruptly shifted course when Fynn yawned. "I'm tired," he mumbled.

Any trace of bitterness fled from the prince in an instant and there, at Moriah's side, was nothing more than an over-tired boy half collapsed against his side with dulling eyes. Moriah's hand combed through Fynn's hair again, ruffling the dark locks. "Close your eyes. I'll be right here."

They stayed side by side beneath the tree in a companionable silence as the day wore on. Moriah's arm had snaked around Fynn's shoulders, securely holding the boy to his side.

For the first time since the day of the funeral, Fynn was able to sleep. He dozed for the better half of the afternoon, blanketed contentedly in the peace the gardens provided. He remembered being lulled to sleep by the warbles of the birds chirping overhead. The boy only roused when he felt someone shaking his shoulders gently and a hand combing through his hair. He didn't want to wake up; he was still so tired. Eyes still closed, he nestled into the warmth of his pillow.

He was shaken again, insistently this time. At last, grey eyes blinked open and found that the pillow was Moriah's chest. As waking dawned upon the prince, he heard the steady beating of the man's heart beneath his cheek and froze. He remembered the last time he had heard that heartbeat. He jolted awake and jumped away from Moriah, eyes having gone wide in terror. He looked around frantically. He quickly realized he was in the gardens and not in the midst of flames. Still, even with that knowledge, Fynn could feel his own heart hammering in his chest. He hated that feeling, the feeling that your ribs would be splintered apart by the pounding of your own heart. He despised it even more when he tried, with every bit of his control, to stop the awful, straining feeling.

"I'm sorry," Fynn mumbled as he forced himself to ease the tension out of his shoulders. He all but crumpled into a heap before Moriah gathered him back into his arms and held him there. Fynn let his forehead rest against Moriah's shoulder, scowling into the embrace as more tears slipped down his cheeks.

Moriah situated the boy in his arms and with astounding grace managed to climb to his feet, boy prince still held tightly. "Let's get inside. It's late," Moriah announced as he took a step away from the tree.

126

"I'm too old to be carried," Fynn protested. However, he made no move to break out of Moriah's hold. Instead, he felt himself melting; his limbs fell limply.

Moriah chuckled. "Right."

Fynn allowed Moriah to carry him back to his room up in the tower. Moriah gently set the boy down on the edge of the bed. The prince looked up at him wearily, the caressing claws of sleepiness still coaxing the boy back towards its embrace.

Moriah tipped the boy's chin up with his forefinger so he could look at him. The man scowled. Dark circles were stretching beneath Fynn's eyes and the spark in the grey depths he had first come to admire earlier that summer were extinguished to mere embers fighting to stay alight. "Go to sleep, little prince," whispered the lord commander.

Fynn made no move to settle himself on the bed. He remained sitting relatively upright on the edge of the mattress, swaying with sleepiness. Moriah huffed. Gently, he pushed Fynn backward and watched, amused, as Fynn fell into the blankets in a tired mass before curling into the softness of the bedding.

At once, he was asleep. Calmness overtook him and he was lost to the world, happily giving way to a soothing quiet, delighting in the vast nothingness of his slumber.

Unfortunately, Fynn's restful sleep was cut haltingly short when his shoulder was jerked repeatedly. His lashes fluttered, tickling his cheek. Pale eyes were assaulted by the sunlight spilling into the room. He groaned, rolled onto his side, and pulled his pillow over his head. Again, his shoulder was shaken forcefully. Still foggy from exhaustion, Fynn grumbled, "What?"

He was surprised when it was Fiona's voice that responded.

"You've been asleep for *two days*. It's time to get up."

Fynn threw his pillow to the side and forced himself upright, blinking away the fuzziness from his vision as he peered blearily at Fiona. She was seated on the edge of his bed looking fretful. He sat up straighter, yawning as he rolled his shoulders.

"That can't be right," Fynn mumbled, feeling the tightness in his back. "Who sleeps for *that long*?"

Fiona reached out and smoothed her hand over her brother's unruly mane. She smiled. "That's what I said, but Moriah *insisted* we let you sleep."

"Have I missed much?"

Fiona shook her head. "Not really." She looked away from him, thoughtfulness in her expression as she studied the far wall. "Everyone's just been moping around really."

127

"And you?"

"Me?"

"How've you been?" Fynn tossed his blankets aside and crawled over to the edge of the mattress, taking up a vigil beside his sister, his stare seemingly fixing on the same nondescript part of the far wall that had so enthralled Fiona's attention. "We haven't talked since...you know."

"I'm fine." Her voice was dull.

Fynn placed his hand over his sister's reassuringly. He laughed when he looked down and noticed that his hand still seemed so small and childlike compared to hers. "I'm sorry." His attention remained on their interlocked hands; he couldn't bring himself to look at her. His voice wavered as he continued, "I'm sorry for acting like a brat that day. You didn't deserve it. I understand why you didn't want to tell me. If I'd found your name written in that creepy book, I probably wouldn't have mentioned it to you either."

"No more secrets?" Fiona ventured hopefully.

Fynn nodded; a tentative smile spread across his features. "No more secrets."

"You'll be heading off soon."

Fynn returned his attention to the wall, his eyes unfocussed as he continued to stare at nothing in particular. "I know."

"Two days."

"Will you miss me?" he asked unsteadily.

Fiona pulled her hand from her brother's grasp, surprising him. She laughed at his shock and then slung her slender arm around his shoulders, pulling him to her side. She rested her cheek atop his head, her hand lazily hanging by his shoulder, fingers twisting circles in the fabric of his shirt.

"Of course, I will." Her voice dropped to a pained whisper. "I'll be all alone, while you're off gallivanting around an island."

"I'll miss you," Fynn admitted.

"Do you want to do anything today?" Fiona slipped from the bed and stood before him, offering her hand to her brother.

He took her proffered hand and climbed to his feet. Fynn's smile was weak, tired, and his eyes were listless. "Can we just walk around?"

"I think I can arrange that," Fiona joked as she pulled him along.

The day passed with comfortable chatter, both siblings reveling in the time they spent out in the gardens. They'd taken their lunch amongst the rose bushes and talked of absolutely nothing of any consequence, choosing aptly to avoid mentioning *The Mortanomicon* or their father's murder at the hand of the masked archer. It was an unspoken agreement between the two that they would spend what time they had left together happily talking about the flowers in the gardens or the shape of the clouds up above, a hobby Fynn stole from Godryk.

The following day continued in much the same manner, finding the siblings sprawled out in the grass of the gardens, watching the clouds slowly creep by. Much like every other day that summer, it was frightfully hot outside but neither paid the heat any mind. Fiona had brought out a basket full of sweets for them to share. They munched happily, enjoying the tarts and candied breads she had procured.

As the sun began to sink behind the castle walls and the bright blue of the afternoon sky gave way to the hazy pink of evening, Fiona sighed and pulled herself up. She towered over her still lazing little brother, watching him for a moment. His eyes had closed, and he wore an utterly peaceful look upon his young face. His black hair fanned out and tangled with the bright green grasses of the castle garden. She toed his hip gently. "Time to get up."

"Just a while longer?" he bartered.

"We've got to get ready for the feast." Fiona nudged him a bit more forcefully this time.

Fynn recoiled from his sister's insistent toe-poking and stood. He brushed the clingy grass from his trousers and shirt. "I'm not much in the mood to be around everyone tonight."

Fiona sighed. "You don't have much of a choice."

"I know," lamented the boy as he raked his hand through his tangled hair. "When do I ever?"

They proceeded back into the castle, ascending the winding stairs of the tower toward their chambers. "The food should be good, at least," offered Fiona by way of enticement.

"Can't say the same for the company," muttered the boy.

"Try and behave," urged Fiona.

He promised half-heartedly, "Right, right." Fynn laughed as he opened the door to his room. He peeked over his shoulder and regarded his sister for a moment. "See you there?"

"See you there," she confirmed.

And so, they did. Fiona and Fynn, rather reluctantly, walked into the dining hall and took in the sight of one morbid face after another. Thankfully, they weren't the last to arrive.

Lachlan was seated at the head of the table, absentmindedly watching the wine swirl in his goblet as he rotated his wrist. At his side was the queen, looking for all the world like she would rather be anywhere else but seated beside her morose husband. Ursalyn's red hair was pulled back, revealing dark half-moons stretching beneath her eyes. She was leaning back in her chair, distractedly staring at the myriad of colors pooling into the room, reflecting off the stained-glass windows.

Ciaran and Hollyn were seated side by side. The brothers wore similar looks of solemnity, their blue eyes looking more tempestuous than usual. Ciaran's normally sunnier disposition seemed overshadowed by the miserable heaviness that had settled over the family. Likewise, Hollyn looked glum and tired, hunched in a most un-princely manner over his empty plate.

James was at Hollyn's other side. His blonde hair was a mess, looking as though it hadn't been properly kempt in days. Much like his aunt, James was leaning back in his chair, staring at the rainbows pouring in, awed by the darkness of the hews, colored so by the fading sun of the late evening.

Fiona and Fynn took their seats. The princess smoothed nonexistent wrinkles from her gown, refusing to look anyone in the eyes, concentrating solely on the self-imposed task of looking preoccupied. Fynn sat, neither leaning back nor slumped forward, but unnaturally straight. His attention was focused on the empty plate situated before him, on the whiteness of the porcelain and the delicate intricacies of the design so carefully painted on the rim. He barely paid any attention to Fiona as she shifted uncomfortably in her chair, her furtive glances chancing their way from Ursalyn to Lachlan, then towards the boys.

By the time Noel and Moriah made their entrance, the royal family was in a state of sublime silence, each one refusing to make eye contact with any of the other statuesque figures seated around the long table. Noel cast a nervous look to his brother before steeling himself for the engagement that laid waiting before them. The brothers took their seats, concerned when no one at the table acknowledged their presence.

Noel fidgeted. He glanced over to Moriah with a weary edginess. "They don't look well," he whispered.

Lachlan's eyes peeled away from the swishing wine. The king carefully set the goblet down and then looked at those assembled. He inhaled deeply, slowly. "It's time we all had a talk."

Every pair of eyes, with great trepidation, forcibly pulled away from whatever they had been occupying their time with to look at the king.

Lachlan drew in another deep breath. Much like his wife, his own features betrayed a certain haggardness that weighed him down. His eyes were dull and hollow, and his skin was sallow. His black hair, normally so much tidier than the rest of his family's, was a mess. He wore the same head-to-toe black garb he had swathed himself in since the day of the funeral.

The king started, "We've had a difficult summer." He took up the goblet once more, sipping heavily from its gold-gilded rim. The wine was bitter and tasted dreadful, but he continued drinking. Finally, he set the goblet down again. "We've lost family." He nodded toward the Mordray siblings. "And we've lost dear friends." Lachlan ran his fingers through his hair. It didn't help tame the black disarray. "But we will carry on as we always do. Tomorrow, the boys leave for Morancy. This should be a happy occasion. We should be sending them off with our best wishes, with words of encouragement."

"What're we going to do about Uncle Felix?" Ciaran asked. He tensely shifted beneath his father's heavy stare. "Are we going to have a funeral for him?"

The king shook his head. "Sadly...*most regrettably*, no. After what happened at your aunt and grandmother's funeral, I don't think it would be best. No need to whip the masses into another hateful frenzy." There was a deadness to Lachlan's voice as he said, "he's been taken to the crypts beneath the castle. You may visit if you choose."

"So, we're just going to ignore what happened? He won't get a proper send off?" challenged Fiona.

Fynn clamped his hand over his sister's. He could feel her hand clench into a fist; knuckles shifted beneath his palm as her fingers curled forcefully.

"We're not *ignoring* what happened," Lachlan replied curtly. "We're being *pragmatic*. It's a tactic I suggest you learn and *fast*."

"What of everyone else? There must have been more casualties," Ciaran continued.

Lachlan exhaled shakily. "There were quite a few losses. The other houses are tending to their dead and mourning. But, as I said, we will carry on as always. We will not let this *incident* dictate how we proceed from here. We are, as we have always been and *will always be*, the Crown. They may be angry now, but the people will take their cues from us. Now, more than ever, we cannot falter. We're under attack from all sides. We can't be seen to be weak, no matter the circumstances."

"What do you mean?" Hollyn questioned. "We've lost three members of our *family* already! I'd say that changes things quite a bit."

"Hollyn!" Ursalyn hissed, immediately cowing the boy. "Not now."

"Fine," Hollyn grumbled, crossing his arms and leaning back into his chair, a petulant gleam sparking in his eyes.

"What I mean to say is that Hollyn, Ciaran, and Fynneas will still leave for Morancy in the morning. James will remain here until Peter returns to the country and can take him back to Bowary Bay. Fiona, you'll be staying here as well until your minder comes for you," the king explained as he reached for his goblet once more.

"My *minder*?" Fiona repeated indignantly.

"Yes, you're *minder*. I'm not sending you back home so far away without someone there with you at all times. Not after everything that's happened. I've found someone suitable to watch over you, so you needn't worry," Lachlan replied shortly.

"My grandfather is suitable enough to watch over me, I should think," Fiona argued.

Lachlan shook his head heavily. "He'll need assistance. Hence, why I've procured you a minder."

The princess demanded, "*Who* then?"

The king laughed lightly. "I'm sure you'll like her."

"Who?" repeated Fiona impatiently.

"One of the Mordray sisters." Lachlan took another sip of wine. "I had to pick someone the Crown could trust and...well...the Mordrays, *for the most part*, have proven themselves to be quite useful to the Crown...if not always *entirely* obedient. If nothing else, you won't be bored. That, I can assure you."

"Our sister?" Noel interjected worriedly.

Moriah pressed curiously, "*Which* sister,"

Lachlan's light laughter turned to a throaty chuckle. "Honestly, need you ask?" He quirked a brow, regarding the brothers coolly. "Mortyma's a mad woman, completely mental, and running around *who knows where* with *who knows who*. Dottie will be at Morancy with all of you. And Rose, *sweet Rose*, I wouldn't trust to watch a *cat*, let alone our *only princess*."

"Emrys then?" Ursalyn asked, a docility to her voice that seemed out of place.

The king set his goblet down on the table, meeting her eyes. "Yes."

Noel chuckled. "Oh, *that* sister."

"Yes, *that* sister," Lachlan noted dutifully.

"Is anyone going to tell me who we're talking about?" Fiona whined.

"Haven't you caught on by now, *princess*? You'll be *minded* by *my sister*," Moriah intoned darkly. He reached for his goblet, greedily drinking down its contents in three gulps. He glanced in Fiona's direction and smirked. "May the gods have mercy on you. You'll certainly need it."

Noel snickered. "Can't say I'm jealous of you, princess."

Lachlan laughed for a moment longer and then calmed, composing himself. "Now that we have those arrangements settled, there is something else I would like to discuss with all of you."

Ciaran looked to his father nervously. Tension gripped the king's shoulders, crippling his normally controlled posture. Ciaran found himself assaulted by a similar force. "What is it, Father?"

"I've made arrangements to adjust Morancy's curriculum." Knowing full well that his latest bit of information wasn't going to go over well, Lachlan waved over a servant and indicated his empty goblet, watching avariciously as the man filled the cup to the brim with the bitter wine.

"The curriculum hasn't been changed in over two hundred years," the queen argued.

"What changes are to be made?" Ciaran asked.

"There are only two primary changes. Though, I'm sure, you'll all find them impactful." He drank down his wine. "Firstly, children will only attend for four years rather than the traditional six." He raised his hand haltingly, already seeing that Ursalyn was close to snapping at him. "For those, like you Ciaran, it won't affect you. You will graduate, as you normally would have. However, the fourth and fifth years will also graduate this year. Going forward, only four years will be required." The king, knowing that the sec-ond change would bother his wife far more, readied himself as he inhaled a deep, strong breath. "As for the *other* change."

"Yes?" grit Ursalyn through grinding teeth.

"The games will be held at the end of the first-year, rather than the second," Lachlan explained sharply.

"What?" Moriah asked, dumbstruck.

"This year, to accommodate the second-years that have not yet competed, the games will be held for both first and second-years," Lachlan elucidated. "The children will be appointed to their respective divisions at the end of first-year. They will spend the next three years training. The studies and training will remain the same, fundamentally, I assure

you. The only difference is the timetable. Their efforts will simply be…
accelerated."

"You've lost your mind," Ursalyn whispered under her breath. She stood from her seat abruptly, slamming her hands upon the table. "You've *actually* lost your mind!"

Lachlan turned to face her, eyes narrowed dangerously. "Mind your *place*, Ursalyn."

She shook her head, disbelievingly. "You've lost all sense!" Her chest heaved. It felt as though she couldn't draw in enough air. "You can't do this." Her blue eyes welled with tears. "They won't be ready! They'll get *killed*, Lachlan."

"Then they don't deserve to be there," the king responded easily. "If they don't survive the games, they weren't *strong* enough to lead soldiers; they weren't *worthy* of the honor."

Ursalyn continued shaking her head. A frantic energy took hold of her; her shoulders quaked as she gripped the table, knuckles turning white with her straining efforts to keep herself upright. "How can you say that? How can you say that when it will be your son and nephew out there? How can you say that after everything that has happened to this family this summer?" She was losing her battle with keeping what remaining composure she had. "At least in their second year they would have completed two years of training. That's *two years*, Lachlan, where they would have been taught how to handle the situations they'll face in the games! *Two years* where they would have had time to grow and get stronger, tougher…ready. They won't be *ready.*"

"They'll be ready," the king assured her. "I've made sure of that."

Ursalyn crumbled. She fell into her chair lifelessly. Hollyn jumped from his place and rushed to her side. He pulled his mother to him, holding her in his lanky arms. He leaned closer, asking quietly, "Mother? Mother, are you alright?"

Her hand reached up and cupped her boy's cheek. "Hollyn?"

"Let me take you back to your room," the red-haired prince suggested.

Ursalyn threw her arms around the boy, her nose burying into the crook of his neck. "He can't have you, Hollyn," she whispered. Her hold on her son tightened. "He *can't* have you."

"Enough!" bellowed the king as he sprang up from his seat. Rounding the table, he pulled Hollyn from Ursalyn's grip, forcing Ursalyn to her feet in the process. He roughly took hold of her elbow, guiding her a few steps away. "Enough of this wailing! It's already been decided."

Ursalyn wrenched her arm from Lachlan's grip, only to find herself quickly pinned to the wall. Both her wrists were stuck beneath his grinding hold, uncomfortably trapping her against the rough stone of the castle wall. She struggled against him, unrelenting to his superior strength. "Let me go, Lachlan!" she demanded.

"No. Not until you stop this. There's no place for this softness," he insisted. "You can't keep coddling the boy."

"It's not *coddling* to want to keep *your son alive*," asserted Ursalyn. She writhed beneath his hold, desperately arching away from the wall and twisting her shoulders side to side. "Now let me go!"

Lachlan made a show of leaning back, away from the queen, and then brutishly throwing her back into the wall. He watched, annoyed, as she slid down to the ground, her legs tangling in the folds of her gown. He looked down at her apathetically. "You'll make him soft." Lachlan glanced back at the table, spying Hollyn still frozen in place beside his mother's vacated chair. "He could be a strong boy, Ursalyn. Don't ruin him."

"*I'm* not the one ruining him," the queen hoarsely insisted.

The king looked back down at his crumpled wife. "What was that?"

"I said *I'm not the one ruining him.*"

Lachlan knelt before the woman. He caught her chin in his grasp and forced her to stare into his stormy eyes. "Ursalyn." He tightened his hand around her chin, undeterred by the reddening of the flesh beneath his hold. "You forget your place."

He let go harshly, throwing her head back against the stone.

Hollyn's eyes widened in horror as Ursalyn's head collided with the wall; a faint speckle of red stained the grey stone as her head lolled to the side. He launched himself from his place and bound toward his father. He caught the man entirely unawares as he locked his arms around the king's shoulders and, with all his weight, pulled them both to the ground in a shouting clatter.

Despite the boy's best efforts, he was prostrate on the cold floor before he knew what happened. Lachlan was kneeling astride Hollyn's torso; large hands held down the prince's shoulders as the boy snatched at the air frantically, trying to push the man off.

"Leave her alone!" Hollyn continued to thrash beneath Lachlan. "Leave her alone!"

Lachlan's hand slowly hovered from Hollyn's shoulder up to the boy's pale throat before settling there, the softness of his thumb tracing gentle figures over the tense column of flesh beneath his touch. The king looked nearly feral as he stared down at his son. "Hollyn, *my boy*, that was not a very smart move." His thumb stopped its idle movements and pressed into the skin beneath as his hand tightened around Hollyn's neck painfully. "You'll learn at the academy. I'm sure you will. You're a smart boy, Hollyn. They'll teach you to use that brain of yours to come up with a better strategy than just rushing an opponent, especially one that outclasses you in all regards." The king's hand released Hollyn's neck and moved to his cheek where just moments ago Ursalyn had so lovingly held him. In stark contrast, Lachlan's hand came down upon Hollyn's face like lightning falling to the earth. "Don't let the woman make you soft, boy." Again, the king's palm flattened stingingly over the prince's cheek. "Don't let her ruin you, Hollyn. You're a tough boy. You'll need to be strong to make it through the games, trust me. You'll need to be strong to make it through Morancy."

The sound of Lachlan's hand smashing against Hollyn's cheek made Fynn squirm in his seat. His stomach roiled with sickening unease. He clenched his jaw and balled his fists. He shook, unnerved at the sight of a grown man striking out against his son with such force and entirely unrepentant. Fiona's hand curled around Fynn's. The gentle firmness of her touch a reminder of how their father used to still his impetuously rash impulses. Another slap sounded and Fynn couldn't help but cringe.

Hollyn stared up at his father blankly. His cheek stung; it would surely bruise. He watched, wordlessly, as Lachlan climbed off of him and seated himself back at the head of the table. Dragging himself back up to his feet, Hollyn approached the fallen queen. "Mother?" he rasped.

Ursalyn looked up at him curiously. She studied the boy in front her for a moment before reaching out her hand. He took it and pulled her to her feet, wrapping an arm around her waist to steady her. Appreciatively, she smiled down at her son, winding her arm around his shoulders for support.

As Hollyn led his mother from the dining hall, he called back to his father, "I'm taking Mother to her chambers. I'll stay with her. Seems like she hit her head rather hard. I don't want to leave her alone."

Almost everyone watched in muted astonishment as Hollyn led Ursalyn through the small door that led to the antechamber. The only one who seemed unphased, entirely too used to the scene they'd all just witnessed, was Ciaran. The prince shook with anger but knew far better than to intervene, to say or to do anything.

Lachlan returned to sipping the wine he so despised, forcing himself to not think about what had just transpired.

Fynn and Fiona remained quiet despite their raging disapproval with what had just happened. Neither had ever witnessed such a thing and neither could imagine that anything of like would have been tolerated at Godsreach.

Noel reached over to his brother, letting his hand fall over Moriah's. He felt the slight twitch of musculature beneath his palm. Lachlan paid them no mind, but Noel could see that Moriah was close to completely unfurling after what he'd witnessed. "Don't," whispered Noel as he leaned closer to his older brother. "Please...just *don't*. Not now."

Moriah stood in a huff. He looked at Lachlan, nodding with as much respect as he could muster, and stated calmly, "I'll be leaving, then. There's a lot to prepare for...knowing that we'll be accelerating the curriculum. I want to be ready." He took a steadying breath. "If you'll excuse me, Your Grace?"

Lachlan waved his hand dismissively, "Yes, yes, go do whatever it is you must." He then turned to the servant who stood silent, wide-eyed, in the corner. "You," he beckoned forth the man with another light wave and then glanced toward his goblet. "More wine."

The farewell feast that was supposed to herald the end of the summer and beginning of the new term at Morancy proceeded in a most somber fashion. James, having remained silent the entire night, picked at his food with mild interest. Noel wasn't much for conversation and chose to rearrange the food on his plate into different assorted piles rather than actually take a bite. Prince Ciaran tried, and failed spectacularly, to draw Lachlan into some semblance of amiable conversation; the elder monarch seemed far too preoccupied with needlessly spearing his pork and gulping down his wine.

When at last they were able to slither free from the stifling atmosphere of the feast, Fynn and Fiona found themselves standing shoulder to shoulder before their father's tomb in the crypts beneath Batsbeckon. It was cool and damp down under the castle. The only light came from torches flickering on the walls, casting a pale, orange glow over the dark, grey stones. The sickening stench of rotting flesh permeated the walls, clinging to every pore in the stone with grotesque resolve.

Fiona was entirely unbothered by the putrid stench of decaying bodies all around them, but Fynn was struggling not to vomit. The coiling, scented tendrils of festering flesh, maggots, damp dirt, and overall rot seemed to claw away at his nose with reckless abandon, their spoiling grasp feeling as though it would melt his nostrils from the inside out. He shuddered, doing his best to control himself.

"It's a travesty," Fiona commented sadly. She ran her hand along the smooth surface of her father's tomb. "It's a damn travesty, Fynny. They aren't even going to give him a proper funeral."

Fynn shook his head, defeated. "There isn't much we can do."

"Why do you think they sent him down here? Why not burn his remains like they did for Gran and Aunt Gemma?"

Neither sibling heard Moriah approach. They hadn't seen him sidle up beside Fiona. The man had stalked up to them like a panther in the night, clinging to the darkness afforded in the crypt as if it were his own mother. "He's not the only one." His voice held a bit more emotion than usual, though it was far from being a sentimental statement. "There are a lot of princes who are buried down here rather than being burned."

Tears began to spill down Fiona's freckled cheeks. She showed no signs of being startled by Moriah's sudden appearance. She had, by this point, grown accustomed to the man just turning up like a phantom sneaking through the walls. "But why?"

"You're right," Moriah commented. "It *is* a travesty." He shook his head, annoyance clear in his strange, green eyes. "The others who are buried down here, they're people of little consequence. Fourth and fifth born princes or lord sons of princesses. Felix deserved better."

"But Uncle Lachlan didn't want to risk it," Fiona thought aloud. "Having another big funeral would likely be dangerous right now. There could be another riot. Or worse."

Moriah nodded solemnly.

"Moriah?" she weakly started.

"Yes?"

"Something's going on." She took in a painfully deep breath. "Something's going on and Uncle Lachlan knows it. Am I right?"

Moriah nodded again.

"That's why he's accelerating the Morancy training, isn't it? He wants everyone as prepared as they can be when the time comes," she continued.

"When the time comes for what?" asked Fynn nervously.

"War," supplied Moriah grimly.

Fynn shook, his chest heaving with the force of his unsteady breathing. "War?"

"There is a war coming. I don't know who it will be with or when it will be, but there is one coming," Moriah assured the siblings sullenly. His attention turned toward Fynn. Moriah's eyes looked even stranger, more eerie, in the dim firelight of the crypts. "You'll need to be ready, Fynneas."

"I know," the prince whispered contemplatively.

"Surviving the games is but one of many steps," Moriah spoke. "There are monsters out there, young prince, and you're going to need to be ready when the time comes to fight them."

Fynn nodded sharply, eyes like burning ice as he stared up at Moriah. "I will be."

A flicker of red splayed across the grey of Fynn's eyes for a moment and no longer. But Moriah had seen it and he recalled, in an instant, the first time he'd ever met Fynn. The lord commander arched a brow inquisitively as he stared down at the prince.

"Very curious," he muttered.

8

THE MORANCY ACADEMY OF MILITARY ARTS

Fynn remembered the day he left Estheria to head to the Isles of Algernon. It was so early in the morning the sun wasn't even up yet; the skies were still an inky black and the waters lashing at the rocky shores somehow seemed even blacker. It was with a great sense of sober melancholy that he stood before his sister, looking up at her and flinching away guiltily when he saw the salty tears roiling in her eyes, the blueness of her irises punctuated by the silver light of the still-reigning moon lingering overhead. He tried his best to smile for her, to offer her some sort of parting affirmation, but all he managed was a weak grin and sad, grey eyes. Fiona had thrown her arms around him and pulled him close and he, as he always had since he could remember, melted into her hold and felt terribly, inexplicably safe there.

"I'm going to miss you," she'd said.

He held onto her with all his strength as if she was his lifeline. "I'll miss you too." He wriggled from her hold and took a step back, forcing himself to look her in the eyes. "The book...well, I don't think you should mention it to anyone. There's something very odd about it and, well I don't know, I *think* it's got something to do with Father's death."

"Fynneas, that doesn't make sense," Fiona argued.

Fynn shrugged. "I know. But...I have a *feeling* they're related. I don't know how. Maybe you...maybe you could look into it?" stammered the prince hesitantly. "You've always been clever about putting things together."

"I'll try and find out what I can. Though, we don't have much to go on."

"Barnaby Lot?"

"Haven't found out anything about him," Fiona said. "Or his family."

"He's got something to do with it. I just know it."

"Don't spend all your time thinking about this," Fiona warned.

Fynn smiled sadly. "I won't. I know I won't have time to think about all this much while I'm away. But I have to know. I have to know what *really* happened that day."

Fiona whispered, "Why?"

"You won't like it."

Fiona's hand had found its way to Fynn's chin. She tilted her brother's head up so their eyes met and she stared at him for a long while. "Tell me anyway."

"Someone needs to pay for what happened."

"I don't like to hear you talking like that." Fiona sighed as she brushed her hand through her brother's hair.

Fynn muttered, "I know." His voice was stronger when he said, "But you and I both know something strange is going on."

She nodded.

"We need to find out everything we can. Well, *you* need to find out." Fynn smirked.

"I will." Fiona smiled almost sadly. "Be safe."

"I'll do my best."

"Do better than that." Fiona laughed.

That was six days ago. The prince sighed before he sat up in his cot and stretched. They'd been sailing for six, long days. His back ached terribly. It cracked as he moved his arms in awkward circles to stretch. He jumped from the bed, pulled on a shirt and his boots, and headed to the deck. He was immediately assaulted by the sunlight.

He sighed irritably. Fynn had learned rather quickly that out there on the sea, nearing the tropical waters of the archipelago, he seemed to burn in just minutes. Presently, his cheeks and nose were bright pink. The sunlight, more than just constantly burning him, also bothered his eyes tremendously. He supposed it was something he would acclimate to, but for the time being, it was an annoyance he was ready to dispense with.

Fynn took to standing on the bow of the ship, leaning over the rail, and watching the water flow by beneath the cutting angles of the hull. He admired the brilliant blue and shimmering turquoise of the waters, so different than the Sea of Esther that ebbed across Estheria's shores. He saw dark shapes—sea creatures—darting in all directions around the ship though, to his dismay, none ever breached the surface. He relaxed, settling his weight onto his forearms as he leaned a little further over the rail, desperate to catch a glimpse of one of the colorful creatures teeming beneath the waters.

"What're you looking at?" asked Hollyn as he sidled up beside his cousin, curiously peering down into the water in search of whatever had caught Fynn's attention. "I don't see anything."

"There're things swimming around the ship," replied Fynn, not bothering to look at the other boy.

"Things?"

Fynn shrugged. "Well, I don't know what sort of things. I can't see them any better than you."

"You can't see them because there's nothing there," contended Hollyn.

Fynn pointed to the water. Beneath a rolling wave, there was a distorted shape swooping this way and that. "There!" He smiled a bit as he watched the wave dissipate and the shape swim along, seemingly riding the current of the rippling sea. "You just have to look harder."

Hollyn pulled himself upright and stretched his arms and back. It was clear he was feeling the effects of being cooped up on the ship for six rather tedious days. He yawned; dull eyes darkened with boredom fell upon Fynn and surveyed him with moderate interest, like a lazy cat studying an unaware mouse. "Your face is burned."

Fynn's nose twitched at the comment, wrinkling some as he said, "I know." He stood, squaring his shoulders, still looking at the sea. "It's the damn sun!" He turned to face Hollyn, grey eyes looking wild. "I can't take it on this ship anymore." He huffed before furiously combing his hand through his tangled mane. "I've had enough of just sitting around here on this damn boat."

"*Ship*," Hollyn corrected flatly.

"Who cares?" grumbled Fynn.

"You should learn the difference," Hollyn added. His voice seemed flat, far more lifeless than usual. There was something eerily familiar about the drawling way in which Hollyn was speaking. His detached, listless tone seemed careless and cold. "I suppose you're not going to be joining the Armada."

Fynn shrugged. "I've never really thought about it."

"Do you think about anything?" came the tired barb as Hollyn smirked.

"So, you're aiming for Armada then?"

Hollyn nodded quickly. "It's tradition, I think. Everyone in the family seems to have been placed in Armada." Blue eyes swept up and down Fynn's lank figure and then he smiled mirthlessly. "You may be the odd one out in that regard. Though, to be honest, that shouldn't come as a surprise."

Fynn reeled his arm back and gave a mighty shove to Hollyn's chest, knocking the other boy back a bit. "What's that supposed to mean?" Fynn whined.

Despite nearly being pushed over, Hollyn had the wherewithal to laugh a haughty laugh and grin, eyes finally lighting up. "What? Can't puzzle that one out for yourself?" He straightened up, relishing being taller than the other prince. "It means, *Fynneas*, that you don't have the temperament to be in the Armada." He eyed Fynn's red cheeks and freckled nose, far more speckled than it usually was. "Honestly, just *look* at you! You spend six days at sea and burn up. You're practically pink."

"Am not!" yelled Fynn, shoving Hollyn again.

Unfortunately, the scenario did not play out as it had before. Hollyn, having anticipated that his jeers would fluster Fynn, caught his cousin's wrist as he was pushed, effectively pulling both of them down in an unbalanced tangle of scrawny limbs, clattering to the deck. Fynn, having landed on top of Hollyn, tried to pin the red-haired prince down but was easily thrown off. Rolling onto his side, Fynn huffed as Hollyn pounced on him, knocking the air from his lungs almost painfully. The row went from boyish wrestling to violent punches and yells, each prince landing a few well-placed strikes to the other; teeth were bared and growling insults were hurled. Small yips of pain escaped tightly clenched jaws until their ruckus attracted unwanted attention.

Hollyn was pulled off Fynn by the collar of his shirt and carefully set to the side. The same slender hand that had snatched Hollyn away quickly dipped back down and grasped Fynn's wrist in its hold, hauling the boy to his feet. Both princes stood before a more than annoyed looking Moriah, neither of them wanting to look the man in the eyes.

Moriah sighed and composed himself before asking, "Do either of you care to explain what was going on here?"

Fynn shrugged and bit down on his lower lip, but his grey eyes burned heatedly as they bore into Hollyn. For his part, Hollyn chanced a glance up at Moriah sheepishly before looking away and, just as Fynn had done, gave a noncommittal shrug.

"Don't do it again," Moriah intoned, his deep voice clashing with the serene whisking of the waters below. The man, remarkably still dressed in an entirely black ensemble, spun around on his heel and took his leave, not bothering to reprimand either boy further.

Dumbfounded, Fynn looked to Hollyn for some assurance that he hadn't imagined the whole encounter. Pleased to see that Hollyn wore an identical look of confusion upon his normally composed, apathetic visage, Fynn smirked. "Well…we should *probably* listen to him," he commented amusedly.

Hollyn nodded.

"Don't want to make *him* mad." Fynn laughed as he cast a final look at Hollyn before skipping off down the deck.

He'd retreated back to his cot below deck, thinking it the last place he would see Hollyn. The afternoon waned into evening. The sun fell behind the horizon; the sky darkened in the wake of the barely-there moon. The gentle rocking of the ship lulled the prince off to sleep, fitful though it was.

Before the sun could rise the next morning, Fynn woke with a start, breathing heavily. He smelt the sickly stench of sweat and soon realized it was his own, feeling the soft material of his shirt, now terribly damp, clinging to his narrow chest. He inhaled shakily, unsure of what had startled him awake at such an hour, but certain it would be there again, waiting for him, if he tried to close his eyes and go back to sleep.

So, it was with that begrudging understanding that there was a nightmare lurking somewhere on the periphery that spurred the boy to groggily slip from his cot and dress himself. He stomped up the stairs to the deck on weary legs, yawning all the while, and rubbing the sleepy haze from his eyes. There were very few people on deck this early in the morning. The quietness of the scene was peaceful.

The wind was salty and smelled of fish, but its tang wasn't entirely off putting. Fynn relished the feel of the cool, morning wind dancing over him, drying the stinging beads of sweat that still clung to his brow and dampened his hair.

"Early morning for you, isn't it?" asked a rather cheery Noel as he sauntered up beside the prince, swinging an arm around the boy's shoulders. "Bad dream again?"

Fynn's eyes narrowed at the question. Defensively, he wriggled free of Noel's amiable gesture. "No. I haven't had a nightmare in a while." He tried to stalk off down the deck toward the bow, but his retreat was impeded by Noel catching hold of his arm and pulling him back. "Let go, Noel," warned Fynn.

The man just smiled a lopsided grin, blue eyes shining in the early morning light. "Everyone has nightmares once and a while. It's nothing to be ashamed of," Noel assured gently. His voice, his tone, were so different than his brother's that it seemed, at times, so unbelievable that they could be related. There was a note of such genuine emotion and compassion, true warmth and sincerity, in everything Noel said. "Let's have something to eat, shall we?"

"I'm not hungry," mumbled the boy as he, once again, squirmed free of Noel's incessant grip.

"Come now, Fynneas, we'll be arriving in a few hours. You're going to want to have something to eat. You've got to keep your strength up," Noel chirped, undeterred by the boy's sour morning attitude.

Fynn grumbled as he continued his march toward the bow. Noel was close on his heels, looming over him like some great, over-happy shadow. The boy huffed indignantly, again trying to rub the bleariness from his eyes. He yawned. "I'm not hungry."

Noel playfully nudged him with his elbow and grinned. "You know, the more time I spend around you, young prince, the more you remind me of a *certain someone.*"

"Moriah?"

"Yes," Noel laughed. "He's also quite the grump in the morning."

"You *clearly* don't suffer from the same affliction," muttered Fynn as he situated himself leaning over the rail of the bow and watching the water splay across the hull as the ship eased through the waves.

"Such cheek is fine for now but do let's remember I will be one of your instructors at Morancy," Noel chided gently. He combed his hand through Fynn's hair, making a halfhearted attempt at smoothing down some wild, errant strands. "You're going to have to learn to mind that sharp tongue of yours."

Fynn chose to ignore Noel's warning and instead leaned further over the rail. His gaze was intense as he scanned the waters, latching onto the sight of dark shapes worming around beneath the surface. "What sort of fish and things are in these waters?" Fynn asked. He looked back up at Noel curiously. "Surely there are different fish in the waters here. It's much warmer this far down south."

Noel smiled affirmatively. "A keen observation. Yes, there are *far* different creatures down here than back up by the mainland shores."

"What kinds?"

"Dangerous sorts," Noel responded flatly.

Fynn returned to staring at the water fixedly. "How dangerous?"

"The *most* dangerous."

"Sharks?"

Noel chuckled. "Sharks would be a welcome reprieve from the sort of creatures you'll find in the southern seas."

"What do you mean?"

"There are all kinds of monsters in the warm waters," explained Noel.

"Monsters?"

The man nodded. "Krakens and mermaids and luscas and basilisks and all manner of other terrible things."

"You're lying," Fynn insisted.

Noel shrugged. "Am I?"

"Yes," argued the prince. "You must be." He shook his head as if trying to clear the very thought of such horrifying creatures from his mind. "They teach us—*children*—to sail at Morancy. There's no way they'd let us in the water if there were monsters like that down there!"

Noel set his hand atop Fynn's shoulder gently. He looked away from the nervous boy and down at the water rushing beneath the ship. His voice was somber. "Fynn, dear child, there are far worse things awaiting you than monsters in the water."

"What...do you mean?"

"Morancy is a cruel place, Fynneas. It was designed that way, purposely structured to ensure only the strongest graduate, so that only the strongest will serve and lead the military. Trust me, young prince, when I tell you that you have a lot more to worry about than what may be in the water."

As the morning wore on, the islands of the archipelago came into view. They were little more than brownish bumps reaching out of the crystalline waters, but they were in sight at long last. Noel had taken his leave from Fynn, having offered no more about the creatures that lurked in the tropical nightmare-scape that were the Isles of Algernon. Fynn, disconcerted by Noel's earlier, rather cryptic warning, remained leaning over the rail of the bow, simply watching for the shapes in the water.

"You're still out here?" asked Hollyn.

Fynn's voice was uncertain, wavering when he asked, "Have...you ever heard of any...*monsters* in the water?"

"What?"

"You know...*monsters*...in the waters down here. Things like krakens and luscas?" Fynn peeked over his hunched shoulders and looked imploringly at Hollyn. "My father...he was in the Armada...but he never talked

146

about it or anything. I don't think he ever spent too much time out at sea and he never really talked about his time at Morancy much."

Hollyn shrugged. "I've heard that there are mermaids around the islands, but the luscas and krakens...and well, the basilisks...they're closer to Erza's shores than the archipelago. That's what Ciaran's said at least."

"You don't seem too bothered by all this," commented Fynn.

"I'm not."

"Why?"

"*Because* that's why we're going to Morancy, *idiot*," snapped the red-haired prince. "We're going to learn how to handle all these monsters and more! It's not like they're going to just throw us out into the wild to fend for ourselves."

"Oh," murmured Fynn embarrassed. "I guess that makes sense."

Hollyn snorted disdainfully. "You really *are* an idiot."

"You've said that already," Fynn hissed. "More than once, actually." He righted himself, springing up from having been hunched over the rail, and spun to look at Hollyn, eyes burning. "I'm getting pretty tired of it," he ground out.

The taller prince shrugged, smirking all the while. "Why don't you run crying to your mother...oh, wait." He grinned darkly.

Hollyn hadn't been prepared for Fynn's fist to collide against his cheek with such force, nor had he been prepared to be pinned to the deck by the utterly enraged boy. Fynn, astride Hollyn's middle, swung again at his cousin's face, growling like a beast possessed as Hollyn's head snapped to the side with the weight of the blow. Fynn pushed down on Hollyn's shoulders, doing his best to keep the other prince contained beneath him. Hollyn, after regaining his composure and assessing the situation, was quick to act. Jerking his shoulders to the side abruptly and thrashing, he managed to toss Fynn off.

Much as they had done the day before, the two princes proceeded to scramble upon the deck, snatching at each other's shirts for purchase, and pulling one another down; they pinned each other, twisted, wrenched, wriggled, and fought viciously. When Fynn's energy began to dwindle, he found himself prostrate upon the deck with a very angry Hollyn poised over him, his shadow looming with unprecedented darkness. Hollyn gave a swift kick to Fynn's ribs, delighting in the sudden gasp of pain that tripped from the boy's split lips.

Fynn rolled to his side. He clutched his throbbing torso and rasped out pained breaths as he tried to calm down. He could almost hear the blood swooshing in his ears, the erratic beating of his heart, the strangled and ragged sounds of his breathing. He heard Hollyn walk away and silently thanked whatever gods there were at play that the other boy had grown tired of their fight. Forcing himself up on shaking legs, Fynn dragged himself back across the deck, descending below to where his cot was situated, and collapsed upon the uncomfortable material in a heap of tired limbs. His chest rattled all the while with every breath.

The prince hadn't realized that he'd fallen back to sleep. It couldn't have been for long, he supposed, since he had been able to see the islands poking out over the horizon prior to his minor altercation with Hollyn. Still, he woke uneasily to the feeling of someone gently shaking his shoulders. When his lashes fluttered open, he saw Noel leaning over him. Fynn smiled grimly at the man and sat up, though the action pained him some.

"Are we there yet?" Fynn asked, rubbing at his eyes wearily.

Noel sighed. "Yes. We're going to be disembarking in a moment."

Fynn watched curiously as a familiar, slender hand pushed Noel aside. The boy felt the cot shift under the sudden weight when Moriah perched himself there at his side. The man, clad in his black-on-black attire, looked a bit more dire than Fynn was used to.

Moriah's feline-like eyes seemed nearly iridescent in the shadowed darkness below deck. He leaned forward, long fingers closing around Fynn's chin, directing the boy to meet his scrutinizing gaze. He frowned. "I thought I told you and Hollyn to cease your senseless fighting."

"You did," Fynn whispered.

"And yet here you are, bruised and bloodied," he continued.

"And yet here I am, *bruised* and *bloodied*," agreed the prince.

Moriah scowled as he leaned closer, bright gaze sweeping over Fynn's face, examining the wounds. There were fledgling purple bruises blooming around Fynn's eyes and nose, his lip was split on one side and still bleeding slightly. There were bruises sprinkled across his jaw and down by his collarbone. Moriah's attention dipped and fell to the hands folded on the boy's lap. Fynn's knuckles were red and swollen.

"Does it hurt?" Moriah asked softly.

"Not really," mumbled Fynn, trying fruitlessly to turn away from Moriah's prying attention. "It was just *Hollyn*. It's not like *he* could really do much damage."

Fynn spluttered in surprise when Moriah's hand slapped him upside the head. Grey eyes widened, begging for an explanation. Moriah drew away from Fynn, sliding from the cot to stand beside Noel. His attention hadn't wavered once during the encounter. "*Clearly* he managed enough."

The boy fidgeted uncomfortably in his bed, shying away from the intense stares emanating from the Mordrays. "Yes…well," Fynn ground between clenched teeth. "I'll get him better next time."

Again, Fynn was surprised when Moriah's hand clipped him sharply upon the head. "You'll do no such thing."

"He starts it," whined the prince.

"You're missing the point," Noel interjected. "You two can't fight all the time while you're at Morancy. It won't do anyone any good."

"Noel's right." Moriah added, "Try and behave, won't you?"

"It's not *me* you have to worry about," muttered Fynn as he finally managed to pull himself from his bed and stand before the brothers who, much to his dismay, towered over him with an unnerving and steadfast resolution.

"*Neither* of you are going to make this year easy on me, are you?" Moriah all but grumbled petulantly as he took his leave and clambered up the stairs to the deck.

"He's mad at me, isn't he?" asked Fynn, hanging his head.

"He *did* tell you not to fight with Hollyn anymore just the other day," Noel expressed, a twinge of exasperation coloring his words. "But you did it again anyway."

There was an awful sinking feeling in the pit of the boy's stomach. Fynn couldn't bring himself to look at Noel. "You're right."

"I know." Noel smiled. "But it won't do to dwell on it. Get ready and come up. You'll want to see this, I promise."

The prince was delighted to find that Noel was, in fact, quite right. Standing out on the deck, looking at the quickly approaching harbor lacing the shores of Dier Island, Fynn couldn't help but grin. The waters were a pale, blue color that waved gently under the weight of the approaching ships, licking at the white-sand beaches of the island shore. There were palm trees that stuck out around the shores with great, green leaves twisting gently in the salty breeze. Large, green covered hills eased into slopes that rolled through the island. And there, as Fynn squinted through the painfully offending brightness of the tropical morning, he saw the towers of Morancy reaching up into the blue sky, looking as though they would scrape against the clouds.

"Wow," Fynn gasped as he bound down the deck toward the bow. He had to stop himself from barreling over the edge of the ship into the waters, such was his excitement. He stared, transfixed by the foreign scene before him. "Wow," he repeated under his breath.

The ship docked and suddenly came alive with movement. Fynn and Hollyn were ushered off the vessel. They stepped down the gangplank onto the awaiting pier. Neither boy could help looking in every direction, drinking in the strange sights all around them. Their things, what little they had been allowed to bring to the island, were gathered up by the servants who had accompanied them on the journey. Meanwhile, the two children were led down the pier toward the shoreline where carriages awaited them. Hollyn and Fynn climbed into one, too distracted by the rush of activity to bother exchanging heated looks or spiteful words.

Once everyone and everything was settled, the carriages proceeded down a small, winding road. They inched along, going at a leisurely sort of pace that allowed the boys to stare out the windows and look at all the greenery, the strange and colorful birds darting between the palm fronds and branches, the oddly-scaled snakes slithering between the bushes, the unusual flowers blooming all around them. Their carriage twisted its way along its familiar route, carrying the two princes up a hill, carefully navigating the turns and divots, until it arrived at the steps of the castle.

Hollyn and Fynn, both overtaken with excitement, jumped out of the carriage and stared, gaping in awe. There, looming before them, seemingly bursting from the ground beneath, was a large castle whose architecture seemed utterly and intrinsically at odds with the natural surroundings. A large, formidable looking, dark, stone archway stretched before them; emerald vines danced along the mortar and stone, twisting and gnarling at odd angles. The doorway to the castle, nestled amongst the arch, was of a deeply colored wood, small nicks and notches marring its centuries old surface. The rest of the castle was constructed of the same, dark stone as the entryway, a familiar building material in Estheria that looked more at home amongst the gloomy, stormy coastlines of the mainland rather than the tropical oasis of Dier Island. The battlements overhead, much like the arch, were overrun with vines and moss that bloomed with the most exotically colored flowers either boy had ever seen. The towers they'd seen from the harbor were, from this vantage point, jutting out from the jungle canopies from wherein the castle seemed to be nestled.

"Alright lads, this way," Noel instructed as he waved. He led them through the great doorway that swung open as if on cue.

They followed on his heels, still letting their attentions dart around to take in everything they possibly could. The light from the morning sun oozed into the entryway, illuminating the long hall, revealing the lines of armor that stood, as if at attention, watching them as they proceeded onward. The stained glass of the peculiarly shaped windows created small, arching rainbows. Their colorful tendrils brightened the space with a mystical sort of whimsy. There were banners with golden stitching proudly emblazoned against deep, purple fields that hung from the vaulted ceiling of the hall denoting the sigils of each of Morancy's divisions.

Noel led them along to a small stairwell that wound in a spiral up to a tower, leading them at last to a door. He opened it and stepped aside to allow the two children to pass before entering into the room himself. There, the boys found themselves in a room far larger than they had anticipated. The chamber was decorated with the division banners, matching purple rugs stretched over the darkly colored stone floor. There were portraits of people Fynn didn't recognize, but each of them looked impressive in their own right, snugged within the confines of ornately embellished, gold-gilded frames.

"This is your dormitory. It will be your home for the next ten months," Noel began, watching with amusement as the two princes marveled at their new surroundings. "To your right is the boys' wing, to the left is the girls'." He gave a nod to a small staircase that led from the center of the chamber. "You won't be spending too much time in here," he continued. "You'll have a great deal to do, so you'll have very little spare time. If I may offer some advice?"

Hollyn nodded curiously.

"When you do have some spare time on your hands, try and use it to get some rest." Noel grinned genuinely. "You're going to need it."

Both princes looked at the man cautiously but nodded in turn at his proffered advisement.

"Your things are being brought up as we speak. Everyone else should be arriving momentarily. I believe I saw their ships docking just after ours arrived. The staff is already here, of course." Noel looked around the room wistfully. "You'll be expected down in the Hall for dinner. Try and be on time." With that, Noel took his leave of the boys.

When the door closed in the man's wake, Hollyn turned to observe Fynn. He raised a brow and smirked. "Nice bruises you have there."

Fynn's mood instantly darkened. "I could say the same to you." Fynn couldn't help but cross his arms over his slight chest, lean back, and gloat at his work. The nasty looking, purple bruise around Hollyn's right eye certainly marred his normally handsome features. "Nice black eye you've got there, Hollyn."

"I'd stop there if I were you," warned the red-haired boy.

"Oh? Or what?"

"Or you'll have a matching one," promised Hollyn threateningly.

Fynn threw up his hands in mock surrender, far too tired to deal with Hollyn's temper. "Fine, fine." He stuck out his hand. "Truce?"

Shadowy, blue eyes observed the hand coolly, disinterest evident in the vacant expression. "Not on your life."

Fynn's hand recoiled, twisting into a fist at his side as he watched Hollyn traipse towards the boys' wing, disappearing up the stairs.

"Bastard," mumbled Fynn as he allowed himself a moment to calm down.

At a loss for what to do to whittle away the time until dinner, Fynn reached for the door leading out of the chamber, only to jump back in surprise when it opened, revealing Godryk. Fynn's lips broke into a crooked, boyish smile as he beamed, "Godryk! You're here."

Godryk laughed as he stepped into the room. "Of course. You didn't think you'd have the place all to yourself for long, did you?"

"Honestly, I was hoping someone would show up." Fynn tilted his head back toward the boys' room. "I don't want to be left with just Hollyn all day."

"He's not the easiest to get along with," Godryk noted with a sour look.

"That's putting it mildly," jested Fynn as he snagged hold of Godryk's arm and pulled him back through the doorway into the tower. "Come on, then! Let's have a look around."

Godryk made no move to extricate himself from Fynn's hold as they wound their way down the spiraling stairs. "Fynn, the last time I let you lead me off somewhere we almost got mauled by a bear."

"Don't worry so much," insisted the prince as he kept their pace quick, pulling Godryk along just behind him. "There *are* no bears out here on the islands!"

"I'm sure there are much worse things than bears out here," mumbled Godryk, but his tone betrayed his good mood, nevertheless.

The boys stepped off the stairs, looking left and right, trying to decide where to be off to for their exploration. The castle was vast, and its halls and towers were not easily navigable. However, the intimidating structure of the great castle didn't deter Fynn's desire to roam aimlessly.

Left it would be. He started off down the hall at a quick trot, excitement spurring him on as he went bounding down the long corridor.

Godryk, the taller of the two, had no problem keeping pace. He asked, "What's down this way?"

"Don't know."

"But, isn't the entrance hall to the right?"

"That's why we went left."

"I don't understand," admitted Godryk.

"Well, we already knew what we'd find if we went right, didn't we?"

Godryk nodded.

"So, we went left!" Fynn was practically bursting with enthusiasm, pale eyes nearly aglow with unrestrained eagerness.

It wasn't long before the two boys found themselves standing before a large, wooden door. There was a shield engraved upon the door, the wood decorated with fine, gold leaf to embellish the sigil. On either side of the door there were banners, the standard purple of Morancy and the intricately designed shield of the Paladin Division set in the center.

Fynn stared at the banners in awe. "This must be the Paladin dormitory." He reached out, tracing his hand along the bottom of the shield etched into the door. "Do you think we can go in?"

Godryk shook his head. "No, they'll kill us!" The young Redmayne nervously chewed on his lower lip. "The Paladins are the scary ones, Fynn. Who knows what's behind the door!"

"*We* will, if we go through," Fynn thought aloud.

Godryk shook his head. "No. No, no, no." He grabbed Fynn's wrist and tried to pull the curious prince away from the doorway but was unable to get the boy to budge. "Fynn, come on." He gave another pull, pouting when he saw Fynn standing his ground firmly. "We shouldn't be here, Fynn. We should go."

The prince cast a glance over his shoulder at the panicking Godryk before looking back at the door. He gave it a push, smiling when it opened. "It's not locked."

"Wonderful, now let's be going." Godryk tried, annoyed.

Fynn shook his arm out of Godryk's hold. "Don't be so scared." He pushed the door open just enough for them to slip through. "Let's just have a little look. We can be quick about it."

"Fynn, no."

"Live a little." Fynn slipped through the opening, disappearing behind the shadows cast down by the heavy door.

Godryk rolled his eyes and sighed. "He's going to be the death of me." He pouted as he followed through the opening.

The two boys walked quietly down the hall that had laid hidden behind the door. There was a long, purple carpet that ran the length of the corridor. The walls were spangled with portraits of former paladins, many of whom Fynn recognized, not even needing to look at the name plates beneath the portraits, as former lord commanders of the King's Guard, the Night Corps, or the Marshals. At the end of the hall, there was a short archway that gave way to a staircase that spiraled downward. The boys stood at the top of the stairs, peeking down into the dimly lit space. The pale-yellow glow of torches lining the curved walls hardly cut through the shadows.

"Do you think their dormitory is all the way down there?" asked Godryk. "Maybe."

"Well, we've had our look. Let's go."

Fynn snagged Godryk's sleeve before the boy had the chance to flee. "Let's take a look."

"We've had a look, Fynn," whined Godryk. "You said we'd be quick about. It's time to go before we get caught."

Not surprisingly, the prince didn't listen. He took one cautious step down the stairs then looked back and grinned up at Godryk. "I don't think it's a long way down. We can be in and out before anyone knows we were here." With that, Fynn crept further down, leaving a very unhappy Godryk in his wake.

The young prince couldn't help the silly smile that curled his lips when he heard Godryk stepping along down the stairs just behind him.

"This is stupid, you know," muttered the young Redmayne.

"Probably," Fynn agreed, not stopping in his quest down the stairs.

"Do you think we're going down to the dungeons?"

"No," Fynn said. "I don't think they'd put the paladins, of all people, in the dungeons. Maybe it's just a lower level of the castle."

"It's cold down here," Godryk commented, rubbing his hands together.

They stepped off the last stair and found themselves in yet another hall. There were torches all over the walls. Golden light spilled over the dark stone of the floors. Before they even took one step, the rather distinct voice of one Moriah Mordray sung out through the gloominess.

"Boys."

Both Godryk and Fynn stopped, absolutely frozen still, when they heard the annoyed, slow drawl of the lord commander. While Godryk had bowed his head, nervously biting down on his lip, Fynn steeled himself and turned around. There, amongst the scant light and shadows, stood Moriah. He had his arms crossed over his chest, head cocked to the side curiously, one thin brow raised. His green eyes - those odd, green eyes - looked as though they were glowing.

Fynn shivered. "Moriah?"

"And what, pray tell, are the two of you doing down here?" asked the man, taking a step closer.

Instinctively, Fynn wanted to take a step away, but he forced himself to remain where he was. He found, however, that he was unable to meet Moriah's unwavering stare.

"We were just exploring," the prince offered, by way of an explanation.

"Exploring?"

"Yes. Just having a look around the castle," Fynn added.

"And you just happened to end up here?"

Again, Fynn answered sheepishly, "Yes."

"Did you notice the Paladin sigil on the banners? The door, perhaps?"

"Yes," Fynn meekly replied.

"And," Moriah's lips twisted like a fox up to no good, "are you a member of the Paladin Division?"

"No."

Moriah took another step closer, towering over the boy prince. "Then, please explain why you thought you could come traipsing in here?"

"I...I," Fynn stammered. "I don't know."

"When, might I ask, do you plan on learning to listen, young prince?"

"I...can do better," Fynn choked out, flinching away from Moriah's harsh stare.

"I know you can." Moriah caught the boy's chin and directed his attention. Their eyes met. "I *expect* it of you." Moriah released Fynn and turned toward Godryk, eyeing him expectantly. "Young Lord Redmayne?"

Godryk turned to face Moriah shakily. He kept his eyes trained on the ground. "Sir?"

"I expect more of *you* as well," chastised the man in black.

The red-hair boy nodded sharply. "I understand, sir."

Moriah nodded toward Fynn. "If you're truly a friend of the prince's, you'd do best to learn to temper his more impulsive proclivities."

"I tried," argued Godryk weakly.

The man's voice was lamely dull as he said, "Try harder."

"Yes, sir," agreed Godryk.

"Now, let's go for a walk, shall we?" Moriah gestured toward the stair-well. "After you."

Fynn and Godryk climbed the stairs, quite mindful of Moriah just behind them. Having the man at their backs was like having the point of a sword needling into your flesh, ready, at any moment, to plunge. Once they'd ascended the stairs and stepped through the large doorway, finding themselves back in the main corridors, they stopped and waited for further instruction.

Moriah closed the door firmly behind him, turning to the boys with an expressionless face. "Let's be going."

Positions were reversed, the boys now following behind the man in black. They continued down the long hall back to the entryway. Though curious as to where Moriah was leading them, neither boy asked where they were going, but chose to silently and obediently follow.

They stepped into the light of day, the sun fully in the sky heralding the early afternoon. It was uncomfortably bright outside; Fynn winced, sure that at some point he would acclimate to the unyielding sunlight of the south.

Moriah stepped onto the walkway, which, like most of the castle, was partially overtaken by wild greenery.

In the full sunlight, Godryk could more clearly see the bruising on Fynn's face and quirked a brow. He whispered, "What happened to you?"

"Fynneas doesn't listen. That's what happened to him," came Moriah's sharp reply.

Startled that the man had heard him, Godryk resigned himself to remaining quiet.

"Where are we going?" chirped Fynn.

"You said you wanted to explore," said Moriah. When he turned to look back at the boys, he was smiling.

The nervous sulking that had taken over Fynn immediately disappeared and was forgotten. There was a spark of amusement in the impossibly green eyes looking at him. Fynn felt that Moriah, just maybe, wasn't angry with him anymore. The wild energy that had led him to trouble in the first place surged back into the prince's slight form and he went skipping up in great bounds to Moriah's side. He looked up at the man, toothy grin in place. "So, where are you going to take us?"

Moriah snorted at the boy's rather childish behavior, ruffling the prince's untidy hair. "You'll see."

Ecstatic, Fynn followed along contently. He took the time to admire the wilderness all around. Everything was so astoundingly different than Estheria. Morancy was situated atop a hill at the far end of the island and if you peered through the thick, jungle canopies that laced around the lesser hills at Morancy's feet, you could see the harbor and the white-sand beaches. If someone were to look over the jungle's canopy, fronds, and branches, they'd see nothing but the amazingly vast expanse of clear waters glinting in the sunlight. Straining his eyes, Fynn saw the distant, fuzzy shape of Green Isle, the island closest to Dier Island in the archipelago.

The boys followed along behind Moriah, who had deviated from the walkway and veered right. They ducked behind a large palm tree and turned a corner, which led them to a ruined looking staircase. The steps were a bit uneven, the stone cracked and old looking. Thick, green moss was overrunning the rocks.

"Is this safe?" asked Godryk as he watched Moriah begin ascending the questionable looking stairs.

"Perfectly," called Moriah, who was presently disappearing amongst the overgrown vines and low hanging tree branches. "Come along, boys."

Fynn had no qualms about darting up after the man in black, but Godryk was far more hesitant. Inhaling deeply, he began climbing up after the two. The stairs were quite steep and slippery, but both boys managed to keep their footing. In just moments, they found themselves standing atop a balcony that was only just slightly higher than the top of the castle entryway. Moriah was leaning over the short, intricately designed, stone bannisters.

The prince joined him, settling in at his side, his shoulder brushing against Moriah's arm. They both looked out, staring in the direction of the sea with a now completely unobstructed view of the harbor. After determining that the balcony seemed soundly constructed and wouldn't crumble, Godryk sidled up on Fynn's other side and joined them in their silent reverie.

There were more ships docking with large, white masts flying the banners of some of the great houses of Estheria. The commotion that was sure to be going on down on the shore didn't reach them, far off and away, perched atop the balcony overlooking the crescent shaped island. The wind was lulling them off, tickling them into a tired stupor. Each of the three took the time to simply indulge in the tranquility of the moment for, with the impending arrival of everyone else, it was sure to be a long time before they could enjoy the luxury of silence again.

"I used to come up here all the time when I attended Morancy," mused Moriah fondly. "It was the only time I could get a moment to myself."

"What's it going to be like?" asked Fynn.

"Managing to complete Morancy's training will be one of the hardest things either of you will ever do in your lives," Moriah answered.

"Seems a bit dramatic," Fynn laughed.

Moriah playfully nudged the boy with his shoulder. "Just you wait, *little* prince."

"My father said there are going to be changes to the curriculum," Godryk added. "Is that true?"

"The king has seen fit to adjust the training time. Unfortunately," Moriah eyed the two boys, "that means your year will be accelerated."

"What do you mean?" the young Redmayne questioned.

"He means the king made some changes to those *games* or whatever they are. We're competing this year instead of next year," Fynn explained glumly. "Aunt Ursalyn was quite...*upset*...by that news."

"You can't...can't be *serious*," stammered Godryk. He looked to Moriah imploringly. "He's joking, right?"

Moriah shook his head. "No. He's very much correct on this matter."

Fynn huffed. "What are these games, anyway?" Grey eyes turned to rove over Godryk's now trembling body at his side. "And why are you so scared by them?"

"Your father never mentioned them?" asked Moriah. "Of course not." He grumbled when he thought better of the question.

Fynn turned to Moriah. "So...what are they?"

Moriah looked away from Fynn, returning his attention to the sea off in the distance, admiring the way the waves glinted in the afternoon light. "The games are designed to weed out any weaklings from the school. They are intended to test all that you've learned, for you to prove yourself worthy of being appointed to a division." He ran his hand through his long, black hair. "Essentially, it's a war game." Moriah's voice deepened with an unusual sense of foreboding sticking to each of his words. "People die, Fynneas. Children die competing in the games." He let his shoulders relax for a moment before tensing again, eyes narrowing. "You're broken into teams. Each member of your team is armed with nothing more than a dagger. Your objective is to sail from Dier Island to Nandulus Island, the last island in the chain. In between, you'll traverse the isles of Green, Middle, and Little.

There are things in the jungles and on the islands that are going to want to hurt you, *kill* you. Not to mention what's in the water."

"But someone will be there if something goes wrong? Right?" asked Fynn hopefully.

For a moment, green eyes turned on the prince and regarded the anxious looking expression shadowing the child's face before returning to staring out across the island toward the shoreline. "No. You'll be on your own. The only people you'll have to depend on while you're out there are your teammates."

"That's madness!" Fynn exclaimed.

"It's the way things have always been," Godryk added weakly, as if hearing Moriah explain the games had somehow made it all the more real.

"We'll all do our best to ensure you're trained properly, prepared as best you can be to go into the games at the end of the term." Moriah leaned back from the bannister and straightened up to his full height. "It's going to be a long year."

9

NAN AND MINNIE

"Welcome, welcome," spoke a commanding, bellowing voice. "Settle down, settle down." Upon a dais stood a man coming along in years. He was of average height, hair that had once been a deep brown was greying, twisting in magnificent curls atop his head. He was tan, more than likely a result of spending all his time down in the southern territories of the kingdom. He was dressed finely in immaculately tailored clothing; brilliant brocades of purple and gold decorated his tight-fitting jerkin, a black cloak snugged around his broad shoulders. "I hope this term finds you all well." He smiled. "Before we proceed with our usual festivities, I would like to discuss some changes the king has seen fit to make, given the current state of affairs in the kingdom."

Evening had taken over and as the sun had gone down, everyone had filtered into the Hall for dinner. There were two chairs on the dais, one for the lord paramount and the other for the vice lord. The dais looked out over the rest of the Hall wherein there were six tables arranged, one for each division and a final one for first-and-second years. Fynn sat beside Godryk and a boy he had only recently met prior to arriving in the Hall, Rory Black-thorn.

The young prince had been curious when he spied the girl he'd met the day of the funeral, Lux, arriving and settling her things in the girls' wing. He hadn't yet had a chance to speak with her, but he couldn't help but catch himself staring at her now and again since they'd been seated at the table.

From the vaulted rafters of the Hall, there hung the banners of each division, five in total, and a last banner bearing the sigil of the school. When Fynn first saw the banner, he'd been transfixed by the design, interested in its origin. Upon a purple field, there was a golden hellebore wrapped in a banner that read 'By Any Means Necessary.' A phrase, Fynn knew, that had once been emblazoned upon the Fog banners. The same design was finely painted upon all of the plates set out before them, delicately done in the same rich, purple color as the banners.

To the left of Fynn's table stood the tables for Armada and Paladin, to his right the tables for Archer Brigade, Cavalry, and the Medical Corps. Those students seated at the division tables certainly held far more curious expressions than the younger children seated at Fynn's table. All eyes were upon the man speaking from the dais, eagerly awaiting the news as to what exactly would be changing.

"For those of you who are here for your first-year, I'd like to introduce myself and your instructors." The man gestured to himself with a proud flourish. "I am Maekon Malcourt, your Lord Paramount of Morancy." He then nodded toward the only other person on the dais, a tall man with thin shoulders and a pointed face. "Standing just there is your Vice Lord, Indigo of the House of Mandark." Maekon smiled, then held his arm aloft and gestured to the first table. "Seated with the Armada Division are Lords Riordan Astor and Drake Shoregore." He gestured back to himself with a smug look in his eyes. "I, myself, belonged to Armada and proudly served in the division in my youth." His meaty hand rolled with bravado. "But, that's a story for another time."

With a tilt of the head, he indicated the next table. "Then of course, we've the Paladin Division, led by your Lord Master of Arms Cort Staghorn, Lord Commander of the Night Corps Moriah Mordray, and Lords Noel Mordray and Nyle Humbert."

Fynn watched as each of the men named nodded and waved in turn, smiling at the students, save for Moriah who looked nearly bored to death, eyes impassive and expression listless. The prince bit back a snort of laughter at seeing Noel positively beaming beside Moriah; it was, the boy thought, harder and harder for him to believe the two were really brothers.

Maekon continued with his introductions, his voice ever so verbose. "It is my honor to then introduce to you the instructors heading up the Archer Brigade, Lady Air Brigadier General Odette Mordray and Lady Gertie Greenfinch. Do note that the vice lord is also a member of the Archer Brigade Division and, as such, oversees certain areas of their education as well."

The mention of yet another Mordray, one Fynn recalled his uncle mentioning at the catastrophe that was their farewell feast at Batsbeckon, drew the prince's attention. He studied Odette and thought her to be quite beautiful, if not rather intimidating. She was tall like her brothers and sat with the same rigidity Moriah often did. Her hair was a golden blonde, short and slicked back; a very odd style for a woman, Fynn thought. When she glanced in his direction, Fynn was almost taken aback with shock by the hardness and severity of her expression. Her sharp features were cold and vicious looking. He shivered and looked away from the woman instantly.

"Ah, and of course, let us not forget the Cavalry Division," cooed Maekon. He grinned, eyes twinkling as he beheld the most populated of all the tables. "Your Cavalry Division is headed by Lord Man at Arms Peragryn Humbert, and Lords Laeton Poisonwood and Benadykt Beckett." An excited whooping came from the cavalry table, their students clapping and saluting at the naming of their instructors. Fynn couldn't help but scoff, instantly knowing the cavalry boys would be the most obnoxious to deal with.

"Lastly," said Maekon, "we would be remiss to not introduce the Medical Corps Division, without whom many a man and woman would die in war time. Your Medical Corps is led by Lady Matron Imogen Blackthorn and Lady Blythe Singer."

The prince noticed that the Medical Corps was the only table comprised of just girls. Fynn couldn't help but smile, liking the dignified way each of the female students surveyed the rest of the Hall, as if knowing they were being judged and not caring in the least. There was, Fynn observed, a quiet confidence to the ladies of the Medical Corps that he found appealing.

Maekon clapped his hands together. "Now that introductions are out of the way, I'd like to again welcome you to Morancy. For first-and-second years, you've a difficult road ahead of you, but I feel certain that our esteemed instructors will guide you toward success. For the rest of you, you are well aware of the challenges that await. Yes, now I did mention that we had some changes to discuss. Right then, after speaking with the king, we've decided it would be best to accelerate the curriculum here at Morancy." A nervous whisper erupted in the Hall, quickly squelched by Maekon clearing his throat. "Fourth and fifth years, your training will be accelerated a great deal. That means more hours training and less hours sleeping. You, along with the sixth years, will be graduating at the end of term."

Before concerned questions could be raised, Maekon continued, "This is a change that will be upheld moving forward. From now on, Morancy will be completed in four years rather than the traditional six." Bracing himself for what came next, the lord paramount paused and inhaled deeply. "Furthermore, there will be a change to this year's games. Instead of second-years competing, both *first and second years* will take part. This means, first-years, courses normally designated for your second year will be introduced. Your training will be accelerated as best as it can be to prepare you. However, to make the games fair, teams will be comprised of first-and-second-year students alike. If everyone is amenable to that suggestion." Maekon paused yet again and then, after seeing the dismayed look in the children's eyes, forced himself to continue. "This means, at the end of the term, first-years will be appointed to their divisions. Does anyone have any questions?"

One boy seated at Fynn's table raised his hand tentatively.

"Yes, Wally?"

"Sir, does this mean there will be a change to how the games work?" the second-year, Wallace Hillwater, asked.

The lord paramount shook his head. "The structure of the games will remain the same. There will be more teams, given the larger number of participants this year, but game play will remain as is."

It was a girl at the same table who raised her hand next.

"Alice?"

"Why are these changes being made?" Alice, another second-year from the House of Hillwater, questioned.

"There have been...*concerns*...expressed by the king and, after much deliberation, we've decided the best way to address those concerns was to accelerate the training," Maekon explained. "As such, to keep the integrity of each division's relative training schedules, we decided to have first-years compete in the games. As I've said, this will be the case going forward."

"But what concerns?" Alice probed.

"It is the king's belief that we've been too easy on all of you," began Maekon. "The faster paced training will, in our opinion, prepare you for what is to come."

A third student, a second-year named Bram Magdolyn, asked, "What do you mean by 'what is to come?'"

All the children turned expectant eyes upon their lord paramount, each silently pleading for answers. The man was undeterred by their persistence. He said, "Unrest, both within the kingdom and abroad, has made it clear to us that you will all need to be ready, should the time come when banners are called."

"So, there's a war?" Alice queried, nervous curiosity shaking her voice.

Maekon held his hands up defensively, insisting, "Calm down, children, calm down. There is no war. Peacetime has been maintained for three generations now. No banners have been called by the king in that time and I do not suspect that they will be called any time soon. This is…just a *precaution*, if you will. We want you to all be ready, should anything go…*awry*."

The students seated at the division tables all looked as though they had something to say, but each seemed to think better of it when they glanced at their instructors. They had been quelled by the stern looks of their superiors, but the unsorted table of first-and-second years had no one to hold them back.

Yet another of the second-years, Oren Bridger, asked, "So, if there is no war, why speed up our training?"

"It is for your own good," the lord paramount declared. "Now then, let us dispense with these un-pleasantries. Eat, children, and enjoy tonight. Tomorrow your training will commence."

Fynn turned from the dais to look at his plate, empty for the time being while they waited for the servants to bring out their meal. His grey eyes flicked up, noticing a boy staring at him curiously. Sitting up a bit straighter, Fynn offered the boy a shy smile. "Hello."

"Oh…I didn't mean to stare." The boy laughed nervously. "You're the prince, though, right?"

Fynn shrugged. "One of them."

The boy smiled and offered his hand. "Albie. Albie Shoregore."

Fynn shook the proffered hand happily. "Fynneas Fog. *Fynn*, actually. I can't say I like how Fynneas sounds really."

"Fynn it is." Albie grinned. He was a fair looking boy with shaggy, brown hair and shining, blue eyes, tanned skin, and a nose that had clearly been broken more than once.

Fynn sat back and studied Albie for a moment. "Shoregore?"

Albie nodded. "That's right."

"So, you're from the south then? In Estherian Erza?"

The boy nodded. "Yes, Red Harbor."

"You're probably really used to this weather then," Fynn commented.

Albie smiled. "Yes. It's not too different from home. Do you like it?"

The prince shrugged. "I'm sure I'll come to like it eventually."

"Different than Batsbeckon, eh?"

"Can't say I'm too fond of Batsbeckon either," Fynn admitted. "I didn't grow up there."

"Oh," the young Shoregore replied. "Sorry, I didn't know."

"Don't worry," laughed Fynn. "I haven't taken offense or anything. I grew up in the north at Godsreach."

"Wow," Albie awed. "That certainly *is* different than here! No wonder you're not used to the weather. It's nearly frozen up there at Godsreach."

Godryk leaned closer to Fynn and whispered, "What do you thinks going on?"

"Don't know," Fynn replied honestly. "I haven't heard much about it."

Godryk looked across the table to see Albie eyeing he and the prince curiously. The young Redmayne smiled at the other boy, a warm and genuine sort of smile. "Sorry. I didn't mean to interrupt." He politely extended his hand. "I'm Godryk."

The brown-haired boy shook Godryk's hand amiably, broadly grinning. "Albie."

"Nice to meet you," said Godryk easily.

"So, do you know what's going on then?" asked Albie.

Godryk shook his head and sighed. "Not at all. Just know that we'll be competing in those death games they've got planned. It's going to be a nightmare."

One of the serving girls had filled their plates during the conversation. Fynn found himself distractedly stabbing at his food. "I don't know," he said as he speared a piece of fish. "I don't think it'll be *so* bad."

With an exasperated snort, Godryk playfully punched Fynn's shoulder. "Oh, what do you know? You didn't even know how the games worked until this afternoon."

"I know," Fynn garbled between bites, "but they don't seem so bad. A *little* dangerous, maybe, but I think we'll be alright."

"Do you really think so?" Albie questioned, beginning to jab at his own piece of fish with disinterest. "From what I've heard, they're *awfully* dangerous and people die sometimes."

"If we train hard, we'll be fine. Isn't that the point of the games? To test what we've learned?" Fynn continued, munching on the candied fruits stacked into a pile on his plate. "We just have to work hard and pay attention and it will all turn out alright." He popped a sweet apple slice into his mouth, enjoying the honeyed taste. "I'm more worried about the monsters in the water."

"Monsters in the water?" asked the boy sitting beside Albie, who up until presently had been engaged in an entirely separate conversation.

Albie turned to the boy. "Haven't you heard about the creatures in the water?"

The boy shook his head. "No."

"The monsters like the warm water, that's why you don't see them by the mainland really. They stay by the islands and Estherian Erza," Albie sagely explained. He eyed the boy next to him before chuckling. "Sorry, I didn't mean to be rude. I'm Albie, by the way."

"Ollie," the boy replied. He was a rounder boy with a wide, pink nose. His hair was brown, shortly cut. His eyes were a muddy hazel. He turned from Albie to regard Godryk and Fynn. Holding out his hand to them, he announced, "I'm Ollie Dangerfield."

Godryk shook his hand first. "Godryk Redmayne."

The prince took Ollie's hand next, boyishly beaming, "Fynn Fog." Ignoring Ollie's look of astonishment that he was shaking the hand of one of the princes, Fynn continued, "So, you're from the mainland then? Danger-fields…you're from Fort Thicket?"

Ollie nodded and looked to Godryk. "Not too far off from you, eh?"

"Not at all," Godryk agreed. "Maybe, what, two or three days ride from Claw Keep?"

"Just about, I'd say." Ollie nodded.

"So, what division do you think you'll be placed in?" Albie asked the other boys. "I'm hoping for Armada," he asserted. "Most my family's been placed in the Armada Division, save for the girls. They've all been in the Brigade. None of them were bright enough for the Medical Corps, I suppose. What about you lot?"

"I'm hoping for Armada too," Godryk said. "My father would be proud if I got placed there. My older cousins, the third and fifth years, they're in the Armada Division. Most our family ends up there. Well, that or Cavalry."

"Well, I'd like Archer Brigade," the young Dangerfield laughed. "It's furthest away from the front lines. Least chance of dying there, I'd think."

"That's one way of looking at it," jested Godryk in good humor. He turned to the prince, "What about you, Fynn? Most the royals go to Armada."

Fynn glanced from Godryk to the Armada and Paladin tables. He saw Ciaran at the Armada table, entirely absorbed in conversation with Riordan Astor. He considered them for a second before his focus drifted to the Paladin table where he saw Moriah and Noel, heads bent together, whispering rather intensely. He let Godryk's question linger for a moment, hanging on palpably quiet air, before looking back to the others. He grinned and said, "I think I'd like Paladin."

"*Paladin?* You must be mad," Albie gasped. "They're absolute madmen in Paladin! They're the best of the best, top marks in every field."

"They're the ones who get the most dangerous posts," added Ollie. "They end up as Marshals or, *even worse*, in the Night Corps."

"They take on the fewest students each year," Godryk supplied. "They've only got three right now."

"Two of them are my cousins," Fynn mused idly. "Not that it matters." He laughed. "I don't think that's what'll get me in."

"Your cousins?" Ollie repeated.

Fynn nodded. He looked over his shoulder, tilting his head toward the two grey-haired boys seated at the Paladin table. "Eckert and Valerian. They're cousins from my mother's side of the family."

"They must be *good* if they're in Paladin," considered Ollie.

"The best," Albie muttered. "They only take the *best*."

Fynn wasn't deterred by their words in the least. He didn't let their skepticism bring down his rather pleasant mood. He asked Ollie, "Archer Brigade, then? Even if you're far away from the front lines, it's still going to be a challenge."

"You think so?" Ollie mused.

The prince nodded. "If a *Mordray* is instructing, I have to assume it's going to be a tough lesson."

"What do you mean?" Albie intoned. "Have you met Odette?"

Godryk shook his head, eyeing Fynn for a moment. "We've met her brother, Moriah."

"You *know* the Lord Commander of the Night Corps?" Ollie seemed utterly astounded by that revelation. "He seems...scary."

"He's not," Fynn assured. "He's like a cat, I think. Comes and goes as he pleases and doesn't really tolerate nonsense or anything like that. But, he's really not bad."

Godryk muttered, "He's utterly terrifying."

"Do you think his sister will be just as bad?" Albie croaked, suddenly quite nervous about their first archery lesson.

Ollie had paled at the description of Moriah, noticeably more anxious than before. "I hope not, otherwise I may try to end up in the Medical Corps."

"Don't they only take the girls?" Godryk joked.

"I'll find a way," Ollie assured with a hearty chortle. "Trust me, if that Mordray lady is as terrifying as her brother seems, I don't want to be anywhere near the Brigade."

"There's another one too – Noel. He's the other Mordray in Paladin," Albie said. "Know him?"

Fynn nodded. "He's…a lot different than Moriah. If Odette's anything like him, you've got nothing to worry about, Ollie. But…I've a feeling she's more like Moriah."

The feast continued on well into the night with easy conversation flowing between the children. When at last their bellies were full, the first-and-second years were led back to the tower and into their common room by the vice lord. He motioned them in, instructing them to gather around the common area. With a pleasant smile, he acknowledged the group of children. "Second years, you're aware of how the school operates. I welcome you back but, as it is getting late, I think you should all retire to your beds for the night. You have an early morning ahead of you."

Indigo watched as the girls and boys scurried up the stairs to their dormitories, some of them casting quick glances back at him over their shoulders. With only the twelve first-years remaining as his audience, the vice lord proceeded, "Let me again welcome each of you to Morancy. You'll find your belongings have already been placed by your beds along with your uniforms. I suggest you all try and get to sleep as quickly as possible. As I told the second-years, you have an early morning. I will be here to gather you all up just after daybreak. Do try not to be sluggish about getting ready; it'll only put your instructors in a foul mood." He smiled an empty smile. "Tomorrow your day will begin with a run to the harbor. There, you will begin your sailing lessons with Lord Drake Shoregore. That should be two hours or so. Following your completion of your day's sailing lesson, you will run back to the castle. You'll eat your breakfast or lunch, depending on when you're back, quickly, and then you are off to Survival Strategies and Tactics or, as we all affectionately call it, Crisis Prevention. That will take the rest of your day. You will return to the castle by evening time and eat your dinner in the Hall. It should be a relatively easy first day. But don't get used to it. Things are only going to get harder. Any questions?"

A tall, gangly boy raised his hand tentatively. "I've one, my lord."

"Name?"

"Hogan Greenfinch, sir."

"Your question, Hogan?"

"Is that to be our schedule every day? What about archery or riding lessons?"

"Very good." Indigo nodded, pleased by the boy's observation. "Your schedules will be similar to tomorrow's. I will have a schedule drawn up for you all by morning. Each day will begin with a run and proceed with either two lessons or one daylong lesson. Those lessons will change from day to day, hence the need for a schedule so you all keep up with where you ought to be." He nodded politely to Hogan. "Mind, children, that your lessons will be both mentally and physically taxing. Sleep, therefore, is integral. With that, I bid you all good night. Go along, then, and get to your beds. I'll see you all first thing in the morning."

The children all watched as Indigo slipped out the door.

Ollie yawned and rubbed his eyes tiredly. "Well, I think we should all be off to bed like he said. It's been a long day." His words were slurred with exhaustion and, as if to punctuate his sentiment, he yawned again.

Hollyn shrugged carelessly. "Whatever. He probably wasn't lying about being here first thing in the morning." The prince was the first to ascend the small stairs to the dormitories.

Ollie looked to his new friends and weakly smiled. "I'm off, lads. See you in the dorms." He turned clumsily and followed Hollyn up to the rooms.

Fynn, who was staring off in the direction Hollyn and Ollie had retired toward, was surprised when he felt someone sharply poke his chest. He turned, head tilted to the side curiously. Lux was standing just in front of him. The boy took a nervous step back, awkwardly composing himself as he said, "Oh, it's *you*. Sorry, didn't see you there."

She furrowed her brow and pursed her lips as if she were about to scold him for something, and then didn't. Her expression relaxed. She eyed him for a moment and then spoke quietly, "I just wanted to say thank you for that day. You were really brave."

An uncomfortable warmth swelled in Fynn's cheeks; he ducked his head, hoping to obscure his face from the girl's perceptive eyes. He stammered, "Oh...right...no, it was nothing. I'm glad you're alright."

Lux playfully punched Fynn in the shoulder. "*Still*...thank you. That was...just the worst day of my life, I think."

The prince's stomach knotted painfully, and his chest grew unnaturally heavy. He recalled, in that moment, the garbled sounds of people screaming and running, the unmistakable tang of blood hanging in the air, the feel of the cobblestones scraping his hands and knees. "Mine too," he whispered. "And...thank you for helping me...in the crowd. Thanks."

Lux took hold of his hand gently. He wanted desperately to pull away from her, to disentangle his fingers from hers, but he couldn't bring himself to move. The terrible, stifling grief he'd been working so hard to keep at bay had suddenly swept over him like an unrelenting wave threatening to pull him down, so far back down he couldn't even breathe. Lux's hand tightened around his, a lifeline to pull him back. Icy eyes looked up and saw her smiling a sad, all too knowing, sort of smile.

"I didn't mean to upset you," she offered.

He shrugged, forcing himself to pull out of her hold. At once, he felt as though that lifeline was gone and he was stranded—painfully, woefully, stranded all alone in the dark. He shuffled for a moment, trying to scramble together, to not look as though he were on the verge of tears. He could already feel the sting in his eyes. He cursed his propensity for over reactions.

"You didn't." He rubbed at his cheeks with his forearm, the material of his shirt rough against his skin. "I'm fine."

"You sure?"

"Yes!" he snapped, rounding on her more forcefully than he intended to. Instantly, he regretted his actions. He took a step back. "Yes. Sorry…it's just been a long day. I didn't mean to yell at you."

Lux stood there eyeing the prince, taking in the redness of his eyes and the pink in his cheeks. She furrowed her brow, wrinkling her nose as she thought for a moment. Choosing not to prolong what had become a rather awkward interaction, she nodded and took her leave, saying, "Good night." Then she was gone.

Every muscle in the prince's young body was spasming with tension, coiling and restricting. His head was abuzz with the screams of so many people rushing through the streets. He was unable to escape the scent of blood that seemed to permeate the air in the room. He was shaking, sweating, breathing heavily. Grey eyes glanced back to the stairs, considering whether he should just retire for the night like everyone else. But the nagging, prickling feeling of knowing that any one of them–especially Hollyn–could see him in such a state made him reluctant to climb into his bed for the night. He looked to the other side of the room, eyeing the doorway that led to the stairs down the tower. It was late. Everyone was asleep. He continued staring at the closed door. He could just slip out and no one would know. He wouldn't go far, only far enough to clear his head before returning to the tower to go to bed.

Fynn pushed the door open, not even realizing he had already somehow managed to clear the distance from where he had been standing to the far wall. He began descending the stairs, unperturbed by the bleakness of the shadows that loomed like watchful monsters in the thin, tower stairwell. He must have been walking quicker than he assumed because, without even realizing he had taken more than a step, he was at the bottom of the tower and rounding the corner into the hall. The castle seemed much larger at night, far more angular in its construction as well.

A rustling sound and soft footsteps caught Fynn's attention. He turned in every direction, trying to find the source of the noise. Spying through the darkness had never been hard for him; he hardly even registered that the only light in the long corridor came from the dying fires of the wall-mounted torches. His lips curled into a smile as he knelt down, arms outstretched. "Dug? What're you doing here? Shouldn't you be sleeping?" He gathered the small animal into his arms, laughing quietly as a furry snout nuzzled against his neck. Fynn smoothed the fur between the fox's ears. "Guess you couldn't sleep either?"

The boy proceeded down the corridor, Dug safely nestled in his arms. As he continued toward the entryway, he looked down at the fox. "I suppose you know your way around here, don't you?"

The fox seemed to grin at the sound of Fynn's voice. Dug uncurled from the boy's thin arms and leapt to the ground, settling into step at Fynn's side, occasionally winding between his legs before returning to a comfortable pace in step with the prince. A long, fluffy tail tickled Fynn's hand. He looked down to the fox once more and quirked a brow. "Yes?"

Dug darted toward a small door beside the entryway. Fynn pushed it open, revealing the vast expanse of greenness stretching out before the castle that was sleepily tucked away in the shadows of the tropical night. Stepping through, Fynn was careful to close the door as quietly as he could. The island looked much different at night. The shining emerald of the foliage was no longer as brilliant in the moonlight, looking more like a faded grey-green. Fynn hurried along the path, stealing onto the roadway that had, earlier that day, carried he and Hollyn up to the castle. Dug remained his faithful companion for the journey.

Fynn saw, in the distance, the glow of fire-lit lamps burning. Curious, he hurried along down the road. He veered to the left where the road forked, knowing that the right would take him back down to the harbor. It wasn't long before the trees became a bit sparser in their vigil along the roadside and he could see, far more clearly, a small town collected amongst towering palms. Fynn remembered someone, probably Fiona, mentioning the small town situated on Dier Island–More Town–but he didn't recall seeing any inkling of its existence on his way up to the castle that morning. Though thinking back, he probably wasn't paying close enough attention to have spotted it.

The town wasn't very large. It reminded him a great deal of Shiver Town, the small township outside of Godsreach. Fynn smiled fondly as he remembered the town where he had once gone on many adventures with his sister, perusing the shops and taverns. He'd known everyone there by name; it was a comfortable place, far flung from the rigid, socio-political maelstrom that was Batsbeckon and the capital. Warmed with the memory of his childhood haunts, Fynn bounded into the town with boyish enthusiasm. The buildings looked very similar to those back on the mainland, but the roofing was sturdier looking, meant to take a beating from tropical storms and still hold together.

Fynn scooped Dug back into his arms, giggling as the fox wriggled free of his hold and settled onto his shoulder; his long tail wrapped around Fynn's neck and draped over his other side.

"I bet you know exactly where we are, Dug," said Fynn. He wandered into the town further. "Do you normally sneak out at night?" The prince grinned when a wet nose brushed under his ear; the small fox chattered away as if Fynn could understand him. "I bet Moriah isn't too happy when you sneak out," the prince mused. He rolled his eyes. "Honestly, I *know* he wouldn't be happy if he caught me out of bed right now." He reached up and scratched at the fox's cheek gently. "It'll be our little secret, alright?"

Thunder cracked overhead, catching the boy's attention. He looked up and, to his dismay, saw dark clouds gathering up above.

"Damn," Fynn muttered as he looked around for a place to escape the coming rain.

He spotted a sign hanging from one of the buildings, 'The Wayward Turtle Tavern.' He eyed it for a moment before snorting, "Stupid name for a tavern." Nevertheless, he ran to the small building and stepped inside just as the first drops of rain began to descend upon the sleeping island. The interior of the tavern was humble. There were wooden floors and stone walls and a few rickety looking tables here and there. An old woman was hunched over one of the tables. She looked bored. Her eyes went wide when she saw Fynn come in and, in an instant, she was at his side.

172

"Child," she said as she pushed Fynn toward the table she had just vacated. "Sit, boy." She smiled as the boy did as he was told, eyeing her reluctantly all the while. Withered looking blue eyes studied the seated boy, fastening onto the animal curled around his shoulders. "Is that Skullduggery?"

Dug's ears twitched at the mention of his name. The little fox pawed at Fynn's shoulder momentarily before jumping bodily to the table face and circling, twisting himself into a little curl and resting his nose against the white fluff of his tail. His bright eyes, despite his relaxed position, watched the old woman seat herself at the table carefully. The fox chattered away as one wrinkled hand descended down upon his head, tickling the base of his left ear.

"That's Dug alright." The woman smiled kindly. "He must be rather fond of you to curl up on your shoulder like that."

Fynn nodded shyly. "I suppose he is."

The old woman straightened in her seat and watched the boy across from her fidget uncomfortably. "I haven't seen you around the town before," she commented. "You must be one of the Morancy boys?"

Fynn nodded again. He smiled nervously. "Yes. First-year."

"Snuck out?"

Fynn looked away quickly, guiltily twiddling his thumbs. "Yes."

"Any particular reason?"

He shook his head. "I don't want to talk about it."

The old lady glanced across the room, worn eyes looking through the misty windowpanes out to the gathering storm, not surprised to see trails of raindrops rolling down the glass. "The storm's come 'round. Don't suppose it'll let up for a while." She returned her attention to the boy. "Hungry?"

He shook his head again.

"Want something warm to drink?"

"No, I'm alright," Fynn replied.

The woman stood up and headed to a back door, disappearing for a moment. Fynn was nervous in the silence. He reached for Dug, carefully combing his hand down the short length of the animal's back repeatedly. The little fox seemed to be dozing but, even then, he leaned into Fynn's touch.

Surprised when the old woman returned and set down a mug before him, Fynn looked to her with a tilt of the head. He eyed the steam rising from the cup.

The old woman grinned, once more taking her seat. "There's a chill in the air with the storm. You could use some warming up."

"Thank you," Fynn whispered as he took the cup, gratefully sipping in the warmth of the freshly brewed tea.

"Now, boy-o, what's your name then?"

He set the cup down. "Fynn."

The old woman held out her hand for him. "Well, Fynn, it's a right pleasure to meet you." She laughed at how tentatively the boy shook her offered hand. "You can call me Nan."

"Thank you for the tea, Nan." Fynn grinned. The tension was quickly falling away. "Is this your tavern?"

Nan nodded. "Been in the family for generations."

"It's nice," the boy commented sincerely.

"It's real shit." Nan laughed. "But it's mine and that's all that matters."

"Right," Fynn agreed. He sipped at his tea, one hand still lazily stroking the fox's red fur.

"Care to tell me how you know Dug?"

"Moriah is a…friend of the family," Fynn explained.

"Oh?"

The prince nodded.

"Moriah must like you."

The boy was surprised. He hadn't expected Nan to announce such a revelation. He pulled away from Dug and the mug of tea and leaned back in his chair. He surveyed Nan for a moment before asking, "Why'd you think that?"

"Dug wouldn't get that close to just anyone," Nan replied surely. "You must be really special."

Fynn shrugged. "I wouldn't say that."

"The fox doesn't lie." Nan chuckled as she traced along the length of the fox's tail.

"If you say so," mumbled Fynn.

"You're a firsty, you said?"

"Yes."

"What do you think of the place?"

"Morancy? Seems alright," Fynn responded somewhat despondently. He wasn't looking at Nan anymore. His attention was stolen by the cracks in the floor. He followed their twists and turns, curiously staring as they branched off at odd angles like lightning strikes. "Island seems alright, too."

"It's dangerous," Nan began, "to be walking around the island alone at night. Especially for a little firsty. There are things out here on the islands… things that wouldn't mind taking a bite out of a small thing like you."

174

"The monsters in the water, you mean?" asked Fynn, still unable to look at Nan.

The old woman grimaced. "There be more than just monsters in the *water*."

"What do you mean?" Finally, Fynn returned his attention to her. His ghostly eyes had gone wide.

"There are things in the *jungles* too, boy-o."

"Like what?"

"Terrible things with claws that tear and snatch and teeth as long as daggers," Nan explained. "There are monsters, Fynn, that are watching."

"Watching?"

Nan nodded. "They're *always* watching. You'd do best to remember that, little lad."

Fynn spluttered. "You…can't be serious."

"Gravely so, I'm afraid."

"That's ridiculous," he insisted. "They wouldn't put us on an island like that with monsters and whatever else is here."

Nan pondered this for a moment. The silence stretched between them. "It *is* a bit cruel, yes. But necessary."

"How is leaving us on this nightmare trap of an island *necessary*?" A certain petulance had crept into Fynn's voice as he pouted, crossing his arms. Any excitement he'd felt toward coming to Morancy was dashed and replaced by an unwavering feeling that everyone in Estheria was suffering from collective madness if they thought this was a good idea.

"Do you enjoy your lifestyle?"

Fynn blinked dumbly, staring at the old woman across the table. "What?"

"Your lifestyle. If you're here on this island, attending Morancy, then you're from a prominent family. Am I right?"

He nodded. "You could say that."

"So, I'll ask you again, boy-o, do you like your lifestyle?"

"Yes," he replied weakly.

"That's your answer."

"I don't understand," he admitted.

"For centuries, Morancy has trained up the boys and girls of the most powerful families in the kingdom. Each generation has consistently turned out the best soldiers there are. Estheria is enjoying an unprecedented time of peace, little lad…peace that was achieved through the efforts of its military. Do you think peace just happens?"

Fynn shook his head. "I suppose not, no."

"Peace is the result of thousands dying. Peace comes about when our soldiers lay down their lives to defend our way of life." Nan's eyes hardened as she spoke. "We achieve that victory through our strength. No other kingdom trains its boys and girls as we do, and so no other kingdom has ever stood as proud as we do now. Morancy will make you strong, boy-o. It will smarten you up and make you strong." There was no question in her tone, no hint of doubt. "What are Morancy's words?"

"By any means necessary," Fynn supplied meekly.

"By any means necessary," Nan repeated. "It may be harsh, but it is what it is. You're not here to be coddled. You're here, all of you are here, to be molded into exemplary soldiers so that should the time ever come when those banners are called, you'll all be ready."

Fynn bit down on his lower lip, rolling it under the sharp of his teeth, as he looked away. "Students have died here."

"They have."

"But that's the point," Fynn muttered shakily, "right? People die in war all the time. It's unavoidable."

"Unfortunately."

"They're just preparing us for it," he continued grimly.

"Child." She held out her hand to him. Fynn's thin hand fell into hers limply. "Lad, you'll learn so much here, I promise you that. But the one thing to remember is that not everyone who starts the journey with you is going to finish it with you. It's a reality of life that you're going to need to come to terms with." She glanced over her shoulder, peering out the rain-battered window. "And the monsters out there in the jungles and the seas, they're not the only monsters lurking." She felt his hand curl into a fist. Nan held on tighter.

"I'm scared, but it's stupid of me. I should be braver...I know, but I'm scared."

Nan turned back to Fynn, staring him down intently. "I would be worried for you, lad, if you *weren't* scared."

"Why?"

"Being scared," she said and squeezed his hand, "makes you *human*."

"Nan?"

"Hmm?"

"Can I ask you something?" he questioned sheepishly.

Nan nodded.

Fynn looked around the tavern before returning his focus to the elderly woman. "You know Dug pretty well, so you must know Moriah pretty well too…right?"

Nan let go of Fynn's hand, placing it once more upon Dug as she began to lightly scratch at his red fur. "I've known him since he was a boy. All the Mordray children, actually. There are nine of them, you know?"

"I've met two," he replied. "Moriah and Noel." He paused before adding, "And Odette is one of the instructors here. I haven't met her yet, though. I've only seen her."

Nan's eyes took on a reflective look as she recalled a time long gone by. There was a certain warmth to her voice that was appealing, welcoming. "They're all so very different. Sometimes it's hard to think they grew up together."

"What were they like?" Fynn leaned forward, resting his weight on his forearms against the table. The terror and unease that had crept into his person, his very expression and mannerisms, was gone and replaced by an unfathomable curiosity. His eyes were positively shining in the scant light of the empty tavern.

"Well, Noel was always the gentle one…always running after his brothers. I'm surprised he ended up in the Night Corps, to be honest." She tapped her chin as she thought. "Yes, never figured that boy for the killing type, but he's done well for himself, grown up a great deal since then, I suppose. Still, he'll always be the kind one."

Nan leaned back in her chair. "Vallon…well, he was always an odd one. Smart boy, that was for sure. He was always quick to temper, though…always picking fights with Noel when they were little."

She traced her hand along Dug's back. "Odette…Dottie is what we all call her. She's always been a bit withdrawn. Aloof, maybe you would say. Poor dear was never good with showing emotion, or *affection* for that matter, but she's got a good heart, she does. Smart, too, like the rest of them. Really smart, actually."

Nan tickled Dug's ears. She continued, "Rose, she's the youngest girl. She's always had her head up in the clouds. I suppose she's the most like Noel. Sweet child, always picking flowers and taking care of stray animals. Not a mean bone in her body, I would say."

The old woman returned to tapping at her chin. "Emrys, well she's the calm one. Level head on her shoulders. Can't say the same for the rest of them. And Virgil, well…he's always been quick to temper like Vallon. A bit more…tetchy, I think, though."

Her hand, apparently unable to be content when idle, returned to scratching at Dug's back. "Then there's Ridley. Oh, my sweet Riddles, he was the most handsome young man. Yes, Ridley is the pretty one. Charmer, he is. Brilliant smile, too." She laughed at a private joke, eyes twinkling with memories.

The tavern keeper shook her head and sighed. "Mortyma, well, she's the oldest of the lot. She's always been…difficult. *Vicious*, more like it."

Her distaste for Mortyma forgotten, Nan smiled back at Fynn. She scooped Dug into her arms and laughed as the fox settled into her embrace instantly. "Then there's Moriah. My Moriah, such a smart boy. Bored easily. That was always his greatest fault, you know. But such a smart lad, clever as can be, and funny when he feels like it. All the girls, you know, were always fawning over him. He has a sort of sinister allure that I suppose some women find attractive. Honestly, I do wish he'd wear something that wasn't black once in a while. He and Dottie *both*. They always look so morbid."

"Emrys is going to be staying with my sister," Fynn said thoughtfully.

"Is she?"

He nodded.

"You must be *real* close to them then, if Emrys is going to be staying with her," Nan surmised.

"I suppose," Fynn answered. "I don't know, really. I met Moriah and Noel only just this summer."

"You remind me of him, you know? Of Moriah."

Fynn laughed, scratching at his hair nervously. "Funny. Noel said the same thing."

"It's true. Well, you remind me of Moriah when he was your age. He's a bit quieter now, I'm sure you've noticed." She grinned, thinking back to a time when Moriah was the same size as the boy across from her, same mane of black hair, snowy complexion, and lopsided, boyish grin. "He grew up to be a fine man, as I'm sure you will too."

"Thank you." Fynn smiled. "I hope I turn out half as strong as him!"

Before the conversation could continue, the back door flung open and a small girl came barreling into the tavern. She stopped, standing just before the table, and chirped, "Nan! Nan!" She was a tiny girl with wild, golden curls that tumbled over her thin shoulders and down her slight back. Her eyes were a deep brown, framed by long, yellow lashes. Her small nose was spotted by pale freckles. Thin lips curled as her grin intensified. "Nan!"

178

The old woman laughed as the girl launched into her lap, tangling her spindly limbs around Nan's neck as she clung to the old woman. Dug leapt away looking ruffled. "Yes, child?" Nan asked, smoothing down wayward curls with a wrinkled hand. "Whatever is the matter, Minnie?"

The child, Minnie, rounded and looked to Fynn while still clinging to Nan. Ignoring the old woman's inquiry, Minnie brightened as she looked at the boy. "I had a dream about you."

"About me?" asked Fynn.

Minnie nodded. "Yes. You're the prince, right?"

Fynn laughed. "One of them, yes."

"No. You're the one from my dream. I remember 'cause of your eyes. They're a weird color."

Nan turned her head to chide the girl for her outburst, but Fynn held up his hand, halting her before she could begin.

"They're pretty strange, aren't they?" He laughed. "I've never seen anyone else with eyes quite like them so, you're right, they're *really weird*."

Minnie's presence was like sunlight, all-encompassing and warming. "Really weird!" she repeated cheerily.

Nan huffed, shifting the child in her arms and glancing back to poor Dug who had been taken by surprise. "Was that what brought you down here?" she asked of the girl.

Minnie shook her head. "No. I came down to say Moriah was coming."

Fynn blanched. He melted back into his seat, making himself as small as possible. "You're joking, aren't you?"

Blonde curls tumbled as Minnie shook her head. "No. Moriah's coming, I know it. I can always tell."

"Wonderful," muttered the prince as he continued to curl into himself, hoping he could somehow turn invisible.

Nan tried her hardest to bite back the laugh that was threatening to erupt from her lips. The boy before her looked absolutely soured by the idea of Moriah finding him out of bed on his first night on the islands, let alone in a tavern down in More Town. He was doing his best to blend into the wood of his chair, as if his skin would meld with the seat and he would simply vanish from sight.

"Come now, you had to know he would catch you?" The tavern keeper laughed.

"Not really," muttered the boy, scowling. "How does he even know? It's like he's got some weird sixth sense or something."

"Dug," Nan said.

Fynn cocked his head to the side, one brow arching. "Dug?"

"Dug followed you out of the castle. He doesn't just go off with any-one, you know. Moriah probably just noticed Dug was gone and figured, rightly so it seems, that you were behind the disappearance."

"You make it sound so obvious." Fynn snorted.

"It is," Nan replied happily. "You should've known better. You don't get much by Moriah."

"I've noticed," Fynn grumbled.

Though his back was to the door, Fynn knew the moment Moriah stepped into the tavern. The door squeaked as it opened. The chill of the storm reached into the room. Fynn could smell the rain. His stomach sank more. He bit down on his lip hard. Then he felt it; Moriah's hand draped over his shoulder. He was trapped. The boy prince forced himself to look up at Moriah and was instantly paralyzed by the coolness of those eerie, green eyes staring down at him. He flinched away from Moriah's touch, but knew better than to try and wriggle free.

"Out for a midnight stroll?" Moriah's deep voice sounded like a lazy purr.

"I didn't want to go to bed," Fynn tried to argue.

"And you decided to leave the castle? Alone? At night?"

Fynn twiddled his thumbs and looked to Nan with pleading eyes. "Yes."

Nan stayed quiet. It was, Fynn realized, Minnie who would be his sal-vation. Upon seeing Moriah sidle up beside Fynn's chair, the child had wrenched herself from Nan's hold and thrown herself fully at the man. Moriah released Fynn's shoulder in time to catch the girl, securely wrapping her in his long arms.

She settled against his chest easily, bright eyes looking up at him joyous-ly. "Moriah!"

As if for a moment forgetting Fynn was there, Moriah snuggled against the little girl in his arms. She buried her face in his shoulder, spindly arms wrapped around his neck with surprising force. He held her close; one hand reached up to run little circles over her back. "You shouldn't be up so late, Minnie," he whispered.

"I knew you were coming." She giggled.

"How?"

"I just knew," she twittered. Minnie tried to burrow against the man's chest even more. She curled into him with such ease, such effortless famil-iarity, that it seemed like second nature for the girl to react so.

180

For his part, Moriah didn't seem at all taken aback by the girl's affections. He held her close. He leaned his head around the girl, peeking back down at Fynn. "You're not out of trouble," the man in black said.

"I know," muttered the boy dejectedly. "I know."

Moriah returned to cooing over the child, tapping his fingertip to her nose gently. She laughed at his antics before resuming her place, comfortably nestled up against his shoulder. When he managed to look away from Minnie, Moriah noticed Nan watching him with a kindly expression.

"I didn't mean to wake her," the lord commander explained.

"I know," said Nan. She gestured to an empty place at the table. "Why don't you sit down and join us for a while? It's still raining out. How you're not soaking wet, I'll never know. When the storm eases up, you can take the little lad back up to the castle."

The storm hadn't eased as the hours wore on. Minnie, after finally allowing herself to be pulled out of Moriah's arms, had settled into Nan's lap and after a few hours of conversation over tea, had fallen asleep. Fynn, likewise, was lost to his dreams not long after. The boy had his head resting against the table; wild, black hair splayed in every direction. Moriah was leaning back in his chair, watching as the last drops of rain rolled down the window glass, distantly listening to the sound of raindrops clattering against the roofing and the road outside. Nan sat, one hand lazily twirling one of Minnie's golden curls while the other held the girl securely to her. She watched Moriah fondly, admiring how his eyes seemed to glow in the easy darkness of the late hour.

"Tired?" Nan asked softly.

He shook his head, not bothering to look back at her. "I napped earlier."

"Of course, you did." Nan softly chuckled and looked toward Fynn. "He's an interesting boy, isn't he?"

Moriah nodded.

"Spritely thing, he is."

"Doesn't listen worth a damn." Moriah yawned.

"Thought you said you weren't tired," joked Nan.

Moriah finally turned toward her, a crooked grin upon his face. "I'm not."

The old woman rolled her eyes dramatically, conceding, "Oh no, of course you're not!"

"The storm's dying down," he commented, ignoring her sarcasm. He glanced back at Fynn, absentmindedly brushing some hair back, revealing the boy's sleeping visage tucked in the shadows. "We should be getting back to the castle. Despite this little outing, the boy still has to be up on time for his first day."

Green eyes intently studied the drowsing prince. The last yellow discolorations from his bruises were fading with every passing hour. The cuts he'd received from his bout with Hollyn had healed already, leaving behind no trace of having ever marred the child's features. Moriah sighed, again combing his long fingers through the black mess of hair. His thumb traced over Fynn's temple, lingering over the barely-there bruise for a moment.

Nan asked, "How'd he get those bruises?"

Moriah's voice was hardly more than a whisper. "He doesn't listen. Unfortunately, neither does Hollyn."

"I see. Well, boys tend to work it out with their fists, I suppose," Nan surmised.

Moriah hadn't looked away from Fynn. "We're going to work on listening to orders."

"You're one to talk, aren't you," Nan prodded. "You only listen when you feel like it, dear boy."

"I suppose you're right." Moriah smirked. "Still, Fynneas needs to follow instructions. It could mean the difference between life and death. Here *and* out there."

"I know," the old woman agreed. A sudden sorrow crept into her voice, like salt into honey. "Don't let anything tremendously bad happen to Fynn. He's too precious a boy. Help him, won't you?"

"The best I can." Moriah's thumb traced the curve of Fynn's cheek softly. "But, eventually, he'll need to do it on his own."

"It's morning, I suspect," Nan observed. She shifted Minnie's weight in her arms and stood. "She was happy to see you."

Moriah rose, eyeing the girl in Nan's arms. "Let me put her to bed."

Dug, having nestled at Moriah's feet some hours ago, sprang to life. He followed after Moriah, who presently held the little girl in his arms once more, through the back door. Ascending the stairs that led to a small room, Moriah knelt beside the bed and, as gently as he could, deposited Minnie onto the bedding. She melted against the softness of her blankets, her cheek nuzzling the cloud-like pillow she now clutched. Moriah pulled the blankets over her, covering the girl up to her chin. For a long time, he remained kneeling at her bedside. She slept so effortlessly; he was jealous. He brushed a few rogue curls from her face.

Minnie's lashes fluttered, revealing sleepy, brown eyes that rolled to look up at the man at her bedside. "Leaving?" She yawned.

He nodded. "I've got to be getting back and you've got to be going to bed. It's far too late for you to be up."

"Night," she mumbled. Her head ducked back down, nose wrinkling against the pillow as she fell back asleep.

Moriah leaned down, tenderly kissing the child's forehead. "Good night, Minnie."

Faithfully, Dug followed Moriah back into the tavern, nipping at his ankles and chattering away.

Nan was standing beside Fynn's chair, watching the boy sleep.

Moriah reached out and shook the prince awake. "Fynneas, get up," he tersely insisted.

Fynn turned away from Moriah's prodding, incoherently gurgling, "I'm up, I'm up."

Moriah shook the prince's shoulder again. "It's late, we need to get back to the castle."

The boy's only response was to twist further away from Moriah. He yawned wearily. "Right, right, I'm up…I'm up, I promise."

"He's a handful, isn't he?" Nan peeped as she eyed Moriah.

The man shook his head and leaned down, gathering the boy into his arms. "You have no idea," Moriah muttered.

Weakly, Fynn beat a hardly curled fist against Moriah's chest. "I'm too old to be carried," he protested, far less than even half awake. "I can walk. Put me down."

Moriah ignored the boy's griping. He spun on his heel and headed for the door. "Thanks for watching him until I got here," he called back to Nan.

"He's an odd boy, I must say. But I like him. Reminds me of a certain someone." Nan winked.

"Whatever," murmured Moriah as he took his leave from the tavern.

The rain had stopped but the sky was still heavy and dark with storm clouds. The moon was waning, its light hardly reaching through the thickness in the sky, starlight barely registering as more than faded twinkles off in the distance way overhead. Moriah held Fynn tightly. The boy's head lolled to the side, his forehead resting against Moriah's shoulder. Dug followed along beside the pair with shining eyes staring up at the tall man in black.

Moriah looked down at the fox and frowned. "You shouldn't give into his stupid ideas."

The fox chattered, bounding off ahead of Moriah a few paces before looking back over its furry shoulder, seeming to smirk all the while.

The man shook his head, exasperated. "You and the boy are going to be the death of me."

10

FYNN'S FIRST DAY

The morning was comfortably warm.

The first-years assembled just outside the castle doors, milling around as they awaited further instruction. They'd woken that morning to the vice lord screaming at them to get dressed and hurry outside and now, as they stood kicking at the dirt below their booted toes, they were bored waiting for him to rejoin their group. There were twelve first-years gathered that morning, all dressed in their uniforms—black, linen leggings, black, leather boots, and long, purple tunics with the Morancy emblem embroidered in gold over their chests. Fynn was seated in the grass, legs stretched out in front of him, idly picking at the green blades poking up all around him. He yawned.

Godryk stood at Fynn's side, arms crossed. He looked down at the prince and smirked. "Tired?"

Fynn lightly punched at the redhead's leg. "You know I am."

"That's what you get for wandering around all night." Godryk laughed and gracelessly flopped down beside the prince. He quirked a brow. "Your bruises are all healed up."

Fynn shrugged.

The young Redmayne shook his head. "Don't get how you do that." He chuckled lightly. "It's sort of weird, you know?"

"Trust me, you're not the first to say that." The prince yawned again.

Godryk nodded toward his right and commented cheerily, "You may look like death warmed over, Fynn, but you still look better than Hollyn. Can't say his bruises have faded all that much."

Fynn combed his hand through his hair, trying to get it to settle into place. He eyed Hollyn, who stood not far from Godryk, arms folded over his chest, looking at the castle rather intently with his stormy eyes. Fynn snickered, seeing clearly in the light of day just how prominent Hollyn's bruises still were. "How *unfortunate*."

Indigo strolled through the castle doors out into the morning; it was still dark out. He rooted himself in the center of the amassed children. The vice lord nodded to each of them, eyes twinkling.

From the moment he saw Indigo earlier that morning, it was clear to Fynn that the man was one of those most-loathed of people, the sort who could be perfectly awake and pleasant at ungodly hours.

"Right children," Indigo said, clapping his hands together, "today is your first day of lessons. From tomorrow on, I will wake you and you will proceed with your day without further guidance from me. Today, however, before you head off to the harbor, I wanted to take a bit of time to discuss what is expected of you. First and foremost, you are each expected to up-hold Morancy's time-honored tradition of excellence. There will be no tears, no whining, no quitting." He surveyed the children with a near predatory expression. "There is no one here to coddle you. You are expected to stand up on your own two feet. Which brings me to my next order of business. Here, at Morancy, you will hold no titles - no lords, or ladies, or princes. Here, you have no family name. You will be called and known by your given name only. There will be no resting on the reputation of your family. Is that understood?"

The children murmured their acknowledgements warily.

"You will succeed or fail based upon your own efforts, your own will. If you get knocked down, you will get back up. If you get knocked down again, you will get back up more quickly. While you are here, you are a unit. The twelve of you will be spending a lot of time together; I suggest you try to get along. There will be times when you are split into teams; but, for the most part, you will remain together. That being said, you are expected to act *as a unit.*" Indigo took in a long breath and then continued, "Retreating, unless otherwise advised by your instructors, will not be tolerated. Surrendering, unless otherwise advised by your instructors, will not be tolerated. There will be consequences for both. Furthermore, there will be consequences for misbehavior, indignancy, petulance, and arrogance. Is this understood?"

Nervously, the children all nodded.

"Arrogance gets people killed in war. It will, above all other things, not be tolerated." The vice lord paramount looked from the gathered children out toward the horizon, eyes falling down to the harbor at the far end of the island. "Now, it's getting late in the morning. The sun will be up soon. I suggest you all get going. You're expected at the harbor for your first sailing lesson. The second-years will be joining you later this morning. Your sailing lessons will be the only lessons your years will share. Like I said, other than that, it will just be the twelve of you. So, best be off. Drake, Lord Drake Shoregore that is, doesn't like to be kept waiting. Do be quick."

Godryk sprang to his feet as many of the others began to slowly lurch from their places and jog down the walkway toward the road. He reached down, caught Fynn by the arm, and forcefully hauled the other boy upright.

Swaying slightly as he yawned yet again, Fynn grumbled, "Thanks."

"Any time," assured Godryk with a broad smile. Seeing that Fynn wasn't doing more than unsteadily gathering his bearings, the young lord sighed and gave Fynn's shoulder a strong shove forward. "Let's try not to be the last ones there, alright?"

Blearily, the prince agreed and the two headed off in the wake of the others. It wasn't terribly hard to catch up and keep pace with their year mates. No one was outright sprinting; rather, they'd all fallen into an unspoken pace, keeping in time with one another quite naturally as they conversed quietly amongst their little herd.

Albie found his way beside the pair, beaming at them all the while. "Sleep well?"

"Great, actually," replied Godryk. He nudged Fynn with his elbow playfully. "Can't say the same for the prince though."

Still fighting off the last remnants of what little sleep he got, Fynn pushed Godryk to the side with a bit more force than he intended. He couldn't stifle the snort of amusement when Redmayne stumbled over his too-large feet. "Don't you worry about me," chirped Fynn.

Godryk huffed. "You heard the vice lord, didn't you? *Arrogance* won't be tolerated."

Fynn quickened his pace ever so slightly, pulling ahead of Godryk by only a few paces. He glanced over his shoulder and grinned smugly. "I'm not being arrogant! I'm simply *confident*, is all."

Albie looked back to Godryk curiously. "I suppose he isn't a morning person, then?"

Redmayne shrugged. "Apparently not."

The three boys once more found themselves in step with one another. Fynn perked up as the jog proceeded, his natural energy easily taking over. His eyes were bright with enthusiasm, shining like ice in the light of the newly risen sun. He was enjoying laughing and joking with Godryk and Albie when he noticed someone missing from their troop. He spied all around him, searching for number twelve but not finding them. He slowed, nearly stopping completely, taking his running mates by surprise.

Curious as to what had brought Fynn to a sudden stop, Godryk and Albie stopped and turned around.

"What is it?" asked Albie.

"Everything alright, Fynn?" Godryk inquired.

Fynn stopped completely, intently scanning the surroundings until he spotted a rounded figure staggering along a good distance behind them. "I think that's Ollie," Fynn commented, still intensely staring back up the road toward the castle. They'd made it about halfway from Morancy to the harbor, the castle standing tall far off behind them. "He's all alone."

"Want to wait for him?" Albie suggested, taking the time to catch his breath. "He should be down here in a few minutes, right?"

"Wait here," instructed the young prince as he took off back the way they'd come.

Ollie shuffled along, round cheeks having turned a speckled red, beads of sweat rolling down his forehead, lingering at his temples. He huffed deeply with every breath, arms still pumping and legs still weakly bending as he tried to keep his momentum moving forward. By the time Fynn reached him, he was doubling over, gasping for breath.

The prince clapped a hand over the other boy's shoulder, watching as Ollie fought to collect himself. "Alright there, Ollie?" Fynn queried.

Ollie straightened up as best he could, brushed the hand from his shoulder, and turned to face Fynn with a sheepish grin. "Sorry," he said, wiping the sweat from his brow. "I don't want to hold you up any longer. I'll be on my way. You don't have to worry about me, Fynn."

Playfully, the prince punched Ollie's shoulder and smiled back. "Don't be daft! Albie and Godryk are waiting for us, I'm sure. Catch your breath; don't hurry. I'll stay back with you." He ran his hand through his own slightly sweaty hair, pushing the errant, black strands out of his eyes. "The vice lord said we were a unit and should act like one. Well, to me, that means not leaving anyone behind." Grey eyes turned away from Ollie and looked back down the road where he saw a third figure come to stand by the two he could now only blearily recognize as Albie and Godryk. Looking back to Ollie, Fynn asked, "Feeling alright?"

Ollie nodded. "Ready," he assured as he began shuffling along down the road.

True to his word, Fynn, despite the energy coiling in his limbs all but urging him to go sprinting off toward the harbor, remained jogging at a slow, steady pace alongside Ollie. The prince's eyes widened and he felt an all too familiar apprehension overtake him when he realized the third person waiting for him and Ollie was Lux; the trio were presently engaged in what must have been a humorous conversation, as Lux was letting the last of her brilliant laugh spring from her lips when she turned to spy the two boys joining them. Fynn bounded up beside Godryk, careful to not look at Lux, as he was all but positive his cheeks had turned an impressive shade of pink. He shifted his weight from one foot to the other, waiting as Ollie took in a few more shaking breaths.

"Ollie, you're looking a bit ill," Albie noted, stepping up to the other boy. He braced his hand upon Ollie's shoulder, dipping his head slightly to get a better angle, watching nervously as Ollie desperately fought to get air into his lungs. "Just breathe, we're not going anywhere."

Godryk looked from Ollie to Fynn. His brows knit together. "He's not looking too good," Redmayne whispered.

"Let's keep our pace slow," Fynn suggested.

Ollie righted himself once more and forced a smile. He noticed Lux standing there, evidently rather concerned about the state of things. He stammered, "I...I don't think...we've been properly...properly intro-duced." He held his hand out to her. "I'm Ollie."

Without hesitation, Lux took the sweaty palm into her hand and smiled warmly. "Lux." She looked toward the harbor. "We'll be late. You feeling well enough to keep going, Ollie?"

He nodded emphatically. "Yes...yes, I'm alright! Let's go, then." Yet again, he began his sluggish shuffle.

Albie took up residence beside Ollie. He decided that engaging the oth-er in a conversation would help take the boy's mind off the physical strain; and so, a muffled chat between the pair commenced.

Fynn remained a few steps behind Ollie, watching intently for any signs that the boy was struggling more so than before. His attention was so fixat-ed on watching Ollie's every move that he hadn't noticed Godryk and Lux jogging up and flanking him. They fell into step with his cadence as if it were second nature to them.

"Lost in your head?" asked Godryk.

"Hmm?" mumbled Fynn, not looking to the young lord.

Lux laughed. "I suppose that answers that question."

When the five-some arrived down at the harbor, their other seven year mates were standing around looking bored, toeing at the ground or gazing up at the clouds. Lux sauntered toward the gathering, breathing heavily, cheeks flushed. She noted that their sailing instructor had yet to arrive. Frowning, she asked, "I thought we were supposed to be meeting Lord Shoregore down here. Where is he?"

Hollyn shrugged. "He hasn't shown yet."

Ollie fell to his backside and stretched his legs out in front of him while he gasped for air. "Right...we'll just...wait for him here, then."

Hollyn snorted, a disdainful look in his eyes. "Have a hard time getting down here, did you?"

"Leave him alone, Hollyn," Fynn warned snappishly, taking up right behind Ollie, looming over the other boy like a sentinel, eyes sharp and dangerous as he glared at his cousin.

Hollyn stared back at them carelessly. Dullness crept into his voice as he said, "Not *my* problem. You're all just lucky Shoregore is later than you."

"Whatever," muttered Fynn as he sat down beside Ollie. His foul mood shifted. He praised, "Well done, Ollie, keeping that pace up. You'll get faster every run, I'm sure."

Godryk seated himself on Ollie's other side. He grinned widely. "Definitely! You'll be beating everyone down here in no time."

All the children snapped to attention at the distinct sound of footfalls approaching. They watched curiously as a man came into view. He was of average height with broad shoulders and wide arms. His complexion was swarthy, coppered from years in the sun and distinctly Erzastran looking. His hair was a pale brown that tumbled in untidy curls in every direction. His eyes were a deep blue. His nose was wide and his jaw was squared. A few pink scars over his forehead stood out strikingly against his tanned appearance. He was dressed in a white tunic and dark trousers; his brown boots looked warn and faded from years of wear. He came to stand before them with a calm smile and said, "Well, good morning, firsties."

"Good morning," they replied at once.

"Right then, I'm Drake Shoregore and, as I'm sure you're all well aware by now, I will be your sailing instructor this year." He clapped his hands together enthusiastically, as if the very mention of sailing had energized him. "There are twelve of you, I'm told."

The children nodded.

"Right, we'll be splitting you up into four groups then." He eyed the first-years for a moment before sighing. "I think it'll be easier if I split you up rather than letting you all fight over it." Chuckling, he waved his hand. "Now then, stand in a nice, straight line."

Complying wordlessly, the children arranged themselves shoulder to shoulder, watching intently as Drake approached them.

"It's early and it's your first day, so I'll make this simple. I'll count you off, you'll be assigned a number one through four. Find the others with your number, get into your groups, and await further instruction. Yes?"

"Yes, sir," they replied in a fair approximation of unison.

Godryk and Fynn grumbled, having been assigned different numbers, and stalked off toward their groups. Though Fynn happily noted that Albie was in his group, he couldn't help but sigh when he realized their third partner was Hollyn. The three boys stood around one another, watching as the other groups collected themselves similarly.

"Right, now that you've all found your teammates for this morning's lesson, follow me." Drake took off toward the shore with a herd of twelve trailing behind him. When at last he stopped, he turned back to the children and proclaimed, "These will be your ships for the day." He nodded toward the rickety looking dinghies resting upon the white sand, worn oars haphazardly thrown about on the shore. "Each group will have their own boat. Go on, pick one out," he encouraged, stifling the laughter that threatened to break free as he watched the children's faces contort into confusion.

Hollyn stepped up to one little boat, peeking over to look into the interior to inspect it for holes. Albie eyed the dilapidated vessel nervously, his attention constantly shifting from boat to water, as if unsure the dinghy could handle their weight and not crumble into a heap of splinters the moment it touched the sea. Fynn bit down on his lower lip, brows furrowing as he contemplated the very same thing. He came up beside his cousin and joined in painstakingly inspecting the dinghy. A nervous itch had found its way to the pit of his stomach.

"Do you think this will hold us?" Fynn whispered to the other prince.

Hollyn shrugged apathetically, eyes never leaving the boat at his feet. "Scared?"

Fynn shoved Hollyn slightly, growling out, "No."

"Here's today's lesson," began Drake. "One of you, take up the oars and sit in the boat. The other two, push the boat into the water and get in.

Not hard, right? Right. Once you're all situated, I will proceed with further instructions."

"I suppose you'll be the one sitting in the boat with the oars?" asked Hollyn as his gleefully sparkling eyes glanced to Fynn. "Don't want the monsters to get you, right?"

Fynn, seething, took hold of one of the oars lying about and tossed it to Albie. "Get in the boat," he commanded, still staring heatedly at the other prince. "Hollyn and I will push."

Clutching the oar to his chest, Albie nodded and, after collecting another oar, gingerly stepped into the dinghy and sat. He shifted nervously as Hollyn and Fynn continued their silent battle of wills, neither bothering to make a move toward pushing the boat into the water. As he watched the other teams decide on their respective positions and begin pushing their dinghies into the shallows, Albie finally spoke, "Do you think we should get started?"

Hollyn was the first to round on Albie. "Just be ready with the damn oars and try not to rock the boat in the water."

Fynn pushed Hollyn, knocking the other boy off his feet. He watched as Hollyn found himself sprawled out in the sand. "Don't talk to him like that," Fynn warned. "You heard the vice lord earlier. There are no titles or anything here. You're not better than anyone else."

Hollyn stood, absently brushing the sand from his clothes. His eyes were ablaze. He barked, "I didn't say I was, you *idiot*!" Hollyn stepped up to Fynn and shoved the other prince backward. As Fynn toppled at Hollyn's feet, the red-haired boy glowered. "And if I were you, *Fynny*, I wouldn't go starting a fight you're not going to win."

Fynn reeled his leg back and gave a solid kick to Hollyn's ankle, laughing when the boy went tumbling to the ground. Sitting up on his elbows, Fynn smirked. "Who said I wouldn't win the fight?" His grey eyes were shining with mirth as he watched Hollyn. He tapped his cheek and laughed. "I'm not the one with a face full of bruises, am I now?"

Like a snake uncoiling, Hollyn twisted around and lunged, pinning Fynn bodily against the sand. One hand perched upon Fynn's shoulder to hold him down. Hollyn was poised over him as he hissed, "Like I said, don't go picking a losing battle."

Fynn writhed under Hollyn's weight. Forcefully, the black-haired boy rolled to the side, knocking Hollyn off balance and sending him spluttering to the ground in a heap. "You were saying?" he asked darkly.

Albie watched, stunned, as the two princes battled in the sand. Still clutching the oars to his chest, he peeked over his shoulder and, stomach sinking, noted that the others—all by this time having successfully managed to get the boats in the water and themselves settled aboard—were watching the row with great interest. When Albie chanced a glance back to his partners, he was dismayed to see them clutching at one another's tunics, rolling around in the sand, overtaking one another before being bucked off; the cycle repeated endlessly it seemed. He couldn't hear what the princes were saying, but he figured based on the tone the words were being snapped in, there was nothing polite being uttered between the two.

A firm voice boomed, "Are you two quite done?"

Albie stiffened, holding tighter to the oars. He peered beyond Fynn and Hollyn to see Drake standing just behind them, arms folded over his broad chest, looking entirely unimpressed with their little display. The instructor leaned down, snatched each boy's collar in a hand, and hauled them to their feet.

"Push off and get in the damn boat," Drake commanded sternly. He gave them a not-so-gentle heave toward the boat and shook his head. "Oh, and boys?" As Fynn and Hollyn were proceeding back to the boat, they paused. Each shuddered before turning back to Drake. There was a humorless smile upon the instructor's face, eyes darkened. "See me after dinner this evening. Yes?"

Both princes nodded affirmatively, duly chastened for the moment.

"Behavior like this will not be tolerated," Drake reminded them sharply.

The little boat rocked gently as Hollyn pulled himself in. He and Albie watched as Fynn remained waist-deep in the water, clutching the hull of the dinghy as if his life depended on it. Fynn's slender shoulders shook; his body trembled in the water despite the warmth. Hollyn sighed and reached his hand out to Fynn and, once the boy had reluctantly taken hold, helped to haul him into the dinghy.

"Are you alright?" asked Albie as he scooted to the side, allowing Fynn a place to sit.

Fynn crawled up and sat beside his friend, looking to the side, refusing to meet Hollyn's quizzical gaze. He nodded. "Fine. I'm fine."

"What happened to *not being scared?*" Hollyn scoffed as he leaned back comfortably.

"Whatever," mumbled Fynn.

"Wonderful." Again, Drake was clapping his hands together enthusiastically. "Now that we're all settled in the water. Let's take a moment to just relax."

Albie quirked a brow. "*Relax?*"

"He's mad," Hollyn muttered. His arm reached over the side of the little boat. His hand lazily dipped into the warm water lapping against it. "Barking mad."

Fynn eyed Hollyn's arm, half expecting some great, watery beast to lurch from the depths and rip the boy's appendage off. His eyes went wide at the thought and his jaw tensed. He could feel the vicious hammering of his heart pounding away at his chest relentlessly, a tightness curled there amongst his lungs making breathing a challenge. Fynn clamped his hand down against the wood of the hull, his arm shook all the while. Biting down on his lower lip, he forced himself to look away from the water.

A hand draped over Fynn's upper back, pulling him from his panicked reverie.

"You aren't looking too good," commented Albie quietly.

Fynn shook his head, insisting, "I'm alright."

"Now that we've acquainted ourselves with the sea, start rowing. Stay in the shallows, mill about where I can see all of you," Drake called from the shore. "Switch off who is rowing every few minutes, yes? Today's objective is to become comfortable in the water. Get used to the waves rocking the boat. Get your sea legs."

Albie, oars lowered to the surface, began churning the spindly, wooden arms against the water. Their little boat was coasting along the shallows gently, moving none too fast. Hollyn's hand was still tracing languid circles against the sea, blue eyes staring into the crystalline waters intently. The water was warm, much like the morning. Small fish darted beneath the boat, little fins beating against the gentle current.

"Wonderful, children!" called Drake from the shore. "You're all doing wonderfully."

"This is stupid," Hollyn groused as he finally sat up straight, drying his hand on his tunic. "How is rowing about supposed to teach us about *sailing?*"

Albie sighed. "Who knows? But, it's not too hard. Honestly, it's rather relaxing. Not a bad way to spend the morning. I was expecting a lot worse the way everyone was talking yesterday."

"I'm bored," Hollyn grumbled as he crossed his arms.

The morning became blisteringly hot as the hour wore on. The children were left to continue their rowing, barely noticing as the second-years strutted toward the beach. It was once again Albie's turn to row, and he found that his arms were feeling weak and stringy. His attention strayed to the shore, as did Fynn's, when the faint sounds of Drake giving the second-years instructions broke the silence. While their year continued with the monotonous task of floating along the shallow waters in oblong circles, the class above them was set to the task of tying knots. Fynn lurched forward, leaning over the side of the boat, and watched as Drake demonstrated different kinds of knots, marveling at the intricacies that were entailed.

"Do you think we'll be tying knots?" asked Fynn to his boat mates.

Hollyn was drowsily leaning back against the edge, head tilted slightly backward, watching the clouds inching by overhead. He yawned. "Who knows."

"Seems boring," Fynn added.

"Can't be worse than floating in this damn thing," Hollyn replied.

"Come on, then, it's not *that* bad." Albie laughed.

Hollyn snorted. "We're not *doing* anything! Anyone can row a boat this small."

They hadn't noticed they were straying too close to another one of the little boats until they clattered against the wood of the other, jostling them from their whining. Fynn and Hollyn were quick to jump to their feet, unsteadying the already rocking boat while Albie clutched tighter to the oars in his hands. Whipping his head round, Fynn saw that the other dinghy had capsized when its occupants, much as he and Hollyn had done, had leapt to their feet in a sudden flash. His eyes went wide when the three children went splashing into the water, their oars floating along over the gentle waves.

Fynn watched, searching the water, as the three resurfaced. Renwyn and Penelope were quick to take hold of the dinghy's underbelly, using it to keep themselves above water. Ollie was the last of his group to breach, spluttering the salty water as he flailed his arms.

Penelope was brushing her dark hair from her face when she caught sight of the panicking Ollie. She instructed, "Ollie, you have to stop splashing like that!"

Renwyn, a strong looking boy, helped Penelope gain a better handle upon the boat before rounding on Ollie, yelling, "Oi! Stop splashing! It'll attract whatever's in the water."

This sentiment only spurred on Ollie's frantic movements as he struggled to snatch hold of the boat, fingers fumbling over the wet wood. He was gasping. "I can't swim!" He turned his wide eyes toward Fynn, seeing the prince still standing in his own boat, staring down at him. "Fynn! Fynn, help!" He continued madly flapping his arms in the soft current.

Albie and Hollyn had leaned over, each doing their best to try and right the other boat. Renwyn was pushing up as the other two pulled, careful to keep a hold of the still-shaking Penelope at his side. When at last their boat was right side up, Renwyn was able to climb in with little effort. Offering his hand to Penelope, he then pulled her in with ease. They looked back to the water, dismayed to find that Ollie had lost his tenuous hold to their boat and was bobbing up and down in a state of total and complete abandon, terror punctuating his desperate gasping.

Fynn watched on, staring at the water, searching for any sign of something swimming near Ollie or the boats. He saw nothing but the pristine, clear water swishing away as the boy continued to splash. Fynn was shoved roughly to the side when Hollyn jumped from their boat and plunged into the water. He watched on numbly as Hollyn swam to Ollie, none too gently catching hold of the other boy's upper body. He hooked his arm around Ollie and then lurched through the water back toward the boats. Ollie was still flailing in Hollyn's hold but had begun to moderately settle when he realized the prince would not let go.

Renwyn reached down, taking hold of Ollie's hand. Hollyn assisted from the water, pushing Ollie up as best he could while the boy tumbled into his boat, panting breathily.

Scowling, Hollyn gracefully climbed back into his own vessel. He watched with dull interest as Ollie moaned and whined. Turning to face Fynn, his scowl only soured further. "Some help *you* were," Hollyn admonished tersely.

The second hour of their sailing lessons proceeded with the first-years diligently watching as Drake demonstrated proper knot tying technique while the second-years went about rowing in the shallows. Not one of the twelve children showed a fraction of the enthusiasm Drake was radiating. He acted as if perfecting each knot was tantamount to finding treasure. While the man grinned from ear to ear, entreating his charges with tales of how he had learned each knot and when each was appropriate to use, Fynn found himself chewing on the inside of his cheek, lost in thought. His eyes were fixed on the water, watching each ripple across the surface as the oars twisted in the paleness of the sea. As the breeze wafted over the shoreline, the distinct scent of salt and fish coloring the air became off-putting. Once Drake had completed his demonstration, he returned his attention to the class still out rowing while Fynn and his year mates set about precisely twisting rope to mimic what they had been shown.

"I take it back. This is worse than rowing," Hollyn muttered as he utterly failed at tying one of the intricate pieces.

"At least we've got some time to dry off," Renwyn grumbled, glancing down at his still-damp uniform.

Hollyn quirked a brow as he looked to his side to stare at Fynn heatedly. "Well, not *all* of us have that problem, do we?" He all but spat each word as if he were tasting poison.

"Sorry," grumbled Fynn, twisting idly at his section of rope. He couldn't quite bring himself to even look at Hollyn.

Ollie nudged Fynn gently, assuredly saying, "Don't worry about him, Fynn."

The prince shook his head. "I should've jumped in to help you." He sighed deeply, sickened. "I...got scared. I'm sorry."

The other boy laughed, peeling the rope from Fynn's claw like grasp. "You're going to ruin it," Ollie muttered. While he took Fynn's section, he exchanged it with his own. "Take mine. Maybe you can work backwards on this one. See how I did it, you know? Then just copy that."

The young royal marveled at the perfectly worked knot he now held. He turned it over in his slender hands curiously, trying to figure out how Ollie had so effortlessly perfected the knot. He tugged at its twists and coils, astounded by how tightly it had been pulled. "How'd you manage this?" When grey eyes roved from the rope in his hands to the twain Ollie now held, he was surprised to see that the other boy had, once again, tied the instructed knot faultlessly. "No way!"

Ollie held his knot aloft for Fynn to inspect, a satisfied smirk upon his rounded features. "It's not too hard, really, once you get the hang of it."

Fynn ogled the knot before laughing. "If you say so, Ollie. *I* certainly can't manage it." He glanced back down to the rope he held and then back to the boy. "Make a deal?"

"What kind of deal do you have in mind?"

"Well...can you teach me how you did this?" He nodded to the knot, keeping his voice deliberately hushed. "You know...when no one's around or anything?"

"What do I get from this deal?"

Fynn shrugged. "What do you want?"

"I don't know yet," Ollie replied sheepishly. "I suppose we'll have to see what *you're* good at that *I'm* not." He turned the knot over in his meaty hands. "But, no matter what, I'll still help you with this."

"You will?"

Ollie nodded. "Of course. We're friends, aren't we?"

Following their late breakfast, the first-years gathered in an open field, once again impatiently waiting for their instructor to arrive. Having exhausted himself with the run back to the castle after sailing lessons and the subsequent run out to the field after breakfast, Ollie was contentedly lazing in the grass, looking up at the clouds. The day had only become progressively warmer as the hours toiled on and, presently, the sun seemed to be at its peak.

Godryk and Fynn stood shoulder to shoulder, quietly discussing how unexpectedly dull sailing lessons were when they were startled by weathered hands clapping down on their shoulders. Both boys wrenched from the hold of those leathery hands and spun around to face the new arrival. The rest of the first-years were equally roused from their griping when Fynn and Godryk had gone spinning around so abruptly. Now, twelve sets of eyes stared intently at the elderly man who had joined them.

Lord Nyle Humbert was a small thing, withered and terribly frail in appearance. His back was hunched, and long, spindly arms hung at his side. Protruding wrists were rather prominent against his twiggy forearms; large hands with splaying, crooked fingers, lazily picked at the material of his trousers. His skin was like sunken leather, craggy looking and weather-worn, splotched here and there with darker marks. His eyes were a muddy brown and almost entirely obscured by the thick, wiry, white eyebrows that nested over them like two rotund caterpillars gone for a nap. Much to the surprise of the children, given the man's skeletal appearance, he seemed to be armed to the teeth; a knife was sheathed on either leg and a long dagger was fixed at his hip. He had a bag slung over his arching shoulders which, the children were certain, held within it nothing pleasant.

He outstretched his arms dramatically and, in a rough and graveled voice, proclaimed, "I am Lord Humbert, Nyle, your instructor for Survival Strategies and Tactics—*do not* call it Crisis Prevention, for there is no preventing *crisis*! Crisis is inevitable! My job here is simply to give you the training and the tools necessary to deal with those crises, lest you be welcomed by Death's embrace." He cleared his throat with a wet cough; it sounded as though his lungs had been dislodged from his heaving chest. He pressed on. "Now, gather 'round children and behold your first lesson…making fire!"

"He's a bit *different*," whispered Fynn as he leaned nearer Godryk.

Godryk nodded dumbly, still astounded by the old man's apparent flair for the dramatic. "Seems so."

Nyle reached a claw-like hand into his bag and pulled from it two, long sticks. He held them up to the children, saying, "These will be your tools for the day. Worry not children, I've brought plenty for each of you." Rather than take the time to hand the children their sticks however, Nyle forcefully shoved his hand back into the bag and withdrew more sticks that he proceeded to hurl toward the children like blunted projectiles. He chuckled as they cringed away, ducking or holding their arms up to keep from being struck. "If you cower at the sight of mere *twigs*, what will you do when you've got an army at your back and nothing but your resolve and a knife as your only allies? *Die*, that's what you'll do. Now, stop your wretched whimpering and pick up your sticks."

Rather reluctantly, the twelve began to gingerly pick up the sticks, holding them attentively while looking back to Nyle. "Yes, yes, you've all managed to listen, well done. Listening will be the difference between being hurled into a shallow grave and making it back home to your nice, warm beds. Do you understand?"

Each child nodded.

Reflexively, Fynn's hold on his sticks tightened for a moment. "He's a loon," he whispered.

Godryk chuckled under his breath.

Nyle knelt down, placing the sticks perpendicular to one another. "You will need to have kindling, of course, for the fire to be effective. Today, you will learn the movement necessary. Today will be *theoretical* fire starting."

"Theoretical?" asked Albie confusedly, staring blankly back at the old man.

Everyone cringed when a small rock was thrown sharply, snapping against Albie's forehead. The boy dropped his sticks and clapped his hands over the point of contact, wincing.

Nyle stood, glaring at Albie. "*Theoretical*, yes. I don't trust the lot of you to try and start a fire without burning the island to the ground." He motioned to the grass whereupon the discarded sticks now lay. "You've proven me right, boy! Look there, you've already gone and dropped your tools."

"They're just sticks," muttered Albie, fingertips ghosting over the blossoming bruise.

No one was prepared for another small rock to be forcefully launched at Albie. Even more astounding was that Nyle managed to angle the small projectile so that it struck in nearly the same place.

Albie glowered. "What was that for?"

"What was that for, *sir*! You will show *respect* to your instructors, you ungrateful little fopdoodle! *Insolence*, of any kind, I can assure you, will not be tolerated." He gestured toward the forgotten sticks. "Pick them up, go on! Gather your tools, boy. What would you do if this was war? Leave your sword discarded on the ground? I should think not, lest you doom your comrades to a most unfortunate and ill begotten death because of your carelessness!"

"What?" Albie asked as he gathered up the sticks from the ground. "They're just *sticks* though."

Despite his decrepit appearance, Nyle moved quickly. The old man was standing just in front of Albie before the boy had time to register the shift and soon he was sputtering as a weathered, old hand smacked him on the side of the head with clipping force. "They are your *tools*, boy, and you will treat them with the respect they deserve."

Albie nodded. "Yes, sir."

"Your name, boy?"

"Albie, sir."

"Short for Albert?"

Albie shook his head. "Albatross, sir."

"A Shoregore, then? Must be. Your house is the only family that sees fit to give its children those ridiculous bird names you're all so fond of. Well, *Albatross*, do you plan on disrupting this lesson any further?"

The boy shook his head. "No, sir."

"Right then." Nyle nodded as he turned to address the other eleven children. "As I was saying, these sticks will be your tools. You will learn the concept behind building a fire. When I believe you can all successfully manage this without burning yourselves to death or reducing the island to ash, I will consider allowing you to practice making real fires. Have I made myself clear?"

"Yes, sir," the first-years agreed.

"Well done, children, well done," Nyle snidely continued. "Now that you've managed to listen—and as I've said, listening can save your *wretched*, little lives—we can proceed with this afternoon's lesson. Right then, so you will place your sticks as so." Nyle returned to kneeling, demonstrating to the class how one properly goes about rubbing sticks together to create enough friction to spark the kindling. "Now, you all try."

Godryk was rather intently working at getting the angle of his sticks just so while Fynn was at his side nervously rubbing his together without any sense or thought behind the action. Pale, grey eyes cautiously looked about, noting that the others were equally enthralled with working on their theoretical fire building under the unnervingly watchful eye of Nyle Humbert, lord of the madmen. When Fynn returned his attention to his sticks, he all but shrieked as his sticks went up in flames. The fire shot upward into the air, violently tearing the sticks from his hold and sending them up in a brilliant blaze of scarlet embers and heavy, choking smoke. Fynn rolled back on his heels, covering his nose and mouth with his forearm as he gasped for breath. His year mates had all ceased their ministrations; eleven sets of stunned eyes stared at Fynn as if he had grown a second head.

Nyle rounded on the boy quickly, snatching hold of his collar and hauling him upright. "You, witless little dalcop, how did you even manage this?" Leathery, twig like arms gestured about wildly, indicating the mass of smoke lilting into the afternoon breeze and the still smoldering remnants of the sticks. "Such carelessness, boy! You would've sentenced your comrades all to death with your inability to follow even the simplest of instructions. By the gods, child, how did you even get such a flame with no kindling?"

Fynn was at a loss. He shrugged, genuinely unsure as he replied, "I don't know, sir."

"You don't know?"

The prince shook his head. "No, sir. I don't know how it happened."

Fynn was stunned when the gnarled looking hand of his instructor slapped against the side of his head with enough force to make him wince. "*I don't know* is not a sufficient answer, boy! Not at all. What would happen if you were in charge of building the fire for your troops' camp, boy? Would you light them all ablaze in some ill effected inferno and turn to your commander and tell him you don't know what happened? Would you, boy?"

Fynn shook his head emphatically. "No, sir."

"Then, pray tell, child, why you think that 'I don't know' is an appropriate answer to my present inquiry?" Nyle pressed heatedly.

"I...I don't know, sir," the boy argued.

Another slap to the head had Fynn clutching at the bruising spot, icily staring back at the old man.

"Did we not just discuss how absolutely imperative *listening* was to your long-term survival?"

"We did, sir," the prince affirmed.

"Then listen with your ears, child!" Nyle was all but snarling as he pinched one of Fynn's ears painfully between his fingers. "The gods gifted you with ears that could hear so, by those very damn gods, boy, use that gift! I said 'I don't know' was not a sufficient answer. Now, how did such a fire come to be?"

"It just happened, sir," explained Fynn. "Honest, I was just rubbing the sticks together and then suddenly…fire."

"Your name, boy?" asked the instructor, quite evidently displeased.

"Fynn, sir."

"Fynneas?"

The prince nodded.

"Fynneas Fog?"

Again, the prince nodded.

Nyle slapped his hand harshly against the back of the boy's head for the third time. He snapped, "Do you think being a prince makes you special, you little loiter-sack? Is that it, planning to get by on that, eh?"

Fynn shook his head. "Not at all, sir." A fourth smack to the head had Fynn seething. "I don't know how it happened; it just did…*sir*."

Nyle took hold of the front of Fynn's tunic and dragged the boy until their noses were only hairs apart. His foul-smelling breath oozed from his dry lips like pus from a festering boil as he spoke, "Then I suggest, *little* prince, that you don't let it '*just happen*' again. Am I understood?"

"Yes, *sir*," Fynn replied coolly.

Nyle jerked his hand away from the prince as if touching the child's shirt had scalded his palms. "Right then, who told you lot to stop?"

The children returned their attention to creating their theoretical fires. This proceeded for the next three hours until each of the twelve felt as though their hands were raw and their shoulders and elbows would crumble.

"Whining, children, will not win wars! Nor will it keep you alive should you be separated from your group, left to fend for yourselves. Will whining keep the beasties from feasting on your little bones? I think not!" screeched Nyle.

"This class is a *nightmare*," Fynn murmured as he continued trying not to set his new sticks aflame.

Nyle sighed, taking in the dismayed expressions of the children. They were each hunkered over their sticks, dutifully trying to prepare their imaginary fires. "You've done well," the old man conceded. "Very well. A few *missteps*, children, but that is to be expected. I suspect that you may be ready for *real* fires next time. Quite the accomplishment!" He twirled about on his heel, tossing his gangly arms to the air, as he said, "Right, children, gather yourselves quickly. Off to the castle! Off you go children! With haste! Eat well tonight, I suspect your lessons tomorrow will be taxing. Go on, go along, children!"

Albie dragged his feet along, rubbing at the prominent bruise now blooming across his forehead, as the group made their way back to the castle. "That hurt," he whined.

"Old loon's a total madman," Ollie muttered, quite thankful that he hadn't borne the brunt of the lesson's devolvement into corporal punishment.

"How's your head?" Albie laughed as he looked over at Fynn.

The prince grunted, "Fine."

Lux sauntered up to the boys, poking Fynn in the side. "Rough first day?"

Fynn shrank away from the girl for only a moment before shrugging. "The worst."

"How *did* you manage to start that fire?" she asked.

"I *really* don't know," he said. "Honest."

Supper proceeded rather pleasantly. The first-and-second-years found themselves alone in the Hall, the divisions either still training or having already dined and retired to their dormitories for the evening. The twelve first-years chose to stay together, seated closely with one another, happily chatting about the day's events.

Renwyn was recounting their capsizing misadventure to a rather enamored-looking Georgina, Georgie as they all called her, while Ollie was stabbing away at the roasted fish on his plate, spinning a tale of how he had almost died during sailing class to a seemingly bored Hogan. Godryk and Fynn sat shoulder to shoulder, Albie and Lux across the table from them. The four laughed about the absurdity of Crisis Prevention, each finding some humor in the lesson's proceedings, even if it was at their own expense.

When ten of the twelve stood, taking their leave from the Hall, only Hollyn and Fynn remained. Hollyn looked down the table to his cousin, sighing as he resigned himself to an evening spent in the other's company. "Wonder what Shoregore has waiting for us," he mused.

Fynn stood, stretching his back and huffing. "As long as he doesn't want us kindling fake fires, I don't care."

"Right," agreed Hollyn.

The boys made their way to the tower wherein the Armada Division's dormitories were situated, seeking out their instructor. He wasn't hard to find; he was leaning against the wall, engaged in a pleasant conversation with Riordan Astor, head of the Armada Division. Both men, upon hearing the boys' approach, turned to greet them. Riordan nodded to them politely before taking his leave, disappearing behind one of the many doors in the corridor.

"We didn't mean to interrupt, sir," Hollyn spoke carefully.

Fynn added, "We were only coming to find you as you instructed earlier, sir."

Drake's energy clearly hadn't waned as the day had progressed, for the man practically sprung from the wall, smiling. "Right, of course! Come along, boys, come along."

The princes trailed behind their instructor as he led them from the tower back out the entrance doors and into the crisp night. They hadn't walked far from the castle, maybe ten or so minutes down one of the winding trails, before Drake came to a decided halt. The boys peeked around him, curious as to what he was looking at. Drake stepped aside, revealing a pile of rocks -large rocks.

"You see those rocks just there?" the instructor asked.

Both boys nodded.

"You're to move them there," he said. He pointed to a lone palm tree just about a hundred feet from the pile. "Once you've moved all the rocks there, you may go to bed." He gave each boy a smile, eyes twinkling, before bidding, "Right, I'll leave you to it."

Hollyn was the first to approach the pile, kicking at it with the toe of his boot. "They're going to be heavy," he noted, observing how the rock didn't shift under the pressure of his foot.

Fynn appeared by the taller boy's side and sighed. "This will take a while." He reached down and curled his arms around one of the large rocks, settling the weight against his slight chest. "They're heavier than they look," he commented as he began to waddle toward the tree. Truthfully, they were much heavier than he cared to admit, but he adamantly refused to let Hollyn see him struggling under the weight of his burden. "Get a move on, then," he called back when he realized Hollyn had yet to move. "I'm not doing this alone!"

The taller prince plucked up a stone and, much like Fynn, found that situating the rock against his chest helped to offset some of the weight. Heaving, he managed to catch up to the other boy with only moderate effort, pleased that he seemed to be handling the weight with a little more ease than Fynn. A moment later, Hollyn was ambling by his cousin, depositing his rock beneath the tree, and turning back to collect another.

"Try not to take all night," Hollyn chuckled as he went by.

Gracelessly, Fynn dropped his own rock under the tree. He lingered for a moment, growling at the ache in his arms. He pulled himself away and headed back to the pile, irritated to see Hollyn already halfway back with another stone nestled in his arms. Fynn pouted before breaking out into a run, skidding to a stop, and scooping up another rock. Ignoring the uncomfortable weight, he did his best to catch up to Hollyn.

Upon seeing that Fynn had all but sprinted up to his heels, Hollyn flung his rock down and rounded with sublime speed, barreling back to the dwindling pyramid of stones. Fynn was quick to toss his rock down and take off in a dash. Soon, the boys were running side by side, jostling for the lead as they went careening toward their punishment pile. Unfortunately for the slighter boy, he tripped clumsily as he sped forward, hurling toward the ground and landing with a painful cry. Hollyn was undeterred by Fynn's misstep, laughing as he stole away from the heap of limbs tangled in the dirt.

As Fynn was climbing back to his feet, his irritation bristled at the sound of thunder cracking. He fell back to the ground in defeat, taking a moment to catch his breath as the rain started to fall lightly. His damp hair hung before his eyes, but he made no move to rectify his mess of a mane at the moment. He watched as Hollyn, too, stopped at the sound of the approaching storm.

"This is going to be harder in the rain," Fynn yelled out.

"What do you mean?"

"It's going to be slippery."

Hollyn trudged back to the still-seated Fynn, standing over him for a moment before offering the other boy his hand. He snorted his derision when Fynn eyed the proffered hand warily before finally taking it and being pulled to his feet. Still clutching the shorter prince's hand, Hollyn said sourly, "This doesn't mean we're friends."

"Wouldn't dream of it." Fynn smirked.

"But it will be easier if we carry the stones together. They won't be as heavy and we'll be less likely to slip," Hollyn reasoned.

"We should be able to finish quickly," added Fynn brightly.

Hollyn nodded his agreement.

The rain began falling with a bit more urgency, splashing against the grassy ground and slickening the dirt into a precarious mud pit. Despite their combined efforts, the princes were still slipping and sliding against the ground as they carried the rocks from the pile to the tree, one by one. Their thin arms were aching painfully, and their backs were pleading their protests, twinging with pain every time they bent down or stood up straight. Their shoulders were strained and their necks were becoming terribly stiff. The rain was chilling them to their bones, their light tunics and leggings doing little to shield them from the persistent assault of the storm. With only seven rocks remaining in the pile, their resolve to finish as quickly as they could intensified. The end was in sight.

As Hollyn and Fynn carefully settled their burden's weight between them, they started for the tree. Angling his foot just slightly too far to the side, Hollyn yowled and tumbled to the ground as he slid in the mud. The weight of the rock forgotten, Fynn could do little more than watch as Hollyn fell bodily into the mud, clutching at his ankle. The red-haired prince was shaking, biting back the whimper of pain that was churning in his throat. Fynn knelt beside the fallen boy, eyeing the injured leg with some concern.

"Hollyn, that looks like it could be bad," Fynn said nervously. He reached out, tentatively prodding at the injured ankle as gently as he could.

"It's not broken," Hollyn supplied shakily.

"Can you move your foot?"

Hollyn threw his head back as he forced himself to stifle a scream of pain the moment he tried to flex his right foot. He turned his head, cheek nestling against the mud. His tears were washed away in the steady rainfall. "No."

Fynn looked between his cousin and the rocks remaining in the pile. Rolling his eyes, Fynn reached out to Hollyn and hooked his arms beneath the other's shoulders, helping him to his feet. Not entirely in the mood to protest, Hollyn allowed Fynn to carry most of his weight as they hobbled toward the tree.

"Stay here. I'll finish bringing the rest of the rocks over," insisted Fynn.

"I'm fine," Hollyn argued weakly. "I don't need you coddling me. Give me a moment and I'll be ready to help."

Fynn roughly shoved Hollyn against the tree. "Just be quiet and stay here. You'd only slow me down with all your limping."

"Whatever," grumbled Hollyn as he settled himself comfortably against the tree trunk, silently grateful to be able to take the weight off his foot.

Not at all amused by having to finish their assigned task alone, Fynn cursed under his breath the entire time, laboring under the weight of the stones and doing his best to keep his footing. The rather simple task of transporting the damnable rocks from one place to another had become infinitely more difficult as the storm progressed. He slipped and staggered but he remained undeterred. His back was painfully pulsing by the time he dropped the final rock beneath the palm tree. He doubled over, hands to his knees, panting for breath as the rain beat away at his back.

"Done...finally," Fynn breathed. "How's your ankle?"

"I'll be fine," Hollyn assured as he carefully stood, keeping most of his weight on his left leg and using the tree trunk for support. "Let's head back."

Fynn nodded but didn't make a move to return. Rather, he remained still and watched as Hollyn delicately extracted himself from the crutch of the tree and tried to take a step before pitching forward. Fynn reacted as quickly as he could, stretching out his arms to catch the boy before he fell face first to the ground. However, being slight as he was, Fynn couldn't keep the two of them from crashing into the mud.

Fresh tears sprung into Hollyn's eyes when his ankle was painfully jostled by the fall. He remained still against the ground, fighting to keep his breathing even. "Damn." He shuddered as the pain lanced up his leg like fire.

"Liar," Fynn muttered as he drew himself up on his hands and knees. "You said you could walk." Dramatically sighing, Fynn leaned on one knee before Hollyn. "Climb on."

"No," Hollyn snapped, shaking his head. "I don't think so!"

Fynn shrugged. "Fine. Then sleep in the mud all night. I don't really care."

Still, Fynn didn't make a move to stand and leave Hollyn behind. He remained kneeling, not bothering to look at the other. When at last Hollyn relented, Fynn felt the other's weight settle upon his back. Thin arms encircled Fynn's neck tightly. The boy stood, wrapping his own arms around Hollyn's legs as securely as he could. "Hold on," he instructed as he took his first hesitant step forward.

The rain was coming down much harder, obscuring the path back to the castle. With his arms presently indisposed, Fynn did his best to shake the hair out of his eyes. His vision was blurred by the constant downpour.

His legs were shaking with the additional weight they carried, knees feeling unsteady with every slow step forward. He felt Hollyn tense against him, so instinctively held the other boy tighter.

"We're almost there." Fynn wasn't sure if his reassuring words were for Hollyn's benefit, or his own.

"Alright," the injured prince replied simply. His voice sounded tired and weak, pained. Hollyn's normally haughty retorts were nonexistent as the nearly crippling pain in his ankle swelled every other second.

"You know," Fynn laughed mirthlessly, "this doesn't mean we're friends."

"Wouldn't dream of it."

11

BUTTONS

Hollyn was limping around, quietly staggering along and refusing to voice any sign of his discomfort. After days of this, the prince was pleased to find that he finally was able to walk without wincing in pain; the barely-there hobbling had waned, and he was back to bounding around with ease. Presently, he found himself gleefully leaning his weight upon his sparring sword like a crutch, propping his weary body up as he listened to Noel's instructions.

The students' day began before dawn. Lessons became more and more taxing over time. Looking around, Hollyn noticed Fynn intensely watching Noel's every move, focused on studying the effortless arc of the sword as it was swung, the rotation of the man's shoulders, the tightening of his grip. Hollyn furrowed his brows as he considered the other prince. Fynn, he'd noticed as the days went on, was the only one of his year mates that watched everything with a penetratingly quizzical stare, as if he was dissecting every aspect of the instructions as they were presented. Sometimes, Hollyn thought, it was almost unnerving the way those icy eyes would appear even colder as Fynn studied and then attempted to mimic the lesson.

"Now, pair up," Noel instructed, casually tossing his own sparring sword to the ground. "The edges and tip are blunted, so don't cringe away from it. It won't cut you."

Godryk and Fynn wordlessly decided upon being partners and turned to one another, each grinning a similarly casual grin.

"I'm not going to go easy on you," joked Fynn.

Godryk rolled his eyes. "I'm stronger than I look. Just mind your own sword and don't go putting your eye out."

Noel stood at the center of the gathered first-years. He instructed, "One of you will attack and the other will parry. Then you'll switch. You'll proceed back and forth until I say stop. Understood?"

"Ladies first," Godryk laughed, readying his sword in his hand.

The prince raised his sword, preparing to strike. "When'd you become so funny?" He lunged and swung, careful to keep control over his weapon.

Godryk easily parried the blow. Fynn, he noted, was not so good at feinting. The red-haired boy smirked. "My turn."

Fynn was taken aback by Godryk's attack, hardly having the time to block. He hadn't expected the strike to come at his side; Godryk had leaned forward, eyes angling toward Fynn's head, before surging toward him and deftly flicking his arm out toward Fynn's ribs.

Watching the prince scramble to parry the attack, Godryk couldn't help but feel quite pleased with himself. "Well then?"

Fynn righted his footing quickly and scowled. "Fine. If that's how you want to play it." He squared his shoulders. A very predatory sense came over him as he jolted toward Godryk. Still lacking the grace and subtlety required to feint to one side, Fynn opted for brute force as his strategy. The blunted edge of his sword slammed forcefully into Godryk's, the residual power behind the attack reverberating up Godryk's shaking wrists.

"How's that?" laughed Fynn.

"Like fighting with a bear," chided Godryk.

"A bear?" Fynn repeated curiously.

Noel's hand came to rest over Fynn's shoulder, keeping the boy firmly in place. His voice was calm and analytical as he spoke, "He means that you're putting no effort into hiding what you're about to do. You just put all your strength into swinging your sword. Might as well have given you a wooden club, the way you're swinging that thing around."

"What do you mean?" puzzled the prince.

Noel pried the sparring sword form Fynn's hands and held it out before him. He angled his arm just so, giving him the perfect leverage with which to strike in any direction—left, right, up, down. He steadied his weight between both feet, bent his knees slightly, and hunched forward. "From this stance, can you tell me where I'm aiming?"

Fynn shook his head.

"That's the point," Noel replied, handing the sword back to Fynn. "Your stance screams your intentions to your opponent. Godryk knew where you were going to hit and thus, was able to block." He reached out and flicked Fynn between the eyes. "Try to use your head."

Noel made his way from the dueling pair he'd just corrected to Penelope and Lux. He eyed them carefully, pleasantly surprised by how well Lux could handle her weapon. She held it naturally. Her attacks were precise and calculated, with just enough force behind each swing to be considered dangerous. Penelope, however, was shrinking back from Lux every time the girl came at her; her offense was no better—probably worse—as she held her sword in her hands as if it were a snake ready to turn and bite her at any moment. Noel sighed, shaking his head with exasperation as he approached.

"Don't be scared of it," he said. "The worst you'll get is a bruise."

"I don't understand why *we* have to do this," Penelope whined, tossing her sword to the ground.

Noel raised a curious brow. "We?"

"Yes. The girls. We all know the only divisions *we'll* end up in are the Brigade or Medical Corps. Why do *we* have to learn how to swing a sword?" Penelope continued petulantly.

Pointedly, Noel reached down and picked up the sword, handing it back to her. "Because you have to be ready for every eventuality. You're right. Girls almost always end up in those two divisions. But that doesn't mean that's all you should learn. What if you're on a battlefield, tending to the wounded and are attacked? It would behoove you to know how to fight back."

"What do you mean *almost* always? I thought it was a rule," Lux piped in. "I thought those were the only divisions we *could* be in."

"No." Noel smiled. "It's not a set rule. It's the way things normally are, but sometimes there are special circumstances and women get into other divisions. It's doubtful you'd ever be placed in Cavalry, given the physicality of the division. Same for Paladin, really. But you shouldn't feel limited. You should do your best in each of your lessons; show us all what you can do."

While Noel continued to help Penelope correct her hold on her sword and stop cringing away from Lux, the remaining ten first-years continued with their practice.

Hollyn held his sword with a lazy grip, easily parrying Renwyn's attacks. Growing increasingly frustrated by the prince's cavalier attitude, Renwyn began wildly swinging with all his strength, hoping to knock Hollyn's sword from his hands. The clattering of the blunted metal drew Noel's attention; it wasn't long before the instructor descended upon the pair with a critical eye.

He watched as Renwyn, yet again, clobbered at Hollyn's sword. The man shook his head. "Not another one," he muttered. He eased the sword from the boy's grasp and explained, "You're supposed to want to hit your opponent. All you're doing is swinging as hard as you can at Hollyn's sword.

You're not going to accomplish anything that way. The idea is to try and find a way around your adversary's defenses and strike. Stop aiming for his *sword* and start aiming for *him*."

Once everyone seemed to grasp the concept of attacking and blocking as best they could in just an hour of one-on-one sparring, Noel returned to the center of the group and announced, "Alright, alright, you can put your swords down for now. Come here and listen closely." He waited for a moment as the children discarded their weapons to the grassy ground and circled around him, attentively staring up at him and waiting for further instruction. "How about a game?"

"What kind of game, sir?" asked Renwyn breathily, still worn out from his one-sided fight against Hollyn.

"Let's see who's the best here," Noel slyly replied. "You'll fight, one on one. The winners will proceed to the next round." He eyed each of them closely, interested to see that, among many of them, there was apprehension evident in their youthful gazes. "You may feel unprepared. You've only had a few lessons with me so far. But such is war. You're never really going to feel prepared going into an actual fight. So, best not to feel entirely prepared for a practice one, right?"

"How do we know who wins each bout?" Albie questioned.

"I'll decide the winner of each match. It won't be one hit and over. A real sword fight wouldn't be like that. You could get hit over and over and still keep going. In fact, that's the exact situation Morancy is training you for. You're expected to keep going until you either win or die. Simple as that." He laughed. "Don't worry though! We won't be doing anything nearly as drastic as that, I assure you. No, we'll just be sparring. I'll let the match go on as long as it stays under control. Once there is a clear victor, I'll end it. Fair enough?"

The children nodded their agreement.

Noel smiled. "Great. Now, spread out in a large circle. That'll be your arena."

The first-years all fanned out as instructed. They eyed one another cautiously, each of them anxious to see who'd they be facing. Noel seemed positively giddy as he made his way to stand between Ollie and Albie. "First match will be Renwyn and Hogan. Go on, boys, step into the center of the circle. Wait for my command before you start."

Renwyn Strangelove was a tall, strong-looking boy. His dark, brown hair was curly, but neat. His eyes were a dark brown color, looking almost black.

He was handsome enough; his easy smile softened his harder features. He held his sword in his right hand tightly as his eyes roved over his opponent.

Hogan Greenfinch was of a far slighter frame than his opponent. The boy was tall, and his arms and legs were gangly. His honey-blonde hair was short, his hazel eyes framed by tawny lashes. He had a long, thin nose and small, round mouth that frowned as he looked at Renwyn. He held his sword with both hands, nervously clutching and unclutching the hilt.

"Ready, boys?" intoned Noel.

Hogan and Renwyn nodded, each drawing their swords up and readying themselves.

"Begin!"

Hazel eyes widened as Renwyn swung viciously at Hogan. The boy hardly had time to move out of the way before Renwyn rounded on him, catching him in the wrist with the blunt edge of his sword. Hogan did well to keep his hold on his weapon, yowling at the impact; he stumbled away. He hadn't time to think of his next step before Renwyn, yet again, came barreling forward and swung. The attack hit Hogan's sword squarely in the center of the blade and with such force that it sent the sparring weapon spinning loose from the boy's grasp.

"Well done," Noel said. "Renwyn's the victor. Alright, you may step back into place. However, Renwyn, do try and listen next time, won't you? You may have won this bout, but you fought clumsily. You used sheer force to overcome Hogan. You may not be able to do that with every opponent you face. Eventually, you'll either be out-maneuvered or tired out."

The instructor took his time surveying the group before proclaiming the next match. "Next, Godryk and Wilder. On my command."

Wilder Dangerfield approached Godryk, standing opposite the future Lord Redmayne, with a smirk fixed to his face. His brown hair was brushed back. His bright, blue eyes teemed with anticipation. He was just slightly shorter than Godryk, but far broader in build. He held onto his sword with effortless strength, easing it up as he slowly began to sink down into a battle-ready stance. He eyed Godryk ferally; every muscle in his body constricted, ready to uncoil at a moment's notice.

Noel ushered the fight's commencement and watched as the boys both took their time, remaining resolutely in their places, staring one another down. Godryk was the first to make a move, darting forward and then jerking to the side, bringing his sword in an arc with him. The blunted edge met with resistance, meeting the defensive maneuver of the other's weapon.

With their blades locked, it became a battle of wills. Each boy leaned forward, hunkering down and forcing all their weight behind their clash. They pushed against one another, each vying for the upper hand only to find, frustratingly, that they were locked in an even match.

Godryk's blue eyes fastened to the site where the two blades tangled, edge against edge, sliding heatedly against each other, the steel screeching. It took only a moment for Godryk to decide upon his course of action. Wilder's shoulders tensed and his arms shook ever so slightly. With his mind made up, Godryk peeled back from the encounter, letting the momentum of the other's attack pull him forward, unsteadying him. As Wilder began to lurch forward, fighting to regain his balance while maintaining his defense, Godryk pivoted. His attack slipped beneath Wilder's blade; the dulled tip of the sword plunged against the other boy's chest.

The first-years watched uneasily as Wilder collapsed to the ground at Godryk's feet, clutching at his chest. He gasped for breath. Tears sprung into his eyes. He bit down on his lower lip, working hard to stifle a cry of pain.

Godryk, without waiting for Noel to proclaim him the victor, cast his sword to the side and knelt beside the fallen boy. His hand came to rest upon Wilder's shoulder. His voice was low and gentle. "You alright?"

Painfully, Wilder nodded. He sounded strained as he said, "I think you just knocked the air straight out of my lungs."

"Better than breaking your ribs," Godryk noted with some concern. He reached out his hand and gently helped his opponent to his feet. He regarded Wilder with some worry, as the other boy had yet to stand straight; he was hunched forward, still fighting for air.

Noel swept from his place and joined the two, kneeling down in front of Wilder. He reached out lightly, running his hand along the boy's sides. "Nothing seems broken," he softly appraised. He felt Wilder trembling under his touch, and he frowned. "I know it hurts," Noel said as he stood, "but it's something you'll have to learn to get used to. I wish I could say this is the worst injury you'll suffer during your training, but I'm not in the habit of lying. It's going to sting for a while, but the pain should dull by dinner tonight. If it doesn't, come find me."

Wilder nodded sheepishly. He allowed Godryk to help him back to the circle of students.

The instructor exhaled deeply. "Godryk is the victor." Noel returned to his place between Ollie and Albie before announcing the competitors for the third round. "Hollyn, Fynneas, you're next." There was an uncomfortable hush that swept over the children as the two newest combatants entered into the center of the circle, dragging their swords behind them. Noel chuckled under his breath at his charges, laughing at the thought of them treating the upcoming bout as if it were a match between two legendary swordsmen rather than two children.

Fynn studied Hollyn for a moment, oddly pleased to see that the prevalent limp that had been slowing the other down for days was finally gone. "Leg's feeling better I see." He grinned.

Hollyn nodded. "Much."

"That's good," the black-haired prince said. "This will be a fair fight, then."

The taller boy raised his sword. "Wouldn't have it any other way."

"Nor would I," agreed Fynn, bringing his own sword up.

"Ready, boys?" Noel asked.

The two princes nodded silently, neither able to draw their eyes away from the other.

"Begin!"

Godryk couldn't help but watch with a stunned expression as Hollyn charged Fynn. The red-haired royal's normally calm and composed nature was gone and instantly replaced by frenzied brutality. Fynn wasn't cowed by his cousin's brazen approach. He bolted forward. Reminiscent of the bout between Godryk and Wilder, the princes' blades clattered together into a lock, smashing into each other with concerning force. Both boys leaned all their weight into the frontal assault, both refusing to give in. Fynn tightened his hold on his sword, angling his shoulders down and forcing himself to take just the slightest step forward, desperate to gain ground. Hollyn, unfortunately, was taller and heavier and the task of pushing him back would not be easily accomplished. The two princes stood their ground, neither flinching back as the power struggle continued on.

"You're not going to win this," Hollyn snapped as he redoubled his efforts, urging his blade forward as best he could, though not finding much purchase.

Fynn growled. "I wouldn't be so sure of that." He felt Hollyn leaning more and more into the attack and so he tensed, freezing his arms into place with all his might to keep his defense strong and unyielding. "I'm coming for you."

"I'll be waiting."

Realizing that he was focusing his weight too far forward to be able to pivot as Godryk had done in this situation, Fynn opted for an entirely different course of action. He continued forcing himself forward, almost leaning so far that his nose was just hairs from his blade. As he settled his weight into his arms and shoulders, still struggling for the upper hand against Hollyn's sword, Fynn kicked out his leg and caught Hollyn's knee.

Everyone looked on, shocked, as both princes fell gracelessly to the ground.

With their swords now disengaged, the battle was once again anyone's fight. Fynn jumped to his feet quickly, scrambling to get a proper hold on his sword as he spun to reach Hollyn. However, Hollyn was not one to be caught off guard easily and also snatched up his sword. By the time Fynn's blade crashed into Hollyn's, both boys were once again standing. Traditional stances and strategy having clearly been forgone, the pair proceeded to mindlessly swing away at one another. The forcefulness of their strikes became more and more violent as each resolved to disarm the other by sheer force.

"You're lasting longer than I thought," Hollyn mocked as he feinted to the right and swung, catching Fynn in the hip.

As the shorter boy staggered forward, ignoring the heated pain radiating from his side, he snapped back, "I could say the same for you." He flicked his wrist, his hold on his sword tenuous, and managed to clip Hollyn's elbow with a grazing blow.

Reeling from the unexpected jab, Hollyn stepped back and righted his sword, holding it aloft before him, blocking Fynn's ability to attack head on. "We shouldn't keep everyone else waiting for their turn." With that, he took off with blinding speed and lunged, the dulled tip of his sword easily twisting by Fynn's defense and catching him in the shoulder - hard.

Having not expected the blunt stab to the shoulder, Fynn tottered backward, falling flat to the ground. His sword, however, remained firmly clutched in his hand. As Hollyn proceeded to throw himself bodily down upon Fynn, Fynn drew up his sword to offset the assault. Once more, both boys found themselves in a heap on the grassy ground.

With great effort, Fynn managed to push Hollyn off and roll away. His shoulder ached and his pulse pounded as he crawled a safe distance away to catch his breath. Fynn quaked slightly with overexertion, but he dismissed the weariness of his body and stood up with unwavering steadfastness, turning to face Hollyn.

"That all you got?" taunted Fynn.

Hollyn found his footing once more, though he was forced to favor his left foot as his newly healed right ankle throbbed painfully. He could feel his skin stretch as the afflicted joint swelled. He was thankful for the tight leather of his boot to keep it from worsening. His chest heaved with effort. The unrelenting heat of the afternoon siphoned his energy.

"Have at it, if you're so tough," Hollyn drawled. His tempestuous eyes looked wicked in the sunlight, shining a dark blue and slightly shadowed by the sweaty strands of scarlet hair tumbling over his forehead.

Too tired to run at Hollyn and knowing his legs wouldn't support a foray, Fynn stood his ground. Truthfully, his arms were beginning to quiver. He wasn't sure how much longer he could keep the fight going. A sense of frantic desire to end the bout quickly seized him and he willed himself to move. Fynn swung his arm in a great arc, crashing his sword down upon Hollyn's. He was too slow. His adversary's sword had come up to meet his, effectively parrying his efforts and casting Fynn's weapon from his grasp. Grey eyes watched, dismayed, as the sword skittered across the grass before he looked back, defeated, to his opponent.

"You win," Fynn lamented weakly.

Hollyn stood before his cousin, watching as all traces of previous confidence ebbed from those familiar, icy eyes, replaced by an uncharacteristic dourness. "Yes," he replied coolly before returning to the circle with a slightly rekindled limp, taking his place like a stony sentinel as he awaited the fourth bout.

Fynn wasn't entirely interested in the next rounds. Penelope's match against Georgie was quick, yielding Georgie's victory within only moments. Likewise, the bout between Albie and Firiel was equally mismatched; Albie emerged victorious after a quick clash of blades, Firiel returning to the circle shaking a nastily bruised hand and cursing under her breath. Yet, Fynn found that he couldn't lose himself in his thoughts once Lux's name was called. He watched as she made her way to the middle, squaring off against Ollie.

"Begin," instructed Noel, an amused look clear upon his features.

Ollie was shaking terribly, his hold on his sword precarious. Lux, however, was absolutely at ease with the weapon in her hands. She made quick work of Ollie; her blade glided over his, easily ripping through his hardly existent defenses, and pegged him sharply in his right shoulder. Fynn wasn't surprised at all when the rotund boy yelped and dropped his sword, immediately yielding the match to Lux. The prince couldn't help the small smile that curled his lips as he watched Lux pick up Ollie's discarded weapon and hand it back to the boy with a warm and genuine nod of acknowledgement.

The next fight between victors Renwyn and Georgie was over far quicker than it should have been. It was evident to all watching that despite Georgie's superior tact and understanding of swordsmanship, she was simply outclassed in terms of raw physicality. Renwyn returned to the circle after hearing from Noel, yet again, that he should not always rely on pure strength to overcome his opponents.

Predictably, the bout between Hollyn and Albie was uneventful. The tall prince hardly bothered to move at all, whilst his opponent flailed, desperate to land a hit on the young royal. Rather unfortunately for Albie, Hollyn had deft control of his sword and, having calmed significantly since his match against Fynn, was easily able to flick his wrist and snap his sword around Albie's, catching the boy painfully in the hand. Once his sword fell, Albie knew he'd lost.

It was the fight between Godryk and Lux that once more captivated Fynn's attention. As the red-haired cousins faced one another, he watched each movement carefully. Godryk clearly had the upper hand where sheer strength was concerned, but Lux was fast and precise. Godryk lunged, sword striking out toward Lux's chest, but the girl parried with effortless precision as she took a step back just out of striking range.

"Not going to make this easy for me, are you?" Godryk laughed as he straightened to his full height.

Lux shook her head. "Not a chance."

Godryk couldn't help the hiss of surprise coupled with pain when Lux's sword made contact with his thigh, nicking him right above the knee. Wincing, he managed to say, "Well done."

Lux shrugged as she pulled back, waiting for Godryk to sort himself out before she continued with their fight. She eyed him with an almost feral, appraising stare as he struggled to put equal weight onto his now bruised left leg. "I thought Uncle Warwyk would've taught you better. You're making this too easy."

The boy huffed, irritated. "Cockiness is unbecoming of you."

"It's not being cocky if you're telling the truth." She laughed, "Ready?"

He gave a curt nod of the head. "Ready."

Gaining the upper hand by sheer strength brought a smile to Godryk's face as he watched Lux struggle to keep her guard up as he swung. He couldn't help but chuckle, thinking that he was fighting much too like Fynn for his liking. But for the time being, the decidedly mindless tactic of wildly swinging with all his might was working well for him. Again, his blunted sword smacked into Lux's, pushing her back a step or so. As he raised his weapon, readying for another impossibly tactless blow, he once again felt the rounded tip of her blade jabbing into his thigh, just above the knee. The unexpected jolt of pain shot up his leg and buckled his knee.

Godryk found himself in the rather precarious position of kneeling before Lux as she raised her sword. He'd expected her to take the opportunity to clobber him upside the head or in the chest, but she didn't. Instead, the flat of her sword was just below his chin, the point just hairs from his throat.

"Do you concede?" she asked sweetly.

He nodded wordlessly.

"Good." She lowered her sword and offered the boy her hand, helping him back to his feet. "Well fought. Though, can I give you some advice?"

Godryk laughed as he curled his arm around Lux's shoulders, allowing the tall girl to help him back to his place in the circle.

Lux leaned closer and whispered so only her cousin could hear, "Swinging like a madman may work for *some* of the boys, but it's not *your* style. Be yourself."

Noel stepped into the circle. His voice was energetic, as it tended to be, but even and firm. "You can rest for a little while." He sighed when he saw how badly Godryk was limping. "Catch your breath and then we'll see who we'll be naming as champion today." He noticed Lux still shouldering Godryk's weight, his arm slung snuggly around her shoulders. "The last bout will be a three-way fight. Lux, Renwyn, and Hollyn—you'll have to come up with new strategies. Two opponents are going to be harder than one."

The instructor retired from the center of the gathered children, who were beginning to disperse and group together, idly chatting as they waited for the last match to commence. Noel knelt down in front of Godryk, tentatively pressing down on the boy's leg, just over his knee. "Here?"

Godryk nodded.

Noel's hand traced over the linen-clad leg, searching for any considerable swelling or bump denoting a broken or dislocated bone. "I don't think it's anything too bad," he concluded, still intently staring at the injured limb, cocking his head to the side. "It'll probably be a nasty bruise though." He stood, clapping his hand firmly over Godryk's shoulder. "Walk around for a little while. The pain should start to dull." He gave the boy a push and watched as Godryk began to gingerly pull away from Lux and start hobbling around in careful circles.

By the time Godryk managed to walk without a limp, Noel had instructed the children to gather back into their circle. Fynn and Godryk stood together, watching as the three competitors made their way to the center.

"Who do you think will win?" asked Fynn, leaning closer to the taller boy until their shoulders seemed to meld together. The prince said nothing as Godryk rested some of his weight against him, clearly favoring his good leg.

"I'd bet my fortune on Hollyn," replied Godryk.

Fynn nodded. "It kills me to say it, but me too."

"Ready?" asked Noel.

The three challengers raised their swords, bent their knees, and leaned forward ever so slightly on their toes.

"Begin!"

Figuring Lux to be the weakest of his adversaries, Renwyn rounded on her and charged. Having not learned his lesson, he swung his sword wildly. The edge clattered against hers as she parried, deftly stepping to the side to offset the sudden force of the attack. Pitching forward unsteadily, Renwyn tried to adjust his course, but found his feet tangling beneath him. Bracing himself with one arm, the boy fell to the ground hard. He yowled as he hit, immediately cradling his left arm closely to his chest. Tears brimmed in his eyes, remaining unshed as he forced himself to not visibly cry. His shoulders shook. His sword lay beside him forgotten.

"Don't just stand there," chided Noel to Lux and Hollyn. "You don't have time to stand around gaping like brainless sods during a real fight!"

Hollyn was the first to regather his senses, entirely unmoved by the clearly injured Renwyn. It was evident that the boy was no longer a threat in the bout, having sustained what looked to be a broken arm and bereft of his only weapon. "You certainly made quick work of him," the prince casually said, nodding toward their fallen competitor.

Lux shrugged. "He did all the work for me, really."

"I don't plan on making it that easy for you." Hollyn smirked and sank back down into an offensive stance, sword angled out before him dangerously.

Lux took a step back, raising her own weapon aloft and steadying her weight, prepared for the coming assault. "Where would be the fun in that?"

"Right you are." Hollyn laughed.

The fight between Lux and Hollyn was more subdued than many of the others. It proceeded with quick forays and well-timed retreats, perfectly executed feints, and well-placed parries. The two, in terms of skill, were perfectly matched. Each looked natural, their movements so effortless, with a sword in hand. Hollyn, however, was quickly gaining the upper hand as time wound on. Lux was unable to outmaneuver the prince, their speed equal in all regards, their blade work of a similar ilk. But the prince was stronger. He was stronger and his attacks had more weight behind them, more raw physicality. She was struggling to keep up. Her defenses became less and less manageable as the fight drew on.

"Give up," Hollyn suggested.

"Not on your life," Lux replied icily.

Hollyn swung again, his wrists twisting at the last minute, sword cutting by Lux's and stabbing her squarely in the left shoulder. The girl pulled back, wincing at the bruising pain of the blow.

"Damn," she muttered, refusing to let her guard down.

Hollyn lunged again, dropping lower at the last moment. He caught Lux's knee, bringing her down. He was upright again within the blink of an eye, his energy and movement frantic. He brought his sword down, intending to catch her right shoulder and knock her sword loose from her grip. However, Lux managed to block his attack, bringing her blade up over her head. The young prince hadn't accounted for the possibility of such a defense and so, his momentum too far forward, he stumbled for a moment.

That moment was all Lux needed to flick her wrist out, letting her sword snap against Hollyn's already weakened ankle. A growl ripped from the boy's throat as he tumbled to the ground, clutching at his wounded joint. He remained holding onto his sword with one hand, but his grip was loose, distracted. His blazing, blue eyes burned viciously when he looked up to meet Lux's stare. Instantly, he clutched tighter to the sword's hilt and tried to stand, only to find that the pain was too great for him to manage.

"Do you yield?" she asked.

"Not on your life." He grimaced.

Lux swung, all her remaining energy put into that final attack only to gasp in surprise as Hollyn reached up with his left hand and caught the blade in his palm. His fingers curled around the sword, wrenching it from Lux's grip. Too shocked by the boy's approach to defense, Lux was frozen in place until she felt her body thrown to the ground. Hollyn was astride her hips, one hand steadied beside her head as he leaned forward, the other bringing his sword down until the dulled edge rested against her neck.

"Yield?" he whispered.

She gulped reflexively. "Yes."

The prince rolled off her. He remained sitting just beside her.

Lux sat up, glancing over at Hollyn. She noticed his scowl and the intense way he focused on the grass as if willing himself not to acknowledge the pain.

"Need help?" she asked.

"I'm fine," he grumbled.

"Sure, you are." Lux huffed as she stood up. Still, she reached out to him and offered her hand.

Reluctantly, he took it and allowed her to help him to his feet. He wanted to scream in pain, but all he did was sharply inhale, screwing his eyes shut for only a moment. "Thank you," he rasped. He tried to set his foot down gently.

"Well, it looks like Hollyn's the victor," Noel proclaimed. "However, let's take a moment to acknowledge that, had those been real swords, that little stunt would have cost him his hand, maybe even his whole arm." He approached the prince, flicking him on the head. "Don't try and catch a sword with your bare hand ever again. Yes?"

The prince smirked sheepishly at his instructor. "I thought we were supposed to win *by any means necessary*."

Noel snorted, flicking the boy's head again. "I'm not going to tolerate cheek."

"Sorry, sir," Hollyn replied sedately.

Shaking his head, Noel scooped the boy up in his arms. "Let's get your ankle looked at, shall we?"

The red-haired prince struggled fruitlessly in Noel's arms. "I don't need to be carried!"

"You can't even stand; how do you expect to walk back to the castle?"

"I would've made it," Hollyn argued.

"Hollyn, I'd like to have someone look at your ankle now, not wait hours for you to drag your carcass up to the castle," Noel replied. "Stop struggling." He glanced back, spying Renwyn standing docilly, arm cradled. "Renwyn, come along too. Let's have that arm looked after."

Hollyn relented, going all but limp in Noel's arms.

"The rest of you, well done. You're dismissed. Return to the castle, get something to eat," Noel instructed the lot.

The remainder of the afternoon and early evening went along without any incident. Most of the first-years were tending to bruises and cuts from the day, grumbling about their aches and pains over their dinner as they stabbed at their food, proper etiquette having long since been forgone by the group of battered first-years.

When the sun set and darkness descended upon the island, Godryk limped up the stairs to the boys' dormitory, aided by Fynn. The pair was weary from the day, both staggering over to their beds and collapsing into the warm embrace of their blankets gratefully.

It wasn't long before Fynn heard Godryk's soft snores emanating from the bed only a few feet from his own. Glancing around, he saw that the others were already asleep. Despite his exhaustion, Fynn struggled to get comfortable. He tossed and turned, kicking his blankets about his person until they finally fell in a linen mountain upon the stone floor. He sighed, falling back against his pillow once more. He closed his eyes, hoping that if he managed to lie still for longer than a minute, he may be able to drift off to sleep.

The darkness that welcomed him was cool and stale. Something was odd about it. His body had gone numb, the familiar heaviness of sleep weighing down his limbs. He tried to blink his eyes open and rid himself of the stifling eeriness of his slumber; he was unable to. In the distance, he heard what sounded like something flying, wings beating against the slowly drifting air. He strained to hear the sound better but found he couldn't discern what direction it was coming from. There was a quiet cry carried upon the wind, lowly howling into nothingness just as it reached his ears. There was something in the darkness with him. He could feel that someone, something, was there.

The prince's heart beat heavily. He felt the way it drummed against his chest. His ribs seemed like they were rattling, strumming along inside him, in time with each beat. He was cold. It was a terrible cold, wretched, like claws raking over his flesh, peels of pale skin churning from his person, hewed from him in the wake of those nasty, snatching claws. He shuddered beneath the dreadful force of their touch.

Those cold claws seemed to reach up and wind their tendril-like fingers around his throat. Whatever breath he had, was gone. The prince choked. His eyes snapped open; piercing grey searched through the darkness of the room. He sat upright, leaning against his headboard. His chest heaved with the effort of every breath. His hair was slicked to his forehead with sweat, the same rancid, cold sweat that drenched his whole body. Fynn ran his hand through his matted locks over and over, scratching at his scalp distractedly as he continued to scan the room for anything amiss, anything at all out of place. He found nothing.

Very carefully, he eased himself from his bed. Dressing and wrapping himself in his black cloak, he slipped from the room and began tiptoeing down the stairs. The common room was dark, the lanterns all extinguished. The unnatural quiet of the familiar space was unsettling. For a moment, Fynn thought, if only faintly, he could still hear the beating of wings and the quiet cry from his dream. Looking in every direction, he saw that he was alone. But he didn't believe it. He was still shaking, still searching for whatever may be lurking nearby.

Hesitantly, Fynn opened the door from the common room into the tower and descended the winding stairs. The tower was dark. The shadows felt heavier than normal. They stretched from the stone; lank bodies of blackness hunched over the stairs. Fynn didn't despair in finding his way, seeing through the shadows had never been hard for him. He peered through their depths with ease; like a cat prowling through a blackened alley, Fynn swept down the tower without missing a step.

A short time later, the boy was silently stepping through the small door beside the far grander entryway. The coolness of the night air was immediate, washing over him like a wave to shore. He listened, just standing there motionless for a moment. He heard it again, the flapping of wings. His head jerked in every direction, searching for whatever could be making that sound. Hesitantly, he took a step forward. He looked back at the castle for a moment, wondering if he should just go back to his bed. But the wings kept beating.

Fynn started off down the walkway toward the road. His eyes roved over the darkness, still finding nothing. He didn't know why he felt so compelled to find whatever it was out there in the night, but something was pulling him along, urging him to keep going, beckoning him to continue his paranoid search. And that he did. He continued down the road, remaining a careful distance from the tree line that denoted the barrier between the civilized world and the jungle, and those beasts within it.

Over an hour of hyper vigilance was beginning to tear away at Fynn's nerves. His senses strained for any indication that there was something out there. The castle loomed in the distance from its hilltop perch, far off back up the road. Fynn spied the wisps of golden light coming from the torches down in More Town and decided to head in that direction. Much like the first time he'd stepped foot into the town, it was quiet and still. He supposed the hour must have been later than he'd previously thought.

He saw a slight shadow move in the distance. Quirking a brow, Fynn remained still as he watched that little shadow scurry forward until the light from one of the lanterns spilled over the figure, revealing Minnie bounding toward him, something cradled in her tiny arms. She came to stop just in front of him. Her beaming smile and bright eyes were trained on him. "I knew you'd come," she greeted sweetly.

"How?" Fynn asked.

"I was calling for you," she replied simply, as if he should have known.

"Calling for me?" he repeated.

"Yes. You heard me, didn't you?"

Fynn's attention strayed from the child's face to the bundle wrapped in her arms. "Minnie, what've you there?"

At the mention of the prize she carried, her eyes brightened impossibly until she was positively radiant with excitement. "He's why I was calling for you."

"He?"

Minnie nodded. "Come with me."

Fynn obediently obliged the child, following her into the tavern. There were a few patrons hunched over tables, goblets of mead or wine clutched in their filth-stained hands, cracked nails idly scraping at the table-face, sketching circles and figures as boring conversation lilted on. Minnie led Fynn to a table in the far corner, settling herself down comfortably. In a most conspiratorial fashion, she leaned over the table and whispered, "Do you want to know what it is?"

"Yes," Fynn replied curiously.

Gently, Minnie set her treasure down upon the table. Her tiny hands carefully unfurled the cloth she'd set down, revealing within its knitted folds a tiny, black creature. Beady, midnight eyes rolled to meet Fynn's inquisitive stare. Its pointy ears twitched. Minnie moved more of the cloth out of the way. Fynn held back a gasp when he saw a delicate wing emerge.

Astonished, he looked back at Minnie. "That's a bat," he said dumbly.

Minnie's curly, blonde head bobbed. "Yes."

"How did you manage to catch a bat?"

"He was looking for me." She smiled. "So, it wasn't hard."

"You think the bat was looking for you?"

"No." Her smile only intensified. "I *know* he was." She reached her little hand down, gently tracing over the exposed wing. "I'll call him Buttons."

"You need to let him go," implored Fynn. "You can't keep a bat."

The little creature of the night, seeming to know he was being spoken about, curled further into the warmth of his blanket, his fox-like nose nestling the material as black eyes closed tiredly. The wing gently curled around the creature's body like a cloak.

Minnie's hand found the bat's ears and began gently petting the tiny animal. "He's hurt. I'm not throwing him out."

"Where is he hurt?" asked the boy.

"His other wing. He had a cut on it," explained the girl.

The prince pulled back more of the cloth, revealing the very wing Minnie spoke of. The bat's right wing had a hole through the delicate flesh, making flight an impossibility it would seem. Fynn's fingertips ghosted over the injury, careful not to aggravate the animal. He pouted. "Looks bad."

"Told you," Minnie huffed petulantly.

"Fine, fine," relented the boy. "We can keep him safe until his wing heals up." His hand moved from the wing to the bat's cheek. His thumb traced over the animal's little snout softly. "Why'd you want to call him Buttons?"

The little girl giggled. "'Cause his eyes look like buttons."

Fynn laughed lightly and kept petting the bat as gently as he could. "Right. Of course." His eyes lingered on the sleeping form of the bat resting between the two of them. His voice was soft when he asked, "Minnie… could I ask you something?"

The girl nodded.

"You said you were calling for me."

She nodded again.

"How were you calling for me, exactly?"

The softness of Minnie's hand was surprising. The warmth of her palm dispensed the chill he'd been feeling all night; her hand draped over his. "I was sleeping. And you were too. I could see you, but you were far away so I had to yell. I was yelling real hard, as loud as I could. I didn't know if you could hear me, so I tried to yell louder." There was an uncertain nervousness in her eyes when she looked back to him. "I'm glad you heard me yelling for you."

"You said you were calling for me because of Buttons? Why?"

Minnie furrowed her brow, nose wrinkling with concentration. "I knew that Buttons was looking for me. I could hear him in my sleep. But he sounded hurt and scared. That's why I was yelling for you. I knew you would come."

"Why was Buttons looking for you, Minnie?"

She shook her head. "I don't know."

"Can I ask you something else?" he chanced.

The girl smiled.

"Do you have these kinds of...dreams...often?"

"No." When her brown eyes turned to regard him, she continued, "Sometimes. They come and they go. They happen only for some people. Some people like you and Uncle Moriah and Uncle Noel and Mama. There are a few others too, but I don't know their names."

Fynn nodded as if he understood, but truthfully, he had no idea what to make of the confession. "I'd like to tell you a secret, Minnie. Do you want to hear?"

"Yes."

"A few days ago, we were learning how to start fires. Nyle, Lord Humbert, he didn't want us actually starting any, so we were just rubbing the sticks together, you know, no kindling or anything like that. But...well...I don't know...I somehow managed to start one. It came out of nowhere, *really*. It just happened. No one believes me, though."

"I do," she whispered shyly.

"You do?"

"When I was tiny, I did things like that too."

"You did?"

"Yes. Nan says I got better, but I used to start fires or hurt people. I didn't mean to. It was an accident."

Fynn turned his hand over; Minnie's smaller one fell into his palm. He held tightly to her. "Minnie, how did I do it? How did *you*?"

Minnie's head shot up like a frightened animal, nervously looking in each direction. Seeing that none of the patrons were paying attention to their table tucked neatly into the shadowy corner, Minnie returned her focus to Fynn. She pulled her hand from his. After a moment of thought, she held out both hands and cupped them together. She closed her eyes. Her voice was small. "You have to think about the hot, see what it would be, feel the warm in your hands. It's like a river from your heart to your hands; it goes down your arms. You have to think of it like that, Fynny, or nothing will happen. It's a river of hot like the water is fire and it stops in your hands."

226

Fynn's eyes went wide as he watched a steady, golden glow build in the child's palms before sparking to life; embers seemingly born from nothing drifted into the stagnant air of the tavern. Then there was the smallest of flames dancing between the girl's pink palms. Fynn reached out, unsure if what he was seeing was really there. But he could feel the warmth of the little fire, the stinging heat as it ebbed out toward him.

"Impossible," he whispered, leaning closer to the flickering flame.

When Minnie's eyes opened, the fire was gone. She laughed at Fynn's expression, giggling, "Silly, Fynny, it's not hard!" She grabbed his wrists and pulled them forward, nodding down to his hands. "You try!"

Fynn cupped his hands together as he'd seen Minnie do. He closed his eyes, steadying his breathing. He recalled the child's instructions and thought of a fiery river flowing from his chest down his arms and into his hands, pooling between his palms. He imagined the warmth that would be there, the way the fire would lick at his skin. He envisioned the embers, the golden glow, the spindly, orange arms reaching out. "Anything?"

"No," Minnie replied.

He thought harder. Instead of a small fire like Minnie's, he imagined a towering column of flames. He thought back to his Crisis Prevention lesson, to how the flames came from nowhere, startling in their strength. He imagined the warmth intensifying to an unbearable heat. The golden glow was replaced by the image of a blinding light. "Now?"

"No."

Exasperated, Fynn melted into his chair. He pouted, annoyed he couldn't manage even a little spark. "Why didn't it work?"

Minnie shrugged.

Fynn combed his hand through his hair. He was becoming more and more tired. The prince glanced back down to Buttons, who remained snuggled peacefully in his cloth nest. "I can take Buttons back to the castle."

"No." Minnie's tone was firm, determined. "Buttons stays here. I'll fix his wing."

"You will, will you?"

Golden curls bounced as Minnie nodded sharply.

"Have you told Nan about him?"

"Not yet," she answered.

Fynn gently folded the cloth around Button's sleeping form, mindful of the injured wing. "If I take him back to the castle, I can ask Moriah to help with him."

Minnie refused to be persuaded. "No. He stays here."

Resignedly, the boy gave in. "Fine. Fine. He can stay here. But let me help you bring him to your room, alright? I'll even tell Nan about him for you. Fair?"

"Fair." Minnie smiled.

Fynn gathered the snuggled bat into his arms, carefully hoisting him and settling the animal against his chest. He made sure to keep a firm hold on him as he stood. "Come on, Minnie." He headed toward the back door he'd seen Moriah go through when he'd last been to the tavern. "Your room's this way, right?" The pair ambled up the stairs, Buttons still soundly snoring in Fynn's arms.

"Fynn?" a voice called from the bottom of the stairs.

The boy looked back and saw Nan in the doorway. "Hello, Nan."

"I thought that was you, boy-o," she said. She came closer. "What've you there?"

All three now stood at the top of the stairs, each set of eyes intently looking from person to person. Fynn chirped, "Minnie found him. She says that he was looking for her. Honest, I'm not making it up."

Nan peeked at the bundle in Fynn's arms, eyebrows raising. "Is that a bat?"

Fynn nodded. "His name's Buttons."

"You named it?" Nan chuckled.

"Minnie did," he replied. "He's hurt. He has a rip in his wing." He chanced a look down to the small girl at his side and then back to Nan. "I told Minnie I'd take him back to the castle, but she wanted to keep him here until he's better. Is that alright with you?" He knew he sounded ridiculous and that his boyish voice was dangerously close to pleading, but he didn't care all that much.

Nan's full attention was on Minnie. "He was looking for you?"

Minnie replied, "Yes. I heard him in my dreams. I knew he was hurt so I had to go find him and I did, and he had a hurt wing. So, I have to help him. We can't throw him out, Nan! We can't. He was looking for us."

"Why'd you name him Buttons?" the old woman asked.

Minnie rolled her dark eyes, annoyed by the question. "'Cause his eyes look like buttons."

"Of course." Nan grinned. "We can keep him here until that wing of his is all better."

Fynn, genuinely surprised the elderly woman agreed to the arrangement, couldn't help but feel happy about it. "Thank you, Nan."

While Fynn situated the sleeping Buttons into a small, wooden crate, Nan pulled the blankets over Minnie. She leaned over the girl as she played with the curls on her head. "Off to bed with you now," Nan insisted, once more fiddling with the blankets as the girl willingly sank further against her mattress. "Sleep well, Minnie."

"Night, Nan." Minnie yawned. "Night, Fynny. Night, Buttons."

Drawing away from Minnie's bed, Nan slung her arm over Fynn's slender shoulders. The two proceeded back to the stairs before stopping. The old woman brushed her hand through Fynn's black hair softly, kindly. "Fynneas, tell me what happened."

"I don't really know," he murmured. "I had this dream, this really weird feeling dream. I heard wings and someone crying, calling maybe, far off. I didn't know who it was, but I could hear it and it wouldn't stop. So...I snuck out of the castle for a look." He shook his head wearily. "I didn't know what I was looking for, really. I was just sort of wandering around. Once I got far from the castle, I just decided to come here. That's when I found Minnie with Buttons." He felt nervousness coursing through him, surging into his chest. "Minnie said she'd been calling for me, Nan. She said she could see me in her sleep and was calling for. That doesn't make sense."

"Minnie is a special case," Nan explained. Her hand settled against the boy's cheek; her thumb traced the curve of his face. "As are you, child."

"What do you mean?"

"There are some people...who are just...*different*. Some people who experience the world in a different way than the rest of us," she replied in a hushed voice. "Some people who are destined for such great and impossible things."

"Minnie said that she only has dreams like that with certain people... with me, and Moriah, and Noel, and a few others...and her *mother*." His icy eyes chilled further as the question escaped from his lips before he could think better of it. "Nan, who *is* Minnie's mother?"

12

FIRES IN THE NIGHT

"Your brother is being a real ass today, did you know?" Benadykt huffed and shook his head.

Odette, presently sitting perched atop the castle battlements, glanced over her shoulder. Benadykt continued toward her, an irritated pout firmly set in place. She smirked. "I know I already know the answer, but I'll ask anyway. *Which* brother?"

Benadykt slid his legs over the battlements until they dangled over the edge. He sat with barely a hair's breadth separating his shoulder from Odette's. He laughed. "Moriah of course."

"Of course." Odette sighed. She returned to looking out over the island, watching as the morning glow slowly seeped away; the gold light that had been pooling over the immense expanse of jungle laid out around the castle gave way to the familiar emerald of the wild and its cacophony of brilliant colors. Freshly bloomed wildflowers were on full display as the final vestiges of dawn's light ebbed away. Morning had come; the children would be finishing up their run and returning to the castle. First-years would soon begin filing into the courtyard for archery lessons. She sighed again. The throbbing of an approaching headache persisted in her temples. "What's put him in a mood?"

"Two of the first-years," Benadykt replied sedately. "As far as I'm told, that is."

"And where did you source this information from?"

"Noel."

"A *valid* source of information on the subject, indeed." The incessant tap-tap-tapping in Odette's temples hammered on. "Names of the nuisances?"

A smirk laced its dastardly way onto the lord's face; he replied, "Hollyn and Fynneas."

"I'm not surprised," Odette mumbled.

She wasn't quite in the mood to teach the children, the lingering weariness from a night spent tossing and turning was weighing her down. Her eyes stung and her vision blurred; exhaustion fought doggedly to bring her down. She couldn't stifle her yawn. "They should be finishing up soon with their run. I suppose I should be heading down. Don't want them shooting each other's eyes out."

Benadykt slid from his perch and offered his hand out to the weary looking woman who'd been so snugly seated at his side. He helped her down, grinning as she so seldom allowed him to assist her in any way – such a treat, it was, to be granted the opportunity to feel remotely useful in her presence. He beamed. "I should be off, too. It's best not to keep Peragryn waiting for too long. He's not a morning person, you know. He gets a bit tetchy."

"Right. I know the sort," the lady grumbled, desperately rubbing at her eyes. "I'll see you later, then?"

"Of course," Benadykt assured as he took his leave.

Odette had only just stepped into the courtyard when she spied the mass of first-years ambling toward her, bows in hand and looking tired. The throng of twelve gathered about, their low chattering a constant rush of noise, steady and hushed like waves over the shore; there was a lulling quality to the way they whispered amongst one another and, for only a moment, Odette closed her eyes and listened to the dulcet tones of their garbled conversations, too far from them to make out every word, but close enough to appreciate the steady cadence. Snapping her eyes open, she focused and approached the children. Odette's stare was as stern as ever. She watched them straighten up as she drew nearer, conversations forgotten.

"Good morning," Odette greeted dully.

"Morning," they responded in turn.

"Today's lesson will be a bit harder than the last few. You'll no longer be shooting while in a stationary position. You'll take your start from one end of the courtyard," she said, while gesturing vaguely in the direction they'd be proceeding from. "Then you'll run across, shoot, and continue on. The goal is to not break your stride. I don't expect you to master it this morning. But I do expect you to be able to at least fire off your shot while moving at a moderate pace. Does this sound doable?"

The children nodded as one.

"Wonderful," Odette intoned in an apathetically bored manner rather reminiscent of Moriah. She waved lazily toward the other side of the courtyard. "Go line up over there. Not you, Renwyn. Not with that broken arm."

With a heavy sigh, Renwyn resigned himself to staying at the instructor's side, watching on enviously as his classmates lumbered in the instructed direction, taking up their bows and arrows as they did. He huffed as he flopped himself down to the ground, making himself comfortable as the others idled across the courtyard.

Odette caught hold of Hollyn's wrist before he'd strayed too far from her. She leaned down and whispered, "How's your ankle? Noel tells me you've hurt it *twice* now."

"It's healed up," the boy replied flatly.

Cat-like green eyes swept over the prince appraisingly. "How long has it been since it was last hurt?"

"Four days," Hollyn responded.

"That's not near enough time for it to be healed sufficiently. I'll not have you stumble and shoot one of your classmates." She straightened to her full height, towering over the boy. She held out her hand, eyeing his bow.

"I'm fine," Hollyn insisted gruffly. "It hardly hurts, *really*."

Her fingers twitched slightly, still holding her hand out to him. "Your bow, Hollyn."

"But—"

"Your bow, Hollyn." Her tone was clipped and icy.

The prince's head hung low as he relinquished the weapon to his instructor. "What am I to do for this lesson?"

"Sit right here where I can keep an eye on you," Odette replied. A blonde brow arched. "I've heard you and Fynneas have become quite the troublemakers."

"From who?

"*Everyone.*"

"It's not true," Hollyn contended. "It's not. We just argue a bit. We're competitive, you know, so we fight sometimes."

Odette considered the boy before her like a fox considering what to do with a cornered rabbit. "Do you think that's acceptable behavior?"

"What do you mean?"

The instructor nodded toward the class milling about on the other end of the courtyard before turning her attention back to the prince. "You and Fynneas, you're princes. I know we tell you titles don't matter here, that your house won't help you succeed, but think about it. One day, you two will be in

232

a position of great power, leading your classmates. If you two keep fighting like you do, no one will learn anything. It's a distraction. I expect better from you...from *both* of you."

Hollyn pouted. "Yes, sir."

The air brigadier general couldn't help the thin smile that wound its way to her features. She'd long since instilled in her students that 'ma'am' or 'my lady' would not be used when speaking to her, that 'sir' would be acceptable, as it was for their male instructors. Pleased, she patted the boy on the shoulder. "Now sit, observe, and learn. Try and glean something from watching your classmates."

"Yes, sir," repeated Hollyn dutifully.

With a wave of Odette's hand, the lesson commenced. Hollyn, seated beside Renwyn now, watched with rapt attention as each of his classmates took their turn; they jogged from one end of the courtyard, made an attempt at shooting the carefully stacked bales of hay used as a target, and then found their place at the opposite end of the grounds. Penelope, he regarded, did a far more possible job than he would have thought her capable of; though his momentary acknowledgement of her meager accomplishments was set aside for genuine astonishment at how well both Georgie and Lux faired during the assignment. Both girls kept up a decent pace and were able to hit the target with relative ease. Albie was disastrously clumsy, pitching forward as he tripped over his own feet and nearly impaling his leg upon the dropped arrow. Ollie, oddly enough, was a fair shot and, though his pace was slow, managed to keep his momentum going the entire time.

When Fynn started his jog forward, Hollyn's attention sharpened. Though the dark-haired prince was graceless in almost everything he did—from running, to riding horses, to tying knots—he was not only capable of moving at an alarmingly quick pace toward his target, but his stride didn't falter, and his aim was true, sinking into the hay in the blink of an eye. Hollyn scowled and turned to stare at the bow clasped in Odette's hands, wishing he could take his turn. He muttered under his breath, cursing his slow-healing injury.

The first-years took their turns in quick succession, completing six rounds each before Odette stopped them. She pulled a man-shaped, wooden figure before the hay, setting it up against the bales. She beheld the gathered class and said, "Your next lesson will be similar. You'll take a running—or jogging—start, take aim, and fire, all while keeping up your pace. This fine, wooden fellow," she wrapped her knuckles over the wood, "will be your target. I'll leave the bales up, just in case you should miss. We don't want arrows flying around wildly. Your objective is to not only hit the target, but to fire a lethal shot. Preferably, I'd like you to hit the head, the neck, or the chest. Arms and legs are fine for now. In reality, those shots would serve to injure your opponent, slow them down. But, when an enemy is advancing on you, you want them dead, not slowed down and angry. Do we all understand?"

"Yes, sir," they replied together.

"Good. Now, line up like before. On my mark."

As the ten children started toward their designated position, Lux lingered near Hollyn for a moment. She poked his knee with the toe of her boot. As he looked up to her, she smiled. "How's the ankle?"

"I'm fine," he grumbled, crossing his arms over his chest.

Her smile didn't falter. "Right. Of course." She started to head to her position but paused for a moment. "Hollyn?"

"Hmm?"

"I hope you'll be back at it soon." With that said, she left him there to consider her words, taking up her place in line behind Ollie.

Penelope didn't fair nearly as well as she had previously. Her arrows plunged into the hay, entirely missing their intended target. Albie struggled similarly. Hogan, Wilder, and Firiel all had a difficult time managing to hit anything at all. Their arrows wavered from their bows and fell, lifelessly, far short of their target. Georgie, with a triumphant smile, managed to embed an arrow in the figure's leg while Lux got one stuck securely in the arm. Godryk and Ollie both struggled to keep their pace and, as a result of focusing more on their forward movement than their aim, managed to only graze the bales of hay.

With his turn finally arriving, Fynn took off with the same energetic speed as before. He raised his bow; his pace never faltered. He drew his arrow back and shot. The boy froze. It was as though time stood still for him. He watched the arrow erupt from the bow; the string vibrated like the wings of a hummingbird. The sound of the arrow cutting through the air was deafening. His eyes went wide when, at last, the arrow found purchase; its viciously sharp tip embedded into the wooden neck of the figure.

Fynn stopped moving. He dropped the bow. It fell soundlessly to the ground beneath. The prince couldn't tear his eyes away from the figure, from the arrow protruding from the splintered, wooden neck. A rush of thunderous sound washed over him, drowned him. He could hear screaming, terrible screaming that would leave throats raw. He heard the beating of hooves over stones, the crying of children, the sickening sounds of lifeless bodies falling against stone, the ooze of blood running through the grooves of cobblestones. He heard people yelling for their loved ones, the clattering of steel against steel, hysterical sobs. He smelled fire burning and the scent of smoke wafting into the air. He felt the embers crackling around him.

He was still. The more he stood there, staring with wide eyes at the figure, the more Fynn felt panic grip and tear at him. His lungs felt as though a thousand clawed hands had clenched around them; his heart felt constricted in his chest. The prince gasped. It was a strangled sound. Before him, he saw blood spilling from the figure's throat, washing down its spindly, wooden body, congealing in a mass of red at its feet.

The boy needed more air; he fought for more, gasping and gulping, but none would come. His lungs were painfully empty; they burned.

Fynn felt the muscles in his shoulders begin to seize. Awful pains shot down his arms; his hands went numb. His back was heavy and tight and standing seemed too arduous an effort to continue undergoing. Finally, his eyes flicked down and he beheld the ground. The familiar green grasses of the courtyard were gone, magically replaced, it would seem, by the blood-stained cobblestones of the capital's roads. Fynn recognized the ground beneath him. He would never forget it. He remembered the feel of the stones as they scraped away at him when he was knocked brutally to the ground, as he tripped and scrambled for safety, as Lux had hauled him away from the maelstrom. Yes, he recognized the ground beneath his feet. He recognized the blood running over the pale, pocked stones.

Fynn's legs shook; his knees were weak. The prince fell to the ground, a trembling mass. Distantly, he heard someone calling his name. The voice—it was familiar but didn't belong there—lilted melodically against the chorus of screams. His eyes flutter closed, and he fell into the welcoming arms of a euphoric numbness.

Odette knelt over the boy's unconscious body. She shook him gently by the shoulders. "Fynneas? Fynn?" She ran her hand through his hair, pushing it from his face. She scowled at the boy's unresponsiveness. "Fynneas? I need you to open your eyes, Fynn."

A coldness gripped Odette when she beheld blood beginning to run from his nose over his lips. She reached out, wiping away the red rivulets, only to be thwarted by more trails spilling out from his nostrils. "Fynn," she called, but she knew he wasn't going to rouse.

Ignoring the alarmed looks and whispers from the children behind her, Odette gathered the boy into her arms and stood. He felt lifeless in her grasp. Only the steady rise and fall of his narrow chest betrayed the still-beating heart pounding away in its cage. "Get back to your dormitory. All of you. Wait there until noon and then proceed with your assigned lessons from there. Now!"

Within the hour, Fynn was soundly tucked beneath heavy blankets in the infirmary wing. Blythe, one of the ladies of the Medical Corps, was clucking around the boy, checking for fever and making sure he was comfortably snugged into the warmth. When at last the woman had decided she could do little more for the boy, she contented herself with looming over Fynn every now and then, her careful eyes sweeping over him for any worrying signs. That evening, she found herself curled up in a rather uncomfortable chair at the prince's bedside, watching as he remained scarily motionless in his bed. Her attention was drawn away when she heard soft footsteps coming closer.

"I hadn't expected to see you here." Blythe yawned and rubbed at her eyes.

Odette stood at the foot of Fynn's bed, staring at his stillness. Her face was expressionless. "Any change?"

"Not yet," Blythe replied. She stood, stretching out her arms. The medical matron eyed the other woman and asked, "What happened out there? You didn't say much when you brought him in this morning."

"I don't know," Odette admitted. "All of a sudden, he just stopped dead. I don't know what happened." She observed the matron, seeing the weariness in her face. "I can stay with him for a while. You look tired, go lie down."

"You're sure?"

Odette nodded sharply. "I'll watch over him."

Blythe took her leave moments before Moriah and Noel crept quietly into the infirmary. Noel, worried by the way Odette remained motionless at the foot of the only occupied bed, hurried over. He sidled up beside his older sister, swung an arm over her shoulders, and drew her closer. He wasn't put off by her lack of response, her expressionless features. Rather, seeing those characteristic mannerisms from her warmed him, if only a little.

"Godryk told us what happened," Noel said softly.

Moriah found his way to the chair Blythe had vacated and settled down. He scooted closer to the bedside, cautiously reaching out to the boy with as much trepidation as if he were handling a delicate heirloom made of the thinnest glass. He smoothed back black hair. "He didn't say much," Moriah added. He withdrew his hand, arms now leaning upon the bedside as he relaxed somewhat. "He just said Fynn shot the target, froze up, and then collapsed." He turned a skeptical eye toward his sister. "What *really* happened?"

Odette shook her head. "I don't know. Just that, I suppose."

"There must be something more," Noel insisted gently.

"No. No, not really. He was doing well. *Exceptionally* well, actually. I wasn't surprised when he managed a lethal shot on the target," explained Odette. "Got the thing right in the neck, just under the chin."

Moriah tensed. His green eyes looked as though they were glowing. His voice was low, like a rumble of thunder lost in the clouds. "The *throat?*"

"Yes," Odette affirmed.

"Felix was shot…*killed*…by an arrow hitting him in the throat," Moriah whispered. "He died right in front of Fynneas." His hand curled around the smaller, motionless hand of the prince. "That *has* to be it. He probably just couldn't take the similarity."

"There has to be more," argued Odette. "You weren't there, Moriah. You didn't see him. I was worried…*me*, of all people. Gods, he just collapsed like he was the one who was shot, not the target. He just collapsed and wasn't responding when I was calling his name. You weren't there." Her voice became chilled, an accusing edge to her words. "You weren't there to see how the blood started running out of his nose. There was so much blood and he wasn't moving. Don't tell me it's just because he was upset. You don't spontaneously collapse and lose *that much* blood from your *damn nose* because you're upset about something."

Noel retreated from Odette slowly, sensing her growing agitation. He cast his attention towards Moriah, noting the man's increasingly detached expression. He chanced fleeting glances between the two bickering siblings before bowing his head. "I think I'll be taking my leave. You two seem like you can manage here without me. I'd only get in the way, I'm sure."

All the talking, both ardent and hushed, hadn't disturbed the boy in the least. Fynn was completely enthralled in his own world, in a freeing sense of darkness where all the anxiety of the morning was left and forgotten. He found himself wandering through a void of nothingness, the blackness rippling at his feet as though he were walking through shallow water. He supposed shallow water would be just the way to describe it, as he felt the rush of something chilly against the soles of his feet, splashing up at his heels with every step. Unlike the last time he'd been in such a place, he couldn't discern the sound of distantly beating wings, or the disembodied call of Minnie flitting across non-existent winds. Now he found himself in a place entirely devoid of sound.

The quiet was, for a blissful moment, a welcomed peace that Fynn embraced; pausing in his aimless walking, he closed his eyes and listened for the sound of the nothingness and smiled when he heard it. But soon that same quietness became maddening and the frantic beating of his heart once more started up. He searched the darkness, eyes straining in the void in search of some direction; but his search was for naught, as there was nothing there. Fynn looked all around, hoping against all reason that he had missed some shining light that would beckon him on. Still, there was nothing.

It was that nothingness that was beginning to gnaw away at him; it was a determined gnawing like termites to wood, slowly whittling down even the most fortified of structures one bite at a time. And so too did he feel as such, like some sort of ill-constructed fort now riddled with the remnants of thousands of tiny tormentors, notches and holes bored into him, leaving him wavering, unsure of his footing, foundations rotting, and pillars crashing down. The unsteadiness made his knees give way; he tumbled down against the darkness accosting him.

His hands burned as though they'd been ripped open. He quirked a brow. He'd felt the same incessant burning in his palms when he'd been thrown to the cobblestone road over and over. Looking down to the darkness under his hands, Fynn shrieked when the blackness began to slip away from his fingertips, receding ever more until there, beneath his hands, were those same pale, porous cobblestones speckled with blood.

Fynn's breath hitched when that awful, coppery scent wafted into his nose. He would never—could never—forget that ghastly fragrance. There was so much of it sprinkling the air as arrows impaled flesh and as swords and knives slashed against skin. The wailings - those awful, mournful sounds - wriggled their way free from the throats of those staggering through the streets. At once, all the blackness was gone and Fynn was there again, there in the road watching as calamity broke loose upon the capital. He was there once more and the sun was shining, the morning heat screaming down fiercely.

Upon realizing and accepting where he was, Fynn reeled around on his heels in search of his father. When his pale gaze settled upon the prone, lifeless form of Felix nary ten feet from where he was hunched, Fynn felt as though—yet again—his world was crumbling down upon him. His eyes met the dead stare of his father's and he couldn't help but cry. The boy felt the warm, stinging sensation of fresh tears spilling unbidden from his grey eyes, tracing down his lightly freckled cheeks. The vacant look in Felix's summer eyes, those eyes once full of life, was earthshattering, rendering his son inert at the sight. Fynn choked back another sob, steeling himself. He stumbled over to his father and collapsed at his side. He placed his hand over the man's chest, but he felt nothing there. There was no beating of a heart, no rise of the chest. There was nothing there beneath his touch but the stony grimness of a corpse lost to a sea of hysteria.

People rushed by, brushing against him, a slight knock here and there. But Fynn couldn't bring himself to move. The awful grief he'd worked hard to rid himself of was once more looming over him, reaching out for him, seizing him. He couldn't shake it off. There was no escape. No, that awful, familiar touch of grief had braced itself against him and wormed ever closer. Fynn could almost feel the fleeting, hot breath of that desolate monster whisper over the back of his neck. He shuddered.

A sudden movement caught his eye and yanked Fynn almost painfully from his wallowing. Just before him, in the distance, amongst the throngs of the frenzied masses, there stood a man staring back at him. Fynn's eyes hardened as he recognized the man almost instantly—it was the man who'd led the funeral service. Incensed, Fynn shot to his feet and ran toward him. To his mounting dismay, the old man began to weave through the hordes of clambering people.

Fynn's eyes were sharp though, and he kept track of the man like a predator rushing through the wood, a wolf chasing down its prey. The prince rushed and dodged through the crowds, pushing people out of his way. He stumbled slightly, falling for a moment and scraping his palms and knees as he tried to avoid landing bodily against the stony ground. Within a moment he was up again, taking off in a sprint after the man. He ran as fast as his thin legs would carry him. He ran as fast as his tired body would allow. He ran so fast he broke free from the grief monster's clutches.

The boy whirled around a corner, almost barreling into a wall as he sought to hunt down the elusive man. He saw, not far up ahead, the man step into an alleyway and disappear. And so too did Fynn step into that same alley. He was greeted there by no one. Fynn stared down the thin alleyway that twisted and turned. He was alone. He looked left and he looked right and still there was nothing. The man had vanished.

Sighing, Fynn combed his hand through his hair. He was about to retreat, to go back and find his father, or maybe Fiona, when something urged him to look back to the alleyway. Deciding to follow the sudden impulse's guiding hand, the prince glanced over his shoulder. Presently, there stood a door attached to nothing. It was just there; just a door in the middle of the alley that had appeared from nothing, stood braced against nothing, and seemingly opened to nothing.

"That's certainly *different*," Fynn mumbled as he stepped closer.

He reached out. His palm fell flat against the door. The wood felt solid beneath his touch. Nervously, he reached to the handle and pulled. He saw therein, instead of the alley stretched out before him as he would have suspected, a small room revealed. "Yes…certainly *different*," Fynn whispered as he stepped inside. He jumped at the sound of the door swinging closed behind him. He whirled around, only to be seized by an indescribable fright when he beheld that the door had gone, vanished without a trace.

"It's been a while," a soft voice said.

It was a familiar voice, but Fynn couldn't quite recall where he'd heard it before.

The prince turned and looked into the room. It was small, comfortably decorated. There was a hearth burning, built into the stone of the far wall. There were tapestries hanging; they looked dingy and thread bare. Upon the floor was a simple, black rug. Two chairs were set there upon the rug in the center of the room, facing one another. Fynn stepped closer. A shadowy figure sat in one of the chairs. The fire flickered and revealed the face of the man Fynn had been chasing.

"Please," the soft voice insisted, "take a seat, Prince Fynneas."

Reluctantly, the boy sat. He stared at the man seated opposite him. He knew that sagging, leathery flesh that clung to bone fruitlessly, wishfully endeavoring to maintain a semblance of its once youthful, supple shape. Watery, blue eyes stared back at him, twinkling in the blinking firelight emanating from behind him. The man's grey hair was as kempt as it was that day, neatly combed back as Fynn remembered. The prince noted, curiously, that in those skeletal looking hands set upon a thin lap, the man still held the unlit candle.

"Who are you?" Fynn asked.

"You don't recognize me?" The old man lightly laughed. "What a pity. I had hoped you'd be smarter than this." He clucked disapprovingly.

"What do you mean?"

"Truly, child, do you not know who I am?"

The boy shook his head.

"Ah, I see. Let me cast some *light* on that for you." A shaking hand arced over the unlit wick of the candle and there, all of a sudden, sparked a tiny flame. The vestiges of the small, golden light reached up to the man's face, further illuminating the curvature of his features. "Still don't know? I suppose I shouldn't blame you."

The same hand that had somehow lit the candle reached up and tugged at a jowl. Fynn was horrified. His stomach churned as the man's skin peeled away from his face. It tore from his cheeks with the ease of tearing parchment from the spine of a book. Revealed beneath the flesh freshly pulled away was another face that Fynn remembered vividly. The man before him continued to dispense with his skin as though it were a mask, stripping back the gnarled, old flesh until nothing was left but the new face looking back at the boy. The same blue eyes stared at the prince heatedly.

"Recognize me now?"

In seeing the face and hearing the voice slip from those particular lips, Fynn gasped. "You're...no...this is impossible!" Fynn protested. He leapt up from his chair. Fear had completely taken him over.

"Say it, Prince Fynneas. Go on. *Say my name.*"

The name slipped from Fynn's mouth like a chilled breath in the dead of winter. He whispered, "Barnaby Lot."

"Close. Though not quite." The man before him smiled wickedly. "Honestly, my little disguise wasn't so different from this face, now was it? I thought you would've pieced this one together, little prince. I suppose I've overestimated you. Seems your sister is the smart one."

Fynn threw his back against the corner; he huddled down into a curled ball upon the ground, drew his knees to his chest and wrapped his arms around his legs. He shook his head and screwed his eyes shut. "No. No, no, no. It's not true. This isn't true. It can't be! This can't be happening!"

The man hadn't bothered to get up from his seat. He leaned back, settling into the plush comfort of his chair. "Now," he cooed, "let's not be so rash." He turned his head ever so slightly to watch as the boy further descended into a fit of hysteria.

Fynn finally managed to calm himself after what seemed an eternity of frantic shaking. He still trembled, but he forced himself to once again meet the watery, blue eyes of the old man. "It was *you* there that day? The whole time?"

The man nodded.

"I don't believe you," accused Fynn, finding the sudden energy to climb back to his feet. He remained pressed into the corner, retreated as far back from the man as he could manage. But Fynn refused to look as cowardly as he felt and so straightened up and squared his shoulders. His gaze was icy, vicious. "You're lying."

"Tell me something, princey-boy." The old man laughed. "Have strange things been happening to you? Around you?"

Fynn remained resolutely silent.

"Aren't you curious, sweet prince, as to *why*?"

Still, Fynn said nothing.

"Tell me, then, why you and your sister have persisted in searching for answers if you are, indeed, uninterested."

"What're you talking about?" Fynn plucked himself from the wall and began inching toward the chairs once more. The man said nothing; Fynn welcomed the momentary reprieve as he gingerly seated himself across from the old man once more. "Tell me."

"How about I tell you something else, eh?"

Fynn wrinkled his nose in confusion, leaning forward as he spoke, "No."

Playfully, the man reached out and poked the tip of boy's nose. A heinous grin spread over his ugly features. "You don't get to make the rules, Fynneas."

Fynn recoiled from the man's touch. "Fine. What did you want to tell me?"

"How about a poem? Do you like poetry, Fynneas?"

Fynn's demeanor quickly soured further. "A poem? That's what you wanted to tell me. *A poem*?"

The old man nodded wryly. "I would be honored if you'd permit me to regale you with my little poem. I wrote it myself."

"Go on," Fynn said flatly. "Let's hear it."

The man coughed, clearing his throat in a needlessly dramatic fashion. "There once was a little prince—that no one has seen since—the castle burned down—and broke his crown—ah, there once was a little prince." He fell back into the softness of his chair, eyes alight with mirth. "So," he said, clapping his hands together enthusiastically, "what did you think?" He tapped at his chin thoughtfully. "A tad rudimentary in its construction, I'd say. But I do think it gets the point across, don't you agree?"

Fynn crossed his arms haughtily. "Your poem makes no sense."

"How so?"

"I assume I'm the *little prince* in question?"

"How observant of you," the man agreed, his voice laced heavily with dour sarcasm. "Aren't you so clever."

"The Crown isn't broken," Fynn argued, adamantly ignoring the verbal jab.

The old man traced the line of his jaw and the arch of his chin, lost in thought. "Oh?"

"My family is still in power. I would say that means the Crown *isn't* broken," Fynn asserted.

"You're looking at this as though it were black and white," chided the man.

Fynn quirked a brow. "Isn't it?"

"Ah," cooed the old man, "poetry is *art* and art is never so blatant, never so black or white, so yes or no, so is or is not." His blue eyes shone eerily in the firelight. "Think like an artist, Prince Fynneas. Go on, princey-boy, and give it a try."

"I still don't think it makes sense. I'm still here! People have seen me since the fire."

The man pursed his lips in dissatisfaction. "You're thinking plainly again, like a commoner. Have some creativity, child!" He leaned forward in his chair. "Tell me, what do you think of time?"

"Time?"

The old man nodded. "Yes, *time*. What do you think of *time*?"

"It's there."

"Another *astounding* observation," the man mused. "Your classmates at Morancy must be ceaselessly dazzled by your wit."

"What am I supposed to think about time?" questioned the boy. "If you're so smart, tell me what *you* think about it."

The man held his arms aloft. "Time is all around us. It's *everywhere*! And yet, here we are, you and I."

"What do you mean?"

Abruptly, the man jabbed his forefinger against Fynn's nose again. He grinned madly. "You know, Prince Fynneas, you ask that question quite a lot. I can't be the only one who's suggested you learn to use your head." He sprang up from his seat, surprisingly nimble for a man so long into his years. "Where do you think we are?"

"In a room."

"Wonderful, simply wonderful! The brightest mind of the age," chortled the man as he went twirling from his chair. "A room, yes. But where is this room?"

Fynn shrugged. He watched the man flounce around. "I don't know. The doorway was in an alley. It was odd."

"Why do you say it was odd?"

"Because the door just appeared," Fynn replied. "It came out of nowhere. Doorways don't just show up in alleys from nowhere."

"You're thinking like a dullard again," admonished the man. He'd come to a stop, standing frightfully still as he stared with glimmering eyes at the boy. "Where are we? Think about it. Where are we in time?"

"The day of the funeral," Fynn answered without thought. "But that's not right." He shook his head and combed his hand through his tangled tresses. "That was this summer. I've been off at Morancy for a few weeks now." He stood on shaking legs. "I can't be here."

"Why not?"

"Because that doesn't make sense!" yelled the prince, stomping his foot. "It doesn't make any sense."

The man reached out his arm, fingers wriggling. Before Fynn had the time to ask what he was reaching for, a door appeared just as it had in the alley. Stumbling back, the prince's jaw went slack with confusion. He watched, utterly dumbfounded, as the man's hand fell upon the door handle and opened it. A blinding, white light spilled into the tiny room.

"I once told you, well *wrote* to you, that all you need do is call my name. I've been waiting. I'll tell you this. You were close with Barnaby Lot. Alas, that's only a name I use when needed. You'll find I use many names when I have to. Though, I have but one *true* name. Think on it a little more, princey. You need only call my name," the man said and then, with a final wave of his hand, he stepped through the door and was gone.

The prince, his presence of mind mustered once more, jumped to his feet in pursuit but was halted when the door vanished again. He was alone. Alone in that room. He was alone and the silence was maddening. His eyes darted about in search of something, anything to help him figure out what he was supposed to do next. Nothing. He saw nothing. He heard nothing. There was nothing there to help him. He was alone and that feeling of nothingness returned with a mighty, rallying cry and again those horrible termites were biting away at him. Fynn crumpled to his knees. Tears welled in his eyes. He beat his fists against the ground, heedless of the pain that shot up his arms as he mercilessly pounded against the stone floor.

"Help," he whispered. His voice sounded weak and frail and he hated it. Again, he smashed his fist into the floor, marveling as the flesh of his knuckles split against the rough stone; warm trails of red traced over the valleys of his hand. "Help…please."

Forcing himself back to his feet, Fynn aimlessly began wandering the room. His hands roved along the walls, finding scarcely more than cracks. His eyes surveyed the furniture decorating the humble chambers, but there was nothing there to assist him. With a final huff, he came to stand before the hearth. He watched, dazedly, as the fire flickered. The gold and orange light sparked and danced before him. The heat ghosted over his front like a warm breath, as if a tired dragon had just sighed. Transfixed by the allure of the light and the warmth, Fynn stretched his arm out and let his hand hover over the fire. He was surprised when he didn't immediately recoil from the heat. Rather, he felt nothing. Upon pulling his hand from the fire, he saw that his palm remained unscathed from the flames.

Curious, Fynn reached out again and found the same results to hold true. His head tilted to the side, intrigue overcoming panic. The hearth was large, its mouth far taller than Fynn and far wider than four men standing shoulder to shoulder. He was easily able to step into the flame. He stood amidst the fire but did not burn. His icy eyes strained, looking for any way out. What he found was darkness there beyond the fire. That darkness was now inviting; it was cool and calm. It was the same sort of darkness he'd found himself in before he wandered back into the worst day of his life.

Fynn sought that comfortable quietness once more. It felt like a lifetime ago that he'd been swaddled in the folds of the soundless void; that very void whose bleakness and eerie silence had driven him mad. But, even in remembering how he had eventually become so uneasy in the silence, he couldn't help but crave it now. And so, Fynn stepped beyond the fire and the room was gone. There was, once more, a vast expanse of blackness in all directions, seemingly unending, unrelenting. At his feet, he once again felt the rushing of the cold, nothingness waters running along like a river leading nowhere.

"He's been asleep for days."

"What should we do?"

"Is he going to be alright?"

"Should we try and wake him again?"

"Fynn, you've been sleeping for a while. You must be rested by now."

"Please be alright."

"He looks so pale."

"He always looks pale."

"Gods, his skin feels cold to the touch."

"He hasn't moved in days."

"This isn't good."

"Does he have a fever?"

"He needs to eat."

"Is he still asleep?"

"How is he?"

Fynn heard them, familiar voices riding the same not-there winds. He tried to remember the people those voices belonged to. He scoured his mind, searching for names, for faces, to assign to those voices. But he struggled. All he found was silence there and an awful fuzziness that made thinking hurt. A nasty throb started in his temples.

"The children are getting worried."

"His friends are asking about him."

"Should we tell Lachlan?"

"Is he looking any better?"

"He's warmer to the touch now."

"His fever is gone."

"Some color has returned to his face. That's good."

"We need to get him up."

Those voices were persisting. They were becoming clearer and clearer. Fynn remembered green eyes distinctly. Green eyes that always seemed alight with some hidden knowledge. He recalled blue eyes. Kind blue eyes that seemed to smile - warm and soft blue eyes. He recalled green eyes that seemed harsher, more distant. Eyes that watched him and studied him, but remained aloof, withdrawn.

"This isn't good."

"His breathing is getting erratic."

"His heart is beating too fast."

"His fever's back."

"He's burning up."

"He's looking worse."

"We need to do something."

"Fynneas, can you hear us?"

The blackness seemed less dense, less cool. The prince stood there, as if on the edge of a precipice. He was surprised that, when he looked up, he saw stars. The night sky was spangled overhead, shining brilliantly. He looked over the constellations he knew, the ones his father had taught him. Fynn smiled fondly. His father used to take him out at night to look at the sky. Felix would point up to the stars and trace figures with the tip of his finger, telling him all about the kings and queens and heroes that lived up in the sky. Fynn's grin broadened when he recalled a specific night, back when he had been no more than five or six years old, when his father had told him that Celestine, his mother, was up in the stars, looking down and watching over them.

"Hello, Mother," Fynn whispered longingly. "Are you up there?"

The stars seemed to shine a bit brighter.

A tear fell from his cheek. "I wish you were here. I don't know what I'm supposed to do. I'm confused…and *scared*, Mother," he admitted shakily. He wiped his tears from his face. "Please…help me."

"The fever's gone again."

"Is he getting better?"

"Finally."

"He looks like he's trying to open his eyes."

"Fynn, come back to us."

"Your friends miss you, Fynneas."

"He's looking better."

"He'll be alright."

Fynn heard them, those same voices whispering. He didn't look away from the stars. "Are you really up there? If you are and you're…watching over me…if you really are, then please…I need your help." He was so tired, so worn. Every muscle in his body ached; even his bones felt sore. "I'm getting tired, Mother. I'm going to close my eyes for a little while." He refused to look away from the stars. "Will you still be there when I wake up?"

Someone was shaking his shoulder. He felt someone shaking him over and over, gently but firmly. His lashes tickled his cheeks for a moment before his eyes broke open. His vision blurred for a second before correcting and adjusting to the light. Fynn was surprised to see Moriah and Noel leaning over him instead of the stars and the blackness. At once, he felt groggy and sluggish. His mind was a mess of jumbled thoughts and memories. The throbbing at his temples had turned into a vicious, stabbing pain. Fynn groaned and leaned his head back against his pillow.

Gently, Moriah's hand swam through the black mane. "You're awake."

Fynn turned into the touch. "What do you mean?"

"You've been in bed for five days," Moriah replied.

There was no note of worry in Moriah's voice. The same dull, bored tone met Fynn's ears, but the boy couldn't help but be comforted in some strange way. He was too tired to grin, to laugh, but he wished he could. "Oh," he rasped.

Noel was jumpy. Fynn was awake but looked rather ill; the pallor of his complexion was worrisome. "I'll go get Blythe and Imogen. And I'll let Dot know Fynn's up." The man practically bound toward the door on legs like springs.

"That bad?" mumbled Fynn.

Moriah nodded. "Everyone was concerned."

The boy's voice was painfully weak. "Were *you?*"

Moriah's thumb traced tiny circles over the prince's forehead while his hand remained steeped in the unruly, black hair. "Yes."

"Moriah?"

"Hmm?"

"Do you remember our talk out in the gardens?" Fynn was beginning to get sleepy. "When I asked about that old man?"

"I do."

"I know who he is. I saw him," Fynn tried to explain. He was struggling to keep track of his thoughts, his words. "I saw him, Moriah."

Moriah tried to quiet the boy, still softly tracing circles over the once-more feverish flesh. "Go to sleep, Fynneas." He pulled the blankets up higher over the boy's prone form. "We'll be here when you wake up again."

"It was the man from the funeral," the boy said firmly. "It was *him*. It was the bookshop keeper, Lot. But...he says that's not really his name. But it was *him*."

"What did you see?"

"I went back to that day," the boy began, exhaustion wavering his voice. "I was there, and I *saw* him. He was looking at me while I was next to my father. He was right there, Moriah." Fynn felt urgency take hold of him and he continued, "He was *right there* that day. I didn't see him then. I wasn't paying attention. But this time, I saw him, and I went after him. And he showed himself, Moriah. He showed himself and it was Lot, or whatever he wants to call himself. He said he's got a lot of names. I don't know what they are."

"What more did he say to you?" the green-eyed man asked.

"He asked me about time."

Moriah pressed, "Nothing more?"

"And that I need only call his name," Fynn recalled. "I don't know which one."

Perplexed, Moriah chose to remain silent.

"He asked me about time and told me to call his name when I knew it, and then he left me alone. I was all alone and I didn't know how I was going to get back. I didn't know how I was going to get out of that place he left me in."

"How did you get back?" asked Moriah.

The pain in Fynn's head was getting worse. The simple act of talking was nearly excruciating. "I walked into a fire."

13

ASHES AND EMBERS

Godryk flicked his wrist and watched impassively as the rock skipped across the glassy waters of the pond. "You know, you're sort of weird."

Fynn, comfortably seated on the shore, the soles of his feet just barely grazing the warm water, shrugged carelessly. "How so?"

"You spent five days in bed, all but dead to the world," Godryk started. He skipped another rock. It skittered across the water easily, splashing slightly as it took the final plunge into the depths. "And then you just wake up and you're fine. It took you what, two…three days to get your strength back and now you're off moping around like the world's ended. It's weird."

Fynn fell back against the grassy shore and stared up at the clouds. "I suppose. I didn't really think of it like that. I'm just glad to be out of bed, really." He yawned.

Though he'd been released from the infirmary over a week ago, Fynn still felt a lingering weariness that seeped down to his bones. He supposed the lack of sleep was probably contributing to his near constant exhaustion. Fynn groaned as another slice of pain cut through his head. He'd been suffering for days with an unrelenting headache that refused to abate. "Were lessons boring without me?"

"Quieter, perhaps," Godryk admitted. He sat down beside the prince and watched the still waters. "Do you want to talk about what happened?"

"No."

"I think you should," Godryk pushed gently. "It was scary, Fynn, the way you just collapsed that day. It was like, I don't know, you just died or something right there in the courtyard. Everyone was really upset. Even Hollyn seemed a bit ruffled."

"So?"

"Don't be like that." Godryk's brow furrowed as he watched Fynn roll onto his side, facing away from him. "You've been acting different since you came back to lessons."

250

"No, I haven't," Fynn protested flatly.

Annoyed, the other boy snapped, "Yes, you have! It's getting really annoying."

Fynn climbed to his feet sluggishly and looked down at Godryk for a moment. His eyes were distant, cold. "If I'm so *annoying*, then why are you still hanging around with me?"

Incensed by Fynn's callous disregard, Godryk jumped up to his feet and shoved the prince hard. "Because we're *friends*, you ass."

The way the young royal regarded the boy lord before him was detached, apathetic. His eyes were vacant. Fynn shook his head; his voice was low. "You wouldn't understand. You can't. Just leave me alone."

Blue eyes watered as Godryk watched Fynn stalk off back toward the castle. He stood, alone on the shores of the pond, lost in the wake of Fynn's retreating footsteps. He cried at the loss of his friend.

Mornings found Fynn running ahead of his classmates, resolutely avoiding eye contact with the rest of his year mates. Afternoons and evenings were similar; Fynn sat apart from the other eleven children, eating quietly—if he bothered to eat much at all. His energetic enthusiasm for his lessons had waned to hardly more than tolerant apathy and he proceeded through each with an aloof lethargy that troubled his peers. Even when Hollyn tried to engage him in competitive antics, sneering or biting out a challenge, Fynn did little more than shrug or sigh before skulking off on his own.

Godryk, having spent days pleading with the prince to speak to him, to share their meals together as they had before, to laugh and joke together, to wander off where they shouldn't be, found himself without his more mischievous half. And with this recent loss, he retreated into solitude. When Fynn would pull away from the group and run ahead, breaking from the herd, Godryk would dawdle at the back of the pack, dragging his feet solemnly. The days where Fynn would act as if he was off in his own world, Godryk would be hunched over, staring off in Fynn's direction with a hopefully pleading gaze. Those nights when Fynn would wake up screaming before darting from the dormitories, Godryk would sit up in bed and wait for his friend's eventual return, only to find himself turned away and shunned when, at last, Fynn would crawl back to bed.

It was afternoon on a most abysmal day; dark clouds loitered in the sky. Thunder clapped overhead. Rain fell steadily. Noel stood before his group of first-years, his expression dour. He couldn't help but observe how Fynn stood separated from the others, arms folded over his chest, eyes dull.

"You've had a few weeks to practice. You've each improved a great deal. I think that it's time for another contest, don't you? Hollyn's held that championship title for too long, wouldn't you say?" Noel forced himself to smile, but he knew the expression was hollow. He gestured with his hand, waving it in a slight circle. "Gather around like last time. Make a circle. Let's see if any of you can best the prince."

Dutifully the children took up their places. Noel watched them assume their positions. Godryk, he noted, continued casting quick glimpses in Fynn's direction, only to look away almost immediately with a soundly defeated expression. The instructor combed his hand through his hair and exhaled sharply.

"Alright, alright," Noel began slowly, "the first match will be Lux and... Renwyn."

The two combatants took their place in the center of the circle, sinking down upon bended knees as they readied themselves. Their eyes were sharp and fierce, sizing each other up as they waited for the command to begin. The moment Noel said to commence, the two launched forwards.

In all the weeks he'd been training, Renwyn had still yet to learn to control the ferocity of his attacks. His movements were quick and strong, but sloppy and uncoordinated. His natural tendency toward wildly swinging at his opponent was only compounded by his hardly healed right arm giving him a bit of trouble. Imogen had warned him he wasn't ready to go back to sparring, but he'd soundly disregarded her medical opinion.

Lux, in that same span of time, had learned to effectively compensate for her lack of raw strength. Thus, as Renwyn swung at her ferociously, she easily parried, making quick work of dismantling his hardly formed defense before the dulled tip of her sword pummeled into his chest, knocking the air from his lungs.

Renwyn fell in a crumpled mess to the ground, clutching at his chest as he gasped. His discarded sword lay forgotten in front of him. "Nice one," he huffed breathily as he forced himself back to his feet. He nodded to Lux, conceding the match to her. "Think you damn near poked out my lung."

Lux scoffed. She gathered the boy's sword for him and handed it over as they resumed their place in the circle. "Don't be so dramatic." She smiled. "When your arm's actually healed, you'll put up a better fight. At least, I hope that's the case."

Not having expected the fight to end so abruptly, Noel nodded as he tried to think of the next pairing. His eyes roved over the children before deciding upon the second round's fighters. "Alright, Penelope and Firiel, it's your turn."

Though she'd not grown so bold as Lux in the weeks she'd spent acquainting herself with close range combat, Penelope had at least managed to learn to hang onto her weapon and not shriek in fear during an oncoming assault. Firiel, Noel had observed, suffered from much the same problem as Renwyn. The two had the same fiery disposition and burning energy needed for frontal assaults, but their attacks were heedless and relied on frantic and frenzied swinging rather than tact and forethought. However, Firiel's over-reliance on manic forays, when pitted against Penelope, worked in her favor. Overwhelmed by the sudden and erratic surge forward by her adversary, Penelope was, in just seconds, disarmed and at sword-point. She held her hands up, yielding the bout to the other girl.

Noel shook his head as he watched Penelope resume her place. The girl's shoulders slumped, clearly discouraged. Firiel, disparately, wore a haughty smirk upon her features, eyes ablaze with the victory. Renwyn clapped a hand over her shoulder, nodding with a grin.

"Right," muttered the instructor. "Round three. Hollyn, Fynn, your turn."

The princes found their way to the center of the circle. They stood toe to toe. Neither had yet bothered to draw their sword. Hollyn looked down the bridge of his nose at the shorter prince and scowled. "I'm getting really tired of this silent act of yours."

Fynn's icy glare stared back into Hollyn's stormy, blue eyes. His expression remained impassive. "Draw your sword, Hollyn." Fynn's tone was uncharacteristically subdued.

The taller boy drew back, raising up his sword and steeling himself. His shoulders curled slightly forward; his head dipped like a predator on the prowl. Hollyn's attention hardened as he beheld his target. "You're not going to win this," he whispered darkly.

Fynn held his sword at his side, not even making the effort to remotely protect himself with his blade. It remained casually pointed downward, the tip grazing the grassy ground. The stony deadness of the boy's personage was eerie. "You're too cocky," he replied. Fynn watched as Hollyn's grip tightened around the hilt of his sword. "Jumpy too, it would seem."

"I'm going to beat you into the ground," threatened Hollyn. "I've had enough of your attitude lately."

The black-haired prince shrugged dismissively.

"Begin!" Noel commanded.

The other ten first-years were absolutely silent as they waited, holding their collective breath to see how the bout would play out.

Hollyn lunged forward. His ankle, having sufficiently healed, no longer slowed him down. He moved with impressive speed and grace, far beyond his years, as he struck. His eyes widened with shock when Fynn's sword slammed into his own. He hadn't even noticed the other boy move, let alone have the time to adequately defend himself. Now, with their swords locked together, Hollyn leaned all his weight forward, pressing against his sword in an attempt to force Fynn back.

Fynn however, had different plans. His grip tightened with unwavering resolve. His shoulders jerked forward suddenly, an unprecedented amount of force behind the movement. The two blades shook for a second before Hollyn's gave way and the prince stumbled back. Fynn couldn't have been surer of his next move. Time seemed to fade away, slipping from the pair like grains of sand from the shore as the tide ebbed away. To Fynn, Hollyn was doing little more than standing still, his guard dropped. Ghostly eyes saw the opening, saw Hollyn's chest and throat laid unguarded.

The blood surged in Fynn's veins, his heart viciously beat against his chest, his breath quickened. But still, time seemed to no longer exist, or—in that moment—didn't apply to the two of them. It was as though he'd been watching the world go by in a blur and, as if at once, his vision was clear and sharp, and he saw things like he'd never seen them before. That was the case, Fynn supposed, as he watched Hollyn standing nearly still before him, his classmates nothing but vague shapes in the distance. The deafening silence rained down on them like the rush of raindrops that beat down upon their backs.

Hollyn was falling back. He was slipping in the gathering mud. His red hair clung to his pale skin; his blue eyes seemed nearly black in the dim light of the tempestuous afternoon. Water clung to his brows and chin; raindrops swept down the milky column of his throat, soaking his uniform until it adhered to his slender frame like a sagging, second skin.

He tried to right himself, to bring his sword up to block the attack he knew was coming. He saw a flash of red strike across Fynn's eyes like lightning through grey clouds. Hollyn's breath hitched.

To Fynn, Hollyn hadn't moved. He was motionless there before him. He looked startled. Coolly, Fynn regarded his cousin. He saw the shock in his eyes, the uncertainty as he tried to think his way out of his situation. Fynn wanted to give Hollyn the chance to compose himself, to fight back, but the other boy looked frozen in time. Fynn was tired of waiting. The searing pain in his head still hadn't gone away. His heart beat like a war drum beckoning him onward. The raven-haired boy stole that moment for his attack; he drew up his sword and swung, easily managing to batter Hollyn's upper chest with a swift cut.

As time returned to them, Fynn watched on with a clouded stare.

Hollyn fell back to the muddy ground with a sickening thump and gasped for air as a nasty pain gripped his chest. He shuddered.

Fynn knew that each breath hurt the other. He stood, towering over his fallen opponent, sword at his side. "Is that all?" he asked lamely.

Noel was about to usher the boys back to their places amongst their classmates when Hollyn, to the great surprise of everyone gathered, jumped back to his feet with his sword in hand and rushed at Fynn. Stepping back, allowing them to continue, the man watched on with concern. Hollyn was breathing raggedly, his chest clearly bruised by Fynn's strike. The look in Fynn's eyes wasn't helping to quell Noel's worry.

The princes, not content with the idea of a quick match, began expertly switching from attack to defense and back again. It was a vicious dance; each knew when to retreat and when to press forward. The precision with which each boy moved, how they bent their arms, their wrists, how their shoulders effortlessly eased and tensed, curled and squared, was oddly beautiful to behold. It was as if the two were lost in their own world, forgetting that they had an audience of increasingly agitated onlookers.

The steel of their swords clashed over and over; a metallic howl sang out with every collision, a beastly chorus melodically intoning with the thunder still bellowing around them. The rain was awash against the mud-slicked training grounds. Their uniforms were muddied and soaked, their sweat mingled and infused with the raindrops as they slid down narrow shoulders and spindly limbs.

Both boys were breathing heavily as their bout wore on, time beginning to take its toll, neither willing to lessen the severity of their efforts.

The inescapable weariness that plagued Fynn since he'd awoken in the infirmary pulled at him, made his arms feel as though they were led rather than flesh and bone. The effort it took to swing his sword was becoming arduous. He saw the fury with which Hollyn persisted; some inextinguishable fire burned within the other boy that drove him forward relentlessly. Fynn was growing exhausted combatting that sort of energy, but he refused to give in.

Hollyn drew back, his shoulders arching in that particular way that denoted a forceful strike on the horizon.

Fynn knew what to do. With speed far greater than Hollyn's, he swung his sword forward. There was a resounding gasp from the spectators as his sword's dull edge slammed into Hollyn's with enough force to crack the blade. It took only one more deftly delivered strike before Hollyn's sword broke cleanly in two. Fynn smirked as he watched the steel split; the upper half of Hollyn's blade snapped and fell to the ground, useless.

Yet again, Noel started to declare the end of the match, only to step back when Hollyn seemed to unexpectedly rally. Though bereft of a weapon, the fire-haired prince was not to be done in. His fist racked through the air. His knuckles wrapped against Fynn's cheek. Their instructor could do little more than gape in astonishment as Fynn, his head snapping to the side with the force of the hit, stumbled back only slightly. It was fair to say that no one had expected Hollyn to forgo the traditional structure of a sword fight and just punch his adversary in the face; but, then again, with Hollyn's ongoing record of unpredictability in a fight, it wasn't all too surprising.

Lurching backward, Fynn sneered. He felt something warm trace down his cheek. Reaching his free hand to his face, he ran his fingertips over the curve of his cheek; he pulled his hand back and watched as the rain washed away the remnants of red from his fingers. His cheek was a grotesque mixture of red and rain. His eyes were trained to the sight of his blood spilling into the mud at his feet. He hadn't looked back at Hollyn. Fynn remained still, forcing his breathing to calm. The pain in his cheek was nothing; it was soon forgotten.

Slowly, he turned to face Hollyn. Blood continued to pour over his freckled cheek. "Fine. If that's how we're going to fight." Fynn tossed his sword aside casually. He rolled his shoulders. His muscles ached. Fynn grinned a lopsided, mirthless grin. "Let's *fight*, then."

Hollyn managed another punch to Fynn's cheek before the slighter boy tackled him to the ground. The two went hurdling earthward, sliding into the mud, sprawling out before gathering themselves up and pounding at one another again.

Each boy wound their hands into the tunics of the other; their fingers snatched into cloth. They desperately pulled at each other until they were just hairs apart.

Using his weight as leverage, Hollyn twisted further downward, bringing Fynn with him. Fynn fell beneath Hollyn's hold and found himself pinned under the other. He tried to reach out, to push Hollyn off, but his wrist was yanked

256

down and trapped at his side. He tried to wriggle loose but could do little with his free arm to dislodge Hollyn from his perch upon his torso. Fynn twisted feverishly beneath Hollyn but was unable to successfully avoid a vicious hit to the head. His world spun and his eyes swam in the blurriness of it all.

Hollyn, realizing he had Fynn cornered, continued. He reeled his arm back before slamming his fist into Fynn's cheek yet again. Fynn's head lolled to the side meekly, but his grey eyes retained a defiant awareness that drove Hollyn mad.

The red-haired royal leaned down and whispered to Fynn, "I'll let you up if you admit your defeat and if you stop acting like such a damnable ass. We're all really getting tired of this lone wolf attitude of yours."

Fynn's cheek was nestled against the cool mud. The rain was still pouring down over them. His black hair, limp and wet, fell into his eyes, obscuring his view of Hollyn. But still, he knew that Hollyn wore a most rancorous look upon his countenance. Alas, Fynn couldn't bring himself to care. He smiled, tasting the familiar tang of blood oozing over his tongue, seeping down his lip. The red mingled with the nearly black mud beneath him. "No. I don't think so," he rasped.

Growling, Hollyn punched his fist into Fynn's head again. He hoped that, even if he were unable to beat some sense into Fynn, he could, at the very least, beat the consciousness out of him. But still, the defiant grey eyes remained twinkling there beneath him. When they turned upon him, nearly glowing in the violent light of the storm, Hollyn felt as if he were staring at something otherworldly. Those ghostly eyes seemed translucent, like every color in the world was bursting from within those irises and yet, at the same time, there was no color at all.

That was the moment Fynn chose to slip from Hollyn's grasp. His left hand swung out; his thin fingers curled into a white-knuckled fist and smashed into Hollyn's jaw. The red-haired prince was sent spinning from his perch, pitching into the mud. As Fynn rolled to his hands and knees, breathing heavily, Hollyn remained prostrate on the ground.

Fynn stood on shaking legs and stumbled toward Hollyn with an anticipated victory just within grasp. He took one more step nearer to Hollyn before the other's hand shot out and seized his ankle, dragging him back to the ground.

"Shouldn't you stop them?" asked Godryk, terrified as he watched Fynn and Hollyn brutally beating each other to bloody pulps as they slipped and slid in the mud.

Noel held Godryk back with a firm hand. He shook his head. "Sometimes, it's hard to watch…but you *need* to. War is messy and it's violent and it's scary; that's what we're preparing you for. That's what you're all here to learn. Fynn and Hollyn…well, this is a perfect example of two unshakable wills meeting." Though Noel felt more than a little apprehensive about allowing the boys to continue, he would not stop them. His grip on Godryk's arm tightened. "Let them fight it out. I think you'll find things will be much better…*for all of you*…once this is over."

Godryk struggled beneath Noel's hold. He shook his head; tears burst into his eyes and rolled down his face. "No! You've got to stop them, sir," he begged. "Please, they'll hurt each other really bad if you don't!"

"Just give up," Hollyn ground out through gnashing teeth as he pushed Fynn back to the ground.

Fynn's arms wildly flailed; one fist managed to graze Hollyn's nose. It didn't break, but the blow was forceful enough to produce a steady stream of blood from the boy's nostrils. "Not likely!" the smaller boy yelled.

Hollyn, fighting back the stinging tears that erupted in his eyes in response to the pain radiating from the center of his face, grabbed Fynn's wrist before he was able to punch him again, wrenching it behind the other boy's back. He twisted; his body weight pulled Fynn's arm up at an unnatural angle. "Give up, Fynneas, or I'll break your arm," warned Hollyn.

With all the strength he could muster, Fynn fought to pull his wrist free of Hollyn's grasp. The leverage, however, was not working in his favor. "Do it then," challenged Fynn. "Go on!"

"Don't tempt me," Hollyn threatened.

"Empty threats don't scare me, Hollyn."

As Fynn continued to fight against Hollyn's grip, the red-haired prince pulled up and back. The wretched, stomach churning sound of Fynn's arm breaking shattered the palpable tension.

Fynn didn't make a sound. Instead, despite the flaring pain shooting up his arm, over his shoulder, and into his neck and back, he jerked his elbow up until the point of his joint hit Hollyn right between the eyes. "You shouldn't hesitate after an attack," Fynn mocked. He rocked forward. He slipped free from Hollyn at last before falling back to the mud.

The taller prince jolted backward, clapping both hands over the upper bridge of his nose. He hissed in pain.

Fynn scrambled back to his feet. He felt tired beyond all belief, more tired than he had ever felt in his life. The weariness that had permeated down to his bones seemed to be festering into his very being, moldering and putrefying like something wicked taking root in his body. Like an infestation, the exhaustion was spreading. Fynn's hands felt numb. His knees shook. He hardly registered the pain emanating from his broken arm.

While Fynn observed Hollyn through half-lidded eyes, the other prince weakly stood up.

Hollyn's hands were still clamped over his face. His voice was muffled as he exclaimed, "You bastard! You've broken my nose." Blood spewed from his nostrils like some macabre waterfall, leaking over his lips, streaming between his fingers, and pouring over his chin, staining his tunic. The rain was doing little to wash away the gory traces of the injury. Furious, Hollyn glowered at the unsteady Fynn just feet away from him.

"Sir, you've *got* to stop this," Godryk tried again. Fynn looked to be on the verge of collapse and the front of Hollyn's purple tunic was reduced to a blackened mess of mud and blood congealing over the knitted fabric. "*Please*, sir."

Still putting pressure over his nose, Hollyn stepped forward. "I'm going…to beat you…into the ground. You'll be nothing but a pile of dust… when I'm done with you." He struggled to catch his breath. "I'm going to knock some sense…back into your thick head, *idiot*."

That odd term of endearment caught Fynn's attention. His eyes snapped open at once and, as if for the first time in a long while, he saw Hollyn standing before him clearly. His senses returned all at once. He saw the people around him, his year mates looking on with horror-stricken expressions; the solemn look upon Noel's face was heart wrenching. Fynn saw the blood coating Hollyn's clothes, the pain sparked in his eyes, the resilience in his stumbling stance. For the first time since he'd woken up, Fynn felt the world around him more wholly. He felt the rain and the coolness as it spread over him. He heard the clap of thunder for all the grandeur that it engendered. He saw the colors of the world all around him with all the brilliance they embodied, rather than through a dull haze as he had done for weeks on end.

Fynn glanced over his shoulder, searching his peers and finding the one he was looking for.

An awful sort of guilt nagged at him when he spied the worried look in Godryk's eyes, when he heard the pleading of the boy's voice as he begged Noel to stop the fight. There was a frantic energy to the young Redmayne as he writhed beneath their instructor's grasp, desperate to get away from the man and stand between Fynn and Hollyn. The remorse Fynn felt was awful and it nearly made him sick where he stood. He choked on his own sobs as he bit them back. He couldn't keep his cries at bay for long. Fynn's tears were lost in the rain.

Hollyn's fist beat into his cheek one last time, knocking him back down. Fynn didn't bother to try and get up. He'd been beaten. His physical exhaustion and emotional despondency collimated dangerously with Hollyn's unwavering desire to win and resulted in Fynn hunched over in the mud weeping unabashedly. His black hair hung in damp strands, swaying in front of his eyes. Cold rain rolled over the curvatures of his face. His clothes stuck to him uncomfortably. Distantly, he could hear the thunder still roaring. Despite his body-breaking weariness, Fynn felt alive – truly so – once more.

"Do I need to hit you again?" asked Hollyn.

Fynn shook his head.

"Are you going to stop acting like an ass?"

Fynn nodded.

Hollyn reached out his bloodied hand and eyed the other boy expectantly.

Fynn slowly peered up. Hollyn looked awful; bruises bloomed across his face, his knuckles were reddened and swollen, tiny cuts littered his pale flesh. Though he wore an impassive expression, his voice ever apathetic, there was a warm gleam in Hollyn's eyes. Fynn outstretched his shaking hand. He smiled tiredly when Hollyn pulled him to his feet in one swift motion.

"Thanks," Fynn whispered. "I think I needed that."

Gently, Hollyn punched Fynn's shoulder and grinned a lopsided, arrogant grin. "I *know* you did. You're a real idiot, you know?"

"I know." Fynn raked his hand through his wet hair. He took stock of his injuries, not entirely concerned about any of them. His broken arm hung limply at his side. "You're going to need to get to the infirmary," Fynn commented dully. He couldn't look away from the awful sight of so much red coloring Hollyn's uniform.

"So are you," replied Hollyn.

"We look a right mess." Fynn laughed.

Smirking, Hollyn agreed, "Like death warmed over."

"You win," Fynn acknowledged.

"Of course," snorted Hollyn. "But there will be other fights."

"You won't win them all," Fynn assured him with a wink.

"That's pretty confident talk coming from the boy who hasn't won a single fight against me." Hollyn's laugh made blood bubble out of his nose.

Fynn shrugged. "For now." His attention roved over Hollyn's form, suddenly realizing that the other boy seemed to have gotten a bit taller. He scowled. "But that doesn't mean I'm not coming for you. I'll be right on your heels."

"Wouldn't expect anything less."

Nodding, Fynn said, "Thank you again…for knocking me out of that… *whatever* it was."

"I'll be here to beat some sense into you any time," Hollyn joked. "Just don't make it a habit, alright? The quiet loner persona doesn't really fit you."

"Right." Fynn chuckled.

As the two boys began to limp back to their places amongst the circle, Hollyn hastily reminded Fynn, "This *doesn't* mean we're friends."

Fynn worked hard to stifle his laughter. "Wouldn't dream of it."

Godryk leaned closer to his instructor and asked quietly, "How'd you know that would work?"

Noel continued staring at the princes as they stumbled over, taking up their places while their shoulders slumped. "When I was younger, my older brothers—Vallon and Virgil—used to get into these really annoying moods. One of them would stop talking to the other, to all of us really, and the other one would reach the point where they'd had enough. It happened so often that we all eventually learned the best way to sort them out was to let them beat the sense back into each other. Honestly, at first, I thought it was horrid to let them hit each other like that. But time and again it proved to work, and things would go back to normal." Noel shrugged. "I supposed it would be the same with Hollyn and Fynn."

Once again, their class concluded with Hollyn's ultimate victory over the other first-years, made even more impressive by his still occasionally bleeding nose and rather pronounced, reignited limp. Upon Noel's declaration of Hollyn's sustained champion title, Hollyn looked as though he were ready to collapse with fatigue. When at last Noel dismissed them, the group of twelve headed back to the castle at a far more sedate pace than usual.

Hollyn grumbled his disapproval as he slung his arm around Fynn's shoulders, settling some of his weight against the slighter boy. Fynn's arm encircled Hollyn's waist, keeping him carefully close as they proceeded up the twisting road. "I don't need your help," Hollyn insisted for the fifth time, though his voice was clearly pained.

"Whatever," groused Fynn, continuing to lever Hollyn's weight against his own body as they slowly continued onward, flanked by the other ten first-years.

"Don't ever fight like that again," Lux warned while sidling up beside the royal pair.

"I wouldn't have had to hit him so hard, so many times, if he didn't spend the last few weeks acting like a damn ghost," Hollyn argued back.

"I'm sorry," Fynn whispered, head hanging. "I'm really sorry. It just... all got to be too much."

"How's your arm?" Godryk inquired, eyeing Fynn curiously. "We all thought Hollyn had broken it. But you seem alright."

"It doesn't hurt, really," Fynn answered. "It's a bit numb, but I can move it some."

"I'm sure Blythe or Imogen will have something to say about this," Albie peeped, gesturing toward the haggard looking messes that were, in fact, royalty. "You both look awful."

"We could just *not* tell them," Fynn suggested half-heartedly.

Hollyn quirked a brow, intoning flatly, "Do you really think Noel will forget? I'm sure the moment he's back at the castle, he'll be telling them. Or *worse*, he'll tell Moriah."

Fynn practically deflated at the mention of the man's name. "You're right. There's no getting out of this mess."

"So," Lux began carefully, "care to tell us *why* you were acting so weird?"

"It's a long story," Fynn answered softly. "And I don't really care to talk about it right now."

As the dozen stepped into the welcoming glumness of the quiet castle, they were taken aback by the little, red fox skipping towards them. But Fynn, Godryk, and Hollyn recognized that fox all too well and their faces went alight at the sight of him merrily approaching, sly smile perfectly in place.

Godryk knelt down, holding his arms out and welcoming the fox to him, cuddling the creature into his chest as he stood. He giggled as a cold nose twitched over his neck; the furry creature curled into his embrace, tiny paws kneading his shoulder. Godryk's hand gently stroked over too-large ears. "Hello, Dug," he greeted brightly.

Fynn's head tilted curiously as he asked, "Dug, what're you doing out and about?"

Hollyn slipped from Fynn's hold. He righted himself carefully, quite mindful of his aching limbs and overwhelming exhaustion. He surmised, "Moriah's close, then?"

Upon hearing his master's name, Dug peeked from Godryk's arms and stared intently at the prince. His ears twitched, paws still kneading. The fox began to chatter as if in response to Hollyn's inquiry.

"I suppose that's a yes," Fynn guessed.

Dug settled back into Godryk's arms comfortably, his long tail swishing back and forth. "So, are you two headed straight for the infirmary? Or back to the tower?" Redmayne asked.

"You should really go to the infirmary wing," Penelope insisted with concern. Her hands fidgeted at her side as she avoided the princes' leveled stares. She added meekly, "You're hurt."

Fynn turned to Hollyn and asked, "How long do you think we can put it off before they get mad?"

"Maybe a few hours?" replied Hollyn after a moment's thought.

"Best to get it over with, I suppose," muttered Fynn.

Hollyn agreed morosely, "Probably."

Godryk started toward the infirmary, Dug still held carefully in his arms. He glanced back over his shoulder. "Well, come on then!"

"Where are you going?" Hollyn questioned, still not making a move forward.

"I'll come with you." Godryk smiled gently. "Otherwise, I don't really trust that you'd both *actually* go. You and Fynn, you have this nasty habit of just wandering off whenever you feel like it."

"Do not," huffed Hollyn defiantly.

"Sure, alright," Godryk laughed. He resumed his path toward the medical wing. "Come on, keep up."

Before either prince had the wherewithal or mindfulness to protest, Lux's arms hooked around each of theirs and began marching them off, dutifully following Godryk. She pulled them along as the two whined their protestations. "Honestly, you two behave like toddlers, did you know?" she grumbled.

When Imogen and Blythe, both working in the infirmary that evening while their charges took their evening meal in their dormitory, saw the four children walk in, their brows collectively furrowed with concern.

Imogen was the first to approach. She looked between Hollyn and Fynn before she asked, "What's happened now?"

Blythe shook her head. "You two are in here more than anyone else."

Lux led the boys by their arms over to two of the empty infirmary beds. The princes settled on the edges of their respective perches and waited for the women to begin their incessant clucking as they checked them over.

Blythe's hand reached under Fynn's chin and tipped the boy's head to the side gently. "Those are some awful bruises you've got," she commented. The pad of her thumb ghosted over his lip. "That looks like it hurt."

"Could you check his arm?" Godryk asked, seating himself beside Fynn. "It looked like he broke it."

Fynn elbowed him. "Really?" He pouted.

Godryk held up his hands defensively; Dug dropping into his lap. "It wasn't like she wasn't going to notice."

Blyth took the injured arm gingerly into her hands and examined it. The boy's wrist was swollen; bruising marbled the snowy flesh. She ran her hand from his wrist to his shoulder, frowning all the while. "Well, it's definitely broken. *Badly* too, it looks like."

As Blythe took her leave from Fynn and began searching for rags, water, and cloth for a sling, Imogen continued her examination of the other prince. She lightly touched the bridge of his nose, careful not to apply too much pressure. "Does it still hurt?" she queried.

"No," mumbled Hollyn, looking away.

"Would you tell me if it did?"

Hollyn said nothing.

"That's what I thought." Imogen stood straight, still staring down at the boy. "Your nose is most certainly broken. It's going to hurt for a few days. I can't do much for it, unfortunately. But," she tilted her head, attentive eyes settling over his heavily bruised jaw and cheeks, "that isn't the only problem. Those are some nasty bruises you've got there. I can't do anything much for them either, but I want to at least clean up your cuts."

Lux sat beside Hollyn. She nudged him gently in the shoulder. "Are you alright?" she asked softly.

He nodded.

"I'm glad you got through to him," she whispered.

"Me too," Hollyn admitted. Catching himself, he added, "I was getting tired of his attitude."

"Right," Lux snickered.

As Blythe tied the sling around Fynn's shoulder tightly, the boy asked, "We won't have to stay overnight in the infirmary, will we?"

"No." She smiled. "Not *this* time." Blythe looked over her shoulder at Hollyn, who was pouting under Imogen's careful ministrations. "You two got lucky." She returned her attention to Fynn. "But you'll definitely be feeling this in the morning."

"Great," groaned Fynn. He ran his free hand over Dug's head softly.

Imogen grinned down at her patient. She announced, "Right, all done!" She gave Hollyn a stiff pat on the shoulder. "Off with you both and try not to get into any more trouble."

Hollyn just stared at the woman oddly before laughing. "I can't make any promises."

Fynn slipped from the edge of his bed and stood. "Same."

Gathering Dug into his arms once more, Godryk nodded to each of the women before proceeding out of the wing, quick to take up pace with the fleeing princes.

Lux raced up to the boys, an annoyed look on her face. "You both need to be heading back to the tower. I'm sure we can have some food brought up. But you two need some rest!"

Hollyn stopped, considering her words for a moment. "You're probably right," he relented. His head throbbed terribly, and he was struggling to breathe out of his damaged nose. "I think I'll pass on food, though. I'm tired."

As the red-haired prince turned to head back to the tower, Godryk jumped over and sidled up in step with him. "I'm off too! It's been a long day." He looked back, regarding the weary Fynn left behind and offered a weak nod. "Coming?" he asked hopefully.

Fynn shook his head. "Not yet."

Shrugging, Godryk called back, "See you later, then."

Lux and Fynn were left standing alone in the corridor. The mid-evening quiet had descended upon Morancy and so, for just a moment, the two reveled in the peacefulness of the unusual silence. Lux stared at Fynn warmly, concern quite evident in her summery stare. "You must be tired," she ventured.

"I am," admitted Fynn.

"Why don't you head off to bed?"

He traced his hand over the coarse fabric of the sling pinning his arm to his torso. "I don't really want to go to sleep yet."

"Hungry?"

He shook his head. "Not particularly. You should go, though. You've got to be starving after your fight with Renwyn."

"Not really," she lied. "With his arm still sore, he didn't put up much of a fight."

"Lux?"

The girl smiled. "Yes?"

"Care for a walk?" Fynn held his hand out to her, waiting.

Taking the proffered hand, she asked, "Where are we off to?"

"I've got someone I'd like you to meet," Fynn replied, leading her back down to the castle entrance.

The two stepped, hand in hand, into the night. It was, like many nights on Dier Island, a comfortable evening with a soft breeze. Fynn led Lux down the walkway before they stepped into the road and headed down its twists and turns toward More Town. As they continued their stroll, Fynn turned his attention skyward, admiring the silvery lights spangling the sky. The storm had gone and, in its stead, left behind a most brilliant array of vibrantly shining stars.

When Fynn finally spoke, his voice was soft and shy, so unlike his usual brashness. "You asked earlier…about why I was upset."

"Yes."

"Do you still want to know?"

He felt her squeeze his hand in response.

"I had this dream. I had this really *awful* dream. Well, it was more like a nightmare, I suppose. It was about the day of the funerals in the capital." He could tell her hold on his hand was tightening even more; his fingers had practically gone numb from the force of her constriction. "I saw it all happen again. I saw my father just…lying there…in a pool of his blood. He was just there, *dead*. It was like I was there again, you know? I could feel the people running by and smell the blood and hear the screaming. It was awful." Fynn lost himself looking up at the stars and, for just a second, he forgot Lux was even there. He continued in a flat, detached voice, "And there was this man I know. He was there too. And he told me things that I don't think are true…and things that I don't think make a lot of sense. It's stupid, really. It was just a nightmare. But ever since I woke up…well, ever since I had gone to Batsbeckon this summer, really…it just feels like there's so much going on around me and no one will tell me anything. It's like everything is just one, big, stupid secret."

Finally, Fynn looked away from the stars. His attention immediately swung down to their interlocked hands. He felt his cheeks burn and jerked his hand from Lux's. Nervously, he looked back at the girl; she was staring at him with an amused look on her face. His cheeks flushed even more. "Sorry! Sorry, I didn't mean to ramble like that." Promptly, he looked away from her and focused on the road. "Sorry," Fynn mumbled again.

"It's alright," Lux promised. "I don't mind. I don't think you were rambling. I think you've just had a difficult few months."

"What?"

"Well, it must be hard. You've lost a lot this summer and then with that nightmare you had, I don't blame you for being upset." She turned to him crossly, her brows pinched together as she warned, "But don't go off on your own again like no one cares because we *do*. You've been absolutely terrible these last few weeks."

Fynn bit his lip anxiously. He muttered, "Sorry."

"I forgive you…*this* time." She smirked. "Don't do it again though."

"I'll try not to." Fynn chuckled breathily. He inhaled for a moment. He readied himself for his next words. "Lux, can I tell you something else?"

"Sure."

He looked back up at the stars, his free hand fidgeted at his side. "It's not something I really want to talk about, but not talking about it is making me sick, I think. Moriah or Noel, they'd be the best to tell, but I just don't want to tell them. Can you promise not to tell anyone? Please?"

Lux's hand shot out in a flash and caught Fynn's, instantly arresting his nervous fiddling. They stopped where they stood upon the road and she looked at him sternly. Her nod was curt, quick but assuring. "Of course."

Fynn's shoulders sagged as the weariness of the day once again fell down upon him. His hand still held in hers, he began once more leading them toward the small town.

He started, "The day of the fire, I didn't remember much of it at first. But lately, I've been having these dreams." He chanced a look at her; his eyes threatened to erupt with the tears he'd been holding back for weeks. "I used to love napping. But lately, well, I just try to avoid sleeping as much as I can. I have these dreams and I suppose I'd rather just be tired than have to suffer through them." The prince tilted his head back, finding solace in the stars once more. "When I'm dreaming, I think I remember more and more of *that* day. I don't know how or why, for that matter, but I think the fire was my fault."

"Fynn, that's impossible," Lux argued.

He shook his head. "I've seen things I thought were impossible happen. *So have you.* Think about it. You were there that day and saw Moriah summon up fire from nothing! All he did was snap his fingers."

"You think…that has something to do with the fire in the castle?"

The prince nodded. "I'm not sure *how*. I've been trying to figure it out. Fiona…my big sister, well she's the one who likes mysteries and she's a lot better at piecing these sorts of things together. I wish she were here. She'd probably have this all figured out by now!" He laughed, thinking of how Fiona tended to throw herself into her research when something piqued her interest. He supposed that was probably what she was doing right now. "I miss her," Fynn lamented.

"You two are close?"

Fynn couldn't help the genuine grin that twisted his lips. "We are. She raised me, really. My father was busy a lot. My grandfather too. Fiona was the one who looked after me when I was little. Well, she *still* looks after me."

"I bet she misses you just as much as you miss her," asserted Lux.

"I hope you're right," Fynn said. For a moment, he looked off toward the harbor as if he could stare far enough across the sea and find Fiona.

"I *know* I am. Now, where are we off to?"

They headed into More Town. The familiar, sleepy nature of the little town was comforting. Fynn led Lux to the Wayward Turtle Tavern and there they found, not at all to his surprise, Minnie rushing down the stairs to greet them. The little girl launched herself at Fynn, painfully jostling his injured arm. He didn't say anything, he didn't even wince. He wrapped his good arm around the little girl. "Minnie! Sorry, I meant to visit sooner," he said cheerily.

Minnie looked up at him, her brown eyes an amber hue in the firelight of the tavern which, as usual, was mostly empty. "I knew you'd come back."

Fynn gently guided her along to one of the tables, Lux at his side. "How's Buttons?"

The child broke into an ear-to-ear grin. "His wing is all better!"

"Really? Has he been able to fly?" inquired Fynn.

Minnie shook her head; golden curls tumbled in front of her eyes. "Not yet. Nan says he still needs to rest a lot before he can fly."

"Buttons?" asked Lux, confused.

Fynn leaned over and whispered in her ear, "It's a long story but, to make it short, Buttons is a bat."

"Oh…alright," Lux nodded, slightly dumbfounded.

"Who is she?" questioned Minnie.

The three settled down at one of the tables. Fynn glanced over at Lux, eyes dazzling like ice in the torchlight. "Minnie, this is Lux." He nodded his head toward the small child. "Lux, this is Minnie."

A tiny hand waved. "Hello. Are you friends with Fynny?"

The older girl nodded. Her voice was warm and sweet like honey as she replied, "I am. I go to Morancy." Lux looked all around the tavern before asking, "Do you live here?"

"Yes!" chirped Minnie. "I live here with Nan."

"Nan?" repeated Lux.

The sound of shuffling was heard, and all three children looked up to not only find the elderly woman in question but, at her side, the familiar, tall form of Moriah looming. Nan regarded the trio fondly, her attention hovering over Lux. She said sweetly, "You must be Fynn's friend. Welcome, welcome, child. I'm Nan and it seems you've already met Minnie." She looked to the window and back to the children. "It's chilly out tonight. Would you like something warm to drink?"

Minnie nodded enthusiastically, bouncing in her seat. "Yes, please!"

And with that, Nan went shuffling off, leaving Moriah to stand there, coolly staring at the children. He quirked a black brow. He sounded predictably bored as he asked, "So, is this what you two do with your free time?"

Guiltily, Fynn averted his eyes and studied a notch in the surface of the wooden table.

Lux's cheeks went red, burning fiercely as she tried to respond. "No... no, sir...it's well...we just were going for a walk...and...and well now we're here."

Amused by the girl's stammered reply, Moriah rooted himself firmly where he stood. He crossed his long arms over his chest and sighed. "Fynneas?"

The boy blanched. "Yes?"

"Should you be out walking around? I heard you and Hollyn got into a bit of a fight this afternoon," drawled the lord commander.

Fynn shrugged, despite knowing the gesture annoyed Moriah beyond reason. "It's only a broken arm. I'll be fine."

"Be that as it may, you really *should* be in bed," the man in black continued.

"Uncle Moriah," Minnie peeped, patting the chair beside her own, "sit."

Lux could do little more than stare in astonishment as one of Morancy's more intimidating instructors obediently followed the instructions of a small child.

Gracefully, Moriah lowered down into the seat. He scooped Minnie into his arms easily and held her there in his lap. His sharp, emerald eyes, however, hadn't faltered and remained staring between Fynn and Lux. His arm curled around Minnie; his hand absentmindedly played with her tawny curls. "How have you been feeling?" Moriah asked. He continued to study Fynn. The boy looked tired. Dark smudges were beneath his pale eyes.

"Better now," Fynn sheepishly answered.

"I see," Moriah muttered dully. "I'm assuming Hollyn at least had the good sense to get some rest?"

"Yes, sir," Lux dutifully replied. "He headed back to the dormitory right after the lady matron tended to his injuries."

"Sensible," Moriah concluded.

"Quite," agreed Lux.

"*Lux* is it?" the lord commander inquired curiously. His chin rested atop Minnie's head. His lip curled at the corner; the faintest beginnings of a smirk squirmed onto his features.

"Yes, sir."

"What compelled you to spend your time out here, all the way in More Town? I would've thought you'd be tired after your lessons."

"I didn't want Fynn to go wandering alone at night, sir. Not after he'd been hurt," said the girl.

The man considered this for a moment. His long fingers rolled a strand of golden hair back and forth idly. "That's quite *thoughtful* of you."

"Thank you, sir."

Fynn fidgeted uncomfortably in his seat. His teeth were practically gnashing over his lower lip, nose wrinkling, cheeks burning brightly. "Moriah?" he chanced.

"Hmm?" Moriah mumbled lazily, turning to look at the boy.

"Were you down here for your own social visit? Or did you know we'd be here?" Fynn asked, still unable to look at the man across from him.

"Clever boy," cooed the lithe lord commander. "Clever indeed." Moriah leaned back, pulling Minnie back with him. The girl leaned against his chest; her head lolled tiredly against his shoulder. He smirked.

Confused, Fynn leaned a bit closer to the table and that's when he saw it. The oh so very familiar red fuzz of a certain fox came into view before the animal leapt up onto Moriah's knees, nuzzling his tiny nose against the girl's outstretched hands. Cheekily, Dug looked at Fynn before happily closing his eyes, enjoying the tiny hands running through his fur.

"Dug," muttered Fynn. "Of course."

Lux looked between Moriah and Fynn. "I don't get it."

Accusingly, Fynn griped, "Dug, I thought you were with Godryk! When'd you sneak off and tell Moriah we'd left the castle? Little traitor, you."

"Now, now, Fynneas," chortled the man as he saw the boy become far more flustered than awkwardly embarrassed. "Don't go blaming Skullduggery because you and little Lady Astor here are bad at sneaking around."

Nan returned, setting down mugs of warm milk for the three children. Seating herself beside Moriah in Minnie's vacated chair, she asked, "So, what brings you out to More Town? Another stroll is it, Fynneas?"

"Wasn't tired," he casually responded before he sipped from his mug.

"If your lessons are so *easy* for the two of you, I can have a word with your instructors. I believe, per the king's request, we were ordered to prepare you much quicker than usual. But it would seem we're still being far too lenient on you lot." Moriah grinned. "What do you think, Minnie? Have we been too easy on them?"

Minnie's small hands grasped Moriah's, yanking with her meager strength as she pouted, "Don't be mean, Uncle Moriah!"

Placatingly, the tall man patted her little head. "I'm sorry, Minnie. I'll try to be nicer to the children."

Minnie's dark eyes shone as she looked back to Fynn and giggled. "You tell me if he's mean to you, Fynny."

The prince nodded the affirmative. "Anything you say, Minnie."

"So, I heard Moriah call you an Astor," said Nan, looking at Lux. "You've two brothers already training at Morancy, yes?"

"Yes. Percy's in his fifth year. Byron's in his sixth. They're both in the Armada Division," answered the girl.

"Good lads," Moriah commented. "Byron's a talented boy, quite smart."

"Percy's always been the fun one, more concerned about the girls around than his responsibilities," Lux added.

"I've noticed," Moriah dryly agreed. Suddenly interested, Moriah asked the first-years, "Have you two given any thought to which division you'd like to be appointed to?"

Lux's hands balled in the fabric of her leggings. She sat a bit straighter and squared her shoulders. Her blue eyes continued to flick from the craggy table, up to Moriah, and back down. "I know women go to the Archer Brigade or Medical Corps."

"Not always," the man noted wanly.

Lux nodded quickly. "Yes. *Not always*. I don't think I'd like either."

Cocking his head at an angle, brows raised ever so slightly, the slender man regarded the girl. "Oh?"

"No. I'd prefer Cavalry, I think."

"There hasn't been a woman appointed to the cavalry in the last forty years," Nan interjected.

"I know. But that doesn't matter." Lux grinned. There was a confidence about her as she spoke of her desire to be placed into the entirely male dominated division. "But that doesn't mean I can't end up there."

"It certainly doesn't." Moriah smirked. "It certainly doesn't at all." He looked to Fynn. "And what about you?"

"Armada, I'd wager," Nan guessed.

"*Anything* but Armada," Fynn whined.

In response to the confusion written all over the elderly woman's face, Lux cheeped, "He isn't one for the water."

Fynn looked up to meet Moriah's steady gaze. He felt a surge of defiant assurance sweep through him. His voice was calm, steady. "I want to be placed in the Paladin Division."

"Is that so?" Moriah asked, a lopsided grin pulling at the corner of his mouth.

The same askew smile punctuated the prince's own features as he nodded with a profound sense of determination. "Yes. I'll *show* you I can do it. Just you watch."

14

TEAM THREEE AND A NIGHT IN THE JUNGLE

"First-years!"

The voice yelling—definitely yelling—was somehow still quite muffled sounding.

"First-years!"

The voice was getting louder. It was a familiar voice, Fynn supposed. But, even with that vague recollection, he didn't care to open his eyes.

"First-years! Get up this *instant!*"

Fleetingly, the boy thought he should obey the command. But his bed was so warm and soft, he didn't want to leave it.

"Enough of this!" The disembodied voice sounded angry.

Before Fynn had the chance to wonder why the voice was so angry, water spilled over him. Eyes snapping open, the boy jerked to the side, only to become tangled in his bedding. He fell in a wet, cocooned mound upon the stone floor. Trying to blink away the bleariness, he saw that the torches around the dormitory were lit. To his left and right, the other first-year boys yawned, disentangled themselves from their blankets, and confusedly rubbed the sleepiness from their eyes as they stretched.

"What's going on?" Fynn asked as he rose to his feet.

"First-years!" The damnable voice was screaming from the common room.

Curious as to who had thrown water over him, Fynn scowled as he looked around the room with newly awake, sharper eyes. Moriah and Benadykt stood amongst the tired boys, empty buckets in their arms and smirks stretched over their faces.

"Figures," grumbled Fynn as he tossed his bedding back upon his mattress.

"Now that you're all awake," began Benadykt cheerily, "Lord Humbert wants you all dressed and ready in the common room." He noted the bedraggled look of the eight children and snorted a laugh. "Best be quick about it. He's already mad."

"Be advised, you'll want to bring your cloaks," added Moriah as he left the dormitory, headed for the commons.

"Right, bring your cloak and bring a knife. That's all you'll be needing," instructed Benadykt, taking his leave from them.

"What do you thinks going on?" asked Godryk.

Renwyn shrugged. "Don't know. But I'm sure, whatever it is, we're not going to like it."

"Why do you think we need our knives?" Hogan wondered aloud.

"We should get dressed," Hollyn said evenly. He was the first to slip on his tunic and lace up his boots before pulling his black cloak over his shoulders. It had been four days since the two princes had beat one another senseless, but the bruising covering Hollyn's nose and just under his eyes was still rather prominent against his normally pale, freckled skin. He combed back his red hair, trying to maintain a semblance of being well kempt, but the crooked lean of his cloak and stained tunic detracted from that image. He fastened his knife to his belt and made his way to the commons, leaving the other seven boys to ready themselves.

Once dressed, Fynn and Godryk, ever curious, went trotting down the stairs in search of Nyle and the others. The girls had already assembled and stood in a semi-circle, Hollyn amongst them, chatting with quieted voices. Moriah and Benadykt stood together; they whispered lowly and cast bemused glances toward the gathered first-years. Nyle was seated in one of the plush armchairs in the common room, a rather annoyed look upon his sagging, old face. Fynn noticed Odette and Noel entering into the chambers from the tower stairway. Noel yawned, brushed his hair back, and shook the sleep from his person with a roll of his shoulders. The last few boys soon joined them, each looking tired and confused.

Nyle clapped his hands and, at once, all eyes in the room fixed upon him. Silence rang. "Right! Now that you've all *finally* joined us here, we can begin." He sprang to his feet with the energy of a man far younger than himself. "Sluggishness, children, will be the death of you! If the enemy descends upon your camp at night, it'd behoove you to move *quickly*, *promptly*, lest you find yourself in Death's most unwelcome, chilly embrace." He skulked around the room, frowning. "As I'm sure you're aware, you were not scheduled to have Survival Strategies and Tactics today. *Alas!* One must always be prepared for the unexpected and, thus, render the unexpected *expected!*"

Fynn rolled his eyes. "It's too early for this," he muttered.

Albie laughed under his breath.

"Now, you've been instructed to bring with you only your cloaks and a knife. Have these instructions been followed?" queried Lord Humbert.

"Yes, sir," the twelve replied in a weary chorus.

"Excellent, children! Well done. Your ability to follow instructions will see that you don't die a most wretched and painful death." Nyle had gone back to standing frighteningly still, his hawk-like eyes piercing each one of them. "Today, your regular lessons have been cancelled. Rather, I should say, for the following week they've been cancelled."

"Why, sir?" asked Ollie.

"Petulant child, I was getting to that!" snapped the old man. "*As I was saying*, your regularly scheduled lessons have been postponed. This morning you will be led to a site predetermined by your instructors. You will be broken into three teams. Your objective, children, is to find the other two teams, reassemble your twelve-man squad, and make it out of the jungle. You've been given a time limit of one week. Should you fail to return to the castle in that allotted time, there will be consequences."

"What…what kind of consequences?" Hogan inquired tentatively.

"We will discuss that should the time arrive," replied Nyle. "Any more questions, children?"

"Do we get a map?" asked Albie.

"Foolish child! You'll not need a map. Will you always have a map should you be lost or separated from your battalion in battle?" raged the old man.

Albie shook his head. "Probably not."

"Exactly, boy! *Exactly*. You will have only your knife and your wits, and I do suggest you keep both sharp while you're out there in the jungle," continued the elderly instructor. Dramatically, he clapped his withered hands together. "Now, it is time to break you into your teams."

Odette stepped forward. She looked rather displeased with having to be up at such an hour. "Team One will be Wilder Dangerfield, Hogan Greenfinch, Oliver Dangerfield, and Firiel Blackthorn." She waved them forward, "Come stand here."

Benadykt was the next to step forward. He announced, "Team Two will be Georgina Belclaire, Albatross Shoregore, Lux Astor, and Godryk Redmayne. If you'll all, please, join me over here."

"Team Three," Moriah began flatly, "will be Hollyn Fog, Fynneas Fog, Renwyn Strangelove, and Penelope Bridger."

Nyle appeared by team three and observed them with a critical eye. He reached out, grasping Hollyn's chin, and pulled his face forward. His eyes narrowed as they roved over the dark bruises muddling the center of the boy's face, the horrid yet healing greenish bruise over his temple, and the scab where his lip had been cut. "How are you feeling, child?"

"Fine, sir," the prince answered evenly.

Nyle huffed and turned his attention to Fynn who, despite feeling as though his arm was perfectly well mended, was still instructed to wear a sling for another few days. The bruising that had marred his features was entirely healed and only the smallest trace of a scar over the corner of his upper lip denoted that there was ever an injury sustained there. "And you?"

Fynn nodded. "Fine, sir."

"Good lads." Nyle smiled. "Strong as steel." He straightened up and said to the twelve, "Now that you've been broken into your teams, you will follow your team leader to your start site. Once there, they will provide you with further instructions. I do *hope* to see you in a week, children."

Noel went around the room, handing each of the instructors a bag. When he came to team three, he stopped and took the time to linger. He yawned, laughing when the infectious action caused his brother to do the same. Noel grinned and said, "Not a morning person, eh? You never were."

Moriah, having snatched the bag from his brother, shook his head and grumbled unintelligibly under his breath. He reached in and pulled out thin pieces of black fabric. "Alright, listen up. You're going to be blindfolded." The tall man proceeded to tie the fabric around each of their eyes, effectively rendering the four children blind. Reaching into the bag once more, Moriah pulled from it four short pieces of thin twine. "Right." He sighed. "Hold out your hands together. I'm going to bind them."

"What do you mean you're going to *bind* them?" Penelope asked nervously.

"It wasn't my idea." Moriah began his work, carefully wrapping the twine around four sets of scrawny wrists.

"Lastly," he said, once his work was completed and each child found their hands tightly bound together. "I'm going to hand you a section of rope. Hold onto it tightly, alright? I'm going to use it to lead you to your start site. Keep hold, I don't feel like having to come back for you if you lag behind. Understood?"

"Yes, sir," each of the four whispered hesitantly.

As instructed, they obediently took hold of their section of the rope and held tightly, too scared to let go. They felt the rope tug forward and so they stepped in that direction; they allowed themselves to be led by the rope like dogs on a leash—blind dogs that is. Team three carefully made their way down the stairs. They could hear the other two teams whispering anxiously amongst themselves. It was once they'd made it outside that the three teams diverged and the distant murmurings of the other eight first-years grew fainter and fainter until they could no longer be heard.

The chill of the morning air began to fade; the first tendrils of sunlight poked through the clouds and reached out to them, but the warmth was fleeting and then gone from them once they entered into the overgrowth of the jungle. The canopy was so heavy overhead that scarcely any light managed to get through the great net of leaves and twisting lattice of branches. It was cold and damp in the jungle. The earth gave way beneath their booted feet more so than it did in the fields or hills of the island. Here, amidst the towering trees and the blooming brush, stepping over the overgrowth of gnarling branches that arched from the earth like dolphins from the sea, they found themselves in an unknown world.

Since they'd all come to Morancy, Nyle had been training them to build fires, find food, make camp, and construct traps to hunt and protect themselves from the wild. But all of this had been done in the fields around the castle, never in the jungle. They'd been told to not wander through the tree line, to never stray from the fields and roads into the foreboding wild kingdom of the tropical forests. And they had all done well to listen, each of the twelve rightfully too scared to go off gallivanting deep into the trees. Yet presently, there they were, working their way through the brush to their assigned starting position.

They'd been walking for what seemed to be hours when at last Moriah stopped and announced, "This is where you'll be starting from." He gathered the rope from their shaking hands and continued, "A word of advice. The quicker you get those blindfolds and restraints off, the better."

"You mean you're leaving us blindfolded and tied up?" Penelope shuddered.

"Yes." Moriah's response was flat; a slight air of annoyance darkened the word. "You're to get your blindfolds and restraints off. That is the first objective. The longer you're deprived of sight, the more danger you'll be in. Once you're all freed, you're going to need to work together." Vibrant green eyes glanced between the three boys, obviously knowing full well that

Penelope was not going to be the problem child amongst the four-man team. "Your goal is to find the other teams. Once you've all regrouped, you'll make your way back to the castle. You have seven days." He glanced beyond them, out to the depths of the jungle. "A word of warning." He looked back to the four children. "Try and get out of here quicker than that."

"Yes, sir." Renwyn nodded.

"I'll be off, then. Good luck, children." As he prepared to leave, he stopped beside Hollyn. He leaned down and whispered softly, "Stay safe."

The prince nodded.

"And keep an eye on Fynneas."

Hollyn nodded again.

Moriah's hand fell over the prince's shoulder and squeezed it reassuringly. "You'll be fine." With that, Moriah left them.

"Alright," Hollyn announced to the others, "let's get started. We need to be out of these restraints and getting a camp ready before nightfall."

Fynn, with his arm still firmly wrapped in a sling, had his hands bound by his side, rather than out in front like the other three. This made twisting his shoulders and using his hands to edge off the blindfold much more difficult. He managed to lean his head down, pushing his good shoulder against the fabric until it fell from his face. The last of the group to get his blindfold off, Fynn sighed as he set to work trying to free his hands. Their position made it a challenge, as did the occasional twinge of pain from his mostly healed arm. He was muttering obscenities to himself when Hollyn approached, having freed his own hands already, and started to untie him.

"Thanks," Fynn huffed, happy his hands were loose.

"You're slowing us down." Hollyn smirked. "Couldn't just leave you tied up, no matter how funny watching you struggle was."

"Bastard," muttered Fynn.

"*Idiot*," snorted Hollyn.

When Hollyn turned to face the other two members of their party, he was calm and levelheaded. "Penelope, Renwyn, go have a look around the surrounding area. See if you can find anything that may be useful or maybe figure out which direction we should head in."

Though Penelope had obediently listened, nodding her head and taking off within sight of the others, Renwyn folded his arms over his chest. He quirked one brow and asked haughtily, "Who put you in charge?"

The ferocity with which Hollyn rounded on the other boy was alarming and Fynn found himself backing away from his cousin slightly, a tad unnerved by the abrupt shift in mood.

Hollyn edged closer to Renwyn; his voice dropped until it was an icy whisper, "Someone needs to keep us organized and on task."

"You think just because you're a prince, you get to make the rules?" Renwyn asked hotly. "Titles don't matter here. You haven't proven yourself any more than the rest of us! If anything, all you've proven while you're here is that you've got a nasty temper." He pointed to Fynn. "Just look what you did to his damn arm! Not the sort of attitude our *team leader* should have."

"Who said anything about a *team leader*?" asked Hollyn blandly. The look in his eyes spoke of his mounting disinterest in the conversation. "And more to your point, Renwyn, what have you done to prove you can lead? All you do in lessons is swing your sword like it's a club or ask Georgie to tie your knots. You couldn't hit the broadside of a stable the way you shoot an arrow and instead of working on it, all I ever see you do is whine about it." Blue eyes narrowed. "Brute strength isn't going to get us out of the jungle. Tact, strategy, and efficient teamwork will."

"All you do is argue with Fynn," snapped Renwyn. He shoved Hollyn hard against his chest. "You broke his arm to win a fight. What does that say about you? He's one of us. Don't you remember what the vice lord said? We need to stick together, act like a unit."

Fynn was annoyed, not at all in the mood to listen to an argument, and one that was growing more heated by the second, so early in the morning. The moment he saw Hollyn stumbled back, Fynn bolted for the other two boys. He steadied Hollyn with his good hand, bracing his palm against the other's back. He scowled over his cousin's shoulder. "This isn't the time for this. We've got to get moving. We have to find the others. The longer we're here, the worse it's going to be."

Hollyn jerked away from Fynn. He hissed, "I didn't need your help."

The smaller prince shrugged his shoulders. "I know you didn't. But I'm going to help anyway."

As Hollyn pulled further away from Fynn, he said, "You know, you're really annoying."

Fynn smiled. "I've been told that before, actually."

Renwyn once again crossed his arms over his chest. His cheeks had gone red. "I think we should take a vote."

"On what, exactly? I think we'd come to the unanimous decision that you're an idiot," Hollyn bid with a glance back to Renwyn and a wry smile.

"That's *my* name," Fynn chuckled.

"Right." Hollyn nodded, still smiling. "You're *both* idiots, then."

"I get it. You call *all* the lads idiots," Fynn snickered.

"What?" chuckled Hollyn. "Thought you were special, did you?"

Fynn shrugged again. He started looking around for Penelope, ignoring the fight that had only just dissipated. "Where's Penelope? I don't see her anymore."

"Hmm?" Hollyn turned and scanned the surrounding brush, not seeing the lone female member of their team. "Penelope?"

"We'll cover more ground if we split up, like Hollyn said," Fynn pronounced, carefully stepping into the overgrowth. "But we should look in pairs. Renwyn, go find Penelope. She can't have gone far. Hollyn and I will go this way." He nodded in the opposite direction. "We'll meet back here. Don't go too far, alright?"

"Fine," grumbled Renwyn as he pushed by Hollyn, purposefully knocking into the prince's shoulder as he did so.

Hollyn and Fynn headed off, side by side. Fynn studied the ground, looking for anything of note. Hollyn's focus was directed toward the trees and sky, searching for any sign of how far from the castle they truly were.

"What do you think started him off?" asked Fynn, toeing at the ground.

"He wants to be the one in charge...the *team leader*."

"I figured that much," Fynn said, looking up from the ground and searching the trees and roots - bored. "He shouldn't have shoved you like that."

"I said I didn't need your help, Fynneas."

"I know, I know," Fynn said. "But he shouldn't have done it. It didn't make him seem fit to lead, you know. Just made him look like a whiney brat."

"How's your arm?"

"Doesn't hurt. The lady matron said I had to keep this stupid sling on for a few more days. She wants to be certain I'm all healed up before I take it off."

Hollyn eyed the arm that hung limply across Fynn's torso. "It really doesn't hurt?"

"Really doesn't."

"That's weird, do you know that? It shouldn't have healed so quickly. I know, for a fact, that I broke your arm." Hollyn stepped in front of Fynn, carefully reaching out and running his hand along the other boy's forearm and up to his shoulder, inspecting it for any sign of injury. He found none. "Can you move it?"

"Haven't really tried," replied Fynn. He flexed his fingers and then began to slowly rotate his wrist. Finding that his movement hadn't been impaired by days of being bandaged, he slid the sling from his shoulder carefully. He slowly moved his arm up and then side to side. "Looks fine to me."

"Weird."

"You've said that already," chirped Fynn, arm still moving in experimental motions and finding no pain. "So, am I to be the *weird idiot*, then?"

"I suppose that would be one way to differentiate you and Renwyn," Hollyn jested. He watched Fynn moving his arm gingerly for a few more moments before deciding that nothing seemed amiss with the appendage and turned away, headed off to scout the area. "Coming?"

Fynn bounded off after the other boy, eyes keenly aware of their surroundings. "How far do you think we are from the castle?"

"Don't know."

"How far away do you think the other teams are?"

"Don't know that either."

Fynn hopped onto a large, moss covered stone and stood tall, easily able to see far more of the jungle laid out before him from such a vantage point. "Do you hear that?"

"What?"

"Water." Straining his eyes in search of the source, Fynn found nothing. But he knew he heard it, the sound of rippling water off in the distance. "There's water nearby."

"A river? Or maybe a lagoon?"

Jumping down from his perch, Fynn nodded. "Either way, it's a good thing. Finding a source of water is always the first step. That and building the fire."

Hollyn agreed, "Let's get Renwyn and Penelope. We'll come back this way. We can set up camp by the water. I'm guessing they couldn't have left the other teams *too* far away from here. They'll be looking for water too. And, if they *are* close, they'll likely find us if we camp out there and wait."

They made short work of tracking down Renwyn and Penelope. The pair had found little helpful information about the site. The look of relief that came over Penelope's face when Hollyn explained they'd found some water was hard to miss.

She slung her arms around the red-haired prince, grinning toothily all the while. "That's wonderful! I knew you'd find something."

Hollyn's cheeks felt as if they were on fire as he stood, frozen with Penelope still hanging from his neck. "Yes…well…let's get going." He managed to extricate himself from her incessant hold and returned to his place in step with Fynn.

Fynn nudged the other boy; a sly smile curled his lips. "I think she likes you," he whispered.

"*Idiot,*" Hollyn muttered under his breath as he stalked off, leading the group. "Left, or right?" he called back to Fynn.

Listening intently, Fynn heard the water again. "Left."

The jungle was a veritable maze with all its overgrown roots springing up, heavy underbrush, dense canopy, and scarce light. The four-man band was careful as they navigated the journey. Ahead, more light spilled through the canopy, and the sound of water grew louder. Chirping birds tweeted from the branches that curled overhead.

Elated, team three knew they must be close. As they were stepping down a rather steep decline in the terrain, the damp soil beneath Penelope's feet gave way under her meager weight and she went smashing down to the earth before careening down the hill.

Hollyn froze when Penelope screamed. He only just had the time to register her falling before he went after her. As she continued her graceless plummet through the dirt, he staggered down the hill in her wake. He yelped when a twisting root caught his toe and sent him pitching forward. A dreadful pain seared through his shoulder at the same time a sickening crack sounded. He was still rolling down, head over heels, but he wasn't quite cognizant of it all. The pain had clouded his focus. He felt terribly nauseated.

The moment he'd seen Penelope go sliding by, Renwyn had already begun to descend down the decline at a quicker pace. Every step was calculated and careful. Fynn, after seeing how hard Hollyn had fallen, disregarded all sense and sprinted after his teammates. His scrawny legs carried him at a pace that seemed incongruous with his awkward, clumsy nature.

Penelope's momentum ceased when she rolled from the dirt; she braced herself over the drop-off where the land disappeared and, just a few feet below, a turquoise-watered lagoon stretched, encircled on all sides by tall trees and emerald fronds.

Hollyn slid down beside her, landing on his back. He gasped for breath. His hand immediately clasped over his right shoulder. Unshed tears lingered in his eyes as he bit back a scream of pain. "Are you alright?" he asked, turning his head slightly to the side to survey Penelope for any outward signs of injury.

The girl scooted closer to the prince before helping him sit up. His wince of pain didn't go unnoticed. "I'm fine. But *you're* not." Penelope sounded worried. "Is it your shoulder?"

He nodded. "It'll be alright."

Just then, Fynn burst from the overgrowth, eyes wide. The moment he saw the pair, he grew frantic, looking between them. "Are you both alright?

"Hollyn's hurt his shoulder," Penelope replied, still helping prop Hollyn upright.

Fynn knelt on the prince's other side. "I've got just the thing." He held out the sling he'd been wearing earlier, the one he was mindful of keeping for just such a situation. "Hold your arm close to your body," he instructed as he began to fasten the fabric tightly around the other boy, quite careful to not bump Hollyn's arm too much. "How's that?"

"Fine," Hollyn answered weakly. He was having a hard time focusing through the pain; his head was beating painfully.

When Renwyn joined the other three, he was quick to rush to Penelope's side. "Are you hurt?"

"No." She looked back at the injured prince. "Hollyn's hurt his shoulder though. Looks bad."

Renwyn studied the now heavily panting prince before scanning his surroundings. His interest was drawn by the lagoon. He stepped up to the edge of the drop-off and gazed down at the water beneath the shoreline. "I think we've found the water."

"A river would've been easier," Fynn thought aloud. "It would've made fishing less of a challenge."

"What do you mean?" a puzzled Renwyn inquired.

Penelope looked down at the drop-off, noting the few feet separating the land from the water. "If we're to fish, we'll have to climb in and out of the water. It can be done; it'll just be harder than simply stepping in and out of a river."

Hollyn stood on shaking legs. Beads of sweat gathered at his brow and rolled down his cheeks. "There's enough space here for us to make camp. I think we should try and find some sticks to make a fire and some kindling, stones too."

"Right," Fynn agreed. "I'll gather up some rocks to line the fire. Penelope, can you find some sticks and something to use for kindling?"

"Yes." She began fanning out from where they'd all landed, looking for dried leaves or fronds to kindle the flames and sticks for ignition.

"So, we're just going to stay here for the day?" Renwyn huffed.

Before Hollyn had the chance to answer, Fynn spun around and stared unwaveringly at the boy. "Yes." He took a step closer, quite aware of the size disparity between he and Renwyn. "If the other teams were dropped off near where we were, they'll be looking for a source of water too. So, they'll probably end up coming this way." He chanced a quick look at Hollyn before returning his intensely focused gaze to Renwyn. "Anyway, Hollyn's hurt. We should give him some time to rest before we start off again."

"Please," Penelope pleaded from the brush behind Fynn. "We shouldn't fight amongst ourselves. That isn't going to accomplish anything."

The afternoon was wearing on when the children finally had constructed an adequate fire pit. Hollyn was resting with his back to one of the many trees that stood vigil around the lagoon; his head tilted to the side as he dozed. His soft snores wilted on the gentle breeze. Penelope sat at his side, ever vigilant. From time to time she pressed her hand to the prince's forehead, each time scowling when she felt that he did, in fact, have a fever and that it was persisting.

"Fynn," she called.

The boy turned around at the sound of his name. He moved closer, hoovering before the two of them, frowning when he saw the flushed look on Hollyn's face. "He doesn't look too good," Fynn commented.

"He still has a fever," Penelope began. "I'm worried."

"Just keep watch over him, alright? Renwyn is going to try and catch some fish," Fynn assured, feigning excited optimism as best he could. "If that doesn't work...I'm sure there are berries or something here we can eat."

"Be careful," warned Penelope. "Please?"

"I'll do my best," laughed Fynn. "We'll find the others in no time! I *swear*. And then we'll be out of here."

Unfortunately, trying to spear fish with no more than just a knife was proving to be a nearly insurmountable challenge. Fynn watched from the shore as Renwyn plunged into the water over and over, knife in his hand, stabbing fruitlessly into the gently rippling waves. It was clear the other boy was becoming restless; his attempts at catching a fish were more and more wild, erratic, and tactless as time went on. After an hour of relentless splashing and yelling, Renwyn climbed from the lagoon to the shore, combed back his matted hair, and used his discarded cloak to dry off.

"Give me a few minutes and I'll go back in and try again," Renwyn murmured before he continued drying himself. "Damn fish are fast."

"Alright," Fynn relented. "We've got time before it starts getting dark. Rest up for a while and then have another go at it."

Hollyn had, in his sleep, changed positions. He was now curled around the far slighter form of Penelope, his head resting against her shoulder. The girl, however, didn't have the luxury of sleeping. Her eyes were trained forward, nervously probing the trees for any signs of danger. So enthralled was she in her sentinel duties that she nearly jumped when Fynn approached.

"Sorry," he said, holding his hands up, "I didn't mean to scare you."

"It's alright, I didn't mean to be so skittish." She blushed.

"Renwyn is taking a break from fishing for now. He hasn't caught anything yet. But he's going to try again in a little bit, just needs to catch his breath," explained Fynn. "How's Hollyn?"

"Still sleeping."

"That's good. Sleep is the best thing for him right now."

Penelope nodded her agreement.

That's when they heard a blood-chilling scream.

It felt as though all the air had been ripped from his lungs when Fynn frantically turned around in the direction of the scream, only to find that Renwyn was nowhere in sight. The prince tiptoed back to Penelope, who now had her arm slung around Hollyn. The injured prince blearily blinked his eyes in confusion.

"What…what's going on?" Hollyn asked groggily.

"Renwyn's gone," Fynn answered.

"Something got him." Penelope shivered, huddling closer to the prince at her side.

"We don't know that," argued Fynn.

"Then where is he?" the girl cried.

Fynn drew his knife from his belt and held it as tight as he could, forcing down the nauseating fear that was festering in the pit of his stomach. He remained staring at the place Renwyn had last been standing, searching for any trace of what had happened. He found nothing. The ground looked undisturbed. There was no sign that he'd simply fallen into the water. Fynn looked in every direction, but he saw nothing out of the ordinary. His hands were shaking.

"Fynneas," whispered Penelope. "Fynn, something got him. *Something's* out there."

"Hollyn," Fynn called.

Hollyn mumbled weakly; his forehead was still pressed against Penelope's shoulder.

The girl began to shake him imploringly. "Hollyn. Hollyn, you need to get up."

Still, Hollyn didn't move.

Fynn rushed to him, seizing him up by the collar of his tunic and forcefully hauling him to his feet. He felt guilty when Hollyn gasped in pain but quelled the feeling as the fear usurped his control. "Hollyn!" Fynn snapped. "I need you to get up. Something got Renwyn. We need to go."

Despite the awful headache lancing through his skull, Hollyn nodded his understanding and reached down to his belt, awkwardly taking hold of his knife in his left hand. "What's the plan?" he rasped.

Fynn felt himself shaking; a niggling terror prickled up his spine, but he resolved to not show fear in front of Hollyn and Penelope. The other boy looked on the verge of collapse and the poor girl was trembling uncontrollably. "Stay together. Keep our guard up," Fynn instructed. He certainly sounded more confident than he felt.

Hollyn held as tightly as he could to the hilt of his knife while Fynn wrapped his right arm around Hollyn's waist, shouldering most of his weight. Penelope took up on Hollyn's other side, her own knife settled in her tiny hand. Each of the three was hyperaware of every sound in the jungle, from the cawing of the parrots to the snapping of twigs in the underbrush. Another throat-tearing scream erupted from the canopy; all three sets of eyes flicked up expectantly, finding only leaves and branches. Penelope pressed closer to Hollyn, mindful not to jostle him too much but desperate to hide in his presence.

"What was that?" whimpered Penelope. Tears spilled from her eyes as she continued searching the trees.

"I don't know," a nervous Fynn responded.

The sound of twigs splitting drew their attention from the treetops to the jungle floor. Something was lurking in the distance. Another scream sounded from overhead and, with that, their attention became split. They didn't know whether to look up or out in front of them for the danger, for it seemed to be coming for them from every direction.

"What do we do?" cried Penelope. She bent her head, trying to hide the tears, but the sob that escaped seemed to echo around them. She buried her head against Hollyn's chest, forcing herself to focus on the unsteady rhythm of his heartbeat.

Hollyn wrapped his arm around her back, still holding tightly to his knife. "I don't know." His voice had lost its usual confidence and, instead, was raspy and weak. "I don't know."

"Hollyn, we have to keep moving," urged Fynn.

The red-haired prince nodded, but he was too tired to actually move. The pain from his shoulder had overtaken him completely and his body felt weighed down; the fever siphoned any energy he had left. He groaned as Fynn, still holding tightly to his waist, began to pull him forward.

"We have to find Renwyn," Hollyn managed to choke out tiredly.

"We'll look for him," Fynn promised. "But we don't know what got him or how."

"Where are we going?" Penelope asked, still clutching tightly to the taller prince as their team of three proceeded slowly through the jungle.

Fynn admitted, "I don't know. I'm just hoping we run into the others. I don't know what else to do. Hollyn?"

"I don't know either," Hollyn admitted. He was having a hard time keeping his eyes open. "They have to be close, right?"

"I hope so," Fynn thought aloud, his voice shaking. "Gods, I hope so."

"It's going to be dark soon," observed Penelope.

"That's not good," mumbled Hollyn. "We'll be at the mercy of whatever's out here."

"We've got to find somewhere else to make camp," Fynn suggested. "And we need to do it fast."

They continued their slow trek through the undergrowth. Hollyn leaned on Fynn more and more, his consciousness beginning to fade until he was all but limp against Fynn's side, slouching over against the smaller boy as they hobbled forward. Fynn, spurred on by the fear of whatever had gotten Renwyn, simply readjusted the taller boy's weight and proceeded on, practically dragging Hollyn with him.

Penelope was just behind them. "I'm scared," she whispered.

"Me too," Fynn lamented.

The darkness of night descended upon Dier Island. Within the confines of the wild, the darkness seemed far more profound. So little moonlight could creep through the canopy; one could only see the vague twinkling of stars beyond the twisting branches overhead. The darkness was heavier in the jungle, as it carried with it the ever-present threat of monsters lurking under cover of the night-time shadows; the chorus of snapping twigs and rustling brush only bolstered the knowledge that there were things creeping all around them, things they couldn't see and, more than likely, could not fight.

Fynn heard a low rumble not far from where team three was standing, catching their breath. His eyes narrowed, having no trouble seeing in such blackness. He searched the jungle floor but saw nothing. But he heard it again, a deep rumble that set him on edge.

"Penelope," Fynn said under his breath.

The girl perked up, instantly at attention. One arm was clutched around Hollyn's waist, trying to offset some of the limp weight from Fynn, the other hand clasped tightly around her knife. "Yes?"

"I heard something."

"What should we do?"

"Crouch down as low as you can. Keep Hollyn next to you, alright? But stay low and don't make a sound," Fynn instructed. He disentangled himself from his cousin and lowered him to the ground as gently as he could.

As Penelope did as she was told, pulling the unconscious prince closer, she peeked up at Fynn. "What about you?"

He held a finger over his lips, quieting her with only a look.

Penelope held onto Hollyn even tighter. Her hand shook; she readied her knife for whatever may come.

Mustering up all his courage, Fynn stood before Penelope and Hollyn, a fleshy, human shield protecting them from the rumbling beast that prowled in the darkness. He drew his knife up in his left hand, readying himself to fight back should anything lunge toward him.

Fynn's eyes widened when he caught sight of golden eyes staring back at him from the darkness. Another rumbling growl echoed all around him.

"Fynn?" Penelope's voice was weak and scared sounding, absolutely pathetic in contrast to the mighty growl that preceded it. She had also caught sight of the glinting eyes staring back at them and her stomach had twisted into knots.

From the shadows a panther leapt. It was as long as a grown man with wicked looking ivory-colored claws curling from outstretched paws. Its pale-yellow teeth shone through the darkness. Golden eyes bore down upon Fynn as the creature slammed into the boy, knocking him bodily to the ground. Fynn brought up his knife quickly, tearing through the animal's shoulder as it wailed viciously. The sound of its shriek reverberated through the jungle like thunder echoing in the clouds.

Fynn screamed, "Penelope, run!"

He was unable to look back to see if she had gotten up. He was too busy scrambling beneath the great cat, wildly slashing at it as best he could, ducking his head down to avoid the violently thrashing paws. A claw grazed over his back, but he didn't have the wherewithal to cry in pain.

Oddly, a familiar feeling blanketed him; it was much the same as the feeling he'd had when he fought Hollyn. It was as though time was slowing down to a crawl. When Fynn's silvery eyes adjusted from the blinding terror, he could see that the beast pinning him down was not moving, but simply frozen in time. One great, big paw was still aloft with claws glinting before him.

Fynn raised his hand.

"Please work," he whispered.

A strong surge of energy bolted through the prince; his blood felt as if it were a river of flames rushing through his veins, and at once a fire sparked in his hand. Soon the flame burned brighter and brighter until his hand was engulfed in the fire. Curiously, it didn't burn him. Fynn hadn't time to think of the sense of the matter. The moment the flame erupted forth from his hand, he swung at the cat and smashed his fist against its jaw. He watched the whiskers ignite and still the cat didn't move.

Fynn twisted beneath the creature until he was free, climbing to his feet quickly and dashing back to where he'd left Penelope and Hollyn. Much like the panther, they seemed frozen—entirely forgotten by time itself. Penelope was draped protectively over a worrisomely pale Hollyn, knife clasped in a white-knuckled hand. Fynn threw himself down beside the pair, hunching over Hollyn like a shield as he peeked over his shoulder.

Time rushed back then, and everything moved far quicker than it seemed it should have. The panther reeled in pain as its whiskers burned out; dancing smoke wafted up into the breezy air. Black fur was singed where Fynn's hand had struck the cat. Frightfully sharp claws raked against the damp dirt as the animal struggled to find purchase, yowling its pain and annoyance as it righted itself once more. Looking back down at Hollyn, Fynn winced when he saw the other boy breathing heavily beneath him. Penelope shook with terror at his side.

When she turned her attention to Fynn, tears were awash over her face. "What're we going to do?"

"Stay here," Fynn ordered. He leapt to his feet and spun on his heels to face the enraged panther. "Is that all you've got?" he screamed into the night. Golden eyes once more flashed in his direction. The prince smirked. "Come on then!"

Fynn bolted off into the shadows, leaving behind Penelope and Hollyn. He ran as fast as his legs would carry him. Though he could see in the dark as plainly as if it were day, stumbling was unavoidable. Roots shot up from the ground at random and the brush would go from sparse to overwhelming, raking at his legs and hips as he rushed by. He heard the cat charging behind him, getting closer and closer. Every breath he took was labored. The panther growled again and Fynn thought his heart was going to rip from his chest. His fear became nearly unbearable.

Spying what he believed to be a clearing, Fynn quickened his pace. He sprinted through the night. He wouldn't chance looking back to see how close the cat was. Its panting breaths came close enough—too close for his liking. When Fynn broke free from the tree line, a startled gasp shrieked forth from his mouth as he went plummeting to the earth. The clearing, in fact, was a drop-off where the jungle floor petered out by way of a steep hill that curled into a ravine. He spiraled down the hill, everything a blur as it rushed by his distorted eyes. Small twigs cut at his cheeks as he tumbled downward.

Fynn splashed into a stream when he rolled free from the earth. He was sprawled out in the shallow water, limbs feeling as heavy as boulders as he heaved a shaking breath. He no longer heard the panting of the panther nor saw the flashing of golden eyes as he stared back from where he'd fallen. Fynn still held tightly to his knife, not completely trusting the creature had retreated. The prince sat up, looking around, watching the water run over him. When he finally stood, the waters barely reached to his knees. The stream stretched far into the wilds, disappearing into heavy shadows off in the distance in each direction.

Fynn coughed throatily. He doubled over, hands braced against his knees. His shoulders shook. Tears burned hot trails over his cheeks. He bit down on his lip until he tasted the tang of blood. He managed to almost stifle a hysterical sob. "Damn it."

He wiped the tears from his eyes with the back of his hand, sniffling. Something warm congealed over his skin and he saw, much to his annoyance, trails of red streaking across his pale complexion. He reached his hand back to his face, ghosting his fingertips over his forehead. He felt a nasty cut stretch from the bridge of his nose up to his hairline. He held his hand before him, scowling at the blood oozing over his fingertips. "Damn it all."

Fynn looked in every direction frantically. He couldn't remember which direction he'd run from. He'd been terrified, not paying attention. He cursed himself for losing track. The water still licked at his legs, chilling him. He shook his head, running his hand through his sweaty hair.

"Calm down," he commanded himself. "You have to calm down." He tried to steady his breathing, but it took far longer than he would've liked before he could breathe easily, steadily. "You can't stand here forever," Fynn chided.

He proceeded to trudge through the stream, following the flow of the water. The sound of the shallow stream trickling over the odd stone or two, rushing by the grassy shores on either side, was like a soft lullaby tending to his jittery nerves. He allowed himself to get lost in the sound of the rushing water, oblivious to everything else. He sheathed his knife. With both hands now free, he outstretched them before him. He cupped them as Minnie had done in the tavern and focused on his palms, envisioning a soft glow and a gentle warmth.

Fynn was delighted when his hands glowed as Minnie's had. There was no flame, just a soft, golden light that poured from his hands, brightening his way. "A little light makes this place less...creepy." He smirked, pleased with himself. Fynn continued on with heavy legs, splashing through the water. The ache in his shoulders grew; his back tingled with fatigue. His eye lids felt terribly heavy. He yawned. Desperately, he tried to fight off sleep, to stave off the uncertainty of resting in the jungle while he was all alone and lost. He forced himself onward, though his legs shook, and his hips began to throb.

"Keep going," Fynn urged himself under his breath. "You've got to keep going."

He stumbled in the water when the depth changed abruptly. He fell forward, plunging chest deep into the chilly stream. He spluttered as he raised his head above the surface, coughing up water. The light had gone out and once more he was in the stifling darkness of the night-time jungle. He sighed, shoulders slinking forward. "Damn it."

Tears came back to his eyes, running down his face. He coughed again, a nasty, wet cough. "Damn it all," he sniveled as he smashed his fist into the water. "Damn it, damn it, damn it!" He sunk down, shoulder deep, into the water. He hung his head, letting his black hair tumble in front of his eyes. "Help." His voice was embarrassingly weak. "Someone...please...help."

"Are you lost, little boy?"

The voice was the most beautiful he'd ever heard. It sounded as though it were made of silk. Fynn's head snapped up, eyes widening when he saw a woman just before him. She was coming from the waters, white hair slick against her back. Her vibrant blue eyes rolled over his shuddering body curiously. He quavered beneath her gaze.

"Are you lost?"

He nodded, not knowing what else to do.

"I can help you."

Fynn stared at her. Her skin was a copper color, not marred by any scars or freckles. Her eyes were a shimmering blue, like ocean waters caught in the confines of her irises. White hair clung to her slender back before fanning out, dancing in the gentle current at her waist. She reached a thin hand toward him; long fingers traced along the jagged edge of the laceration he sported upon his forehead.

"This looks like it hurts."

"It doesn't," Fynn whispered, pulling away from her touch.

"It's bleeding quite badly," she continued, undeterred by his reaction.

"I'm fine," he insisted uneasily.

Her hand caught his chin and hauled him forward until he could feel the chill of her breath when she spoke. "I think you're lying."

Fynn struggled in her hold, unable to wrench himself free from her grasp. Her hands felt corpse like, cold and clammy. There was an unnaturalness about the woman that was frightening. Her eyes were haunting, glowing in the blackness of the night.

"I'm fine," he said again, still trying to get free.

Her nails were like claws that easily ripped the soft flesh beneath her hold. Small trails of red seeped over her fingers. She drew her hand back. Fynn watched, utterly mortified, as a bizarrely long tongue shot from her pale lips and lapped at the blood greedily, her eyes never leaving his face. Her silken voice spoke, "Are you here alone?"

Fynn he was unable to answer. He tried to edge back away from her, but she caught hold of his wrist and pulled him closer.

"Where are you going?"

"No…nowhere?"

She tapped him on the nose in an almost playful manner before smiling a most toothy grin. "That's what I thought. Come, let me help you, little boy."

She dragged him closer. Fynn shook his head. "Really…I'm…I'm alright." He thrashed against her grip, but it tightened painfully around his wrist; those nasty nails dug into his pale flesh. "Please…let me go."

"No."

The woman turned in the water and lunged forward, submerging herself up to her shoulders. That's when Fynn felt something scaly brush against his side. A fish tail flicked from the water, its scales a brilliant shade of purple. He would have found it a dazzling sight, had he not instantly realized that the tail belonged to the woman who, presently, was dragging him through the increasingly deep stream-turned-river.

"You're a mermaid!" Fynn wailed when realization finally dawned.

"Very clever," she quipped.

"Please," yelled Fynn hysterically, twisting erratically in her grasp. He was pulled deeper into the water; it rushed in his mouth, up his nose. He coughed, gasping for air as he soon found himself having to swim to stay above the surface rather than being able to walk. "Let me go!" He kicked in the water, wriggling like a fish on a hook. "Let me go!"

The mermaid turned in the water. She pressed against him, leaning dangerously close. She flicked her tongue over the deep cut on the prince's forehead, reveling in the taste of blood stinging at her tongue. "Don't be afraid, little boy." She drew back, her forefinger tracing the curve of the boy's cheek as he tried to get away. Her hand came to rest over his throat, feeling the strong pulse strumming under her palm. "Don't be afraid."

Fynn's panicked breathing increased tenfold when the mermaid's hand lightly curled around the column of his throat. His eyes bore into hers pleadingly. He reached his hand from the water, tentatively laying it over hers. He was mindful to keep his legs gently kicking, his other arm treading water, to stay afloat and not drown in her clutches. He nodded, maintaining eye contact with her. "Alright." He slowed his breathing down, focusing intently on the task at hand. "Alright. I'm not afraid. Where are you taking me?"

"You'll see."

He didn't know what happened. He didn't know how she'd managed it. But all at once his vision failed and blackness - solid, unwavering blackness - crept into his sight until he saw no more. A blessed numbness stole him away as he lost consciousness.

15

THE IBA-JII

Cold water splashed over Fynn's face. His lashes fluttered; pale eyes opened, adjusting to the dark. He sat up, finding that his hands had been bound behind his back. There was stone all around him - dark, dripping stone. A few feet from where he sat, water ebbed over the rock.

"A cave?" marveled the prince as he slowly stood up. Dizzy fuzziness roiled in his head, but he continued taking careful steps around the stony enclosure, searching for signs of light. He found a scant amount breaking through cracks overhead, reflecting off the greenish water pooling in the center of the cave. Vines entangled with the stones; red flowers bloomed from the lanky green twisting up the cave walls.

"You're awake."

Fynn went rigid; he froze where he stood. He recognized that filthily silken voice from earlier, all too quickly recalling the siren who'd caught him in the river. He turned to face the source, eyeing her suspiciously from where he stood. "I am," he said flatly, doing his best to imitate Hollyn's abject indifference.

"Aren't you curious where you are?"

"I'm in a cave," Fynn surmised.

"But don't you care to know why?"

"Not particularly," he drawled slowly. "I assume you brought me here."

"Well, you're no fun." She pouted. The woman—mermaid—was peeking from the pool. She leaned her elbows over the stone of the cave; her head settled in her hands as she continued watching her captive. "You're not in the jungle alone, are you?"

Fynn backed up until he was flush against the cave wall. "Why does it matter?"

"I'm only asking," teased the mermaid.

"It *doesn't* matter," insisted Fynn adamantly.

"Ah, so you're *not* here alone!" She smirked. "You wouldn't be getting so upset about it if you were. Tell me, little boy, where are your friends?"

"I'll answer your question if you answer one of mine first," bargained the boy as he sat down, back braced against the cool wall of the cave. "Deal?"

"Alright. Deal."

"What other creatures are in the jungle?"

"What sort do you want to know about?" she asked curiously.

"One of my friends—there, I've answered your question—disappeared earlier. He was standing just behind me and then all of a sudden he was gone, but I could still hear him screaming for a while after he vanished." Fynn's eyes narrowed dangerously. "So tell me, what took him?"

"Was he in the water?"

The prince shook his head. "No."

"The thick of the trees?"

"No." He sighed. "We were by a lagoon. I turned my back. He was standing by the shore, and then he was gone. He didn't fall into the water though, I checked."

"It was probably the Iba-Jii then," explained the mermaid.

"Iba-Jii?"

The mermaid's lips curled. "Oh yes, didn't you know? Terrible little beasties, they are. They enchant the vines and the roots. They're far too small to take on a human, even one as tiny as you. But they're tricky little things, as I'm sure you've noticed."

"Where would they have taken him?"

"You can't go after him."

Fynn jumped back to his feet and snarled, "Why not?"

Brilliant blue eyes shone with amusement. The mermaid laughed, "How're you to go after your little friend when you're my prisoner?"

"What?"

"Well, haven't you noticed? Your hands are tied. You're in a remote cave all alone. What did you think you were here for?"

Undeterred by the woman's cavalier attitude towards his detainment, Fynn fumed. "You can't just keep me here!"

"*Little boy*, I'm doing just that," she cooed as she slipped beneath the water, leaving him all alone in the dank cave.

Fynn felt terribly tired. His head ached from where he'd been cut. His back stung where the panther's claw had ripped his snowy flesh. His whole body tingled with twinges of pain from his fall down the hill. He leaned his head back against the stone, focusing on drawing in slow and steady breaths.

"You're going to be alright," Fynn assured himself in a hushed, weary voice. "It's going to be alright. You'll get out of here." He opened his eyes, peering through the darkness, studying his surroundings. "Think. Just think. Everyone's *always* telling you to do it, so why not give it a try now?"

Splashing drew his attention, shattering his meager focus. From the green waters, white hair emerged. As a body surfaced from the pool, Fynn was surprised to see that it wasn't the woman who'd abducted him and left him in the cave. Rather, the woman—another mermaid apparently—who arose from the waters seemed much younger, her face rounder, blue eyes gentler. She blinked; water dripped from long, white lashes.

Looking at him, she sighed. "What're you doing here?" she asked, not unkindly.

"I…I don't know," stammered the prince.

"Did Attika bring you here?"

"Who?"

She rolled her eyes. "Well, never mind. I can't think of anyone else who would leave a boy tied up in a cave."

"Does this happen…frequently?" Fynn worriedly asked.

"No. Usually you humans are smart enough to stay out of the water."

"Well, it's not like I had much of a choice!" he asserted sharply. "Can you get me out of here?"

"You've been rather rude," the mermaid chided.

"Well, pardon me," Fynn said seething, "if I'm not in the best mood after being tied up and left in a *damn* cave in the dark."

She waved her hand and called, annoyed, "Come here. I can't very well get to you all the way over there."

"How do I know you won't do anything bad once I get close?"

"You don't," she answered evenly.

Not seeing that he had much of a choice in the matter, Fynn gathered himself and ambled over to the water's edge, kneeling down before the mermaid. He turned his back to her, showing the aquatic siren his bound wrists.

"Do you have a name?" Fynn asked.

She worked on unfastening his wrists, tied as they were by the torn remnants of his school cloak. "Ophelia."

"That's a nice name," Fynn admired absentmindedly. He felt the bindings fall from his hands and he grinned, stretching his arms out before him, flexing his wrists. "Thank you." He turned around to face her, grinning ear to ear. "You didn't have to help me. So…thanks."

"I wasn't going to leave you here. Rude as you are, I wouldn't do that. Attika has a bad habit of playing with her food," Ophelia explained. Her eyes took on a certain lost quality as she looked into the murky, green water. She looked back to him, smiling weakly. "What's your name?"

"Fynn." He held out his hand to her politely. "It's a pleasure to meet you." His hand remained lingering between them. He laughed. "You're supposed to shake it."

"Why?"

"Well," he said, as his hand recoiled, "I don't know. You just are, I suppose."

"So, Fynn, why are you out here in the jungle all alone?"

Fynn combed his hand through his matted hair. He felt himself shaking again, guilt gnawing at him unrelentingly as he thought of Renwyn. "I wasn't alone. One of my friends was taken. One was injured. We got separated and then that other mermaid… Attika, was it? She found me and I just woke up here." His eyes were warm with tears as he continued, "She said…she said he was probably taken by the Iba-Jii!"

"Oh, that *is* most unfortunate." Ophelia grimaced.

"Please, Ophelia, is there a way out of this cave?"

"Only by water."

The water lapped at the stone. The cool trickle of droplets from overhead splashed down into the pool. There was the faint whistling of a breeze somewhere beyond the cracked, stone walls of the cave. Fynn knew, just beyond the stony prison he found himself in, that there was air and there was light. He craved the expanse of the island and wished to be liberated from the oppressive dankness of the cave.

But when he looked back at the water, gently rippling with every motion Ophelia made, every sigh of her chest or sag of her shoulders, his anxiety mounted. It was a twisting sort of feeling that began in the pit of his stomach and took root, firmly latching to his core while vines of fretfulness curled their way upward until they tickled his lungs, transforming each breath into a nervous hiccup. The muscles in all his body seemed to clamp down and strain almost painfully. His heart thudded harder and harder until he could hear the pounding, like drums, echoing in his ears. He couldn't look away from the water, but the longer he remained staring, the more sickened he felt.

"There has to be another way out," choked Fynn.

Ophelia shook her head. "There isn't." She nodded to the pool, eyes staring at something far below the surface. "You'd have to swim through there."

He shook his head emphatically. "I can't."

"Well, then you'll be stuck in here."

Fynn's breathing was heavy and labored, but he forced himself to lean closer to the pool. Hesitantly, at first, he reached his hand out until his fingers brushed over the cool surface of the water. Slowly, he dipped his hand in, making gentle circles as he whirled his wrist. He furrowed his brow as he continued the motion. The water felt so light against his hand. It was chilly, calming in a way. The soft sounds of splashing began to ease the uncomfortable hammering of his heart until, at long last, he could breathe more easily. Fynn closed his eyes and evened his breathing. He thought about the water, about its mutability.

A thought struck him. He let his senses focus on his hand. He concentrated on the rush of the water over his flesh, the splaying of his fingers against the pool. As he rolled his hand just beneath the surface, the tiny waves he produced dove just further. His breathing was slowing. Fynn extended his concentration from his hand up to his arm, thinking of how the blood sloshing in his veins was like water in a river. That feeling extended up to his shoulder until he focused on his heart, pumping the blood down to his hand.

"Please work," he muttered softly. "Please work." He opened his eyes and found that the water had pulled away from his hand, leaving a hollow in the pool where water dared not flow. He smiled.

Ophelia stared, dumbfounded. "How'd you do that?"

"Not sure." Fynn shrugged. He didn't let his focus waver from his hand. If he moved his hand left, the water withdrew from him. If he moved it to the right, it did much the same thing. Wherever his hand wandered, the water would not flow; it seemingly flinched away from his touch as if burned.

"What *are* you?"

Fynn pulled his hand back, examining it as if it were a puzzle. "What do you mean?"

"I've never seen someone do *that* before," Ophelia insisted.

"Honestly, that's the first time I've tried it." Fynn laughed. "Well…the first time I tried it with water. I've managed fire a few times."

Ophelia leaned back over the rocky edge to observe the boy as she commanded, "Show me."

Obligingly, Fynn cupped his hands, holding them out for Ophelia to see. He willed the feeling of warmth to congregate in his palms, visualizing the golden glow he'd utilized before. And, in a flash of brilliant light, Ophelia found herself gaping at the small, flickering flame settled in the boy's hands.

"I can't do much more than that," Fynn lamented, watching the fire slowly fade to nothing before turning his attention to the mermaid. "But I'm getting better at it!"

Ophelia's cold hand fell into his as she reached out to him, pulling him nearer. "You said your friend was taken by the Iba-Jii?"

Fynn nodded. "Well, that's what Attika said."

"The Iba-Jii don't like fire," Ophelia elucidated. "There's no saying whether your friend is still alive. The Iba-Jii don't take prisoners mostly. But they *hate* fire."

"You're saying I could still save Renwyn?"

"What I'm saying, little boy, is that the Iba-Jii hate fire. Your friend may be alive. He may be dead. But with fire at your fingertips, you could take your revenge quite easily."

Fynn yanked his hands from Ophelia, curling them at his chest. His eyes hardened; his voice was sharp. "Why would I care about *revenge*?" An uncomfortable weight lurched over Fynn's shoulders with such force that the boy thought he'd be bowled over bodily. He remained as he was, but a niggling tremble insinuated its way down his back.

"They might have killed your friend. Don't you care?"

"Of course, I care!" he snapped. "But if he's dead, revenge doesn't get me anything. He'll still be gone." Fynn looked down, considering the hands he clutched to himself. "But if he's alive…if there's even a *chance* he's alive…I need to try and find him." Imploringly, he looked to Ophelia. Fresh tears streamed down his face. "Can you take me to them?"

"To those little monsters? No. They don't stay by the waters. They know better." Softly, carefully, she placed her hand over the boy's knee. "But I can help get you out of here. I can make sure Attika doesn't kill you."

"Alright." He'd made his decision and so slowly slid into the water. Though Fynn hated how the water reached up to his shoulders as he waded, dreading the depth of the pool with every paddle of his arms, he forced himself to remain calm. "Don't leave me?"

"Take my hand."

Fynn held to Ophelia's hand with desperate resolve. He bit back his fear, squelching it in the pit of his stomach, using his roiling, tense energy to be productive. With his free hand, he began slowly waving the water back and forth, concentrating on the motion, the feel of the water against his hand, the push and pull of the pool under his touch. The water began to flee from him, pulling back as he sank deeper, retreating from his fingertips. Ophelia sank deeper with him, his hand safely in hers, remaining within the confining walls of water, watching Fynn command the tides from his person, parting the pool before him as they descended.

The pool, the prince noted, gave way to a small, under water tunnel that he supposed led back out of the cave, to where the waters once again met the open air of the jungle. The light, what small amount there was, gave way where the tunnel opened, and blackness consumed the passageway. He couldn't tell how far it went on or how deep it went. Ophelia tugged him toward the tunnel and though he knew prior to getting into the pool and embarking on his grand escape that he would likely encounter such an obstacle, seeing it there before him horrified him to his very core. Ophelia continued pulling his hand, urging him to follow her into the tunnel, but he jerked away from her hold.

He shook terribly and as he screamed, the terror broke his resolve. The water he'd parted came crashing down all around him. Finding himself all at once submerged in the murky tides of the pool, Fynn frantically beat his arms. Bubbles scurried in every direction, racing around his flailing limbs. He gasped, only for his scream to be stolen by the waters. A bubble erupted from his lips. He had spun to the side as the force of the water crashed over him and as he peered through the greenness of the water, he couldn't tell which way was up. Unnerved by his disorientation, Fynn continued his frantic paddling; his fingertips clawed at the water as if he could climb from the depths and to the surface. They caught nothing but the chill of the pool that gave way as his fingers curled fleetingly.

Ophelia snatched hold of the panicked prince once more and easily pulled him close to her as she swam toward the tunnel, soon engulfed in the all-encompassing blackness of the passage. Fynn curled closer to the mermaid, screwing his eyes shut, shaking against her. He felt her ribs move slightly as her body arched and twisted, expertly navigating the turns of the tunnel. Her heart beat under his ear and he found that focusing his attention on the steady thumping was soothing.

The water slipped away. Fynn could finally breathe again as they breached the surface. The boy opened his eyes and beheld, with more happiness than he could remember ever mustering before, the sunlight peeking through the canopy, glistening over the water as it rushed by, reflecting off its surface in a thousand shades of blue. He smiled, swam to the bank of the river, and clambered out of the chilly water.

Fynn greedily sucked in air as he flopped onto his back. "Thank you!" He laughed as he rolled onto his stomach. "Thanks, Ophelia."

She swam to the edge of the bank and leaned over the grassy shore, brushing the prince's black hair from his eyes. "Glad to be out of there?"

"You have no idea." He leaned into the mermaid's touch. She continued combing her long fingers through his hair. "Is there anything *I* can do for *you?*"

She shook her head, errant white tresses curling in front of her eyes.

"Are you sure? You really helped me. Let me return the favor."

"I've nothing to ask of you."

"Ophelia?"

"Hmm?"

Fynn sat up. Ophelia's hand fell away from him. "Why did you save me?"

"I didn't want Attika to kill you."

He quirked a brow. "But why?"

"I don't condone the killing of children for a snack," she answered sourly. "It doesn't sit well with me."

Fynn laughed. "Thanks, Ophelia."

"You're a special little boy, Fynn."

"What do you mean?"

The mermaid grinned softly and, with a voice like honey, answered, "You're capable of amazing things. I saw you in there. I've never seen a human do that before. You must be *someone* special."

"Well," he snickered, "I *am* a prince."

"Are you really?"

Fynn nodded. "Yes. But, I'm not the prince that'll be king." He playfully scratched at the back of his head, ruffling his soaked hair. "But that's alright with me. I don't think I'd want to be."

"You'll be so much more; I can tell."

"Can I ask you something else?" His head cocked to the side.

Ophelia nodded her agreement.

"Are there more mermaids around?"

"Here? Not so much. Attika prowls the waters around the island the most. Me too sometimes. The others like the warmer waters to the east. There are some more of us out near the harbor, but not too many."

"Do the others…abduct humans to…to eat them?"

"No. Let's suffice to say that Attika's practices are not well received amongst the rest of us," Ophelia retorted dourly, as if speaking of Attika put a sour tang upon her tongue. "But there are plenty of other beasts in the waters, Fynn. I'd advise you not wade into the deep."

"I don't plan on it," he assured. "Trust me."

"Can I ask something of you, Fynn?"

"Of course," he answered enthusiastically, leaning closer to the water expectantly.

"How old are you?"

"Twelve."

"How long will you be here, on the island?"

"I'll be training at the castle until I'm sixteen," he explained. "I'll leave for the summers, I suspect. But I'll be back for ten months every year for the next four years."

"Can you promise me something, Fynn?"

Unsure, he nodded hesitantly.

"One day, when you're big and strong, can you hunt down the monsters that live in the deep? The awful ones that kill mermaids. The ones that sink ships and eat their crews? Those nasty ones?"

Fynn held out his hand to the mermaid with a confident smirk. "I'll get them for you. I promise. It'll be a while until I'd be ready for it, but when I am…I *promise*."

She eyed his hand confusedly for a few moments before her own hand outstretched slowly, taking the boy's and shaking it. She laughed. "I still don't understand this human custom."

"If I find out why we do it, I'll be sure to come find you and let you know," Fynn joked.

"See that you do." Ophelia laughed. "Best be on your way, Fynn, before Attika comes back."

"Will she be mad at you? You know, for letting me go."

Ophelia assured the boy firmly, "You needn't worry. I'll be taking my leave as well. She won't know it was me."

"If you're sure?"

"I am. Don't worry about me, Fynn. Run along and stay out of the waters. Go find your friends and get out of the jungle, alright?"

He jumped up to his feet in one, swift motion. "I will." He turned, readying to leave when he stopped and glanced back at his savior. "Ophelia?"

"Hmm?"

"Um, which way should I go?"

"If you're going after the Iba-Jii, straight ahead would be the most certain course."

He waved as he sprinted off, calling back to the mermaid, "Thanks, Ophelia!"

Fynn ran through the jungle until his lungs burned and his legs shook. When he stopped, he doubled over with his hands braced against his knees as he panted tiredly. His back stung from where he'd been clawed; his head pounded from the nasty cut there across his forehead, but he did his best to ignore what he deemed, presently, to be nothing more than minor inconveniences.

Something rustled in the undergrowth not far from him. He tensed, reaching for his knife and preparing himself, his muscles coiling like springs. Fynn listened carefully. Then he heard it, familiar voices chattering through the dense foliage.

The sound of Godryk's voice nearly brought fresh tears to the boy's eyes. Fynn yelled out, "Godryk! Godryk, is that you? Gods, please tell me it's you! Are you there?" He darted into the brush, jolting forward, heedless of the nasty thorns scraping at his legs as he burst through into a small clearing. "Godryk? Lux? Albie? Georgie? Where are you! Godryk, it's me! It's Fynn!"

Fynn heard their voices clearly; the sound of their footsteps drew closer. He sheathed his knife, fell to his knees, and couldn't help the steady sob that nearly choked him. "Godryk!" He beat his fist into the jungle floor over and over. "Godryk!"

They were coming closer. With each second that fell away, with every moment they drew nearer, a sense of selfish relief flooded within the boy. Fynn cried. He didn't know why he was crying, just that, in that moment, letting out a scream made him feel a bit steadier, a bit calmer. "Help…help, please!"

Fynn smelled the salt of his tears as they rolled by. He felt the familiar burn of their trail from his eyes to his jawline. He wiped at his face until his cheeks were red, matching the sclera of his eyes. "Godryk! Lux! Albie! Georgie!" He yelled for them over and over, desperate for them to find him there, collapsed in the dirt.

Exhaustion, fear, guilt—they all came crashing down over the prince. He couldn't take it anymore and so allowed himself to fall to the ground. The damp earth felt soft against his cheek and, for a few moments, he was able to imagine he was back, safely in his bed in the castle. He heard footsteps break through the undergrowth. Huddled around him, muffled voices that sounded worried began to cry. A hand draped over his shoulder and began to shake him, but Fynn couldn't bring himself to open his eyes. The darkness was too soft, too comforting for him to push it away.

The feeling of water brushing over his face woke Fynn up. He jolted upright, expecting to be back in the cave. He saw, to his delight and confusion, that he was amongst the trees. There was a small fire burning in front of him. People were huddled around it, talking in hushed voices. Fynn's vision was muddled, but when he managed to blink the fuzziness away, he saw Lux leaning over him. Her hands clamped over his shoulders, pushing him back down. Something soft was under his head. A folded cloak served as his pillow.

"You've been out for a while," Lux whispered, quite cognizant of the headache he more than likely had.

"It's dark," Fynn commented idly, his voice raspy.

"It's the middle of the night."

"It was bright earlier."

"We found you collapsed and unconscious this afternoon," she explained.

His head was wet again. His grey eyes flicked upward and watched as Lux dabbed the blood crusting over his forehead with a damp cloth.

"Does it hurt?" she asked worriedly.

"No."

"Fynn...what happened? Where's Renwyn? Where's Penelope?"

"Penelope?" he repeated. "What happened to *Penelope*?"

"We don't know." Lux sighed. "We found Hollyn, but the rest of you were missing."

"Is Hollyn—? How is he?"

"We think his shoulder's broken. Other than that, he's just tired and shaken. He had a fever for a while, but he seems to be doing better."

"When did you find him?"

"Yesterday. He was alone, wandering around. He couldn't tell us what happened to the rest of you. We were...I don't know, really...just scared for you all."

Fynn wanted to talk to her for longer. Truly, he did. But the warmth from the fire burning at the center of their campsite and the lilting chords of birds chirping overhead, the whistling of the night breeze swirling through the branches, all came together and lulled him to sleep. He knew, too, that he was dozing. He felt himself fall over the edge of consciousness into the welcoming arms of sleep, and he smiled as he tumbled head over heels into that embrace, escaping, for the time being, the terrors of the jungle.

The next time Fynn woke, it was bright - far too bright to be early in the morning. The heat that assaulted him was, he noted ruefully, indicative of the midafternoon. Grumbling, he tried to sit up, only to fail and flop back down, nuzzling against the softness of the cloak pillowed under his head. Someone nudged his side and, groaning, he forced himself awake and slowly sat up, wincing slightly in discomfort.

"You were mumbling about mermaids in your sleep."

Fynn snorted. He rubbed the sleepiness from his eyes and yawned. "Good morning to you, too."

Godryk laughed under his breath. He pulled off his cloak and wrapped it around the prince, fastening it carefully. "You should keep warm. You've been dead to the world for a while now."

"Great," groused the prince irritably, drawing the cloak closer to himself. It smelled distinctly of Godryk. "Where's Lux?"

"She and Albie went to look for something to eat."

"And they left you?" Fynn arched a brow.

"Georgie and Hollyn are hurt. They certainly weren't going to go out foraging. Someone had to stay here with the lot of you."

"What happened to *Georgie*?"

"Hurt her leg," Godryk answered. He glanced out toward the campsite where the fire smoldered, its smoke long since extinguished. Georgie and Hollyn were each curled into their cloaks, still resting soundly. "At least *they* don't talk in their sleep."

"I suppose Lux thinks I'm strange, then? Great. Just wonderful." Fynn huffed.

Godryk elbowed the boy, happily laughing all the while. "Trust me when I say I'm sure she thought you were strange *long* before you started talking about being abducted by mermaids in your fever dreams."

"It happened, you know," Fynn asserted testily. "Really. Two of them. One helped me escape."

"What do you mean?"

"The mermaids. There are mermaids in the waters here."

"I've never heard of mermaids in rivers and streams or even lagoons away from the main shorelines," Godryk mused. "You sure?"

"I know it. Ophelia. That was the one who helped get me out of the cave. She said the mermaids don't normally come this way but that she and another—Attika—they hang around these parts sometimes. She warned me to stay out of the water."

"Seems like you've certainly had an eventful time out here," commented the young Redmayne. "So, what happened to Hollyn's shoulder? And where are Renwyn and Penelope?"

"The first day," Fynn began, "Penelope fell down a hill and Hollyn ran after her. He fell and that's when he got hurt. It looked broken. We found a lagoon and figured that your team or Ollie's would come by eventually for the water source, you know? We were there for a few hours when Renwyn just vanished. We heard him scream. I don't know where he went. But we could hear him screaming." Fynn's eyes momentarily took on a rather distant quality as he finished his story. "The screaming was awful."

"Could he have fallen into the water? Maybe a mermaid got him if he fell into the lagoon," suggested Godryk.

Fynn shook his head. "I checked the water. He wasn't there. The screaming was coming from up high, in the trees, I think. The mermaids," he continued nervously, "they told me, both of them, about the Iba-Jii."

"You think there are Iba-Jii out here?"

Fynn shrugged. "I know there are. Ophelia and Attika both talked about them. They said they enchant the jungle…the vines and the roots…that's how they prey upon people wandering around."

"Did they, by chance, happen to tell you where to find the little beasts? Or how to fight them off if they're enchanting the jungle against us?"

"Fire."

"Fire?"

"Ophelia said they hate fire," Fynn explained. "Godryk, if there's a chance Renwyn is still alive, I've got to go find him."

"Do you think—? I mean, you heard screaming, right? Do you think he's still alive?"

"I don't know," whispered the prince. "I don't know, but I can't leave without knowing for sure. I can't leave him. I can't leave him here to die. We're a team, even if he is an ass."

"But he may already be gone, Fynn."

"But he may not be!" Fynn lowered his voice to a pained whimper. "I don't even know what happened to *Penelope*. Last time I saw her, she was with Hollyn while the panther was coming after me."

"The *panther*?" Godryk asked incredulously.

Fynn nodded numbly, not quite seeing the absurdity in his statement. "I was distracting it so Penelope and Hollyn could get away."

"Of course, you were," muttered Godryk. "Always have to be the hero."

"Didn't work though," Fynn mumbled, dejection evident in his voice. "*She's* gone too." He shook his head. "There's still a chance for them, Godryk. I can feel it. We can't abandon them. We can't!"

"You're right." Godryk slung his arm around Fynn's shoulders and pulled the other boy close, rather concerned that Fynn was allowing himself to be coddled in that moment. "You're right. *You're right*. We can't leave them. When Albie and Lux get back, we'll figure something out. We still have to find Ollie's team too. We're going to get out of here and we're going to do it together, *all* of us. We're *all* making it out of this alive. No matter what."

"Moriah said something to us before he left," Fynn whispered. He curled closer to Godryk, resting his head on the other boy's shoulder. His eyes became vacant as he spoke, recalling the man's words. "He told us that we had seven days to complete the mission, but that we should try and get out of here faster than that."

"Don't think too much about that," Godryk warned. He held onto Fynn tightly. "They just want us to stay focused and not dawdle while we're stuck out here."

"No," croaked the weary prince. "No, I think Moriah was warning us. I think he knew. They all know. I think the jungle…I don't know, really… but I think the jungle does things to you and plays with your mind. I don't know if it's the Iba-Jii doing it, like one of their enchantments or something like that, but I think the jungle plays with your head the longer you're here."

"What do you mean?"

"Do you know where we are? Which way to go? Where you just were, even?" Fynn's demeanor darkened the more he thought on the matter. His voice was hoarse. "I've been running all over and everything looks the same. I swear. Really, it's like every time I start running, I don't find anywhere new, just the same trees everywhere I go. It's maddening."

"I think you're just tired," Godryk argued gently.

"I hope you're right."

"Ollie's team can't be far, right?"

"I hope not." Fynn relaxed against Godryk.

Godryk held onto his prince tighter. "Me too. Me too."

It was another hour before Albie and Lux returned to camp. They came back toting an assortment of berries wrapped in their cloaks. While Albie set about to cleaning their finds and divvying them up, Lux joined Godryk and Fynn. Her red hair was a mess, sticking out in every direction. Dirt and grime and a bit of blood were smeared across her freckled face; her left eye was badly bruised; her lip was cut. She didn't seem bothered by the state of her being. The moment she saw Fynn was relatively awake and aware, she positively beamed.

Lux settled down close to the boys and kept her voice low. "How are you feeling?"

"Tired," Fynn murmured.

"Does anything hurt?"

"No." He pulled himself up from Godryk's shoulder. When he saw the dried blood caked over the girl's chin and the purple bruise blossoming under her eye, he cringed. "You're hurt."

"I'm alright." She smiled despite the nasty cut over her lip.

Fynn pressed, "What happened?"

"Tripped over some roots, I think. I don't know for certain. I just fell really hard, hit my head."

"They're playing with us," Fynn noted dreadfully. "They're just *playing* with us."

"Who?" asked Lux, perplexed.

"Fynn said that mermaids told him the Iba-Jii got Renwyn," answered Godryk flatly. "I'm inclined to believe him. They might be behind Penelope's disappearance too."

"What're Iba-Jii?" the girl questioned. "I've never heard of them."

"They're pixies or gremlins or something like that," Fynn answered, yawning. "They haunt wild areas like forests and mountains and apparently tropical jungles. I remember my grandfather mentioning them some when I was little, but he never said much. Just cursed the little beasts and that was all." He ran his hand through his hair - back and forth, back and forth. "Ophelia said they enchant the vines and the roots to catch their victims."

"Who's Ophelia?" Lux inquired.

"She's the mermaid who rescued me," replied the prince easily. "It's a long story, I suppose. I'll tell you when we get back to the castle." He shook his shoulders, forcing the feeling back into his body. He'd been asleep for too long, he'd wager; his arms and legs felt stiff and numb as a result. "We need to find Renwyn and Penelope. And we need to do it *quickly*."

The girl implored, "Do you know where they are?"

"No." He glanced in Godryk's direction. "We need to come up with a plan. We need to find Ollie's team, get Renwyn and Penelope, and get out of here."

"We should all rest one more day. We're tired and hurt and we'll be no good to anyone if we're all limping and yawning through the jungle. We won't be alert enough to sense danger or prepared to fight it off." Lux was adamant about resting one more day, her brow lowered seriously. "We rest for the day, yes?"

The battered prince knew that he would struggle to keep the fear and guilt at bay if he spent the rest of the evening doing nothing but idling, waiting for sunrise, but he knew Lux was right. Looking at the girl, he could practically see the fatigue radiating from her body. Her eyes, normally so very full of life, seemed hollow and weary. Godryk appeared as though he was fairing no better. Fynn nodded his assent. "Let's eat and rest up best we can. But, we should all stay close."

"Why? What do you know that you're not saying?" Lux asked, tensing.

"Fynn thinks that there are more than just enchanted vines and roots at work here," Godryk answered.

Fynn added, "I think the Iba-Jii have done something more to the jungle. The longer we're here, the less likely we are to get out."

Hours wore on before Hollyn woke with a start at the sound of shuffling. His shoulder still throbbed horribly, but the pain, as time wore on, was lessening, dulling ever so slightly. He sat up from the comfort of his cloak-made-cocoon, watching blearily as Lux staggered by.

"Lux?" It was dark. He figured it must be night. The girl continued creeping by him. He was louder this time. "Lux?"

The sound of Hollyn's mildly nervous voice struck through Fynn's slumber like lightning tearing the night sky asunder. His eyes snapped open as he pulled himself up, watching as Lux crept across the campsite. Hollyn was watching her, blue eyes alight by the dying fire's embers.

"What's going on?" Fynn asked. He slowly stood up. Though he felt weak, he remained resolute in his course and stole across the camp toward the girl. He caught her by the wrist and pulled her back. "Lux?"

Hollyn was trying to stand, but he struggled with one arm so tightly bound. His balance was hindered, but he managed to rock to his feet and wobble until he was upright. He found his way beside Fynn. "Luxy, what's wrong?" he asked shakily.

The eyes that looked back to them were foreign. Gone were the vibrant, blue eyes of the girl they'd come to admire and in their place were eyes lost in a daze. She didn't seem to recognize them or really even realize they were there. Fynn tightened his hand around her wrist, but she didn't make a move. She stood there, swaying gently as a breeze blew by, tousling her red hair. It tumbled over her face. She made no move to push the tangled curls away.

"Lux? Are you awake?" queried Fynn.

When she spoke, her voice was haunted and distant. "Can you hear it?"

Hollyn reached out, brushing Lux's hair behind her ears. He tried to look into her eyes, but the girl looked away from him. He kept his tone even, calm. "Hear what?"

She whispered, "They're getting closer."

Fynn, startled, took a step back. He released his hold on the girl's wrist. Horror struck the boy as he watched a vine shoot from the darkness and entangle itself around Lux's slender ankle. As it went taut, it pulled her to the ground. She shrieked, clawing frantically at the earth beneath her fingertips, nails splitting in her dogged effort to escape the clutches of the vines. They were tightening with such force she believed her bones would splinter soon.

Hollyn lunged forward, catching one of her hands in his; he pulled back with all his failing strength. Lux screamed the most terrified scream either prince had ever heard. Fynn could recall a similar scream from Renwyn when he vanished. He couldn't bring himself to move. Hollyn was just to his side, desperately trying to pull Lux free.

"Fynn!" cried Hollyn. "Fynneas! Help!"

Yanked from his petrified reverie, Fynn grabbed hold of Lux's other hand and, like his cousin, tried to root his weight in his heels, leaning back and pulling. "We've got you!"

"Don't let go!" she pleaded. "Don't let go!"

"Godryk!" yelled Fynn. "Albie!"

Footsteps rushed nearby. Fynn glanced back, seeing someone darting forward. Soon he recognized the blurring shape to be Godryk. He heard the boy cry out, "Georgie!"

Vines snapped and wiggled like snakes, tearing through the jungle with ease. They caught Georgie's ankles and began dragging her from the campsite. Godryk and Albie, each having been roused from their sleep at the sound of the princes screaming, scrambled to try and catch hold of Georgie before she disappeared into the seemingly unending darkness of the night.

"Georgie!" Albie, on the verge of absolute hysterics, screamed. "Georgie! Where are you? Georgie!"

"Don't let go!" Lux sobbed. She was holding onto the boys' hands with all her might. "Please!"

Fynn looked to Hollyn who, despite only being able to use one hand, was doing a fair job of keeping his ground. "Don't let go!" Fynn shouted. He pulled his knife from his belt and crawled to Lux's ankle. He began to saw away at the vine. "I won't let it get you, Lux! I won't let it."

Every time the green fibers ripped beneath the sharp of his blade, they grew back within an instant. Fynn was mortified to see the vine intensify its hold around the girl's ankle. He could all but hear the sound of her bone quaking under the pressure. "No!" he shrieked.

Lux's hand ripped away from Hollyn's as something dragged her into the undergrowth. She disappeared amongst the foliage, lost to the expansive sea of shadowed jungle all around them.

Hollyn pitched forward at the loss of contact, sprawling out painfully upon the ground. He cried into the dirt. "No...no, no, no!" A wash of salty tears drowned his freckled cheeks.

Godryk, having raced across the site, wrapped his arms around Fynn's shoulders and pulled him a safe distance from where Lux had vanished, forcibly hauling him back to where the firelight was able to reach them, where the gold of the flames extended like a protective barrier fighting off the unnatural forces that had stolen the girls. He held the prince tightly, knowing that if he loosened his hold for even a moment, Fynn was liable to bolt after Lux.

"Did you see that?" whispered Godryk.

Fynn croaked miserably, "They got her."

"Georgie too," Albie shakily added.

Hollyn pulled himself upright from the dirt. He staggered closer to the other three boys. He stared unwaveringly at the darkness, believing that if he stared hard enough, he would will Lux back into being, hoping beyond reason that she would appear there before them unharmed. "We have to go after them," he said.

"We will," assured Fynn icily. "We're not leaving without them. *All* of them."

"Do you...do you think...whatever that was...do you think it's going to come for us, too?" Albie asked.

Fynn watched as the firelight danced over the earth. The dim, golden glow stretched only a foot or so beyond where they were all huddled. "No. They don't like fire."

"What?" Albie questioned.

"We're safe if we stay close to the fire," Fynn replied. "That's how we'll get them back."

Godryk pulled Fynn closer, still not entirely convinced the other boy wouldn't run off on his own. "We have to find Ollie's team first," he advised. "We *have* to find them. Hopefully they haven't lost anyone."

"We find them. First thing in the morning, we find them. Then we go get Penelope, Lux, Georgie, and Renwyn," Fynn agreed. "We're all going to make it back. No matter what."

16

KING OF THE JUNGLE

Wilder's limp became more pronounced as the morning waned into the afternoon. Firiel, with one arm slung around the boy's waist to steady him as they continued their aimless slog through the jungle's undergrowth, sighed wearily. Blood was caked over the side of her face, having gone spilling down her temples when she'd been struck in the head by a vine that seemed to move of its own volition. That was yesterday and the entire ordeal had frightened team one so much that they had unanimously decided to keep marching through the night in hope of finding the other teams.

Hogan's shoulders were slumped forward as exhaustion threatened to overcome his weak constitution. He chanced a glance toward Ollie, who remained resolutely in step with Wilder and Firiel despite how worn he was. Despite a moment where he had a near emotional breakdown following Wilder's unfortunate tumble over the side of a rather nasty, rocky hill, Ollie had remained relatively optimistic. As they proceeded further into the nightmarish wilderness, he had not stopped encouraging them, offering sound words of comfort and assurance despite their increasingly concerning circumstances.

"Let's stop for a moment," Firiel suggested. She began to carefully lever Wilder to the ground. "He can't keep on walking with his leg like that." The boy was carefully propped against a tree and gingerly stretching his leg. Firiel knelt in front of him. She removed her cloak and began to gently dab away at the still-bleeding gash just under Wilder's knee. "We all need a break. We shouldn't stay long. But we should take the time to catch our breath."

Ollie flopped down opposite his cousin, watching as Firiel proceeded with what meager medical treatment she could offer. The cut had torn deep into Wilder's shin and, much to Ollie's dismay, the flesh around the wound was an angry red. Deep purple bruising marbled the exposed knee and shin where his leggings had been torn away by the sharp of the rocks. Ollie frowned. "That doesn't look good."

"We need to find the others and get out of here as fast as we can," Firiel asserted, still doing her best to keep the wound clean. "How bad does it hurt?"

Wincing, Wilder responded through bit back sobs, "I'll be fine 'til we get back to the castle. Don't worry."

"We're *already* worried." Ollie sighed, concerned, as more blood trickled down the injured boy's leg. "But we're going to get out of here."

Hogan seated himself beside Ollie, combing his hand through his sweat-matted hair. "The others *have* to be close."

"I think you're right," Ollie said.

"Let's hope," Firiel mumbled.

A rustling in the branches above caught their attention. Instantly, they were tense, none of them forgetting the terror of watching the jungle move on its own as if possessed. The four each reached for their knives, readying themselves for another assault. None came. As time went on and still no offensive foray of vines lashed their way, they began to relax a little. Something rustled again. They stared all around them, waiting for something, anything. They didn't expect a small bat to tumble from the branches and land just before them, gazing back at them with beady eyes.

"Is that a bat?" asked Hogan.

"Looks like it," Ollie said.

"But out in the middle of the day?" Firiel questioned, staring curiously at the small creature.

"Maybe it's lost?" Wilder suggested.

The tiny creature crawled forward; its wings braced against the jungle floor. Its movements were careful but confident and soon it stopped just in front of Ollie; one tiny wing outstretched and rested over the boy's knee. The impossibly black eyes stared up at the boy, pleading. Tiny ears twitched; its nose wrinkled. It gave a flap of its wing as if beckoning Ollie into action.

"Hello there." Ollie smiled as he gently reached out his hand to the creature.

Surprisingly, the bat allowed the boy to stroke its head.

Ollie looked back to his teammates and said, "It's like it isn't scared of humans."

"Weird thing, it is," Wilder huffed.

"What do you think it wants?" Hogan thought aloud, watching the bat leaning into Ollie's idling hand.

"Why don't you ask it?" snorted Firiel.

Hogan shrugged, grinning. "Hello there, little bat. What're you doing out here? Shouldn't you be in a cave somewhere sleeping?"

The bat remained staring up at Ollie with deep, imploring eyes. It flapped its wing again. As softly as he could, Ollie took hold of the creature's wing, pulling it back from his knee. He saw upon the black membrane of its dainty wing, a pinkish scar in the shape of a crescent moon. "You've been hurt," Ollie mused sadly.

The bat pulled its wing away, baring its tiny teeth in aggravation. As if to prove it was perfectly capable, the creature of the night beat its wing a few times before, once again, resting it over Ollie's knee.

"I see, it's all better now, I suppose?" Ollie took to brushing his meaty fingers over the bat's head again, stroking over the black fur carefully. "Don't you lot normally travel together? I've never seen a little bat like you off on its own before…and *certainly* not during daylight."

The four children watched as the bat leapt up, beating its wings fervently until it steadied itself in flight. They watched as the creature swung in low gyres around them, looking back down at them now and again. He continued his flight path, never straying far from the team.

Hogan didn't miss the way the bat kept glancing down at them. "I think it wants us to follow it," he speculated.

"We're not taking directions from a bat, Hogan," Wilder snapped.

"Do you have any better ideas?" asked Ollie.

"No, but we're not following it," argued Wilder.

"It may lead us to water or maybe food," reasoned Hogan.

Ollie stood. "I think Hogan's right. We should follow it and see where it takes us."

Firiel, shaking her head in disbelief, laughed. "I can't believe I'm saying this, but I think you're right. Let's give it a try, at least." She offered her hand to the injured Wilder, smiling warmly. "We don't have a lot of options left, Wilder. Come on, then."

Taking the girl's hand, despite his opposing thoughts on the matter, the wounded Wilder was pulled to his feet. He resumed his place against Firiel, her arm curling around his waist, his slung around her shoulders. "This is stupid," he grumbled.

She chuckled, "Probably."

Hogan sprung up to his feet and began leading the group in pursuit of the bat. They followed dutifully as the tiny creature weaved through the air above them, mindful to never fly off too far from them. They kept a steady pace, the bat seeming to know just where to lead them so as they didn't encounter any dangers or particularly stubborn obstacles along their sojourn through the jungle.

"Do you hear that?" Hogan asked, looking back to the other three.

"People." Ollie nodded. "Up ahead."

Delighted at the prospect of finding the others, Hogan rushed ahead, yelling, "Hello? Hello?"

Bursting through the brush, he found the remnants of teams two and three. Godryk was the first one he saw, and his jaw went slack at the sight. The red-haired boy had blood smeared over his face and tunic; mud and sweat matted his hair. There was a cut by his hairline and another striking over his chin. His uniform was in tatters; mud and filth stretched over his knees where his leggings had been ripped apart.

When Godryk turned, hearing Hogan's approach and beholding the other boy, his blue eyes went alight with tears.

"Godryk," Hogan whispered. He ran up to him and didn't hesitate to throw his arms around the young Redmayne. "You look awful."

As Ollie, Firiel, and Wilder came into view, Godryk smiled. He pulled away from Hogan, nodding. "I've been better."

Albie sauntered closer. His face was covered in dirt, as were his tunic and leggings. His cloak was torn and ripped nearly to shreds. Blood stained the arms of his tunic; both of his hands were wrapped tightly with pieces of his cloak, red creeping through the knit of the fabric. He smiled. "Glad to see you all."

Hollyn and Fynn came closer to the group, each prince inching toward them on shaking legs. Hollyn's red hair was sticking out in all directions; blood and dirt covered almost every inch of his pale face and tunic. His leggings were ripped and bloodied. His eyes didn't hold their normal fire, but instead looked tired and scared. One arm was tied tightly to his body with a sling. Fynn looked no better. His black hair was slicked back with sweat and reddened with dried blood. There was a laceration to his forehead that looked as though it was healing nicely, but the crusted blood from the wound coated most of his face. More red was splattered across his front; his uniform was almost unrecognizable.

Fynn smiled a crooked smile at the sight of team one. "You're all still together. That's good."

"You four weren't all on the same team," noted Hogan warily.

Albie shook his head. "No. Our team," he indicated Godryk with a wave of the hand, "found theirs. Well, we found Hollyn. Then we found Fynn."

"Renwyn and Penelope disappeared," Fynn explained. "Then Georgie and Lux were taken."

"*Taken*? By what?" Firiel asked insistently.

"The Iba-Jii," replied Godryk.

"That explains what happened yesterday," Hogan began, turning from the boys to look back to Firiel. His expression softened. "When that vine got you. We weren't imagining it; the vine really did attack you."

"The Iba-Jii enchant the jungle. That's what we've heard. It's a long story, though. But that makes sense." Fynn's grey eyes stared back to the girl, an unreadable expression twinkling in the icy depths. "Are you alright?"

"I'll be fine," Firiel assured.

"Good." Fynn smiled.

"Well, what're we going to do? I mean, four of us are missing. We can't just leave them," Ollie said. "What do we do?"

"We're going after them," Fynn replied sternly. "No one is getting left behind. We're leaving here *together*."

Ollie grinned. "Right. What's the plan?"

"The Iba-Jii hate fire," Hollyn started. "The vines and roots, everything they enchant, I suppose, won't come near us when there's fire close by."

"So, we make torches," Fynn added.

"Makes sense," agreed Wilder.

Albie, as he had been curiously looking about the gathered group, chirped, "How'd you all find us anyway?"

Ollie laughed. "Oh! We forgot to tell you." He looked up and then pointed to where a tiny bat wrapped in a cloak of black wings hung in the branches. "You won't believe me, but a bat led us to you." He remained regarding the creature as he continued, "Tiny thing, he is. He's got a nasty scar on one wing. I'm surprised he was able to fly so well."

At that, Fynn's head snapped up and he couldn't help the elation that burst into his eyes as he smiled, calling out, "Buttons!"

"Buttons?" Hollyn repeated flatly, quirking a brow.

Fynn, ignoring the other prince, held his arm out and watched, positively enthralled, as the small bat unwound its wings from its tiny body and fluttered down, clinging to his arm. Soft wings curled around the boy's spindly limb, clasping tightly as a tiny nose nuzzled at the prince's elbow. Fynn slowly curled his arm to his chest and laughed as the bat crawled from his perch, little claws twisting into the fabric of his tunic, tiny head nestling against the crook of his neck. He held the bat close.

"Hello, Buttons," Fynn whispered. "Looks like you're all healed up. Did you lead our friends to us? What a good boy."

"Great," drawled Hollyn, as he flung himself down and sat, watching Fynn. "He's making friends with animals now...*talking* to them, too."

"Fynn?" Ollie ventured. "Do you *know* this bat?"

Fynn nodded, looking back and stifling a laugh at the absolutely perplexed looks angled his way. "Yes." He drew closer to the group, letting them all have a good look at the creature held protectively in his arms. "His name's Buttons."

"Buttons? Not the most intimidating name." Firiel laughed as she observed the tiny creature. "What about Night Stalker? Or Black Danger?"

Fynn leveled an irritated glare her way and repeated, "His name is *Buttons*." He sighed. "Look, alright, I didn't name him, but that's his name and I'm not changing it."

"Alright, alright." Firiel held up her hands in mock defense. "Don't get so worked up!"

"Right, but how did Buttons know how to find you?" asked Hogan.

"He's a special bat, I suppose," Ollie figured.

"You've no idea," joked Fynn.

"Let's get to work," Hollyn grumbled. He turned to Fynn, determination darkening his stare. "*Idiot*, can that bat of yours scout the area for us?"

Fynn turned, still grinning impishly, to regard the taller prince and nodded happily. Glancing back down to the bat, he kept his voice soft as he asked, "Buttons, can you have a look around?" He chuckled as the bat fluttered its wings in his arms before it let go. "Have a look, see if you can find out where our friends might be!" He watched, quite amused, as the little bat took off, disappearing amongst the twisting canopy on his orders.

"Right," Hollyn said. "Wilder, your leg looks a mess."

"It's alright," growled Wilder as he staggered toward Hollyn, seating himself opposite the prince.

Hollyn wore a bored expression; his eyes lost any bit of light they had before. His voice was flat and dull as he said, "Right, all the same, why don't you stay here and bleed all over the place rather than tracking blood through the jungle and attracting whatever is out there. Alright?"

Wilder grumbled, crossing his arms over his chest. He nodded. "Fine."

"Great, now that we've gotten that out of the way, Ollie, Albie, Hogan, Firiel—you gather together sticks, rocks, and kindling. We're going to make another fire. Godryk," he turned slightly to eye the others warily before continuing, "and Fynneas, you two try and find some large sticks or fallen branches and bring them here. And stay close by. Within earshot at the very least, alright? At the first sign of danger or anything *abnormal*, come back here."

"Understood," agreed Fynn as he started off on his task. "Hollyn? What're we going to use the branches for?" he asked, while he continued forward slowly.

"Spears and torches," Hollyn answered. "We'll sharpen the ends of the sturdiest ones."

"Right," Fynn acknowledged. "*Smart.*"

It was evening before the children had completed their tasks. A fire burned between them as they huddled around, sticking close to the pale, orange glow, finishing their final task of sharpening fallen branches into spears.

When the last branch was sharp - the final spear complete - Fynn set it down in his lap and smiled. "Finally."

As if sensing that the time had come for his return, Buttons fluttered down and clung to Fynn's back, his small head peeking over the boy's shoulder down to the makeshift weapon settled over his legs. The prince reached up to scratch the bat's cheek, softly humming as he did. When the animal settled, Fynn asked, "Find anything?"

"Are you expecting him to answer?" Hollyn chuckled. "You *do* remember he's a bat?"

Buttons bristled at the red-haired prince's derisive tone, tiny teeth baring as his wings beat and he took to the air. The eight children watched as the small bat, a mere black speck amongst the growing evening-darkness, swooped in grand, oblong twists, before coming back to the campsite. He settled on the ground before Fynn, peering up at him with bright, black eyes.

"Did you find them?" Quirking a brow and smirking, Fynn suggested, "Flap your wings once for yes and twice for no. Do you understand that, Buttons?"

The small creature's wings flapped—only once.

Fynn turned to Hollyn, a rather self-satisfied smirk firmly in place on his visage. "*Yes*, to answer your question, I *do* expect him to answer. And *yes*, I *do* know he's a bat."

"Buttons," Ollie started, "did you find them?"

Buttons' wings beat once.

"Are they far?" Albie asked.

Two beats.

"Are they in danger?" Ollie questioned.

One beat.

Fynn's brow furrowed. "Are they all still alive?"

One beat.

Hollyn asked, "Can you lead us to them?"

One beat.

The red-haired prince's confidence returned; though the weariness from his lingering fever persisted, he was determined. "Right. They're all still alive. We know they're in danger, so we'll have to be smart about this."

Hollyn's stormy, blue eyes swept over the gathered group. Wilder was looking pale; sweat clung to his forehead. His leg was still leaking blood and he stifled gasps of pain every so often.

"Wilder will stay back. We can't afford him going in and getting even more injured." Seeing the boy's look of sheer displeasure at that statement, Hollyn continued, "I know you're plenty strong. I understand. But right now, you're hurt and a liability. Arrogance isn't going to get them back. It'll just get more of us hurt or killed. So, you're staying back. Understood?"

"I don't see why you get to make that decision," argued Wilder vehemently. "I can help!"

Fynn looked toward his cousin. Hollyn, himself, was in obvious pain. It was plain in his eyes and in the set of his posture. But he knew that Hollyn was right and that he wouldn't budge on the declaration. That much was clear by the tight line of his lips, the dip of his brows, the narrowing of his eyes.

"Hollyn's right. You'll only get in the way. No one is saying you're not plenty strong. We know you are. We've all trained with you. But right now, strength isn't going to save them, smarts will." Fynn smiled warmly. "You won't be here alone. Hollyn will stay back too. With his shoulder as bad as it is, he won't be any help to us. Just like you, he'd be a target."

Hollyn nodded dismally. "He's right for once. I'll be staying back too. I'm no good to anyone with just one arm."

"We shouldn't leave you two here alone. One of you is down a leg, the other down an arm. If anything happens, you'd be hard pressed to fight back," Fynn continued. "Ollie, why don't you stay back with them?"

320

"Right," Ollie readily agreed. "I can do that."

"Hogan, why don't you stay with them too?" suggested Fynn.

Hogan nodded. "Right."

"Now that that's settled," Hollyn began weakly, feeling the fatigue clawing at him relentlessly, "let's set out a plan to get the others back." He inhaled deeply, slowly. Fynn's hand draped over his shoulder.

Looking to the black-haired nuisance, Hollyn fought back the urge to roll his eyes when his cousin nodded reassuringly, and instead said, "Right. Fynn, Godryk, Albie, and Firiel will find the others. If they're hurt, that means there's at least man-on-man coverage to help carry them back. Let's hope they're not hurt though." He ran his hand through his messy, scarlet hair. "If you each carry a torch, you'll be too weighed down for much else. Two of you should take a torch, and two should take a spear. You each have your knives with you as well. Stay close to the fire. That's important. Albie, you should go with Fynn. Godryk, take Firiel. Albie, Firiel, you two should carry the torches. Between the four of you, Godryk and Fynn are the best with close combat. They'll most likely handle the spears best. Fair?"

Firiel nodded. "Fair."

"Right, so you'll need to be quick about it. The faster we get our teammates back, the faster we can find our way out of here," Hollyn reminded.

"We'll go get them, bring them back, and start finding our way out. We won't make camp for the night. It's too dangerous. A lot of us will need to go to the infirmary. It's best that we try and get out of here as quickly as we can," Fynn agreed. "Wilder, how's your leg?"

"Still bleeding," he answered painfully. "Can't really move it."

"Ollie," Fynn instructed, "while we're gone, try and tend to Wilder's leg as best you can. Wrap it up tight, but not too tight." Fynn unwound the cloak from his shoulders, tossing the bundle to Ollie. "Clean it best you can first, then wrap it. Once we get back, one of us will help him out of here. If it's worse, we can carry him."

"Understood." Ollie kneaded at the cloak in his hands nervously. "You'll all be careful, won't you?"

"We'll do our best." Firiel smiled.

"Godryk," Hollyn called.

"Yes?" responded the young Redmayne.

"Make sure Fynneas doesn't do anything *exceedingly* stupid, won't you?"

"I'll do my best, but I can't make any promises," Godryk jested.

Fynn stood up, taking his spear in his hand. "Let's be off, then."

As Firiel and Albie lit their torches and Godryk gathered his spear, Fynn looked back to Hollyn. Their eyes met for a moment, a fleeting second wherein Fynn could see the worry, the genuine concern, flickering in the stormy depths of blue. Despite his own fear, his own trepidation about their venture, Fynn forced himself to smile. He forced himself to smile and be confident, to believe that they would return and make it out of the jungle.

"We won't be long," Fynn promised.

"We'll be here when you get back," Hogan assured with a smile.

"See you soon." Fynn waved as he paired up, standing beside Albie. "Don't have too much fun while we're gone!" he joked as they disappeared from the campsite, stepping into the darkness of the early night.

Following the bat's lead, the foursome made its way through the jungle. The trees seemed to be closer and closer together, leaving them little room to twist and turn their way around as they carefully stepped above the overgrown roots. Firiel and Albie diligently kept their torches high; Godryk and Fynn remained within the dim glow of the light, their spears held firmly in their quaking hands. Fynn kept his eyes on Buttons, leading the way for the others. The night was cool, and starlight broke through the canopy.

"Fynn," whispered Albie. "I'm scared."

The prince reached back, taking hold of Albie's free hand. Grey eyes seemed to glow in the darkness, glistening in the firelight, as they turned to regard the frightened boy. "Me too," Fynn admitted softly. "We all are. But we're going to get out of here tonight."

"Where's Buttons?" asked Godryk from just behind the pair. "I can't see anything."

Fynn released Albie, stepping apart. He scanned the night, searching for the fluttering wings. He found the bat quickly enough. Nodding his head in Buttons' direction, he called, "Follow me."

Again, they were off, sifting through the undergrowth. Within the hour, they came upon a clearing where the trees seemed to form a semi-circle and gave way to a large expanse of grass; an emerald sea stretched out before them, speckled by wildflowers and fireflies. Here, there was no canopy, nothing obscuring the vastness of the night sky looming over them; the stars were blindingly bright, and the full moon was unobscured by clouds. Fynn was the first to step into the clearing, initially hesitant. He looked left and right but saw nothing there.

"Buttons, are you sure this is the right place?" he asked. The bat glided down from the sky, perching upon Fynn's shoulder, wings clinging to the boy's back and upper arm as he peered around, nuzzling Fynn's neck for only a moment before tiny ears twitched. "I suppose that's a yes."

"I don't see anyone here," Godryk said.

"Me either," Firiel agreed, stepping a bit closer to the clearing.

Albie, standing just behind Fynn, swung the torch side to side, looking across the clearing expectantly. "Same."

"They've got to be close," insisted Fynn as he proceeded to step further into the clearing.

It felt strange, he thought, to be so open to the sky. They hadn't been in the jungle for more than a few days, but already it felt as though he'd forgotten what it was like to be free, to see the sky as it was with all its grandeur laid out so spectacularly above him. He'd forgotten what it was like to look up and see stars instead of twisting, gnarled branches and leaves. The sight of the night sky set him at ease; it made him feel as though someone were watching him. He leaned his head back, his whole focus on the sky.

"Hello, Mother," he began. "I know you're probably not really up there…and you probably can't hear me…but if you can, if you're anywhere out there…I need your help." He took another few steps forward, heedless that he'd left the safety of the torchlight. "Some of my friends were taken. I need to get them back and make sure they're safe. I know they're here, *somewhere*, but I need your help, Mother. Show me, please, if you can. Show me where they are."

The wind blew, as if urging him forward. Obligingly, Fynn continued. He could hear his friends just behind him, faintly calling for him to return. He focused on the feel of the wind pushing him along. When the wind stopped, Fynn looked down. The ground beneath his booted feet was dead. The grass, so green before, was grey and black beneath his soles. It was contorted and wretched. It crackled beneath his feet as he stepped forward. The fireflies wouldn't fly near where he stood. No flowers bloomed here. He looked around and found the place he stood to be utterly dismal.

Looking skyward, Fynn asked, "They're close, aren't they?"

The wind swam through his black hair, ruffling it. He smiled, the feeling reminiscent of those times his sister or father, Moriah or Noel, would run their hands through his hair affectionately. He closed his eyes, reveling in the sensation for a moment longer. When he again opened his eyes, he was startled to see a woman standing at his side. A tear leaked from his eye and slowly - painfully slowly - crawled down the side of his face.

"Hello, darling," Celestine greeted. Her voice was like a melody playing just for him, silky and refined.

"You heard me, then?" Fynn asked. There was sadness in his voice.

"I always hear you," she replied.

"Can you help me?"

She nodded. "You're looking for your friends."

"Yes."

"You'll find them here," she said. Celestine took a step forward but stopped when she saw her son was not following. She reached her hand back for him. He took it. She smiled. "Follow me and I can take you to them."

Before following her, Fynn stopped. "Wait." He pulled his hand from hers and looked back. "I need to tell them where we're going. They should come! They can help me get my friends back."

"No," she said, shaking her head. "You won't need them. Not yet."

Turning toward his mother, Fynn's voice lowered. "They're not here. Are they?"

"No."

"Buttons, he led us here." Fynn scowled. "I shouldn't have trusted a bat. Hollyn was right."

"No."

"No?"

Celestin smiled. "No."

Fynn stepped closer to his mother. He looked up to her, eyes pleading. "He led me here on purpose?"

She nodded.

The boy's hand reached up, gently stroking the bat's fur. "He led me here to see you."

"Yes."

"How could he have known? That's impossible."

Celestine drew away from Fynn's side to come to stand before him. She reached out; her ghostly hand traced over Fynn's as she, too, gently stroked the bat's fur. Her smile was small, sad. "He's a special bat."

"His name is Buttons."

"A fine name." The late princess laughed.

"How did he know...how *could* he know you'd be here?"

"We're acquainted," she said.

"What?"

"Let's just say, he's a *gift*…for you."

More tears began to flow freely down the boy's cheeks. His voice wavered, "You…sent him?"

"Do you not like him?"

"No. No, it's not that," Fynn stammered. "But…how…*why?*"

"Because," Celestine began as she knelt before her trembling son, "I can't be here to guide you and to help you. I thought you could use a friend who could be there. One who could see when you could not, who could lead you when you're lost." She combed her hand through the boy's hair, her touch as cold as frost.

"You sent him for me?"

"Regrettably, on his way, the poor dear was injured." Her hands came around the boy's back and pulled him closer. "Minnie was good enough to take care of him until he was ready to come find you."

Fynn allowed himself the moment to rest his head upon his mother's shoulder. He couldn't help but let slip a quiet sob as she ran her hand in gentle circles over his back. "Thank you," he whispered.

"Now, darling, I believe you came here for a reason. Some friends of yours were taken?"

He cuddled closer to her, unwilling to relinquish the contact just yet. "Yes," he said softly. "The Iba-Jii got them."

"Nasty creatures," Celestine proclaimed, leaning into her son's embrace. "But you can beat them."

"I promised I would. I won't leave my friends here to die," Fynn vowed.

"You're a good boy, Fynneas."

"Where can I find them?"

Celestine extricated herself from her son gently. He'd grown since she last came to visit him at Claw Keep. She cupped her hand over his cheek; her thumb brushed away his tears. "They're just beyond this clearing. Go beyond the trees and you'll find a cave. Your friends will be there."

"How do I get them? I know the Iba-Jii don't like fire, but all we've got are torches and these spears." He nodded down to the weapon he held limply in one hand at his side. "Can we do it? Can we get them out?"

"Fynneas." Celestine's voice was gentle and calming. "Darling, can I tell you a story?"

He nodded.

"Do you know why I gave you your middle name? Why I wanted to call you Draekon?"

The boy prince regarded his mother, thinking. After a moment, he answered, "Father said you always liked dragons. That you'd read stories about them all the time. That you used to read Fiona stories about them before bed every night."

Celestine's eyes grew distant and fond as she thought. Again, she brushed tears from her son's cheek. "I had a dream just before you were born. I'd been so sick. All I'd done for days was sleep, but I never dreamt. It was just blackness when I slept. But one night I had a dream." She traced the curve of the boy's cheek, trailing her fingertip over his jaw. "I had a dream that there was ice all around. That the castles all across Estheria were frozen. The skies were black. There were no stars. Everywhere I looked, there was just snow and ice. And then I saw a dragon come from the black and he was huge, *magnificent*. I saw this dragon right in front of me and I reached out and I swear to you, Fynneas, I could feel his scales against my hand. He looked at me and I saw his eyes, right there…so close. They were this color…like ice, staring back at me. This dragon, he was so black it was as if he were the night itself come to life." She tapped the tip of Fynn's nose with her forefinger. "And as I stood there and watched, he breathed fire and all the ice melted. It was like everything came back to life and the sky was there again and it was sunny and blue. The snow was gone, and the ice was gone, and the grass had come back. And then I turned to look at the dragon, and he was still there, staring back at me with those icy eyes." She slung her arm round her son's shoulder, mindful not to knock Buttons from his perch, and pulled the boy as close as she could. "So, I asked the dragon its name and do you know what it said? It whispered to me its name…*Draekon*." Celestine leaned away from the boy and stared into his eyes, so like her own, and continued, "And when I woke the next morning, I told Felix I would call you Draekon. We'd already decided, you see, that if you were a boy, we'd name you for one of the kings. Felix liked the name Fynneas, thought it was strong. I agreed. I think the name suits you well. But I insisted you'd be named Draekon also and he agreed to it. And I think that name suits you just as well."

"Those stories you'd tell Fiona. What were they about?" asked Fynn.

"So often we hear stories of the princess in the tower, kept prisoner by the dragon, until a knight would come to save her and slay the beast,"

Celestine wistfully started. "But I would never tell my daughter such silly stories. I told your sister of the princess who protected the dragon from the knights. I told her the stories of the princess who raised the dragon until he was strong enough to fly on his own, strong enough to fight those vicious knights off. I found that Fiona liked those stories best."

"Mother," Fynn whispered as he gazed back at her, "what should I do?"

"A dragon, my darling, is born from fire." She smiled. Celestine stood then, raking her fingers through his hair one last time. "A dragon emerges from the fire, Fynneas."

"You're talking in riddles," whined Fynn.

"No."

"Yes, you are!"

"You'll be alright, Fynneas. Remember *who* you are, and no one will be able to stand against you," she said.

The wind began to blow and with it, Celestine turned her back and began stalking off. With every step, she grew more faint, as if she were dust being carried off on the breeze.

"No!" Fynn cried, rushing forward. "I don't understand! Please, come back! Come back."

But she was gone.

A hand braced against Fynn's shoulder and pulled him around. Godryk shook him, "Fynn!"

Blinking as if clearing his vision, Fynn looked up to the boy. "Did you see that?"

"See what?" asked the young Redmayne.

Fynn looked back over his shoulder, straining through the night in search of his mother. "Nothing...nothing at all."

"Are you alright?" asked Godryk. "You just wandered into the clearing and stared off at nothing for a while. We were yelling for you, but you just kept staring. It was like you couldn't hear us at all."

"I'm alright," replied Fynn absently. "I know where they are. Where they're being kept." He nodded off in the direction Celestine had pointed him in. "They're just beyond the clearing. They're in a cave."

"How do you know?"

"Just trust me?"

Godryk nodded. "Always."

"Good." Fynn smirked. "Ready?"

"Ready."

Fynn shrugged his shoulder and Buttons took flight from his perch, jolting into the sky. "Lead the way!" yelled the prince.

With renewed vigor, the four trudged across the clearing. They entered back into the tangle of jungle and headed further into the lair of the wild. Fynn kept his eyes trained on Buttons while Firiel and Albie worked to illuminate the way.

There, mingling with the trees, vines crawling up the fine, stony archways, was a cave whose mouth stretched large before them like a black void. They stood before it, firelight barely grazing the magnitude of blackness before them, upon the precipice of the unknown. Once more, Buttons had descended from among high to clamber over Fynn's back, clutching at him forcefully.

"They're in there," Fynn said.

Markings were etched upon the archway of the cave. Albie lifted his torch and ran the flame over the curve of the cave's lower walls, revealing carvings of strange symbols none of the four had ever seen before. Frightened, Albie asked, "Are you sure?"

Fynn nodded. "I *know* they are."

"Then let's go," Firiel said resolutely. She stepped forward. "Stay together."

They entered into the cave shoulder to shoulder. All around them tall walls of black stone jutted upward, arching over their heads. There was a steady dripping sound that kept pace with the sound of their heart beats. Vines reached up from the dark soil like the tentacles of an earthen kraken, creeping up the walls, reaching into crags unseen by the searching sets of eyes. The ground began to slope and bring them downward, so far down that they could no longer look back and see the opening. Presently, they were there in the belly of the cave with nothing but the flickering torchlight to show them the way.

It was cold in the cave.

There was a chill that permeated every inch of its innards, stinging the children as they continued, undeterred, into the depths of darkness. From far off in the distance, down in the bowels of the subterranean labyrinth they'd wandered into, came the faintest sounds of laughter. Fynn, peering far further into the shadows than his comrades could, saw the end of the stony corridor. He urged them on, silently taking up the lead, heedless of the dangers that may lurk at the end.

The cave tunnel gave way to a large chamber of stone. In the center there was a throne made of vines that curled forth from the earth; wildflowers of every color bloomed brilliantly despite the lack of light and warmth. Thorns decorated the throne's back, jutting from the green vines like sunrays. There was no light there, save for the glow of the children's torches, but they could see a thousand golden eyes peering through the darkness back at them. And, from the black, there strode a dark figure far larger than the rest, far larger than any human they'd ever seen.

The beast, whatever it was, approached through a throng of staring little eyes and appeared to be a monster the likes of which they couldn't even imagine. It stood two men high, a creature with the legs of a goat, furry and curved. Its body was that of a man, except for the face, which was elongated and animal like - its eyes like slits, gold irises burning in the darkness. Upon its head twisted two horns which bore the same markings they'd seen on the mouth of the cave outside. The creature regarded them thoughtfully before stealing from their firelight to sit upon the throne and, from its regal seat, returned to staring at them.

With a wave of a clawed hand, the cave chamber was alight with thousands of fireflies darting in every direction. The chamber became golden and the darkness was chased away. The children huddled together at the sight of spritely little creatures amassed all around them—the Iba-Jii. Their skin was grey, and their eyes were tawny and far too large for their tiny, beaked faces. They wore garments fashioned from fronds and held tiny spears in their three-fingered hands.

Fynn squared his shoulders and set his back perfectly straight. Stepping in front of his three companions, he said, "We've only come for our friends. Are they here?"

None of the Iba-Jii replied.

"Please. We've come for our friends. They have names, you know. Lux…and Renwyn, Penelope, and Georgie. They've names and families and friends. Please, are they here?" persisted the prince.

A clawed hand strummed against the arm of the throne as the beast watched the prince before him. Gold eyes narrowed and, at last, the monster spoke. Its voice was like thunder, rumbling in the cave. "You come seeking your friends?"

"Yes." Fynn was sure to keep his voice steady. "Are they here?"

"They are."

"Will you let them go?" Fynn asked. The monster before him straightened in its throne, leaning forward slightly, baring teeth. Amongst the Iba-Jii, this monster must be their king, Fynn realized. Desperate to get his year mates back and out of harm's way, Fynn sharply inhaled. He lowered his head and bent his knee until he was there, kneeling before the monster and its wild throne. "Please, we've only come for our friends. We mean you no harm."

The monster laughed.

Fynn remained there, head bowed. He knew better than to look up and challenge the monster. "Please. Give us our friends and we'll leave."

"You come making demands?" the monster asked.

The boy shook his head. "No. I ask it of you out of the kindness of your heart. I wouldn't think to make a demand of you here, amongst *your* people, as you sit upon *your* throne."

"Smart child," commented the creature.

"I can see you are a king, are you not?"

"I am."

"Then I stand by what I said. I wouldn't make demands of a king."

The creature leaned further forward to regard Fynn and asked, "And who is it who is so smart as to know not to make demands of a king?"

Still staring at the ground beneath him, Fynn answered humbly, "My name is Fynn. And, as I've said, I come here only seeking to get my friends back so we may leave and go home."

"Tell me, *Fynn*, how have you come to be so wise as to know how to talk to a king with such ease?"

It was then that Fynn chose to raise his head and level his gaze upon the monster. "I am Prince Fynneas Draekon Fog of Estheria." He rose to his full, though meager, height. His eyes lingered, gazing thoughtfully into the gold abyss of the creature's stare before he threw out his arm and cast his spear to the ground. "I've not come to fight."

"A prince?" The monster rose from its throne and started toward Fynn. "Come all this way to speak with me?"

Fynn nodded.

The great beast stood with its hooved feet just hairs from Fynn's booted toes. It towered over the boy like a mountain would a pebble, eyes hungrily gleaming as its head dipped to regard the boy. "Do you know who I am, Prince of Estheria?"

"No."

"I am Drusus, king of this jungle. And you, tiny, mortal prince, have come a long way for nothing. I have no intention of returning your friends."

"Why not?" Fynn asked sharply.

"I don't owe you a reason."

"I'm asking for one anyway," insisted the boy.

Drusus reached out a hand and placed it over the boy's shoulder. His thumb stretched and spanned across the boy's neck. Tilting Fynn's head just to the side, Drusus chuckled, "I could snap your neck in two with the flick of a finger and you dare ask me to explain myself?"

Choking back his mounting fear, Fynn replied flatly, "I do."

"And why is that?"

"Because, as you said, I've come all this way for my friends." His eyes flicked down and chilled as they saw the thumb braced against his throat. "And I don't plan to leave without them."

"You're either very *brave* or very *stupid*, Prince of Estheria."

Fynn laughed darkly, mirthlessly. "I believe if you ask most people, they'd say very stupid."

"And if I asked you?"

Fynn smirked. "I'd be inclined to agree with them."

Drusus withdrew his hand and pondered the prince at his feet. He retired from the boy's proximity and returned to his throne, still mulling over the children who stood before him. "Tell me, Fynneas Draekon Fog, what would you give for your friends' safe return?"

"What would you ask?"

It was Drusus' turn to smirk. "Your life."

The words stole Fynn's breath from him. He felt heavy. But there was something peaceful about the suggestion. Fynn, for all his short life, had looked at his time as granted, nothing special. Life was a given, never to be questioned—never having been questioned. And yet, presently, with that very granted gift at stake, the prince felt oddly calm. He looked back and saw the horror etched upon Firiel and Albie's features. He saw Godryk, with his eyes gone wide, looking at him, shaking.

Godryk stepped forward, his hand grabbed Fynn's shoulder. He shook his head, pleading, "Fynn, *no*. There has to be another way."

"Ah," grinned the king of the jungle, "but there isn't. You asked what I wanted in exchange for the lives of those I've stolen from you and I've offered you a fair bargain."

"No!" cried Godryk, shoving Fynn behind him. He shook his head; tears spilled down his face, leaving hot trails in their wake. "No. You won't kill him."

Fynn stepped before Godryk, eyes icy in the yellow light. "It's alright." He turned to Drusus. "I want to see my friends first. I want to see that they're alive."

"Have we a deal then, Prince of Estheria?"

"If my friends are alright," began Fynn carefully, calmly, "and you promise them safe passage out of here, out of this cave and the jungle? Then yes, we have a deal."

"Bring out the prisoners," Drusus ordered.

Firiel and Albie, clutching to their torches like lifelines, watched as a few of the Iba-Jii stole away into the darkness, down another twisting, shadowy corridor of the cave. They weren't left waiting long, for soon the limping forms of Renwyn, Lux, Penelope, and Georgie appeared before them. Each of the four was filthy, covered head to toe in dirt and blood, shivering in the cool atmosphere of the cave. When they realized where they were, who they stood before, none of the four could hold back their sobs and tears.

"You came for us," Penelope whimpered.

Renwyn trembled as he looked at Fynn. "Are the others alright?"

Fynn nodded solemnly.

"What have they done to you?" asked Albie as he ran toward his year mates.

Lux stepped forward. Her attention was drawn to Fynn and Godryk the very second she stepped into the cave chamber. It had not escaped her notice that there was a monster seated at a throne far too close to the two for her liking. "They haven't done much. We were tied up, stored away in a cage made of vines and sticks. But we're alright. No worse, really, than when we were taken."

"Are you satisfied, Prince of Estheria?" asked Drusus cheerily. "Your little friends are well."

"May I speak with them before...you know?" asked Fynn softly.

Drusus grinned. "You may."

Both Godryk and Fynn joined their friends. The eight circled around each other, throwing their arms over one another's shoulders, sobbing and clinging and going weak from exhaustion, stress, and the cold.

Lux peeled herself from Godryk's embrace, then threw herself at Fynn. Her cheek pressed against his shoulder as she bent her head, allowing herself to cry for only a moment. "You came for us."

Fynn wrapped his arms around the girl. His forehead rested against her head as he whispered, "You're all going home."

Lux jerked away from Fynn, eyes narrowing accusingly. "What do you mean *you're* all going home?" She looked between Fynn and Godryk frantically. Her eyes trained upon her cousin. "What does he mean, Godryk?" She rounded on Fynn. "*You're* coming with us."

The prince shook his head. "I can't."

"What do you mean *you can't?*" Lux demanded.

Fynn forced a smile. "It was the terms of your release."

"What do you mean?" Penelope asked, stepping forward. Her hands clutched over her hysterically beating heart. "*You're* coming too, Fynn. Right?"

"I can't," he repeated in a hushed, broken voice.

"If you would prefer," cooed Drusus, "you may join your friends back in their cage. If not, then please, let us continue with our bargain. A price must be paid, Prince of Estheria, you understand."

"I understand," Fynn lamented as he returned to stand before Drusus and his throne. "I wouldn't go back on my word."

"Ah," chuckled the beast, "for what is a king without his word to stand by?"

"I'm no king," Fynn argued pointlessly.

"But you are, Fynneas Draekon Fog. For, what is a prince if not a king yet uncrowned?" Drusus' long arm reached back and Fynn watched disgustedly as one of the Iba-Jii handed their monster king a goblet filled with what he could only assume was some sort of poison. "And what is a king who is not prepared to lay down his life for his subjects?"

"No king at all," replied Fynn. He took the goblet from the monster, marveling at how heavy it was in his hands.

"Very wise," Drusus nodded. "You're very *brave*, Fynneas Draekon Fog."

"Why all the formality?" Fynn snidely scoffed. "You're going to kill me; you might as well know me as my friends do. *Please*, call me Fynn."

Drusus nodded. "If that's your wish. Then please, *Fynn*, drink your fill."

The boy prince stood unmoving, staring down at the colorless liquid sloshing in the curved gullet of the goblet. "You swear that my friends will be allowed to leave unharmed?"

"I swear."

"I believe you."

Fynn braced himself. He stole one last breath from the air, relishing the way his lungs felt as they expanded within the cage of ribs. He felt the soft thudding of his heart. Then he took a sip from the goblet, then another, and another until there remained no more liquid in its confines. He waited. He waited for the sting of poison, the pain of his oncoming death, the unwavering stillness of his final moments, the merciful numbness of his demise. He waited and waited. He chanced a final, sad glance to his friends. He waited. Still, nothing happened.

He looked down into the goblet, reassuring himself that he had drank everything. There was nothing there. It was, indeed, empty. Fynn looked back up to Drusus questioningly, only to see the monster king smiling back at him. "I thought…well…why am I not dead?" Fynn stammered.

Drusus rose as a powerful figure from his throne and stood before the boy. "Only someone who expected to die but, nevertheless, drank the poison willingly could survive." He reached down, plucking the goblet from the boy's hands. "You're alive, Prince Fynneas Draekon Fog, because you were ready and willing to die for your comrades, your subjects."

"So, I'm *not* going to die now?"

"No."

"You'll let us go?" Fynn whirled around to his friends, relief washing over him. He ran to them and fell into the grateful embrace of Godryk, who clung to him frantically. When at last Fynn managed to disentangle himself from the other boy's arms, he turned to look to Drusus and asked, "But why take them in the first place?"

"We were hungry," Drusus admitted simply. "And you and your friends were easy prey. It wasn't hard for my Iba-Jii to capture them."

"Then why not kill them once you caught them?" asked Godryk bravely.

"We were saving them," Drusus answered as though it were plainly obvious.

"For what?" pressed Fynn.

"Never mind that now," grumbled the monster. "We'll go in search of something else to serve our purposes." He gently flicked Fynn's back, hurling the boy forward. "I keep to my word, Prince of Estheria, just like you. Your friends and *you* are free to go. You'll have safe passage out of my jungle."

"Sire," Fynn began humbly, "thank you for your mercy." He bowed. "May I ask something more of you?"

"You may."

"Can you tell us how to get out of the jungle? We're a bit turned around, you see. We're not really sure how to get back out." He sighed, nervously combing his hand through his hair.

"I shall do more than just point you on your way," Drusus replied. "I shall give you a guide." He waved his hand toward the darkness and, as another figure began to emerge, he continued, "In his company, I can assure you, nothing in this jungle will pose any threat. They wouldn't dare."

The eight children watched in fascination as a far smaller creature appeared beside Drusus. Much like the king of the jungle, the new arrival had goat-like legs and twisting horns, a man's torso, and gold eyes. But his face, unlike the king's, was rather human looking. His features seemed young and fairly attractive; a light smattering of blonde hair covered his chin, an aquiline nose hooked over pale, pink lips. He shifted his weight from hoof to hoof, nervously fidgeting at Drusus' side.

"This," the king said, nodding down to the smaller, "is my son, Gaia. He'll guide you out of the jungle." He gently pushed his son toward the eight Estherians.

Fynn was the first to greet him. He offered Gaia his hand amiably. "Thank you for helping us, Gaia."

The fawn prince shook Fynn's hand reluctantly. "Right." He proceeded to trot toward the twisting cave tunnels, beckoning the eight to follow him off with a wave of his hand. "This way."

Fynn lagged behind the group. He couldn't help but run back to Drusus, stopping a few paces from the once-more-seated king.

Eyeing the child curiously, Drusus asked, "Is there something more?"

"No."

"Then why do you not follow your friends?"

Fynn bowed to Drusus once more. "Thank you."

"Rise, Prince of Estheria. You needn't bow here."

The boy stood. His eyes were hard, but not unkind. "I won't forget this."

"In the annals of your human history, this will be but a story soon forgotten," Drusus mused.

Fynn shrugged. "Maybe so. I can't say for certain. But I can promise you that I won't forget this."

"Don't think more of my actions than they were," cautioned the monster. "I was willing to let you die."

"I don't believe you."

"Oh?"

Fynn smirked. "No. I don't."

"And why, pray tell, Prince of Estheria, is that?"

"Because you knew I'd live," asserted the boy.

"I knew no such thing."

Fynn countered, "You knew how the poison worked. So, you knew, the moment I agreed to your trade, that I wouldn't *really* die."

One long, heavy index finger tapped Fynn's head softly. Drusus chuckled, "And you say your friends think you're stupid."

"I have my moments," boasted the prince.

"I'm sure you do," jested the king. "Now, be off with you, child!"

"I *meant* it," Fynn maintained. "I meant it when I said I wouldn't forget."

"I believe you."

Fynn rejoined the group, happily grinning as they emerged from the mouth of the cave. They followed along behind Gaia, keeping relatively quiet. They chattered amongst themselves, relieved to once again be in one another's company. Lux was beside Fynn and Godryk flanked the prince's other side.

Lux kept her voice low when she asked, "What were you thinking?"

"That the rest of you would get out of here," Fynn replied.

"You could have died," she continued.

"It would've been worth it to save all of you," Fynn contended. "I don't regret my decision."

"Well, you would have saved all of *their* lives." Godryk laughed, attempting to lighten the mood. "Hollyn would've killed me. I promised him I wouldn't let you do anything *exceedingly* stupid."

"I think willingly drinking poison qualifies as *exceedingly* stupid." Lux jabbed her elbow into Fynn's side. "Wouldn't you agree?"

"Probably," Fynn relented.

"I'm glad you're not dead," she mumbled.

"Me too." Fynn grinned.

Buttons thrashed against Fynn's back for a moment before his wings twitched, then beat against the cool air of the approaching dawn. He took flight, looping in the air just ahead of the band of first-years.

Lux watched the bat merrily twirling about, stretching its wings. "Is that Buttons?" she asked.

"You know the bat too?" Godryk asked, disbelievingly.

"Clearly," Lux drawled in what, Fynn believed, was a perfect approximation of Hollyn.

Buttons led the party to the campsite where they'd left the remaining four of their dozen. It was early morning, just beyond dawn, when they regathered. Upon seeing Gaia emerge from the undergrowth, welcomingly gathered amongst the eight sojourners, Hollyn stood and raised a skeptical brow. His attention, however, immediately fell away from the bizarre creature and to the worn looking first-years as they came to encircle the little camp.

"Hollyn!" cried Penelope as she rushed forward.

The prince held back a yelp of pain when the girl threw her arms around him, crying hysterically into his shoulder as she held to him tightly. "Penelope, you're alright?" he asked.

"I am," she choked, balling her fists in the filthy fabric of his tunic. "Are you better?"

"Much."

Wilder wobbled to his feet; Ollie grabbed him around the waist and levered his weight as the other stood. Both Dangerfield boys felt a swell of relief upon seeing their year mates looking dreadful, but alive.

"What took you so long?" Wilder joked.

"It's a long story," Godryk said with a heavy sigh.

Fynn approached Hollyn. Penelope had wormed her way to the boy's side, doing her best to act as a crutch for him. Fynn nodded to her, but his focus was wholly upon his cousin. "I told you we'd be back."

"Who's the monster?" Hollyn asked.

"You probably shouldn't call him a monster," Fynn muttered. "He's here to guide us out of the jungle."

"How'd you manage that?" inquired Wilder.

"The *idiot* probably went and made friends with it," grumbled Hollyn.

"His name is Gaia," Fynn explained, ignoring Hollyn's pointed remark. "He's going to help us get back." The prince turned to the fawn and smiled a toothy smile. "Lead the way!"

The journey back through the jungle was a slow one. Most of the Morancy children were staggering, slowed down by hunger, exhaustion, and injuries. Gaia led the way, Fynn at his side. The others maintained a wary distance from the strange beast, but no one dared utter a word against Gaia's presence. They were simply grateful to be headed home.

"The boy with the red hair," began Gaia.

"Which one?" Fynn asked.

"The one with one good arm," snorted the fawn.

"Hollyn."

"He seems—"

"He's an ass," Fynn interrupted, "but he grows on you. *Slowly.*"

"If you say so."

"Thank you again," Fynn started, "for showing us the way out of here."

"Do not thank me. It was my father's decision."

Fynn rolled his shoulders carelessly. "Still. Thank you for doing it. We would've never made it out of here."

"No, you wouldn't have." Gaia, having observed the spear that Godryk still toted, asked, "Were you really planning on fighting my father and the Iba-Jii?"

Fynn nodded. "If that's what it took to get our friends back, yes."

"You would have lost."

"Probably," agreed Fynn. "But that doesn't mean I wouldn't have tried."

When Gaia came to a halt the others followed suit. He looked to them with a flat regard and said, "This is where I leave you."

The jungle canopy gave way as the trees became only slightly less dense in their standing. The sunlight beamed down upon the island. Based on the sun's position, the children figured it was no more than mid to late morning. The first-years began slowly creeping out from the tree line, emerging into the full, pristine, daylight. Fynn was the last to step free from the jungle's grasp and he did so with a slight turn, watching the retreating back of Gaia as the fawn stole back into the green clutches without another word.

It was a warm day, like all days on Dier Island. It seemed ages ago that they'd all been led into the jungle for their test of survival, yet it hadn't truly been that long. No, they'd made it out of the jungle before their allotted week was up. They gathered together, sharing in a collective silence wherein they reflected, each abundantly happy to be free, to be headed back to the castle, to see the sunlight fully. When Fynn looked up to the sky, he smiled when he saw small, black wings casting a shadow over the group as Buttons swooped above them.

"Will you come with us?" called Fynn to the bat.

The eleven watched as the bat lingered above Fynn for a moment longer before jolting skyward and twirling, dropping low before curling back upward and flying toward More Town.

As Buttons left them, Fynn's arm shot up and he waved. "I'll see you soon!"

"Let's head home," suggested Hollyn.

And so, the twelve of them began their walk to the castle, quickly finding the winding road from where they'd emerged. They stumbled their way back. What normally took no more than half an hour, took them almost triple the time. They were worn and beaten, but their spirits were ever high as they finally crossed the threshold through the castle entrance. The sunlight spilled through the stained glass; rainbows were thrown across the stony ground. Everything seemed so warm and inviting. The total absence of anything green and tree-like was a welcome sight.

Starved and currently feeling the pangs of hunger far more acutely than any other ailment, the children wandered their way toward the Hall. Though they were bleeding, some sporting broken limbs, others splattered with disastrous bruises. They held their heads high. Godryk pushed open the doors to the Hall, allowing the others to walk in first. They were startled to find the Hall full as the other years had gathered for their mid-day meal.

All eyes turned toward the first-years as they appeared a most wretched sight, covered from the top of their heads to the soles of their boots in muck, blood, and all manner of grime, their flesh hewed and bruised, their gaits staggered and limp.

Lord Paramount Malcourt sprung from his seat at the high table, astonished. "First-years?"

Nyle slowly clapped his hands in approval. His one-man chorus of claps was swiftly joined by Noel. Both men stood from their chairs, eyes betraying their mingled concern and pride.

"Well done!" called Nyle from across the Hall.

"Here, here!" cheered Noel.

Fynn's eyes searched the Hall, seeking out one man in particular. When he found the one he sought, he quirked a smile. Moriah looked back at him and nodded. He stood, ever so regally, and clapped slowly for them.

"Well done," Moriah added at a far more subdued decibel than the others. "Well done."

Ciaran stood from the Armada table. When Hollyn limped forward, supported by Penelope, Ciaran went cold. He darted from his division and rushed to his brother. He stopped just short of running straight into his younger sibling. He stood, more than a head taller than Hollyn, looking down upon the prince. He wavered in his decision for a moment and then, without another thought, threw his arms around his brother and pulled the boy flush against his chest.

"You're hurt," Ciaran murmured, so low Hollyn had to strain to hear him.

"Just a broken shoulder," Hollyn answered.

"You made it back."

Hollyn nodded. He allowed Ciaran to embrace him, but his own good arm remained limp at his side. He hung like a rag doll in his brother's clutches.

"You're embarrassing me," Hollyn croaked.

"I'm sorry."

"No, you're not," groused the younger prince.

"You're right. You may not believe me," Ciaran pulled back just slightly from Hollyn, "but I was worried for you."

"I'm not surprised," Hollyn retorted shortly.

"You're not?"

The younger brother shook his head and scowled. "You've always been the sentimental one."

Ciaran arrested a laugh in his throat. He stepped back from his brother. "I suppose you're right." He thumbed his nose at Hollyn. "But can you blame me? You're my baby brother."

"I don't think Father would share your sentiment," Hollyn said, passing by Ciaran on his way toward the first-year table. The others had begun shuffling that way. Many of the older students came forward and pat them on the backs and smiled cheerily.

Ciaran caught Hollyn's wrist firmly, jerking him back toward him. "Don't make the mistake of thinking I'm like him."

"It doesn't matter," muttered the younger as he tried to free himself. "Just let me go, Ciaran. I'm starving."

"I *am* happy, you know. I'm happy you're back…and you're alright. A broken shoulder? It could've been much worse."

"I know," Hollyn acknowledged glumly. "I know." He stayed put, lingering in his brother's proximity, as he glanced toward the first-year table where Fynn sat; the other prince was lost in conversation with their year mates. "The *idiot* got me back here. He got us *all* back here."

"Fynneas?"

Hollyn nodded. "He's smarter than he looks."

17

COMMISERATIONS

Days had come and days had gone since the first-years' return from the jungle. What praise they'd won for their triumphant adventure through the wilderness was quickly squelched in favor of a more rigorous training schedule. Where once their days began at dawn, the children were now roused from their fitful sleep hours before the sun rose and herded along to their lessons. Morning meals, which had once been a time to relax and prepare for the afternoon's training, had been forgone in favor of longer, more arduous sessions with their instructors.

Their afternoons were now spent dragging their fatigued bodies through the motions of the day's instructions, being yelled at to do better, work harder, stop whining, and show, in general, as little emotion as possible. Per their instructors, cumbersome emotions such as fear, sympathy, mercy, and exhaustion had no place on their island.

The first two weeks following the children's emergence from the emerald inferno that was the jungles of Dier Island saw Wilder and Hollyn relegated to the infirmary. Hollyn's shoulder, regrettably, was in fact broken; a fact the boy bemoaned as he found himself confined to a medical wing bed with little more to fill his days with than reading historical tomes on long-since concluded battles. Wilder was also stuck, bored and in bed. Though, he'd managed to emerge from the ordeal far luckier than his royal counterpart; Imogen and Blythe, after both had seen to his care, had concluded that the wound to his leg was not a break. He'd spent two weeks huddled up in his blankets, whining and moaning while Hollyn read, until, at last, the matrons decided he was well enough to begin putting weight on his leg.

The following week saw Hollyn watching with bitter rage as Wilder began taking his first shaking steps across the medical wing chambers. He would shuffle and limp, but each day his strength and coordination seemed to improve. By the end of the week, Wilder was walking quite well, though his pronounced limp had yet to fade completely. So, while Wilder was permitted to return to the dormitories, Hollyn grumbled his jealousy. When Wilder had gathered his things, offering Hollyn a parting wave and promise to be by to visit, the prince could do little more than scowl over the pages of his most recent historical text.

Hollyn spent another two weeks, now alone, stuck in the infirmary. He had little company during the day. The silence gave him ample time and opportunity to pore over different writings he'd found interesting. Moriah would usually come by in the mornings, groggy and not at all in any sort of humor to engage in conversation, bringing with him a stack of scrolls or full texts on different subjects. The man, ever consistent about stopping by, would bring history and military texts predominantly, though there were times where he seemed to opt for something a bit lighter, choosing songs and stories from different regions collected during Estherian military campaigns in Erza. Hollyn didn't much care for those as much as the war texts but understood the necessity of appreciating the cultural backbone of their offshore province. It wouldn't do for a prince to be dismissive of such things, but that didn't mean he had to like it.

So, Hollyn's mornings were spent in comfortable, albeit sparse, conversation with Moriah. He'd appear in the infirmary just before dawn, waking Hollyn with a gentle shake of the shoulders, insisting it was necessary for the young prince to maintain his sleep schedule, even if he wasn't presently participating in his lessons. He'd stay for an hour or so, explaining which texts he brought for the day, and which he found most interesting, before taking his leave to go instruct.

Nightfall would usually herald Fynn's appearance in the ward. At first, the other prince's presence was like the sun bursting through on a cloudy day. Despite how tired Fynn was from his lessons, his still abnormal energy levels were refreshing. He'd pull a chair up to Hollyn's bedside and tell him everything they'd covered in the day's instructions. He'd regale the other boy with tales of their classmates' triumphs and failures and whatever ludicrous thing Nyle had done to them that day. During that time, Hollyn found Fynn's stories amusing and motivating. But, as the weeks wore on, the visits were less pleasant.

The matrons said that Hollyn would be stuck in bed for at least five weeks. Once they'd entered into the sixth week, Fynn had all but become despondent at the loss of Hollyn's presence in their lessons. His visits were more subdued, far quieter, and less animated than they'd been previously.

The more Fynn began to mope, the more Hollyn became frustrated. He, himself, could feel the muscle he'd been building at the beginning of their term slipping away, seeping from his slender body like rot. He hated it. He hated all of it. What made it worse was that he could see Fynn's progress, what strides he'd made since first clumsily stepping onto the island, failing him. Despite everything Hollyn said about and to his cousin, he knew that Fynn was a quick study. His mastery of all the intricate knots Drake had taught them, albeit after Ollie had tutored him some, was evidence enough of the boy's ability to catch on. What's more, Fynn had demonstrated his ability to, if not gracefully fight with a sword, learn to counteract Hollyn's far more controlled and practiced strikes. Fynn's efforts were not a mirror image of what his instructors were teaching, but the boy had an uncanny ability to compensate for his pronounced lack of deftness and fluidity with creative solutions and an iron will to succeed. However, as the days wore on, that will seemed to be waning for want of the only opponent who truly, in every sense, could challenge him.

Hollyn descended into a fouler and fouler mood as the days continued to drag on. Lux and Penelope would often times come visit before lunching. The girls would sit by his bedside, as Fynn would at night, and tell him about the day and their year mates. Hollyn's scowl intensified when Lux recounted how Fynn's behavior had suffered a marked change. The red-haired prince was unsettled to know that he was not the only one noticing Fynn's shift in mood. As it was related to him, it was not so much the listless despondency that had accompanied the raven-haired prince following his episode during archery practice months ago, but more a bored, distracted sort of disinterest that had begun annoying many of the instructors. Penelope supplied Hollyn with tales of Fynn's two consecutive victories in their class tournaments during Noel's instructions, with Lux adding in that Fynn seemed to beat the others with pronounced ease. When Hollyn asked how Godryk had held up against Fynn, he was shocked to hear that the young Redmayne had been defeated in only moments, though he'd made it to the final round both times.

Hollyn was secretly delighted when Nan and Minnie would come to visit. The first time they came to see him had been in the company of Moriah on a rare afternoon visit from the man. Minnie had been seated happily upon Moriah's shoulders when he came in, Nan quick on his heels. They'd pulled up chairs by the prince's bedside and Nan, having brought a small feast with her, set about to arranging the food for the four of them to share.

After introductions were properly made by Moriah, Hollyn found he quite liked the presence of the old woman and the little girl. And, it seemed to all involved, Minnie took to Hollyn much the same way she'd taken to Fynn. After the first visit, the two More Town residents made a point to cheer Hollyn up with occasional afternoon visits, usually bringing sweets and other treats in tow with them.

Ciaran came by the wing to check on Hollyn's progress a few times. He'd stop by, a tentative smile in place, asking the younger prince how he was feeling and if he was in any pain. Most times Hollyn responded with indifference or a casual 'I'm alright' or 'don't worry' before dismissing Ciaran with a wave of the hand and assurance that he truly needn't be concerned. Hollyn's apathetic attitude toward him didn't deter the older prince entirely. Ciaran made a habit of, if not talking to Hollyn himself, asking Imogen or Blythe how the boy was doing, how he was progressing. And those times when he couldn't hunt down one of the two matrons to inquire about his brother's health, Ciaran would stalk through the castle until he found Moriah before demanding of the man to tell him how Hollyn was fairing.

By the middle of the seventh week, Imogen was unwrapping the sling that had been binding Hollyn's arm for the better part of a month and a half; he'd been allowed, after careful checking and monitoring of his progress, to take it off for a few hours every day so as not to stiffen the joint and cause further problems. Day by day, the matrons would come by when they'd finished their instructions and work with him, each time getting his range of motion back just a little more, each day helping increase his strength and flexibility little by little.

When the day came that Imogen decided Hollyn was well enough to return to his dormitories and start attending lessons, he couldn't help but feel positively elated. He was gathering his things together when Nan and Minnie came through the doors, beaming smiles ablaze upon both their faces. Minnie came running up to Hollyn, arms thrown out as she encircled his legs in a great, big hug. He ruffled her hair affectionately as she congratulated him on finally being able to get back to his training.

"You're all better!" Minnie squealed happily as Hollyn bent down to give her a gentle hug, quite mindful of his still-healing arm and shoulder.

He nodded, a genuine smile upon his face. "Well... not all better but getting there. Good enough that I can go back to my lessons, at least."

"Are you happy?"

"To be getting out of here?" He hugged the little girl tighter and laughed. "Minnie, you have *no* idea!"

"I'm happy too," she added cheerily.

Hollyn stood when Nan approached. The old woman enveloped the prince in a soft hug, careful to not jostle him unnecessarily. She patted him on the head gently as she cooed, "You'll be back at it in no time, I'm sure."

"Thank you." He smirked. "Let's hope I haven't been away for *too* long. Can't have Fynn's ego getting too big, can we?"

At the mention of the other prince's name, Nan sighed. "How is he? Do you know? We haven't seen him around the tavern for the last couple of weeks. I've started to get worried...but Moriah says I'm just being dramatic."

Hollyn's expression soured as he answered, "He's been *really* annoying lately. Moping around like the world's about to end. You'd think *he* was the one who's been laid up in bed for weeks." The boy snorted. "Guess I'll have to beat it out of him again."

"Boys," Nan said with a huff, "you always have to settle things with a fight. Can't ever just talk about it, can you?"

"Well, I don't know about everyone else, but our family isn't a 'talk about your feelings' sort of family."

Exasperated, Nan relented, "I've noticed."

Not desiring to spend any more time in the infirmary than absolutely required, Hollyn insisted that they take their lunch out on the balcony. It was the balcony that Moriah had shown him and, Hollyn later found out, also shown to Godryk and Fynn. He didn't mind so much; he could understand it. He'd noticed how Moriah favored Fynn, much like he favored Hollyn. Though, Hollyn mused, Moriah certainly handled the two princes differently. He shrugged at the thought, thinking he'd come back to it later with a more critical eye. At the moment, he was hungry and just plain happy to be out of the infernal infirmary. So it was that he, Nan, and Minnie found themselves bathed in afternoon sunlight, enjoying flat breads and lemon tarts and talking about everything and nothing all at once.

Hollyn wasn't the only one who had suffered through seven weeks of loneliness and tedium. Fynn was feeling rather isolated. It wasn't the same, he knew, as when he'd woken up in the infirmary and found himself emotionally displaced from those around him. It was a different sort of loneliness that clutched him this time, one that he couldn't remedy no matter how hard he tried. Yes, this time was different. He didn't spend his time consciously separating himself from his classmates. Rather, he actively sought out their company most of the time, desperate to drown his own internal conflictions in the easy conversation that flowed between he and his year mates. But he still struggled.

Classes had intensified. The lord paramount had explained to them, "Your survival test in the jungle was the first step. Now that you've all proven you're capable of passing such a test, your classes will begin to test you more and more. You're ready for it. You've shown us all that you're ready. We won't be treating you like children any longer. You'll be treated like soldiers and, thusly, expected to act as such."

When they'd asked in tentative, shy voices if they'd be given any sort of reprieve to recuperate and tend to their injuries, their inquiries were met with the icy grumbles of the lord paramount, saying, "In war you won't always have time to recuperate, to tend to your injured, to regroup yourselves physically and emotionally. You'll have to learn to work through it. We expect you to keep going. When you fall down, you get back up… *no matter what.*"

The lord paramount added with stern certainty, "Morancy's motto is, and has always been, 'By Any Means Necessary.' We intend for you to live by those words. You are to win at all costs. Failures will not be tolerated. I hope that is understood."

And so, with those words of wisdom and expectation imparted upon them, the first-years were herded along to the first of their many nightmarish lessons.

With the help of Ollie, Fynn became more and more proficient at knot tying. However, that accomplishment garnered him little reprieve from what had quickly become his most hated class. Where once he had been bored by the idea of tying knots and rowing in a dinghy, he now wished to return to those simpler lessons. The children had recently been learning to manage small sailboats, navigating the ins and outs of the sails, celestial navigation, and the tide. They spent many of their mornings skittering through the crystalline waters, dodging around manufactured obstacles and running both standard tactical, naval formations and emergency maneuvers.

Likewise, Survival Strategies and Tactics had gone from building imaginary fires to becoming a living nightmare. Nyle, not the most well balanced of the instructors from the start, was now described by the students as being stark, raving mad. He spent his afternoons with the first-years hurling rocks at them for any imagined slight or failure and screaming their inadequacies at the top of his lungs until his throat was raw. He'd harangue them for the most minor of infractions, asserting that they'd somehow doomed the entire class and condemned them to an imminent and quickly approaching demise. Ollie, unfortunately, tended to bear the brunt of Nyle's temper, though there were days where the old man's frustration was angled toward Hogan and Albie.

The day came upon them where, an hour or so before the sun rose heralding the dawn, the first-years were awakened by a rather annoyed looking Benadykt who stood, arms crossed over his chest, in their common room as the twelve shuffled down the stairs from their dormitories to stand at attention, or what could pass for attention at such an hour, before their instructor. Hollyn was welcomed back with a terse nod of acknowledgement from Benadykt before he continued his surveying of the rest of the herd.

Benadykt sighed wearily before saying, "Right, your schedule is being rearranged today. Rather than sailing this morning, you'll have it this afternoon. *I'll* be teaching you lot this morning. So, go on and get your run done. I expect you assembled and ready for lessons within the hour. Am I understood?"

With a collective nod, the children all shambled by their instructor down the winding stairs of the tower to begin their morning exercise. Godryk nudged Albie and whispered, "He seems in a bad mood today."

Albie nodded. "Wonder why."

Ollie, coming up beside the pair, shrugged. "Who knows? He and Moriah seem to both be in foul moods recently."

Albie agreed, saying, "Too right you are. Well, I'd rather deal with an annoyed Benadykt than an annoyed *Moriah*. Wouldn't you?"

"Any day," Ollie laughed.

"*Definitely*," agreed Godryk.

When the class emerged from the castle, it was still dark. The morning was cool, which made their jog comfortable. They'd kept a steady pace, all twelve staying fairly close. Wilder had improved quickly; his limp dissipated after his first week back to lessons. He was still a bit slower than he'd been when it came to running, but Imogen had assured them all he'd be back in form within a few more weeks. Months of running around the island saw Ollie presently managing to keep pace with the rest of the group, though his gait was still reminiscent of an awkward waddle.

As they proceeded down their usual route, Lux cast a glance back to see Fynn intently staring at Hollyn. For his part, Hollyn would occasionally look to the other boy before looking away, a scowl quite firmly fixed upon his face. Lux turned back, keeping pace with Renwyn and Firiel. She shook her head.

Georgie sidled up beside Lux. She tilted her head to the side as she asked the other girl, "What's the matter?"

"Fynn and Hollyn, that's what. All they've done since Hollyn got back yesterday was stare at each other," Lux answered.

"So?"

"It's getting annoying, don't you think?"

Georgie shrugged. "I suppose I haven't really been paying attention." She peeked over her shoulder, maintaining her pace, and caught sight of Hollyn glaring at Fynn. Giggling, she looked back at Lux, saying, "Guess you're right."

"Honestly!" Lux glowered, spying the boys still fixedly sizing each other up. "I thought we'd gotten past this a while ago."

"Boys will be boys," joked Georgie.

"*Idiots*," muttered Lux. "The *both* of them."

The sun began to crawl its way over the horizon and, as such, pale flushes of yellow streaked across the sky just as the children gathered around the stables. Their morning runs had gotten longer since their jungle adventure—far longer. Presently, they surrounded the stables, still panting, sweat trickling from their brows, dampening their bed-mussed hair. As they caught their breath, Benadykt came sauntering toward them and, much to their dismay, still looked quite perturbed.

"Good run?" he asked curtly.

"Yes, sir," they answered.

The instructor leaned his long back against the stable, crossed his arms over his chest, and tilted his head back as he watched the sun rise. For a long stretch of time, the man seemed to ignore the presence of the dozen children in his proximity in favor of watching the clouds meander across the sky. "Lovely day, isn't it?"

"Sir?" ventured Lux curiously.

Hollyn looked around, glancing from the stable, to the assembled first-years, to the instructor. He quirked a black brow and asked, "Sir, are we waiting for anything?"

"Yes, in fact we are," came the clearly irritated response as Benadykt pulled himself from the stable wall, rolling his shoulders. "For today's lesson, we'll be splitting into two groups. It'll be easier to manage that way."

Pouting petulantly, Benadykt continued, "To do that safely and to make sure you get it right, we need a second instructor. *However*, it seems *punctuality* is *not* his *priority*."

Fynn couldn't help the ghost of a smirk that found its way to his lips. He knew, simply by the annoyed manner in which Benadykt referred to the day's second instructor, that he must be talking about Moriah. Secretly, Fynn wished Moriah would show up and offset the monotony of more of their lessons. The man had a way of making classes a bit more interesting than the other professors. Fynn lamented frequently since more often than not, Moriah didn't usually come to teach the first-years.

Footsteps drawing nearer sounded and the class collectively craned their necks to see who was approaching. Fynn perked up for a moment, searching for the familiar stalking, black figure of Moriah only to be disappointed when, instead, a slighter, blonder figure emerged from around the corner.

Odette approached, eyeing the children distractedly as she headed toward Benadykt. Fynn's attention was riveted to the woman as she came closer, studying the way she walked–so very much like her brother and yet distinctly different.

"Lady Odette," greeted Benadykt stiffly, "good morning." He set his mouth to a thin frown as he continued evenly, "What're *you* doing here?"

"I was led to believe you needed a second instructor for today's lesson," she replied flatly.

"Yes…that is why *Moriah* was supposed to be here," Benadykt retorted sharply.

Odette asked, "Am I not to your satisfaction?"

Clearly flustered and apparently taken aback by the question, Benadykt stuttered, "N-no. No, that's not it at all… *honestly*." Righting himself, he continued, "I just wasn't expecting *you*." Curiosity getting the better of the man, he asked, "Pray tell, where is your *dear* brother?"

"Dear brother? I was under the impression we were discussing Moriah, not Noel," jested Odette as she settled amongst the gathered group.

"Clever," drawled Benadykt in a pale approximation of Moriah's usual bored tone. "Truly, though, where is he?"

"Not sure."

"But you're his *sister*," argued Benadykt.

"Yes. His *sister*, not his *keeper*." Odette combed a hand through her already perfectly well-kempt, blond locks. "Honestly, I don't know where he is. Noel woke me this morning and asked if I'd be willing to come out and help with your firsties' cavalry class. So, alas, here I am." She yawned with the drama of a lion tired in the tall grasses. "Tell me now if my assistance is not needed and I'll gladly go back to sleep."

"Yes, yes, you're needed," Benadykt groaned. Squaring his shoulders, he proceeded into the stables, a dozen children following behind obediently. "Right, saddle your horses and get yourselves ready. We'll split into two groups when you're done."

While the children went about their tasks, Odette slid closer to Benadykt, their horses already prepared. Taking the reins, the two instructors headed out of the stables and back into the fresh, morning light. Benadykt stood, his calloused hand gently stroking his horse's neck.

Odette mounted hers, looking down at the cavalry instructor, a certain chilliness in her green eyes. "Ben?"

"Hmm?"

"Care to tell me what your problem is?"

Finally, he looked up at her. He was more snappish in his response than he cared to be, but he didn't let himself feel too guilty over the matter. "Don't worry about it."

"I'm not *worried*," Odette corrected. "*Curious*, maybe … a little *annoyed*, too." She sat up straighter in her saddle, surveying the surroundings with indifference and cool detachment. "But you and Moriah have been oddly quiet and when you're together, well… I'm really not in the mood for this. What has he done to upset you *this* time?"

"Nothing," Benadykt bit as he climbed into his own saddle, pleased that he was once again higher than she. Peering down his nose with a sneer, he continued, "If you're going to talk the whole time, I'll send you back to the castle and do this myself."

"Benny," purred Odette gleefully, "it's not much of a threat to tell me you'll send me back when I don't want to be here to begin with." With that said, she gave her horse a gentle kick with her heels and trotted off into the nearby field beyond the castle walls where the cavalry trainings were conducted.

"Insufferable woman," muttered Benadykt as he waited for the children to emerge from the stables.

By mid-morning the first-years were split into two groups of six. One group had followed after Benadykt to one side of the large field while the others remained with Odette. Fynn was only half listening as Odette proceeded to explain the day's third drill. Cavalry lessons had never really captured his attention, but he found that recently they seemed even more boring than before. Idly, he ran his hand through his horse's mane, playing with the brown locks, twirling them between his fingertips. When he tired of that absentminded activity, he peered up to the sky and watched the clouds roll by. As the morning had gone on, the clouds overhead began to darken and look heavier and heavier, until it was quite apparent that it would rain soon.

"Fynneas!" Odette snapped.

Jarred from his reverie and silently wishing that it would, indeed, rain soon, Fynn turned back toward his instructor with a sheepish smile, apologizing wordlessly with only a pitiful nod and moderately more focused attention. Odette continued on with her instructions, but he found her voice droning and monotonous and all at once he lost interest again. His attention wavered; he shifted his grey stare from Odette to his classmates. He smirked, noting that Albie looked just as bored as he did. Penelope and Lux were paying rapt attention, both girls having taken to cavalry training from the very first days of their instruction. As always, Hogan looked rather uncertain about being perched atop the animal, his constant furrowing brows and anxious clutching of the reins a tell-tale sign of his discomfort.

But it was Hollyn who most interested Fynn. The red-haired prince sat calmly atop his horse, comfortably situated in his saddle, one hand lightly holding to the reins while the other rested limply upon his thigh. He seemed to be listening to Odette's instructions with characteristically insistent attention, so much so that he didn't even notice how Fynn appraised him with almost feral interest.

The morning was spent performing different drills. The children were instructed to acclimate themselves to riding close to one another and in formations. It started with slow trots and worked toward outright gallops. Penelope and Hogan were reluctant to get up to speed so close to another horse; Penelope, though, was quick to become accustomed to the action and took to it rather well. Hogan, unfortunately, still blanched at the thought of accidentally being thrown from his mount to the ground. An understandable fear, Fynn mused, though one he couldn't personally relate to. Of all the things that could happen to him, he figured falling from his horse seemed the most mundane and, as a result, frightened him the least.

When the two groups finally rejoined, Benadykt dismissed them back to the stables. The twelve did as they were told, having gotten used to being ushered back and forth between instructors, heedless of their weariness.

They dismounted and began the painstaking process of removing saddles and cleaning up, brushing the horses, and resituating each in their stalls. Fynn emerged from his stall, hay sticking up from his hair, grumbling. His shoulders ached terribly but, as he glanced around and saw the tiredness apparent upon his year mates' faces, he knew better than to complain. So, it was with lead-like legs that he dragged himself from the stables and began the run—more like painful lurch, as it was evident that exhaustion was slowing them all down— toward the harbor.

For the first time that day, Hollyn came up beside Fynn and spoke. His voice sounded tired, more so than everyone else it seemed. His stay in the infirmary, clearly, had worn his stamina down. "Why were you staring at me?"

"Didn't think you saw," admitted Fynn, keeping a slower pace to stay in step with Hollyn.

"You're not very subtle."

"Wasn't trying to be."

Hollyn drawled, "Clearly."

"How are you feeling?" Fynn asked.

"Fine."

"Liar."

"Why do you ask?" Hollyn questioned suspiciously. "Don't think because I've been laid up in bed that you're suddenly going to start beating me at everything."

"Wouldn't dream of it." Fynn snorted. "You just look tired. Are you sure you're alright?"

"Yes."

"Would you tell me if you weren't?" Fynn quirked a brow expectantly.

"No." Hollyn laughed.

"Didn't think so."

"You've gotten better on a horse," Hollyn commented.

Fynn shrugged. "You've been gone a while. I've gotten better at a lot of things."

"We'll see about that," the taller prince challenged coolly.

The shorter smirked. "Don't be *too* upset when I win, alright?"

"Don't get too cocky, Fynneas. Hubris is unbecoming."

"I'll keep that in mind."

"Do."

Sailing lessons that afternoon went by with the same back-breaking demands as cavalry class did and yet, just as its predecessor, failed to capture

Fynn's whole attention. He only vaguely heard Drake screaming at them to do better, to tie their knots faster, more precisely. He only caught hints of Drake yelling at them from the shore, insisting they handle the sails better, get a grasp on the mood of the sea, focus. Fynn didn't really pay much attention to any of that. What he did notice, however, was that, despite Hollyn's time imprisoned in the infirmary, the boy's natural ability to catch on after only having something explained to him once had not at all been impaired. Fynn hunched over in his small sailboat, grumbling upon realizing that, of course, Hollyn was still the model student when it came to the old adage 'watch and learn.'

Sun-beaten and inexplicably irritated, Fynn stepped from his boat as it slid against the sand of the beach when class ended. He groused as he watched Hollyn gracefully descend to the shore. His internal grumblings were broken when he heard the all-too familiar crack of thunder bursting from the clouds. Fynn smiled a genuine smile for the first time that day as the first drops of rain came spilling down over them. It wasn't long before cool drops were descending upon the island in sheets of pale silver, washing from the highest hill, whereupon Morancy loomed, all the way down to the harbor.

The rain was relaxing. It was cool and fresh and washed away the foul, stagnant scent of fish that always clung to their uniforms following a sailing lesson. Fynn brushed his hair from his face as the group began heading toward the castle. The others were bemoaning the rain, hating that they would more than likely be called upon to suffer an evening run in the downpour. Fynn, unlike the others, couldn't help but grin at the prospect. The rain helped him unwind, eased his tension, helped him focus on something. The steady sound of the water smashing over them was soothing and peaceful.

Upon stepping up the walkway leading to the entrance, ten of the twelve retreated into the warm, dry safety of the castle walls. Only Fynn and Hollyn remained outside, both of them watching as the winds picked up force and speed, blowing through the lush greenery all around.

"Aren't you tired?" asked Fynn casually.

"No." Hollyn turned his deep, blue eyes toward Fynn. "Aren't you hungry?"

"Not really."

The two princes remained in the rain, each simply standing there like statues frozen before the castle doors, allowing the rain to pour over them as if it would, or could, wash away everything troubling them. Fynn finally broke the spell of silence that had enveloped them when he asked, "Should we head inside?"

"You can." Hollyn's focus was transfixed skyward. "I'm going to stay out here a while longer."

"I'll keep you company," Fynn said.

Hollyn looked back down from the clouds and turned to Fynn. All of a sudden, the smaller boy was right next to him, staring up at the sky as the rain washed over his face. "Why?"

"You were gone for a while."

"Fynneas." Hollyn snorted derisively. "I saw you almost every day. Or have you forgotten?"

Fynn shook his head. "No. I know. But that's not the same."

Hollyn looked to the sky again. For a long while, each boy was caught up in their own thoughts, too entrenched in their individual musings to continue speaking. Hollyn let the rain fall over his face, blinking away some of the blinding drops, feeling the cool trail left in their wake as they slid over his temples and down his face. "I like the rain."

"Me too," agreed Fynn.

"Lux and Penelope said you've been acting off."

"Did they?"

Hollyn gave a barely perceptible nod. "Yes." He pushed his hair from his eyes. "I didn't entirely believe them until today."

"That so?"

"Last time you got into a mood, I had to beat it out of you."

"I remember."

Hollyn sighed. "I don't really have the energy to do that again right now."

"You won't need to."

Hollyn looked back to Fynn, quirking an eyebrow in sheer confusion. "Oh?" Finally, Fynn looked away from the clouds and back to his cousin. It never ceased to unsettle Hollyn how Fynn's eyes seemed to glow at night. "Is that so?"

"You're back." Fynn shrugged, smirking. Abruptly, he rounded on his heel and headed into the castle. "I'm going to get something to eat. Are you coming?"

"I thought you weren't hungry," Hollyn replied.

"I lied." Fynn headed inside.

Hollyn shook his head as he followed suit, smiling. "I knew it."

The following morning the children were roused again just before dawn. As they always did, they ran along their new route, engaging in weary conversation in a feeble attempt to fully wake up. Just after sunrise, they gathered in the training field, waiting for Noel to arrive. As usual, the dozen arranged themselves in a small huddle, whispering amongst themselves to keep boredom at bay.

Godryk nudged Fynn, a smile on his face. "You seem in a better mood today."

Fynn offered a non-committal shrug and lopsided grin.

Hollyn took up the place on Fynn's other side. He leaned closer to the other prince and whispered, "I've been told you won the last two tournaments."

The black-haired boy nodded.

"Don't expect to win a third."

"Is that a challenge?" asked Fynn with a sly look in his eyes.

"A *promise*."

"I do believe it was *you*, wasn't it, who mentioned *hubris*?" chuckled Fynn.

Noel joined the small group, pleased that they seemed to all be in a relatively easy humor this morning. He was delighted to see Fynn and Hollyn engaged in what appeared to be friendly banter, rather than the normal, typically heated arguments which, much to everyone's dismay, usually ended in one or both of them bloodied.

Clapping his hands together enthusiastically as he settled in amongst their huddle, Noel began, "How is everyone this morning?"

They nodded and smiled and tiredly grumbled their morning pleasantries.

"Right," Noel continued, "well, it's been a while since we've had a bit of friendly competition. Two weeks? More? Well, since the whole group is back together again, this seems like just the time." He stepped back and with a flourish of his hand, instructed, "You all know the routine by now. Gather round, big circle, yes, yes…alright." Noel strategically stood on Hollyn's other side, glancing down to the newly healthy prince cautiously. "Right, first match will be Hogan and Wilder."

As the boys stepped to the center of the circle, Noel pronounced the beginning of the bout. Once swords were brandished, he leaned toward Hollyn, keeping his voice low, and said, "I don't expect you to participate just yet. I know you're not quite ready for a fight."

Scowling, Hollyn answered, "I'll be fine."

Noel shook his head. "No. I don't want to chance you hurting your arm or shoulder."

"Then I'll fight with the other," countered the prince. "I'll use my left."

"You'll put yourself at a disadvantage," advised Noel.

Hollyn turned his full attention, sharp as it was, upon Noel. He asserted, "The lord and vice lord paramounts...they were the ones who reminded us to live by Morancy's words. *By any means necessary*, they always say. I can do it, sir."

"You're sure?" asked Noel, leaning back away from the boy to watch, albeit distractedly, the bout presently raging.

"Yes."

Relenting, Noel replied, "Fine. But you'll fight Penelope or Georgie... *maybe* Ollie."

"No."

Noel laughed, turning to look back to Hollyn. "No?" he repeated incredulously.

"No, *sir*." Hollyn's eyes narrowed. "Let me fight Fynn."

"No."

"*Sir*," implored Hollyn.

"No, Hollyn. No. I've seen you two fight. You get riled up, the both of you. You'll get hurt. We can't risk you hurting yourself further this late into term."

"Sir, please," begged Hollyn boyishly. "*Please*."

"You *are aware* he's won the last *two* competitions we've had?"

Hollyn nodded. "I am."

Noel favored the boy with a studious look. "No one is going to think less of you if you hold off on fighting him. Everyone knows you were hurt, Hollyn. Take some time to heal and get better. You haven't even swung a sword since going into the jungle."

"Sir, please." The prince's gaze leveled upon his instructor. "Let me do this."

"Fine." Before Hollyn had the chance to rejoice in his victory, Noel continued, "But if it looks like things are getting out of control...like they tend to with you two...I reserve the right to stop the fight."

"That's fair, sir," agreed Hollyn.

The bout ended with Wilder, unsurprisingly, emerging victorious after having disarmed Hogan. Noel congratulated the boys as they resumed their positions in the circle. Before announcing the next match, he sighed deeply and looked back, one last time, to Hollyn questioningly.

Resolutely, the prince nodded.

Noel rolled his eyes as he said, "Match number two... Hollyn and Fynn."

A hushed note of trepidation echoed through the circle as the children looked from one another, then to the two announced combatants, before turning questioningly toward Noel.

The instructor shook his head defeatedly, continuing, "Go on, boys, take your places."

Hollyn strolled into the center of the circle with a confident air about him. His blue eyes viciously steeled as he watched Fynn smirk. When the two princes stood toe to toe, Hollyn drew his sword and held it in his left hand. Despite the strange feeling of wielding the sword in his weaker hand, he betrayed no hint of the awkwardness he felt. His eyes didn't waver from Fynn's.

"Left-handed?" Fynn asked, cocking his head to the side.

The taller boy nodded. "Yes."

"Right arm's not entirely healed?"

"It's a safety precaution," Hollyn assured. He nodded toward their instructor. "Noel wouldn't let me fight otherwise."

"Right." Fynn drew his own sword into his right hand.

Hollyn smiled. "Right-handed?"

Fynn shrugged. "I figure if you're going to use your weaker hand, I'll use mine."

"I don't need you going easy on me," Hollyn growled.

"I wanted you back because I wanted a challenge. It's not much of a challenge if I use my dominant hand while you use your weaker, now is it?"

Noel called, "Ready?"

"Ready," they replied together.

"Begin!"

Both boys hoisted their swords to the ready, each a bit unsteadily. One handed swordsmanship didn't quite come naturally to either child yet. Hollyn tried to balance his sword as he normally would, holding it out before him, strategically blocking his body with the blade. Fynn took a step back, clumsily drew up his own sword, and levered it forward toward Hollyn very slowly.

"Come on then," baited Fynn. "Have at it!"

Hollyn lunged forward, wincing slightly as the sudden motion and lean of his torso caused a twinge of residual pain to lash through his upper back. Fynn saw the momentary flash of pain and took the opportunity to clatter his blade against Hollyn's. Unsurprisingly to everyone watching, the bout between Fynn and Hollyn quickly escalated to their swords clashing wildly, blades locked against one another. The two princes were, presently, forcing their weight forward, heatedly pressing all their effort against the other.

"I thought this would be harder," Fynn taunted. "I suppose all that time in bed made you weak."

"Funny," Hollyn teased as he flexed his strength, smiling as his blade inched forward, forcing Fynn's back a fraction. "From where I'm standing, I look to be winning."

"Not for long." Fynn laughed as he side-stepped the deadlock.

Hollyn, all his weight having been intently trained forward, stumbled as his sword no longer had purchase against Fynn's. Quick to right himself, Hollyn rounded on Fynn with the ease of a practiced swordsman. He swung, catching Fynn in the leg with enough force to impair the others forward motion.

Effectively halted, Fynn turned squarely to face Hollyn. Within a moment, the two were once more locked together, leaning forward with blistering force. The rattling of steel smashing and bracing against blunted edges was the only thing that was heard. The rest of the world seemed to fall silent.

"Clever move," Hollyn noted. His lip twitched upward, a smirk born as he whispered, "but not clever *enough*."

Fynn's eyes went wide when Hollyn kicked his leg out, his foot catching against Fynn's ankle, knocking the shorter off balance. Suddenly thrown backward and fighting with his weaker hand, Fynn desperately swung his sword while his left arm shot out to break his fall. The dark-haired boy fell in a heap to the ground, his fingers uncurling from the sword's hilt. He watched, dismayed, as the weapon tumble over the grass and came to rest more than an arm's reach from where he lay. When he looked back to his opponent, Fynn was not surprised in the least to find Hollyn looming over him.

The tip of Hollyn's sword was ever so gently grazing the paleness of Fynn's neck.

"You cheated." Fynn pouted.

Hollyn drew back with a crooked grin. He held out his hand, waiting expectantly for Fynn to take it. When the boy did, Hollyn pulled him to his feet with a heave of his arm. Once more toe to toe, Hollyn shrugged, wryly replying, "No I didn't." He looked down to the sword he held flimsily in his left hand. "I used my weaker hand, same as you." Peering back to Fynn, he continued cheekily, "I didn't say I'd *never* fought using my left hand before."

"It was implied," Fynn muttered.

"No. You just *assumed.*"

Softly, Fynn punched Hollyn's good shoulder. "I'll get you back for this."

"You can try," Hollyn replied dismissively.

"I'll do more than *try.*"

Hollyn couldn't help the competitive fire that ignited in his stormy eyes. "I welcome the challenge."

18

TEAM MORDRAY

The first-years were huddled in a field, yawning as they rubbed the sleep-iness from their eyes, blinking in the first light of the day as the sun began to slowly make its way over the horizon; amber light trailed the darkened sky. No clouds hung around to obscure the fresh dawn.

Godryk rolled his shoulders back. He blinked blearily, his vision still a bit fuzzy from only a few hours of sleep. His voice was scratchy, weary when he asked, "What do you think they've got planned for us this morning?"

Lux, who had taken to stretching her arms and shoulders in a desperate attempt to ease her already sore muscles, replied, "I heard from the second-years that they make us play some sort of war game. They didn't tell me anything else though…no details."

"A game?" Penelope repeated curiously.

Firiel snorted, annoyed. "Weird."

"What do you think it could be?" Albie asked.

Ollie sighed. "Whatever it is, I hope it isn't another trip into the jungle."

Albie nodded his agreement. "Hopefully it won't be as bad."

"What do you think?" Hogan asked, turning toward Hollyn.

The prince shrugged and threw himself down to the ground, sitting comfortably. His shoulder and arm were still sore, occasionally twinging with pain that ranged from tolerable to nearly debilitating. He surveyed the group for a moment and then looked back up the hill toward the castle. "Who knows," he grumbled.

Renwyn paced back and forth, stomping the grass beneath his feet, leaving a patch of upturned earth in his wake as he continued his endless lumbering. Hands on his hips, he pouted. "I hate when they rush us out of bed and then *they* show up late."

"They do it on purpose," Hollyn noted flatly. "To get in your head. They know it's annoying; that's why they do it."

Renwyn ceased his anxious trek and reeled toward Hollyn, scoffing. "*Of course,* you'd have all the answers."

Rolling his eyes, Hollyn didn't deign to respond to the obviously frustrated boy. Instead, he looked to Lux and queried, "You sure you didn't get anything else from the second-years?"

Lux shook her head. "No. They said they weren't allowed to tell us anything."

"Great," muttered Hollyn.

Fynn, still yawning and quite tired from nights upon nights of restless sleep, hadn't bothered to enter the conversation. He was content with standing beside a still stretching Godryk, listening to the group's weary deliberation; he scowled when Renwyn tried to goad Hollyn into an altercation. Fynn straightened, his back aching in protest, and scanned the field. He spied a few figures coming toward the huddled group and announced, "I think that's them." He pointed; the others followed his indication with moderate interest. "Five of them... odd."

"That *can't* be good," Hollyn groaned as he climbed to his feet.

Albie shook his head. "Never is when there's a bunch of them together."

"Can you see who it is?" Godryk inquired, glancing at Fynn.

"Two of them look tall... I'd guess Benadykt and Moriah," Fynn answered thoughtfully.

"Moriah?" Hollyn repeated, quirking a brow as he considered Fynn for a moment. "He doesn't normally bother with us. First-years aren't his priority."

Fynn shrugged. "Looks like him—tall, dark, thin. I can't think of anyone else that could be."

"If Moriah's here, that must mean it's something hard," Ollie commented sourly.

Hogan hunched forward and droned defeatedly, "It's going to be a *long* day."

The children remained respectfully quiet when their five instructors joined them in the field. The sun had risen, and the day was proving to be, as always, blisteringly hot. Nyle stood at the forefront of the instructors, the other four quietly assembled at his back; he regarded the dozen children with cool attention.

Nyle clapped his hands together and began, in a suitably dramatic voice, as he was wont to do, "Children, come closer, come closer!" And when the children did as they had been instructed, he continued on, "You've all done well thus far, you have. I can honestly say, children, I'm surprised! When I first met you lot, I was sure at least one of you would be killed off in the jungle. But you've proven your mettle, children! I'm so proud of all of you." He beamed. "You've shown you can take instruction and orders *relatively* well. We'll work on it some more, but I must say, I'm quite pleased with how you're all coming along!"

The first-years, not at all used to Nyle praising them, remained awkwardly still and silent. Their eyes occasionally flicked by the old man and lingered on those instructors standing just behind him, before quickly snapping back to attention.

"Right, so today you've another chance to prove yourselves, to prove to me and your instructors what you've all learned thus far." Nyle gestured a wrinkled hand outward, waving the other instructors forward. They assembled, two on either side of the skeletal man. "You know your instructors, have worked with each of them at least once. Today, children, you'll be working *alongside* them. You'll be split into two teams of six each, headed by two of your instructors." The old Lord Humbert smiled a sly sort of smile as he continued, "But before we break apart, I'd like you to get to know each of your instructors a little more. How does that sound, eh?"

Nervously, the children nodded but remained quiet.

"I think it's best that you get to know exactly who they are, what they've accomplished. I've noticed a distinct lack of admiration amongst you, children, and I must say I'm displeased. Absolutely, *displeased!* You should be honored, you little cretins, honored to be instructed by Estherians of such a caliber."

"Yes, sir," the dozen first-years intoned.

"Right then." Nyle nodded tersely. "First, Lord Benadykt of House Beckett from the Cavalry Division. He graduated second of his year in Cavalry, served three years on the Estherian Erza borders, and spent another four years training middle and low borns at Fort Briar Hollow." As Benadykt gave a little nod of acknowledgement, Nyle continued, "During his time on the border in the east, he was named Cavalry Commander of the Thirteenth Unit. Additionally, children, he was titled Lord Man at Arms while at Briar Hollow. He's an asset to Cavalry and you should all count yourselves grateful to be under his tutelage."

Nyle grinned warmly as he continued, introducing the feats of the next instructor present. "Lord Drake of the House of Shoregore from the Armada Division. Drake graduated third in Armada. He was stationed for a year at Port Zarya, overseeing the completion of the naval fort on the coast. He served three years at Saia Shores where he was titled Lord Commander of the Fleet, overseeing the construction of the Estherian Erza war ships that would remain stationed in the east. Moreover, he instructed at Fort Briar Hollow for two years, being named Lord Commander of the Sails during his tenure there. He is a master of ships and the seas. There is no man better, I can think of, to train up you firsties, to ready you for the perils of the deep!"

Angling his head to his right, Nyle nodded toward the third instructor present. "Lady Odette of House Mordray from the Archer Brigade, respectfully referred to as our most beloved air brigadier. Odette finished first of her year in the archer's division. A unique case she was, children. Though she graduated from the Archer Brigade, she was drafted into the Night Corps after serving only three months with the archery unit. She then served six years with the Night Corps before returning to the archery unit, where she was then given the title of Lady Air Brigadier General for her services to the Crown. A remarkable woman, children, and a shining example of what tenacity can accomplish."

A genuine grin bloomed across Nyle's face when he introduced the final instructor's accomplishments. "Lastly, Moriah of House Mordray, Lord Commander of the Night Corps. Of the instructors assembled before you now, Lord Commander Mordray holds the highest title…and *rightfully* so! Moriah was named champion of the games at the conclusion of his second-year. Following his graduation from Morancy, Moriah was immediately placed in the Night Corps, where he still serves. A brilliant lad, truly remarkable! The best of the best," cooed Nyle fondly as he nodded toward an apathetic looking Moriah.

Turning his attention back to the students, Nyle again clapped his hands enthusiastically, pronouncing the conclusion of introductions. "Now that you have all been rightfully humbled by the accomplishments of your superiors, I hope you've been spurred on to strive for equal greatness. Show us what you can do, children! Show us all you've learned." He held out his hand wherein Odette placed a small bag. Nyle continued in a steely fashion, "In this bag, there are slips of parchment. Each slip bears one of your names. Your instructors will each pull three names from the bag. That is how you will be divided for this assignment. Am I understood?"

Hesitantly, each of the twelve nodded.

"They don't sound all that impressive," whispered Fynn, leaning closer to Godryk so only the other boy could hear.

"What do you mean?"

"Well…it's not like any of them are war heroes."

Godryk nudged Fynn's side with his elbow. "Hollyn's right," he joked, "you're an idiot sometimes."

"What do you mean?"

"We haven't been to war in a really long time. *Of course*, none of the instructors are war heroes," Godryk explained. "They're all far too young."

"Oh. Makes sense then."

Godryk shook his head and grinned.

"Right, before we choose names, let us choose team leaders! Dottie, *my darling*, you may choose who you'd like to serve on a team with. Choose wisely, Lady Air Brigadier General. This is a competition, let's remember; you'd do best to pick a strong partner," said Nyle.

As she stood beside her elder brother, Odette looked so remarkably like Moriah that Fynn thought that, if not for Odette's blonde hair, the two could have been twins. She was elegant in her appearance, swathed in tightly fitted black garb from head to toe. Her hair, golden and shining in the morning sunlight, was slicked back, twisting to its end just above her shoulders. Her eyes were calculating and analytical, rather cold looking despite the warm, golden glow of the day reflecting in those eerie, emerald depths. The corner of her lip pulled into a wicked curl as she decided upon her teammate.

Nodding toward Nyle, she said, "I choose Moriah."

Benadykt noticeably blanched at the declaration before regaining himself and bristling. Odette, having noticed his reaction, only smirked more as she regarded the cavalryman.

Moriah slung his arm over his sister's shoulder; he turned toward Benadykt with an identical looking smirk, the same chilly, mocking-green eyes narrowed. "I accept," he replied dully, turning from Benadykt and glancing down at Odette. "Should be fun."

"The *most* fun," she quipped; her own attention never having wavered from Benadykt.

"Gods, she's just like him." Ollie gulped as he frantically looked between the entwined Mordrays, silently praying that he wasn't chosen for their team.

Albie nodded dumbly; his eyes wide with fright. Clearly, he was raising up the same wordless intonations to the deities that watched over them.

"Right," Nyle clucked, "now that that's settled, and a fine choice I might say, let's choose the teams. Drake, go on, pick a name!"

After gingerly reaching into the bag, Drake called out the name on the parchment. "Wilder."

Odette chose next. "Lux."

Lord Beckett reached in and drew. "Albie."

Moriah, who seemed entirely disinterested with the whole ordeal, sighed as he reached into the bag. "Ollie."

Firiel and Hogan both found themselves on Benadykt's team while Penelope and Georgie nervously shuffled toward the Mordrays. They cast anxious glances toward the siblings, who paid them no mind, before being comforted by Lux's assuring presence.

"I don't think it will be *too* bad," Penelope whispered shakily.

Georgie smiled sheepishly; turning to the other girl, she giggled. "At least Moriah's not too hard on the eyes."

"Always the optimist," joked Penelope.

Drake drew his fifth team member, saying, "Renwyn."

Odette was next, smiling when she pulled out her parchment slip. "Hollyn."

Fynn and Godryk, the only two left, turned to one another dourly.

"We won't be on the same team," bemoaned the young Redmayne.

The prince hung his head, feeling defeated by the team choosing process. "Looks that way." Forcing himself straight again, he levered a grin toward Godryk. Playfully, he punched the other boy in the arm, espousing, "I'm definitely going to beat you."

"It's a *team* game, Fynn," groused Godryk.

Fynn shrugged. "Well, *my* team's going to beat *yours*."

"Don't be so sure about that," challenged Godryk with a smile.

"You're on," Fynn laughed.

Benadykt reached into the bag, withdrawing the penultimate slip. "Godryk."

As Godryk joined his team, Fynn bounded toward the Mordrays and his classmates. He offered Moriah a cheeky grin. He snickered. "I suppose that means I'm yours."

Moriah stared back at the prince with indifference while Odette regarded him with little more than tepid interest.

"So, it would seem," Moriah drawled in a deep, monotone voice.

"Try not to make a mess of everything," Hollyn mumbled, shaking his head as he regarded this still-grinning Fynn.

The teams settled in amongst one another, mulling about for only a moment or so before Nyle continued his instructions. "Right, right, children, now that we've our teams assembled, let's go over your objective. Each team will have a flag. You may place it where you like; the entire island is fair game but keep out of the jungles! Right then, your objective is to guard your flag and capture the other team's. Once you capture your opponent's flag, you are to reassemble your team, gather your own flag, and return to the castle. Only then will you be declared the victors." His keen eyes roved the small crowd, grinning excitedly he continued on, "Your team leaders will lead you back to the castle and outfit you with the appropriate weaponry. You'll have shields, swords, and arrows at your disposal for this task."

"Arrows?" Ollie asked nervously. "We'll be shooting at each other?"

"Listen, child! Don't interrupt." Nyle harrumphed irritably, brows knitting together as he eyed the round boy. "As I was saying ... the arrows you'll be given are specially made for this task. Their tips are blunted and wrapped in linen. If you're shot, it will hurt, make no mistake. Pain is inevitable in battle, children! Remember that. Do not run from it; accept it as it will come. Right then, as I was saying, your arrows are *blunted*. If you're shot, they will not break the skin. But, children, mark my words, you will find yourselves with nasty welts and bruises by the game's conclusion."

"Great," grumbled Fynn under his breath.

Moriah, his green eyes glancing down to Fynn, quickly arrested the amused smirk tugging at the corner of his lips. "You've had worse," he whispered irreverently.

"Now that you've been given your assignment," Nyle asked, "are there any questions?"

When none of the children said anything, they were dismissed to follow their team leaders. Team Mordray headed toward the castle in a close-knit huddle. Moriah and Odette led their band of six; shoulder to shoulder, the siblings headed up the hill, heads leaned inward toward the other as they whispered amongst themselves. Penelope and Georgie followed closely at their heels, giggling behind cupped hands as they chanced quick glances toward Moriah.

"I don't think they're taking this very seriously," commented Lux.

Fynn chuckled. "I think they've found something more interesting than the game."

"Looks that way," muttered Hollyn.

Ollie nudged Hollyn softly with his elbow. "Jealous, are you?"

Hollyn snapped his head to the side, leveling Ollie with a heated glare. "Of *what?*"

Fynn and Lux couldn't help but laugh at the prince's reaction.

"I don't know," Fynn began.

"Maybe that Penelope isn't paying you any attention," Lux added. "Neither is Georgie for that matter."

"Don't be ridiculous," Hollyn huffed incredulously, stomping by the other three to make his way toward the still-giggling girls.

Ollie watched, amused, as Hollyn sidled up beside Penelope. It wasn't long before he had struck up a conversation with the girl, occasionally peeking over his shoulder with smoldering eyes narrowed upon the trio.

"I think you made him mad," Ollie said.

"You're the one who mentioned it," Fynn countered, smiling boyishly.

"Oh, was that me?" Ollie sniggered. "My mistake."

Lux shook her head and sighed. "Try not to get him riled up, Ollie. He's more useful to us if he's focused."

Once within the walls of the castle, the group headed toward the armory. The other team, it would seem, hadn't yet come by. Fynn, eyes alight at the sight of all the weapons strewn about the room, went bounding toward a rack of swords. He skittered to an abrupt halt when Moriah warned, "They're not practice swords. Don't cut yourself."

Odette began gathering the bows and blunt-tipped arrows. She looked to her brother and asked, "What do you think? Three archers?"

Moriah didn't bother to turn to face her; he continued rummaging through a secondary collection of swords all clustered together. He pulled out practice swords, setting them gently upon the table that stretched along the far wall. "Three will be sufficient." He ran his hand through his well-kept hair, straightening up and turning to face the group. "Dot, you can handle the archers."

She nodded, filling quivers with the selected arrows, counting them out one by one as she made sure each of the children were given ample ammunition. "What's the plan?"

"I'm sure Benadykt is going to take charge," Moriah began. He started prowling through the room in search of light-weight shields. "If I had to guess, I'd say they'll utilize an aggressive strategy."

"So, we'll need a strategy to counter," Odette finished.

Moriah nodded. "Drake will probably stay back with their flag."

"Hogan and Albie are the obvious choices to stay back with him," mused Odette aloud. "Firiel, Wilder, and Renwyn all have more aggressive, straight forward personalities. They're the ones who'd do best with Ben. Godryk…I don't know about him. I could see him used for defense *or* offense."

The elder sibling shook his head. "He'll be hanging back with Drake. I'm rather sure of that."

"Right." Odette nodded. "So, they're using three back and three forward. An equal split for offense and defense." She paused for a moment, considering her opponents and their strengths, their weaknesses. "Drake isn't particularly good with a bow."

"Neither is Benadykt," Moriah commented flatly. "Knowing those two, they won't rely too heavily on long-range attacks."

"But they know *we* will," Odette replied.

"Exactly. They *know* we will."

Odette arched a brow curiously, a rather wry look in her cat-like eyes. "What did you have in mind then?"

Moriah smirked. "We'll do exactly the opposite of what they suspect."

"Clever."

"But of course," drawled Moriah silkily. "They won't know what hit them."

"What's the plan?" asked Fynn. He inched closer to the two siblings; the other five circled around him and their team leaders.

"They think we'll leave three back, just like them, but stationed out of range, probably in the trees. They're expecting us to rely on long-range strikes for defense, to attack out of their range and slow them down. They're expecting archers to be defending the flag," Odette explained. "Naturally, they'd expect Moriah to go forward with three of you, all of you with swords and shields. They'd expect us to break apart three by three."

"So, we're not splitting three and three?" Lux questioned, confused. "I thought you said we'd have three archers, and the rest would be swords?"

Moriah leaned his long back against the wall, folding his arms over his chest. He regarded the children with tepid interest; his voice was low and sharp when he spoke. "Nyle told you all that the assignment was to capture the other flag, regroup, and return to the castle. That's the only way to win."

"He never said anything about splitting into offense and defense. He never told you how you had to defend your flag or take the other," Odette added.

"Your opponents will likely be utilizing a very aggressive strategy. They're best bet in a frontal assault would be to catch us in the open."

368

Moriah glanced down to his sister who'd flattened her own back against the wall just at his side. "So, we won't give them the chance."

"Tell us, what's the first step to winning a battle?" asked Odette.

The children looked between one another questioningly, their eyes brightening as they raked through the information they'd been given since arriving at Morancy so many months ago.

Hollyn was the first to realize what Odette was trying to say. He turned back to his instructors, a knowing look upon his face. "Knowing your enemy."

The lady air brigadier general nodded, pleased. "Very good."

"So, tell us. What do you know about your adversaries? We've already told you what we think of Drake and Benadykt, how they're likely to lead their team," Moriah started.

His sister continued, "But, what do you know of the other team? You've spent months together. Tell us how you think they'll behave in this situation."

"Firiel and Renwyn are the cockiest of the lot," Lux asserted. "They're the ones most likely to charge their opponent without thinking first. They'll leap before they look every time."

"Hogan and Albie are smart, and they're capable when they remain calm… but they're easily overwhelmed," Hollyn noted evenly. "If we take them by surprise or come at them harder than they anticipated, they'll panic. It'll be easy to get their flag."

"Wilder's strong," Ollie said. "He's tough, that's for sure. But he isn't the sort to think things through all the way. He needs direction. If he's without a commander, he won't know which way to turn. It'll be easy to out-maneuver him."

Fynn jumped into the conversation, eyes narrowed and fixed on the swords resting on the table. "Godryk is smart, very smart. And he's strong. He's a good fighter, hand to hand and with a sword. But he's sort of nervous. He won't jump into a fray without proper coaxing from his commander. He'll look three times before he *ever* leaps."

"Well done." Odette nodded. "Very thoughtful assessments from each of you."

"Now then, what's the second step to victory?" Moriah inquired.

Fynn turned to look the man in the eyes, his own icy gaze unwavering. "Knowing yourself."

The man nodded sharply. "Exactly."

Odette folded her arms over her chest. "So then, analyze yourselves as you did your opponents. Tell us what we should know about this team."

"What do you want to know?" Ollie ventured. "What sort of information?"

"Assess your team the same way you did your opponents," Odette answered. Her tone was clipped when she continued, "You did well in judging your enemies' strengths and weaknesses. We want to know what yours are now."

"Lux is good…well, *great*…with a sword," Fynn chirped. "She doesn't just wildly swing. She's quick and precise." He eyed the girl for a moment, lamenting having to disparage any of her qualities. He paused, then continued, "But…physically…she lacks the size and strength to beat Renwyn. She could win as long as the bout remained quick…hit for hit…but if their blades lock…he can overcome her easily."

"Ollie is good with a bow." Lux smiled fondly at the boy and said, "You've got great aim." Her eyes returned to the instructors, glancing between the two. "But his sword work is lacking and his ability to fight hand to hand is near non-existent. He isn't the sort to fight someone in close quarters. He's better suited to long-range assaults."

Fynn chimed in, "Hollyn is the tactician amongst us. When we were in the jungle, even when he was hurt and everything was going wrong, he kept his wits about him. He was giving us instructions, helping us come up with a plan of attack. He kept calm even when it seemed like everything was against us."

"He's good with a sword too," Penelope added. "He's strong. But he's also really precise with his attacks."

Stormy, blue eyes, alight with interest, regarded Fynn raptly. When, at last, Hollyn voiced his part, his tone was even and analytically cold. "Fynn should be on the attack. He's too impulsive and jumpy to stay put if you leave him back to defend the flag." The boy had to smoother the petulant grin threatening to crack his cool façade when he saw the scowling pout Fynn dawned, spurred on by the assessment. "That being said," Hollyn ventured slyly, "he's not *entirely* useless. He's still a bit sloppy with a sword, but he's *strong* and he's *fast*. He can outpace all of us. And if it comes down to hand to hand? Well, the only one who's beaten him is *me*…and we're on the same team this time. I don't think there's anyone on the other team who'd be able to stop the idiot."

"Georgie's smart," Ollie peeped. "She's brilliant in our medical lessons. She's not much of a fighter, but she does well in archery. I think she'd do best with a bow."

Georgie, energized by Ollie's somewhat favorable analysis, beamed. "Penelope's good with a bow also! She's got great aim."

Hollyn nodded. "She does. She's also really good at knowing how to help out when things go wrong. She can transition, I think, better than most of us, from one post to another."

Moriah pulled himself lazily from the wall. He rolled his shoulders back as he straightened up. He felt the tension pooling in his sinews, the excitement for the coming game beginning to stir within his muscles. It'd been a while since he'd been allowed to go out and run around, get some real exercise, and he longed for it. The anticipation for their war game was beginning to gnaw at him; he found himself fighting off the feeling of restlessness that was pawing within. There was a bit more bite to his voice when he spoke, "Dot, is it settled then?"

She nodded.

"So, here's what we're going to do. We'll send Fynn and Hollyn out first to scout. The rest of us will stay back, surrounding the flag, but out of sight. We'll establish a perimeter around our flag on both the ground and in the trees. Once Fynn and Hollyn return with the location of the other team's flag, we'll begin our attack. First, Fynn, Hollyn, and I will engage the enemy's offense. We'll keep it brief. We'll break away and make a run for it, in the direction of their flag," Moriah said.

"Ben will think you'll know where their flag is. He won't chase you; he'll want to beat you at your own game. He'll come for our flag, following the direction you came. That's when we've got him," Odette wickedly explained, an excited glint igniting in her eyes.

"What do you mean?" Lux asked.

"Moriah, Hollyn, and Fynn won't really be going for their flag. Instead, they'll double back, out of sight, toward *our* flag. Once Ben and his team advance on our flag, thinking that it'll be an even fight, we've won. They'll have their attention so focused on getting by us that they won't anticipate a strike from behind their lines."

"We'll come in behind them, effectively trapping them." The same malicious fire burning in Odette's eyes now sparked to life in Moriah's as he spoke about the plan, the lust for a bit of a fight clearly thawing his normally chilly demeanor. "They'll be hit from all sides, surrounded. They'll panic. Dot and Lux can come at them with swords from the front. Penelope, Georgie, and Ollie will be in the trees, pelting them with arrows. Fynn,

Hollyn, and I will charge them from the rear with swords. They'll be too confused to acclimate quickly enough to fight back."

"Then what?" Fynn questioned excitedly.

"Then we neutralize the threat. We'll tie up their offensive force. Georgie and I will stay back, guarding the flag. The rest of you will advance with Moriah to *their* flag. You'll outnumber them. That should make capturing their flag easier," elucidated Odette.

Moriah nodded. "Exactly. Once we've overcome their defense, we'll do the same. We'll neutralize them so they can't follow us back. We'll tie them up, take their flag, regroup with Dottie and Georgie, and then head to the castle. Then, we've won."

Hollyn furrowed his brow thoughtfully, asking, "Do you think they'll anticipate this sort of plan?"

Odette shook her head. "Not at all."

It was eerie to the children the way Odette and Moriah seemed to allow a conversation to flow so easily between them. It was as if, the children thought, the two siblings knew exactly what the other would say next, making completing one another's thought process frighteningly simple.

Moriah cocked his head to the side, an impish grin upon his features, eyes burning. "They won't know what to expect. That, children, is the virtue of not using the same tactics at every opportunity. Creativity will usually throw off your adversary."

"And even if they do, by some miracle, figure out what we're planning," Odette assured, "Moriah and I are rather adept at thinking on our feet."

"It's one of our many shared talents," insisted Moriah. "Trust us when we say out-thinking the other team is not going to be much of a challenge."

"Out-muscling them, though, may be," joked Odette mirthlessly.

Moriah shoved her lightly, pouting, "Sister, you *wound* me. Surely you don't think *Benadykt* is stronger than me."

She smacked his arm sharply, laughing, "He's got a bit of weight on you, Moriah. But, if it comes down to it, I'd bet on you, *darling* brother."

"Flatterer," Moriah muttered.

When they'd gathered their supplies, swords fixed to their belts, quivers strapped to their backs, bows in hands, and bags slung over their shoulders, the team made their way from the armory and back outside. Emerging from the castle, they saw the sun reigning supreme overhead. It was late morning and still very hot.

"Moriah," called Odette from the front of the pack.

At the sound of his name, Moriah perked up, looking over the six heads wading in front of him. "Yes?"

"I know where we should place our flag."

He nodded, waving his free hand. "Go on then, lead the way."

And so, Odette began to lead her band of first-years through the grounds. They shuffled along obediently behind her, chattering amongst themselves like eager ducklings toddling in a malformed line.

"Where do you think we're headed?" Ollie asked.

Lux shrugged. "Don't know. We don't normally come around this way."

"Right," Georgie agreed, while looking around curiously. "There's never much of a reason to come this way."

There was a vast expanse of open land where they walked, stretching all around them until it gave way to clusters of trees with overgrown fronds and vines that twisted their way up the trunks like snakes. They'd long ago left the path and the road the children normally stuck to when running off to their lessons. They were slowly descending down a hill; Morancy castle loomed over them, ever watchful. The team was careful to keep quiet, each of them occasionally letting paranoid eyes flit across their surroundings, searching for anyone who may be spying on them. They never saw anyone.

Upon their successful descent down the hill's slope, they began delving through the thickness of brush that speckled the area. They sifted through the roots and vines and undergrowth. Occasionally their clothing snagged on thorns or twigs. Still, they watched where they stepped, hyper aware of snapping twigs drawing attention to their location. The eight continued on deeper into the trees where the sunlight could hardly claw at them anymore and, instead, the shadows weighed down upon them.

The north side of the island, where they found themselves presently, wasn't wild with jungle. Nor was it sparse by any means. The trees here weren't clumped so thickly as the jungle and there was no canopy to blot out the sun, only some twisting branches overhead that stretched out like a lattice; the leaves were scarce, and the now-afternoon sky was still quite visible.

"Not much further," Odette assured them from the lead position.

"How does she know about this place?" Fynn wondered aloud.

Moriah was quietly stalking up just behind the prince. He chuckled. "We used to come out here when we were children, back when we attended Morancy."

"Why?" Lux asked.

There was a certain light that flashed in the fathomless, green eyes of the lord commander. It was the sort of light that normally didn't live in those eyes. Moriah's lips curled into a smile as he said, "It was quiet and peaceful."

Fynn slowed, his attention far too focused on Moriah and what he said. As such, he found himself being ushered forward by Moriah's hand as it found purchase upon his back, pushing him along.

"Don't dawdle," Moriah whispered to the prince as, a bit more roughly this time, he urged him on.

Odette came to a halt not too long later. She stood, stock-still, surveying the area. She nodded, as if affirming to herself that she had, indeed, found the place she was looking for. She threw her bag and the flag down to the damp earth, rolling her shoulders and stretching her arms out. When she turned to face her team, there was a competitive gleam in her feline eyes and a malicious smirk upon her features. "Right. We'll set up here."

"Where *is* here?" Penelope inquired, looking all around and wondering how in the world Odette and Moriah could have found this place when they were students.

The woman comber her hand through her sweaty hair. "Does anyone know the story of Dier Island?"

When Lux nodded, Odette smiled in her direction and implored her to explain to her team. The girl began, "The island was a kingdom. Well, all the islands in the archipelago were part of the kingdom. They belonged to King Algernon and that's why they're called the Isles of Algernon now. Estheria won them in a war."

"Very good," praised Odette. "What else?"

"Morancy was the king's castle," Georgie added. "It was their capital castle, like we have Batsbeckon."

"Correct." Odette brushed the sweat from her brow with her sleeve. "And what lies beneath castles? Especially big castles like Morancy? Castles that are the focal point of a kingdom?"

A collective puzzlement came upon five of the six children, but Hollyn caught on quickly. He looked about to the left and to the right before he saw what he was looking for. Not too far from where they stood, there were vines growing at a particularly odd angle. They crept down from arching stones and hung like a curtain over what seemed to be a tunnel leading to nothing but perpetual blackness. "Catacombs," the red-haired prince answered.

"Creepy," shivered Georgie.

Moriah strode through the small throng of children. He stood beside Odette, dropping his things down beside hers. He stretched his lithe back, luxuriating in the unwinding of tense muscles. "Very good," he replied flatly. His own eyes traversed the area until they, too, rested upon the curtain of vines and the mouth of a small cave. "Not many people know where to find the entrances to the catacombs."

"*Entrances?*" Hollyn repeated. "So, there's more than one?"

Moriah nodded, a sly grin creeping across his features. "I do believe you've found one before."

"When?" asked Georgie.

"I think we'd remember that, sir," Penelope added.

Lux shook her head. "I know." When the attentions of her year mates turned toward her, Lux continued, "That cave Drusus had us in…that's one of them, isn't it?"

Odette nodded. "Yes."

"Why here?" Fynn asked, confused. "Why pick by the catacombs for this? Am I missing something?"

"When're you not?" muttered Hollyn.

Fynn elbowed the other prince in the side. He frowned. "If you're *so* smart, then you tell me. Why here?"

Hollyn nodded toward the catacomb's entrance. "Look there. What do you see?"

"A cave," Fynn answered sharply. "Obviously."

"Look up from the cave and tell me what you see," prodded Hollyn, nearing exasperation.

Fynn looked. His eyes roved from the arching entrance of the cave where from the vines dangled, up to the rock juts that formed about the entrance. Vines and moss clung to the rock, climbing up and up, higher than some of the trees. "Rocks."

"Think about it. The cave is there." Hollyn pointed to the archway and then gestured all around. "That means no one can come at us from that side. That leaves only three possible directions for them to attack from." He walked by Odette and Moriah, standing to the side of where they'd set their things. He looked into the brush, the denseness of it all. "But if they came from the sides, it would slow them down. It's too dense in that direction. They'd make too much noise trying to sneak up on us." He turned to face the group, blue eyes piercing down the way they'd come. "That way is the only feasible direction to approach. So, if we keep to the sides in the brush or up in the trees, we can see them, but they won't be able to see us."

Lux caught on and grinned. "We'll be able to see them long before they can figure out where we've hidden."

"Exactly," Odette grinned. "Well done, children." She reached down and picked up the flag. She plunged its pole into the ground, making sure it was secured in place. Their red banner hung limp in a furl; it looked meek and un-interesting amongst all the trees, perfectly passable and not drawing attention. "They won't realize they've walked into an ambush until it's too late."

Moriah began prowling the area, keen eyes darting in every direction, inspecting the site for anything that may give them away too easily. "Ollie, Georgie, Penelope."

When he said their names, each child straightened into perfect posture, clearly on edge.

He had to suppress a grin as he said, "Gather up the bows. You'll be stationed in the trees. I'll help you up."

One by one, the children collected the bows, quivers having already been strapped to their backs and filled generously with arrows. Moriah helped them clamber up the trees. Once they were amongst the branches, he stood at the base of each of their perches and assessed whether or not they were effectively hidden. Once satisfied that his archers were practically invisible to on-comers, Moriah returned to the remaining group.

"Lux and I will each take a side," Odette said. She lightly brushed her fingers over the hilt of her sword, absentmindedly reassuring herself it was in place where it ought to be. "I'll take the left. Lux, go right."

Lux bustled off into the brush, hunkering down amongst the shrubber-ies. "Can you see me?" she called out.

To the others, it seemed her voice was disembodied.

"No," Hollyn answered.

Odette nodded, pleased. "Right." She kneeled over the bag she'd brought along. She reached in. "Come here," she murmured as she wrestled with the bag's contents. Suddenly, she pulled from it a round, furry creature with beady eyes.

"What *is* that?" Fynn asked, aghast.

Odette dropped the animal at her feet as she stood, brushing off her hands. "*That*...is Mischief."

"Mischief?" Hollyn laughed as he bent his knees and leaned down clos-er to the animal. "What is he?"

"He's what's called a raccoon," Odette replied, an unfamiliar warmness to her voice.

"I've never seen one of these things before," cooed Fynn. He knelt beside Hollyn to get a closer look.

Mischief was round. His fur was a pale grey, dark rings of black decorated a rather fat, fluffy tail. His paws looked more like hands; tiny fingers kneaded at the ground. His ears were small, twitching with every sound. Encircling his shining, little eyes was what appeared to be a black mask. His nose was long and thin; whiskers protruded in every direction.

"That's because they're not native to Estheria," elaborated Moriah with the air of someone explaining the most obvious concept in the world.

"Where'd you get him then?" Fynn asked, reaching out his hand to the odd creature. He giggled when a tiny, cold nose brushed over his palm.

"Erza." Odette stretched her arms. "There was an exotic meat market. I saw this little guy in one of the cages. He had his hands wrapped around the bars like a tiny, fuzzy prisoner."

Moriah knelt on Hollyn's other side, affectionately running his hand over Mischief's head. He toyed with one of the animal's ears between his thumb and index finger. The smile he wore was soft and gentle, reminiscent of the way he often looked upon Skullduggery. "She *simply* couldn't leave him there." Moriah snorted. "That's what *she* said, at least. She came to me, *crying*, about this *cute* little animal she had rescued." He tapped his finger over Mischief's nose. "Then she showed me *this* thing. Cute? I'm not so sure about that. But he's proven himself to be useful."

"Useful? What do you mean?" Hollyn inquired. He leaned back on his heels and looked up to Odette expectantly. "Is that why you brought him?"

Odette nodded. "You and Fynn will take him with you."

Fynn turned his own nonplussed expression toward Odette. "What does he do?"

"He *does* many things." Odette stepped around the boys; placing her hands on her brother's shoulders, she leaned over his back and peered down at the small creature she doted upon. "But, for this mission, he's going to help you track down the other team."

"How?" Hollyn asked. He climbed back to his feet.

"He'll catch Ben's scent and lead you straight to their camp." Odette grinned wickedly. "He shouldn't have a hard time finding them."

Fynn stood. Mischief settled in a comfortable mound at his feet. "How'd you train him to do that?"

Moriah stood slowly, pulling Odette up with him. He gave her one last moderately interested look before peeling away from the group and settling in the cover of the bushes beside Lux.

Odette regarded the boys for a moment before answering them dully, "I didn't have to train him. He just figured it out, I suppose." She continued, "You've both got your swords? Good." She placed a hand upon each of their shoulders and pushed them along, back the way they'd come. "Let's not waste any more time. You two take Mischief and go find the others camp. When you have, come back here as quickly as you can."

"Understood," Hollyn replied dutifully. He let his hand rest over the pommel of his sword. Looking down, he smiled softly at the animal curled around Fynn's feet. "Mischief? Lead the way."

Mischief took off, bushy tail waggling happily.

The princes followed Mischief for the better part of three hours, winding their way across the island, keeping close to the shade, careful not to remain out in the open for too long. They heard the sounds of other lessons being conducted, of the Cavalry Division out training in the fields on horseback, of the archers yelling from the battlements about the shots they'd missed. The day had only grown hotter, and the lack of clouds made for a particularly bruising heat that was beginning to wear both boys down. Still, they forged along, neither willing to take a break. The two were mindful of keeping quiet, not wanting to draw any attention to themselves that may tip off the other team.

Mischief led them down another hill. By this time, they were far off from any of the heavily traveled paths or roads. They'd have easily become lost if their guide wasn't so sure footed as he scampered through the grass and the brush. The odd trio ducked into the trees. Much like where they'd staked their own flag, this part of the island was littered with trees and shrubberies and large stones; the mid-afternoon sun was obscured by large palm fronds that swayed in the soft breeze. The beginnings of the jungle canopy were encroaching upon the area, casting long and dark shadows that helped cool them off.

Hollyn and Fynn stopped suddenly when they heard, muffled by the distance and the wilds, the distinct sounds of voices speaking in hushed tones.

Fynn immediately recognized Godryk's voice amongst the group. He whispered, "It's them."

Hollyn nodded. "They probably aren't too far away."

"Should we head back now?"

"No." Hollyn took a few tentative steps onward, crouching as low as he could. "Let's get a look at how they've set up before we head back. The more information we can gather, the better prepared we can be."

"Right," Fynn agreed as he, too, crouched down low and began stalking into the denseness.

The pair weeded their way through the greenery. The voices of the other team were growing louder, closer. Mischief kept quiet, inching along between the two boys. They stopped when the voices were just a few feet away.

Peeking through the leaves, Hollyn studied their opponent's encampment. "Godryk, Albie, and Hogan," he stated softly.

"I see Drake just a way behind them," added Fynn astutely. "That means Moriah and Odette were right about their strategy."

Hollyn shook his head. "We don't know that for certain." He turned to face Fynn, eyes serious, mouth set in a firm, thin line. "The others could be hiding out of sight…just like we planned to do."

"Do you suppose they anticipated what Moriah and Odette would plan?"

Shrugging his shoulders, Hollyn sighed. "I don't know. Maybe."

Both boys stiffened instantly when they felt the blunted tip of steel pressed against the napes of their necks. Their shoulders and backs went rigid. They never heard the footsteps of their foes approaching. But now, as their breath had hitched in their throats, they could hear two people standing just behind them, breathing rather heavily.

"Yes." It was Renwyn speaking; both princes recognized his voice as soon as he spoke. "We did guess what you would do."

"Clever," Firiel cooed. "But, unfortunately for your team, not clever enough."

"Stand up," commanded Renwyn. "Hold out your hands."

Very slowly, both boys stood. They held their hands out, palms up. They didn't turn around to face their captors. Rather, they stood staring toward the enemy camp. They could see the blue of the flag amongst the thick of green stretched out before them. Fynn's silver eyes glanced sideways toward Hollyn.

Seeing Fynn's conspiratorially look, Hollyn smirked. He nodded ever so slightly. "Now!"

The princes whirled around at a spectacular speed, each of them drawing their swords and slamming their steel against their adversaries'. Hollyn forced his weight forward, trying to overpower Renwyn despite the awkwardness of his foray, his right side still weakened from his shoulder injury. Fynn was luckier; he'd managed to catch Firiel off guard and then easily overpowered her by means of raw physicality. In just a moment's time, he'd knocked her to the ground and kicked her discarded sword away and out of arm's reach. Seeing Hollyn struggling, the raven-haired boy launched himself at Renwyn.

His sword forgotten, tossed to the ground, Fynn brought Renwyn down in a tackle. They fell in a painful cluster of limbs upon the ground, wrestling for supremacy. Renwyn kicked Fynn from atop him. When the smaller boy was prostrate, dazed, upon the ground, Renwyn hopped astride his torso and bore his weight down over him. He pinned Fynn's wrists down with his own hands, forcing his superior weight down even further with bruising strength. Fynn thrashed beneath Renwyn but made little progress in escaping.

Hollyn, regaining his footing after Fynn's tackle nearly brought him down as well, threw himself into Renwyn's back. Knocking the offending enemy off of Fynn, Hollyn jumped back to his feet. He reached down, snatched Fynn by the collar of his tunic, and hauled him upright. "Run!"

With Mischief at their heels, the boys burst from the scene of their tussle and into the trees. They ran deeper and deeper until they realized that they'd found themselves in a never-ending expanse of green. They stopped. They were breathing heavily, sweat prickling at their temples, falling down to their jaws, dampening their tunics. Their chests heaved as they struggled to regain their breath. When they looked around, they were mortified to find that, in every direction they could see, there was little more than greenery shaded by a heavy, twisting canopy splayed overhead.

"This isn't good," Hollyn said, still gasping for breath. "I think we went further than we intended."

Fynn was spinning in place, desperate to find a way out or hear the lilting of voices in the distance. He heard nothing but the chirping chorus of birds as they dipped and dove between the branches. "I think we're back in the jungle."

Hollyn raked his hand through his scarlet hair. He shook his head. "It can't be." Looking around, he saw that it was true. Thick-trunked trees towered all around them, vines climbing up their bark, roots up-turned from the damp earth and cresting over the dirt like whales breaching the surface of the sea. "We weren't *that* close. There's no way we could have run this far without realizing it," he rasped.

"I agree." Fynn sighed. "It doesn't matter what we think though. We're here. And we have to get out. And quickly."

"Mischief," Hollyn called, kneeling down before the animal. He held his hand out and watched fondly as the tiny, hand-like paws of the creature took hold of his fingers. "Can you get us out of here? Can you find Odette?"

Mischief uncurled his paws from Hollyn's fingers and steadied them against the earth, feeling it sift beneath his meager weight. He sniffed, whiskers jumping as his nose twitched. He began to turn in circles, ears twitching back and forth, searching for a familiar sound or voice.

"I think the jungle has him confused," Fynn offered.

"For once, you may be right," a resigned Hollyn relented as he stood. "We should keep moving. If we stay in one place too long…well, you know. The vines have a tendency to start moving."

Fynn reached down and scooped Mischief into his arms. He held the creature tightly to his chest, smiling when the fluffy tail draped over his arms and the tiny nose nuzzled against his collarbone. "Hollyn, everything looks the same. Which way do we go?"

Hollyn had been trying to figure that out since they realized where they were and, presently, didn't have an answer. He furrowed his brows; his nose wrinkled as he concentrated. "You're right." Again, he combed his hand through his hair. "Let's just start moving."

Nodding, the smaller boy followed along after his cousin as they started their journey through the trees. The sound of birds got louder, the air got cooler, and everything around them got darker. The canopy became so thick they no longer could see the daylight peeking through. An unwanted, all too familiar, nervousness settled in the pit of Fynn's stomach. He recalled, not at all fondly, the last time he'd been beneath the oppressive hold of the jungle's canopy. He shuddered at the thought.

Hollyn grumbled, "Damn it. I think we're going the wrong way."

"How can you tell? Every way looks the same."

"Because we've gone further into the jungle," Hollyn snapped. Calming himself down, the prince squared his shoulders and held his head up high. "Let's turn around and go back that way."

Yet, as they ventured in the opposite direction, they were unsettled to find that they weren't making any progress in their escape. Everything was still dark and chilly. There were no signs of breaking free from the greenness and stepping into the sunlight.

Fynn saw something wriggle in his periphery. He tensed, his hold around Mischief tightening. "Hollyn," he whispered.

"What is it?"

"I think I saw a vine move," Fynn choked out. Biting down on his lower lip hard, he turned and watched as, indeed, one vine snaked along the spine of a tree until it slithered to the ground and began creeping toward them. "It's getting close."

Hollyn's eyes went wide as he watched the jungle's tendril advance towards he and Fynn. "We've got to make a run for it."

"Alright," Fynn bit out.

"Ready?"

"Ready!"

They darted forward and began to run as fast as their legs would carry them. They dodged and weaved through the trees, heedless of the thin branches that smacked into their faces, cutting their pale skin. All they could hear were the sounds of sticks shattering beneath their feet, of leaves rustling as they ran by, of branches clattering against their sprinting forms, and of their own, heavy breathing thunderously echoing into the green void.

A vine ensnared Fynn's ankle and went taut, bringing Fynn smashing into the ground as he pitched forward face first. Mischief had just enough time to wiggle free of the boy's hold and avoid being trapped beneath his weight. Fynn moaned in pain as his chest collided with the earth, all the air in his lungs forcefully expelled, leaving him gasping. The prince scowled when he felt the eerily familiar sensation of warmth oozing down his face—blood. He propped himself up on his elbows, still struggling to catch his breath. Wiping the blood from his face with the back of his hand, Fynn was a tad disconcerted to see just how much red he saw. "That can't be good," he groaned as he tried to get up.

Fynn was brought back down as the vine tightened and began dragging him backward. He reached out with both hands, scraping and raking frantically at the ground, ripping small trenches into the earth with his nails. "Hollyn!" he screamed.

Hollyn reeled around on his heel. He hadn't seen Fynn fall, so when he looked back to where the voice had come from, he saw nothing but trees and undergrowth. "Fynneas?"

"Hollyn! Help!"

"Where are you?" Hollyn called back. He rushed in the direction of the voice. "Fynneas!" He erupted from the brush partitioning him from Fynn and shrieked when he saw Fynn being dragged deeper into the jungle. He lunged forward, tossing himself bodily to the ground, and caught hold of Fynn's wrist. "Idiot! You let yourself get caught."

"Yell at me later," whined Fynn as he held onto Hollyn with all the strength he could muster up. "Help me get loose first!"

Hollyn leaned all his weight back. He succeeded in slowing down the vine's progress of wrenching Fynn into the depths of the jungle but became concerned about their current situation when he found himself being pulled along with Fynn.

Mischief clambered over to the vine and began gnawing away, tiny teeth hewing the green.

"Try kicking your legs out," Hollyn suggested. He continued doing his best to pull Fynn free. "Kick!"

Fynn's legs jerked in nervous, spasming motions as he tried to break free of the jungle's grasp. But with every movement of his leg, he felt the hold around his ankle tightening painfully. "It isn't working."

"Damn it, damn it, *damn it*," Hollyn cursed. He lurched forward, leaning around Fynn, and began to claw at the vine, anxiously trying to unknot it from the other boy's ankle. "Damn it!" He was making slow progress, but he could feel it giving way under his efforts. "Fynn, when I say so, pull your leg up. Got it?"

"Alright."

Hollyn continued wringing the vine in his hands, pulling and twisting until he saw a gap appear between the green of the vine and the black of Fynn's boots. "Now!"

Fynn jerked his leg up and rolled to the side, free of the afflicting tendril at last. As he scrambled back, Mischief jumped into his arms. He watched Hollyn wrestle free of the vine himself. Both boys were seated in the dirt, shoulder to shoulder, panting and with wide, frightened eyes watching everything around them.

"Are you alright?" wheezed Hollyn.

Fynn curled his arms around Mischief more, burying his face into the animal's back for a moment, letting his tears be brushed away by the soft fur. "Yes."

Hollyn slung his arm around Fynn's shoulders and pulled him along to his feet. "We have to keep moving."

Fynn nodded. He asked shakily, "Do you think that was the Iba-Jii's doing?"

"Don't know, probably," mused Hollyn. "Maybe your little truce with Drusus was a one-time deal."

Fynn shook his head. "Or maybe there are other things in the jungle we should be worried about."

"Whatever the case is, just stay close."

They were more careful this time, cautious as they proceeded quickly through the sea of green. Both boys made certain to keep the other near, shoulders always just a hair's breadth apart. They heard rustling around them as if the vines were following, heatedly hunting them down. In response, the princes quickened their pace.

Within minutes they were once again sprinting through the jungle's undergrowth. Terror spurred them onward. They didn't notice their shortness of breath or the way their legs quaked with every step. They staggered along as fast as they could, stumbling over the roots.

Fynn inhaled sharply when, all at once, Hollyn pitched forward and disappeared. Having been just a step behind his cousin, Fynn didn't have time to stop his own forward momentum or redirect his course. Within the blink of an eye, he too was careening down the side of a rock-strewn hill.

By the time he came to a rolling stop at the bottom, Fynn was wincing in pain. His lean, little body had been pummeled by the rocks; cuts and bruises littered his arms, legs, and face. Mischief had broken free of Fynn's hold before being crushed between the boy and the earth. Presently, the creature scampered up to Fynn, brushing its tail along the boy's flank. The prince groaned lowly; he ached all over. A fresh cut on his temple leaked blood down the side of his face. He wiped the blood away with his sleeve, scowling. "Again? It's *always* my face."

Hollyn was just a few feet to Fynn's left. He was sitting, legs stretched out before him, shoulders hunching forward. "Why is there *always* a damn hill?" he seethed.

Fynn scoffed. "You have the *worst* luck."

"Me?" Hollyn turned his blue eyes toward Fynn. "If you hadn't noticed, you're down here with me."

Fynn shrugged his shoulders carelessly. "True. But you're the one who seems to go down the hill first every time." He eyed his cousin carefully, scanning his figure for any tell-tale signs of injury. He bit down on his lip when he noticed Hollyn favoring his left side; his right arm hung limply. The boy's left hand came up shakily before clamping down on his shoulder, fingers curling into the fabric of his tunic.

Fynn observed, "You're hurt."

Hollyn nodded. "My shoulder."

"Same one?"

"Yes."

Fynn crawled over to the other boy. He settled down just to Hollyn's side, facing him. He reached out and softly set his palm against Hollyn's shoulder at the apex where the joint met his neck. He felt a bump, the skin beneath his touch was warm. "You really have the *absolute worst* luck."

"Seems that way," muttered Hollyn. His voice was strained; pain laced over his words. "I suppose I'll be back in the hospital wing after this."

"Probably," Fynn agreed glumly.

Hollyn snorted, leveling his gaze upon Fynn's battered body. "That doesn't mean you get to mope around again."

"Whatever."

"*Really.*" Hollyn's tone was firm, resolute. "You need all the practice time you can get if you think you're ever going to beat me."

"Don't flatter yourself." Fynn kept his hand over Hollyn's quaking shoulders, gently running it along in search of any other anomalies. "You're already no match for me."

"Is that so?"

"It is." Fynn laughed humorlessly.

"We'll see," Hollyn sighed. He tried to move his right arm but found that it was almost entirely numb. The pain was racing through his shoulder, shooting up his neck. It was a throbbing, heated pain that was siring a headache that pounded in his temple and behind his ear. He hung his head and tried to keep calm, forcing himself to take slow, deliberate breaths. "This isn't good, Fynn."

"I know."

"We have to get out of here."

"I know." Fynn's hand pressed more insistently upon Hollyn's shoulder, eliciting an accidental yelp of pain from the boy. "Sorry."

"It's alright," Hollyn weakly assured. "It's no worse than last time."

"We have to keep going," Fynn lamented. He readied himself with strong, assured breaths. Then he hooked his arms beneath Hollyn's and hoisted him up. They stood, toe to toe, Hollyn shaking before Fynn, head still bowed. "Look, I'm going to help you, alright? I don't care that you don't want my help. I just want to get out of here and I'm not going to have you slowing me down. Got it?" said Fynn.

"You wouldn't leave me." Hollyn chuckled. "Don't even try to pretend it crossed your mind."

"You're right." Fynn smiled. He shuffled up beside Hollyn, wrapping one arm around the other's waist while Hollyn draped his left arm over Fynn' shoulders. They clung to one another for support, Fynn shouldering Hollyn's taller, heavier body as best he could.

For the first time since they'd fallen down the hill, Hollyn saw the blood painted across Fynn's face and splattered over his tunic. "You're hurt too."

"Don't worry. You know me. It'll heal pretty quickly."

"Right." Hollyn arched a brow and smirked. "It's weird, you know? *You're* weird. The way you can get hurt and just be fine so quickly."

"I suppose," Fynn agreed as they took their first few, hesitant steps forward.

They hadn't walked very far from where they'd fallen. Mischief kept pace with them, trotting along beside Hollyn. Fynn's eyes roved their surroundings, paranoid as they swept in every direction, alert to all the very present dangers around them. Those same, pale eyes saw something dark in the distance.

"There's something there," Fynn said, nodding his head forward.

"Another cave?"

"I think so," Fynn replied.

They headed in that direction.

"Moriah *did* say there were a lot of entrances to the catacombs," mused the taller boy. "They're probably all caves."

"Do you think this one leads into them?" asked Fynn.

"Maybe."

"The island isn't too big," mused Fynn aloud. "So, the catacombs probably aren't too big... nothing like the ones beneath the capital, at the very least. Right?"

"Right. What're you thinking?"

"I'm thinking that we could find our way back to our camp if we follow the catacombs," Fynn answered. "Think it'll work?"

"Maybe. But it could also take us deeper into the jungle... to Drusus' cave or something like that," countered Hollyn.

"True. But, if we end up finding Drusus, we could just ask him to have Gaia get us out again." Fynn smiled. "You know...maybe the truce isn't a one-time thing. They could help us."

Hollyn was getting tired. Pain, he had learned since arriving on the island months ago, wore a person out very quickly. "I don't think we have many options. It's either try the cave and the catacombs…or stay in the jungle and get even more lost…or *worse*."

"So, the cave, then?"

"The cave," Hollyn agreed.

They found that this cave was much like the one that marked the entrance to Drusus' dwelling. Whereas the mouth of the cave that rested behind their flag was covered by a thick curtain of weaving vines, this one sat bare and vast, the blackness seeming to seep from its mouth like cold breath. They stood on the precipice of the foreboding darkness, staring into the seemingly never-ending expanse of blackness sweeping out in front of them. Mischief nervously pawed the ground beside Hollyn's feet.

"I don't like this," Hollyn whispered.

"Me neither," muttered Fynn.

"We don't have a choice," reasoned Hollyn.

Fynn shook his head, "No…not really."

They took their first step, breaching the threshold between the chilled air of the jungle and the downright frigid air within the cave. The walls arched around them, engulfed them in the bleakness of the dark stone, swallowed them into the throat of the cave. As they continued on, the feeling of oppression intensified, as if the relentless shadows of the cave's confines were physically weighing them down, forcing them to hunch forward and curl towards one another as they limped onward. There was no light there in the pit of the cave; it was just a long and deep expanse of nothing as far as their eyes could see.

"How far do you think it goes before we get into the tunnels?" asked Fynn.

Hollyn's voice was weak, his pain continued to siphon the last vestiges of his energy. "I don't know."

They were ambling along at an agonizingly slow pace. Hollyn's weight became heavier and heavier as he began to grow more tired, leaning more and more on Fynn as a crutch. Fynn stopped a few times to adjust his cousin's weight but found that he was struggling with every passing moment— they both were.

"Hollyn?"

"Hmm?"

"How are you feeling?"

"Tired."

Faintly, in the distance, a pale, orange glow licked at the darkness, rebounding off the craggy surface of the stone.

"I think I see something," Fynn announced hopefully. His pace quickened as he and Hollyn tottered forward. "It looks like firelight."

Before them, there were torches mounted on either side, their dancing flames bouncing over the stone walls, casting just enough light to see about ten or so feet deeper wherein a second set of torches were mounted. From therein, the cave lost its intimidating darkness and gave way to a tunnel of orange and gold and red and yellow lights all flickering in the coolness of the cave's innards.

"I think we're heading into the catacombs," Fynn asserted. He led them deeper.

"Who…or *what*…do you think lit the torches?"

Fynn soured at the thought. "Don't know."

"Wasn't the Iba-Jii."

"They hate fire," agreed Fynn.

"But I'm sure they're not the only things down in the caves."

"What else do you think is down here?"

Hollyn answered grimly, "I don't think I want to find out."

Mischief scurried along just a few paces in front of them, casting nervous glances back to the boys, waiting for them to catch up before hurrying along again. Fynn felt the earth shift beneath his feet, angling downward. They were headed deeper into the tunnel system carved out below Dier Island. The cave wound down in a spiral like one of the stairways in the castle towers. Carefully, cautious not to jostle or drop Hollyn, Fynn slowly proceeded further and further.

When they came to the end of their descent, it was far colder. The air was pungent; its ghastly stench crept into their noses and stung. Fynn fought hard not to gag at the scent. He shuddered. He felt Hollyn do the same.

The same torch system seemed to be set upon the walls down in the depths; golden light crawled up the manmade walls. That's when Fynn stopped, his eyes as wide as they'd go, pupils dilating. The cold hand of dread seized his heart and he was sure, in that moment, that there was a distinct possibility he may just die of fear right then and there.

"Hollyn."

"What?" Hollyn groaned tiredly.

"Hollyn, you've got to stay awake," Fynn insisted. "Please. Don't leave me alone here." His voice was hardly more than a childish plea. He didn't care. "Hollyn?"

The taller prince's eyes fluttered as he forced himself to remain conscious. "Yes?"

"The walls. They're made of bones."

19

THE SKELETON LABYRINTH

Fynn pulled Hollyn closer. He wasn't sure if it was for Hollyn's benefit or his own but knowing the other was there was comforting. He heard the hitching sound of Hollyn's breathing as the other boy bit back a cry of pain. He felt his cousin's shoulders shaking, the tensing of his upper body as he tried to keep the pain at bay and failed.

Even in knowing Hollyn was hurt, that he was anguishing with every moment they were standing there, Fynn couldn't bring himself to offer the other boy his full attention. No, his own attention was riveted by the realization that the walls of the catacombs were constructed of bones—human bones. The distinctive skulls gave away their origin; lifeless, empty holes where eyes once were nestled stared back at the two boys who cowered there in the tunnels, clambering to remain in the steady glow of the firelight.

"I'm scared," whispered Fynn.

Hollyn's arm tighten around Fynn's shoulders. "I know…me…too. But we have to keep going. Can't stay here."

"I know," Fynn croaked. A warm tear slinked down his cheek. He bit down on his lip, hard. His eyes glinted like melting ice in the light of the torches. He glanced down to the raccoon. "Mischief, do you think you can find the way back to our camp? Can you find Odette?"

As the little creature pawed across the earth, fluffy tail limply scraping against the dirt, Fynn followed. Hollyn grumbled at his side; occasionally he'd hiss in pain or tense before going limp again and staggering along. Fynn adjusted the weight against his shoulders. His back was beginning to scream its protest as they continued through the winding catacombs. Again, he shifted Hollyn against him to ease the pressure on his own shoulders.

"How are you?"

"Fine," Hollyn mumbled.

Fynn shook his head, snorting, "Liar."

"You're right."

The smaller prince smiled mirthlessly. "Now I know you're in bad shape, if you're saying I'm right about something."

Hollyn coughed. "Must be worse than I thought." He hunched his shoulders forward. The pain was becoming less and less tolerable, the headache it spawned only making the journey through the catacombs more difficult. The world seemed to be spinning by Hollyn, the walls melting and dancing around him. Everything was off kilter.

Fynn saw the other prince blinking rapidly in his periphery. He lowered his voice as he said, "You must have hit your head on the way down too."

"Must've," rasped Hollyn groggily. "Everything's a bit blurry."

"Just stay awake. Alright?"

"Alright."

Hollyn's docility was becoming alarming. Fynn stifled any comment he may have had, focusing instead on keeping their forward momentum steady and ongoing. The pair found that the catacombs stretched along much deeper than they would have anticipated. The amber glow kept their path illuminated, chasing away the darkness from the cave up above and the creepiness of the atmosphere. But it was little comfort.

Instead of being trapped in the shadows, they were surrounded by empty eyes that wouldn't look away, jaws that hung open, ribs that jutted out from the walls and curled at unnatural angles. The passageways beneath the island were twisting and unending, turning and winding. There were some corridors that lead to dead ends. It was becoming readily apparent to Fynn that they had been purposefully designed to be disorienting. He wasn't sure why, but he had a hunch that he didn't really want to know the reason behind the intentionally confusing maze.

They'd wandered around in the skull-lined tunnels of the catacombs for hours. Fynn had come to accept the ever-watching skulls. It was, instead, the silence that was beginning to unnerve him. He heard little more than the crackling of fire, the scraping of Mischief's paws against the ground, their feet shuffling in the dirt, and the ragged breathing of the red-haired prince balanced against his side. At first, Fynn thought the silence was welcomed and peaceful. Now it was maddening.

Fynn heard the thumping of his heart. It was erratic. Not at all soothing. He could hear the swoosh of his breath as it was expelled from his nostrils. He most hated the wretched sound of his teeth grinding over one another, his gnashing jaw acting as the jailor to the unspoken cries of fear he swallowed back every few seconds.

Something on the wall caught the boy's attention. He slowed his pace; Mischief followed suit. Edging a bit closer to the skeleton wall, Fynn stared at the markings. There, painted in red upon the pale ivory of the skulls, was a nine-pointed star.

"What is it?" Hollyn asked, adjusting his eyes to the meager light, straining to see what had stopped Fynn in his tracks.

"Hollyn, please tell me that wasn't painted in blood." Fynn nodded at the star.

Despite the numbness Hollyn felt in his right arm, he managed to will the limb to move. His hand was shaking terribly as he reached to the wall; his fingers ghosted over the red star. "It looks like blood, Fynn."

"But *whose* blood?"

"I don't think I want to know," Hollyn admitted fearfully. "We've got to get out of here… *fast.*"

Steeling himself as best he could, Fynn asked, "How's your head?"

"I'll be alright," Hollyn assured weakly. His eyes looked unfocussed. "I *have* to be. We have to get out of here." When Fynn made no effort to move, Hollyn asked, "What's the matter?"

"I've seen that symbol before," Fynn said evenly.

"Where?"

"It's a long story. We need to leave."

Concerned by Fynn's demeanor, Hollyn tried to straighten to his full height. The pain that struck his back and shoulder, however, prevented him from doing so. Instead, he crumbled further against Fynn. "How far do you think we are from the camp?"

"I don't know," Fynn whispered. He began withdrawing from the wall, stepping back into the middle of the tunnel. "Hopefully we're close. We've been walking for a while now."

"Let's keep going," urged Hollyn.

Fynn nodded. "Right."

They took up their task of staggering on through the chambers of the catacombs. While Hollyn drifted in some middle ground between consciousness and total blackout, Fynn was lost in his own thoughts. He hadn't noticed he was shaking until Hollyn moaned in pain as he was jostled uncomfortably.

"Sorry," murmured Fynn.

The quietness was still frightful. It was taunting, Fynn thought. It was mocking them, daring them to imagine some nonexistent noise emanating from an imagined threat or danger. It was intended to trick them. The olfactory overload from the pungent stench that permeated the catacombs, the golden glow of the torchlight illuminating the pallid skulls and bones, the purposefully maze-like structure, the silence, it was all intentional. That's when he knew. The catacombs were as much a trap as they were used to get around beneath the castle and under the island. They were as much to ensnare their prey as they were to help the castle's occupants escape from predators. The catacombs, he reasoned, were designed to make a person go mad.

"We're lost," Fynn whispered.

"Don't say that," Hollyn argued, but the bite of his tone was mollified by the haggard sound of his voice. "We're going to get out of here."

"Hollyn," Fynn began tearfully, "I don't think we're going to get out." Salty trails streaked down Fynn's cheeks, washing away strips of blood and dirt that still clung to his lightly freckled face. "We're trapped down here. We're lost."

Hollyn wrenched himself from Fynn's hold and stumbled back a step before lurching forward with none of his usual grace and precision. He slammed his fist into Fynn's jaw. Glassy, blue eyes watched dully as Fynn tumbled to the ground.

"Stop it," snapped Hollyn.

The smaller boy pushed himself up on his elbows. The nasty metallic taste of blood, like copper, stung his mouth. Fynn narrowed his eyes as he glared up at his cousin. "What was that for?"

"Now ... isn't the time to panic .... you *idiot*," wheezed Hollyn through a fog of newly erupted pain and dizziness.

Fynn didn't bother to get up. Instead, he let his arms go limp and just fell to the ground. He felt the dirt, cool and damp, against his cheek. He wished it were his pillow; he wished that the chill that washed over him was the warmth of a blanket. He was shivering; his shoulders jerked; his teeth chattered. He'd been spending so much time, all of his effort, on making sure Hollyn was tended to, on getting them down the cave and into the catacombs, that he hadn't noticed the severity of his own injuries. Now that he was prone against the ground, he took the time to assess the damage.

His head ached. The fresh laceration to his forehead was still leaking a bit, but he knew well that head wounds always bled the most. His back was sore as a result of hauling around Hollyn's nearly dead weight for hours. He noticed a new pain; one he hadn't realized until presently. There was a nasty stinging in his leg that spanned from his knee up to his mid-thigh.

"That's probably not good," Fynn judged. His hand reached down, grazing over his leg. His leggings were ripped and damp. "Blood," he bemoaned.

Hollyn, who'd been watching Fynn take stock of his injuries, knelt beside the boy. His eyes maintained a worrisome, far-off look to them as he stared down at Fynn. "You're leg's bleeding." The unnatural detachment in his voice was alarming.

Fynn struggled to sit upright and relented to bracing his back against the wall. He did his best to ignore the bones that jutted at uncomfortable angles. "I don't think it's too bad," he replied. Though he could see that there was, in fact, a fair amount of blood spotted over his black leggings. He could make out the cut digging into his pale leg, punctuated by the reddening of the skin around it. "It doesn't look bad."

"Does it hurt?"

"Not really," Fynn answered flatly, shaking his head. "I didn't notice it until now actually."

"Idiot," mumbled Hollyn as he tried to clear his head and make himself useful. He leaned closer to Fynn's injured leg, hissing when he saw the wound up close. "I'm surprised you were able to keep walking this long."

Fynn shrugged. "I'll be alright."

"Liar."

Mischief snugged close to Fynn's side, tiny nose nuzzling the boy's ribs. The prince's hand came to rest upon the animal's head. His thumb traced small patterns over the grey fur. He turned to look back to Hollyn who'd taken to seating himself at Fynn's side, his back leaned against the wall, shoulders curled forward, head tilted back.

"Where do you think all these bones came from?" asked Fynn.

"Who knows."

"Do you think they were prisoners? Or the bodies of a defeated enemy army?"

"Could be," Hollyn answered distractedly.

"Do you...do you think anything else is...down here with us?" The small boy couldn't keep the fear from his voice. He knew it.

Hollyn knew it.

Neither of them mentioned it.

"I don't think so." Hollyn grunted. He tried to shift and get more comfortable. "Well, maybe not around here. It's been really quiet. I haven't heard anything down here with us."

"But we know that Drusus and Gaia and the Iba-Jii live in a cave like this," contended Fynn. "I still think that Drusus might help us again…get us out of here."

"Maybe," whispered Hollyn tiredly. "Let's hope that's the case."

"And that nothing else is down here this far," added Fynn.

"Exactly."

The fatigue was becoming more noticeable; its wicked, grasping touch was more pronounced as it raked over both boys. Hollyn's eyes fluttered shut and his face went slack as unconsciousness claimed him. Fynn, barely awake, kept his eyes trained on Hollyn. The blood matting his red hair was concerning; the frightful pallor of his skin was more so. To keep himself awake and moderately alert, Fynn contented himself with tracing shapes in Mischief's fur. The prince coughed. The action rattled his chest painfully.

"We've got to get going," Fynn wheezed. He tried to straighten himself up. He shakily climbed to his feet, wincing. "We can't sit here any longer." He tottered over to Hollyn, kneeling down in front of the unconscious royal. Gently, he shook him by his good shoulder. "Hollyn. Hollyn, wake up."

"Just a little longer," whined the prince, as he turned his head away from the other's voice.

Fynn inhaled deeply. "Hollyn, we have to get up and start moving. We need to get out of here." His pale eyes roved their surroundings. "I don't like it here, Hollyn." He felt sick as he choked back his own mounting discomfort. "I'm scared."

"We've talked about this already," grumbled Hollyn. He finally opened his eyes. "We're *both* scared." Despite the blinding pain radiating from his shoulder, Hollyn leaned into Fynn's hold and allowed the smaller boy to help him to his feet. "But crying about it isn't going to help."

Nodding, Fynn tried to calm down. He resumed his position at Hollyn's side, once more transforming himself into a human crutch. "Ready?"

"Ready," Hollyn said with a decided nod.

Their progress was meager and tedious. Their footsteps were hardly more than limping shuffles. Mischief kept close to their heels when he stopped, fur bristling, and trilled a high-pitched, frightful trill of fear. The raccoon darted back behind the boys, clinging to the back of Hollyn's legs with his tiny paws, black eyes wide in terror. Then they heard it, the sound of claws scratching against the bone walls.

"Hollyn." Fynn shuddered.

"I know. I heard it too," Hollyn said hoarsely.

Their tears were warm when they tracked down their faces, leaving muddled streaks of dirt and blood and filth smeared messily over their cheeks and jaws.

Fynn's voice was strained and low when he asked, "What do you think that was?"

Hollyn trembled against Fynn, unconsciously leaning closer to the other boy. "I don't think we want to know."

Fynn tightened his hold on his cousin, taking comfort in the other's presence. "Hollyn, what do we do? We can't fight back."

Determined, though glassy, blue eyes turned to regard Fynn with cold, methodical reason. When Hollyn spoke, there was a steely resolve in his voice that had been absent since they'd first walked into the mouth of the cave. "You have to run for it."

The smaller boy jerked backward, raising his brows to his hairline in alarm. "No!" Fynn narrowed his eyes challengingly. "I'm not leaving you here alone. Are you mad?"

"Look…it's not ideal—"

Fynn seethed, "It's a lot more than *not ideal.*" He shook his head heatedly; filthy, black hair tumbled over his eyes. "You must've hit your head harder than I thought." He pulled Hollyn closer against his flank. "I'm not leaving you. We're here together. We're getting out of this place *together.*"

"Don't be stupid," argued Hollyn while trying to extricate himself from Fynn's grasp. "I won't be able to outrun it…whatever *it* is. Everything's blurry and spinning. There's no way I'll outrun it. But you can, Fynn. Get out and find Moriah and send help."

"I am *not* leaving you," Fynn insisted. The piercing look he leveled upon Hollyn brooked no argument. The discussion was moot.

Hollyn huffed, irritated, before looking away from Fynn and back down the palely lit corridor of the catacombs. "What do you think *it* is?"

"Sounded like claws," Fynn replied quickly.

"Claws?"

Fynn nodded. His own attention was fixed to the same point, vaguely angled down the passageway, peering at nothing but waiting with rapt attention for something to appear. "Yes. Claws," he whispered, "I'm sure of it."

A screeching sound echoed from down the chamber, reverberating off the bones. They seemed to almost shake under the pressure of the dreadful shriek. Instinctively, both boys clung to one another desperately, neither looking away from the direction in which the sound originated, neither daring to blink. Mischief held so tightly to Hollyn's calf he thought the little creature's tiny claws would scrape through the leather and get to his skin.

"It's getting closer," Hollyn said weakly.

"That's not good."

Shaking his head, Hollyn agreed, "No. *No* it's *not*."

There were shadows that dulled the light some thirty feet from where the princes stood. They were lengthy shadows that obscured the pale flicker of the torches, creeping shadows that traced like long fingers over the curves of the bones, falling into hollow darkness where the empty eyes of the skulls looked out. The sound of sharp claws scraping over bones seemed thunderous in the oppressive silence of the catacombs. Then another wail, louder than before.

"It's here," Fynn whimpered.

"Get ready," Hollyn commanded. "No matter what, we fight back with all we've got."

"Right." Fynn glanced to Hollyn and offered him a small, weak smile. "We came in here together."

Hollyn nodded and finished the sentiment, saying, "We're getting out of here together."

Both boys gulped back their fear when they saw the source of the sounds illuminated in the firelight. Long, muscled arms stretched out of the walls. Clawed toes left trenches in the ivory bones beneath its touch. There was a large head, made longer by a toothy snout that jutted out with snapping jaws; a pale, forked tongue protruded and lashed at the chilly air. Eerie, green eyes searched in the darkness but seemed to trace over the boys with little recognition. As it crept forward, poised on the wall at a most peculiar angle, a long tail snapped back and forth, the tip cracking small fragments of bone from the wall.

"What *is* that?" Fynn gasped quietly, shrinking back against Hollyn.

"It looks like—"

"A giant lizard."

"Exactly," agreed Hollyn.

The creature haunting the catacombs continued closer and closer until it was scuttling by the boys, paying them little attention. The pair had to stifle a cry of terror when the thing, again, shrieked loudly. They jumped back, scooting around the beast and pressing themselves as firmly as they could against the far wall, heedless of the bones that poked out at them.

"I think it's blind," Hollyn deduced. "It hasn't reacted to us."

"So, we just need to keep quiet."

Hollyn nodded and then began to slowly peel himself from the wall. He was hyperaware of everything around him, mindful not to make the slightest noise. He kept his breathing slow, controlled. His stormy eyes never wavered from the figure of the creature that had, rather unfortunately, stopped its prowl through the passageway and fixedly remained just a few feet from them. When he was at last free from his place against the wall and safely distanced from the creature, he stared back at Fynn imploringly, silently willing the other boy to move.

Seeing the pleading look in Hollyn's eyes, Fynn began to follow suit. He leaned forward, rolling his shoulders toward his chest and away from the jagged wall. One of the protruding bones snagged his tunic. The sound of the bone breaking was like thunder, the sort of thunder that clapped with such boisterous force it was strong enough to shake the earth. Fynn froze, not daring to move a single muscle, no matter how small. His eyes were trained to the creature.

When the reptilian stare flicked in his direction, Fynn felt as though all the blood rushing through his veins down each extremity froze. His heart seemed like it might have actually stopped beating. His chest restricted painfully. The lizard-like monstrosity, easily three sizes larger than both the boys, slowly turned its head until its nose was hairs from Fynn's. Its jaws opened inch by inch, revealing sharp, yellow teeth that glittered with slick saliva. Its tongue slithered from its mouth and darted out. It was warm, disgustingly so, as it traveled the curvature of Fynn's face.

The prince's lip trembled but he stayed quiet.

The creature's tongue continued its course down the side of Fynn's face, curling over his cheek, and then traveling the line of his jaw until it slinked down his neck, lapping at the pulse pounding away beneath its slimy touch. Hot air puffed out of slatted nostrils and ruffled the boy's dark hair. Its jaws opened wider; silver strands of saliva slowly slipped from its teeth and clung to its black lips, oozing over its lower jaw and falling in globs to the dirt ground beneath. Languidly, the slippery tongue proceeded to make its way back up Fynn's throat, lingering just below his jaw, before traveling back up his face and lapping at the fresh blood pooling over his head wound.

"Hollyn," Fynn screamed, "run!"

Fynn ducked away from the monster's mouth and bolted toward Hollyn, snatching hold of the other's tunic and dragging him along. He didn't dare look back. He heard the creature's tail whipping back and forth angrily, claws smashing into bones. Then, as it gave another ear-splitting screech, the torch lights lining the passageway all went out.

There was nothing but darkness in every direction, no differentiation from the walls or the ceilings to show openings or dead ends, turns or straight sections. Everything was dark and cold and the only sounds that could be heard were those of the catacomb-crawler racing toward them. Fynn's fingers curled tighter in the material of Hollyn's tunic, forcibly hauling the other boy closer to him.

Not knowing what to do or where to run, Fynn tried to stagger forward. He was too frantic to look through the darkness, to see what was around him. All he knew was that staying still wasn't a viable option for their survival. Hollyn stumbled along with him, clumsily tripping through the shadows, head still spinning. They were both breathing heavily, panting as they moved as quickly as they could in the never-ending bleakness.

It felt as though it were getting colder; the ghastly stench of the air lessened as the dank chill began to bite at their skin. Hollyn shook, exhaustion and pain overcoming him more and more with every passing moment. Fynn's own breath was ragged; his back was throbbing. His leg stung, and his head pounded with raging force. Still, the scraping sounds of claws came nearer. They kept on moving. As Fynn made another effort to lurch further into the shielding embrace of the darkness, something whipped into his back with enough force to send him to the ground. He lost his hold on Hollyn. He heard the other prince grunt in the distance before the sound of a stomach-churning scream exploded.

Prostrate on the ground, Fynn felt a searing pain burst over his back. The creature's tail had lashed against him with the speed and force necessary to shred the woven fabric of his tunic and hew the flesh beneath. Though hot tears pricked his eyes, Fynn arrested the cry before it left his lips. He bit down on his lower lip. For the second time that day, he tasted the coppery tang of his own blood awash in his mouth. Shaking uncontrollably, Fynn pressed himself lower into the dirt, trying to blend in with the ground as best he could.

The creature bellowed again, that same, detestable, high-pitched wail that sent a shiver down Fynn's spine. He heard the claws once more scraping at the bone and felt the cutting of the air breeze over him as the long tail swished back and forth only a foot or so above where he lay.

Another violent scream of pain. It was Hollyn's, Fynn knew, and it echoed through the blackened passageway. The knot that had twisted in the pit of Fynn's stomach seemed to tighten, nauseating the boy. He forced down the bile that welled in his throat. As he heard the creature take its leave further down the corridor, Fynn balled his hand into a fist and beat his knuckles into the ground. He punched the dirt over and over, his arm trembling with the effort.

The torchlights flickered; their wicks once more ignited. The orange sparks were soft at first, hardly bright enough to see the pale contours of the bones constructing the walls. But it grew and grew and soon the flames were as they had been before, casting out a golden field of light that chased away the darkness. Pulling himself up to his hands and knees, Fynn coughed. His coughing turned to heaving and then to acrid-scented bile that churned from his mouth, clinging to his chin and the front of his uniform. Mucus ran from his nose and clung to his barley-parted lips; tears ran rampant down his face.

The creature was gone. Hollyn and Mischief were gone. Fynn was alone and the silence was once again maddening. He wanted nothing more than to lay down and close his eyes, to pretend everything had just been a bad nightmare and he'd be waking up in the comfort of his dormitory soon. But he knew that wasn't the case, it wasn't true, and so he urged himself to stand, despite the protest from every muscle and nerve composing his slender body.

More tears, fresh-salty beads that betrayed the anguish he refused to cry over, rushed from his watery, pale eyes when he beheld the blood on the walls, the speckles of red against the dirt floor. There was a handprint with long, smeared finger marks, as if the hand had been dragged across the bony wall. Stumbling forward, Fynn reached out and placed his hand over the red stain and grimaced. The blood was warm, fresh.

"Hollyn," Fynn croaked. Yet another onslaught of tears spilled down his already filthy face. "Hollyn!" he screamed. His throat felt raw. "Hollyn!"

Fynn's hand fell from the wall, his fingertips coated in red. He wobbled forward on legs that felt as though they'd give way at any moment. He struggled to breathe; his lungs felt heavy and empty all at once. His chest hurt. His head hurt. The stinging pain in his back was becoming nearly too much. Eventually, after managing ten or so weak and weary steps, he was driven to his knees by a culmination of fear, exhaustion, and raw pain.

Once more his face was pillowed against the damp earth. He laid one palm flat against the dirt, feeling it shift beneath his touch. He couldn't focus on much else. He was too tired.

"Hollyn!" he yelled out as best he could, but his voice was no more than a pained rasp. "Hollyn."

The awful silence had encroached upon him, taking him over. The tunnels were deathly still, eerily calm after the horror that had taken place. He strained to listen for the scratching and scraping sounds, but there was nothing. He couldn't hear Hollyn's breathing or his footsteps either. The silence was deafening. Resignedly, the prince closed his eyes, his lashes dampened by the waterfall of tears that leaked into the dirt beneath his head. His lip was bleeding from where his teeth had gnashed through the pink tissue. He could taste the dirt mingling with the metallic sourness against his mouth. Fynn scowled.

"Hollyn," he whispered. The sound of his voice was muffled as he nuzzled his nose against the soft ground. "I'm scared." His breathing hitched. "I'm scared. Come back. Don't leave me here … alone."

The sound of crumbling lanced through the haziness that had befallen Fynn and his eyes, at once, snapped open. Disregarding his fatigue, he pushed himself up on hands and knees, then rocked to his feet and stood, wavering, one hand braced against the wall beside him. He followed the sound with just his eyes, rolling his gaze to the side where he saw the bones of the catacombs shifting. Fynn pressed himself backward against the opposite wall and watched, utterly mesmerized, as a skull and bones leapt free from the wall and clattered to the ground before, seemingly of their own volition, assembling themselves into a rickety approximation of a human skeleton.

"Oh… that can't be good," Fynn wheezed as he retreated as far as he could.

His eyes went wide as the skeleton began advancing toward him, wobbling back and forth on legs unsupported by muscle or tendons. The bony stalker crept ever closer. Fynn pulled back until he was flush against the catacomb wall, the blood trailing from his back injury sticking sickeningly against the porous surface.

He screwed his eyes shut and shook his head, repeating over and over, "No. No, no, no, no, no, no! This can't be happening. This isn't happening! No. No, no, no. This isn't real. This can't be real. Hollyn! Help! Someone … *please*, help. No. Not real. This isn't real."

His trembling was arrested when the bones at his back broke free of the wall and wrapped around him, ensnaring him in a skeletal embrace; cracked-bone fingers wrapped around his torso and clamped over his mouth. Fynn tried to pull free, jerking his shoulders left and right, desperate to wrench himself from the inhuman hold. He watched as the skeleton before him continued forward until its palms slammed into his chest, pushing him backward as the arms around his body, encircling his limbs and middle, began pulling him back. He was disappearing into the wall, into a heavy darkness.

Fynn shook his head violently. The hand clamped over his mouth shook apart, fingers falling to the ground in a mess around his booted feet. "No!" His voice didn't sound like his own, it was higher and frantic. He screamed, "Hollyn! Hollyn! Help!"

Everything fell away into the black then. The feeling of the bones pressed against him was gone. He was free. He turned around quickly, only to find more blackness stretched out in every direction. But it was different than the darkness of the tunnel. This was a different all-encompassing void. One he'd been to before. He looked down and was not at all surprised when he saw rippling beneath his feet, like he'd stepped into shallow water. He was certain of it now; he'd been here before.

"Not this place again," Fynn groaned as he continued forward. The blackness was splashing with every step.

"Hello? Please…is anyone there?" Fynn turned in circles, desperate for any sign of which way to go.

The water, if it was in fact water, was getting deeper. His legs seemed to disappear into the blackness just below his knees. He continued to wade forward, dismayed as the liquid shadows overtook his middle section, rising up to his shoulders. Soon only his head was above the darkness, his movements slowed and labored.

"Hello!" He was growing more panicked. "Hello! Please, someone, help! Hollyn!"

Then he was drowning in the blackness. There was nothing all around; he wasn't standing amidst the void, but floating in it as if he'd been washed away into a midnight sea. The way the shadows oozed by his body, washing over him like soft waves, rocking him gently as he sank deeper and deeper, was—in a most peculiar way—quite relaxing. The sensation was fondly reminiscent of the way Fiona would rock him to sleep when he was a child and had been awoken by a nightmare. He could almost feel the way she'd wrap her arms around him and pull him into her lap. He thought he could hear the sound of her voice, hushed in the deadness of night, as she sang him a lullaby to usher him off back to the welcoming embrace of slumber. But he knew better than to believe she were there, that he was safely in her arms.

Fynn had the distinct and very firm belief that he must be sinking further and further down. His arms and legs seemed weightless, suspended in the black. He didn't bother to struggle, to kick out his arms and legs and fight to breach the surface. He reasoned that there wasn't really a surface, just a confusing and endless nothing all around. Whether he was standing upon the rippling blackness or drowning beneath its depths, it didn't matter much. No matter which way he looked, all he saw was nothing.

He didn't know how long he'd been floating—sinking—but it felt like ages. His back finally contacted something solid, smooth. His limbs gently floated down to follow. Fynn, lost in his thoughts, wondered if this was what lying upon the sea floor would feel like, with the infinite swell of thousands of waves crashing overhead, miles from where you rested, gazing up at a surface you could no longer imagine being real. It was peaceful. His breathing evened out; the pain and fear slipped away from him, like sands lazily pulled from the shoreline as the tide ebbed and flowed. It felt good; it felt easy to be washed away.

"Fynneas."

He knew that voice. He longed to hear it again.

"Fynneas."

"Hello, Mother," he drowsily answered.

"Fynneas, you need to open your eyes."

He hadn't realized they'd been closed. "Can't I just stay here?" he asked.

"No. Fynn, darling, you've got to open your eyes." Her voice was imploring, urgent even, but still soft and silky and undeniably warm, familiar.

"Alright."

His eyes fluttered open. He was assaulted by sunlight he hadn't anticipated. It was a burning light, as though it were early in the day. He blinked repeatedly to clear away the bleariness and adjust to the sudden, unexpected brightness. Sitting up, he realized he wasn't resting in the black waters of nothing anymore, nor was he in the catacombs.

"*Not* again," he whispered.

Fynn felt the cobblestones beneath his hands and the wind brushing through his hair. He could smell the scent of fire and smoke, could hear people screaming and hooves smashing into the road.

"Please," Fynn begged as he stood up, "*not* this again."

People were nothing more than blurs as they rushed by. The sound of steel slamming into steel was loud, crackling in the background, joining the chorus of chaos ringing out through the capital. He took a deep breath, knowing what he'd find when he turned around. Slowly, he looked back and through the crowd and, at that unfortunately precise moment, he watched the arrow slink through the sky and embed in his father's neck. He looked on with teary eyes as the man he loved so dearly crumpled to the ground, soon lying in a pool of his own blood, choking as specks of red leapt from his parted lips.

He knew he couldn't change it, knew it would never be different no matter how many times he watched it happen. Still, Fynn sprinted forward until he was at his father's side, kneeling beside him, hands braced on his chest. He felt the nearly imperceptible rise and fall with each strained breath that his father took. Fynn looked on, absolute despair welling within him. But he wouldn't cry again; he couldn't bring himself to. He remembered begging his father to get up, though he knew in his heart of hearts that Felix wasn't going to make it out of that road. He had told his father that he'd be alright and that he'd get up. He knew better and, he supposed, Felix did as well.

Felix's hand fell limply from his throat, his red-stained palm a terrifying reminder of the blood loss. The arrow remained there, protruding from his pale, white throat. Ghastly scarlet trails trickled from the corners of his mouth as he choked on his own breath. His eyes fluttered open, straining to focus on the boy crouched over him. "You've got to be…strong." Felix's voice was little more than a wet wheeze, blood still oozing from the corner of his mouth.

Though Fynn told himself he was stronger now and that he'd come to accept what had happened that awful day, it was an empty assurance. Hearing those words from his father in the same breathy, dying voice from month's before, broke something inside him. His shoulders quaked as he bowed his head. He clung tighter to his father's chest, shaking him ever so gently as he sobbed.

"Fynn," Felix implored tiredly.

The boy whispered faintly, "Don't go. Don't leave me. Stay with me, please." Fynn's hold upon his father tightened. "I won't let you go!"

"You don't have a choice." Felix coughed, flecks of red bespangling his now too-pale lips.

"No! Please, no. Please … don't leave me," the boy begged.

Felix smiled. "I'm proud of you." His eyes dulled; his chest stopped moving.

"No!" Fynn screamed as he doubled over, forehead resting against the motionless chest of his father. Hysterical cries racked his frame, and he shook. "You left me all alone … and never told me how to survive this - this *nightmare*. You have to come back! Come back and *help me*. Please. I'm not ready to be on my own like this. I'm not ready. Come back! Come back and show me what to do."

A gentle hand perched upon Fynn's shoulder and squeezed softly. "Fynneas, it's time."

Fynn didn't make a move to get up. He buried his head deeper against his father's chest, dismissive of the blood that now brushed against his forehead. "No."

"Fynneas." Celestine's voice was insistent but kind. "It's time." She gave his shoulder another squeeze. "You've got to get up. You can't stay here."

"Will you stay with me?" Fynn asked as he mustered the wherewithal to pull himself away from his father's corpse. He couldn't look away from the dead eyes that stared, unseeing, skyward. "Please?"

"For as long as I can," Celestine promised softly.

Fynn stood and turned to his mother. She looked pristine as ever, just as he remembered her from the last time they'd spoken. Her hand was still upon his shoulder, holding him at arm's length, regarding him with sad eyes—eyes so like his own in so many ways. Fynn was still shaking but he managed to wipe the tears from his eyes. "Promise?"

"I promise."

He launched himself against his mother. In response, her arms curled around him and held him close. He welcomed her touch, smiling sadly as he nestled against her. "I don't know what to do," he admitted helplessly.

"I'll help you all that I can."

"You said I couldn't stay here?"

Celestine smiled down at the boy, smoothing the hair back from his face affectionately. "You have to keep moving forward."

"Like last time I was here?" he asked curiously.

Celestine nodded.

"I have to follow the same path as last time?" He didn't wait for her response. He wriggled from her arms, staying close still, and turned to look down the road. "You'll come with me?"

She remained silent, but she took his hand in hers firmly. Her thumb brushed against his bruised hand.

He smiled. "Thank you."

Mother and son proceeded like specters through the maelstrom as they weaved their way down the road, heedless of the mania exploding around them. As they continued on, Fynn felt sadness blossoming in his chest, a reluctance to keep moving through the scene, a desire to turn and hide instead of continuing onward. He squelched the feeling, taking solace in his mother's hand holding his.

Fynn turned a corner and came to the alley. It was a thin alleyway that twisted and turned and soon fell to shadow. No one was there. He looked left and he looked right. "Nothing," he said dully.

"Just wait a moment longer," Celestine urged. "It'll come."

And then, with a whirl of warm wind, a door appeared before them. It was just there, just a door in the middle of the alley that had appeared from nothing, stood braced against nothing, seemingly opened to nothing. He reached out. His palm fell flat against the door. The wood felt solid beneath his hand. He reached down to the handle and pulled. He saw therein, a small room revealed. Stepping inside, Celestine at his side, he wasn't surprised when the door closed behind him.

He remembered this place. It was small, comfortably decorated. There was a hearth built into the stone of the far wall. There were tapestries hanging; they looked dingy and thread bare. Upon the floor was a simple, black rug. Two chairs were set there upon the rug in the center of the room, facing one another.

His eyes lingered upon the empty chairs, remembering when he sat facing the man who occasionally called himself Lot, discussing a subject that still baffled him. But this time, the man wasn't there.

The room was empty.

Looking away from the vacant seats, Fynn's attention then landed on the hearth. The fire was burning, just as he remembered. Letting go of Celestine's hand, he stepped up to the stony hearth and peered into the flames. "What is this place?"

"It's not really a place at all, I suppose," Celestine replied.

"Then what is it?"

"The best way to describe it is a place between places."

He shook his head, sighing. "I don't understand."

"You will … in time."

Fynn nodded to the flames. He could feel their warmth dancing over his dirty skin. "Last time I walked into the fire to get out." He glanced over his shoulder to Celestine, who stood at the center of the room, watching him with interest. She smiled. He continued, as he returned to staring at the fire, "There was no other way."

"Do you remember what I told you?" She drew closer, her hand once more resting on his shoulder. "About the dream I had. About your name."

The prince nodded. "You said dragons were born from the fires."

"Exactly."

"I'm no dragon." Fynn snorted humorlessly.

"Not yet, anyway. Are you ready?"

"You'll stay with me?"

"I will." She took his hand in hers once more. She held it tightly.

Fynn stepped into the fire, his mother just behind him. The flames didn't burn. They almost felt gentle against his body as they lashed angrily all around him. He didn't know what to expect as he stepped through. He dreaded going back to the blackness. But that had been what laid beyond the fire last time. He supposed it wouldn't be so bad this time around; he had his mother with him, and she wouldn't abandon him there.

The prince was surprised when he wasn't greeted by the bleak nothing or the starry sky, but instead found another room laid out around him. This room was far larger than the last, and far less inviting and cozy. The stone walls were white. The tapestries were a pale purple and hung, partially obscuring large, arching windows decorated with elaborate stained glass. Light reached into the room; daylight turned into a rainbow as the glass colored the pale tendrils that illuminated the space.

There was an ornate rug laid out on the ground. It was blue with a white owl emblazoned in masterful stitching; its lavender eyes bright against its white-threaded feathers. There was a large bed against the wall to Fynn's left. A pale, blue canopy was draped from its four posts. The bedding was of the same fair blue; small owls were woven into the fabric upon the pillows. It was well kept, as if someone had just tidied the room.

A cradle beside the bed caught Fynn's attention. He walked over to it, peeked inside, and found nothing but blue and lavender blankets. He heard his mother come nearer until she stood beside him. Celestine reached into the cradle and pulled out the blue blanket; she held it to her chest fondly. She smiled.

"The owls…the color of everything…this, well, it looks like Gods-reach," Fynn mused. "But I've never seen *this* room. Where are we?"

With her other arm, Celestine pulled her son close to her side. She ran her hand along his side absentmindedly. "This was your room…a long time ago. You were born in this room." She withdrew from him slightly and clutched tightly to the blanket she held to her. "This was your cradle."

The tall woman left Fynn and climbed gracefully into the bed. She sank against the thick pillows. Leaning her head back, she closed her eyes and relaxed into the softness. She brought the blanket back to her chest, balling it up over her heart. With her free hand, she tapped the bedding beside her. "Come here."

Fynn crawled into bed beside his mother. They sat shoulder to shoulder. He tried to smile, but sorrow had nestled its way into his heart and when he spoke his voice was pained and lost. "I wish you would've been here…with me. I wish I had had you around when I was little. It would've been nice to sit with you like this every night before bed." Fynn tried to brush the tears away before they became too apparent. "But Fiona…you'd be proud of her, Mother, really. Fiona sat with me every night. She'd tell me stories or sing me songs until I fell asleep." His ghostly eyes, a mirror image of Celestine's, looked up at her. "But I still wish it was *you*."

"I wish it were me too," she whispered. She fingered the blanket's soft fabric thoughtfully. "But I'm glad Fiona was there for you."

The boy prince's voice was low, strained. "Why are we here?"

"I don't know why it's brought you here, darling."

"What is *it*?"

"Fynneas, there are secrets." Celestine finally managed to look at her son. "Estheria…the Crown…has secrets. People did…we *all* did…terrible, awful things, Fynneas. We've tried…all of us…we've tried to keep those secrets hidden…buried so deep no one would ever find them. But they're all starting to surface…and you, darling…you will find yourself at the center of the storm when it hits. And for that, Fynneas, I am so very sorry."

"What're the secrets that you're hiding? That everyone's hiding? And who *is* everyone?" Fynn inquired nervously. He chewed on his lower lip, fidgeting beside Celestine. "And why *me*?"

Celestine enveloped her son in her arms and pulled him as close as she could, burying her nose in his hair. "I'm so sorry, Fynn. I'm so, so very sorry."

"Mother," the boy whispered as he cuddled closer to her. "Tell me. Please."

"Your ancestors…they did *things*… *things* to ensure that Estheria would be safe…*strong*. But those *things*…they were *unnatural*…*dark*." She ghosted the pad of her thumb over her son's cheek. "And *dark things* often have consequences. I don't think they ever intended, or could have ever imagined, what would happen. None of us could. And I don't know what *will* happen…but there are consequences for our actions, Fynneas. When you trespass against the natural order of the world, you must pay the price."

"Mother…*what happened?*"

Celestine remained thoughtfully silent.

"Can I ask you something else then?" He didn't bother to wait for her response. "I saw something in the catacombs, a symbol I've seen before. I saw it on the wax seals sent to me by that man, or *whatever* he is, Lot. It's a nine-pointed star. That means something, right?"

Celestine choked down her reply before her long-fingered hand reached out and clasped Fynn's chin, forcing him to stare directly into her eyes.

The gesture reminded Fynn of Moriah.

"Promise me something, Fynneas."

"Anything," he swore.

"No matter what, remember that I love you and that there are so many people who love you. And no matter what, my darling, stay true to who you are. Don't let anyone change you or *use* you."

"I promise," he answered warily.

Celestine released him; her hand fell from his face slowly. "You have to go."

Fynn shook his head emphatically. "No! No, you have to tell me what's going on. You can't just tell me to go! Please. I have so many questions! Nothing makes sense."

His mother nodded to the side, eyes glancing away from him. "Look."

Fynn followed her line of sight and gaped, stunned, as the white walls began dripping with globs of red that snuck from the cracks and pores of the stones and spilled like deathly tears down the walls, pooling on the floor, reaching so far into the chambers that the gorgeous owl rug was swallowed in the sea of churning redness, gone from their sight.

"What is that?" gasped Fynn. He huddled closer to his mother fearfully.

"Blood."

"Blood?" He crawled even closer. "*Whose* blood?"

"Can you swim?"

He nodded sheepishly.

"Hold your breath."

The prince hardly had the time to register what his mother had said before a wave of gore crashed over the bed, sweeping him from the safety of Celestine's arms and into a violent sea of crimson that twisted and turned and crashed with waves of frothing, warm blood. Had Fynn not been so focused on holding his breath and not drowning, he thought he'd probably vomit. The scent, all-too familiar for his liking recently, was overpowering. His thoughts were muddled as his senses were overtaken. The scent, the horrific sight of his mother disappearing in the abhorrent sea of carnage, the sound of the blood roiling around him - it was all too much.

He was pulled deeper. It was like something beneath the surface had taken ahold of his ankles and was dragging him downward. He could no longer see the rainbow light that had brightened up the white room, nor could he see the pristine canopy of blue silk that had been draped over his mother's bed. His arms shot upward, hands frantically snatching at the pool trying to pull himself to the surface. His lungs were burning, his air running low. The depths were thick and dark and what had once been red clouding his vision had turned to black. No longer was there any light left for him to fleetingly cling to. And once more, he realized with a most heavy heart, he was alone.

The force of the waves that sloshed around, above the surface, were forcing Fynn downward. He was spiraling in the sticky, red liquid. He could no longer keep his eyes opened. They burned. He couldn't breathe. He'd gasped and expelled what little air he'd been holding in. This wasn't like floating in the blackness. Being washed away now was terrifying; anxiety and a burning desire to live, to breathe again, usurped his consciousness and he began flailing his arms and legs, trying to swim to what he believed would be the direction of the surface.

After a valiant struggle, Fynn breached the surface with a thankful and air-starved rasp, greedily breathing in as much as he could. He thrashed his arms, splashing in the gore, desperate to find some purchase, somewhere around, and claw his way free of the sublimely grotesque waves. While madly lashing out his limbs, one hand came upon something smooth and cool, something that felt distinctly like rocks—long, smooth rocks. He dug his fingers deeper, nails scraping against the surface of the shore he clung to, and pulled himself from the carnage, leaving in his wake a trail of deep crimson that glistened in the pale firelight he found flickering all around him.

"Fynneas?"

Still gasping for breath, Fynn looked up and nearly broke into tears of sheer elation at the sight of Hollyn crouching before him. His cousin looked dreadful. He was covered - his face, his arms, his uniform - entirely in red. He'd clearly just pulled himself from the same pool of sickeningly metallic-scented blood. Hollyn reached out, catching Fynn's wrists in his hands, and pulled the other boy free from the mess. Despite the burning pain in his shoulder, he was steadfast in his resolve to pull Fynn ashore.

The raven-haired boy collapsed beside a crouching Hollyn. He rolled to his back and gulped in the chilly air. "Hollyn?"

"Hmm?"

"Is that really you?"

"Yes. Who else would it be, idiot?"

"Yes." Fynn chuckled breathily. "That's certainly you."

Fynn leaned to his side and propped himself up, taking a moment to gather his bearings, and then rose. Hollyn followed suit. The boys stood upon the uneven ground that banked the blood well they'd emerged from. Fynn's hand found Hollyn's shoulder. He didn't remember if it was the good or bad one; he just squeezed to reaffirm that the other boy was really and truly there, standing beside him.

"I thought you were gone," whispered Fynn.

Hollyn leveled Fynn with a piercing glance. "I thought I'd lost you. Thought that *thing* got to you."

Fynn shook his head, sickened when red droplets dripped from his hair. "I heard you scream. I thought you were dead."

Hollyn reached up to his shoulder and covered Fynn's hand with his own. He didn't look away from the haunted grey eyes that studied him. "It slashed me up, but I got away in the dark. I couldn't find you." His tempestuous, blue eyes took on a far sullener look. "And then…I don't know? I…I saw *things*. There was this darkness and then…I saw *things* that…that I wish I didn't see…and then? And then I was here in all this blood, drowning."

Fynn, having never heard Hollyn stammer so badly, was taken aback by the other prince's reluctance to provide any detail to what had happened. But he understood, knew all too well that there was a sort of moroseness to this place—this dreadfully dark, dank place—that siphoned the energy from you, leaving you unable to really communicate what was going on. He admitted softly, "I saw *things* too." He hung his head, not wanting Hollyn to see him cry any more than he already had. "I want to get out of here."

"Me too," whispered the taller prince. "Let's go."

"Where to?"

Hollyn looked away from Fynn, nodding just head of them. "It looks like we're back in the catacombs."

"I hadn't noticed," Fynn murmured as he sidled up beside Hollyn and, as he had done earlier that day, took his weight against his side, acting as the other's crutch.

Hollyn snorted. "That's because you don't pay attention."

"You're probably right."

"I usually am."

"Humble too," groused Fynn. "Guess you're feeling at least a bit better, then."

As they took their first step toward the entryway where the tunnels seemed to resume, jutting off from the horrid, bloody chamber they presently stood in, they heard a crunch. They both looked down, aghast when they realized they stood upon a bank of bones heaped atop one another.

Fynn inhaled deeply, settling himself. "Where do you think all these bones came from?"

"I don't want to know."

"I don't think I really do either," agreed Fynn with a scowl.

The boys continued forward, trying not to focus on the snapping and scraping and crunching of bones beneath their weight. Hollyn looked around, trying to distract himself from the morbid scene. "Where's Mischief?"

"I thought he was with you," Fynn answered.

"Maybe the creature got him."

"I hope not," mumbled Fynn dejectedly.

Hollyn nodded, a sad frown pulling at his lips. "Me too."

They stumbled their way up the bank and to the passage's entrance. The dim light of the torches reached into the winding bowels of the catacombs. Passing through into the cramped confines of the tunnel, once more surrounded by the unseeing caverns of skulls where once eyes looked out, they carried on in wordless companionship, taking comfort in the others presence. A scuffling sound just ahead caught their attention and they stopped, both tensing, both leaning closer to the other.

"What was that?"

Hollyn tried to keep calm, replying, "I don't know. Stay quiet."

The sound of shuffling, of the earth shifting beneath the weight of something, grew louder. The boys withdrew to the wall, pressing themselves against it and trying to make no noise, hardly chancing to even breathe.

When Fynn saw Mischief emerge from around the corner, he couldn't help but break out into a toothy smile. He scoffed, "I think we'll live."

Hollyn smirked, eyeing the raccoon as he came closer. "Well, well, well…where have you been, eh?"

Mischief scuttled over to the princes, preening at their feet, beady eyes staring up at them.

Fynn reached down, scooping the fuzzy animal into his arms. The raccoon clambered up Fynn's chest and perched on his shoulder, tiny hand-like paws clutched at the blood-slicked fabric of his tunic, bushy tail wrapped around his neck.

Returning his attention to Hollyn, Fynn slinked his arm around the boy's waist and stood still, allowing the other to settle himself comfortably before they started off down the tunnel again. "How long do you think we've been down here?" Fynn asked.

"Too long," muttered Hollyn.

"Feels like days."

"After everything," Hollyn began tiredly, "it seems like capture the flag was a lifetime ago."

"I know what you mean," Fynn acknowledged. "I know *exactly* what you mean."

They knew better than to keep their conversation going. They knew that the sound of their voices would once again attract the wall-crawler that had found them once before. Neither wished to repeat that particular experience and so kept staunchly quiet as they continued their adventure through the long and winding tunnels of the catacombs beneath the island.

It seemed like hours later that they felt the ground shifting; their muscles strained as they began to ascend. Voices were flitting off in the distance, far off it seemed, but there.

"Hollyn," Fynn whispered.

"I hear it too." Hollyn couldn't help the tired smile that found its way to his lips.

"That's Ollie's voice." Fynn smiled broadly. "Do you hear him?"

Hollyn nodded. "I do." Tears seared a salty path through the grime that masked his face. "We made it."

"We did."

They continued their climb upward until the unmistakable sight of light breaching a curtain of vines was before them. Hollyn, puzzled, knit his brows together. "There's no way it's still light outside."

"What if it's tomorrow?"

"Maybe," Hollyn mused. "It's odd though, don't you think?"

Nodding slowly, thoughtfully, Fynn replied, "I've seen a lot of odd things since we came to Dier Island." The arm that ensnared Hollyn's waist tightened its hold. "I don't think I want to tell them *everything*."

Hollyn sounded sure of himself when he said, "You won't have to."

"They'll ask," argued Fynn.

"But you don't have to tell them," contended Hollyn.

"Maybe one day," Fynn whispered.

Hollyn smiled darkly. "Maybe one day. But not today."

Fynn's hand reached out shakily as it moved the vines from their path. The two princes, wrapped up in each other's arms for support, stumbled into the light. The brightness was painful in its brutal assault. They saw both teams fighting around their flag that still stood - stalwart, un-captured. They took another wavering step forward, both fearing they'd soon be pitching face first to the ground.

Blunt-tipped arrows were flying, and dull-edged swords were clashing. Moriah was the first to notice their appearance. He stopped, frozen in place, when he beheld the princes emerging from the forgotten cave. His breath caught in his throat. The boys stood just a few feet from him, Hollyn draped partially over Fynn's side, Mischief perched upon the shorter boy's other shoulder. They were coated, head to booted toe, in blood and grime; the whites of their eyes stood out in stark contrast to the crimson masks clinging to their faces. Lacerations glistened beneath the blood that stained their entire persons. Their uniforms were torn and muddied - sleeves ripped off, the knees of their leggings shredded open, exposing more bloodied and bruised flesh beneath.

"Gods," gasped Moriah.

Everyone stopped at the sound of the man's mortified exclamation. Slowly, each of them turned and gaped at the two.

Penelope shuddered. Tears sprung into her eyes. "Hollyn? Fynn?"

Moriah tentatively stalked toward the boys and when he came to stand just before them, he knelt and threw his long arms around them, drawing them both to him as tightly as he could. His voice was low and mournful sounding, the usual silk and glibness gone. "You need to tell me what happened."

Hollyn replied, exhausted, "Can we go back to the castle first?" He looked into Moriah's abnormally green eyes, silently pleading for a reprieve from the horror they'd encountered. "Please."

Fynn, finally free of the labyrinth of nightmares that stretched beneath the island and assured that he and Hollyn were safe and in the comforting presence of Moriah, allowed himself to give in. He'd been so intently focused on escaping that he'd been ignoring his body's screaming protests since he'd emerged from the pool of blood. His back stung painfully, his leg hurt, his head was throbbing. The corners of his vision were blurring. He cast one last look at Moriah, pleased beyond reason to see him once again, and then let the darkness take over. He collapsed limply against the man's chest, bringing Hollyn forward with him.

Moriah held both boys tightly in his arms, refusing to let them go. "You're safe," he whispered.

Hollyn's lips curled into a final smile before he, too, allowed himself to give into the exhaustion and lose himself in Moriah's grasp. His forehead rested against the man's chest. The beating of Moriah's heart lulled Hollyn into a peaceful, much needed sleep.

20

THE PALADIN

Fynn stretched his legs out, careful not to kick Hollyn's stomach, as he lifted his arms over his head and yawned. He combed a hand through his messy hair tiredly. When Hollyn kicked his own leg out, jamming his heel into Fynn's hip, the shorter boy jerked awake, eyes wide. "What was that for?" he yelped.

"You're tired," Hollyn replied dully.

"Well, of course." Fynn shrugged. "It's been a long few days. Can you blame me?"

"Go to bed," Hollyn offered. "You don't want to be dead on your feet tomorrow."

"I'll be fine," Fynn argued as he adjusted himself against the mattress. "You need the company. Don't want you stewing over whatever has you in a mood."

Looking away, Hollyn muttered wearily, "What? I'm not allowed to be upset?"

"No."

The taller prince couldn't help the mirthless snort that escaped before he had time to school his emotions. "It's nothing."

Fynn stared at Hollyn intently. "When we were in the cave, you told me I wasn't allowed to sulk just because you got hurt."

"You're not," reaffirmed Hollyn.

Fynn gently kicked Hollyn's covered leg with his toes. "But that doesn't mean *you're* allowed to sulk."

Hollyn still didn't look back to Fynn. "Why not?" His voice was low and weak. "I'm the one that's stuck in this damn bed...*again*."

Fynn's smile broadened. There was warmth in his pale eyes as he spoke resolutely, "You being stuck in bed again isn't *all* bad."

"Oh?" Finally, Hollyn looked at Fynn. "Enlighten me then?"

416

"Well, it gives me time to catch up to you…Godryk too. We're good, but you're still better."

"A little selfish of you, don't you think?" joked Hollyn as he leaned his head back against the headboard of his infirmary bed.

"Just a bit," Fynn laughed.

"You two need all the help you can get." Hollyn grinned.

"Exactly!" Fynn settled comfortably against the footboard of the bed. "Can I tell you a secret?"

"Go on, then."

"Godryk's getting pretty good."

"I *knew* that."

"Want to know something you *don't* already know?"

Hollyn nodded curiously.

"I'm still better than him." Fynn smirked.

Playfully, Hollyn kicked Fynn's hip again. He shook his head. "You're insufferable."

"You wouldn't change me for the world," insisted Fynn, feigning indignation.

"Well," Hollyn conceded, "you certainly make life interesting."

The jovial atmosphere that had blossomed between the boys slowly wilted as both princes felt themselves relent to the persistent urge to commiserate about what had transpired just two weeks ago in the catacombs. When they'd finally made it out, Moriah had brought them back to the castle; there was a worrisome look in Moriah's eyes that betrayed an underlying, roiling sense of dread and fear, and dare they say, genuine concern. Fynn had been confined to bedrest for only two days before being allowed to rejoin his year mates; Hollyn didn't fare nearly as well. But, while Hollyn was confined to his infirmary bed, Fynn came by every night after supper.

By the end of the first week, Hollyn and Fynn came to the decision to tell Lux and Godryk about the strange happenings in the catacombs. This discussion inevitably led Fynn to divulging that he'd, in fact, seen the nine-pointed star before, on the wax seal of the letters he'd received during the summer.

Hollyn was the first to speak again. He kept his voice soft. "Fynneas?"

"Hmm?"

"What do you thinks going on? It can't be a coincidence that the wax seal on your letters had the same markings as down in the catacombs,"

Hollyn reasoned. "There's got to be something more to all this, something we're not thinking of. Something's missing."

"I think you're right." Fynn inhaled deeply. When his eyes sought out Hollyn's, they bored into the deep, blue depths imploringly, urgently. "I need to tell you something. It's something I didn't mention before. I didn't think it was important, I suppose. But now I think it probably is."

"What is it?" asked Hollyn.

"My mother," Fynn whispered shakily, "when she was talking to me in that place, she said that the Crown did things to keep Estheria and all of us safe." An unknown dread crept over Fynn like a thousand small spiders with spindly legs made out of impossibly sharp needles. He shivered. "She said those things were dark and unnatural."

"What do you think she meant by that?"

Fynn shook his head. "I don't know. But whatever is going on, it's been happening for a while."

Hollyn thought for a moment and then ventured, "When we head back to Batsbeckon this summer, I think I know where to look for answers."

Curiosity piqued, Fynn straightened up and leaned forward. "Where?"

"I've heard Ciaran mention a place in the castle," Hollyn began slowly, "that no one ever talks about." He brushed an errant, ruby strand from his face. "There's a portrait of our grandfather. It's in a room no one uses. Ciaran says that behind the portrait there's a secret passage." He laughed. "I didn't believe him when he told me. I thought he was just having a laugh. But now, I don't know." He shook his head and sighed. "I think he may have been telling me the truth. If there is information about...*whatever* it is we're looking for...I think they, and I don't know who *they* are so don't ask me, would have hidden it there."

"When we get back, first thing we do is try and figure this out," Fynn said. "We go find that portrait and see if anything is really there."

Hollyn, his right arm wrapped tightly in a sling, extended his left arm, hand outstretched. "Agreed."

Fynn shook his cousin's hand, nodding the affirmative. "We'll figure it out."

"*All* of it." Hollyn smiled.

"Together."

"*Together.*" Hollyn leaned back against the headboard. His own weariness was catching up with him. "It's late. You *really* should get some sleep. You look awful."

"Flatterer," mumbled Fynn as he rolled from the bed, careful not to bump the other boy. "I'm going to head up. Try and sleep, won't you? If *I* look awful, then *you* look like death warmed over."

Fynn took his leave from the infirmary and wandered his way through the castle toward the tower when he saw a shadow flit across the stonework of the corridor. Stopping, he watched as the long shadow marred the already rather dark stones before rounding the corner. Moriah stood at the far end of the hall, not moving. Swathed in black, he blended into the midnight darkness easily, save for glimmering eyes that shone brilliantly in the scant light. At the sight of the man, Fynn smiled.

Walking up to the lord commander, Fynn stopped when he stood nearly toe-to-toe with the man in black. He craned his neck to meet Moriah's eyes and laughed tiredly, "Can't sleep?"

Moriah sniggered, "I could ask the same of you. Coming from the infirmary?"

Fynn nodded.

The lord commander's hand fell upon Fynn's shoulder, squeezing gently as he urged the boy to turn around and head back the way he'd come. Fynn made no move to protest and so obediently walked in-stride with the far taller Moriah.

"Where are we going?" the boy asked.

"I've been looking for you," Moriah answered. "I wanted to speak with you after supper, but you were off to visit Hollyn. I didn't want to interrupt." He glanced down at the prince and quirked a brow. "I just didn't think you'd be there for so long."

"Sorry," muttered Fynn.

"No matter."

By the time the pair arrived at Moriah's intended destination it was after midnight. The apartments in the bowels of the castle, those that belonged to Paladin, were cool and dark. Moriah leaned into the heavy cushions of a thick chair in his private chambers, the fire in the hearth burning gently, warming him as he relaxed. Fynn sat opposite him in a chair quite similar. There were pieces of clothing tossed here and there; no real order to the way things were kept. However, Moriah's swords, of which he had many, were well-kept and tended. They were racked on the far wall, each with gleaming steel, freshly polished. His armor was beside them, resting on a small table. There was a shield leaning against the wall at the table's foot. The lord commander's bed was at the center of the room; its ornate headboard stretched proudly over the dark stone of the walls. The bedding was dark, and the mattress was littered with thick, fur blankets and a multitude of pillows scattered about. The blanket that sat atop the others, partially folded up and messily curled around as though Moriah had seen little use in straightening his bedding before leaving the room when last he was there, bore the Mordray insignia upon it in fine, intricate stitching. There was little else in the room that seemed personal to the man to whom it belonged.

Fynn watched curiously as Moriah seemed to melt into the comfort of the chair, the tension easing from his shoulders, rigidity leaving the taught line of his back. When, at last, the man spoke in his impossibly deep, purr-like voice, Fynn was pulled quickly from his reverie.

"I've something for you."

"What is it?" Fynn asked, one brow raised inquisitively.

"It arrived today. Nan brought it over," Moriah explained. Letting loose an exasperated sigh as he was forced to peel himself from the comfort and warmth he had previously been luxuriating in, he strode across the room to his bed where a trunk had been set. He called back to Fynn, "I wanted to give it to you earlier, but you had your lessons and I didn't want to have to pull you out of them. They're important." When he returned to the hearth, he set the trunk down gently in Fynn's lap before resuming his place in his plush chair. "And, I thought you might want to talk." His green eyes shone fiercely in the firelight, "Talk…far away from prying ears."

Fynn ran his hands over the smoothness of the trunk. It wasn't particularly spectacular looking to behold, but he knew better than to judge contents by their container. Reverently, he undid the fastenings and slowly opened it. There were multiple letters sealed with wax embossed with the royal insignia, all tied in twine and neatly awaiting his attention. There was a small parcel set beside the letters and next to it was a small, black velvet pouch tied with a red silk bow.

"What is this?" asked the prince.

"They're from Fiona."

"Fiona?"

Moriah nodded. "It's a few days late, but I believe these were intended to be gifts for your birthday."

Fynn smiled. He'd been missing his sister. His time at Morancy had been full of friends and adventures, but nothing could truly replace his sister in his day-to-day life. She'd been a constant, the one who'd raised him, and all of a sudden, he'd been forced to accept living a life where she no longer featured as a prominent player. It pained him. "She remembered," he said fondly.

"Of course, she did," scoffed Moriah.

"I miss her."

"I know." Moriah once more was on his feet, stalking through his room like a cat on the prowl as he searched for something. He was sifting through his wardrobe on the far side of the room as he began distractedly saying, "You know, she'll be coming for a visit soon."

Fynn turned in his chair and watched Moriah lean into the wardrobe, clearly intent on finding something. "She will?"

"Yes. I know you've lived your life in that gods-forsaken, wintery nightmare up north, far away from the rest of the kingdom, but by now, Fynneas, that's no excuse for ignorance. Everyone who's anyone comes to the archipelago for the games. It's tradition."

"Oh."

Fynn reached into the trunk and plucked up the velvet bag. He turned it over in his hands for a moment before unfastening the silken bow. Reaching inside, he withdrew a deck of cards. They were old, some of the edges torn, and the intricate designs painted upon them were faded and weathered. Fynn drew a card and stared as he asked, "Tarot cards? Why would she send me these?"

"I see my sister has gotten the princess interested in fanciful flights," murmured Moriah. "Truthfully, Fiona didn't seem the type to take an interest in such things."

Fynn shook his head. "It's certainly not something I would've thought she'd like." He turned to look back at Moriah, eyes shining with humor. "Do you know what the cards mean? Surely, if Emrys likes them, she would have imparted some of that knowledge on you."

Moriah shook his head, still intent on looking for something. "Noel, more so. I was quite adept at avoiding her any time she felt like telling our futures or whatever it is the cards are supposed to do."

"Why? Didn't like what she predicted?"

Moriah huffed. "There's only so many times your own sister can predict your brutal and dramatic demise before you tire of it all."

Fynn returned his attention to the cards, marveling at the detail painted before him. "Nine of Swords," he read aloud, while fanning the cards out in his hands. "Wonder what it's supposed to represent." He plucked up the card and held it out.

"Don't know," Moriah said. "Sounds a bit grim though, doesn't it?"

The prince shrugged as he placed the card back in the deck and then the deck back into its bag, carefully tying the bow once more. As he set it back in the trunk, Fynn asserted, "I suppose as long as it's not the Death card, it can't be too bad, right?"

Seemingly finding what he'd been looking for, Moriah paused. "Speaking of our dear sisters, Emrys says that she'll be bringing Fiona by a little earlier than everyone else. It seems she's missed you just as you've missed her."

He returned to his chair; Fynn watched him with barely contained, yet muted, interest.

Upon Moriah's lap there now rested a small box. Long, pale fingers ghosted over the lines and angles enclosed within his hands, his eyes intently latched upon Fynn. "This is a gift from me." After a moment's hesitation, he handed the box to the boy.

Much like the trunk, the box was outwardly nothing special. But when he opened it, Fynn's eyes went wide. In the velvety confines of the container there rested a pendent strung upon a silver chain. It was a dragon coiled in on itself, eating its own tail, with rubies for eyes. The boy reached out, plucked the magnificent piece from its box and held it aloft, watching with rapt interest as the firelight sparked in the red eyes of the dragon.

"Thank you," Fynn cooed in awe, twirling the necklace in his grasp as he continued admiring it. "Why a dragon, though?"

"You know the answer," Moriah intoned. He leaned forward and stole the necklace from the boy's grasp and with a wave of his hand, beckoned Fynn to come closer.

Fynn obliged wordlessly. He rose and stood at Moriah's feet. He bowed his head, allowing the man to easily clasp the chain around his slender neck. The pendant fell over the center of his chest, just by his heart. The dragon's eyes gleamed up at him, as if watching, knowing. Fynn touched his fingers to the cool metal of the pendant and smiled. "Where did you get this?"

"It was always yours," Moriah replied. There was a hitch in his voice, as though some foreign emotion had wormed its way into his normally flat, bored pitch. His eyes flicked upward from the pendant to Fynn, realizing that, as he sat before the prince, they were now eye to eye. Presently, for the first time, Moriah saw that Fynn's eyes truly were like ice, absorbing and reflecting all the light and colors around them. They shone brightly; the happiness from the boy's smile extending into them.

"I got it for you when you were a baby…for your first birthday." He brushed Fynn's hair back, away from his face. He was almost tempted to smile, but refrained and leaned back into the chair, turning from the boy and gazing into the fire. "I asked my sister, Emrys, to have it found and sent here. I wanted you to have it finally. I never got the chance to bring it to you then. So, I'm giving it to you now."

The fingers that had been tracing along the intricate grooves and curves of the pendant suddenly ceased their ministrations and wrapped, with white-knuckled strength, about the dragon. "She told you?" Fynn surmised. "My mother told you about her dream?"

Moriah didn't chance a look back at Fynn. "Felix thought it was just a dream brought on by fever and all that." He sighed again. The tension returned to every sinew that stretched along his back and shoulders, coiling almost painfully. "I *knew* it wasn't."

Fynn reached out to Moriah beseechingly, hand balling in the leather of the man's black jerkin and pulling him insistently, silently beckoning him to look back. When he did, Fynn let his hand fall away. "How did you know?"

"Some people see things," the man whispered, "and some people see more than others."

There was a forlorn look to his expression, a world-weariness that Fynn had never before associated with the man, but now found utterly impossible to dismiss.

"I knew when Celestine told me about her dream, that it wasn't just a normal fever dream. It was something more." He shook his head, muttering, "I don't know what it meant, Fynneas. But I knew—I *know* it meant more than I wanted to admit." Moriah reached out and placed his hand over the fist that once more encircled the pendant; long fingers curled over Fynn's straining knuckles. The boy's hand shook beneath his palm. "Your mother was very special, Fynneas. As are you." His hand fell away; he rose to his feet slowly. "And, as I'm sure you've figured out by now, you're not the only special one."

Fynn nodded. "Minnie…and you and your brothers…and sisters, too?"

Nodding, Moriah smirked. "They're certainly *different,* that much is for certain." He strode languidly toward the hearth and there he stood, motionless, staring into the depths of the flames with an almost desperately searching gaze. "But there are more."

"Who?"

"I'll tell you one day, maybe one day soon. But right now, it wouldn't do for me to let you know," Moriah explained. He waved his hand and paused, waiting expectantly for the boy to come over. He wasn't surprised when the prince complied and joined him before the hearth, staring into the fire.

When Fynn spoke after a long stretch where both figures stood frightfully still and quiet before the gently crackling flames, his voice was even and calm. "My mother said dragons were born from fire."

Moriah nodded.

"I walked into the fire the first time I was in that…*place*," the boy said.

"And you found darkness waiting," Moriah continued.

"Yes."

"What more?"

Fynn's hand tightened around the pendant again. He felt as though there was an unseen force, some sort of strength, resting within, that he imbibed every time he touched it. "The first time I was scared. And when I did walk through, there was darkness everywhere and then I saw stars. The second time, I wasn't scared any more. My mother was there, and she said it would be alright." He held the necklace tighter, drawing solace from its presence. "That time, when I walked into the fire, there wasn't darkness on the other side. It was light… white, I suppose. I was in my mother's room back at Godsreach." He smiled fondly at the memory. "I was in her room…the room I was born in."

"The room she died in," Moriah added in a rasp.

"It's weird, don't you think?"

"What is?"

"That I was born in the room she would later die in," Fynn replied. There was no sadness in his voice, just flatness that belied the detachment he was forcing upon himself. Wordlessly, Fynn inched closer to Moriah until his shoulder pressed against the man's side.

"Life and death often go hand in hand," Moriah said as his arm snaked around Fynn's back; his hand draped over the boy's shoulder. He never looked away from the fire.

He wasn't sure why he was reaching toward the fire, but as he did, Fynn felt quite at ease. His hand scooped into the flame and he felt no pain, no searing agony as one would expect; and when he withdrew his hand, there was a small fire still blinking in the curled confines of his palm. "Can I ask you something?"

"Yes."

Fynn turned his hand over and watched mildly as the little flame wiggled around his thin hand, never once burning him. "Was the fire at Batsbeckon my fault?"

Moriah shook his head. "No."

"But it wasn't a normal fire, was it?"

"No."

Gently, Fynn leaned closer to the flame and flicked his wrist, setting the little fire free to join the blaze within the mouth of the hearth. He drew back, nestling closer to Moriah's side. "Do you know what happened?"

"I have an idea."

"Will you tell me?"

Moriah turned away from the fire and knelt before the prince. Both hands clasped over the boy's shoulders, forcing him to face the lord commander head on. "I don't think it's my tale to tell. But I suspect, you'll find out soon enough."

Fynn pouted petulantly, grousing, "Why does everyone always talk in riddles?"

As he was wont to do, Moriah seized hold of Fynn's chin and turned the child's face back toward him. "I think you'll find we don't talk in riddles." He laughed. "We simply answer your questions evasively."

"That's not any better!" argued Fynn.

The hand that had seized Fynn's chin climbed its way up until thin fingers of the palest white combed through hair of the darkest black, pushing the messy tresses away from the boy's face. "That may be true, but, *alas*, it is what it is."

"You're the worst," grumbled Fynn.

Moriah stood up and chuckled. "Most definitely." His hand found its way to Fynn's upper back, fingers splayed between the shoulder blades, as he pushed Fynn away from the fire. "Now, it's late. You need to get to bed." He nodded to the trunk that sat almost forgotten beside one of the chairs. "And take that up with you."

The boy stopped before the trunk, staring at it thoughtfully. "Moriah?"

"Hmm?"

"Can you…walk me back to the tower?" Fynn turned quickly, eyes wide, brows furrowed in question. "Please?" Chewing on his lower lip, he whispered, "I'm not *scared*. It's not like that. But…it's just a lonely walk."

"A lonely walk?"

Fynn nodded sheepishly.

With the trunk settled in Fynn's thin arms and pendant neatly tucked beneath the hem of his tunic, the prince and the lord commander made their way from the Paladin apartments and headed toward the tower. The castle was dark, torches not lit. It was quiet, comfortably so.

Fynn scooted closer to Moriah as they headed along down the corridor. "How long is Hollyn going to be in the infirmary this time?" the prince asked.

"I thought Imogen told you already," Moriah replied.

Fynn shrugged, ignoring the snort of annoyance the action garnered from the man at his side. "She did, but I wanted to know what you thought. I get the impression she didn't tell us everything."

Sighing, Moriah shook his head. "It's funny."

"What is?"

"That this is the time you choose to be observant." Moriah laughed lightly. "But you're right." His expression sobered until there was a noticeable solemnity to his normally vibrant eyes. "I think she wanted to spare Hollyn from it, but he's going to be stuck in bed for a while. And when he's up, he'll still have his arm wrapped and immobilized. He took a nasty knock to the head too. It's going to take a lot longer for him to heal up this time."

"Oh," Fynn murmured. "That bad?"

Moriah nodded. "Hollyn isn't stupid by any means; he's a smart boy. He likely already knows the extent of the damage that was done."

"Will he be able to compete in the games?"

"No."

That one word alone tore through Fynn's very being like a lance piercing through armor and plunging into his heart. His breath was expelled with a sudden, shaking gasp. The warm prickle of tears began to well up in his eyes and then, to his mortification, wet trails streaked down his cheeks. His lip trembled as he stifled the cry threatening to break loose; he bit down, but it didn't help. His shoulders shivered, racked by the guilt of it all. "Are you sure?" he asked meekly.

"Yes." Moriah reached out, snatching Fynn by his tunic and pulling him back until they stood side by side in the corridor, the tiny boy quaking at his side. "I spoke with Blythe and Imogen about it." He knelt, carefully taking the trunk from the child's arms and setting it down. Slowly, he enveloped the prince in his arms until the boy's forehead was set against his shoulder. "It's not your fault, you know. He's going to be alright. But he isn't going to be able to compete. If he did, he'd risk permanently damaging his shoulder."

"I should've done more," Fynn weakly protested. He wanted to wriggle out of Moriah's embrace, but the warmth and security of the gesture had him, instead, curling closer. "I should've helped him more."

"There was nothing more you could've done, Fynneas," Moriah assured. One hand traced lazy circles over the boy's shaking back, the other softly

426

combed through Fynn's hair. "It's no one's fault, and he *will* be alright. It will just take some time."

"Will he still be placed in a division?"

"Yes."

"Do you know which one?"

"I do." He held Fynn tighter. He felt the boy shivering against him; he heard the muffled sniffles buried against his shoulder. "It was decided once we knew he would be unable to compete."

"Will you tell me? Hollyn said once he hoped for Armada, but I don't think that's true anymore."

"You're quite right. I think you already know where he'll be placed," Moriah replied gently.

As Moriah withdrew from Fynn, still kneeling before the boy, the prince straightened up. He blinked away his tears, wiping any traces of his perceived weakness from his cheeks with the back of his hand roughly. Squaring his shoulders, calming down, and regaining himself, the boy faced the man before him with a more resolute, even stare than he would've been able to muster up only moment's prior. "Paladin."

The man in black nodded.

"Only the best of the best are chosen for Paladin," Fynn said.

Moriah's face remained rather impassive; his eyes dull. He nodded again.

"Hollyn deserves that."

"He's a talented boy," remarked Moriah. "He's proven his worth in every subject and shown his capacity to lead others on more than one occasion…to think through situations calmly, rationally."

"He'll do well there," Fynn agreed.

Curiously, Moriah cocked his head to the side, one brow arched. "Not jealous?"

Fynn shook his head, smiling agreeably. "No. Not really."

"Didn't you say *you* wanted to be in Paladin?"

The boy shrugged, yet again choosing to ignore how the action irritated Moriah. "Yes." His eyes brightened as he continued, "I do. But there's no rule that says only one student can be picked for Paladin every year."

"No, I suppose you're right. Normally, however, that *is* the case."

The boy prince affected a cheeky smile, replying coyly, "I think you'll find I'm not overly fond of being *normal.*"

"No. I think it's more that *normalcy* isn't overly fond of *you*," Moriah joked as he stood. "Now, let's head to the tower. No more dawdling in the halls. You've got a hard day ahead of you tomorrow."

Collecting the trunk, Fynn laughed. "Oh? Any insights you want to share?"

"No. Not particularly."

"Noel's lessons are tomorrow," Fynn speculated. "You must know what he's planned for us."

Moriah continued down the hall in long strides, not bothering to look back as he said, "I know exactly what you'll be doing tomorrow. That doesn't mean I need to tell you."

"You're the worst," grumbled Fynn as he followed along after the man.

"I relish the title," the lord commander slyly mused. He stopped, waiting for the boy to catch up to him. Once Fynn was happily trotting along at his side, Moriah brushed his hand over the boy's messy, black hair and smiled down at him. "And by the way...happy birthday, Fynneas.

"Thank you," Fynn whispered. He leaned closer to Moriah; his eyes closed softly at the feel of the hand brushing through his hair. There was something fondly reminiscent of the gesture, something that reminded him of his father. "Thanks for walking back with me. I appreciate it, just so you know."

"I will never leave you alone if you ask me to be there."

The comment was so soft, Fynn could scarcely hear it. But he was certain it had been said. "Thank you," the boy replied.

They came to a stop just before the winding stairwell that led to the common room and dormitories for the first and second-years. Before heading up, Fynn stopped and looked back at Moriah with shining eyes and a lopsided, childish smile. "I'll be seeing you, then."

Moriah nodded.

"Thank you again...for *everything*."

"You needn't keep thanking me," Moriah intoned flatly.

"Still," muttered Fynn, "thank you."

Moriah flicked his wrist, waving his hand insistently. "Be off with you, little prince, you've a long day ahead of you."

Grousing petulantly, Fynn grumbled, "*Every* day here is exceedingly long." He ascended the stairway, following its twisting path until he could no longer look back and see Moriah. "Night," he whispered before continuing further up the tower.

Upon entering the common room, there wasn't a sound to be heard. Fynn crept up the short stairs and turned into the dormitory, carefully closing the door behind himself. The other boys were fast asleep; gentle snores lilted along in the silence of the still-dark, early morning. The prince tiptoed over to his bed, set the trunk down beside it, and climbed in. Nestling into the warmth of his blankets, burrowing his cheek into the softness of his pillow, Fynn allowed himself to drift off into a relatively comfortable, nightmare-free sleep.

That sleep, however, did not last nearly as long as he would've liked. It wasn't long after Fynn had fallen into the perfectly quiet, calm lull of a deep slumber, that the sun began creeping over the horizon and Nyle could be heard screaming at them from the common room, beseeching them all to get up immediately, lest there be most dire and dramatic consequences. Fynn groaned, rolled onto his side, and pulled his pillow up over his head to drown out the old man's shrill yells. He was doing a fine job of willing himself to ignore the commands being continually shouted from the common room until he felt someone shaking his shoulder.

"Fynn," Godryk called.

Fynn curled away from his friend's touch, leaning further into the warmth of his bedding.

"Fynneas," Godryk implored more forcefully.

The prince batted Godryk's hand away with a lazy slap before rolling onto his stomach, his pillow now firmly clasped over his head; he snuggled deeper into the blankets that were twisted around his lank form.

Shaking his head and with an exasperated roll of his eyes, Godryk, rather unceremoniously, shoved Fynn over the side of the bed. He couldn't suppress his amusement when Fynn clattered to the ground in a heap of blankets and gangly limbs. When the prince finally peeked his head over the side of the bed and glared in his direction, Godryk broke into a fitful peal of laughter. The boy looked decidedly un-princely with his black hair an absolute mess, sticking out in every direction, and the dried remnants of drool still clinging to his chin.

"What's so funny?" snapped the prince.

"You," Ollie joked as he walked by the pair. "You look a mess, Fynn."

Albie was quick to come bounding over, giddily beholding the sight of Fynn so disheveled. He snickered. "You don't have long to get ready before Nyle comes up here and drags you out. Best get your uniform on."

"Quickly," Godryk added.

"What help are you?" Fynn huffed as he stood, collecting his blankets and tossing them on his bed.

"I woke you up, didn't I?" The young Redmayne laughed. He left Fynn to get ready for the day.

By the time it was early in the afternoon, Fynn was breathing heavily. He wiped the sweat and grime from his face with a spare rag proffered by Lux. Tossing it to the bed at his side, he brushed his hand through his sweat-slick-ened hair in a fruitless attempt to tame it. He was smiling; the warmth of the expression reached his eyes, igniting them with an amiable spark. De-ciding he no longer wished to stand, he collapsed into the chair he'd pulled up beside Hollyn's bedside. Fynn eyed Hollyn, wincing a bit when he saw the bandages that laced both his arms, covering the nasty lacerations he'd received from the cave-crawler in the catacombs. He soured even more so at the sight of the sling that firmly bound Hollyn's arm to his torso.

"How's the shoulder?" Fynn asked.

Hollyn narrowed his eyes, taking on an expression quite reminiscent of Moriah when he was deliberating a response. "Sore." He settled for not expounding upon his retort and rather settled back into the amply fluffed pillows that propped him up against the headboard. He took the time to survey his companions. Despite making an attempt to right himself, Fynn was filthy. Mud stained his tunic; his leggings were ripped at both knees; his face was streaked with sweat and all manners of filth. Even so, he still had an overall happiness to him that seemed to have infected the rest of the foursome.

Godryk was leaning over Fynn's chair, his hands resting over the back, shoulders hunched forward. Like Fynn, he was covered in filth. His red curls were a wild mess. Lux, seated at the foot of the bed, appeared somewhat better. A painful bruise bloomed over her cheek and there was a bit of blood speckled over the collar of her tunic, but, other than that, she seemed to be, relatively, the most pristine of the three.

"Rough day?" Hollyn asked.

"You've no idea," Lux laughed.

"Enlighten me," Hollyn drawled flatly.

Fynn, Godryk, and Lux had decided to take their afternoon meal in the infirmary and keep the injured prince company, much to Hollyn's secret delight. And so, as they happily munched on their lemon cakes and spiced flatbreads, Godryk regaled them with a recounting of the day; he talked endlessly about how dramatic Nyle tended to be when it came to the most minor of infractions, how Noel had them compete against each other once more and how, after the longest bout they'd ever had, Fynn had defeated Godryk in the final round and come out on top, yet again.

"Don't get too comfortable at the top," warned Hollyn.

Fynn glanced up from his lemon cake, smiling a toothy grin. "Don't worry. I'm just waiting for you to come join me there."

"How very gracious." Hollyn smirked.

"I've been known to be," joked Fynn as he took another bite of his cake.

The easy companionship the four had acquired amongst themselves continued on for the proceeding weeks. Hollyn was getting stronger day by day. Moriah would come visit in the mornings before taking his leave, allowing Hollyn his time to read or, as the days had progressed, begin walking around the infirmary to regain his strength. His legs, at first, were wobbly and weak, but it wasn't terribly long before he could make the rounds around the medical wing without being so out of breath that he felt near collapse. His injury still pained him, but he forced himself to straighten his back and do his best to square his shoulders; sacrificing his perfect posture because of an injury was simply out of the question.

Quite often Hollyn was chastised by either Blythe or Imogen for his insistence when it came to a speedy recovery; on the very worst days, he found himself on the receiving end of both women scolding him for being stubborn and difficult. He had been told, by no less than five people already, that he would not be participating in the upcoming games. It was made quite clear to the ailing prince that, should he be allowed to participate, he would be risking life-long injury to his shoulder, arm, and back. Such a thing, he was assured by everyone, would be detrimental to his future, as well as the future of the kingdom. The lord paramount said it would simply not do for him to be an invalid, that it would be bad for the kingdom, for his brother, for the Crown.

Hollyn scoffed; though he understood the implications associated with being a cripple, he didn't want to admit to himself that such a thing was a possibility. And though he wanted nothing more than to compete alongside his year mates in the games, he knew deep down it was an utter impossibility. Not only did he know because everyone felt the need to constantly remind him, but he could feel that his body would simply not be ready when the time came. And it was that, more than anything else, that frustrated him the most.

However, much to the delight of Godryk, Hollyn's frustrations did not manifest themselves in the same impossibly broody manner as Fynn's.

Rather, Hollyn was far more adept in recognizing and handling the adversity that he'd been dealt. His days were spent resting, though he'd admit that resting for so long was becoming maddening. When he wasn't resting or reading, he was strolling around the wing or, on the very best of days, Nan and Minnie would visit and keep him company. Those were the days the prince looked forward to the most.

It was just such a day where Nan had her chair pulled up to the side of Hollyn's bed, a tray of lemon cakes set upon her lap. Minnie was curled up next to Hollyn.

"Does it hurt?" the little girl asked.

"Not terribly," Hollyn said. "It's only a bit sore."

"Good." The child nodded; her golden curls tumbled over her tiny shoulders as she did so.

"I'm sorry to hear you won't get the chance to compete in the games," Nan started, eyeing the boy, careful to ensure she didn't strike a nerve.

He accepted the choice of topic for their evening conversation. He plucked a lemon cake from the tray as he sighed. "It's alright." Taking a bite, he savored the tang of the treat. "Moriah was by just after I was told I'd be staying in the infirmary for a while. I was upset...you know, about it all. But he told me that I'd still be placed in a division. That helped me not worry so much, I suppose."

"Oh?" cooed the elderly woman. "Did he tell you which one you'd been picked for?"

The self-satisfied smirk that bloomed over the boy's handsome features was devoid of any arrogance and, instead, sired from a strong sense of pride. He answered, "Paladin."

Nan pat his leg softly, grinning all the while. "That's wonderful! You must be pleased. Not many get chosen for that one."

"I'm happy about it," agreed Hollyn. He was pensive for a moment, considering the topic. "Fynn's been at the top of the class in Noel's combat lessons."

"I've heard," Nan acknowledged. "He's come by the tavern a few times. Minnie is always so happy to see him. He says he's been doing really well under Noel's instruction but says it's too easy without you there."

"No one left to give him a challenge, I suspect." Hollyn laughed. "Godryk's good though."

"Not as good as you?" Minnie asked sweetly.

Hollyn ruffled the girl's curls. "Nowhere *near* as good as me."

"Have you heard that the princess will be visiting?" the old woman questioned.

"The *idiot* hasn't stopped talking about it," said Hollyn.

Later that night, like many of the nights Hollyn had spent in the infirmary recently, he was joined by Lux, Godryk, and Fynn. They discussed the day's events and what they suspected waited for them the following morning. The night gave way to the dawn and the hours fell away, days went by with relative quiet, nothing nightmarish occurring since the fateful game of capture the flag.

It was just after sunrise; the golden light began to leak in through the windows, rousing the prince. As his eyes fluttered open, he saw Moriah seated at his bedside. Yawning, Hollyn shifted to a more comfortable position amongst his many pillows. He laughed lightly. "Do you *ever* sleep?"

"Too often, so I'm told," Moriah answered. "Though not enough, in my opinion."

"You're here early," Hollyn commented.

"How astute of you. Tell me, has Fynneas been instructing you in the delicate art of observation?"

As Hollyn had come to expect, Moriah was none too pleasant this morning. His usual drawl had a frightful bite to it, each word dripping with over-tired malice.

"Not a morning person, right." Hollyn nodded. "How could I have forgotten?"

"Not at all," griped the man in black.

"Is everything alright, then? Why're you here so early? I mean, you're always by in the mornings, but never quite *this* early." His eyes grew marginally wider, asking, "Is anyone hurt? Did something happen."

Moriah's hand fell to Hollyn's blanket-clad knee. Green eyes flicked in the prince's direction. "No. Everyone's fine." Moriah's hand withdrew as the man stood to his full height, now towering over the infirmary bed. "I thought you'd like to know you're going to be allowed out of this horrid place."

Excitement ignited in the boy as he looked up to meet Moriah's eyes. "Really?"

Moriah smiled a barely-there smile, but it was gone as quickly as it had appeared. He continued flatly, "You still can't participate in lessons. But that being said, Imogen thinks you're strong enough to go back to your dormitory and take your meals with your year. That is, if you feel up to it."

The prince was already making his way from his bed to standing up, tall and straight, still nodding enthusiastically at the man's words. "I'm ready."

Moriah's lip curled at the corners as he watched Hollyn right himself, pleased with the boy's willfulness and his stubborn strain of tenacity. For one so young, Hollyn was quite adept at schooling his emotions, controlling his expressions. There before Moriah stood a boy with a smile that shone in his eyes and with an expression that betrayed none of the pain he was more than likely still experiencing, a child who was smiling with such utter certainty, forcing down the anxious thoughts that had been simmering below the surface. "Yes," Moriah agreed evenly, "you are."

When Hollyn slid into his place beside Ollie in the Hall, joining his year mates for breakfast after returning to the dormitories to dress in his uniform, there was a raucous reception at the very sight of him.

Instantly seeing that Hollyn's arm was still wrapped and fastened in a sling, Ollie set to work piling food onto the prince's plate for him. "How hungry are you?" he asked.

"Very." Hollyn smiled, ogling the bowl of fig pies just to Ollie's right. "Thank you."

"So, Imogen let you out?" Albie asked.

"She said I was well enough to leave the wing, but I can't return to lessons." Hollyn began daintily picking at his food.

"Does your shoulder still hurt?" queried Lux.

Frowning slightly, the prince answered, "It's sore. It's getting better every day, though."

"How are those nasty cuts?" Godryk questioned, eyeing the bandages that were still wrapped around both of Hollyn's arms. "Healing alright?"

"I'll have some scars," the prince replied impassively, "but that's no matter. They should be fine in a few more days, I suspect."

Fynn had been watching Hollyn carefully from the moment his cousin arrived. He seemed paler than usual, his skin having taken on a rather unhealthy grey tint during his stay in the medical wing. His eyes, Fynn noted, had regained their usual stormy energy; thankfully, they were no longer dull and tired looking. There was life to Hollyn again, more so than he had seen in the last few weeks. When Fynn finally spoke, he couldn't contain the smile that swept over his face. "I'm glad you're back," he admitted.

Hollyn hadn't been looking at the others much. He'd spared a glance to Penelope and Lux but hadn't really focused on anyone since his food was thoughtfully doled out. He'd been picking at his pie, happily munching and enjoying the relatively easy conversation with the others. But when Fynn spoke, Hollyn's attention was garnered. He looked up and was pleased, though he couldn't exactly understand why, with what Fynn had said. "Me too."

"Have you told them?" asked Fynn.

"Told them what?" Hollyn wondered, curiously arching a single brow.

Fynn clarified, "What division you'll be in once you're all mended up."

"No."

Ollie's mouth went slack as he gaped at the prince to his side. "You know what division you'll be in? How?"

"I won't be able to take part in the games," lamented Hollyn. "So, they've told me which division I'll be in ahead of time. Seems they decided about it pretty early on."

"Well," Ollie insisted, gently nudging Hollyn's side imploringly, "tell us, then."

"Paladin," Hollyn said, deftly working to keep the proud smile from over-curling his lips.

Albie's eyes went wide as he cooed, "Wow! That's amazing. Well done."

Hollyn nodded briskly. "Thank you." He averted his eyes, returning his attention to his plate full of food.

The clambering in the Hall grew louder as the meal drew to an end. The instructors, those who had bothered to join the students, were shuffling from their seats and headed to their afternoon lessons. The children, having come from their jog around the island and morning instructions prior to eating, were still sore and, thus, grumbled as they reluctantly stood up and prepared to head off for their afternoon classes. Hollyn, too, climbed to his feet and, as he prepared to head out of the Hall, cast one last look at Fynn, who lingered behind the herd of first-years.

"Fynneas," Hollyn called.

Fynn turned to regard his cousin, drawing closer as the other ten first-years made their way into the main corridor. "How are you *really*?" he asked softly.

"As well as can be expected."

Grey eyes were riveted by the sight of the sling. Fynn frowned. "You'll be out of that thing soon. Won't you?"

"Not for another six weeks, so Imogen says," corrected Hollyn dutifully, but dully.

"But you'll get out of it and be stronger than ever," asserted the smaller boy.

Hollyn snorted with amusement, "Rest assured, Fynneas, the moment they tell me I'm able to swing a sword with my right arm again, I'll be back to training. Can't let you have all the fun."

"Beating me won't be as easy as you think," warned the black-haired prince.

"I never said I thought it would be easy," countered the other.

"Is that so?" Fynn gently elbowed Hollyn's side.

"Yes. It's certainly *doable*. But I doubt you'll make it easy," replied Hollyn with a smirk worthy of Moriah. "You don't make *anything* easy."

"I'll see you back at the tower tonight then?"

Hollyn smiled. "You will."

"Right. Well, I best be off."

"What lessons do you have now?" asked Hollyn.

Fynn replied, "Archery with Odette."

"Should be fun."

Rolling his pale eyes, Fynn laughed, "Oh, the *most* fun!"

The injured prince insisted, "Best get going, you don't want to keep the others waiting."

Fynn agreed before scampering off, leaving Hollyn in the Hall alone to watch him bound through the entryway and join the others. He couldn't help but smile a small smile at Fynn's infectious energy.

Out in the corridor headed toward the courtyard, Fynn skittered to a halt after bursting into the huddled first-years, grinning. "Well, what sort of mood do we think Odette is in today?"

Penelope laughed. "I think she'll be in a fine humor, really."

Georgie added, "I think so too. She almost smiled this morning, did you see?"

Penelope grinned. "Of course, I saw! She was smiling at Benadykt, so she must be in a good mood."

Lux shook her head and grumbled, "We should head out to the court-yard. If she *is* in a good mood, I'm sure us all being late will sour it." She reached out, snatched Fynn's wrist and pulled him along. "Stop dawdling."

"Alright, alright!" Fynn chuckled. He let Lux lead him along.

The group of eleven proceeded through the corridor. They stayed close to one another as they often did, making quiet conversation as they headed to their lesson. Lux remained at Fynn's side. She ducked her head closer to his. Keeping her voice low, she asked, "How do you *really* feel about Hollyn being chosen for Paladin?"

Taken aback, Fynn said, "Fine."

"*Fynneas*," Lux implored sternly.

"Really," he assured quickly, "I'm fine. I'm happy for him. He deserved to be placed in Paladin. He's the best in every lesson."

"Are you worried?"

"About what?"

"That his placement there means you may not end up where you wanted to be," she clarified. "Are you worried that you won't make Paladin?"

At that, Fynn turned to face Lux fully. There was a fierce resolve evident in his expression. "No. Not at all."

"Oh?"

"I really am happy for him, you know. He deserves it." His voice took on a steely edge as he continued, "But that doesn't mean I won't work myself into the ground to make sure I'm placed there as well."

21

VERY STRANGE THINGS

Godryk's shoulders were slumped forward; his whole-body ached. Fynn clapped his hand over the boy's back, smiling all the while. "Come on, it wasn't *that* bad," the prince cheerily insisted.

Just behind the pair, Ollie dragged his feet along as he groaned, "It was the worst sailing lesson of the year!"

"I thought it would never end," Albie added with a disdainful snort.

Penelope was doing her best to straighten out the mats in her hair, smoothing back errant strands as best she could, as she groused, "I think he was trying to kill us all."

"Come off it." Lux laughed. "You know it wouldn't be in Drake's best interest if we *all* drowned."

"She's right, you know," Fynn agreed, before he peeked over his shoulder and graced Lux with a broad smile.

Renwyn trudged along, sweeping by the girls and pushing past Godryk and Fynn. "You all complain too much," he snapped. "If that were a real naval battle, we would've all died. You should try and take it more seriously."

Hogan was catching up to the group, having been ordered by Drake to check the boats once more before rejoining the others on their way back to the castle. He breathed heavily; sweat inched along the curves of his cheeks. He caught up to his peers and wheezed breathily. "Gods be damned, that was the *worst!*" he bemoaned.

Georgie nodded. "I agree."

Ten of the first-years snickered and shared amiable looks of assent. Renwyn crossed his arms over his chest and shook his head. "You lot are going to be the death of me."

Fynn and Godryk straightened, standing shoulder to shoulder. While Godryk's blue eyes surveyed the group, Fynn's attention was garnered by three black figures in the not-so-far-off distance, winding their way down the road that led from Morancy to the harbor. Squinting in an attempt to ignore the sunlight and further spy who was approaching, Fynn quirked a brow in confusion when he saw the three Mordrays huddled together heading toward them.

"Do you see that?" he asked the others, gesturing in the direction of the castle. "Where do you suppose they're going?"

The atmosphere of the small gathering immediately sobered; all the first-years turned their attention toward the road and the three persons traveling along it.

"Looks like they're coming this way," Lux said.

"All of them?" Godryk asked. "That's odd. They don't normally wander out together like that."

Georgie nodded. "You usually only see two of them together at a time."

Penelope noted, "I don't think I've ever even seen them *all* eat together."

Like every day on Dier Island, it was swelteringly hot. While the children had the sleeves of their tunics rolled up as high as they could to keep cool, the three Mordrays were swathed in black from their jaws down to the tips of their toes. Everyone was quite well accustomed to seeing Moriah and Odette dressed in such a fashion, but to see Noel in similar attire was cause for speculation.

Moriah was at the front of the Mordray herd, his customary impassive expression well fixed to his features, though there was an unsettling glint in his eyes that belied his outward affect and denoted the tidal undercurrent of annoyance churning just beneath. His garb, Fynn thought, was odd, even for him. Normally the man chose to wear black boots, black trousers, and a black tunic; on some occasions, he'd wear a black, leather jerkin to complete his morbid look. Today, however, he was elegantly clad in well-tailored clothes that clung to him as though they were a second skin; a long-sleeved, black jerkin with dramatic shoulders stood out most. Golden snakes were embroidered over the shoulders of the piece, green-stitched eyes ablaze against the leather. He wore a cloak, which must have made the temperature near unbearable; it was wrapped about his shoulders and fixed with a pin of gold in the likeness of a coiled serpent.

At his back was Odette who, as had come to be expected, was not attired in a dress of any sort. Much like her brother, her clothes clung to her like a second skin fashioned of black leather. A thick, gold necklace stood out against the high-collared tunic she wore. It was fashioned in the likeness of a snake eating its own tail; its emerald eyes glinted in the afternoon sunlight.

Her blonde hair was swept back, making her sharp, angular features stand out remarkably. Despite the heat, she, too, wore a cloak - one of very similar fashion to her brother's.

The third of the herd kept close on Odette's heels, clearly looking for all the world as though he wished to be anywhere else but where he was. His normally soft, floppy, brown hair was slicked back in well-done mimicry of his elder siblings. His black tunic was closely fitted, though stretched looser than Odette's, as his sleeves still wrinkled in the slight wind. Golden gauntlets were affixed to both wrists; coiled snakes with sapphire eyes decorated the pieces in a most dramatic fashion. His cloak, much like Moriah's, was affixed with a snake pin; it bellowed out behind him as the wind started to pick up its efforts.

"They don't look happy," Penelope whispered.

The rest of the first-years found themselves in silent agreement, choosing to dumbly nod as they watched the small procession continue closer.

"Where do you think they're off to?" Fynn asked.

"Looks like they're dressed for a funeral," Albie commented wryly.

Godryk shrugged. "Moriah and Odette *always* look like that."

"Noel normally doesn't," Georgie argued. "If they've got him dressed like that, I think it's because something's going on."

"I think I know what it is," Lux commented.

The children all turned to regard the tall, red-haired girl curiously.

Renwyn quirked a brow and queried, "What then?"

Lux turned slightly, pointing out toward the shoreline whereupon there could be seen a ship quickly approaching the island. "Look at the banners they're flying."

The ship approaching was grand in its dimensions; its large, black sails fluttered in the afternoon sea-winds. From its masts, there flew banners that furled in the salty spray, bearing upon their black fields the golden snake of House Mordray.

Fynn shuffled through the group and peered insistently toward the harbor. "Mordray banners," he said to no one in particular as he remained, squinting through the sunlight, regarding the ship as it continued its approach.

"What's a Mordray ship doing here?" wondered Albie, crossing his arms over his chest and watching the ship sail closer.

Without another word, Fynn took off in a sprint toward the harbor, heading back the way they'd just come. He was mindful not to trip over the cobbles of the road that led back down to the docks, but his excitement was spurring him on with such force that he couldn't help but clumsily stumble here and there. He sped along, racing toward the docks until he was stopped by Drake snatching his shoulder and hauling him backward.

"Sir?" Fynn asked as he whirled around to face his instructor.

"And where are we off to?" Drake inquired dutifully.

Having been released, Fynn made a show of smoothing the wrinkles of his tunic, not looking his instructor in the eyes for some while. When he did, there was still a lingering air of sheer and unbridled happiness. "I saw the ship from the road and wanted to be here when they arrived," explained the prince.

"Oh?"

Fynn nodded. "Moriah…I mean, the lord commander, told me my sister would be arriving earlier than everyone else for the games." He looked in the direction of the ship and continued, "She's been staying with Emrys Mordray. I assumed, given the banners I saw, that she'd be on that ship." He bit down on his lower lip, chewing anxiously as he toed at the stony ground beneath his boots. "It's been a while, sir, since I've seen my sister, you see."

"It's been a while since any of your year mates have seen their families," Drake countered. Gone was his usual geniality, replaced by a dourness Fynn was finding most unappealing. "Shouldn't you be eating in the Hall by now? You realize, whether she arrives now or not, you will still be attending *all* your lessons?"

Nodding respectfully, the boy assured, "I do, sir."

"I thought you'd be hungry after our little sailing lesson," commented the instructor idly.

Fynn shrugged. "I am, sir. But…well, I just want to say hello to her before I head back up to the castle. If…if that's amenable to you, sir?"

"As long as you arrive to your next lesson on time," Drake began, "I'll allow it."

The boy beamed. "Thank you, sir!"

Before Fynn could race off, he felt his tunic once more ensnared in Drake' hold, keeping him still. "You'll wait here, however. I'm sure the docks will be busy while they get settled."

"Right," mumbled Fynn resignedly. "I'll wait here, sir."

"Good lad." Drake smiled before taking his leave.

Fynn remained where he'd been apprehended by his instructor. He was on the edge of the harbor, still standing upon the last remnants of the cobbled road that lead to the castle. He was close enough to the water to smell the salt sprinkling the balmy air. The breeze blew through his sweaty hair, washing over his warm skin, cooling him immeasurably and making the afternoon's weather a bit more tolerable. He sat, legs extended out in front of him, and watched as the ship drew nearer.

"Waiting for your sister, eh?"

"Nan!" Fynn smiled in greeting, seeing the old woman tottering toward him and Minnie skipping along at her heels. "Minnie." He held out his arms for the girl.

She didn't disappoint. At the sight of the prince sitting upon the ground with his arms wide, Minnie jolted forward and lunged, throwing herself into his welcoming arms and clinging to him, tiny arms curling around his neck. "Fynny!" she squealed with glee.

Fynn allowed the girl to settle on his lap, her arms still slung around him, as they both set about to watching the waves lazily roll over the shore. Gently, Fynn pushed a stray curl from Minnie's face, watching as her eyes lit up when she saw the ship inching closer, the golden snake emblazed upon its black banner now positively shining in the sunlight. Nan remained standing just behind Fynn, towering over the children as she also watched in delight as the ship approached its destination.

The three Mordrays made their way down the road and as they headed toward the docks, they spied the trio before the harbor watching the ship draw nearer. Moriah stopped at the sight of Nan and Minnie, adjusting his course to approach them. With a nod and a smile to the old woman, Moriah knelt before Fynn, eyes twinkling as Minnie broke into a toothy smile at his arrival. The prince relented his hold on the girl and she clambered with enthusiasm to Moriah, crawling into his arms as he straightened up, adjusting her weight comfortably against his side; her tiny arms were thrown over his shoulders and her cheek nestled against his chest.

"Minnie, darling," Moriah purred, running a hand through her honey hair, "how are we this afternoon?"

She grinned happily. "Great!"

"Glad to hear it," the lord commander said softly.

Odette found her way to Moriah's side. She reached up to absentmindedly trail her hand through the blonde curls tumbling over Minnie's slender back, her green eyes cast outward toward the harbor. "They'll be docking soon," Odette commented dully, still watching the ship, lulled by gentle waves and a fair push of wind, creep closer to the harbor.

Noel was the last of the three siblings to find his way to the huddled group, comfortably insinuating himself next to Nan with a beaming grin upon his fair features. "Nan, it's been a while," he said easily.

The elderly woman nodded. "You don't come 'round to the town much these days."

The young man chuckled warmly. "Entirely my fault, really," he assured. "I'll be sure to make more of an effort to stop in."

A wrinkled hand settled over Noel's back, softly tracing circles as she replied, "It's been a long few months for all of you, I'm sure. But Minnie certainly misses you."

At the mention of her name, the girl's head whirled around from the pillow it'd found upon Moriah's chest; deep, brown eyes lit up at the sudden appearance of Noel. Her arms disentangled from Moriah's shoulders and spread out, hands clasping at the air, beckoning Noel forward. He obliged and with a shake of the head, Moriah deposited the child into his brother's waiting arms.

Much as she'd done with Moriah, Minnie clutched tightly to Noel's neck, her legs wound around his sides, her cheek smashed comfortably over his chest. "Missed you," she whispered.

"Missed you too." Noel smiled as he held the girl tightly.

Fynn stood and straightened, eyeing Minnie for a moment longer before sidling beside Moriah. Softly, he nudged the man with his shoulder, nodding his head toward the approaching ship; he kept his voice low. "I suppose you're the welcoming party?"

Moriah's hand fell over Fynn's shoulder; long fingers curled in the material of the boy's uniform. He gave the prince a gentle shove forward, urging him on. As the two started by Odette, departing from the group, Moriah leaned down and whispered into his sister's ear, "Stay here with them. I'll take the boy to the docks. We'll head back to the castle together."

Odette nodded, eyeing Moriah for a moment longer. She watched her brother and the prince proceed to the docks, steadily getting further and further from where they'd all huddled.

Once alone with the prince, Moriah's features took on a rather more amused look, his green eyes sparkling as he asked, "Shouldn't you be attending a lesson?"

"Sailing just finished. Everyone was headed back to the castle." Fynn shrugged. "I told Lord Shoregore that Fiona was arriving, and I wanted to meet her when she got here."

"And that excuse was enough for Drake?"

"Well," Fynn continued sheepishly, "I promised I would make it to my next lesson on time, no matter what."

A fine, black brow arched as Moriah prodded, "Do you plan to keep that promise?"

Fynn bit down upon his lower lip, smirking as he did so; pale eyes rolled upward to meet Moriah's unwavering stare. "Do you plan on making me?" the prince ventured boldly.

"It wouldn't do for you to miss lessons," reasoned the man in black.

Deflated, the boy sighed. "So, you'll be sending me along, then?"

"I never said as much," argued Moriah flatly.

"Oh."

"If you're late, I'll escort you." The lord commander smiled coyly. "Your next lesson is with Nyle, yes?"

Fynn nodded.

"Then it shouldn't be a problem."

Fynn's voice pitched lower as he muttered, "I wouldn't say that. That man doesn't exactly *like* me, if you haven't noticed."

"Oh," chuckled Moriah darkly, "I've noticed. But really, Fynneas, he doesn't *like* most people."

"Seems to like you," grumbled the boy.

"Yes." Moriah nodded curtly. "Yes, he does. Which is exactly why your late arrival won't be much of an issue if I arrive as your escort."

"Thank you."

Moriah gave Fynn another push forward, dully saying, "Don't make being late to your lessons a habit."

"I won't," assured Fynn as his pace increased.

The ship was docking; large ropes were tossed down from the deck to the piers, people bustled about, there was shouting from all directions coming from the docks and the deck alike. It all served to stoke the boy's enthusiasm. With a last glance to Moriah and an approving nod from the man, Fynn took off in a dash toward the ship. He went bounding recklessly into the harbor proper, careening from the structures lining the shore to the docks, deftly dodging the rope laid about and the people rushing this way and that. The gangplank was lowered, and people began disembarking at just the moment Fynn arrived before the ship.

In all his excitement, Fynn hadn't noticed that Moriah had caught up to him. Though, Fynn couldn't quite picture Moriah hurriedly sprinting off anywhere. He was more than a little curious as to how the man seemed to always just appear places but pushed the thought aside for another time. The prince stood, eyes wide and shining in the sunlight, eagerly anticipating his sister's appearance. Moriah stayed just at his back, standing stiff and resolute, a tall pillar of black set against the crisp emeralds and golds and sapphires of the island's tableau.

The first noble to make their way down the gangplank was a small woman, slender in build with light brown hair that wound in limp curls over her thin shoulders and down her back. The paleness of her skin was accentuated by the deep black of her dress and the long, tightly tailored sleeves stretching down her arms, revealing only small, long fingered hands with nails stained a dark red. The thin, pale column of her throat was adorned by a golden necklace in much the same fashion that Odette wore, though the eyes of the snake hereupon the woman's neck were a shining sapphire rather than Odette's emeralds. The slender neck gave way to a rounded face with pink cheeks and full lips; large, blue eyes like a doe's sat beneath thin brows.

There was a familiar sharpness to the woman's eyes that caught Fynn's attention and he made the connection. He leaned backward, closer to Moriah, and whispered, "Your sister?"

"Yes. Emrys."

Fynn guessed, "Older?"

"Yes."

Just behind Emrys trailed the familiar personage of Fiona. Whereas Emrys looked like a shadow gliding down the plank, Fiona was like the summer born into human form. Her pale blue gown matched the sea, her black hair was pulled back and tamed as best it could be. As if sensing Fynn's attention upon her, her warm blue eyes sought him out there, waiting upon the pier. She smiled fondly at the boy and hastened to meet him.

Both women approached, Fiona with a blossoming grin with all the warmth of the afternoon sun in the south, and Emrys with a reserved expression verging on disinterest.

All at once Fiona was upon Fynn, scooping the boy into her embrace in a crushing hug, burying her forehead against his shoulder as she held to him tightly. "You've grown!" she cooed as she drew back from him, combing her hand through his sweaty hair. "You've grown so much! Oh, and happy birthday!"

Laughing, Fynn shook his head. "I haven't grown *that* much, Fi." He wiggled out of her hold, cheeks burning with embarrassment. "I'm still the shortest in my year."

"Never mind that," Fiona chided, slapping him on the shoulder. "You'll shoot up soon enough! But just look at you, Fynny. You look so much older."

As Emrys approached Moriah, he smirked. When she stood not a hair's breadth from him, he quirked a brow and glanced toward the royal siblings who still continued to fawn over one another as if they'd been apart for decades. "What? No hug for your dear, darling, little brother?" Moriah drawled, his deep voice all but dripping with sarcasm.

"We're not the hugging sort," Emrys replied coolly.

"I think Noel would have something to say about that," Moriah argued listlessly.

"Noel's always been a bit *odd*."

"Right you are there."

"And where, pray tell, *is* Noel?" Emrys inquired, peeking around in search of her more wayward sibling.

"With Dottie."

"And *where are* Noel and Dottie?" pressed Emrys, her annoyed gaze levering upward to meet the amused expression now adorning Moriah's visage.

"Just back a way," Moriah explained, still riveted by the meeting of Fiona and Fynn. "I told them to wait for us and that we'd all head up to the castle together."

"Surely you don't mean for me to walk all the way there," Emrys said.

"I think a little walk would do you some good," Moriah answered.

"A *little walk*? Morancy is on the other side of the island."

"A *long* walk then." Intense, green eyes rounded on the woman before him. Moriah's voice dipped lower as he whispered, "We've a great deal to discuss."

"More so than you know," Emrys added.

"Is that so?"

The elder of the siblings nodded back to the ship. Her gesture was keenly followed by Moriah's searching eyes, his curiosity quelled and replaced by vitriol at the sight that now greeted him. There upon the gangplank, making his way down at a most languid pace, was Ridley.

"What's *he* doing here?"

A note of unabashed detestation rang soundly in Moriah's question; so pungent was his displeasure at the sight of Ridley that Emrys found herself reeling closer to her brother, snatching his hand into hers tightly, and eyeing him evenly. *"Don't."* With her meager size and weight, she leaned against Moriah's side, imploring him to take a steadying step backward.

He relented without much prompting, though his piercing stare never wavered from Ridley's approaching figure.

Emrys' free arm snaked around Moriah's waist, holding him still. "Let's not make a scene," she softly urged.

As Ridley drew closer, Fynn peered past Fiona and watched the man coming their way. He knew instinctively that Ridley must be another Mordray. From the high collar of his shirt to the tip of his booted feet, he wore all black. Golden gauntlets encircled his arms; embossed snakes embellished their already lavish appeal. He was tall; that was for certain. Though not quite as tall as Moriah, but easily taller than Noel. His shoulders were broad, more muscled than either of his brothers. His jaw was more squared, harsher in its angles. His nose was long, straight. Thick, black hair was haphazardly combed to the side, though still managed to stick out in odd directions here and there. There was, Fynn thought, a far less controlled air about this man. His eyes, the prince noted steadfastly, were near as unsettling as Moriah's had been the first time he'd met the man. Though not the piercing, unnatural green of his brother's or Odette's, Ridley's tawny, nearly golden, eyes shone beneath thick, black brows. In the sunlight that bore down, they sparkled like two embers, crackling in stark contrast to the ghostly white complexion of his countenance.

The young man stopped before the prince and princess, bowing his head to Fiona with the most meager of smirks worming over his lips before turning to look down at Fynn. He bowed more acutely before the prince, humbling himself as was his place to do so. Though, his features retained an amused twinkle about them that bore his humility to be false. "My prince," he greeted. His voice was as deep and cool as Moriah's. "It's an honor to meet you at last. I've heard nothing but great things from your sister." He glanced in Fiona's direction, smirking more so, before once again looking to Fynn. "I do apologize for my rudeness, sire. I seem to have forgotten my manners. It was a long journey, you see," he offered casually. "My name is Ridley, Ridley Mordray."

"The pleasure is mine," Fynn dutifully replied.

And with that, Ridley stole by and headed toward his siblings. Fynn watched carefully, observing the way Ridley chanced one more parting glance over his shoulder toward Fiona before decidedly turning away. And he observed, with mild annoyance, the way Fiona's cheeks flushed at the hint of attention. "Right," muttered Fynn. He didn't look to his sister again, not caring to see the doting look ebbing into her summer eyes as she watched Ridley traipse by. "We should be heading back," the prince said as he followed in Ridley's wake.

It was Odette who saw the procession of figures, most of whom clad in black, headed toward them. "They're coming," she announced.

Nan was just behind her and began to bustle and coo, pleased at the thought of seeing Emrys again after such a long while.

Noel, still holding Minnie, held on just a bit tighter as he edged closer to Odette. Side by side, the two watched as the small party crested over the line of piers and crossed the harbor toward them.

"Is that…Ridley?" asked Noel quietly.

Odette nodded; her eyes narrowed.

"What's *he* doing here?"

"I don't know," she answered dully. "But he isn't our problem, is he?"

"What do you mean?"

"If Emrys saw fit to bring him along, then he's all *her* responsibility," Odette replied as she started forward to meet them.

"Let's see how that works out," grumbled Noel, shaking his head. Both he and Nan followed behind Odette, keeping a few steps between themselves and the irritated looking lady air brigadier general.

"Did I see Riddles along with them?" Nan wondered softly.

"Yes," Noel responded, distracted.

"Were you expecting him?"

Noel murmured, "Not at all."

Emrys, still holding tightly to Moriah, brightened when she saw Odette. Peeling herself from her brother, she greeted her sister with nod. "It's been a while."

Odette stopped just in front of her sister, towering over her elder sibling as it were. She brushed an errant hair behind her ear as she smiled her agreement. "Two years."

"Is that all?" jested Emrys.

"So, it seems." Green eyes flitted over Emrys' shoulder to rest upon Ridley. "I see you've brought *him* along."

"I have." Emrys wasn't the least bit ruffled by her sister's obvious displeasure.

"Any particular reason you'd like to share? Or did inciting further chaos on this island seem like a fun bit of sport for you?"

"Come now," chided Emrys dully, "you're acting almost as childish as Moriah."

"Nonsense." Odette smirked, still watching Ridley closely. "Ridley still seems to be in one piece, so Moriah must've behaved quite well."

"For now," muttered Emrys as she proceeded to greet Noel and Nan, combing her hand through Minnie's hair affectionately as she began a muted conversation with the two.

"Big sister." Ridley sauntered over to Odette, arms outstretched. "It's been too long."

As her brother's arms enclosed around her, Odette did little more than stand still as a statue, rigid in his embrace. "Ridley."

"Oh, has living on this *dreadful* island with Moriah made *you* frigid as well?" Ridley laughed.

Fynn was quietly watching the uncomfortably cold welcoming take place when a familiar hand closed around his shoulder, stealing him away. Looking up, he wasn't surprised to find Moriah looming just behind him, pulling him back. Fynn sighed, turning to Fiona he offered a small smile. "I've got to get back to my lessons, Fi. But I'll see you later."

The princess once more ran her hand through her brother's hair, smiling down at him. "I'll see you for supper, yes?"

"Promise." He grinned as he turned around, following Moriah's beck as they headed up the hilly path toward Nyle's lessons.

The prince had a hard time keeping pace with Moriah as they headed back, getting closer to the castle. The man's strides, always having been long and elegant, seemed rushed and far more stilted than they normally were. Fynn hurried and noticed, when he chanced a peek up at Moriah, that the man's eyes were narrowed, and his brows were knitted together. There was a tension, too, that had gripped his shoulders and over-straightened his back.

"Moriah," Fynn began carefully.

"Hmm?"

"Are you...alright?"

"Fine."

Fynn nodded. "Right, then."

Nyle's insistent yelling could be heard not far off from where the pair continued in silence closer to the clearing. The furtive grumbles of ten first-years soon followed in the withering wake of Lord Humbert's ravings. As they had anticipated, Moriah and Fynn came upon the lesson late. All eyes turned expectantly toward the duo, curiosity sparking in many of them as they noticed the murderous look emblazoned upon Moriah's normally apathetic visage.

"Moriah," Nyle said, spying the man coming closer, the small prince trailing just behind him. "I see you've brought the boy along for his lesson?"

"Yes." Moriah reached back, snatched Fynn by the collar of his uniform and all but threw him before Nyle. "I apologize for his tardiness, my lord. It was, you see, entirely my fault. Please don't blame him."

Nyle's leathery hand closed over Fynn's wrist and pulled him along, shoving him toward his year mates. He waved with a flourish of his wrinkly hand. "Not at all, my boy. No harm done."

Fynn stumbled uneasily over to Godryk, nervously looking back between Moriah and Nyle. The red-haired boy took up beside the prince; leaning close, he whispered, "What did you do to make Moriah so mad?"

"It wasn't *me*," insisted Fynn with a fervent shake of the head.

"*Who* then?"

"I've got *so* much to tell you," Fynn replied quietly.

"After lessons then?"

Fynn nodded.

The afternoon pressed on in much the same fashion that all of Nyle's lessons proceeded; a great deal of screaming was had on the part of the instructor who, on occasion, saw fit to lob rocks at the children when he felt their attention was not wholly trained on the task at hand, which was creating an emergency shelter that would be sustainable for a week's stay.

When at last the torture of Lord Humbert's lessons concluded, the children were shooed off back to the castle with a flippant wave of the hand and a tersely snapped, "I expect better of you all next I see you! Lest you'll all die of exposure because of your ineptitude! Now, be gone with you, children."

The band of eleven trudged along in a closely-knit pack, most of them huddling close to Fynn with excited expressions.

Godryk was the first to speak, breaking the anxious whispering as he asked, "Well, where were you off to earlier?"

"My sister's come to the island a bit ahead of the rest of the nobles," Fynn said. "She wanted to get to see the island and spend some time here before the games started."

"If that's all, why did Moriah look so mad when the two of you showed up?" asked Georgie. "He's never looked *that* angry...that I've seen anyway."

Fynn shook his head, brushing back sweaty strands of hair as he answered, "I never said *that was all.*"

Penelope elbowed him playfully, asking, "What then?"

"My sister didn't arrive alone," the prince answered. "She was staying with Moriah's older sister Emrys. I knew as much before I left from Batsbeckon. But I suppose no one anticipated that Emrys was going to bring along their brother too. Moriah looked a bit…furious, I suppose, when he saw him. Odette didn't look too pleased about it either."

"*Another* brother?" Firiel questioned.

"Is he…well…handsome like Moriah and Noel?" Georgie asked, a pink tinge coloring her cheeks.

Penelope inquired, "Dark hair and green eyes like Moriah? Or brown hair and blue eyes like Noel?"

Albie snorted. "Why does any of *that* matter?"

Georgie shrugged. "Only curious, is all."

"*Well,*" prodded Penelope.

Shaking his head, exasperated, Fynn huffed, "Black hair…gold-ish eyes."

"Gold?" repeated Firiel. "That's curious, isn't it?"

"Well, what was *this* one like?" Ollie asked.

"Don't know, really," Fynn said. "Didn't get a good sense of him. I was trapped, really, between my sister and Moriah for most of the walk back from the docks. I didn't say more than hello to him."

Godryk mused, "So is *he* the reason Moriah looked ready to tear someone's throat out?"

"I think so," Fynn speculated. "They didn't seem to get on too well, like I said. But Ridley, that's his name by the way, didn't really *do* anything."

The first-years walked through the entryway, still chattering in hushed voices amongst themselves. They continued on through the corridor, headed toward the Hall where they collectively stopped upon seeing Hollyn standing by the doors. He had his arm bound in a sling, the other arm noticeably still bandaged. There was a far healthier color to him than there had been recently; his normal spark of keen interest once more glinting in his dark eyes. The first-years stopped, waiting as the prince darted over to them. Seamlessly, they enveloped him into their ranks, heads all bowed together, eager to hear whatever information Hollyn had been waiting to impart.

"I take it you know, then?" asked Hollyn, his question directed toward Fynn.

"About Emrys and Ridley's arrival?" Fynn ventured.

"More so about Moriah's mood," Hollyn corrected.

"We've been told," Georgie commented.

Penelope added, "Fynn says he's mad about Ridley?"

"They don't get on well," replied Hollyn.

"Do you know why?" Renwyn questioned.

"No more than you lot, I suspect," Hollyn answered flatly.

"Have you seen them?" asked Hogan.

Hollyn nodded. "Moriah, Odette, and Emrys are in the Hall. I haven't seen Noel or Ridley."

"Should we...go in?" Ollie, fidgeting nervously as he peeked over the group toward the Hall's closed doors, inquired.

"Well we're not going to stand out here and starve, are we?" Renwyn snorted as he righted himself, pulled from the group, and headed toward the doors. "Stop being so dramatic, all of you."

When Renwyn pushed through the doors, he hadn't expected the graveyard-like silence of the Hall to smash over him like a wave crashing into a rocky shore. He was staggered by the uncomfortable, stifling stillness of the room, which normally would be bustling and loud as everyone gathered to eat. He stood, stock still, waiting for the others to join him. And they reluctantly did so. As a group, feeling more comfortable in their dozen-strong flock, they carefully made their way to their usual seats.

Each of the twelve sat down almost gingerly, too unsettled by the tension-filled silence of the room to do more than pass anxious glances between themselves. Plates were placed before each of the children and soon their meals were set down, piles of meats and fruits heaped onto the saucers and their goblets filled with water. Still, not one of them made a move for their food.

Penelope looked around and then asked, "Fynn, where's your sister? I don't see her."

"Does she look like you?" Georgie wondered aloud.

Fynn shrugged. "I don't know. I don't think so, really." He glanced around the Hall in search of Fiona but came away disappointed at the realization that she was, indeed, absent.

However, Fynn's now wandering gaze found Moriah seated at the Paladin table, arms braced against the surface, shoulders tensed as though he were ready to pounce forward at a moment's notice. Pale eyes lingered for a moment and then shifted to the Archer Brigade's table where he saw Odette staring blankly at a plate full of untouched food, one hand white-knuckle-curled around her knife. Unsettled by the sight of the lady air brigadier general glaring her meal to death, Fynn's attention shifted to Odette's right where Emrys sat. The woman, unlike her siblings, seemed to be enjoying her meal easily enough. However, the same gripping unease that seemed to have usurped both Moriah and Odette had also clearly, to Fynn's minor surprise, taken a firm hold of Benadykt, who presently sat at the Cavalry table with a look of strained frustration, eyes narrowed and nearly feral looking.

"Did Moriah, by chance, murder Ridley while we were out?" whispered Firiel.

Renwyn nodded shakily. "They certainly are acting as though someone's died."

"Or they're *plotting* a murder," interjected Hogan.

"Could go either way," mumbled Albie. "Look at them. I'm not sure who looks more ready to kill—Moriah or Odette."

"Is that Emrys, then, beside Odette?" asked Georgie.

Fynn nodded.

Lux mused aloud, "She looks a bit like Noel."

"Why does *that* matter?" Godryk asked, quirking a brow.

Shrugging her shoulders carelessly, Lux answered, "It doesn't. I've just always thought it odd that none of them seem to look anything alike."

"She's right," agreed Penelope.

"Odd really," commented Georgie.

"Where do you suppose Noel and Ridley are?" asked Ollie.

"If I had to guess," began Hollyn, eyeing the scene unfolding all around them, "Noel's probably doing his best to keep Ridley as far away from Moriah as possible. That would be the *smart* thing to do."

The sound of the doors creaking open was tantamount to thunder as it echoed through the impossibly quiet Hall. Every student snapped their attention towards the newest arrivals as they entered. Noel did his best to make himself seem as small as possible, hunching his shoulders even more so when he caught Moriah's burning eyes tracing over him. He inched his way down the Hall as silently as possible, refusing to look his sisters in the eyes as he seated himself at the Paladin table, nervously shifting his weight in his seat across from his brother. But it was the second arrival that ignited the curious whispers of the onlooking students.

Ridley strode into the Hall with none of the passive trepidation that Noel had exhibited; rather, the young man stood straight and walked with the same ethereal elegance and long strides the students had come to equate to Moriah, more so than the other Mordray siblings. And so, they watched with rapt attention as this young man clad all in black and adorned in brilliant gold gauntlets, with wildly untamed, black hair, and frightfully sharp, amber eyes, strolled in amongst them. Much to their collective surprise, he seated himself beside the still fidgeting Noel.

"Well," Hollyn lamely drawled as he watched the entrance of one Ridley Mordray unfurl before his very eyes, "no one ever accused Noel of being the *smart* one, I suppose."

"Moriah," began Ridley easily, nodding toward the quite full plate before his eldest brother, "you haven't touched your food at all."

"I'm not hungry," Moriah answered wanly.

"What a waste," admonished the youngest Mordray.

Moriah pushed his plate before Ridley. "Have at it, then."

Idly picking at a piece of fruit with plain disinterest, Ridley sighed. "Alas, I can't say I'm terribly hungry either."

"Come now, Ridley," cooed Moriah with feigned concern. "You've had a long journey here. Surely you *must* be hungry."

With an exaggerated flick of the wrist, Ridley cast the plate aside, uncaring as food spilled from its porcelain surface unto the table, some fruit rolling from the surface's edge and falling to the ground. "No really, I'm not *hungry* at all. I've come for your *company*, of course, big brother."

Noel's hand clapped over Ridley's, fingers curling around his younger brother's wrist tightly. He turned blue eyes toward his sibling, wordlessly willing him to behave. His silent pleas, however, were met with chilly indifference.

Jerking his arm free of Noel's clutches, Ridley shrugged boyishly. "No matter." He sighed. "You've never been the best of company to keep, now have you?"

"No, I suppose not," the elder Mordray answered, bored.

"Well, see," beamed Ridley, "there's *something* we can agree on, at long last." Eyes that had previously seemed muted now bristled with light as they settled upon Moriah. A certain depth laced Ridley's voice as he whispered, "It's always nice when we can get along."

The day proceeded much the same as it had prior to the arrival of two more Mordrays and a princess and, for that, many of the instructors found themselves eternally grateful. Though Moriah and Odette continued to skulk about with furious expressions as the day wore on, everyone else seemed to ease into a comfortable sense of normality.

The lord and vice lord paramounts busied themselves with talking end-lessly to Fiona, much to the annoyance of Fynn, who grumbled his way through his later lessons and evening meal, disdain clouding his normally sparkling eyes when he noticed that Fiona was noticeably absent from the assembly in the Hall. Though he happily found that none of the Mordrays were present either and, though he was curious as to what the relationship between the siblings was like, he was quite pleased to enjoy his meal without the palpable, nearly oppressive, tension that had taken hold earlier that day. Yes, he quite enjoyed the easy conversation he held with Ollie, Albie, and Godryk about the upcoming games and what they thought it would be like. Fynn found himself even more delighted, though he fought quite hard to keep his expression as impassive as he could, when Hollyn arrived, only a few minutes late, and seated himself at Fynn's left.

Pushing his plate away, Fynn sighed and leaned back in his seat. The day, truly, had been a tedious one, and so he found himself wanting nothing more than to retire to his bed and sleep it off. With a shake of the head, he knew that was not how his evening would unfold. Rather, he supposed, he would go off and try and find, or need be rescue, Fiona from the para-mounts. He'd missed her and he realized that he missed her more so when she was in the very same castle but seemingly not permitted to join the stu-dents for their supper. He combed his hand through his hair; it was sweaty, smeared and matted with dirt and mud from a day full of lessons out in the heat and the wild. He stood, nodding to his friends as he took early leave of the evening meal and headed toward the tower.

Intent upon changing into something less grimy, Fynn stopped by his dormitory. As he carelessly tossed aside his ratty tunic, he spotted the trunk full of Fiona's letters and presents tucked neatly beside his bed. Kneeling before it, he traced his hand longingly over the sharp angles of the box, smiling warmly as he recalled reading each and every one of her letters to him. Standing, he quickly sorted through his clothing and slipped into one of the few tunics he had remaining that did not bear stains of mud or blood, or rips and holes. Pleased that he looked moderately presentable, Fynn swept from the room, down the stairs, across the commons, and out the door. The liveliness of his steps increased as he wound his way down the tower and burst into the corridor, bouncing down the hall and rounding the corner.

Fynn had a hunch as to where Fiona may be, and found that he wasn't so sure of arriving, unannounced and uninvited, to the paramount wing.

Steeling himself, he continued along through the castle, deftly making his way through the stony labyrinth of impossibly similar walls all spangled with vibrant portraits of war heroes, monarchs, mythical figures, and monsters. He'd never been to the paramount wing in all his many months attending Morancy; there had never been an occasion. He knew where it was; they all did. But, to go there seemed an entirely new sort of adventure.

Fynn supposed that he must have arrived at the correct place when he saw the subjects of the many portraits hanging upon the walls change to the likenesses of the many lords and vice lords paramounts who had run the school. Thick curtains of deep purple hung from golden valances set over large, arching windows. There were long stretches of the corridor floors that were adorned by narrow carpets of dark purple, golden helle-bores embroidered all over them. There were vases of gold with brilliant purple flourishes painted over their smooth surfaces; black roses bloomed from their curved brims and stood proud, statuesque, in the multi-colored moonlight that had begun streaming in through the stained-glass windows.

A large, arched doorway loomed at the far end of the corridor. Fynn hoped it was the door that would lead him to where Fiona may have found herself stashed away. Approaching, Fynn's attention was fixed to the in-scription that was carved into the dark wood of the door, 'At All Costs.' The prince quirked a brow at the motto. Similar as it was to the Morancy motto, it seemed to bear an almost darker meaning. Shrugging it off, Fynn knocked on the doors and waited.

One door opened only so, permitting the prince the smallest sliver of a face peeking from the other side.

"Yes?"

"Umm," Fynn began, unsure. "I'm here to see my sister?"

"Your name?"

"Fynneas Fog."

The door opened enough to allow the boy to enter and so he did, cross-ing the threshold and nearly jumping out of his own skin at the booming sound of the door closing just on his heels. A frail looking man stood beside the door. He was tall, bent over some with humped shoulders and long, skeletal arms that dangled nearly lifelessly at his bony sides.

The man eyed Fynn for a moment longer and then asked, "The prince?"

Fynn nodded. "I am. Well, one of them, at least."

"Your sister is dining with the lord paramount and vice lord paramount presently," the man said, his hazel eyes lazily trailing from Fynn toward a small notch in the endless line of pale stones wherein Fynn spied a smaller doorway. "Should I be telling the lords you've called, or would you prefer me to announce your presence?"

"The latter," Fynn replied a smidge unevenly. "If you would."

Nodding, the man began shuffling toward the smaller door, calling back to Fynn, "Wait here."

Left to himself as the stooped skeleton of a man disappeared behind the smaller door down the hall, Fynn took the time to look around. He stood in a rounded room of pale stone floors whereupon more garish purple rugs were set about, more vases and more roses lined the pale walls that hosted the stern looking features of people Fynn didn't recognize. As he waited, he toed at the ground and gave an audible sigh, scowling as moments drew into minutes and minutes trailed by, leaving him bored. He brushed his hair back from his face as he shook his head with exasperation.

The sound of the small door opening drew Fynn's attention. He whirled around, greeted by the sight of the stooping man holding the door for the lords and his sister, who ambled through in a most sour looking procession. Fiona seemed the most irritated of the lot as they approached. Though, when she finally noticed that it was her brother who'd come calling, her eyes lit up and she darted to him, pulling him close.

She leaned down and whispered, "They said someone had come asking for me, but he didn't have the decency to tell me it was you." She huffed, leaning away from Fynn and righting herself. "I'm sorry I couldn't meet you for supper."

Fynn shrugged, smiling as he stayed close to Fiona's side. "It's alright. I understand."

"Awfully boring, they are," she murmured as she gave the demurest nod she could manage in the direction of the far slower approaching lords.

"You've *no* idea." Fynn laughed.

Maekon Malcourt and Indigo Mandark, their heads bowed together as the muttered amongst themselves in hushed tones, drew closer to the royal siblings until they joined the duo. Peering down at the two curiously, Maekon quirked a brow as he watched Fynn shift his weight from foot to foot.

"Fynneas," greeted the lord paramount. "What brings you here at such an hour?"

"I didn't mean to intrude, my lord," began the prince carefully. "I was only looking for my sister. This seemed the most likely place she'd be. I didn't mean to interrupt anything."

Maekon grinned a lopsided sort of grin that unsettled Fynn as he took a step closer, clapping his large hand firmly over the boy's back. "Nonsense!" He turned his beaming eyes toward Fiona for a moment before once more studying the boy. "We've kept her far too long, wouldn't you say, Indie?"

Indigo nodded curtly. "Yes. We didn't realize the late hour."

"Not at all." Fiona smiled coolly.

"Well," Maekon said, taking Fiona's hand in his, bowing gallantly, and placing a chaste kiss to her knuckles, "it's been a pleasure to finally meet you, princess. We hope you'll do us the honor of dining with us again during your stay."

"Of course, my lords." There was the slightest tinge of frustration coloring her voice, but Fiona did well to maintain a sort of put-upon smile, her eyes flicking between the two men.

"Have a good night, princess," bid Indigo.

"You as well," she replied.

Her arm snaked around her brother's shoulders, turning him away from the lords. They headed toward the large, double doors. The stooping man with his gangly arms was quick to dart across the small hall and open the door for the siblings, nodding politely as they went by, and then closing the door sharply at their heels. Fiona laughed under her breath. "Lovely, isn't he?"

"Which one?" grumbled Fynn with a shake of his head.

"Malcourt is certainly an odd fellow," began the princess. They proceeded from the paramount wing. "It's my estimation he's more interested in prestige than anything else." She tapped her chin with her forefinger thoughtfully, continuing, "Mandark, well he seems more involved with the school than Malcourt. Although, I can't say I'm *overly* fond of him either." She laughed. "But it's that servant fellow, Chippy, I think Mandark said his name was, that I *really* don't like. He's a bit creepy."

"Honestly, I've never even *seen* him before," Fynn commented. "But I've never been to this *wing before* either."

"Really?"

Fynn nodded. "There's never been a reason to come this way."

"Oh," thought Fiona aloud. "I hadn't thought of it that way." She looked all about the corridor, fleetingly casting a glance to the portraits all around them with their eyes that seemed to follow the pair as they continued their journey from the wing. "Do you *have* a favorite place in the castle?"

"Not *in* the castle, really," joked Fynn. Noticing Fiona arching a black brow, he added, "I could show you. If you *like*, that is."

Her arm disentangled form him and her hand stole into his, keeping him at her side. Though Fynn hadn't grown much, Fiona did notice that he walked a bit straighter, his shoulders more squared, strides more purposeful and less bouncy, less childish. It was a subtle change, she knew, for there was still that blinking bit of mischief that glimmered in his eyes here and there, and the same cheeky smirk she'd seen occasionally gracing his features since she'd arrived on the island. But, as she regarded the boy at her side, he certainly wasn't the same boy she'd seen off months ago.

She smiled fondly. "I think I'd like that." With a firm squeeze of his hand, she said, "Lead the way."

Their trek through the many intersecting halls of the castle was carried out at a most leisurely pace; the time was spent in amiable conversation, mostly focused on the many subjects of the varied portraits and how they pertained to history. When they'd reached the doorway that stood tucked away in the shadows just beside the far larger, far grander entryway of the castle, they slipped through into the night.

The stars above seemed endless, coloring the sky in a glinting silver, gleaming and glittering even more so as the moonlight flashed over the bejeweled sky in full once it wormed its way through the few clouds that lazily crept through the deep, blue night and the tangle of emerald leaves that canopied so much of the island. The summer was approaching and so the nights didn't bring about the same barely-there chill that Fynn had begun to miss. Instead, the air was warm and damp feeling; a slight breeze whistled by and ghosted over them.

Fynn, his sister's hand still in his own, led Fiona down the same pathway that Moriah had led him on his first day on the island. They climbed the same mossy stairs and came upon the balcony that the prince adored. The boy settled himself against the bannister; he looked out over the island and to the harbor on the other side, the sea spread out before them, the moonlight falling over blackened water, white light splashing over rolling waves in the distance.

Fiona stood beside him. Her breath hitched in her throat at the sight. "It's beautiful," she muttered as she leaned against the bannister with him, bracing herself on her elbows with her shoulders curling forward. She watched the island sleep, stretched out before them.

"I've missed you," Fynn admitted shyly, not looking at her.

"I've missed you too. But I wrote you letters."

Fynn nodded. "Moriah gave them all to me for my birthday. Thank you for writing to me. It—Well, it means a lot." He shifted his weight from foot to foot uneasily, not entirely sure how to proceed. There was a weightiness in his chest. He tried to swallow down the lump in his throat that threatened to strangle him. "It hasn't been easy here." He shook his head, continuing quickly, "I do like it. I've got friends. It's great to have so many people my age around. I like it, I do. But there have been times…that have been hard."

"What's happened?" Fiona asked. She laid one hand over his; her thumb gently traced indistinguishable patterns over his snowy skin. "Were you hurt?"

"You know I heal up fast." He laughed. There wasn't anything genuine in the laughter that tripped form his lips awkwardly; it was breathy and fake, and he hated it. "How much do you know about Morancy? Or…I suppose…how much do you know about Dier Island?"

"I suppose not as much as I should," she replied. "Why?"

"There are things here that scare me."

"What sort of *things*?"

"I've seen *things*, Fi." Fynn shuddered. "I've seen mermaids and skeletons and strange visions of strange people and strange places…visions of people I know and places I know…and there was this symbol I saw, too, that I can't stop thinking about."

"Mermaids live in the warmer waters," Fiona said as though it were the most obvious thing in the world. "Skeletons?"

"Well…not *skeletons*," Fynn said. "There were these bones and they… well…formed into a skeleton that attacked me."

"You're talking mad," Fiona chided, shaking her head and clucking with annoyance.

"No, really!" insisted Fynn. "Hollyn was there too. He can tell you. We were down in the catacombs…not on purpose or anything, but that's where we were when it happened."

"You said you had visions of people you knew?"

Fynn nodded.

"Who?"

"I saw Father," whispered Fynn weakly. "I saw him a few times, actually. And Mother."

Prodding more, Fiona asked, "And the symbol?"

"A nine-pointed star," he replied dully, not entirely expecting her to believe him. Sometimes, he too, found it hard to believe everything he'd seen since arriving on the island. "I saw it on the wax seal of the letters from Lot or *whatever* his name is. I saw it again, the same star, in the catacombs here under the island."

"I believe you." Fiona's voice was hardly more than a breathy whisper.
"What?"

"I *believe* you, Fynneas."

Stunned, Fynn's eyes went wide as he watched his sister at his side.
"You do?" He ran his hand through his hair. "I'm glad! Really…I am. I just
thought, well…I didn't think you'd believe all that."

Fiona stood straight, still staring out at the slumbering island, eyes lost
in the distance. "After all the strange things that happened at the capital?
How could I *not* believe you?"

"After the incident in the catacombs," explained Fynn, "I knew something was going on, something dark. It's something no one wants us knowing. I just don't know what. But Lot, that's not his name I know, but I don't
know what else to call him. He *knows*. I don't know what it is he knows, but
he knows more than he's telling me."

"You talk as though you've seen him since the bookshop," Fiona noted.

Fynn nodded. "I *have*. I told you, Fi, I've seen things…people…visions.
Call it what you want. I don't care. But I've spoken to Lot while I've been
here. He found me in a dream or something, but it felt so real. It *was* real. I
don't know what it is, but something's going on and he's involved."

"I may have found something," Fiona admitted quietly.

"You did?" Fynn inched closer to his sister, nudging her side with his
shoulder. "What was it?"

"I don't think Lot is who we should be looking for. Well, not in the way
we thought. You're right. He's involved in something, with whatever is going
on, *somehow* at least. But he's not who we *think* he is. It's *strange*. In all the
ledgers I looked over, any time anything particularly out of sorts happened,
there always seemed to be mention of a man involved. But it's never the
same *name*."

"What do you mean?"

"A merchant ship was destroyed, and the only survivor of the accident
said his captain, Braxas Linklatter, seemed to just have disappeared right
before the accident. Then there was a strange fire years ago at Lions Bay.
One of the dock boys said an old man saved him from the flames, an old
man he said was named Brandon Leatherby. Then, I found reference to
the murder of a family in the lower quarter. The man who reported the
murder to the King's Guard was named Branagh Luster. There was an incident outside Shiver Town many years ago. A man said he bore witness to
a stranger leading children out of the township with nothing more than a

song. Children that were never seen again. His name was recorded in some records at Godsreach. His name was Burt Limby. Strange, isn't it?"

"I don't get it," admitted Fynn.

"The names, Fynny. All of them have the same initials. B.L., just like Barnaby Lot from the bookshop that apparently never existed," Fiona explained.

Fiona reached into the sleeve of her dress and pulled from its material confines a crumpled piece of parchment. She handed it to her brother, still not looking to him. Her movements were chilled, almost as if she expected something frightening to bound out before her at any moment. "I kept looking all this time. I kept trying to find out what was going on. A few days before we left, I found this on my pillow."

Fynn looked down curiously at the mashed piece of parchment he now clutched. "What is this?"

"Read it."

The prince uncrumpled the parchment and held it out. He read—

Prettiest Princess Fiona,

You're so close. It's only a matter of time before you find the B.L. you're looking for.

Still staring at the parchment, Fynn said, "How are we supposed to know who the *right* B.L. is?"

"That's just it." Fiona beamed. "We know already!"

"We do?"

The princess nodded. "We do. Think about. Who's the monster Father used to tell stories about when we were little? The same stories *he* grew up hearing."

"Biel," Fynn answered numbly. "But he's just a story. *Ghosts* don't exist, Fi."

"Really? Everything odd that's happened to you and ghosts is where you choose to draw the line of disbelief? Come now, it makes sense. Biel was always a trickster in Father's stories. He always played games with people before he killed them or caused some sort of calamity."

"You *really* think it could be him?"

Fiona nodded. "I think so. I *really* do."

"Fiona," Fynn began. A dreadful weightiness came upon him again and breathing seemed a frightfully difficult endeavor. Each breath stung him; his lungs burned. "If it *was* the same Biel from Father's stories, do you think Father knew *he* was real and not just a fairytale? Do you think those stories were lessons...warnings, maybe?"

"Maybe." Fiona exhaled warily. "In those visions you had, what did he say to you?"

"Time." Fynn held onto the bannister before him as if it were a lifeline, as though at any moment there stood the remote possibility that he may slip from the very earth and be thrown into the emptiness of the space above. He didn't like that thought at all and so clung even tighter, knuckles going white as could be, to the bannister. "He told me about time. It's all around us...and yet, *we're here.*"

"That's very peculiar," commented the princess.

"Yes. I thought so too." Fynn hunched forward slightly. His heart beat thickly, drumming, thundering. He hated that feeling almost as much as the weightiness, the feeling that his heart would break apart his ribs like glass and rip right through his chest in some gory display of dramatics. Yes, he really hated the feeling. "I haven't really thought about it much since then. But it scared me, you know? It really scared me because he was right. Time is everywhere for all of us, it's always there...always existing...and yet, here we are...right here...right now...and we know nothing different, nothing more or less." Fynn was shaking. His shoulders jittered as he drew in long, suffering breaths. "I'm scared because I don't know what to think about all that. And I'm scared because I don't know what to think of everything else that's happened...things, *everything...nothing...*things won't ever be the same, Fi." Fynn's black hair tumbled in front of his eyes, obscuring his sight for only a moment before he brushed it back again. "Everything was so simple and then we went to Batsbeckon and it went to shit."

"That's certainly one way to phrase it," Fiona agreed.

"Have you seen things too?"

She shook her head. "No."

"Did you bring the book?"

"It's in my trunk. I've hidden it. No one knows I've brought it or that I even have it."

"Did you find anything else in it?"

The princess turned away from her brother and once more found herself drawn to looking out toward the sea. The hour was late and the waters before them, stretching off from the shore and the harbor at the far end of the island, seemed black. From where they stood high up on the balcony of the castle, it looked as though the island simply gave way into a vast expanse of blackness. It was as though the island were perched on the very edge of the world.

When Fiona spoke, her voice was low. "Hollyn's name was in the book."

"Hollyn's?"

"I saw it there as plainly as I saw your name." She drew in a lung-stretching breath. "I saw the Mordrays there too. *All nine* of their names are written in the book."

Fynn pondered, "The Mordrays make sense. But, why *Hollyn*?"

22

ROCKS

Fiona was lying in bed. It was late. The days she'd spent on Dier Island seemed somehow so much shorter than those back home. She'd enjoyed watching Fynn train when she could, though she was sure to keep her distance and not distract him. She found that she liked many of the instructors who taught there, particularly Drake, who had shown her all the different knots that one could tie. Honestly, she didn't think there could be so many. But it was the man's sheer enthusiasm for the subject he taught that had warmed her to him and so she'd found herself, on many an occasion, down by the harbor watching the students sailing, skittering through the crystalline waters.

The princess liked to keep herself busy; idling about made her anxious and she preferred to keep the dastardly tendrils of chilled anxiety from closing around her. Though, walking around Morancy at night with her brother tended to make her feel as if she were being watched by some unseen throng of eyes. Yet, despite her constant busyness, she wasn't quite tired enough to sleep. Her body was weary, but her mind kept working as though she'd had plenty of rest. And so, there she was in her bed, staring up at the ceiling, counting the cracks and divots in the stonework by the pale light of the moon and stars that bled in through the window glass.

She wasn't entirely sure how long she'd been lying there awake, but she reckoned it must have been more than a few hours. When she'd settled in for the night, having escaped another miserable dinner chat with the lords paramount and vice paramount, she could still hear the faint murmurings of the goings-on of the rest of the castle.

It was silent now. Little was heard other than the faint whimper of wind from outside and the occasional call of a bird or two. Though she normally liked the silence, she found that the quietness of the island seemed abnormal and put her on edge. A cold sweat prickled over her skin and traced down the fine curves of her face. Fiona scowled.

With a deep sigh, she tossed herself onto her side, gathered up the blankets in fisted hands, and hauled them over her head. She would force herself to sleep, she'd decided. Walking around looking like death warmed over, brain fuzzy and addled from sleep deprivation, simply wouldn't do. The blankets were thick and warm and, within an instant, she could see no moonlight or starlight, or even faint torchlights from More Town far off down the island still burning at such an ungodly late hour. It was pitch black beneath the blankets and the heavy warmth was beginning to help lull her to sleep.

Her sleep wasn't to last long. Within an hour she emerged from her blanket cocoon, yawning and rubbing at her eyes, her slumber interrupted by the incessant fluttering of wings at her window. She rolled from her bed and levered open the window glass to find a bat staring back at her, beady eyes glinting in the moonlight. To her surprise, the bat didn't seem disturbed in the least by her presence; rather, it fluttered its wings and leapt from the sill, hoisting itself into the night air and swinging in oblong gyres not far from her window, peeking back at her now and again as if beckoning her outside. Shaking her head, Fiona closed the window and huddled back in bed, determined to get at least a few hours of sleep that night.

Alas, it was not to be, for the bat once more fluttered at her window glass and, once again, when she opened it the creature took off and twisted about in splendid spirals, waiting for her to come and join him outside.

With a heavy sigh, the princess relented. Dressing herself, Fiona stole from her chambers and through the halls and to the entrance way; she stepped cautiously into the warm, island night. Looking over head, she spotted the long wings beating against the night air. Obsidian eyes reflecting with starlight stared down at her. The bat swooped down, dipping toward the ground before curling back into the air, flying just an arm's length over Fiona's head. She followed without question, thinking that this was actually one of the least strange things that had happened to her since the summer, and continued on down a path until she came across a stairway she recognized with a fond, little smile.

Carefully ascending the mossy stairs, Fiona was greeted by the sight of her brother seated atop the vine-wound bannister, staring off toward the shore at the other end of the island.

"Couldn't sleep?" she asked as she crossed the balcony and climbed atop the bannister beside him. "It's late. You should be in bed."

Fiona marveled as the bat appeared overhead in an instant, before slowly descending to them until it clambered over Fynn's upper back; silken wings clung to the boy's shoulders and a fuzzy nose nestled against the prince's nape.

Absentmindedly, Fynn reached up and began stroking the creature's head softly. "Not really tired."

"Do you *know* this bat?" Fiona asked.

"His name's Buttons."

"Buttons?"

"I didn't name him." Fynn huffed.

"He seems quite attached to you."

"You've no idea." Fynn laughed under his breath. He turned to regard Fiona, who sat to his side curiously eyeing the bat perched atop his thin shoulder. "What brings *you* out here?"

"Buttons, as it were," she replied. "He kept popping up outside my window. Wouldn't leave me alone."

"Sorry about that."

The princess shrugged. "No bother, really. I wasn't able to get to sleep."

"Not tired?"

"*Dreadfully* tired, actually. Just couldn't sleep, I suppose."

"The games are coming up," Fynn muttered.

"They are." She took a moment to appraise her brother; concern crept into her chest when she saw the worn look of his face and the red rimming his eyes. "How are you?"

"They've been working us longer than usual," he answered. "They want us ready for the games…as ready as we *can* be."

"Do you feel ready?"

"I don't think so."

"I think you'll do fine," offered Fiona. "You know, your instructors have nothing but good things to say about you. Well, Lord Humbert isn't thrilled with you, but all the others tell me you're one of the best in your year."

"Thank you, Fi." Fynn smiled.

Her hand draped over his and she whispered, "You've an early morning to be ready for. Off to bed with you."

Fynn complained childishly, "Oh, come off it, Fi! I'm not tired."

"To bed!" She laughed as she dismounted the bannister. Her brother's hand still in her own, she tugged him down after her and, hands braced over his back, shuffled him along back down the stairs as they headed toward the castle's entrance. "You don't want to be tired during your lessons."

Shaking his head and grumbling, Fynn said, "I'm *always* tired for lessons. You get used to it."

The pair walked into the castle, instantly embraced by the sleepy shadows of the corridors. "Be that as it may, Fynny, you really need to try and get a few hours of sleep," admonished the princess. Fiona retired to the paramount wing with a final nod toward her brother.

Fynn trudged his way up the tower to his dormitory. Buttons still clung to his back and as Fynn ascended the stairs quietly, he reached up to the creature and tickled his cheek softly. "You'll keep watch for me during the games, won't you?"

Buttons snuggled closer against Fynn's nape, damp nose brushing over the pale flesh beneath.

Fynn smiled. "I'll keep a look out for you, too. Promise."

Sliding into his bed and wrestling the blankets over himself, Fynn settled against his plush pillow. Buttons climbed from his shoulders and swept into the rafters overhead; he hung over Fynn's bed, wrapped in a cloak of delicate wings. Both boy and bat closed their eyes, thankful as sleep took hold.

Just before dawn, Fynn woke to someone shaking his shoulder. He blinked blearily, peering up into the face that loomed over him. With a mighty yawn, Fynn sluggishly pulled himself upright, rubbing at his eyes with the heel of his hand. "It can't be morning already," he whined as he swung his legs over the edge of his bed.

Godryk stepped back from Fynn's bedside, combing his hand through his wild curls. He offered the prince a lopsided grin. He replied, "Unfortunately."

"*Morning* people," Fynn muttered as he stood, stretching his arms out over his head as he, once more, yawned. "You're the worst."

"It's not my fault you wander around the castle and grounds at all hours of the night." Godryk laughed as he returned to his own bedside, pulling on his tunic and lacing his boots.

"What do we have this morning?" asked Albie as he came around to Fynn's side.

"Archery," Fynn answered.

"That's not too bad," chimed Ollie happily.

Hogan shook his head. "Depends what mood Odette is in, really."

"Let's hope it's a good one," Fynn grumbled.

"Is it ever?" joked Albie.

The boys shuffled from their dormitory into the common room, not in the least surprised to see the girls already assembled. They made their way out as a herd of twelve, chatting pleasantly as they twisted their way down the tower. Hollyn bid them their leave with a nod and left to the paramount wing while the rest of the first-years headed out into the warm clasp of the morning. The heat, as summer was drawing nearer, was intensifying. Rolling up his sleeves, Fynn set his shoulders back, delighting in the crack and pull he felt as he did so.

"Ready then?" asked Firiel as she surged to the head of the group.

"Ready," the other ten chorused.

They proceeded down the roadway two by two, jogging shoulder to shoulder, keeping close to one another, Firiel at the head of their trotting troop. As the months had gone on, the first-years fell into a steady rhythm, a comfortable comradery that made their group activities more bearable. And so, it was with that closeness that they eased down the road at a well-practiced pace.

Fynn looked to his left and smiled; Lux was jogging beside him this morning. Her red hair was braided, pulled back from her face, save for stray, fiery strands that tangled by her ears. Her eyes seemed to sparkle in the fresh morning sunlight. Fynn felt heat erupt in his cheeks, though he told himself it was due to the warmth of the day and nothing else.

"Up late again, were you?" Lux asked.

Fynn easily replied, "Wasn't tired."

"You're *never* tired," she insisted.

He snorted a laugh. "I'm *always* tired, I just don't sleep much anymore."

"Bad dreams?"

"No."

"Would you tell me if you *were* having bad dreams?"

Fynn considered Lux for a moment. There was a certain warmth, a genuine note of sincerity, to her words that calmed him. In that moment, he wasn't worried about everything else that was happening around him, to him, because of him. Rather, in that moment he felt serene, peaceful even. The burning in his cheeks seemed to intensify tenfold, but he ignored that as best he could. His heart pounded away with that nasty feeling he normally so hated; but, just then, he didn't hate it so much.

"Yes," he answered simply.

"Do you promise?"

"I promise."

To Fynn's surprise, he noticed a smattering of red creep over Lux's cheeks. She seemed to notice too, for she instantly looked away from him and focused rather intently on the cobbled roadway beneath their feet. The boy smirked, satisfied by the flustered expression Lux bore as they hustled along.

Once they'd returned from their jog, the eleven made their way to the courtyard where they found Odette leaning against one of the castle archways, arms crossed over her chest, eyes narrowed. They shuffled in quietly, heads bowed together as they muttered amongst themselves, quietly mentioning that their instructor for morning lessons did not, in fact, seem to be in a good mood. Lining up before the lady air brigadier general, they readied themselves for a frigid lecture from the woman.

None came.

Odette pulled herself from the wall and stood upright before them, arms still folded tightly over her chest. She leveled her gaze over them; the unnatural greenness of her eyes even more eerie as the tawny light of the day set them ablaze. Shadows from the archways and shrubberies laced over her face, accentuating the sharpness of her features. She looked even more austere than usual.

Fynn's stomach sank. He fidgeted in place, looking away from the fierce greenness that roved over each of them.

When at last Odette spoke, her voice was low and dangerous sounding, like the rumbling growl of a wildcat. "The games are in a week. Do any of you feel as though you are *truly* ready?"

Unsure if the question was rhetorical or not, not a single one of the first-years spoke. Instead, they looked from one another and back to their instructor questioningly, an inkling of genuine fear gnawing its way into the core of each child.

"I didn't think so." Her arms disentangled; her right hand fell over the hilt of a sword she had fastened to her waist. A sword, Fynn noted, that he'd never seen her carry before. "Today's lessons will be a bit different. All of your lessons, from now until the games, will be modified. You've learned as much about basic archery as I can teach you. The same can be said for your equestrian skills. For the next week, you will train in survival and close combat only. These are the skills most necessary for keeping yourselves alive during the games. As such, today we will have a competition to gauge where each of you stand. At the end of the week, we will have another competition to see if any of you can make progress, to see if any of you are *truly* ready."

Fynn watched as Odette drew her sword. The gleam of the steel was nearly blinding.

"This will not be like the little tournaments my brother holds for you. You will not only be fighting one another; you will be squaring off against your instructors." There was a concerning viciousness that sparked in the emerald depths of Odette's eyes; a feral grin crept its way over her countenance. She held her sword aloft and asked the first-years in a flat voice, "Which of you will go first?"

Lux stepped up, squaring her shoulders. "I will, sir."

"Very well then. You'll find practice swords just there." She nodded to her right, where behind one of the courtyard benches there was a mound of dull-edged weapons.

They'd formed a circle in the courtyard and at the center stood Odette and Lux. The instructor held her sword almost lazily, the predatory expression still firmly fixed to her features as she watched Lux tighten her hold on her weapon's hilt, shifting her weight from foot to foot.

"Begin!" commanded Odette.

Within a moment, the woman lunged forward. Her blade caught Lux's, easily sliding against the blunted edge and nearing the girl's chest. With a twist of the wrist and a surge forward, Odette's blunted end embedded against the coarse fabric of Lux's tunic just on her shoulder, knocking her back. With an animalistic smirk, the instructor watched as the girl fell to her backside, sword clattering just beside her.

The lady air brigadier general reminded, "If this were a real fight, little girl, you'd be dead right now."

Lux huffed. She rubbed at her bruised shoulder as she collected her discarded weapon and stood. "Yes, sir."

"Right, join the others." Odette reeled around on her heel, eying the remaining ten combatants fiendishly. "Which of you is next? Come now, don't be shy. You'll each be having a go before the lesson's over."

Firiel stepped forward and drew her sword. "I'll have my turn now, sir."

"Good girl." Odette smiled. They stood face to face. The instructor announced, "Begin!"

Firiel's fate was much the same as Lux's. She hadn't anticipated the speed with which her instructor could move, never having seen her wield a sword until today. And so, within just moments, Firiel was sprawled out on the ground, sword easily cast aside by Odette. Staring up at her instructor, Firiel scowled. The girl stood on shaking legs, picked her sword up, and shuffled off to rejoin the circle.

The proceedings continued in a similar ilk, with each of the first-years staring down the tip of Odette's blade as she loomed over them, not a single golden hair out of place. The penultimate match featured a nervous Godryk standing before Odette, eyes wide as fear crawled its way up his spine. Having seen nine of his year mates fall before their instructor within only moments of their bouts beginning, Godryk supposed he had little hope of besting her.

"Begin!" she yelled. As she'd done nine times before, she lunged forward with feline-like grace.

Godryk reeled back and twisted, avoiding the piercing blow of her sword. Stumbling, he lashed out with moderate control, his blade swinging just by Odette's cheek. The blunted end of his sword caught her jaw enough for her eyes to widen in surprise. Unfortunately for the young Redmayne, his fair fortunes were not to last long. As he continued his momentum-fueled jerk forward, Odette shouldered his side and knocked him further off kilter. As he staggered to right his footing, Godryk felt the keenly painful blow of a dulled-edge barrel into his ribs. Spluttering for air, he fell to his knees, wheezing as his arms encircled his torso.

"Godryk's done the best so far," Odette announced as she stood over the crumpled boy. She twirled her sword in her hand, bored, as her green eyes turned toward the only remaining combatant. Smiling, she said, "Fynneas, I believe you've yet to have a turn?"

Nodding, Fynn proceeded forward. He stopped just beside Godryk, offering his hand to the boy and hoisting him to his feet. "You alright?"

"Fine. Fine," rasped Redmayne.

"She got you pretty hard," whispered Fynn, grey eyes peering down to where Godryk still clung to his ribs. "That'll be a nasty bruise."

"I've had worse," Godryk assured breathily. He clapped his hand over Fynn's shoulder, pulling the smaller boy nearer. "I managed to just get her in the chin. You got to do better than that, otherwise I think that means I win."

Fynn chuckled. "You're getting rather cocky."

"Am I?" Godryk laughed.

"Most certainly. It doesn't become you, you know?"

"Are you saying cockiness looks better on you?"

Fynn shrugged. "I wear it well."

The prince stood before his instructor, his hold on the hilt of his weapon white knuckled. He forced himself to calm his breathing. He'd seen the last ten matches; he knew what Odette was likely to do and was all too aware of how quickly she could manage it. Fynn planted his feet, weight evenly distributed. He'd seen the way his year mates had shifted and fidgeted nervously beneath the heavy stare of their instructor and how that ill-distributed weight resulted in them being tossed around like ragdolls. Drawing in another steadying breath, Fynn squared his shoulders, bent his knees, leaned forward slightly, and drew his weight toward the balls of his feet. He would be ready for her when she came for him.

"Begin!" Odette yelled.

He'd anticipated her lunge forward and so when it came, he stepped just to the side. He had resolved he wouldn't be caught off balance as Godryk had. No, he kept himself steady as he side-stepped another blow. He watched as she straightened, a look of intensity blazing in her eyes as they narrowed, staring him down. Fynn smiled.

There was something about close combat that Fynn enjoyed more than anything else. Archery was impersonal and he found he disliked sailing class, but that was mostly because of his trepidations about the nasty beasts that lurked in the depths of the water. He'd found, over his many months on the island, that he excelled in cavalry lessons, but he didn't much enjoy it. Yes, it was close combat that Fynn relished most. He supposed it was the way everything slowed down, how his breathing seemed to even out effortlessly; the anxious nerves melted away as a calming warmth blossomed in his chest. He didn't understand it, really, how everything seemed to slow down, how the external world melted away and left only he and his opponent.

Watching Odette turn and ready another attack was like watching smoke waft into the wind; he knew she was moving quickly, far more quickly than any opponent he'd faced before, but she seemed to do little more than float slowly, elegantly. Her arm drew upward, bringing her sword along with it. It came striking down with speed like lightning, but Fynn saw every minute movement as plainly as if he were staring at nothing more than words on a page. He brought his own sword up; rippling power lanced up his arms as Odette's blade clattered against his own. His wrist quaked beneath the force almost painfully.

Fynn took a step back, unsettled by the strength of the attack. He kept his sword raised, poised to parry another blow. None came. Odette stood in front of him, cocking her head to the side as she studied him. Fynn drew in a long, deep breath. Without another thought, he lunged forward and swung. He wasn't surprised when she blocked his attack but was pleased that she seemed to be so intently focused on his sword that she neglected everything else. Seizing the opportunity, Fynn kicked out one foot and tried to catch Odette's ankle and knock her off balance.

His plan was unsuccessful when he failed to notice her attention flicker down from the interlocked blades to him. She'd anticipated his action and reacted before he had the chance to notice. She stepped away, disengaging their swords.

As the boy pitched forward, Odette leaned back, drew her leg up, and kicked him square in the chest. She grinned, pleased, as he went down.

The air was forcibly expelled from Fynn's lungs. He crumpled, dropping his sword carelessly. His hands flew to his chest as he heaved, desperate for air. Tears welled in his eyes. He bit down upon his lip, hard, and choked back a sob. The boy's shoulders trembled with the effort of drawing in breath. His lungs burned, still deprived of much needed air. He gasped.

"Well done," Odette said dully, "but you'll need to be faster than that if you want to make it out alive."

All Fynn could think to do was nod. He was still shaking when a hand wrapped around his upper arm and pulled him up. He turned watery eyes to his aid and found Lux looking at him, stare full of worry.

"Thanks," he wheezed, trying his best to compose himself.

"She got you good," Lux said.

"You're telling me," he muttered breathily.

"How bad does it hurt?"

Fynn stubbornly insisted, "I'm fine." He winced and held to his chest tighter.

Lux's hold around his arm tightened and she pulled him closer.

"That's not what I asked," she reminded him harshly.

"It hurts," he admitted softly. "But I'll be fine."

"Promise?"

Still wheezing, Fynn nodded. "Promise."

Their afternoon was little better than the morning had been. After demanding that each first-year try their hand at a second round, Odette had finally released them from their morning lessons, a smirk firmly etched across her features as the eleven children stalked off, some still limping, back to the castle.

Presently, they were huddled around Benadykt who, much as Odette had done hours previously, espoused the necessity of being as prepared as possible for the games. As such, the afternoon was a repeat of the morning, with the children pitted against their instructor in a hopeless match of dulled-edged swords.

Godryk toppled to the ground, panting. He turned weary eyes toward the sword he'd discarded when Benadykt flung him backward as if he weighed no more than a feather. Red hair tumbled before his eyes, slicked with sweat. He sighed. Pulling himself up on quaking knees, Godryk turned his attention to his instructor. The man seemed far too amused with himself to offer any condolences to the boy he'd mercilessly defeated in a matter of seconds. With another sigh and a shake of the head, Godryk returned to stand amongst his peers.

Fynn clapped his friend on the back, offering him a slight smile. "Well, you managed to last longer than Renwyn."

"Renwyn was down and out after only one hit," muttered Godryk.

The prince shrugged. "Still, you lasted longer."

"Right." Godryk chuckled.

Benadykt waved his hand, calling, "Hogan, your turn."

The boy looked stricken at the mention of his name and, with a look that betrayed his remembrance of how Odette had so thoroughly beaten him that morning, he headed toward his instructor. Drawing his sword, the boy readied himself.

Benadykt, the class had realized, fought nothing like Odette. Where she was swift and quick and precise, he was brutally strong and little more. Still, that had proven to be enough to beat them.

And so, it was little surprise when Hogan was disarmed within the blink of an eye; nor was it any surprise when Benadykt snatched the boy's wrist and twisted his arm behind his back before dropping him like a sack of rocks.

"That looked like it hurt," murmured Ollie.

Albie nodded. "Looks like it's going to *keep* hurting for a while."

"Wilder, you're up," proclaimed the instructor, self-satisfied grin firmly in place.

With profound trepidation, Wilder stepped up to face his instructor in close combat. He managed to stay on his feet longer than Hogan had, but not quite as long as Godryk. Thus, it was with a deep huff and shuddering breath that Wilder drew himself upright after having been thrown down.

Unlike his predecessors, he'd managed to somehow retain his hold on his weapon. Upright once more, he leveled his sword to his instructor and prepared for his bout to continue.

While the swords clattered against one another, Godryk leaned closer to Fynn and whispered, "I didn't expect Wilder to do so well."

"He's been getting better," Fynn commented.

"Well," noted Godryk, "as it stands, he's lasted the longest so far."

Smirking, the prince said, "I'll best him."

"Arrogant as always," sniggered Godryk.

Elbowing the taller boy in the side, Fynn corrected, "*Confident* as always, you mean."

"Of course," conceded Godryk. "How could I forget?"

Wilder was sprawled out on the ground, sword far flung from his grasp. His chest heaved, rising and falling erratically, as he struggled to catch his breath. The boy crawled to his hands and knees before raising himself up slowly. Rejoining his year mates, he grumbled, "Hits a lot harder than Odette, that's for sure."

"Fynneas," called Benadykt. "Come on, lad. It's your turn. Have at it."

Benadykt stood before Fynn, towering over the prince. He held out his sword, ready for the match. Fynn did the same, taking a long, steadying breath. He smiled. As Benadykt took a step forward, swinging his sword at Fynn's flank, the boy managed to lever his blade downward and block. The resulting reverberations shook his spindly arms, but he refused to let Benadykt think he'd gotten the upper hand. Knowing full well he couldn't overpower his opponent, Fynn took a step back and withdrew his blade from his instructor's.

Smirking, Benadykt took another quick step forward. This time, he swung downward toward Fynn's head. Again, the boy blocked the strike. His wrists quaked beneath the force of the blow, but Fynn maintained a fierce hold on his sword.

Narrowing his eyes, Fynn tried to find a way around Benadykt's offense. He retreated back another step, keenly spying how Benadykt moved with a lot less speed than Odette when preparing for each strike.

As the instructor raised his sword, Fynn took the opportunity to dart forward and stab toward Benadykt's chest. The man had just the time needed to step back and avoid the full force of the foray but scowled when he felt the subtle brush of the blunted tip graze his chest just beneath his collar.

Fynn smiled once more.

"He's doing well," noted Godryk.

Albie agreed, "Better than the rest of us, at least."

"Are you really surprised?" asked Ollie incredulously.

"Not at all." Godryk grinned.

Fynn lunged forward, intending to sneak his attack in just under Benadykt's blade. His eyes widened in alarm when his wrist was snagged by the man's large hand and forcefully pulled from the hilt he'd been holding with an iron grip. Fynn watched, annoyed, as he dropped his own sword to his feet.

Benadykt pulled the prince forward, knocking the boy further off balance. With Fynn's wrist seized in his grasp, he easily managed to toss the prince to the ground. And so, Fynn fell in a heap, rolling to his side, frowning.

"Not bad," Benadykt admitted. He turned his attention from the crumpled royal to the ten children gathered around, addressing the group. "You have one week left to prepare yourselves for the games. One week to be ready to fight off whatever may be out there, waiting for you. If this is the best you've all got, I'd best be off to tell the lord paramount to prepare eleven little caskets. From what I've seen, not one of you is going to be able to survive your final test. Not *one* of you." He kicked Fynn's discarded sword toward the boy. Shaking his head, he lowered his voice and commanded, "Again!"

The sun was falling behind the horizon, its golden glow lost amongst the seemingly endless array of green blanketing the island. Evening was fast approaching and still the first-years were facing off against their cavalry instructor.

Firiel was on hands and knees, head bowed as she gasped for air. Renwyn pulled away from the group and approached, helping the fallen girl to her feet. She offered him a tired smile. "Thank you."

"Any time." He grinned as he helped her back to their herd.

Benadykt folded his arms over his chest, shaking his head irritably. "This is pathetic." All eyes turned toward him, pleading looks of exhaustion coloring each of them. "After supper tonight, you'll all be moving rocks."

"Moving rocks?" Ollie asked.

Fynn shuddered, remembering his first day of classes at Morancy and the time he and Hollyn had spent the night moving rocks in the rain. "How many, sir?" he asked knowingly.

"How many what?" inquired Benadykt as he sheathed his sword.

"Rocks, sir. How many rocks will we be moving?" clarified the prince.

"There's eleven of you," began their instructor. "I'll have Noel ready fifty."

"Fifty?" Albie gaped.

"*Sixty*," Benadykt barked. "There will be no more complaining, no more *whining*. This is for your own good."

"Yes, sir," the eleven chorused.

Benadykt dismissed the class.

As the children lumbered back toward the castle, Renwyn shoved Albie.

The smaller boy fell to the ground, too exhausted to muster the effort to fight back.

Renwyn snapped, "You just had to open your damn mouth and get ten more added on?"

Picking himself up and dusting the dirt from his hands and knees, Albie said, "Sorry. I didn't *mean* to."

Renwyn shoved Albie once more, far harder than the first time. Fynn was there, ready for it, and caught Albie before he could tumble back to the ground. The prince growled, "Leave him alone."

"No." Renwyn took a step nearer the two. "I don't think I will. This is *his* fault."

Fynn pushed Albie aside, stepping toe to toe with the far larger Renwyn. "No, it isn't. We were in trouble anyway. Ten more rocks aren't exactly a *huge* difference."

"Then *you* carry the extra ten alone...or have Albie help you. But I'm not bothering with them," asserted Renwyn. His breath was hot and foul as it wafted over Fynn's nose.

"That isn't how it works, and you know it," Fynn contended.

"All I know is that after the first fifty, *I'm* done."

Fynn narrowed his eyes dangerously; the early moonlight reflected in the paleness of his irises. "You'll help until we're done, just like everyone else."

It was then that Renwyn swung his fist, catching Fynn in the jaw and knocking him to the ground, hard. As he loomed over the fallen prince, he sneered, "No. I don't think so."

Cupping his bruised jaw, Fynn looked up through tearing eyes at his assailant. He bit his lip, tasting the disgustingly familiar tang of blood as the sharp of his teeth gnawed through the pale, pink flesh. Though he felt the sting in his eyes, he refused to make any sound. He wouldn't give Renwyn the satisfaction. Worn and weary from the day's trainings, Fynn didn't quite have the strength to jump to his feet and swing back. He remained laying on the ground, propped up on one arm, holding his hand to his now slightly bruising jaw, glaring up at Renwyn.

Godryk, unlike Fynn, overcame his sluggishness instantaneously and lunged forward. Hand balling into a fist, he swung and struck Renwyn square in the face, feeling a nasty sensation of something crumbling beneath his knuckles. Standing over Fynn, wide-eyed, he watched in silent horror as Renwyn reeled back with a wretched screech, clamping his hands to his face. "That's not good," muttered Godryk under his breath, as he beheld the sickly sight of blood oozing from between interwoven fingers, trickling down Renwyn's chin, splattering over his uniform.

"*Really* not good," Fynn whispered as he stood, peeking over Godryk's shoulder and watching the morbid scene of Renwyn's newly broken nose splashing blood out in front of them.

Firiel rushed to Renwyn's side, pulling the boy's hands from his face to get a better look at the damage. "Oh," she said, as she saw the bruises beginning to blossom beneath his watery eyes and the full extent of the gore pouring from his nostrils. "That's probably broken."

"I gathered as much, thanks," snapped Renwyn.

"You should have Blythe or Imogen take a look," Georgie chirped. She shuffled a bit closer to the injured boy. "Maybe they can get the bleeding to stop before supper."

Renwyn wiped some of the blood away with the sleeve of his tunic as he pushed by the girls, stalking toward Godryk and Fynn. "You're not always going to be around to come to his defense, you know," he warned, while eyeing Godryk.

Godryk squared his shoulders as he stood before Renwyn. "It doesn't matter. I *was* this time."

Fynn sidled up beside Godryk, looking up to meet Renwyn's feral gaze. "I can fight for myself, thanks."

"Really?" mocked Renwyn.

The prince nodded tersely. "*Really.*"

"Prove it."

"Fine."

Renwyn took a step back, gesturing at the space between them. "Alright, then. Let's have it. We've got all the room we need right here. Do you really think you'll win?"

Fynn was about to take a step forward and accept the challenge when Godryk caught hold of him, pulling him back. He held tightly to the prince as he warned, "Don't."

The smaller of the boys wrenched his arm free from the other; spinning to face Godryk, he insisted, "I don't need your help! Let me go. I can beat him."

"I know you can." Redmayne sighed. "*Everyone* knows it, Fynn. But we're all tired and hungry. We're all in a bad mood. Why bother? What'll it solve?"

Fynn snorted. "That's not the point."

"What's the point, then?" challenged Godryk.

"He's always picking a fight with me," contended Fynn. "I've had enough."

Godryk turned an imploring look toward the prince, furrowing his brows as he whispered, "*Please*, let's just head back inside and eat. This is stupid."

"No one's keeping you here," argued Fynn sharply.

"Well, it's not like I'm going to just leave you."

Fynn shrugged, "That's *your* choice."

Godryk breathed tiredly, exasperated. "It is."

Fynn turned to face Renwyn and said, "Fine. Have at it."

Both boys raised their fists and began to circle one another, neither wanting to make the first move, but neither wanting to look cowardly as they took the defensive. Renwyn, it seemed, had far more energy than the prince, who wound his way around the boy with a slight limp. Taking advantage of the barely perceptible stagger in Fynn's gait, Renwyn burst toward the prince and swung. His fist caught Fynn's side and had the desired effect of doubling the boy over.

Smugly smirking and pleased with his work, Renwyn hadn't expected Fynn to launch himself into his middle. As a result, both boys fell backward to the ground. Fynn, astride Renwyn's chest, swung his fist down, smashing his knuckles into the larger boy's jaw. His head snapping to the side with the brunt of the blow, Renwyn's eyes went wide with alarm. He tried to struggle beneath Fynn's weight but found himself hit once more in the jaw by the small prince's fist.

Fynn drew his arm back, ready to strike Renwyn again when a hand shot up from below him, bundled in the fabric of his tunic, and yanked him sideways. Yelping as he hit the ground, Fynn didn't have the time to fend off Renwyn as he leapt up and pounced, pinning him prostrate to the grassy earth beneath his back.

A tight fist struck Fynn's nose and, at once, the prince knew damage had been done when something distinctly very warm began trailing from his nostrils and over the curve of his lips. Inhaling sharply, Fynn sat up in a flash and pushed Renwyn off him. As the boy fell backward, Fynn descended upon him once more.

The two boys were a flurry of fists; a frightful melody of growls and yips and curses spilled forth from the tangled mesh of limbs tumbling this way and that.

Godryk shook his head, annoyed. "This is *so* stupid."

"Shouldn't we…well…I don't know, stop them?" asked Georgie, clearly concerned as she watched Renwyn and Fynn roll around at the center of their gathering.

"Maybe they'll beat the stupid out of each other," Wilder noted optimistically.

Firiel sighed. "I don't think that's how it works."

Fynn was once more atop Renwyn, pinning him down and beating his fist into the other boy's raised-arm defense.

Renwyn yowled when a fist hit his cheek and, as his anger swelled, he surged upward and knocked Fynn to the ground once more. Jumping atop the prince, he yelled, "I'll *kill* you!"

"Not if I kill *you* first," Fynn protested as he pushed Renwyn off.

Once again, the two were interlocked in a heated tumble, twisting and yelling as they swung at one another wildly.

Lux arched a brow. "This is getting nowhere fast."

"I'm quite hungry," Penelope commented.

Lux crossed her arms over her chest. "Me too."

"We can't just leave them," asserted Godryk, nervously shifting from foot to foot as he watched the fight commence. He was more than slightly alarmed by the amount of blood now staining the tunics of both combatants, as well as the purple splotches marring their complexions.

"You're right," Georgie agreed.

Before Fynn could punch Renwyn again, Godryk caught the prince's arm and hauled him up to his feet. Wrapping his arm around Fynn's middle, Godryk tugged him away from the fallen Renwyn. "Alright, enough. Let's go back."

Fynn wriggled free of Godryk's hold. "I was winning."

"Who cares?" Penelope snapped.

Firiel pulled Renwyn to his feet. Her fiery stare turned to Fynn as she said, "Satisfied? You two look awful now. Let's just get back inside and get something to eat. We still have to move those damn rocks afterwards. Save your energy for that."

Renwyn smudged the blood from his lip as he scowled. "Fine."

Godryk took hold of the prince again, restraining Fynn, making absolutely certain the boy couldn't bolt forward. "Fynneas?"

The black-haired prince shrugged. "Alright. You're right."

The eleven huddled together once more, lugubriously climbing their way up toward the castle. Godryk tilted his head to the side, whispering to Fynn, "I don't think you won that time."

"What do you mean?" Fynn smirked cheekily. "I would've had him if you didn't stop us when you did."

Slinging his arm around his friend's shoulders, Godryk shook his head. "Of course, Fynneas. Of course."

"You don't believe me?" Fynn accused.

"No, no. You *definitely* seemed to have the upper hand." Redmayne chuckled.

Following a rather quiet and, thankfully, uneventful meal, the first-years were outside once more. It was a delightfully warm night with a whispering breeze that cooled them down as they stared, forlorn, toward the mountain of rocks awaiting them.

Hollyn seated himself between the stack of rocks and the all-too familiar tree he, himself, had once had to stack rocks under. "Right," he said to his year mates, "Lord Beckett wants you to move those rocks from their stack just there to under that tree." He tilted his head, indicating the lonely looking tree about a hundred feet from where he sat. "You have to move all sixty before you can head to bed."

"I take it you're in charge of making sure we get it done?" asked Renwyn.

Hollyn smiled dully. "I am."

"Wonderful...just *wonderful*," grumbled Renwyn as he proceeded toward the stack of quite large looking rocks.

Fynn ran his hand through his sweaty hair, wincing when his palm grazed a tender bruise.

Hollyn, hearing the quiet hiss of pain from his cousin, turned to regard the boy. There were two distinct bruises beneath Fynn's eyes. His nose was swollen and the red stains from where trails of blood had tracked still

482

colored his normally snowy flesh. A cut at the side of his mouth looked to have reopened; a tiny trace of scarlet swept down over his chin. His left cheek was a deep purple, the right was only slightly discolored. A jagged cut breached the distinct line of his black eyebrow.

"What happened to you?" asked Hollyn.

"Nothing," Fynn replied tersely.

"Does it have something to do with why you're all out here hauling rocks?"

"No." Fynn huffed and proceeded to join Renwyn at the tower of waiting stones.

Godryk shook his head. "Fynn and Renwyn got into a fight."

"Again," added Ollie.

"*Idiots*," Hollyn mused.

"Yes," agreed Godryk. "They are." He smiled down at the Hollyn.

Renwyn wrestled one of the stones into his arms, heaving with great effort to right himself and begin the arduous trek to the tree. Fynn hefted his own rock into his arms and, after a moment of watching Renwyn waddle along, trotted off after the other boy. Easily catching the taller boy, Fynn looked up at Renwyn, smirked, and sprang off toward their destination. Seething, Renwyn hastened his pace. Depositing his rock before Renwyn had the chance to catch up, Fynn spun around and headed off toward the pile quickly, impishly grinning at Renwyn as he went by.

As Renwyn and Fynn proceeded to turn what was intended to be a punishment into a competition, Godryk stood resolutely beside Hollyn. Both red-haired boys shook their heads, frustrated.

"They've turned this into a game," Redmayne noted distastefully.

A small smile touched Hollyn's lips as he remembered his first night as a student at Morancy and his own evening spent lugging rocks with Fynn. He recalled it beginning quite similarly. He chuckled lowly, "Idiots."

"Right, well I don't want to be here all night," Godryk said as he stole away from the injured prince and headed toward the stack of stones.

Ollie and Albie each took a rock and, far more calmly than two of their year mates, proceeded to walk from the pile to the tree.

"These things are much heavier than I thought," whined Albie.

"This is the worst," Ollie complained.

Albie watched as Fynn rushed by in a blur. "I don't know how he has that kind of energy."

"Odd," Ollie noted.

"*So* odd," Albie laughed.

23

BROTHERS

Emrys leaned back in her chair. It was mid-afternoon. The Wayward Turtle Tavern was barren, save for a bustling Nan attending to a chattering Minnie.

The little girl sat across from Emrys at the small table, happily sipping at a cup of warm milk. Her golden curls were braided, a few stray wisps fell over her forehead. Bright, brown eyes peeked over the rim of the cup and stared back at the woman. Emrys raised a brow, causing Minnie to smirk as she sipped.

Nan tottered over and took a seat beside Minnie. The old woman smiled, her cheeks red. "It's been a while since you've been back to the island," she said.

"A few years, yes," agreed Emrys.

"It's good to see you…and Riddles, of course." Nan grinned fondly, a spark of warmth in her eyes.

"He was always your favorite."

"He has a way about him," chuckled the old woman.

"I think Moriah and Dottie may disagree with you," Emrys commented coolly.

"They'll sort themselves out," assured Nan confidently. She combed her hand through Minnie's hair softly. "They always do."

With a heavy sigh, Emrys rose slowly. She regarded her companions for a moment, allowing herself a subtle grin and nod as she said, "I've enjoyed our morning together. Alas, it's past midday and I should probably look in and make sure the children are alright."

"They have you watching the children? Which year?"

Emrys shook her head, laughing, "I was referring to my siblings."

"I see." Nan wrapped an arm around Minnie's little shoulders. "You're probably right. It was good to see you, Emrys. Your visit most certainly made Minnie's day."

The little girl nodded enthusiastically. "You'll come back?"

"Yes," Emrys answered dutifully. "I'll stop by when I can."

She took her leave from the tavern and walked into the sunny streets of More Town, instantly greeted by the sight of people bustling around their little shops, happily stopping and chatting about this and that. There was a calmness to the town that Emrys had always found quite appealing. It was the sort of cheeriness that was so lacking from most Estherian cities and towns. A few of the townspeople spotted her; she nodded politely, waved to those she recognized, and then continued down the road and back toward the castle.

Halfway back, she was strolling by the large field used for training exercises, usually small cavalry practices or combat, when she heard yelling. Stopping, Emrys listened for a moment and then frowned. She recognized the voices within moments. Her frown deepened. Exasperated, she shook her head and adjusted course; veering from the road back to the castle, she began her trek across the field to the huddled mass of people on the other side.

She was not at all surprised when she saw Moriah and Ridley standing nearly toe to toe with one another, a nervous Noel between them doing his best to keep them from lunging at one another like starved dogs going for a slab of meat. Emrys quirked a brow when she noticed that the audience the two were throwing their collective tantrum before was, in fact, the first-years.

Twelve children watched, huddled with morbid fascination, as their instructor valiantly endeavored to keep his brothers from tearing at each other wildly. Noel had one hand pressed to Moriah's chest, urging his older brother back. Moriah, the far taller of the two, leaned over Noel's shoulder to continue glaring at Ridley with murderous intent. Noel's other arm was employed in the attempt to restrain Ridley; his forearm draped over his younger brother's torso like a fence corralling an unbroken horse.

Ridley, taller than Noel by two inches or so, was not having near the luck Moriah had when it came to staring viciously over Noel's shoulder. Rather, he was huffing and puffing, eyes narrowed, as he listened to Moriah and Noel argue.

Emrys settled in amongst the collection of first-years. "What's happened here?"

Firiel shrugged. "Don't know, my lady."

Moriah pushed back against Noel, shoving his brother into Ridley with the motion. As Ridley caught Noel and threw him aside effortlessly, Moriah seemed to glide forward and was suddenly upon Ridley. Their noses were just more than a hair's breadth apart as they set to squaring their shoulders and narrowing their eyes; each brother scowled an identical scowl.

Noel did his best to right himself, preparing to head back into the fray and pull the two off one another when he spotted Emrys amongst the crowd of children. His eyes brightened, hope ablaze in them once more. He rushed over to her, a pleading expression usurping his panic.

"Emrys!" He nodded over his shoulder to Moriah and Ridley, who remained bristling, each of them seeming as though they were embroiled in an internal conflict with whether or not to physically strike the other. "Thank the gods you're here. I need your help."

"What're they fighting about *this* time?" she asked.

"I don't rightly know," Noel replied sadly.

"What happened?"

"I was teaching the firsties. I wanted to have an easy day with them, you know? The games coming up so soon and all...and then Moriah appeared...and then Ridley did...and then it was—"

"Chaos?"

"Chaos," Noel confirmed.

"I've always found it best to let them just beat it out of each other," she said, clearly amused.

"I don't think that'd be best," Noel argued. "It works for Vallon and Virgil, but Moriah and Ridley are completely different."

"It's worked before and it will again. Just let them get in a few good punches, maybe a stab or two, and they'll be alright." She turned from watching her brothers posturing to regard Noel. Smiling, Emrys added, "Better yet, darling, make it a teachable moment for the children! Yes, I like that idea."

"A teachable moment?" Noel repeated incredulously.

Emrys nodded, slyly smirking. "Yes. I think it's a wonderful idea, really."

Noel turned to face his brothers, watching with dismay as they continued hissing thinly veiled threats to one another. He sighed, "Children?"

The twelve children gathered around Noel and Emrys, curiosity having been piqued. "Sir?" they asked.

"We're going to play a game to start your lesson," Noel said.

"What sort of game, sir?" asked Ollie.

Noel looked to Emrys expectantly. His sister began, "Right, you'll all get to make a choice. Think of Moriah and Ridley as two armies. Which one do you want to support? Team Moriah, gather to my right. Team Ridley, gather to my left. We'll let them fight it out. You will watch and observe their techniques. At the end, whichever team loses—"

"You'll get to move rocks after supper," Noel chimed in, a smirk well fixed to his features all of a sudden. "Fair?"

"Is that all we'll have to do today, sir?" asked Hogan.

"No." Noel rolled his shoulders back; tension made them sore. He continued, "You'll still have your regular lesson once this mess is taken care of. Think of it as a reprieve. You'll still get to learn something, but you'll all get a most deserved rest."

Hollyn snickered, "This should be interesting."

Nodding dumbly, Fynn agreed, "I'll say."

"I don't think this will end well," Godryk sighed.

"There'll definitely be bloodshed, if that's what you mean," Albie said.

Clapping his hands together, garnering the full attention of his class once more, Noel urged, "Go on, then, pick your sides. Moriah to the right, Ridley to the left."

"Who're you for?" asked Ollie.

"Moriah, of course." Albie laughed.

"I don't know," Hogan countered. "Ridley looks a bit stronger."

Renwyn nodded. "I'm for Ridley."

Fynn crossed his arms over his chest, stomping off to the right and planting himself there firmly. "I say Moriah will win."

Godryk remained, eyeing the two unsuspecting combatants carefully. Shrugging, he joined Fynn. "Same."

Hollyn was quick to take Moriah's side, smirking as he watched the Mordray brothers still snapping at one another, neither of them having made the move to strike just yet, both apparently oblivious to the wager going on around them. "Moriah will kill him."

"I don't think he'll *kill* him." Albie laughed, taking up beside the red-haired prince. "But I definitely think he'll win."

Shuddering as he watched Moriah seethe in the distance, Ollie sidled up beside Albie. "I'm just happy we're not the ones who have to fight them."

Renwyn, standing to the left of Emrys, chuckled. "What? Scared, Ollie?"

Rounding on Renwyn, Ollie nodded. "Of course, I am! You'd have to be mad to want to fight Moriah."

Firiel and Hogan joined Renwyn in the pro-Ridley camp. The girl commented, "I don't know, Ridley looks like he could put up a nasty fight."

Wilder, joined the team to the left. "I certainly don't want to fight him."

Georgie shuffled over beside Wilder. She couldn't look away from the feuding brothers. "Ridley looks well built. I think he has a chance at winning."

Penelope and Lux joined the princes in support of Moriah. Lux shook her head, arguing, "Moriah's fast and strong. Ridley doesn't stand a chance."

"Great," muttered Noel as he stepped forward, "now that you've all chosen a side. I'll let our fighters know they're…well…going to be fighting."

Not particularly enthused with the way the afternoon was progressing, Noel stalked toward his two brothers with a great deal of trepidation. He pushed his way between them, doing his best to cajole the two with an affected humor to his mood, though the feigned lightheartedness didn't reach his eyes. His voice rang hollow when he asked, "How would you two like to fight?"

Moriah withdrew slightly, arching a brow curiously. "Where are you going with this?"

"Emrys and I," Noel began, nervously glancing back at his older sister before returning his attention to his brothers, "thought we could play a game with the children. She called it a *teachable* moment."

"Do tell," Ridley drawled.

The look of boredom that overtook Ridley's features was eerily similar to his eldest brother's. The likeness to Moriah unsettled Noel for a moment. The middle brother explained, "You two fight with *practice* swords, obviously. I can't have you going about lopping each other's arms off. Dot would be mad if she found out."

"We wouldn't want that," groused Ridley.

"Agreed," Moriah grumbled.

"Right. So, you two will fight with *practice* swords. The children have picked sides, you see. We told them they had to study your techniques during the fight. I'll have them do a tournament afterward, see if any of them picked up something useful from you two." He looked from his older brother to his younger, concerned by their lack of response. "Well?"

"I'll do it." Ridley smirked.

Rolling his eyes, Moriah consented, "Fine."

"Wonderful." Noel smiled. "It'll be just like when we were younger."

"Not at all." Moriah snorted as he turned to head toward the group of students. "Father isn't here for Ridley to go running to when I win."

Watching his brother's retreating back, Ridley bristled and tensed. He would've lunged forward and tackled Moriah just then, but Noel managed to ensnare him in his arms and haul him away.

"Not yet. At least wait for your proper match to start, yes?" Noel beseeched.

Shrugging free of his brother's restraining arms, Ridley huffed, "Fine."

The children sat in their groups; eager eyes turned toward the brothers who stood before them. Emrys remained between the two teams of children, her eyes bored, her expression slack. Noel, now at her side, remained taut with anxiety as he awaited the inevitable disaster that was about to play out before him.

Noel's voice quavered as he said, "Ready?"

Moriah raised his sword in one hand, leveling a wooden shield before his chest and left flank with the other. Ridley did likewise, his shoulders settling into a tense line, his muscles curling like a coiled snake ready to strike at any moment.

"Begin!"

Ridley jerked forward in a flash. The brothers were a clash of quick movements and deft strikes, smashing their blunted blades into the other's shield over and over. In a moment of deadlocked blades, the brothers threw tact to the wayside and forced their weight forward, willing the other to slip up. When neither sword gave way, Ridley huffed and took initiative. He pressed forward with more vigor.

Moriah tactfully stepped back and whirled to the side. The blades disengaged, leaving Ridley to pitch forward unsteadily before regaining his footing. In that moment, Moriah rounded on his brother and swung. Unprepared for the assault, Ridley had little time to dodge.

"I thought Ridley would do better," whispered Penelope.

"Me too," agreed Georgie.

The children were startled at the thunderous sound that erupted before them when both Moriah and Ridley slammed their wooden shields together. It was, at that moment, that the first-years came to understand that neither Mordray brother was terribly concerned with fighting well and with any modicum of proper technique. The goal became obvious — winning. The shields shuddered against one another. With burning eyes, both Mordrays glared over the shields' top edges.

"I'm going to rip your arm off," threatened Ridley.

"I'd like to see you try," Moriah mocked dully.

Once more, they swung their swords at each other. The speed at which they both struck was akin to lightning, silver bolts of steel whipping this way and that; clattering smashes sounded as they collided and parried and struck.

Despite forgoing skill and years of well-honed swordsmanship, Moriah and Ridley still fought with a sort of innate grace that none of the children had really quite witnessed before. They'd never seen Noel swing a sword with this sort of poise, nor Benadykt, for that matter. It was like a dance - a vicious, violent dance.

"This is lasting longer than I expected," said Lux.

Fynn nodded.

Moriah's sword slashed at Ridley.

The younger brother swung back. Ridley carelessly discarded his shield to the side and flung himself forward. He curled his left hand into a fist and beat it against his brother's shield, splintering the wood.

Tossing his own shield to the side, Moriah imitated Ridley's newest tactic. He reeled his own left hand back and punched his brother wholly on the jaw, knocking him to the ground. In an instant Ridley was up again, this time throwing his sword to the side in favor of his bare fists. And, as before, Moriah obliged to fight Ridley on fair terms.

They were clawing at one another, raking nails across cheeks, hurling insults, smashing knuckles into heads. It wasn't long before they were on the ground, wrestling one another for ultimate supremacy. Though Ridley had more weight to him, he was unable to hold down the feline-like Moriah, who seemed to wriggle free with ease. It was like his body was little more than smoke that simply curled away from Ridley's snatching grip.

Moriah pinned Ridley down at last. His brother prone against the ground, Moriah kneeled over him, ready to hit him once more when Noel yelled, "Alright! Alright! Moriah wins. That's enough. Good show."

Running over to his brothers, Noel all but tackled Moriah from atop Ridley, hauling his older brother off the younger, hands smoothing over his shoulders as he whispered calmly, "I think you've won, Moriah. No need to rub salt in the wound, right?"

Ridley climbed to his feet. Smudging blood from his split lip, he spat, "You're *always* interfering."

"If I didn't step in, he'd be beating your head into the ground. Is that what you want?" Noel turned to face his younger brother, leveling a nonplussed expression his way.

"No," muttered Ridley.

"What was that?" Noel asked, smirking. "I didn't quite hear you."

"I said *no*," Ridley snapped as he stomped off. He brushed by his brothers, certain to shove Moriah aside as he began hiking back to the castle.

Emrys was quick to take up at Ridley's heels, calling back to Noel, "Never mind him! Carry on with your lessons."

Fynn grinned a lop-sided, rather pleased little grin as he regarded Renwyn. "Told you Moriah would win."

Noel ushered Moriah over to the group of gathered first-years, placatingly patting him on the shoulder and offering a timid little smile. "Well done," he cooed. "Why don't you stay for the lesson?"

Fynn brightened at the mention of Moriah staying, turning his wide, grey eyes toward the man.

Moriah caught the look and, for the briefest of moments, his dulled expression broke and gave way to something resembling warm sincerity before returning to its normal flat, bored mask.

The prince watched as the tall man settled down, sitting in the grass with his long legs stretched out before him.

Cocking his head to the side, he noted Fynn still watching him. "Whose side were you on?" Moriah asked.

The boy snorted and smirked. "Whose do you think?"

"Good boy," chuckled Moriah.

As Noel gathered the first-years together and chose who would fight in the first bout—Hogan and Ollie turned out to be his pick—Hollyn sat down beside Moriah. He'd been spending more and more time outside of the castle, though he was still forbidden to participate in his lessons. The nasty cuts that marred his arms and shoulders had healed well enough, leaving behind only the barest hints of scars. Hollyn's shoulder, unfortunately, was still in a bad way; his arm still hung in a tightly fitted sling. Truthfully, his back and neck were starting to ache and the ever-present exhaustion that he'd been unable to fight off was once more back to wreak havoc upon his young frame. Hollyn yawned, blinking away the tired bleariness that was clouding his vision.

Moriah queried quietly, "How're you feeling?"

"Better," Hollyn replied.

"I'm sorry you won't be able to compete in the games," Moriah offered.

"Me too." Hollyn turned his head to face the man. His dark, blue eyes lit up. "But I'm happy I'll be in Paladin next year."

"I thought you'd like that."

The prince nodded. "What division will Fynn be in?"

"That remains to be seen," the man answered.

"He wants Paladin."

"I know."

Hollyn breathed in deeply. The air was warm, crisp, clean. It felt good, he thought, to be out of the dingy castle. "I think you should consider it."

"Oh?" The sunlight flitted over Moriah's angular features as he regarded the prince at his side; golden rays were seemingly trapped in the depthless, emerald gleam of his eyes. "Is that so?"

"He deserves it." Laughing mirthlessly, Hollyn continued, "He isn't the most naturally talented by any means, do understand. He's not the best at anything water related either...honestly, he's mostly useless when it comes to our sailing lessons. But he's good with a bow and arrow...decent with a sword, too."

"If this is your endorsement," Moriah began, "you may want to work on it."

Hollyn's eyes took on a sort of seriousness that seemed to conflict with his thirteen-year-old features. His voice lowered as he said, "Paladin is the division for those who excel in all areas. I understand that. So, does he. What I'm saying is, you can teach him to get better at sailing. Or you could just not put him on a damn boat. But the fact of the matter is, *sir*, that Fynneas *is* strong and he's brave. He's a good fighter, and when you *actually* can get him to listen, he does quite well."

"I've noticed," Moriah commented dully.

"He's odd, there's no denying it, but he'll surprise you," Hollyn finished.

The lord commander inquired thoughtfully, "How do you think he'll do in the games?"

"He'll win."

"*Win?* You seem quite confident about that."

"I am."

Moriah brushed a lock of his hair behind his ear, turning his attention from the prince beside him to the rest of the first-years. Hogan had just disarmed Ollie in a spectacular display of near-skill-less swordsmanship. "If memory serves, it wasn't too long ago that the two of you were at each other's throats."

"People change."

"No, they don't."

Hollyn arched a brow, curious. "What do you mean?"

"People don't change, Hollyn. Circumstances change people. Tragedy changes people. Triumph changes people. *People* don't just change for no reason."

"This island changed us," Hollyn said.

"It changes everyone," whispered Moriah.

The afternoon wore on and as the tepid glow of sunlight became a more burnished copper, the final bout of the lesson's tournament arrived. Godryk, some blood dribbling down his chin and a nasty bruise flowering over his cheek, stood ready for the match. He held his sword in his hands surely, but weariness was warring with his conviction, making retaining such a grip a bit of a challenge.

Fynn, standing opposite the young Redmayne, looked no better. The foul bruises he'd been bequeathed by the brunt of Renwyn's knuckles a week prior had faded to nearly non-existent; conversely, in their place, new bruises from the day's exercise had formed. His broken nose had healed well, leaving no crookedness or bump to distinguish the injury, but his nostrils flowed red with blood from a recent hit to the face, courtesy of Wilder two fights prior.

The small prince held tightly to his sword, staring down his friend with gleaming, silver eyes. "Ready?"

Godryk nodded, red hair tumbling over his forehead in sweaty waves. "You're not going to win this time."

"That's what you say *every* time." Fynn lightly laughed.

At the sound of Noel commencing the bout, Godryk lunged forward and swung. Within a moment's time of the match starting, both Redmayne and Fog were locked in a fierce competition. Their normally matched skills were fading, leaving in their wake only sheer willpower as tiredness from a weak of non-stop combat lessons and survival training began to strip them, piece by piece, of any remaining strength and technique. No, rather than a match to display what each boy had learned during their months on the island, Godryk and Fynn were reduced to little more than savagely smashing steel into steel, each fighting with every last twitching muscle in their slender frames, trying to overpower the other.

Once more their blades locked. Blue eyes met silver as they each peered around the steel, glaring at one another as the heat of the exchange boiled beneath their skin.

Godryk threw all his weight forward, bearing down against Fynn's sword with everything he could. "I told you I would win this time," he mocked as he pressed on, delighting in the slight give against his blade when Fynn shuddered, the prince's wrists trembling against the heavier weight.

"Don't bet on it," contended Fynn, smiling all the while.

Whilst the struggle between Godryk and Fynn continued, effectively enrapturing everyone's attention, Hollyn returned his focus to the lord commander at his side and asked very softly, "How do *you* think he'll do in the games?"

Moriah's reply was similarly quiet, his voice sorrowful and dreary as he said, "I've done all I can for him, all I can to ensure he makes it out alive."

"It's going to be bad, isn't it?"

"The hardest thing any of them will likely have to face." He paused. "I hope."

"Moriah," Hollyn said. His chest tightened. His breathing was labored, heavy. He looked from Moriah to the scene before him, focusing on the rash, yet powerfully energetic, attacks from Fynn, the way his cousin smiled, the way his eyes shone like ice in the sunlight. Hollyn's chest felt like it would cave in at any moment. "Moriah...let me go with them."

"No." Moriah's voice dropped lower. "I thought you were convinced Fynneas would win?"

"That's not it," Hollyn supplied pitifully, his own words sounding worn and tired, a frightful dread dripping from each syllable. "I think...I *know* Fynn will make it out alright. The others—Moriah, he can't watch over them *all*. Please, talk with Imogen and Blythe, convince them to let me go with my year mates. They're...well? They're my *friends*. Please."

"You can't." Green eyes turned to the boy, sweeping over the now trembling frame.

The prince turned once more to face him, to stare him in the eyes with a pleading, hopeful expression.

Truthfully, it was the most Moriah could recall seeing Hollyn ever emote. "You'd risk permanently damaging your shoulder. More than that, you'd be putting all your friends in danger. They'd be too worried about you to pay complete attention to their surroundings." Shaking his head, he added, "You've been out of practice for months now. You're not ready."

"Please," Hollyn implored. Desperation found a way to color his words with the most bitter shade of regret as he whispered, "*Please* let me go with them."

"I'm sorry."

Hollyn stood. Biting the inside of his cheek, he reeled away from Moriah and began stalking off toward the castle. The stinging prick of tears welled at the brim of his eyes and he tried fruitlessly to blink them away, succeeding only in aiding their swell before they eventually spilled down his cheeks. With one last glance over his shoulder, he saw Fynn knock Godryk's sword to the ground; the little prince pounced on Redmayne like a feral cat. There was a tug at the corner of Hollyn's mouth, an inadvertent smile crept over his morose expression. But soon it fell, and an awful, most dreadful feeling overcame him.

His legs felt heavy as he trudged back to Morancy, slouching pitifully as he crept through the entryway and made his way toward the Hall. He was stopped at the sight of his brother coming toward him. Hollyn stood still where he was; he swiped the heel of his palm over his cheeks, brushing the tears from his face, and straightened up as tall as he could.

Ciaran came bounding forward, looking out of breath, his cheeks pink, red hair darkened with sweat and grime. He came to a halt just before his brother, catching the pallid wake of fresh tears and the tinge of red to his brother's eyes, but said nothing of the matter. He knew better. Combing his hand through his hair and catching his breath, Ciaran asked, "Back for the day?"

Hollyn nodded.

"Some of the nobles have arrived," Ciaran continued. "Redmaynes and Astors and Belclraires. The others should be here by tomorrow."

"Father will be along by tomorrow, then?"

Ciaran's feigned joviality slipped, and he frowned. "That's what I wanted to talk to you about. It worked out, as it happens, that you're here when you are. Come for a walk with me?"

"Do I have much of a choice?" grumbled Hollyn.

"Please?" Ciaran looked almost hopeful.

The younger prince acquiesced and joined his brother, who turned him around with a gentle push; soon, the pair were stepping back into the late afternoon sunlight.

"Where are we going?" Hollyn asked as he followed a step or two behind his brother.

Ciaran didn't answer. His only response was a fleeting glance over his shoulder and a slight nod. They walked along the pathway, steering away from it after a while and headed toward a shallow pond, one which Hollyn recalled Godryk and Fynn often snuck off to, to skip rocks and grouse about their day. It was a quiet place, the young prince observed, to have a talk without prying eyes and ears peeking in on you. There were shrubs all around, but not dense enough to draw any sort of legitimate concern about Iba-Jii; so too were the waters of the pond shallow enough to ward off any lingering thoughts of mermaids running afoul.

Ciaran sat on the bank of the pond, staring out at the mirror-like surface of the water, whereupon a few lily pads flittered, causing little more than a ripple or two beneath their barely-there weight.

Hollyn sat beside his brother and watched the colorful shadows of fish lazily passing just below the surface. "What did you want to talk about?"

"Father isn't coming."

Hollyn heaved a deep breath; his lungs expanded at the intake of air, hot and warm. He exhaled, shuddering, doing his absolute best to keep the wretched feeling of disappointment from rearing its ugly head. "I see."

"*Mother* is," Ciaran explained. "Father sent word with Lord Redmayne. Warwyk says that there's been some more unrest in the capital and that Father thought it best if he stayed to handle it."

"Alright." Hollyn's voice was flat, bereft of anything resembling an emotion.

"He'd be here if he could, Hollyn," Ciaran offered sincerely. He couldn't quite bring himself to look at his brother, far too aware of the broken look that would be on the boy's face if he did. "*Really*, he would."

"No." Hollyn reached out and dipped his hand into the water, intently watching as the ripples he'd created jostled the lily pads and stirred the fish. "No, he wouldn't."

Ciaran couldn't take it and, as he huffed, he angled himself toward his brother and scowled. "*Yes*, he would." His words seemed darkened by acute frustration as he said, "You're his *son*."

"But I'm not *you*," whispered Hollyn. He waved his hand slowly through the cool water, still watching the ripples shatter the once serene surface.

"That doesn't matter!" protested Ciaran as he jumped to his feet, glaring down at his younger brother. "You're his son as much as I am. He'd be here to see you if he could!"

The sound that stumbled from Hollyn's lips seemed foreign, as if the voice speaking weren't his own; it was far too weak and wavering to be his. "He *wouldn't*, but that's alright."

With a put-upon sigh, Hollyn wearily stood. Everything ached. But most importantly, his shoulder throbbed, and, at that moment, he understood that he wouldn't be able to join his friends during the games, that he wouldn't be there to help them along, to make sure each of them made it out alive.

"I didn't really expect him to come. I'm sure once he got word that I'd been hurt...that I wouldn't be able to compete...well, he had an excuse, then, not to come." Hollyn heard Ciaran fuming just behind him, but he didn't bother to look back and see the sight for himself. He added, "It's alright, really. I don't think I mind much."

"He doesn't love you any less," asserted Ciaran. There was no certainty in his voice; his words rang hollow.

"He does." Finally, Hollyn turned around. He stared back at his brother with empty eyes; vacant, blue pools bore within them the dying embers of a fire that had been lost to a storm. "I'm not *you*, Ciaran. I never will be." He took a step closer to his brother. "That's alright, I think. I'm *me*. I can't be anyone else." He chuckled joylessly, a dark and cavernous sort of chuckle that set Ciaran on edge. "He doesn't much care for that, I suppose…for *me*. I can't do much about that. I've tried." He turned those pitiful eyes up to his brother.

Ciaran saw the last of the embers burn out and die, leaving behind nothing more than ash in dark eyes.

"I *really* tried, Ciaran. I did. I *swear* to you that I tried. But it's not enough. *I'm* not enough."

The older boy set his hand upon his brother's uninjured shoulder carefully; fingers curled around the slight frame gently. "*I'll* be there."

"I know."

Ciaran pulled Hollyn to him until his little brother's cheek was settled against his lower chest. Hollyn seemed nearly limp in his hold, but he refused to let the boy go. "I'm *proud* of you, Hollyn. I'm proud that you made it into Paladin and that you've done so well in all your lessons. All the instructors talk about how talented you are and I'm *proud* of that. I'm proud that it's *my* little brother who's doing so well."

"I'm sorry," whispered Hollyn as he nuzzled his face against his brother's torso. He felt the rough scratch of Ciaran's uniform brush over his cheeks, but he didn't care. His shoulders shook; arrested sobs crackled in his throat as he bit back, refusing them liberation. "I'm sorry."

Ciaran wrapped his arms around his brother, as tight as he could without harming him. "For what?" he asked quietly.

"I should have done better," Hollyn admitted, choking back yet another sob.

Ciaran ran his hand through his brother's hair, admiring how the red of those locks was so like their mother's. "You've done so well, Hollyn. You've nothing to apologize for."

"I should be competing with everyone else in the games."

"You got hurt."

"I *shouldn't* have." Hollyn hissed and added, "I should've been stronger."

"It wasn't your fault," Ciaran quickly asserted. "Accidents happen, Hollyn. No one blames you for not being able to compete."

"It was stupid of me to get hurt like I did."

Ciaran continued softly raking his fingers through the mess of red beneath his touch. "No, it wasn't." Pulling back from Hollyn slightly, Ciaran knelt before his little brother. He smiled sadly. "I'm sorry you did. I'm sorry you got hurt and I couldn't do anything to help you."

"I was awful to you," the boy confessed.

Ciaran snorted. "Yes, you were. But what are brothers for if not to be awful to one another sometimes?" His thumb brushed away a tear that fell down Hollyn's cheek, despite the boy's desperate schooling of his emotions. "But I'm not *mad* about that."

"Promise?"

"I promise on my life, Hollyn."

Settling himself, Hollyn asked, "Ciaran…what sort of *unrest* is there exactly?"

"Warwyk didn't say."

"It's *bad*, isn't it?"

"I don't know."

"You're lying," muttered Hollyn as he pulled from his brother's hold and sat back down on the bank.

Ciaran took up his place beside his brother, slinging his arm around Hollyn and holding him close to his side. "I don't know what's going on, honest."

"But it's bad?"

Ciaran grimly stared off into the distance. "I think so."

"There's going to be a war, isn't there?" Hollyn looked up at his older brother, arching one brow questioningly. "That's why everyone wants to train us up so quickly. It's because they think we'll need to fight. Father said they'd come at us from all sides, that it was only a matter of time."

"You won't be fighting," Ciaran said flatly. "It doesn't matter how much they've accelerated your training. You're all too young to fight in any war."

"What's going to happen to us?"

Ciaran held his brother tighter. "We'll be fine."

Hollyn protested weakly, "You don't know that."

"I won't let anything happen to you," vowed the older prince. "*Nothing* will happen to you." He smiled fondly, a soft, tentative sort of smile. "You're my little brother. I won't let anything happen, Hollyn."

"You act like I can't' do anything for myself," grumbled Hollyn.

Ciaran shook his head. "I know you can. I know you're plenty strong. But that's what big brothers are for, to protect their little brothers from as much as they can, for as long as they can."

The royal siblings returned to the castle just before supper, joining their peers in the Hall.

Hollyn sat beside Fynn, nudging the other boy. "You won?"

"I did." Fynn bounced in place. He looked over to Godryk, who sat across from him, and beamed. "Godryk put up a great fight though!"

Supper proceeded quite uneventfully. The first-years passed their time in the Hall with conversations about the fight between Moriah and Ridley and theatrical retellings of each of the bouts culminating, at the end, in the apparently quite dramatic give and take between Godryk and Fynn.

Fiona, Fynn noted rather glumly, was spending her supper, once again, in the paramount wing. Disheartened by her absence, he rose at the conclusion of the meal, intent on snuggling into the warmth of his blankets and getting as much sleep as he could, only to have his wrist stolen away into Hollyn's tight grasp.

"Something the matter?" asked Fynn.

The other first-years had begun their journey back to their dormitories high up in the tower, passing by the two princes with sparing glances, none of them bothering to inquire as to why the two had stopped so suddenly, breaking from their little herd.

Hollyn waited until the ten had filtered out of the Hall, watching as they proceeded on their way. When it was only he and Fynn, Hollyn urged Fynn forward with a slight push to the back. And so, the pair took their own leave from the Hall and began making their way, at a far slower pace, back to the dormitories.

"I wanted to talk to you," Hollyn said.

The corridors leading back to the dormitory were eerily still; all the eyes of the portraits hanging from the walls seemed to be following the two princes as they continued on. The stillness was calming, the ambient torchlight lending itself to the gentle feeling of the early night.

When Hollyn spoke again, his voice was even, calm. "The games will be here in a matter of days, Fynn."

"I know," the other agreed dully. "Two more days and then…well…I suppose I'm not entirely sure what to expect."

"According to everyone I've spoken to, you should expect something quite nightmarish."

"Wonderful." Fynn laughed.

"I've got something for you," Hollyn began, reaching to his waist where, hidden by the folds of his cloak, there was fastened a dagger nestled within a red sheath. He held it out to Fynn, eyes steadily fixed to the other boy. "I want you to have this."

Taking the dagger from his cousin, Fynn admired it. It was a fairly good-sized weapon; golden bats with dangerously spread wings decorated the red sheath; their ruby eyes glinted in the torchlight. He curled his fingers around the hilt, pulling it from its scabbard to reveal that the blade, instead of being straight as one would think, was curved oddly, like a slithering snake. The metal was black. His pale eyes flicked back up to Hollyn. "What's this?"

"It's a gift, of course. I want you to have it. You're allowed a knife during the games. So, I want you to have *this* one."

Re-sheathing the strange blade, Fynn looked back down at the weapon he held in his hands. "Is it yours?"

"Grandfather gave it to me before he died. I was six at the time, if I recall." Hollyn stepped closer, joining his cousin in admiring the intricate decorations of the sheath. "He said the blade was curved so it would cause more damage. Sounded brutal to me."

"Very brutal," noted Fynn. He looked up from the knife, watching the captivated way in which Hollyn's dark eyes roved over each detail, as if memorizing them. "Why're you giving it to me?"

"I already told you, *idiot*, I want you to have it for the games."

As Hollyn peeled himself from Fynn's side and stood before the shorter prince, Fynn couldn't help but grin boyishly, light sparking in his eyes, cheeks going pink as he beamed. "I think this means we're friends now."

"We are not."

"Yes," chirped Fynn cheerily, "we *are*."

"Not on your life," drawled Hollyn in an affected recreation of Moriah's voice.

Fynn bounced back from Hollyn, combing back his black hair, sheepishly smiling at the other prince. "You *like* me! You know it. That's why you gave me our grandfather's dagger."

"You're being ridiculous," argued Hollyn flatly.

"Just admit it, Hollyn." Fynn laughed. "Just admit you *like* me! We're *friends.*"

"I do *not* and we're *no* such thing." Hollyn huffed rather indignantly.

"You *do*," Fynn protested, still smiling a lop-sided smile. "You know it."

"You're an *idiot*, Fynneas."

Fynn playfully punched Hollyn's good arm, all the while laughing. "I'm *your* idiot now."

Shaking his head and grinning the subtlest of grins, Hollyn laughed wanly, "*Lucky* me."

24

A NIGHT ON THE TOWN

The first-and second years gathered in the common room, having been woken earlier than usual and told to sit quietly and await further instruction. They were seated in various chairs and plush pillow-tops and lounges, none of them knowing why they'd all been called together. It was quite a rare occurrence, outside of their joint sailing lessons, that they'd all be gathered at the same time.

The door from the tower steps into the common room opened, revealing a parade of instructors who trudged in, each looking wearier than the last. Odette and Benadykt took to leaning against the wall, folding their arms over their chests, and fighting back the encroaching desire to fall back asleep. Noel and Moriah stood, moderately more alert, side by side, though looking rather grim and dour, the dark rings of lost sleep coloring the pale flesh beneath their eyes. Drake, appearing as though he hadn't slept in days, collapsed into an open seat and leaned back, blinking away the bleariness infringing upon his vision in a vain attempt to wake himself up.

The vice lord paramount was the only one of the lot who appeared cheery, as he always did in the mornings, and ready for the day. He stood at the center of the common room, beaming a smile at the gathered children, eyes dancing in the pale firelight of the torches.

"Good morning, children," he greeted brightly. "We wanted to gather you all here this morning, before the festivities begin, to discuss the games. Firstly, we wanted to go over the matter of teams. Usually, as you're aware, only the second-years compete. As such, we just divvy up the year into equal, or equal as can be, squads. This year, with the firsties competing as well, things are a bit different. It was our intention, initially, to mix you all together—to have teams comprised of first- and second-year students. But, as the games require steadfast teamwork in order to make it through, we are not entirely sure if that's the right approach." Indigo drew in a deep breath, then continued, "We'd like to hear your thoughts on the matter. Would you prefer mixed teams, or would you prefer to be split up with only your year?" He waved his hand. "Go on then, the floor is yours."

A mousey looking second-year named Alice Hillwater was the first to stand. Her voice was as meek as one would expect, coming from such a waif of a girl. "I'd prefer to stay with my year, sir."

A boy at Alice's side, Aldus Singer, nodded his agreement. "I think we'd do better that way, sir."

Tulip Malcourt, a tall girl with a wan sort of twinkle in her pale eyes, stood to Alice's right. She was far more confident in her speech, as she asserted, "We've spent much more time with our year mates, sir. We know how each other thinks, how we work, how we fight. I think it best, sir, if we stay together."

Indigo turned to regard the twelve first-years. He asked them pointedly, "What do *you* all think?"

Lux, casting a quick glance around her to her fellow year mates, turned to the vice lord and said, "I agree with the second-years, sir. I think we'd do better staying together, rather than mixing the years."

"I agree," Fynn said, stepping up beside Lux. He chanced a shy smile in her direction, before fixing a confident look to the vice lord. "We're close; we can think like one another, anticipate what each other will do. We know each other's strengths and weaknesses."

Godryk chimed in, "I think we'd stand a much better chance of making it to the end if we stay together, sir."

Clapping his hands together, Indigo declared, "Right, then it's settled. Second years, you will be split into three teams of five. Firsties, you will have one team of five and one team of six, as Hollyn won't be competing. Does this seem fair to everyone?"

The assembled students all nodded.

Indigo shuffled over to Noel, who handed him a large, leather pouch. Returning to stand before the students, the vice lord explained, "On to the second matter of business this morning— picking your teams. You will each be assigned a color. I will call each of you up, you will place your hand inside the bag and pull out a tile. The color of your tile will be the team you are assigned to. Later this morning, you will go to the paramount wing and Chippy will provide you your uniforms for the games."

The black, white, and blue teams were comprised of second-years. Once they'd been picked and neatly assembled in their groups, only green and yellow tiles remained in the bag. Fynn, the first of the first-years to be called to select his tile, was nervous as he stood before the vice lord. He stared, for just a moment, into the shadow of the pouch, before reaching in and plucking out a tile. Yellow. The prince stepped to the side, waiting for the other ten of his year to pick their tiles. He was delighted when Godryk, the second to pick, also pulled a yellow tile.

By the end of the selection, the yellow team was comprised of Fynn, Godryk, Albie, Ollie, and Penelope. The prince looked over to the green team, watching as Lux and Renwyn discussed something between the two of them quietly, heads bowed together. He frowned, a creeping agitation finding purchase in his chest as he watched the exchange.

Fynn was pulled from his melancholic reverie by Godryk shaking his shoulder, whispering, "Are you paying any attention?"

"What?"

"I thought not," sighed Redmayne.

Indigo tossed the now-empty pouch aside and said, "Now that you've all been placed in your teams, please settle back down. I've one last thing to discuss with you before you're dismissed to pick up your uniforms." He paused, watching amusedly as the children all huddled around, still arranged in their new team formations. "I want to explain to you exactly how the games will work. Tomorrow morning you will assemble on the docks, divided into your teams. Each team will be given a boat. Your team boat will be marked with sails of the appropriate color. You will each be allowed a knife and nothing else. There are three islands between Dier Island and Nandulus Island. Upon each of those three islands, you will find a flag with your corresponding team color. Your objective is to collect all three flags and arrive at the amphitheater on Nandulus Island within a week." His spritely morning cheer was waning as he continued to detail the specifics of the endeavor, saying, "You will sail to Green Isle and collect your flag. You may then be tempted to sail to Middle Isle, but I would advise against this. There is nowhere on the island to safely dock and recover your boat. There is, however, a land bridge that appears just before dawn that stretches between the two. If you're quick, it is your best option to get between Green and Middle. Just helpful information. Use it if you wish. Now, once you arrive on Nandulus Island, you will take the main road to the amphitheater. There, you will wait until the week is up. At such time, you will then be paired off into matches. You will compete in the amphitheater in close combat against one another until one of you is named the victor. Are there any questions?"

Tentatively, Ceral Belclaire, a second-year, raised his hand. Once acknowledged by the vice lord, the boy asked, "What happens if our team doesn't make it to Nandulus Island within seven days?"

"You will be disqualified from competing in the final stage of the games. Which, I know, may not sound too terribly bad to you now. But, let me say this—it would be a great dishonor to your house to not compete, to be considered a weak link in the chain of your family. Is that understood?"

The children nodded wordlessly.

"Any other questions?" pressed Indigo.

Another nervous second-year, Haemish Stonecraft, asked, "Is it a race?"

Shaking his head, Indigo said, "Not necessarily. There is no prize for your team getting to Nandulus Island first, if that's what you're asking. The advantage, however, is great should you finish before the others. The quicker you collect your flags and arrive at the amphitheater, the longer you have to recuperate before the tournament begins."

No more questions were voiced by the hoard of nervous looking children gathered about the common room. The vice lord and the accompanying instructors, who'd all remained silent during the interaction, poured out of the chambers and into the long, winding staircase that led down the tower.

Left then, in a cold silence loudly punctuated by the mounting dread as the sheer reality of the situation sunk in, the children sat silently, no one chancing a glance at one another for fear of seeing their own mounting terror reflected in the eyes of their peers.

The second-years, slightly more accustomed to the workings of Morancy, gathered themselves quickly and in their assigned groups proceeded out of the commons and in search of the paramount wing to gather their uniforms for tomorrow's games.

Once more left alone in the oppressive silence, the first-years fidgeted under the weightiness of the trepidation that, in that moment, seemed far more tangible than anything else, far more lifelike than one would possibly ever care to imagine.

Fynn sat frozen in his chair, staring off at nothing in particular. He'd known about the games, yes, from the very day he'd set foot on the island. Conversations focused on the games had been bandied about all throughout his stay at Morancy. It was always there, lingering like a storm on the edge of the horizon, the sort of storm whose dark rainclouds only poked the barest brim of their makings over the horizon, a speck of grey against the blue of the sky—there, simply, but far off enough so that you wouldn't truly be worried over it. But now, as Fynn remained motionless in his seat, it seemed as though the storm clouds, all at once and without him having realized their approach, had gathered over the sky and darkened everything around. It was raining, for sure, and the prince wasn't sure he was ready for the storm, wasn't convinced he could weather the tempest. So, he sat there, unable to bring himself to move, staring off at nothing at all.

Hollyn nudged him gently, sinking down in a seat at Fynn's side. They sat, shoulder to shoulder.

Fynn, still staring off, didn't acknowledge the other prince's presence. He remained motionless, quiet.

Again, Hollyn nudged him, harder this time. He bowed his head towards Fynn's and whispered quite softly, "You're going to be fine."

"You don't know that," Fynn answered.

"I do." Hollyn's hand dropped over Fynn's, curling around the other's like a shell. "I wanted to go, you know."

"I know."

"I asked Moriah yesterday, even. I wanted to go with you...with everyone. But they told me I couldn't."

Fynn's head lowered, his eyes fluttering shut. His black lashes ghosted over white flesh. His shoulders shook, but he remained quiet.

"Do you know what else?" Hollyn smirked.

"What?"

"Moriah asked me what I thought of you...how I thought you'd do."

Fynn straightened at that, turning to face Hollyn with eyes that swelled with unshed tears. "What did you say?"

"I said I thought you'd win."

The smaller boy shook his head. His voice was raw, shaken sounding, as he said, "Liar."

Hollyn squeezed Fynn's hand. "Not at all, *idiot.*"

Fynn couldn't help the small smile that tugged at the corner of his lips. "Hollyn?"

"Yes?"

"I don't know if I can do this...if I'm ready," he admitted.

"Fynneas, I *know* you can." Hollyn's voice lowered; seriousness overtook his expression. "I know you can and, more than that, you *need* to."

"What do you mean?"

"You need to do well, Fynn, because they all need you." The prince discreetly nodded toward the rest of the gathered first-years, who still looked as though they were awaiting their execution. "They need you, Fynn. So, even if you're not ready, at least pretend to be, alright?"

"They don't need me," argued Fynn weakly.

"They do." Hollyn's hold on his cousin's hand became impossibly tight as he continued, "They do, Fynn. Do you think Georgie, Penelope, Hogan, Albie, and Ollie would survive this without you? Godryk may, yes, but he's far too sensible." Hollyn laughed under his breath, "He's far too cautious to just go running into the fray. You, whether it's a good or bad thing I'm not quite sure really, will go running in where no one else dares. I haven't quite figured out if it's bravery or stupidity, though I suppose it's a little of both."

"Funny," Fynn said, looking up at Hollyn, "Drusus said the same thing."

"I bet he did. You know, even if the others aren't on your team, you still have to look out for them, if you can. Renwyn, well, he probably won't want your help. Wilder probably won't either. But Hogan and the girls…? Fynneas, just try and keep a watch on them."

"I will. I'll do my best." Fynn couldn't help the stinging feeling in his throat that darkened his words as he whispered, "Hollyn?"

"What is it?"

"I'm scared," confessed Fynn.

"Everyone is."

"What if something happens?"

"Fynneas, listen to me." Hollyn drew in a deep breath. "I have no doubt that something *will* happen. It's the nature of the games. And, truthfully, you attract disaster like no one I've ever met before. So, don't be scared of *something* happening. Just be ready for it when it does."

Nodding, Fynn stood. He still felt a creeping numbness, a sort of distasteful paralysis of the body that allowed him to keep moving but feel nothing at all. He supposed it was the fear and anticipation culminating, but he wasn't quite sure. Nevertheless, Fynn found that he was the first to have stood up, the first to break free from the spell they'd all fallen under, the icy hands of the encroaching solemnity gave way. He felt, for just a moment, freer.

But, as he looked into the faces of his year mates, he spied what he had dreaded before. In their visages, he saw his own reflection - stricken expressions of trepidation and doubt, horror and resignation. Combing his hand through his hair roughly, Fynn forced himself to find his voice. He did, but he didn't quite recognize the nervous croak that sounded as he said, "Right! We should head off and gather our uniforms."

Hollyn smiled, watching as Fynn crossed the room, albeit on shaking legs, toward the door. He rose, waving his one good arm, gesturing for the others to get up. "Come on, you don't want to spend all day here moping about. Get a move on."

Godryk stood next, offering up a small smile for Hollyn before crossing the room and joining Fynn. Standing beside the prince, the young lord said, "I'm glad we'll be on the same team."

"I had a feeling we would be." Fynn smiled.

"No matter, I'm still glad for it."

"Me too."

Upon the first-years' arrival to the paramount wing, the second-years had already left. There was no trace of them having been there, save for the rather irritated look on Chippy's face when he led the eleven children into a small room to gather their uniforms.

As the skeletal man was fussing about, sifting through the mess of the room to gather the green and yellow tunics, Fynn asked, "Chippy, why is it that you never leave this wing?"

The other children, overhearing the inquiry, turned their attention to the man, each of them unable to mask the curiosity that had just been piqued.

Chippy, noticing the rapt attention being paid to him, sighed as he gathered a bundle of green tunics and turned around, tossing them to Renwyn unceremoniously. "Do you really want to know why?"

Fynn nodded, followed shortly by the hesitant nods of the other first-years.

"They don't let me."

"Who?" questioned Fynn.

"The paramounts, of course, daft boy," hissed the man.

"Why?" asked Lux.

"You'll find, little girl, that if you know too much, the *noble* sort don't want you walking about freely. Scared that what you know may get out, as it were."

"What do you mean you *know too much*?" asked Albie.

"Don't matter," Chippy huffed as he tossed the yellow tunics into Godryk's arms. "Be off with you now." He gave a dismissive wave of his hand, shooing them all out the door. "Prince Fynneas, boy," called the man as the children were leaving.

Fynn stopped, whirling around to face the attendant. He quirked a brow. "Yes?"

"I was asked to relay a message to you."

"Alright?"

"Your sister would like you to meet her before the feast. Says she'll meet you on the balcony. I'm supposing you know which balcony she's referring to."

"Thank you for telling me." Fynn shifted his weight between his feet, anxious to get going.

"Right," snorted Chippy irritably, "off with you, boy."

Smiling, the prince scurried out the door. He was quick to catch up with most of his year mates, finding them shuffling through the main corridor leading out of the castle. Running, Fynn assembled back into the fold, the tension of the early morning finally starting to dissipate.

Fynn was beside Lux as they headed outside. It was a quiet morning, warm and sunny, red sky fading and giving way to blue. The first-years milled about, waiting for the remnants of their group to rejoin them.

Fynn sat, pleased when Lux followed suit and sat beside him. He smiled shyly as he asked, "How are you?"

She shrugged. "Fine, I suppose. Maybe a little nervous. What about you?"

Lux looked at him so expectantly, so openly, that Fynn wanted nothing more than to tell her he was deathly terrified of tomorrow. But still, he could see the niggling fear in her blue eyes, and he stopped himself, hauling back the desire to once again voice his own anxieties. Rather, he brushed back his black hair, feeling his cheeks go warm as their color turned from white to pink in an instant. "I'm fine," he said simply.

"Ready for tomorrow?"

"As ready as can be, I suspect." He tried to straighten up, to square his shoulders, to level the girl with a confident look. He failed, and instead his voice wavered when he asked, "What do you think of your team?"

"I think we'll do well together. That is, if Renwyn can leave his ego behind." Laughing, she added, "I'm a little disappointed you're not on my team."

"Really?"

"Really. You're very good, Fynn. You'd have been an asset! But I think we'll manage."

"I'm sure you'll do great." Fynn grinned. His face felt nearly on fire, his cheeks burned brightly. "Your team has *you*, of course, so they'll have no problem." He wrinkled his nose, sneering comically. "You're right about Renwyn though; try and get him to put his arrogance aside, won't you?"

"I'll do my best. No promises though."

Fynn chuckled. "Understood. I'll be around, anyway, so you won't be stuck with him on your own."

"I think that's a good idea." She brushed an errant, red strand from her face. "We should all keep together. We'll do much better that way, I think. What do you say?" She held her hand out to the boy expectantly.

He took it, shaking it with a wide smile. "Agreed."

Penelope rounded on the pair, whining, "What's taking the others so long?"

Fynn looked up at her and shrugged. "Don't know."

"They'll be here in a moment, I'm sure," placated Lux as she stood up.

Georgie chimed, "What should we do the rest of the day?"

Hogan added, "She's right, we haven't any lessons today."

Fynn stood, stretching his back, delighting in the cracking that came of his odd contortions. Yawning, he offered, "Why don't we go to More Town? We could make a day of it."

"I second that," Lux chirped.

Not bothering to pay attention to the rest of the exchange, Fynn simply watched as Lux settled in amongst the group. He felt his heart thudding in his chest; it wasn't the painful sort of thudding he hated, the sort that made his ribs feel like they were shaking, or his chest feel like it would explode. Rather, it was the sort of thudding that brought an inexplicably stupid grin to his face, the sort that set his cheeks aflame, the kind of thudding that made him feel light and free and weightless, like the wind might just carry him away. He decided he liked that sort of thudding in his chest, the happy sort. Though Fynn didn't catch any of the details, so enraptured in his own thoughts was he, it seemed that the group had agreed to head off to More Town.

He hadn't noticed Hollyn, Godryk, and Renwyn rejoining them. He hadn't heard them decide upon their destination. He hadn't heard more than a low buzzing, a lulling sort of sound that seemed fuzzy and distant. The boy was brought out of the depths of his thoughts by Lux snagging his arm with hers and pulling him along, laughing at the bewilder expression he shot her at the gesture.

"We're going to the tavern in More Town. Weren't you listening?" She laughed again, still pulling the prince along down the road.

"Of course, I was!" protested Fynn.

Shaking her head, Lux argued back, "Liar."

Arriving in town, the first-years soon discovered that most of the townspeople had already made their way to Nandulus Island for the games. Pouring into the Wayward Turtle, Fynn was delighted to spy Nan bustling around behind the counter. As his year mates seated themselves around the many tables, Fynn went bounding toward the old woman, Hollyn following at a far more sedate pace.

"Nan!" greeted Fynn warmly.

Hollyn, sidling up beside the small prince, grinned. "Hello, Nan."

"Boys." She smiled as she ambled over, throwing her arms around them both genially, mindful of Hollyn's shoulder. "What're you lot doing here?"

"We've the day off from lessons," explained Fynn.

"The games are tomorrow," added Hollyn.

"Yes, yes, haven't forgotten them," Nan clucked.

Looking about, Fynn fixed Nan with a quizzical stare. "Where's Minnie?"

"Oh, I'm sure she'll be down. She'd have heard you all come in by now. I'm sure of it," the old woman supplied. Nan laughed as she was quickly proven right. The door swung open at the far wall, revealing the dashing form of a small girl with a head of curly, blonde hair. "See what I mean?"

Minnie flung herself at Fynn, encircling her small arms around his thin frame. "Fynny!" Peeling herself from the boy, she rounded and clung to Hollyn. "Hollyn!"

The red-haired prince messed the girl's hair and knelt down before her. He cocked his head to the side and asked, "And how are we today, Minnie?"

Her cheeks went pink at the sight of the boy and she giggled. "Great!"

Hollyn leaned back a bit, relaxing as he nodded. "That's good to hear."

"You're still hurt?" she asked softly, spying the sling that bound Hollyn's arm.

Glancing at the offending piece of material, Hollyn scowled. "Not hurt, don't worry. But I have to keep my arm in this thing for a little while longer."

"Why?" asked the girl.

"Well, because I want my shoulder to heal properly so I can go back to beating Fynn at everything," joked Hollyn as he stood up.

Shaking his head, Fynn scoffed, "Don't listen to him, Minnie. He's hit his head a few too many times. There's no way he can beat me!"

Playfully punching Fynn's arm, Hollyn said, "You just wait, Fynneas, and we'll see about that."

Fynn couldn't help but smile back at Hollyn, saying, "I look forward to it."

The late morning and afternoon were spent in companionable conversation amongst the tables at the Wayward Turtle Tavern. Nan was generous enough to supply the children with food and drink. Minnie settled herself on Godryk's lap, having taken a quick liking to the boy. Early evening found the first-years settling down, their conversations becoming less lively, less animated. Minnie had curled at Godryk's side, head resting against his chest as she dozed lightly, lulled off to sleep by the quiet sounds of the children's conversations. The anxiety that had affixed itself to their little group returned as evening reared and had only persisted in becoming steadily more palpable as the hours wore on into night.

Fynn, for the entirety of the day, had been seated between Hollyn and Lux, equally enjoying the dry, sarcastic comments of the prince and the warm, genuine musings of the girl. There hadn't been a time, he thought, where they'd all been allowed to relax and act their age since they'd come to the island. Fynn was mentally preoccupied by the approaching games, but couldn't help but feel calm, relaxed. Looking around at all the faces gathered, even as the day had dulled and muted their energy, he decided that he was happiest with them. It was something new for him to realize, really.

Back in Godsreach there weren't many children around for him to socialize with, play with, train with, learn with. He'd had his sister, but she had always been a shepherd in his life, not a friend. He'd had his cousins, but they were older and less inclined to indulge the youngest amongst them with any attention. Presently, amongst the other first-years, Fynn finally realized how terribly alone he'd been before. He smiled with the knowledge that he wasn't any more.

Again, distracted by his own thoughts, Fynn heard little of the conversation. Everything seemed a blur of sounds, soft and quiet and curious musings that danced around like a cloud, no defined shape or reason, but there hanging around, nevertheless.

It was the sound of whistling that garnered his attention. The whistling was piercing, defined, and cut asunder the blanket of noise like a blade tearing through wet parchment, such was the ease of its sharpness. Perking up, Fynn craned his neck toward the sound, searching for its origin. There was no one else in the tavern; the first-years, Nan, and Minnie comprised the whole of the Turtle's populace for the night.

Without a thought, Fynn rose, pale eyes sweeping through the interior. He supposed, for a moment, it could be the wind whisking by the windows. That thought was squelched, however, when the sharp whistling sounded once more, a distinct tune being carried out. A spark of recognition ignited within the prince's mind, though he didn't know why he knew the song. Still, the wick of his attention had been lit and there was little hope of extinguishing it now. A quick glance back to his year mates found that they hadn't yet noticed his mounting suspicions. They were all too engaged in their own conversations. Fynn extricated himself from the group quietly, nodding his reassurance to Godryk when the boy fixed him with a curious look.

Stealing from the tavern and into the night, Fynn stepped out onto the street. Looking both ways, he saw little more than cobbled stones glowing a pale silver in the moonlight.

"Hello?" he called into the darkness of the town. "Anyone there?"

The whistling had gone.

Undeterred, Fynn stepped further into the street. "Hello?"

The whistling returned; the melody beckoned Fynn. The familiarity of the rhythm was undeniable though the boy still couldn't recall where he'd heard it before. He turned down the road, heading further into town. The stillness of the town that night was eerie; not a single torch was lit. The only light guiding the boy's way was the moon, full overhead, and the stars spangling the blackness of the sky. Still, the light that fell upon the town was little more than a dim glow that cast jagged, haunting shadows onto the pale, grey surfaces of the walls all around.

A crack sounded and then another. Looking skyward, Fynn saw greyness, weightless and heavy all at once, begin to dot the sky off by the horizon near the castle. Storm clouds, spindly as they were presently, were beginning to collect. A flash in the sky denoted lightning and another solid crack of thunder dispelled any doubt that there would soon be rain. The air that night was warm, the wind little comfort.

Still, weaving its way through the rumblings of thunder and the whispering of the near-summer winds, the whistling cascaded over it all, hanging in the air, suspended in time, urging Fynn onward. He obliged the beck and call of the melody and pressed on further into town. Looking back, he could no longer see the tavern. No, he'd gone too far and now there was nothing but the night and the bleakness it carried with it.

"Hello?" Fynn called out into the town.

There was no sound, save for the whistle that had grown faint and tired.

"Who's there?" the prince asked.

513

The whistling stopped and, all at once, everything seemed impossibly still, quiet, lifeless. Another crack of thunder boomed; it seemed loud enough to shake the earth, possibly to split it. The lightning struck with such vicious brightness that Fynn had to close his eyes. As they fluttered open, he saw, standing only ten or so feet before him, a figure in the darkness, little more than a shadow. Fynn spied features he thought to be familiar, though wasn't sure if his weariness was simply playing tricks on him.

"Hello?"

There came no response.

Lightning streaked through the sky once more; the flash of its presence illuminated the figure. It was only for an instant, but Fynn was sure he recognized the man standing there before him. Spurred on by the realization, Fynn jolted forward and ran toward the man.

"You can't be here!" he yelled desperately. For once, Fynn was struggling to see through the darkness.

The man had fled at Fynn's approach, retreating into the shadows and rounding a corner, lost to the gloominess.

Fynn followed, but when he reeled around the corner, he saw nothing but a thin alleyway stretched out before him, barren. The boy stood there, motionless, staring off down the alley, searching for any hint of movement.

"Hello?" he called out once again.

A tapping on his shoulder, so light it was nearly imperceptible, caught his attention, startling him. Jumping, the boy jerked around and came face to face with a pair of pale, watery, blue eyes that leered back at him through the night with an all-too-familiar glint of malicious amusement. The voice that sounded was, likewise, known to the prince and made him shudder.

"It's been a while."

Fynn retreated from the touch as though he'd been burned by the contact. His eyes narrowed, piercing through the night. "You can't be here."

"Alas, here I am," the man said jovially, gesturing about with a coy air to his movements. "Standing here before you, real as the stones you stand upon."

The boy steeled himself, tensing as he glared back to the man. "*Why* are you here?"

"Ah, a good question," the man cooed. He was beside Fynn before the boy knew what happened; a slender arm slung around the prince's shoulders, fixing the boy firmly in place. "A good question indeed."

Fynn was unable to pull away from the man's hold. The prince relented and allowed himself to be ushered further into the alley. "Where are we going?" asked Fynn.

"My, my, full of questions tonight, aren't you?" The man continued along, urging the boy forward at his side. "Never mind that, princey. Do come along, won't you?"

"Have I a choice?"

"Fynneas," drawled the old man dramatically, "you wound me so. You *always* have a choice."

They came to a decided stop before a door. It was an unspectacular door, looking like all the doors in More Town. They were far from the beginnings of the town, wherein the Wayward Turtle Tavern was situated. They were long past the center of town where the square and the merchants were found. They were, Fynn noted with a hint of dread, in a part of More Town he'd never been before. It was dark, far darker it seemed, than the rest of the town. Here, the shadows reigned supreme, holding dominion over the narrow, winding streets.

The rain clouds had gathered; cold droplets began their descent.

The man gestured at the door. "Go on," he encouraged, "open it."

Fynn reached out, his hand shaking as it pushed the door open. He stepped through the threshold into a place he'd rather not be. He entered a room. It was small, comfortably decorated. A fire burned in a hearth that was built into the stone of the far wall. Dingy and thread-bare tapestries hung on the walls. Upon the floor was a simple, black rug. Two chairs sat upon the rug in the center of the room, facing one another.

The prince looked back to the man, who remained lingering in the doorway; the pale vestiges of moonlight that managed to creep through the clouds illuminated his silhouette.

"Why do you always bring me here?" Fynn whispered.

The old man entered, closing the door behind him. He crossed the room and seated himself in one of the chairs, motioning for Fynn to do the same. Fynn sank into the chair opposite him.

The man asked, "Tell me something, little prince. Tell me, have you given any more thought to *time*?"

"Time?"

The old man nodded. "Yes, princey, *time*. I do recall we discussed it before, yes?"

"You told me it was everywhere, all around us."

"And?"

"And that, even though it's everywhere, we—you and I—*are* where we *are*." Fynn looked across to the man warily. "I still don't understand."

"Child, tell me, where in time *are* we right now?"

"It's nighttime."

"Nighttime when?"

Fynn shrugged. "The night before the games."

"Good." The man arched a brow. "I'd like to ask you another question."

The boy sighed. "I don't see how I can stop you."

"You and your sister have continued your little search for answers, yes?"

"Well...*she* did. I didn't do much, really."

"And what has she found?"

"Your name."

The man smiled a most wicked smile; his pale, blue eyes shone eerily in the golden light cast out from the hearth. "Very good." He reached into the pocket of his trousers and pulled from its confines a piece of parchment. He handed it to the boy. "Go on, boy, and say it. Say my name."

"Biel," rasped Fynn.

The face of the old man melted away and there, revealed beneath as if a mask had been pulled off, was the face of a far different sort of creature. Gone was the aged, leathery skin, and in its place was a smooth, fair complexion. The eyes, once a watery blue, were now the deepest black, gleaming in the firelight. Wispy, white hair fell away and was usurped by deep, dark black. Biel smiled a toothy smile, teeth sharp as a shark's and just as frightening. When he spoke, his voice was the same as it had always been. "Go on, princey, read the letter."

Fynn held it, immediately spying the familiar scrawl writing out 'FDF'. He unfolded the parchment, revealing the words:

I'm glad you've found your present. Give it a look.
You're sure to have questions.

He scowled. "This is the note Sir Jaeryn brought me. It's from you. But I knew that."

Biel continued, "And so, do you have questions?"

"None that I'd trust you to answer honestly," Fynn hissed.

"Ah, little prince, you're learning. It's about time." Biel sighed, smoothing a youthful hand over his black hair. "But we can talk about all this at a later time, I suppose. For now, I'm curious, how've you been?"

"Don't act as though you care," sneered the boy.

"I have a professional interest in your life and well-being." Biel chuckled. "Or, have you not noticed? I can't say I just hang around you for the fun of it."

"No," snapped Fynn, jumping to his feet. He stomped one foot like a petulant child, carrying on, "I can't say I've noticed! Every time I see you, it's because something bad has happened." His eyes went wide, jaw slackened. "But nothing bad *has* happened recently." His gaping turned into an accusatory expression as he glared. "Something bad is *going* to happen, is that it?"

Holding his hands up in mock defense, Biel assured, "Please, I'm no harbinger of things to come, no foul omen, if that's what you're thinking."

The prince folded his arms over his chest. "Well, what am I supposed to think? I've grown up hearing bedtime stories of how you eat children and plot chaos. Not the most endearing qualities, *Biel*, that's for sure."

Biel rose in one fluid motion, appearing before Fynn in a whirl. He flicked the boy's forehead as he whispered, "Ah, dear boy, that's hurtful to hear. I'm far more than that. Alas, it's up to you, Fynneas, to decide what to think. I can only help you along the way."

"What…what do you mean?" croaked the boy.

Biel withdrew from the prince and stepped over to the hearth. He stared into its flames. When he spoke, his voice was flat, cold. "What's on the desk?"

Fynn turned away from Biel and paced over to the desk to find a book atop it. His hand fell over the tome, feeling the defined tracks of wear upon the leather. He traced his finger over the lettering - a dark, blood red, that read *The Mortanomicon*. "Why's this here?"

"Go on. Open it," encouraged Biel.

The prince turned the binding, revealing the fragile looking pages of the old book. He flipped through them until he stopped at a page that said nothing more than:

Fynneas Draekon Fog

"Your tricks aren't going to work, Biel." Fynn closed the book with a snap. "I already know my name is in the book!"

"Ah." Biel peered into the soul of the fire. "But have you asked yourself *why* it is?"

"Yes," whispered the boy. His attention was fixed to the red lettering. "Many times."

"And have you come up with an answer?"

Fynn shook his head. "No. Not yet."

"Might I offer you a suggestion?" Biel turned to face the boy, black eyes nearly glowing in the firelight.

The prince nodded.

"Ask those closest to you. I guarantee, one of them knows."

"Which one knows, Biel?" demanded Fynn.

"Darling child, if I told you that, there'd be no sport in you finding out for yourself. *Really*, you must learn to be a bit more independent."

Fynn growled, "Tell me."

"I'm not the one to ask," cooed Biel. "But I think you know who it is."

"Please," begged Fynn.

"I can't. I made a promise to someone a long time ago, you see, and so I find myself in the terrible position of being unable to tell you any more than I have."

"You've told me nothing!"

Biel shrugged. "So, it may seem."

Fynn surged forward, intent on tackling the man to the ground. He threw his weight toward Biel, blinded by a frightening rage that absconded with all his sense. Biel merely stepped aside, watching with a smirk as Fynn tumbled into the fire within the hearth.

As the flames stole Fynn away, Biel waved cheekily. "Until next time, little prince!"

The flames didn't burn, but they licked over Fynn's frame and pulled him deeper and deeper until he could no longer make out the details of the room, and deeper still until he no longer saw anything around him but various shades of gold and orange and red and yellow. He continued to tumble until the comfortable warmth of the flames was gone and replaced by a soft breeze ghosting over him, tousling black hair from his face.

Blinking, Fynn saw beneath his hands and knees, not the jumping embers or clawing flames, but a cobble stoned road. The boy raised himself up and stood, his legs quaking beneath his meager weight. Looking all around in every direction, Fynn concluded that he was once more standing in the darkened streets of More Town.

It was raining. The cool droplets beat down over the boy relentlessly. The light of the moon and stars was all but obscured by the now-very-thick storm clouds that had amassed. The roads were darker, a sinister presence fixed to their existence; haunting, non-existent eyes watched Fynn as he slumped, wrapping his arms around his body as he stalked off into the night. The wind intensified, chilling the cool rain. Thunder cracked overhead, but its roar was dull and faded; it seemed as tired as Fynn felt.

He wasn't quite sure what force led him back to the tavern, but Fynn was silently grateful for it pulling him along in the right direction. Upon entering the tavern, the prince was greeted by a chorus of worried questions, curious glances, and concerned chiding from Nan.

Hollyn studied Fynn quietly, not joining in with the others demanding to know where Fynn had been off to.

"Where were you?" Nan inquired.

"Nowhere." Fynn shrugged as he seated himself.

"You must've been somewhere! You've been gone nearly an hour," the old woman reprimanded.

"I was just off for a walk," offered the prince.

"At night? All alone? In the rain?" Nan pressed.

"I suppose," muttered the boy.

Lux shook her head, flustered by Fynn's avoidance, but said nothing. Instead, she grabbed him by the collar of his tunic and pulled him up to his feet. She cast a glance to Nan and said kindly, "Thank you so much for your hospitality, but we really should be heading back to the castle. We have to be up for the games in the morning. We shouldn't have stayed out as long as we did."

"It's raining," said Nan. "You'll catch your death out there in that rain."

"We'll be quick about it," Godryk assured with a smile.

"Fine, fine, be off with you then. But no dawdling. Get back to the castle quick as you can. Yes?"

"We will," promised Penelope.

True to their word, the first-years hurried back to the castle. They ran the better part of the way back up the hill toward Morancy, the rain pummeling them as they went. They burst through the castle entrance, tracking mud and muck into the hall.

Renwyn, trying to wring the water from his drenched tunic, frowned. "Great, just great. Well, I don't know about all of you, but I've had enough fun for tonight. I'm headed to bed." He went trudging off through the corridor, sleepy looking Hogan and Wilder fast on his heels.

Penelope bid goodnight to the group and then hurried off after the boys, catching up with them and whispering, her words lost to those who remained standing in puddles of their own designs.

Hollyn shook the water from his hair. "I don't think the storm will be gone by the morning."

"Do you think they'll let us get a later start?" Georgie asked hopefully.

The red-haired prince shook his head. "I doubt it."

"Oh," the girl lamented.

"I have to go see my sister," Fynn stated to the remaining first-years. "I'll be back up to the dormitory after I talk with her. I'm late as it is."

25

LET THE GAMES BEGIN

He was tired. There was certainly no getting around that.

Fynn had met his sister out on the balcony, finding her huddled up under the angled stretch of the tower to avoid the rain. After having a laugh at her predicament and dutifully apologizing for his tardiness, the siblings retired to the warm and dry confines of the library. There, he regaled Fiona with his interactions with Biel, of his time in the catacombs, and of the details of his strange experiences - the room and the hearth being mentioned more than once. They'd stayed together all night in the darkened expanse of the library with little more than a dying candle flame to shed some light; stacks of books were piled high, scrolls set aside in flimsy hills of rolled parchment. Fiona told him, more than once, to go off to bed and get some rest, that he'd need it in order to do well for the upcoming competition. Fynn hadn't listened. It wasn't that he had boundless energy or that he wasn't tired, in all honesty he was tired enough to collapse where he sat opposite his sister. But he couldn't bring himself to go to sleep. There was a nagging fear pulling at his mind and he worried that if he fell asleep, it would burn from an ember to a flame and he wouldn't be able to extinguish it. So, he remained awake, wearily reading through tomes of Estherian history in search of something, any sort of hint that could help him piece together all the clues he'd been handed.

As dawn approached, Fynn had yawned his farewell to Fiona as he took his leave of both her and the library. She'd drawn him into a tight hug, smoothing the messy, black hair from his eyes. She'd cried and her tears dampened his shoulder as she bowed her head, burying her face at the crook of his neck. He tried to console her, but he knew well that she worried for him, for what was to come, and that there would be little that could be said to quell that sisterly concern. So, he let her hug him, let her cry for him. He'd wrapped his arms around her, tried telling her that he'd be fine, that he'd see her at the amphitheater. She still cried and so he continued to let her hold him.

When he'd manage to extricate himself from his sister's teary embrace, he'd clambered back to the tower and joined the first-and-second years in dressing - each of them garbed in tunics of their team color. He thought the yellow of his own uniform a bit garish, frowning at the brightness of the shirt with distaste, but said nothing. There was a noticeable trepidation latching itself onto the occupants of the common room as the twenty-six children waited to be collected by the vice lord. No one spoke. No one wanted to be the one to break the silence, to stain it with the sound of their inevitably nervous voice.

Everyone stood around, their own nervous energy keeping them from lounging in the plush seats and sofas about the room. They shifted their weight from foot to foot, some stared off at nothing at all, just allowing themselves to get lost in their own thoughts.

Still, no one spoke.

Fynn touched the dagger fixed to his belt, tracing the intricate patterns of gold with his index finger. It was cool to the touch and smooth. He smiled, remembering that it was Hollyn who'd gifted it to him. He missed the other's presence. He'd gone off earlier that morning with many of the instructors to sail to Nandulus Island, to join the other nobles and the queen, who'd already arrived and begun the festivities. Hollyn's absence in the room was noticed by all the first-years, but it struck Fynn almost painfully.

Presently, the prince stood beside Godryk, who himself was running his hand over the hilt of his own dagger, tracing his finger over the detailed work of the golden, lion's head pommel, flicking over the ruby eyes and then back down the carved mane. Fynn sighed a rattling sigh. Though he was delighted Godryk was on his team, he missed the calming effect Hollyn's presence usually brought with it. Now, bereft of the other prince, Fynn felt his whole body jittering; instead of absentmindedly shifting from foot to foot, the boy was nearly bouncing back and forth, biting down on his lower lip, narrowing his eyes as he watched the door.

Indigo arrived, stepping through the doorway into the common room with a profound air of grandeur; sweeping his arms aloft he said, "Good morning, children. Right, come along this way."

All twenty-six children remained quiet, obediently following the vice lord paramount out of the commons and into the tower, trudging down the stairs wordlessly, and proceeding just as silently into the corridors. They came to a stop before the entrance of the castle.

Indigo turned to face them. His voice was somber as he said, "This is where I'll leave you. From here, head to the harbor. There will be dinghies waiting, five in total. You'll know which one is your team's by the color of the sails. You're as ready as you can be for this, children. I've nothing more I can do for you now. It's up to you. You have seven days. Don't dawdle."

Stepping outside, Fynn couldn't help the groan that escaped when he realized it was still raining. The storm hadn't dissipated much since last night, but thankfully hadn't intensified either. The rain was consistent, falling in chilly patters over the children as they made their way down the road.

Godryk came up beside Fynn, ducking his head, letting the rainwater slide down his temples, his cheeks, his jaw. "Ready?" he asked with a heavy exhalation.

Fynn nodded, determination darkening his pale eyes. "As I can be. You?"

Godryk shrugged. "Does it matter? Not much we can do about it now, is there?"

"No," Fynn grumbled.

Godryk elbowed Fynn playfully, a boyish, lopsided grin gracing his features. "We'll be alright. We'll all stay together. It'll be fine."

"We're going to make it out. I won't accept anything less," Fynn declared.

"And when we *do* make it out," Godryk started, "it'll be you and I in the finals at the amphitheater. You're not going to win this time."

"We'll see about that." Fynn chuckled.

Godryk elbowed him in the side harder. "Yes. Yes, we will."

Ollie hastened his steps, catching up to Fynn and Godryk. He walked at Fynn's side, keeping pace. "Fynn?"

The prince turned to Ollie, quirking a brow. "Hmm?"

"I just...well...I just wanted to say," Ollie began, twiddling his thumbs anxiously, "that I'm glad I'm on your team."

The black-haired prince smiled broadly, eyes lighting up. "I'm glad I'm on yours too, Ollie."

"Seriously. I'm happy it's you," the boy admitted sheepishly.

Fynn slung his arm around Ollie's meaty shoulders, proclaiming brightly, "Ollie, don't be so nervous! Sure, it's scary. But we're all together and we're all going to *stay* together. Nothing is going to happen to you. I promise."

"You don't know that for *certain*," Ollie protested.

"No," Godryk said, "but we know for *certain* that we won't leave you, Ollie."

"That's right," agreed Fynn. "No one is going to be left behind. If anything *does* happen, Ollie, I promise I'll come running."

"Me too," assured Godryk warmly. "No matter what."

Once at the harbor, the second-years made quick work of clambering into their boats, setting the sails, pushing off, and heading into the shallows. The waves were mild, though erratic, in their rolling. The wind picked up, howling by, wrinkling the sails as it carried the three boats further from shore. Watching the black, white, and blue sails creep further out, they seemed little more than blotches of ink spotting a dark canvass.

The water was dark, and the sky was darker, melding into one another so that you could scarcely tell where one ended and the other began. It was, as Fynn stared out toward the sea, a chaotic cacophony of greys all mingling together, accented by the sharp silver of raindrops hurling downward.

The green team headed to their boat, arranging the ropes and readying the sails as they climbed in; they pushed off from the harbor and headed into the waters. They stilled, casting an expectant look back to the yellow team, waiting as their counterparts embarked their own vessel and joined them.

Fynn was the last of the yellow team to board, still rather wary of the sea. He forced down that fear, refusing to let it show on his face or in his eyes. Settling in beside Penelope, he gave Albie and Godryk, who had taken up manning the sails, a decisive nod, and they were off.

The green and yellow sailed vessels petered along through the water, side by side, carried on the same waves. Dier Island grew smaller in the distance behind them until they could hardly see the harbor or the looming shadow of Morancy at the top of the hill. No, now there was little more than grey all around and screaming winds that jostled their boats, knocking them this way and that. The rain was coming down harder, the drops pelting them like small pebbles falling from the skies. The waves lashed at the meager hulls of the sailed dinghies, thrashing away at the wood. Sea spray splashed over their faces, stinging their eyes.

"Stay close!" called Firiel from the green-sailed boat. "The rain's getting worse!"

Fynn's stomach leapt into his throat when their boat lurched, cresting over a wave shakily. Turning his eyes toward the sails, he felt his insides knot as the yellow sails shuddered in the violent winds, flapping and dancing sporadically. They were veering left and right, unable to keep a steady path through the water. Again, they crested over a wave, rocking uneasily as they splashed back down. Water sloshed into the boat, splashing them as they tried to right their course.

At their side, not too far off, the green-sailed boat was facing troubles of its own when navigating the worsening waves. It was leaning left and right, sails fluttering. Waves barreled against the hull, drenching the students as they scrambled to keep their craft on course. Renwyn and Wilder manned the sails. Lux was perched at the bow, staring off in the distance in search of the other boats.

"We're taking on too much water!" Georgie cried as she leapt up, cupping her hands and frantically trying to bail the water out of their boat. "How are the sails?"

The wind worsened, screeching over the waters and cutting at the green fabric. The sound of the wind and the rain was near deafening. The waves continued to batter the boat.

"They're holding up!" Hogan yelled over the chorus of the tempest.

At the sound of yelling, Fynn craned his neck to spy the other boat being pushed off course. "We need to help them," he said, looking back at his team. "They're falling behind."

"We can't do anything for them," Albie lamented. "We're having our own problems."

Just then, Fynn was thrown to his knees as a wave beat into the side of the boat, knocking him from his seat. The water slapped his face; his eyes went wide. He gasped, coughing up the salty spray as he heaved. "Shit," he hissed as he forced himself back up, only to be knocked down once more by another violently crashing wave. "Damn it all."

Godryk struggled with the lines; the force of the wind made righting their sails a near impossible task. He, too, was thrown unceremoniously to the belly of the boat when their vessel was struck once more. The wind goaded the water and soon the dinghy was jolting over higher and higher waves, rocking up and then crashing down, water spilling over the bow. Godryk tried to stand, tried to do something useful, but every time he rose, he was knocked back down. Still on his hands and knees, he yelled, "Is everyone alright?"

The green-sailed craft came back into view; the vibrantly colored sails stood out in stark contrast to the empty greyness of the open waters. The rain hung like a curtain, persistently falling down, nearly blinding. The green-sailed vessel was thrown by a wave before crashing back to the surface, its bow tipping just beneath the water's edge for a moment before rocking back up once more. The boat's occupants were clinging to the hull's lip with white-knuckled grips, straining to keep their purchase upon the wood and not be thrown overboard.

Over the roar of the storm, Fynn heard Lux scream, "Hogan!"

Staring through the rain, Fynn saw Hogan tossed from the boat and into the churning grey waters. His head disappeared as waves rolled over him, but his arms still clawed at the air frantically. Those arms were the last Fynn saw of him.

The prince forced himself up; leaning over the edge of his boat, he yelled, "Hogan! Hogan!"

Renwyn and Wilder were doing all they could to keep their boat upright, their attentions fully affixed to the sails. Firiel did her best to dart between the boys, assisting when she could, and to the bow of the boat, searching the seas for signs of Hogan. Georgie and Lux, however, were both leaning over the edge, searching for their lost teammate.

Lux cried, "Hogan! Where are you!"

"Hogan!" Georgie wailed desperately.

A hand breached the surface, fingers curled at the air, grasping at nothing. It was gone in an instant, lost once again beneath the roiling waters. Without another thought, Fynn launched himself into the water. It was only when his body plunged into the depths, lost in the swirls of grey, that he remembered what exactly lurked beneath the surface, what sort of beasts he'd heard tales of.

Spluttering as water filled his mouth, Fynn called, "Hogan! I'm here! Where are you?"

Hope burst into his chest when he saw Hogan break the surface, gasping for air, coughing up water. He was pulled back under. The waves were getting higher and higher. The rains came down like needles.

Fynn was thrown to the side by a gust of wind that soared over the vicious waters before being pulled under as a wave crashed over his back. His eyes went wide when he was submerged. He'd expected to see nothing but darkness, a vast expanse of nothingness. He was surprised, then, when he saw he could see clearly. Schools of fish rushed by, tails flicking expertly from side to side, navigating the current with ease.

As a wave erupted over head, the force pushed Fynn down deeper. His lungs burned as what little air he had left was failing him. Frenziedly, he looked around for any sign of Hogan. He spotted the other boy quickly enough. Hogan seemed limp in the water, like he was a feather floating on a gentle breeze, simply suspended in the middle of the expanse of sea all around. He wasn't moving. His eyes were closes. His fingers were no longer clawing for life.

Seized by the sight of his friend so still, Fynn tried to push himself forward. Another wave pulled him deeper before the current yanked him back up. As Fynn broke the surface, he gasped for air desperately. His chest felt tight, heavy. Black hair clung to his forehead, dripping in front of his eyes. He took a deep breath, deep as he could, and dove under.

Once more amongst the weighty depths of the water, Fynn caught sight of Hogan. He was sinking. With everything he could muster, Fynn forced his arms and legs to move accordingly, directing himself toward Hogan, forcing the water back as he swam closer and closer. The current worked against him. It pulled him back, pulled him under, tossed him from side to side as waves up above slammed down.

The prince's lungs seared once again, their air supply lost. With a mighty struggle, Fynn swam to the surface. He had little time to do more than take a breath before he was forcefully thrown back under.

Hogan was sinking further down. Fynn strained, swimming deeper and deeper. He caught Hogan's wrist and simply refused to let go. He pulled, drawing the other boy closer. The weight of another wave bursting over the surface forced them down. Presently, Fynn wasn't sure if they'd ever make it back above water. His eyes burned from the salt, his lungs on fire from lack of air, his heart pounding in some last effort to keep him alive.

Still clinging to Hogan, Fynn began a frantic ascent upward. He kicked out his spindly legs and waved his free arm, forcing water back with splayed fingers. He heard the muffled sounds of yelling. The dark shape of something swerved by overhead. With a final great effort, Fynn broke the surface, wheezing; Hogan crested over the water, lolling limply at his side. The prince curled his arm around the unconscious boy's waist, holding tightly as he treaded water.

Through the thickness of the rain, Fynn saw the yellow and green sails peeking through, not too far off. His lungs were filling with more water than air. Fynn spluttered, choking on the sea.

"Godryk!" he cried before being pulled under. He beat his arm against the waters, holding steadfastly to Hogan. He broke the surface once more, wheezing and hacking as more and more salty water splashed down his throat. Fynn choked out, "Godryk! Help!"

The sound of Fynn's pleas were faint, hushed under the yowling of the wind and the beating of the sails, the splashing of the waves and the pattering of the chilly rain. It was wearing into mid-morning now, but the sunlight was still nowhere to be seen. Godryk, wrestling the lines and attempting to right the vessel, strained his eyes through the bleakness to spy Fynn bobbing in the water, one arm flailing while the other clung to a limp Hogan.

As the rainwater flew from his brow with a sharp snap of the head, Godryk yelled to his teammates, "There! Just there, do you see them?"

Ollie was up to his feet in an instant, searching for where the prince had drifted to. In the distance, just a few feet from where the green-sailed boat tottered, he, too, spotted Fynn struggling to remain above water. He pointed out and cried, "He's there! He's there!"

"Ollie, help Albie with the sails," ordered Godryk. Handing the lines off to Ollie, Godryk perched one foot atop the brim of the hull, coiling his muscles and preparing to jump. "Try and get closer to the other boat."

Ollie obediently took over where Godryk had left off, nodding his assent to the command. Knowing he couldn't stop Godryk, Ollie bid, "Be careful, won't you?"

Redmayne nodded dutifully. "Steer closer to the other boat. You'll need to help us back aboard once I get to him."

"Right," Penelope agreed, taking up vigil over the sea. She could only just see Fynn splashing in the waves.

Godryk steeled himself, frightened by the waves curling over the boat, beating against the hull, splashing into the surface of the turbulent seas. The wind was blowing them off course. It was clear Ollie and Albie were struggling but still, Godryk hoped that the two would manage to right their way and they'd all make it to Green Isle soon. Despite the wretched feeling of his innards churning about in the pit of his stomach, Godryk jumped from the boat into the water. He swam with all the urgency of the moment, desperate to get to Fynn before the prince was pulled under once more. "Fynneas! I'm coming. I'm coming!"

The waves lifted the green-sailed boat and then dropped it back down. It swayed in the water. The girls clung to the side fearfully, the boys fought to keep the sails from catching the wind harshly and splintering the fragile mast.

Fynn plunged through the surface once more, eyes widening in alarm as he watched the dinghy careen toward him. He tightened his hold on Hogan, curling around the unconscious boy, placing himself between the boy and the boat. Everything went black with the sting of a sharp pain lancing through Fynn's head. As his vision failed him, as his arms went numb and slipped from Hogan, ceasing their frantic paddling, Fynn could faintly hear Godryk calling out to him. The boy sounded terrified; a horror-stricken note darkened his cries; but Fynn couldn't understand why he'd be so upset. In that moment, as the prince fell into the depths further, he could hear little more than the continued, distant cries of Godryk and the lulling sound of the waves splitting over the boats, of the rain falling down, and then the sound of water rushing by his ears until there was no sound at all.

He was sinking, drowning in the sea.

His vision had gone dark.

The stinging in his head was gone as quickly as it had come, and he felt a pleasant sort of numbness come over him. As he fell deeper into the clutches of the sea, Fynn could faintly recall feeling something quite similar once before. Down in the catacombs, he remembered drowning in the blackness. It struck him that this was much the same feeling. Once again, he believed the sensation was fondly reminiscent of the way Fiona would rock him to sleep when he was a child and had been awoken by a nightmare. He could almost feel the way she'd wrap her arms around him and pull him into her lap. He thought he could hear the sound of her voice, hushed in the deadness of night, as she sang him a lullaby to usher him off back to the welcoming embrace of slumber. But he knew better than to believe she were there or that he was safely in her arms. No, he knew he wasn't safe in the embrace of the sea, but for the time being, he couldn't bring himself to be bothered by that realization.

He was sinking.

He didn't bother to struggle, to kick out his arms and legs and fight to breach the surface. No, he knew he was falling deeper and deeper. But the weight of the water was calming, motherly in its caress, as he allowed himself to give way to the pull of the tide. Fynn didn't know how long he'd been floating—sinking—but it felt like ages. He remembered back in the catacombs, he'd been wondering if the vast expanse of nothingness all around while he floated there, suspended in the blackness, was what the sea floor would be like. Now, he reasoned, he may find out. For, as it were, he was once more surrounded by the blackness and falling quickly to what he presumed would be his imminent death. And, as before, he couldn't quite bring himself to want to fight it. There was a pleasant ease to the way he was sinking, the way he was floating like he was little more than a fallen leaf, wilting down to the ground.

It was when he heard his name spoken, spoken by a voice he longed to hear more of, that his eyes snapped open.

"Fynneas."

Then he was searching through the darkness, looking for the one who'd called to him. But he couldn't see her. No matter, he thought, as her voice lilted in the water like a melody on the breeze.

"Fynneas."

He knew his mother's voice instantly; he'd heard it before when it seemed his life was in peril. She had great timing, he supposed.

"You have to swim, my darling. You'll drown."

His eyes were stinging madly from the salt, but he continued staring blindly into the void of water rushing all around. Where he was, wherever that was, the chaos from above hadn't yet reached. He couldn't hear the yelling of his year mates or the howling winds and ripping raindrops, nor could he feel the pressure of waves forcing him down or the pull of the current. It was comfortably still where he was. He looked on through the darkness. His heart was aflutter when light shone around him; a brilliant, silvery sort of light that twisted and curled and formed the wispy, ethereal shape of a woman floating by his side.

She smiled and said softly, "Hold out your hand, Fynneas."

He did so. Every movement, he realized, was a struggle. His lungs felt as though they'd simply burst, his heart pounded away in the cage of his chest like a feral beast longing to be set free. His limbs felt as though they were composed of lead, weighing him down. But he held his hand out at his mother's request, watching in awe as her ghostly hand draped over his. He couldn't feel her touch, but it felt, to him, as though she were right there with him.

Celestine's silver hand curled around her son's. Her voice was firm but kind as she said, "Now, darling, relax. Feel the water all around you. That's it. Now, think of it moving, parting before your hand."

In his foggy-mind state, Fynn could hardly focus on what his mother was saying. But he splayed his fingers, nevertheless, and felt the water rushing all around him, felt the weightlessness of his present existence. He thought back to the day Minnie explained how to call upon fire, how one must feel the blood in their veins turn to heat and ember and lava before the fire would appear in your palm. He thought back to when he'd first, albeit accidentally, moved water at his will when escaping the cave Attika had left him in. With Minnie's instructions and the comforting knowledge that he'd done it once before suitably present in his mind, Fynn willed his body to calm even further, to sink into a pleasant lightness. He imagined the blood flowing from his heart and down his arm to be water rushing through a river, splashing at the banks as it surged by. He felt the sensation pool into his palm, extending up to each fingertip. He thought of the water parting before him, the waves like soldiers lining the roadway for a military procession wherein Fynn was the triumphant general returning from battle, basking in the lauds of his men.

Before him the water started to swirl and twist unnaturally. As if acted upon by an unseen force, it moved from his fingertips and pulled away from him until it curled all around him like a tunnel, cascading at his sides, tumbling towers of water swirling, pulling apart in a sublime expression of something so gloriously beyond the bounds of nature's laws. He couldn't help but watch in awe. Fynn smiled when he saw his mother's ghostly hand still entwined with his own.

She returned the gesture, warmly smiling as she whispered, "Well done, darling. Well done."

Lux and Firiel had only just managed to haul Godryk and Hogan into their boat when they watched in abject fascination mingled with horror as the sea gave way, waves splitting asunder before their eyes, parting like a great chasm in a mountain face. Towers of water were sent spiraling over them, twisting and churning and roiling as they upended from the surface and shot skyward. The rain still fell in sheets, clattering over them, all but blinding the children as they watched the abnormal phenomenon unfold before their awe-stricken eyes. The green-sailed boat was pushed by the waves and sent sailing through the waters, waves still crashing and smashing into its sides, knocking it this way and that, tossing the occupants about with every blow.

The yellow-sailed vessel soared over a wave before plummeting back down, knocking its sailors to their hands and knees as they clung to the boat with all their might, fearful of being thrown overboard into the strange waters. More waves licked against the boat, splintering the wood.

Penelope shook, warm tears mingling with the cool rain as the water slipped down her cheeks. "We're going to die," she whimpered, shoulders quaking.

Ollie wrapped his arm around her shoulder and held her close. His own voice shook as fear warped his words. He said, "We'll make it to the shore. Once we hit land, we'll be alright."

The waves sloshed violently in all directions. Godryk, having been thrown onto his back, sat up. He was nearly startled into shock when he saw a pale hand clamp over the edge of the boat, clinging desperately.

Chest heaving, Godryk yelled, "Fynn! Fynneas, is that you?"

The hand still clung but was at once joined by another. Godryk launched himself to his feet; leaning over the edge, he took hold of Fynn's scrawny wrists and leaned back, hoisting the prince into the bowels of the little boat. They both fell back in a heap, Fynn draped over Godryk's legs, coughing up mouthfuls of water as he gasped.

Godryk placed a hand upon the boy's shoulder and shook him gently, "Fynneas?" He felt the tears pricking his eyes and a smile curling his lips. "You're alive!" He clung to the prince, wrapping the smaller boy in his arms as he cried, his own shoulders shaking with the force of the emotion. "You *idiot*!" His forehead nuzzled against Fynn's shoulder as he continued to shake. "You *stupid idiot*! Are you mad? Gods, but you're alive!"

The boat still rocked and turned and jumped and fell; there was no real control anymore and no one kept up the pretense that there was. They were all knocked about, tipping and sliding and doing all that they could to not fall into the water. Renwyn and Wilder were once more wrestling with the sails and the lines, working hard to keep the boat from capsizing. Georgie clung to the still unconscious Hogan, while Lux and Godryk kept a firm hold on Fynn, who remained dazedly staring back at them with unblinking, silver eyes.

"I see the island!" yelled Renwyn to the group.

"It's just there!" confirmed Wilder eagerly. "We'll make it!"

The yellow-sailed boat cut through the waters; Albie and Ollie managed to expertly direct their craft alongside the green team's. They coasted by, close enough to see Fynn snugged in Godryk's arms, Lux leaning over the two, keeping watch.

"Are they alright?" yelled Albie to the green team.

"They're both breathing," Godryk answered.

"Land's just there," Wilder announced to the yellow team. "We're not far."

Fynn trembled in Godryk's arms, coughing up more water. Blinking, the bleariness cleared from his eyes. He looked down to his own chest weakly, only to see the sight of blood washing down his neck, staining the yellow collar of his tunic. "I'm bleeding," he rasped. He reached his hand to his head, pulling it away only to watch as the rain washed the remnants of blood from his fingertips. "That can't be good," he mused tiredly.

"What's the matter?" Godryk questioned, having spied Fynn curiously touching his hand to his head and pulling it back over and over. "Are you hurt?"

Fynn regarded Godryk with a vacant stare, his eyes holding within them none of their usual spark of life. Torpidly, he nodded. "I think so. I just seem to be bleeding."

"Where?"

Fynn pointed to his head. "Just there."

Godryk ghosted the pad of his thumb just at the side of Fynn's head. He felt the telling warmth of oozing blood. "Damn."

The edges of Fynn's vision remained rather fuzzy. He couldn't make out a great deal of detail. He saw the green sails fluttering overhead and the yellow sails keeping pace at their side. The rain was beating down on them with frightful intent, washing the blood from the prince's face and neck nearly as fast as it spilled. He was thankful, however, that he was able to breathe once more, unencumbered. It was a simple delight – air - that Fynn hadn't known he'd been taking for granted. But, as he breathed in each shuddering breath, he smiled at the feeling of his lungs filling up, extending, full of delightful air.

Lux had gotten up, joining Wilder, Firiel, and Renwyn in their endeavor to keep the sails steady and the boat somewhat on course. "We're getting closer!" she cried out, spying the sight of land loping over the sea just beyond.

Another wave smashed into the side of their boat, forcing them sideways, careening into the yellow team's vessel. The two boats collided forcefully - wood splintered; sails fluttered. The mast of the green team's boat shattered in half with the force of the collision and the wind ripping at it, sending it piercing into the yellow team's sails, tearing the fabric to shreds as they tangled further. The wood continued to buckle under the weight of the impact. The first-years were all sent sprawling to their backsides, watching with terror in their eyes as the sails fell limply into the turbulent waters; wooden splinters drifted over the waves.

"What do we do?" Georgie yelled.

Ollie shook. "I'm not a good swimmer!"

"We *can't* swim for it. We'll drown!" Albie asserted.

Renwyn gathered himself up, frantic as he looked about in every direction, desperate to find a way out of the situation. Jumping in and swimming for shore was out of the question. Albie was right. With the waters as volatile as they were, none of them stood a chance of making it to the island alive. Panic was setting in, taking control of the boy as he began breathing sharply, shallowly. "What do we do? What do we do?" he whispered. He continued his fruitless search for a way to save them all.

Fynn, his head still foggy, rasped, "I've an idea." He struggled to sit up straight, peeling himself from Godryk's arms weakly. "I think I know how to get us to the island."

Incredulously, Renwyn asked, "How?"

Fynn lurched forward, crumpling over the edge of the boat, looking down into the waters that continued washing against the hull. "Ophelia!" the prince yelled. His voice was weak and paling. "Ophelia! Ophelia, it's Fynn! Help! We need your help!"

"Who's Ophelia?" asked Georgie.

Lux smiled knowingly. "The mermaid from the jungle!"

"Smart," Godryk said. "It takes him cracking his head open to come up with good ideas."

"What're you all on about?" Renwyn demanded.

"You'll see," Godryk said hopefully.

Yelling was straining Fynn's already tired body; his throat felt raw, his lungs fragile, his heart heavy. "Ophelia! Please…if you're there…we need your help."

He was fading quickly; he knew. He wasn't sure how long he could keep yelling. Each word took a bit out of him. He was exhausted, slumped over the edge of the boat, one arm dangling over the side precariously. His head felt immensely heavy, as though he were balancing a boulder upon his neck. He set it down against the crook of his arm. His eyes began to flutter closed. He couldn't stave off the blackness claiming him.

"Ophelia," Fynn wheezed half-heartedly. "Ophelia!"

Godryk looked on, mounting fright gripping his chest as he watched Fynn's eyes roll back and close, his head lolling to the side, the rain washing blood down from his black mess of hair over the hull and into the sea where it mingle with the tides like smoke to the wind.

"Fynn," whispered Godryk. He crawled over to the prince's side, hand falling over the boy's slight shoulder. He shook gently. "Fynneas," he implored with another shake. "You need to get up."

Lux felt as though she'd been kicked in the chest; all the air was expelled from her as she watched Fynn slip away into unconsciousness, still slumped against the brim of the boat, wet hair obscuring his face. Her voice seemed to catch in her throat. She could do little more than rise to stand, then nothing more than tremble silently as she watched Godryk shaking Fynn's shoulder, pleading for the prince to wake up. "We have to try," Lux finally managed.

"Try what?" asked Wilder, still grappling with trying to stand as the boat swayed dramatically.

"Ophelia," said Lux. "If Fynn thinks she'll come to help us, well...I believe him."

Renwyn shook his head, "He's cracked his damn head open, Lux! He's out of his mind, *delirious*. Have you seen this mysterious mermaid Ophelia before?"

"No. But I know she'll come." Lux tried to blink away her tears but failed. "I *know* she will."

Godryk pulled Fynn away from the edge, resting the boy against his shoulder, arm slung around the prince's middle protectively. He fixed Lux with a steely gaze and nodded. "I agree. Fynn seemed pretty sure she'd help us if he called for her. We have to keep trying. It's that or drown."

"Ophelia!" screamed Lux. "Ophelia! If you're out there, *please*, Fynn called for you. Please! If you can help us, we need you." Her knees buckled and she fell, kneeling at the edge of the boat. Another large wave poured over the hull, soaking her to the bone. Shivering, Lux leaned over and yelled to the sea, "Ophelia!" The girl recoiled in surprise when the surface broke and a white-haired woman emerged from the depths of the water.

The mermaid's strange, iridescent eyes fixed upon the startled Lux. Tilting her head to the side, she asked, "Is the odd, little boy here? I smelt his blood in the water."

Lux couldn't help the nervous laugh that escaped her. She nodded, "You *must* be talking about Fynn."

The mermaid's hair dripped into the water. "I smelt his blood in the water. Then I heard someone calling for me. Is he here?"

Scuttling back over to the edge, Lux nodded. The rain washed her red hair in front of her eyes; her green tunic clung to her like a sagging, second skin. She looked far smaller than usual, far frailer and younger and more fragile.

Lux said, "He's here. He's *hurt*. Please, we got caught in the storm. Fynn thought you might be able to help us. If you can...well...*please*. Our sails are destroyed, we're trapped out here."

Ophelia peered through the curtains of rain and spied the second boat rolling over the waves just beside the first. She nodded. "Have you any rope?"

Wilder was quick to toss a line to her. "Here you are."

"Have them," she pointed toward the yellow team's boat, "throw me some as well."

Albie hurled his rope into the sea just at the mermaid's side. She took it up in her other hand. Returning her attention to the lot of children adrift in the storm, she instructed, "Hold on, little children. I'll pull you to shore."

Lux fell back into the belly of the boat, sidling up beside Godryk. She bowed her head next to his and whispered, "Are we being pulled to shore by a mermaid, or have I gone and hit my head too?"

Dumbly, Godryk shook his head. "No…no, we're definitely being pulled along by a mermaid."

Lux quirked a brow, chuckling, "Should we be concerned about the company Fynn keeps?"

Shrugging, Godryk replied, "No."

"You don't think it's *odd?*" pressed Lux.

"Honestly, if it were any other person who called a mermaid for help, yes, I'd probably think it's odd. But since it was Fynneas, I can't say I'm terribly surprised."

"True," agreed Lux. She peeked around Godryk down to the limp Fynn resting against the boy's other side. "How is he?"

"Unconscious," Godryk whispered. "His head's bleeding pretty badly." He looked away from Fynn and back to Lux. "How's Hogan?"

"Still out. Georgie's doing a good job minding him," Lux retorted. "He's still breathing."

"Good."

"Godryk?"

Redmayne glanced back to his cousin curiously. "What is it? Are you hurt?"

Lux shook her head quickly, "No, no. It's not that."

"What is it then?"

"I'm scared." She couldn't look him in the eyes any longer. Her gaze averted, sweeping up and looking skyward at the heavy, black clouds congealing together overhead. "The games only just started this morning and already it's a disaster. I'm scared. How much worse will it get, do you think?"

Godryk's free hand clasped Lux's, holding tightly. "I can't imagine it will get any easier," he lamented. "But we're here together, all of us. And I know Fynn won't let anything get to us if he can help it. And I won't either. I swear."

"Me too," Lux assured. "We're all making it to the end." She smirked, elbowing the boy gently. "And when we get to the amphitheater, just know that you don't stand a chance."

"Funny." Godryk smiled. "I said the same thing to Fynn earlier."

"Luxy!" Ollie yelled. Their boats were drawn closer as Ophelia pulled them through the stormy waters. "Luxy!"

The red-haired girl popped up, clambering closer to the yellow team's boat. "What's wrong?"

Ollie pointed toward the white-haired head bobbing through the water, the glinting tail splashing over the surface with effortless flicks. "Is that a *mermaid?*"

"It is," the girl answered. "You only just noticed?"

"A *mermaid* is pulling us to Green Isle?" Albie chimed in curiously.

"That she is," Lux replied. "Try to be more observant, you two."

"How did we come to garner the assistance of a *mermaid?*" Penelope asked.

Lux shrugged. "Apparently she's acquainted with Fynn."

"Should've known." Ollie smirked happily.

At last, the rain was beginning to dissipate, lightening up as they approached the shoreline. Ophelia breached the surface once more and called back to the children, "This is as far as I can take you. The water gets too shallow from here until shore."

"Thank you, Ophelia," said Godryk. "Really...thank you for rescuing us."

The mermaid spun in the water and faced the two boats filled with first-years. Her voice was even, calm. "Get to shore as quickly as you can. The storm will die out soon. Keep Fynn out of the water. If I could smell his blood, so can the others."

"The *others?*" inquired Renwyn.

Ophelia nodded, eyes narrowing as she glanced at the water, seemingly peering into the darkness that swam beneath the troubled surface. "There are all manners of creatures in these seas. Until he stops bleeding, don't let him in the water."

"Alright," Penelope agreed. "Understood."

"This is where I leave you," Ophelia reiterated. "Tell the little prince I wish him well."

Godryk grinned. "We will."

The nine children watched with interest as the white-haired mermaid disappeared amidst the rolling waves, gone into the depths and darkness within a moment's breath. Before they could question how they were to get to shore, the bottoms of their boats burrowed into the sands of the shallows, marooning them in the sand bar.

Renwyn squinted, searching through the rain and spying the shore only thirty feet or so from where they were stopped. "We can make it to the shore from here. The water is shallow. It'll be no higher than our waists."

"What about Fynn?" asked Penelope. "Ophelia said to keep him out of the water."

"I can carry him," Godryk said confidently. "Let's just get to shore as quickly as we can."

From the shore of Green Isle, a weather-beaten blue team emerged from the tree-line. Maeryk Redmayne, a cousin of Godryk's, spied the first-years staggering through the shallows toward the shore. Instantly, he saw that at least two of their group were injured, if not entirely unconscious. He saw familiar red hair, recognizing Godryk at once, even from the distance. The boy, without a word to his teammates, bolted from the tree-cover toward the shore. He rushed into the waters, splashing as he slogged through the shallows toward the herd of first-years. "What's happened?" he asked. He hurried to help Godryk better balance Fynn's weight.

"Fynn and Hogan are hurt," Penelope whimpered.

"And our boats are wrecked," added Albie.

"How'd you manage it all the way here, then?" asked Maeryk.

"A mermaid," said Georgie.

"A *mermaid?*" Maeryk repeated disbelievingly.

Lux nodded. "Trust me, it's not the oddest thing that's happened to us since we've been at Morancy."

Sparrow and Crane, twins from a branch family of House Shoregore and cousins to Albie, met the troop on the beach. Sparrow ran to Renwyn, helping the boy shoulder some of Hogan's limp weight.

Crane bustled over to Albie, worriedly asking, "Are you alright?"

Albie assured, "I'm fine."

Crane beckoned the group to follow him and so led them into the dense jungle of the island wherein the canopy provided adequate shelter from the rain. "We had just started setting up camp," he said, as he led the first-years into the wood, "when we heard you lot sloshing in the water."

"You're setting up camp already?" Georgie inquired. "Isn't it early?"

Crane shook his head. "Until the weather lightens up, there's no point in searching the island for the flag. It's better to dry off and keep warm best you can."

"Ransom was working on a fire," Sparrow added. "It should be ready by now."

"A fire? In this rain?" Penelope asked skeptically. "How are you keeping it lit?"

"The canopy keeps a lot of the rain out," Sparrow began.

Crane added, "And we found a spot just up ahead that's plenty dry."

Indeed, just up ahead, flickering fire crackled. Around it were two more boys, Haemish Stonecraft and Ransom Blackthorn. They rose immediately at the sight of the group approaching. Maeryk helped Godryk lever Fynn to the ground softly; Sparrow and Renwyn did the same for Hogan.

Maeryk knelt beside the prince, frowning when he saw the steady trickle of red slipping down the side of the younger boy's head. He reached down, brushing his hand through the matted, black hair. The older Redmayne was alarmed by the amount of blood that stained his palm when he withdrew his hand. He shifted his attention to his teammates and said, "They're going to be making camp with us. They're tired and hurt. Their boats are wrecked, totally useless now."

"Alright by me," Sparrow nodded.

"Me too," agreed Crane.

Ransom and Haemish nodded their assent, turning to busy themselves with tending the fire. The first-years, after being sufficiently assured that both Hogan and Fynn were still breathing and adequately close to the fire to dry off, seated themselves in a circle around the small blaze. They huddled together, clinging to one another for comfort and warmth.

"Thank you for helping us," Lux offered shyly.

"You're family," Maeryk contended. "I wouldn't just leave you out there."

Maeryk was a tall boy with fair features, a squared jaw and straight, thin nose. His eyes were a hazel sort of color, muddy looking in the scarce light. His red hair was a wild mess of curls, currently weighed down by the salt-water that clung to every crimson twist. He was comfortably settled down beside Godryk. He engaged the boy in conversation, occasionally glancing down at the unconscious prince at his cousin's other side with an air of curiosity and fascination, concern flickering in his eyes.

Crane and Sparrow were not quite identical, but they bore a striking resemblance to one another. They sat side by side, happily chattering away amongst themselves. Their pale, brown hair was cut short at the sides, the top left long and curling over their foreheads. Their eyes were strikingly blue, shining brightly in the meager glow of the campfire. They seemed pleasant enough; from time to time they'd try and draw their cousin, Albie, into light-hearted conversations. Each time to no avail.

Haemish was as austere in his appearance as all the Stonecrafts. Dark, brown hair was cut short; beady, brown eyes sat glimmering beneath thick, black brows. His face was squared and his nose wide and crooked. But, despite his more hardened aesthetic, he seemed the gentlest of the blue team. Upon seeing how distraught Penelope was, he had taken to sitting next to her, telling her stories about all the adventures he'd been on during his first-year at Morancy. It didn't quite manage to calm the shaking girl down, but it distracted her enough to ease the tension from her quaking shoulders.

Ransom was a far quieter figure than his four teammates. Tall and pale, he sat stretched out before the fire, watching the flames dance and squirm. His dark, brown hair fell to his shoulders, slicked back by the rain. His eyes were a deep blue; they would have appeared black if it weren't for the golden glow of the fire brightening them. He seemed lost in thought as he crept ever closer to the flame for warmth. He didn't bother engaging the others in much conversation, preferring to keep to himself.

Lux addressed the group, asking, "If you're the blue team, have black and white already been through?"

Sparrow furrowed his brow as he looked to Lux. "We don't know."

"Haven't seen them," Crane explained.

"Their boats aren't on shore as far as we could find," Sparrow continued.

Crane said, "We're not sure if they've made it to the island. We only just made it before the rain got too bad."

Penelope's voice was quiet and meek. "So…do you think…they're still out there? On the water?"

Sparrow shrugged. "It's a possibility."

"If they are, they best hurry and get to shore," Crane commented.

"If they're still out there," Maeryk started, "they're far off course. They were ahead of us when we left Dier Island…I don't know how we could've overtaken them without knowing it."

"We can have a look when the rain dies out," Haemish offered.

"I agree." Maeryk nodded. He turned to look at Godryk, tilting his head to the side curiously. "So, are you going to explain how a mermaid came to be pulling you all to shore?"

Godryk combed his hair back with an absentminded brush of his hand. He sighed. "I wish I could explain it, really. I don't quite understand myself. I don't know. I suppose Fynneas just has a way about him."

"What do you mean?" Maeryk asked, peeking back to the prince huddled at Godryk's other side.

"You'll see when he wakes up." Lux laughed. "It's hard to explain."

"Odd one, he is," grumbled Renwyn.

Maeryk chortled humorously. "I suppose that anyone who keeps company with mermaids wouldn't make a habit of toeing the line of normality."

"That's certainly one way of looking at it," Wilder huffed.

26

THE EYES IN THE TREES

Someone was shaking his shoulder, but he wasn't sure he wanted to open his eyes and wake up. The shoulder shaking persisted until, at long last, Fynn's eyes fluttered open. He forced himself to sit up from his prone position, feeling the ache in his back, the heaviness of all his limbs. His head felt fuzzy; a fog had descended upon his mind. He blinked the blurriness from his vision and wasn't at all surprise to see the vast expanse of empty darkness stretching out all around him, no end in sight.

However, he was taken aback when he saw who had been shaking his shoulder, rousing him from whatever sleep he'd fallen into this time. Fynn's heart felt like it would leap from his chest into his throat, it felt like it might just vault clear into his mouth, like he'd choke at any moment. His eyes stung; his cheeks were suddenly dampened by the warm trail of tears striking down the pale curves of his face. His voice was little more than a rasp as he stared at the man hunched over him. "Father?"

Felix drew himself upright, towering over his seated boy as he looked down, smiling at the prince at his feet. "You've been asleep for a while."

Jumping to his feet, Fynn launched himself into his father, quickly ensnaring the man in his shaking arms, burying his cheek against his father's middle, heedless of the outright display of such hysterics. He screwed his eyes shut as he shook, silently delighting in the feeling of the man's arm curling around his shoulders, holding him close.

"What're you doing here?" asked the boy as he trembled in the embrace, tightening his hold around the older prince, terrified that if he were to let go, Felix may just slip away into the darkness and leave him.

"I've come to get you," Felix replied simply. "I've come to take you back. You can't stay here for much longer."

"Can't I stay just a *little* longer?" the boy beseeched. Fynn pulled away from Felix and looked up into the familiar, blue eyes he missed so greatly. "Please."

"I'm sorry," Felix whispered. He reached out and combed his hand through his son's hair. His smile was small, somber. The light in his eyes sparked, but it was a solemn sort of spark that seemed almost chilly, sorrowful as it crackled. "Come with me."

Fynn obliged as Felix guided him along. They walked side by side. The boy noted, with some distant feeling of anguish, that he seemed to come up higher at his father's side than he had last time he'd been able to stand so close to the man.

The thought alarmed the boy; his stomach knotted and churned at the remembrance of his last day with his father. He'd relived it too many times now, the images of the morning forever burning in his mind's eye. But, when he glanced up at Felix, the man looked just as he always had. There was an inherent easiness about his person that Fynn envied. As the boy prince scrutinized further, he noticed there was no blood pooling from Felix's neck. Rather, all he saw poking out from the collar of a black cloak was a white column of throat, unmarred by any murderous arrow.

"Usually, I see Mother when I'm here," Fynn commented absently. "Is she here too?"

Felix shook his head. "She's around. But she thought it would be better if I came to speak with you. I've missed you, you know?"

"I've missed you too," Fynn answered quietly. He struggled to keep his emotions from his voice, to maintain some semblance of control over his words, his tone. "Can I ask you something?"

Felix nodded.

"Dying…did it hurt?" He looked up at his father expectantly, curiosity brimming in the icy confines of his quizzical gaze. "What was it like?"

"It was…quiet," Felix answered slowly. "It was like everything just slid away at once. It hurt…the arrow…but it stopped and then everything just melted away and it was *quiet*." A small smile crept onto his face as he continued, "Nothing hurt. Nothing hurt at all. I didn't feel anything anymore. There was no more pain or fear. I wasn't scared about it. It just happened and before I knew it, I was gone, and I found myself somewhere strange. Well, I suppose you'd call it the land of the dead."

"This place?"

Felix shook his head. "No, this place is something different. I'm not really sure. It's like the place you go between life and death. Death is different than all this."

"Oh," Fynn muttered. He couldn't help the small chuckle that sounded. "You know, you're the first person I've spoken to here who's given me a normal answer. Everyone else just answers in riddles or just stays really vague about everything. It gets annoying."

"I could imagine." Felix laughed lightly. "Fynneas?"

The child cocked his head to the side, curiously looking up at his father as they continued further into the depths of the blackness. "Yes?"

"Let's talk about something else, alright?"

Fynn agreed.

"Tell me, how are you liking Morancy?"

All at once with the mention of the school, Fynn was broadly smiling. A warmth erupted in him as he thought about his time on the island, of the friends he'd made. "I like it."

At the thought of his friends, he recalled the waves breaking overhead and the deafening sounds of the storm wailing all around them. The warmth he felt faded, chilled, and he was left wondering if they made it to shore alright, if they were all still alive. Something about the thought of losing them, even Renwyn, profoundly disrupted something within the prince and he winced, frightened by the prospect of returning only to find they'd all been swept out to sea, drowned, or ripped apart by one of the monsters in the water.

"I have friends," Fynn continued shakily. "I need to get back to them."

"You will," assured his father. "Tell me about them."

Nodding numbly, Fynn began telling his father about each of his new comrades. He talked at length about how Georgie and Penelope always gawked at Moriah when he was around, at how Firiel was the scariest girl he knew, about how Hogan was a kind and gentle soul who probably should be as far away from the battlefield as possible. He regaled his father with how Ollie had started their term frightful and nervous, but how he had worked hard to keep up with the rest of their year mates, of how well he'd done in sailing and how he'd taught Fynn to tie the different knots. Fynn talked about Albie's easy-going nature and Wilder's more brash tendencies, about how Renwyn was always trying to lead the pack.

He said, "And Godryk's been great. I suppose he's my best friend, really. He's the one who's been there. Even when I was awful to everyone, Godryk still stayed around. He's gotten really good with a sword too. He beats me sometimes, but I win more than I lose." Fynn smiled. "For now. But I've been working hard too, you know? I can't let him win."

"And Hollyn?" prompted Felix.

"He's, well…I don't know. I hated him, really. We'd fight all the time. But now? I certainly don't hate him." Fynn laughed, "He's like my brother now. We fight and argue all the time still, but it's different. He's made me better. And even though he isn't competing, he still tried to make me better. He told me he thought I'd win, you know? He actually said he told Moriah he thinks I'll win the tournament at the end." Feeling embarrassed, Fynn looked away from Felix's bright eyes and stared down at the blackness passing beneath his feet. He smiled as he continued, "I want to win. I want to win for *me*, to prove to *myself* that I can do it. But I want to win for *him*, too. I suppose…well…I want to *show him* I can do it."

"It seems like you've made good friends," Felix commented. "It sounds like Godryk and Hollyn have been quite good for you."

"They have." Fynn's cheeks burned like flames as he looked at his father, knowing full well the pale white of his complexion had gone pink. "There's this…*girl*."

"A *girl*, eh?" chuckled Felix.

Nervously, Fynn chewed on his cheek as he nodded once more. "Yes. She's in my year."

"What's she like?"

"She's really strong. And brave. And she's smart. She's so good at everything. She's really good on a horse and with a sword. Sometimes, I only barely win against her when we spar. She's quicker, I think." He raked his hand through his hair. "Her name's Lux."

Felix quirked a brow as he looked down at Fynn. There was a sort of pride swelling in him as he noted, "You didn't mention anything about what she looks like."

The boy shrugged, saying, "Oh, you're right. Well, she's got red hair and blue eyes and freckles. But what does that matter? I didn't tell you what anyone else looks like."

"True," mused Felix. "But, from what you've said about her, it seems like you don't think of her like you do everyone else. Is that a fair conclusion?"

Fynn shrugged again. "I suppose. I probably pay more attention to her than the others, but I still don't see what it matters."

"Well, do you think she's pretty?"

"*Pretty?*" Fynn repeated uncertainly. "What does that have to do with it?"

"Well, usually boys notice if a girl is pretty," started Felix with an amused smirk. "You're telling me you haven't noticed?"

"Georgie and Penelope are *much* prettier," Fynn replied confusedly.

Rolling his eyes, Felix instructed, "Maybe don't mention that to Lux. Yes?"

"I don't pay attention to her because I think she's the prettiest girl around," Fynn protested. "Being pretty has nothing to do with who a person is." His tone bore a stubborn, nearly indignant quality to it that further amused his father. "Georgie and Penelope are nothing like Lux! She isn't the sort of girl who worries about how her hair looks or if she's dirty or anything like that. Georgie and Penelope are just silly girls most the time—they're my friends, of course—but they aren't...well...like Lux."

"I look forward to hearing more about her one day," Felix said.

"One day?"

Felix nodded. "Unfortunately, Fynn, our time together for now has run out. This is where I must leave you."

"Do I have to go? Can't I stay just a little longer with you," pleaded the boy.

Felix sighed. "No."

"Please!" cried Fynn, throwing himself at his father. His arms wound around the man once more, hot tears springing into his eyes. "Please? This wasn't enough."

Felix's hand smoothed over his son's messy hair. "You'll never think it was enough."

"I miss you," whimpered the boy, burying his face against his father's torso. "I don't want to go."

"I don't want you to go," Felix admitted softly. He pushed Fynn away slightly, kneeling down before the boy. They were eye to eye. He could see the darkness shading Fynn's luminous eyes, the ghostly light of them paled in the shadows, as if overcome. "I'll miss you, Fynn. But know that I'm proud of you. I'm so very, very proud of you."

Silvery tears fell, unrestrained, down Fynn's face. They poured over his cheeks, sloshed from his jaw and wet the collar of his yellow shirt. He shook his head. Black hair tumbled over his eyes. "I don't want to go."

Felix's hand cupped Fynn's cheek; his thumb brushed away the tears. His voice dropped to a rasping whisper as he said, "I know. I know."

"Don't make me," Fynn whispered.

"You know you have to go back." Felix sighed. "Your friends need you, don't they?"

Reluctantly, Fynn nodded slowly. "Yes."

"You can't just abandon them for your own selfish desires, Fynneas," Felix chided hollowly. "No matter how bad you may want something, would it be right to sacrifice others to obtain it?"

"No," Fynn replied.

"You're not alone in all this." Felix smiled sadly. "Your mother and I are here. We'll always be here."

"Will I see you again?"

His father brushed another tear from Fynn's face. "I hope so."

"I'll do my best," vowed the small boy, his shoulders trembling as he curled his hands into fists. "I promise."

"I know you will." Felix laughed. He pulled his son into his arms one last time, resting his chin on the boy's shoulder. "You'll do great things, Fynny." He rubbed his hand in circles between the child's shoulders. "I know you will."

"Love you," murmured Fynn, burying his head against his father's chest. He couldn't hear the sound of any heartbeat.

"And I love *you*," Felix assured. He couldn't help his own tears from falling. "Be good."

Fynn pulled away languidly, swiping the tears from his face with his hand. "I will."

"Goodbye, for now."

"Bye for now," Fynn solemnly repeated.

The blackness crawled up Fynn's ankles, creeping like a thousand spiders over his legs. The black tendrils pulled him down as the waters of the sea had, when the waves had crashed overhead. He was sinking further and further and soon could only scarcely see his father looking down, watching him being pulled under. Fynn reached up, straining his arm as far as it could go, grasping at nothing but wishing with everything within himself that his father would reach down and catch his hand and pull him back to stay for a while longer. But Felix didn't and so Fynn continued to sink down and down and down until he no longer saw his father there, watching him. He no longer saw anything but the endless darkness all around. Once more he was floating there in the dark, alone in the silence of it all.

He let himself relax against the caress of the heaviness that washed over him like lolling waves, softly passing over his thin form as he floated in the abyss. His arms and legs felt light, airy. He was certain this was what flying must be like. It was a peaceful sort of numbness that settled over him, calmed him as the blackness pulled him deeper and deeper.

"Fynn?"

He strained his eyes to peer through the darkness and saw nothing. But he knew he had heard Godryk say his name.

"Fynn? Are you waking up?"

It was Godryk. He knew it was. Though the voice sounded distant and faint, as if the other boy were calling from some place far off and away, Fynn knew it was Godryk.

"Fynneas? Does anything hurt?"

Nothing hurt. Truthfully, Fynn couldn't feel much of anything at all. He felt so totally and completely weightless, like he was nothing, like his body were composed of wafting smoke. No, certainly nothing hurt. What an odd query.

"Fynn, wake up."

Godryk's voice seemed more imploring now than it had before. Strange, thought the prince as he continued to sink. He tried, truly tried, to find where Godryk was. The voice was coming from all around, echoing from every direction. Still, he couldn't see the red-haired boy.

"Please. Please, you have to get up. Fynn!"

Godryk was begging. He sounded desperate, frantic. The frenzied nature of the boy's pleading worried the prince. Fynn's heart beat faster and faster until he could hardly breathe. Something landed on his shoulders, beating down over him, shaking him.

"Wake up!"

Fynn's eyes flew open and at once were assaulted with green all around; cold raindrops rolled from the leaves overhead and plopped down atop his head. The air was warm and damp; the distant sounds of thunder rumbling up in the clouds poked through the canopy. He heard the crackling of a fire, saw the tawny glow of its light, the twitching flickers of the embers as they jumped up. Then Fynn's eyes focused on Godryk beside him, hands clamped over his shoulders, blue eyes wide with panic.

"Godryk?" mumbled Fynn as he sat up wearily. It was a moment later that a terrible pain lanced through his head, hammering viciously. His vision was blurry; everything swam in and out of focus.

The red-haired boy threw his arms around Fynn and pulled him close. He held tightly, shaking against the prince. "You're up," Godryk whispered softly, uncertainly. "We didn't know how long you'd be out."

"Out?" asked Fynn. He felt dreadfully groggy. He could feel Godryk trembling. Slowly, one arm rose to curl around the other boy, patting him on the shoulder. "Don't be so upset," Fynn insisted tiredly. "I'm fine."

When Godryk withdrew, disentangling himself from the prince, Fynn was surprised to see the sheer emotion that swelled in the boy's eyes, how the blue of his irises seemed infinitely bluer than before.

"Really…I'm fine," cajoled the prince.

Godryk remained kneeling before Fynn, red hair a mess as it tumbled and curled in every direction. He wiped at his tear-stained cheeks forcefully, leaving them red when his hand pulled away. He coughed, his own sob catching in his throat as he bit it back. "You hit your head really hard. Well, the boat hit you. And you almost drowned. There's no way you can be *fine*. I mean even *you*, of all people, wouldn't be alright after something like that." He shook his head, no longer looking at Fynn but intently studying the ground, as he said, "You've got a nasty looking gash on the side of your head. Does it hurt?"

The grogginess was abating, but as it ebbed the pain flowed in, stronger and stronger with every passing second. The lancing sting that'd slashed at Fynn's head had calmed, leaving in its vicious wake a dull, but quite painful, throbbing. It pooled from where he supposed the gash was, radiating toward his left temple, making his left eye feel as though it would explode at any moment. Moreover, his vision remained concerningly blurry, the edges of his sight a hazy fog. He tried to blink it away, but his vision remained muddled, dulled, and distorted. "Head's sore." Fynn tried to shrug but the movement made it hurt more. "I'll be alright."

Tentatively, he reached his hand to his head. He was alarmed by the blood that stained his fingers but forced himself to maintain a neutral expression. He could see the blue eyes burning, staring back at him woefully. He wouldn't worry Godryk if he could help it.

"Still bleeding, but head wounds always bleed more than anything else. Don't look so scared, Godryk." Fynn shifted, stifling a yelp of pain before it could sound, and then asked, "How's Hogan?"

"Alive."

"That didn't sound too promising. Is he alright?"

"He hasn't woken up yet," admitted Godryk quietly. "It's almost nighttime. We've been here on Green Isle for a few hours now. He should've been up."

"Give it time. *I* only *just* woke up, remember?"

"He didn't have his head smashed in by a boat," countered Godryk.

Choosing to not argue more, Fynn pulled his bleary gaze away from Godryk and surveyed his surroundings. It was getting dark. The rain was still falling, but it was a gentle pour rather than a raging tempest. Godryk, Fynn, and Hogan were the only three that were around the campfire.

Arching a brow curiously, Fynn inquired, "Where's everyone else?"

"Gone looking for food and water," Godryk replied evenly.

"When do you suspect they'll be back?"

"Soon, I think."

As if summoned by Fynn's words, Lux emerged from the shadows that hung amongst the trees around the camp. She held thick sticks in her arms, her red hair a matted mess, dirt smudged over her freckled cheeks. She took another few steps closer, seemingly lost in her own thoughts, before she noticed Fynn sitting upright beside Godryk. Her eyes ignited when she saw him. Dropping the sticks, she jolted forward toward the prince, skidding to a stop just before him and crumpling to her knees as she knelt. Her pale arms, exposed by the torn sleeves of her green tunic, curled around the boy tightly. Like Godryk had done not long before, she pulled him close and trembled against him, the force of her own tears shaking her whole body as she clung to Fynn with the sort of desperation one would a lifeline.

"You're awake," she whispered, her cheek firmly set against his shoulder, tears crawling through the grime that stained her snowy flesh. "You're awake."

The corners of Fynn's lips curled upward into a smile as he gently pat Lux's back. "I am. And I'm fine." When she pulled away from him, eyes narrowed incredulously, he nodded with certainty despite the pain. "*Really*, I'm fine."

The sound of footsteps drawing nearer caught Fynn's attention. He peered over Lux's shoulder and watched as a second-year he recognized from sailing lessons, Ransom, emerged with sticks in his arms. He stopped just short of the trio, staring at them with a blank expression.

"I see you're awake," he commented. "Good." Ransom's attention strayed to Lux, still curled closely to Fynn. He furrowed his brow but didn't speak. Striding by the group, he set his sticks down by the fire and took a seat opposite them.

"I'm glad you're alright," Lux whispered quietly, looking away and toward the fire. "I don't believe that you're *fine*, but I don't feel like arguing with you."

"If only Godryk was as sensible." Fynn snorted. "I don't need to be worried over constantly like I'm an infant. I'm *fine*."

"It's only because he cares." Lux huffed as she stood, retreating from the prince.

Godryk laughed, playfully punching Fynn's arm as he said, "Brilliant."

"What did I do?" Fynn asked genuinely, eyes going wide when he looked back to Godryk. "What did I do?" he repeated.

"She was worried about you," Godryk explained. "You could pretend that you appreciate her concern."

"I do!"

"Weird way of showing it," grumbled Godryk.

"*You* didn't leave," contended Fynn, "and I wasn't any better to you."

"*I'm* not a girl," Godryk rebutted. "*Try*, just *try*, and use your head *for once.*"

The remaining first and second-years soon returned to the campsite, each of them commenting about Fynn having woken up, and then settling down in a circle near the fire. When they were all returned, cooking the rabbits they'd managed to catch over the fire, Fynn asked, "Is this everyone?"

Maeryk nodded. "We don't know where the black and white teams are."

"Not at all?" Fynn questioned.

Sparrow rubbed at his eyes. "No. Haven't seen them or their boats since we got here."

Crane added, "Could be lost at sea."

Fynn, comfortably seated between Godryk and a worn looking Ollie, settled into the easy silence shared amongst the three teams as they ate. He looked at the piece of meat skewered on a sharpened twig that had been set in his lap. He wasn't hungry. He reached down to the twig, twirling it between his fingers, admiring the morsel impaled upon it. He still wasn't hungry. The scent of freshly roasted meat wafted into the air, a gentle and alluring fragrance tantalizing all the children who'd been at sea that day. Still, Fynn wasn't hungry. He set the twig down upon his lap once more, choosing to simply relax in the blissful silence for the moment.

The sound of a stick snapping behind him caught Fynn's attention and he whirled around, jumping to his feet. Instantly, he knew he shouldn't have done that. His vision blurred more, angling dangerously as if the world was suddenly off kilter. His head felt as though someone had buried in axe in it. He could practically feel the blood rushing in his head. Swaying, Fynn continued glaring into the darkness around their campsite until he caught the distinct flicker of an eye alight by the pale glow of the fire, peering back at him.

"Something's there," Fynn said. "Watching us."

Godryk leapt to his feet, now shoulder to shoulder with the prince. He took a careful step forward, standing between Fynn and the trees. He narrowed his eyes, staring into the shadows until he, too, saw the glowing eyes looking back at him. He shuffled to his side a bit more, fully standing in front of Fynn, carefully edging the injured prince closer to the group. Godryk squared his shoulders; his hand reached to the blade fastened to his belt. He whispered, "You're right."

The others climbed to their feet, each of them holding their hands at the hilts of their knives, waiting for the moment to draw and fight.

Ollie snatched ahold of Fynn's wrist, dragging him back and away from Godryk, pushing him closer to the others. He murmured, "Look, I know normally you'd go running off straight at whatever that is, but your head's split open so just stay here. Alright?"

Fynn scowled but stayed quiet. He knew, better than the rest of them at present, that there was no way he would win any kind of a fight at the moment. Everything still seemed to be tilted to the side. Worried, he noted that he could scarcely even see out of his left eye. He hadn't realized that his hand had flown from his side and clamped over the afflicted eye until Ollie squeaked with concern, rushing to Fynn and gathering the prince up in his arms.

"What's wrong?" the boy asked, prying Fynn's hand away from his face. All the air seemed to abscond from Ollie's lungs, for he stood before Fynn gaping and wheezing. His own eyes had gone wide as he studied the prince before him. "Your eye," he muttered. "That *can't* be good."

The pain was intensifying, striking from the laceration at the side of Fynn's head all the way down a jagged path to his temple, burning his left eye. Simply blinking felt as though someone were dragging a blade over the plush softness beneath his lids. A scream was brimming in the back of his throat, but Fynn fought hard to keep it at bay. As it were, he doubled over in pain, eyes screwing shut as he gasped, struggling for air. He crumpled to his knees, shaking terribly. Sweat ran from his forehead down the angles of his face.

At once, Ollie was kneeling beside him. Fynn could only faintly hear the other boy talking. His lashes fluttered and then he could see the blurry shape of Ollie at his side, but the other boy's voice sounded so distant that it seemed impossible he could be so close.

"Hurts," Fynn hissed as he bowed his head.

Ollie's arms wrapped around the prince's shoulders, pulling him snug against his side before helping him to his feet.

Lux watched in stunned horror as Ollie hauled a practically limp Fynn closer to the group. The prince was sweating, shaking almost violently in

Ollie's arms. He was clutching the left side of his face. To her absolute terror, she could see red rivulets stretching between Fynn's fingers, slowly crawling down his hand and to his wrist, staining his already tattered shirt. She swallowed back the fear that had arisen and turned her attention to Godryk, who stood closest to the trees, resolutely still as he stared back at the iridescent eyes that had affixed to their group.

Mustering what strength she had left, Lux sidled up beside her cousin. This close, she could see the vibrant green of the mysterious eyes staring from the shadows. Lux kept her voice low, quiet. "What do you think it is?"

"I don't know," Godryk replied. Slowly, carefully, he drew his knife. "It's just watching us."

Lux nodded numbly, drawing her own knife. "Are there Iba-Jii on *this* island too?"

"Maybe." Godryk shook his head. "But I don't think whatever that is, is an Iba-Jii. Looks too big."

Another pair of inhuman eyes blinked into existence beside the first. Then a third set, and a fourth. More and more eyes appeared until the children realized they were surrounded. Ollie, with Fynn still held protectively in his arms, knelt down and pulled out his knife. He levered the blade out before him, ready to fight back should something lunge from the darkness. Fynn could do little more than slump further against his friend, his head hanging down, chin braced against his chest as he struggled to breathe.

"We're surrounded," Ollie said. His arm tightened around Fynn reflexively as the fear began to wash over him. "Whatever happens, don't go running off."

The prince nodded silently, still shaking. The pain wasn't getting better. It was blindingly agonizing as it seared through his head.

"What do we do?" Lux asked, looking expectantly toward Godryk.

The boy drew in a quaking breath. "Be ready."

"For what?"

"I don't know," he answered.

Lux shuddered. "Right." Her grip around her knife intensified. She drew it up, level with her shoulders, and held it out, prepared for a fight. "Ready?"

Godryk smiled. "As I can be. You?"

She grinned back at him and said calmly, "No matter what, we're all making it out of this."

Someone screamed. The blood curdling shriek drew the collective attention of the children gathered around the fire. Lux and Godryk reeled around on their heels in time to see Firiel pulled to the ground by something darting from the trees. She was screaming, kicking her legs out and hissing as she swung her dagger wildly. Long fingers were curled around her ankle, dragging her into the darkness. She continued screaming, fighting, clawing at the ground to get away. By the time she was gone, the only trace of her that remained were the deep marks in the dirt where she'd raked frantically, long scars in the earth that extended into the trees and disappeared into the darkness.

"What was that?" Lux cried, trembling. She held her knife in juddering hands. "What was that!"

"I don't know, I don't know, I don't know," Godryk kept saying, shaking his head as if he were trapped in a nightmare, willing it not to be real.

"Ollie," moaned Fynn. The world around him continued to melt away into a colorful mess of swirls.

"It's going to be alright," the boy said. Ollie's shaking voice betrayed him. "I won't let them get you."

At once, creatures leapt from the trees and descended upon the children. Godryk buried his knife into one of them, fear stricken as green blood jumped from the wound and splattered over his face. Spluttering, he tumbled backward, falling to the dirt and watching as the creature whirled around to face him with wild eyes. It had the body of a man, dressed in animal skins. Its complexion was copper-like, muscled arms were braced for a fight, back rigid. Its face was angular in composition; a short and stout nose protruded at the center, flanked by burning, green eyes. Its ears were abnormally pointed at the tips. There was a feral sneer upon its face, revealing sharp teeth that shone frighteningly white in the flickering light of the fire. About its head, vines were twisted to create a crown. It stared, looking back at Godryk maliciously, as emerald blood streaked down its taut back.

"What-what is that?" stammered Godryk. He tried to scoot away, knife still in hand. "What is that thing?"

Chaos found the children.

More and more of the island's creatures lunged at them from the trees, seemingly appearing from nowhere as they burst through the shadows and toward the campfire. Lux managed to cut one, slicing at its palms as it reached for her. The same thick, green blood Godryk now wore as a mask oozing down his face, was presently clumped in the girl's red hair. She yelled as she stabbed at another, plunging her knife into its thigh. It retched in pain, one hand striking out and smacking her across the face. Lux fell limply to the ground, her eyes fluttering closed. The last thing she saw was little more than a brilliant cacophony of colors ablaze in every direction; she was lulled to sleep by the chorus of screams and growls and the low crackling of the fire.

Albie watched, paralyzed, as one of the creatures pulled the still-unconscious Hogan into the darkness. He was shaking in place, knife in hand, as he watched the listless body disappear into the darkness. His heart threw itself into his chest over and over. He could practically feel his blood gushing through his veins with the force of every heartbeat. His eyes were wide when he turned and saw Lux, limp upon the ground, dragged into the shadows. It was the sound of Penelope's scream that caught Albie's attention next. Turning, he saw the girl twist away from the hold of one of the creatures, its arm shooting out in an attempt to grab her. Without another thought, Albie rushed forward and drove his arm down; his knife's blade sank into the forearm of the monstrous assailant.

His triumph was short lived when, from just behind him, Penelope screamed again. When Albie turned to look for her, he saw nothing but the dancing of shadows as another creature, presumably with Penelope in tow, fled from the campsite. Panicked, he'd forgotten the creature he'd wounded. He felt something, a hand perhaps, curl around his neck and lift him from the ground. Albie dropped his knife. His hands flew to his neck, fingernails frantically clawing at the fingers curled around his thin throat like a murderous collar. He kicked his legs out as he wriggled, hysterically wheezing and gasping as air failed to reach his lungs.

Wilder launched himself at the creature, stabbing its shoulder so deeply it let go of Albie. The boy smashed to the ground in a heap, panting for air. As Albie struggled to compose himself, he watched weakly as Wilder tried to fend off his attacker. It wasn't long before the boy fell to the beast and Albie could do little more than watch as his friend was pulled away until he was far from sight.

The vociferous hysterics mounted until Albie couldn't make out anything distinctive. It was little more than waves of sounds, undistinguished and muddled, breaking over him. His head felt light and heavy all at once as he rolled to his stomach and began crawling toward the vague shapes he saw not far from him. His chest heaved with the strain of breathing; his lungs felt like they were burning with every breath. He continued his strained attempt toward his comrades, his arms feeling wobbly and unsubstantial as he made his way.

"The fire." Fynn coughed. He saw little more than pale colors all around, presently. He heard nothing more than a faint buzzing and distant crackle. He felt Ollie tense against him, the arm supporting him and keeping him from pitching face first into the ground tightening even more, securing the prince in place. "The fire worked last time...maybe...this time too." Every word was a struggle, every syllable increased the nausea that had recently begun roiling in Fynn's stomach, knotting his insides.

Ollie nodded "You think it'll work?"

"We have...to try." Fynn coughed, tasting bile on his tongue.

"Right," affirmed Ollie solidly. He gathered the prince against him fully and hefted the boy back up to his feet. He shifted the weight of the smaller boy against him until he could safely begin staggering toward the fire, never letting his attention stray from the onslaught for too long. He winced when he saw Haemish, one of the second-years, struck in the leg and then dragged off.

"Almost there," Ollie said.

Once within arm's reach of the campfire, Ollie eased Fynn to the ground gently. He saw, at once, the sticks piled by the fire. He tipped one into the flame, delighting in the end catching alight quickly. Ollie swung his arm out; the yellow light of fire streaked the night air, burning brightly. He continued waving the stick, letting the heat of the flame lick the skins of the creatures who'd descended upon them.

As he continued thrashing his arm this way and that, he saw Albie crawling toward him.

"Albie!" Ollie screamed. The other boy looked up to him, his eyes glazed and unfocussed. "Albie!"

Fynn heard Ollie yelling, calling out to Albie. He tried to look up, to force his eyes to focus, but he still couldn't see anything but colors, shapeless blurs flitting across his line of sight. But he knew that things were going horribly wrong for them; the strained, throat tearing cries had sent a shiver down his spine, the sort that shot through his legs and left him feeling numb, useless, stricken down by an overwhelming emotion that had seized every muscle in his small frame. Through the cloudiness of colors, Fynn saw fire alight, swaying right and left just before him. Ollie had gotten the fire; that simple realization calmed the prince, though only marginally. The continued cries of the others as they fought with everything they had to fend off their attackers still unsettled Fynn.

"Albie!" Ollie cried. Tears poured down his face.

The growls were getting closer, as were the sounds of claws scratching against the earth. Shakily, Fynn reached out one hand toward the fire and dipped his palm down into the flame. He felt no pain; his hand didn't burn. Closing his eyes, Fynn drew in a deep breath and then exhaled flatly. Focusing, he let his breathing even out, willing his heart to stop thudding so violently. He did his best to ignore the pain in his head, to register it only as a peripheral annoyance. Calming down, he thought of the fire reaching all around his hand, his wrist, his arm. He felt the heat racing up his arm, like blood flowing in his veins, igniting in his chest. "Please...*please* work," he murmured.

The fire swirled in a column, reaching upward toward the canopy like a pillar made of flame. Embers sparked in every direction, raining down over the campsite. The feeling of intense heat warmed over Ollie's back; the resounding hiss of flames as they erupted caught his attention further. He whirled around only to remain there, stunned, as the fire burst upward. He dropped his knife, letting it clatter against the ground as he watched the fire continue reaching, stopping just shy of igniting the lush canopy. Unnaturally, the flames reached out and swirled around the camp, staying clear of burning any of the remaining children, but doing well to chase off the offending creatures until they rushed back into the safety of the trees and the darkness, disappearing from sight and leaving the scared children to wonder how the fire had managed to act thus.

Fynn collapsed to the ground. His cheek rested upon the earth. It felt cool and damp and soothing. His whole body seemed impossibly heavy, weak. His head still felt as though it may be bleeding; those fears were confirmed as he watched the dirt beneath his head dampen and darken; blood washed down his face and onto the earth below. He saw shapes rushing toward him, but the fire had gone out, the night took hold, the rain streaked down. He was tired. Fynn let his eyes close and, at last, gave into the easy embrace of unconsciousness.

Penelope, covered from head to toe in dirt and grime, blood staining the knee of her trousers where she'd sustained a minor wound, inched closer to the limp prince. Her whole body ached dreadfully, but still she knelt carefully at Fynn's side. Her hand settled over his shoulder. Rolling him over, she gasped when she saw half his face reddened from the laceration on his head. She felt his neck, smiling softly when she noted the pulse, slow and weak, striking against her fingers. She looked up from Fynn and saw Ollie huddled over Albie, checking the other boy for signs of life. Penelope called over, "How is he?"

"Alive," Ollie answered. He nodded to the sprawled mass at Penelope's feet. "And Fynn?"

"Alive," she assured. "Bleeding…but alive."

Ollie looked right, then left. "Is anyone else here?"

There was a pause.

It was a frightening pause, fraught with the heavy reality that the four of them were the only remaining Estherians in the area. Penelope set her palm over Fynn's chest, relishing the feeling of it rising and falling beneath her touch. Her cheeks felt damp from more than just the rain. Her sleeved arm scratched across her face, forcefully removing the tears that clung at her cheeks. "We're the only ones left," she said direly.

Ollie, Albie's semi-conscious body at his side, arm draped over his shoulder, approached. Easing Albie to the ground, Ollie settled beside Penelope. He glanced down, spying her hand, now resting over Fynn's heart. His own hand draped over the girl's and he gave a light squeeze. "We'll be alright."

"You don't know that," she argued.

The boy felt Fynn's chest rattle beneath their hands, as though he were struggling to breathe. He sighed, fearful of the condition the prince would be in when he woke again. He remembered, with absolute clarity, when he'd turned to Fynn earlier, when he'd pried the other's hand from his face. He shivered at the image that materialized in his mind's eye, the sight of Fynn's normally ghostly pale iris having gone a violent scarlet. His left eye, where silver should have met Ollie's gaze, was a deep, unnatural red. His left eye seemed to glow with the same burning intensity of the campfire. Moreover, strips of red peeled from his waterline, spilling down his cheek like a macabre wash of tears.

Shaking his head, Ollie tried to banish that memory. It was, he believed, one of the most frightening things he'd ever seen. "We'll do our best; that's all we can do," he lamented.

"Do you think they're all dead?" asked Penelope.

Ollie shook his head. "No."

"Really?"

He nodded. "*Really.*"

"Where do you think they are?"

"I don't know." Ollie sighed. "But we're not leaving until we find them."

27

BLACK, WHITE, AND THE CASTLE IN THE PIT

The storm had stopped. The light of morning stretched through the still-heavy cloud cover, almost gently falling over Green Isle. Tulip Malcourt, a second-year from the black team, clawed at the shore of the island, pulling herself from the failing grip of the tides. She breathed heavily, coughing up pools of salty water into the sand. She shook as she continued raking her nails against the shore, dragging herself further out of the sea's clutches. The sound of splashing just behind her caught her attention, but she was too tired to look back and see who it was.

Aldus Singer, a member of the white team, staggered from the shallows of the water toward the shore. He could see a body stretched out in the sand; the tide was lapping at the girl's ankles. The boy forced himself forward, tripping in the knee-high waters but refusing to fall. He trudged through the shallows up to the shore, collapsing just beside the girl and breathing raggedly. He turned blue eyes toward her, noticing she'd lost consciousness, cheek pressed to the rough sand. Reaching out slowly, he shook her by the shoulder. "Tulip, you have to wake up. We can't stay here."

Tulip coughed; more sea water splashed from her lips to the sand. She opened her eyes and saw Aldus leaning over her, shaking her shoulder. Pushing herself up on hands and knees, she retched more and more until all the water that sloshed in her lungs was expelled and she could, once again, breathe normally. She turned her bleary, brown eyes toward Aldus and asked weakly, "Did anyone else make it?"

The boy shook his head. "I haven't seen the boats. You're the only other one here, far as I can tell."

She nodded weakly. "What do we do?"

"We keep going. Maybe some of the other teams got here first."

"Maybe," she whispered as she stood on wobbly legs.

He rose too, taking her hand in his and keeping a tight hold. "There's no going back now," he said firmly. "We have to keep going. We'll make it through."

"I hope you're right," she relented, allowing him to pull her along toward the trees.

"I know I am." He smiled. "I can't afford to be wrong."

Hand in hand, the pair walked into the tree-line and welcomed the coolness brought about by the heavy canopy blocking what little sun there was. Water slid from leaves and fronds all around, dropping down on them as though it were still raining like the night before. Tulip pulled closer to Aldus, attaching herself to his side as they trudged through the dense foliage. Yellow rivulets of light managed to stretch into the denseness of the green wilderness, throwing weird strains of sunlight and casting jagged shadows in every direction. Birds chirped up in the branches; feral melodies squawked from their curved beaks.

"Do you think there are...*things*...here?" she asked.

"Like back on Dier?"

"Like that, yes."

"Probably," Aldus answered thoughtfully. Fear began tickling his heart, making the pounding increase until it was erratic; his breath hitched in his throat as he tried to calm down. "But we're together. We're going to *stay* together."

"Promise?"

"I promise," he assured, continuing to lead her further into the labyrinth of trees.

Tulip drew in a deep, steadying breath. "Aldus, do you really think any of the other teams made it through the storm?"

"For our sake, I hope so."

The proceeding hour was spent with the two carefully stepping over thorny bushes, around poisonous plants, cautiously keeping their skin exposure to the environment at a minimum. The sound of something thrashing in the bushes stopped both second-years where they stood. Simultaneously, Aldus and Tulip rooted themselves in place, clutching at one another's hands as though it would somehow save them. Eyes going wide, riveted by the rustling, both watched as a long, folded shape unfurled itself from the bushes and stood, mostly obscured by shadows, staring back at them. Burning, green eyes blazed through the shadows, never blinking, never looking away.

"What…what is that…*thing?*" stammered Tulip.

"I don't know." Aldus shuffled closer to the girl, melding against her until they were a meshed lump of jittering frailness standing dumbly, staring at the eyes that never wavered as their own welled with stinging, hot tears.

The shadowed body moved, shifting its weight. Its eyes still made no effort to cease their lingering. Rather, the vibrant green intensified as the creature stepped forward, hunching slightly as it continued its restless eyeing of the second-years.

"I think we should run," Aldus said.

"What? No." Tulip shook her head. "We should stay still. Maybe it will leave us alone."

"I don't think it's going to go away," the boy countered. "I think it's getting ready to come for us."

"Where should we run? Back to the beach?"

"We can try, but there's nowhere to hide if we're on the beach."

"I'm scared," Tulip admitted softly.

"Me too." Aldus' hand flexed around Tulip's. "We have to try and make a run for it."

"Alright," relented the girl. She choked back the fear threatening to strangle her. "If we get separated—"

He interrupted, "We won't."

"*If* we do, we try and find some help. We can't be the only two on the island," she rationalized.

"Agreed."

"Ready?"

He nodded. "Run!"

Still holding tightly to Tulip's hand, Aldus bolted away from the eyes that had been watching them. He heard rustling and bustling behind them and knew, without any doubt in his mind, that whatever had been watching them was now, in fact, chasing them. He leapt over fallen branches and careened around trees, deftly avoiding divots in the earth and maneuvering with frighteningly precise grace around all manner of hazardous foliage. Tulip was pulled, or rather she was dragged, along. Aldus was heedless of her tripping, far more concerned with keeping them moving and ducking and dodging, maintaining a distance from whatever was coming after them, and keeping far from its striking range. The feeling of his arm pulled downward broke through his hysterical trance and he glanced back to see, in that moment, Tulip pitch forward and smash to the ground.

She squealed in horror as she collided at full speed with the earth, dirt thrown up and coating her face and hair, staining her uniform, roughening her palms as she slid to a decided stop. There was a fierce pain in her leg. Her eyes watered as she glanced down at the offended appendage, only to see that her linen leggings had been torn at the knee, blood evident as it shone in contrast to her pale skin. She reached a shaking hand toward her knee, bracing her palm over the nasty looking gash there, feeling the warmth of her own blood seeping through her splayed fingers.

Aldus jumped back, kneeling at her side, clapping his own hands over her knee and staunching the blood flow. He shook, shoulders practically convulsing as he hunched forward, pressing down harder, nervously looking from her and then back at the endless expanse of green and shadows, of curling trunks and twisted branches.

"How bad is it?" he asked quickly.

"Bad," she rasped, falling back, prone, to the dirt and juddering as she took in another breath. "Hurts." Tears freely fell down her face, making tracks through the dirt that gathered there. She felt red stickiness streaking down her shins, lapped up by the material of her trousers, staining the tops of her leather boots as it continued downward. "Hurts really bad," she hissed as she screwed her eyes shut.

Aldus pulled his tunic over his head, ripping a sleeve from the shirt. He wound it around over Tulip's knee, knotting it tightly. The white of the garment quickly turned an alarming shade of pink as it sopped up the blood. Anxious, he pulled the other sleeve clean from its stitching and tied it over the first bandage, knotting it a bit tighter than he had before. Pulling the tunic back over his head and combing his hand through his sweaty hair, he said, "That should keep the bleeding down. We've got to go. Can you stand?"

She shook her head. "I don't think so."

Looping his arm around her waist, Aldus struggled to pull Tulip to her feet. "You'll have to try," he bit out as he adjusted her weight against his body, letting her head loll at his shoulder. "Come on. Left then right."

They staggered forward, not nearly as quickly as they'd been hurrying along before. Glancing down, Aldus grimaced when he saw the layers of white linen over Tulip's knee going a deeper shade of pink. "Try not to put too much weight on it," he instructed. He shifted her again, letting more of Tulip's weight settle against him. Despite the added burden of balancing the girl, Aldus steeled himself with gnashing teeth and pressed onward.

The sound of something hastening toward them set both second-years on edge. Aldus felt Tulip tense against him, rigid in his arms. His own fear was mounting, settling like a rock in the pit of his stomach. He tasted bile rising in his throat; the threat of vomiting from his own firing nerves was now a quite real possibility. He held Tulip tighter, refusing to let her fall, refusing to let her go. It was only when the ground beneath their feet gave way and they plummeted downward, tumbling head over heels down a remarkably steep hill, crashing over stones and twigs, that he finally relinquished his strained hold on her.

The world spun by at all manners of strange angles, a blur of colors of various shades of brown and green. Up was down and down was right and there was no more down, only constant spinning and turning and the appallingly ghastly feeling of one's stomach leaping into their throat and strangling them as they continued to twist and plummet and turn and careen at such a quick pace. Distantly, they felt the twigs shattering beneath their weight, limp as it was as they no longer struggled against gravity. The sharp of rocks tore their clothes and hewed some flesh when they struck just right; the abrasive earth peeled away some skin as they slipped and slid and fell further and further into the belly of the island, a pit-like cavern so far down one could scarcely believe there was a canopy stretched above at all; it seemed nearly black overhead, the distance from the bottom of the pit to the winding green canopy so great that the leaves and fronds and branches looked no more distinct than the bleakness of the night sky.

When Tulip felt her body stop moving, she thought it best not to open her eyes. She felt as though they'd been falling for an eternity and was certain, as she laid there numb against the earth, that if she were to open her eyes the world would still be off kilter and askew. After a moment, finally realizing that she was, truthfully, no longer falling, she opened her eyes and saw Aldus at her side. He wasn't moving. She could see his chest rise and fall. He was filthy - dirt all over, blood trickling from his nose, nasty cuts on his face and arms and hands. Tulip reached out her own quavering hand and gave him a push, calling, "Aldus? Aldus, you've got to wake up."

When he gave no inkling, not even the smallest iota, of registering what she'd said, Tulip chose to use that time to take stock of her own injuries. Her leg was still bleeding. That much was readily apparent to her as she felt the blood still weeping from the wound. But her ankle hurt now, worryingly so. She tried to flex her foot but had to stifle a scream of utter agony at the small motion. Her hands were bruised, palms cut up here and there. Her back ached, her neck throbbed, and her head felt as though it might explode.

"It's going to be alright," she assured herself softly, choking on her words as she said them. "It's going to be alright." Her mantra wasn't helping, much to her dismay.

She gave Aldus another shake. Her voice was far more desperate this time, a broken quality sharpening each syllable with a frenzied urgency. "Aldus! Aldus you *need* to get up. We have to get out of here."

The sound of the ground giving way beneath heavy feet caught Tulip's attention instantly. She peered past Aldus weakly only to see a great, large beast of a creature stomping toward them. Her heart seemed to freeze. It was like time, itself, had stopped as the horror radiated from her core and struck every nerve within her frame, wracking through her violently until she was left hyperventilating.

The creature continued its approach. It stopped just before Aldus. Tulip could see the hair of its legs, far thinker than any human's would be, but not so thick and lush as a fawn's. The creature reached down with one, long arm; black-clawed fingers ghosted over Aldus' cheek before its hand curled around the boy's middle and hefted him up, slinging the unconscious second-year over its shoulder. When the second hand descended upon her, lifting her from the ground upon which she had wished she could melt and hide, and flung her about its sinewy shoulder, Tulip gasped. Pain shot all throughout her at once and she cried out, almost ashamed of the pitiful sound of her anguish ripping from her throat and past her cut lips.

From her perch, limply slung over the monster's shoulder upside-down, she watched as the world went by with lurching jolts as the creature trudged. She saw that they were surrounded on all sides by steep hills, the canopy of the tropical island-jungle far up over head. There was, at the center of the pit, what seemed to be a wild castle constructed of trees and vines and stones. It was large, stretching up toward the canopy, parts of it breaking through and disappearing overhead. Towers were made from hollowed trees - trees larger than Tulip had ever seen before. Vines with nasty thorns the size of her arm curled around the towers, looking deathly in the faint light.

The entrance, a large stone door expertly carved and adorned by runes she couldn't place, opened and admitted the monster and his findings into the feral halls of the island castle. The halls, like the rest of the construct, were shades of earthy tones. The ground was dirt, the walls were bark, and there were leaves of brilliant emerald that sprung out from tiny crevices here and there. It was cool within the confines of those barked walls, relaxing almost. The chill of the air, so far from the sunlight, lulled Tulip into a restless sleep as her head tipped side to side with every step her captor took.

When Tulip opened her eyes again, she was in a cage. That much was clear. That was just about all that was clear to her. Everything hurt. She groaned as she let the world around her come into focus. Her hands were bound behind her back, restrained. She twisted and wriggled, but found she was unable to slip free. She sighed and let her eyes fall closed.

"You're awake."

Snapping back to attention, she searched for the sound of the voice. In the pale glow of firelight, she saw one of her year mates from her team looking back at her with worried eyes. Rory, bound and bruised and bloodied, looked hopeful. Tulip nodded. "Yes," she croaked, "so it seems."

"You've been out for a while," Rory said.

"Few hours I think," added Wallace, another black team member.

Upon closer inspection, Tulip found that the entirety of the black team was with her in the cage. "I thought you all...well...I don't know, really. I thought you all drowned during the storm." She wheezed. Her chest felt heavy. Her inhalations came in short gasps.

Ceral shook his head. "No. When we ended up in the water, we couldn't see you. We thought maybe, well...*you* drowned. We tried to stay close, all of us. We washed up on shore and wandered into the wood. That's when *they* caught us."

Ox, the fifth and final black team member, added, "We're glad you're alright."

Tulip scoffed, "I don't think I'd say *alright*."

"Well, *alive*, at least," Ox corrected.

Taking in another shaking breath, Tulip asked her teammates, "Have you seen Aldus? We were together when that *thing* got us."

Ceral nodded to the side, "He's in the cage next to us with the white team."

"They've split us up by teams," Rory explained. "Must've been able to tell by our shirt colors. Clever."

"It's a test," Ceral elucidated. "They were never going to actually kill us. Morancy has been holding these games for centuries. The fairies...we figured it out after a few hours here, when you see them, you'll know too... they're working with the school. This is a test."

"A test?" asked a groggy Tulip. "What're they testing us *for*?"

565

Ceral looked around, watching the white team huddle together and, more than likely he thought, explain the same thing to the now-waking Aldus. "Us. All of us. They're testing us to see how we react to a crisis like this, to being taken captive. There are a few missing. Blue, green, and yellow are here too. Well, *one* yellow. Apparently, they were all together when they were attacked. There are four yellows still out there."

"I think they want to see if we can break out," said Rory thoughtfully.

Ox added, "Or if those four yellows can break *in*."

Tulip let her head fall back, resting against the branch-made bar jailing her and her team.

"Great," she mumbled, eyes closing wearily.

"Your leg looks bad," commented Ceral, admiring the red-tinged wrappings around Tulip's knee with mounting concern. "When'd you hurt it?"

"Just after I washed up. Aldus and I were running away from…*whatever* brought us here…a *fairy* you said, or whatever," she replied faintly. "Hurts."

"I can imagine." Rory frowned.

"Yellow boy," Ceral called, looking toward Godryk's lonely cage.

Slumped against the bars, alone in a cage, Godryk perked up at the call. He looked through the bars, across the small room toward the black team cage. "Yes?"

"What're the chances your teammates will come and get us out of here?" asked Ceral.

It was Lux who responded resolutely, "They'll find us. I know them. They won't leave us behind."

"She's right," added Georgie. "Fynn would *never* leave without us."

Renwyn snorted indignantly. "He wasn't exactly in any position to go gallivanting around after us, in case you hadn't noticed his head being cracked in two."

"Wonderful," grumbled Rory, dejectedly settling against the bars and trying to find a moment's respite. "Our only hope has smashed his head in."

"He's not *alone*," snapped Godryk.

"Right. Tubby, the crying girl, and a Shoregore are going to manage to not only find this place, but break in and rescue us?" Ceral laughed. "Maybe we should start thinking of a way to break out."

"We can't break out of the restraints," sighed Rory. "There's no way for us to get out."

"Don't give up just yet," encouraged Ox. "There *has* to be a way."

The sound of wings fluttering overhead drew all of their attention. They watched curiously as, from the shadows, a shape unfurled in the blackness. Its soft wings spread as it swooped down, landing decidedly upon Godryk's cage. Claws curled around the branchy bars as it slipped between the gaps and landed gracelessly upon Godryk's folded legs. The boy's blue eyes lit up instantly, a smile widening across his face. "Buttons!"

"Buttons?" repeated Ceral.

"It's Fynn's bat," Georgie explained happily.

"He has a bat?" asked Ox, confused.

"It's a long story." Lux laughed.

Godryk bowed his head, staring into the bat's beady, black eyes. "Can you get my hands free?"

The only response Buttons gave was a quick flap of the wings and a twinkle of the eye. Climbing over Godryk's lap, the bat set to work gnawing at the thin twine binding the pale wrists together.

Leaning forward to allow Buttons more room to work, Godryk glanced toward the green team's cage. "Once my hands are free, I can try and break out of the cage. Buttons can take me to my team, and we can come back and break you all out."

"You can't just leave us here!" cried Bram from the white team.

"I'm not *leaving* you." Godryk assured, "I'll come back."

"How do we know you won't just leave us here? You could collect your flags and make it to the end long before we even have the chance to get free," argued Oren, another white team member.

"He wouldn't do that," Lux insisted heatedly. "Don't be daft! He won't just leave us."

"Why can't he help us *all* get out of the restraints and then we can *all* break out?" questioned Ox.

"Because twenty-two of us sneaking around is going to be a lot more noticeable than one," Lux retorted tersely. "If they notice, we'll have to fight our way out."

"That didn't go so well last time," grumbled Firiel.

"Exactly." Lux nodded. "If it's *just* Godryk, he can slip out before anyone notices he's gone."

"I don't like this plan," groused Bram.

Ceral huffed. "Well, it's the only plan we've *got.*"

When Godryk felt Buttons clambering up his back, holding tightly to his shoulder, he knew his hands must be free. Flexing his fingers and turning his wrists, he delighted in the feeling of the twine slipping from its purchase around his hands. "Buttons, I need you to find me the key to get out of here. Can you do that?"

"He must be mad. He's talking to a damn bat," muttered Rory.

"It worked the first time," Ceral said dully.

Godryk watched as the bat slipped through the stick bars and took off, disappearing upward into the shadows of the small room once more. He hoped beyond all hope that Buttons understood, that he would return with a key to the cage. While Godryk waited, he once again settled his back against the wooden bars and let himself have a moment to calm down. It had only been last night that he and his friends had been set upon by the fairies, last night that they'd been snatched away in the darkness by monsters with claws and fangs and glowing eyes and brought to a castle in a pit. Just thinking of the ordeal soured his mood further. But he couldn't help but ruminate on the subject of the attack further. Mainly, his thoughts were drawn to Fynn. When he'd looked back, he saw Ollie holding Fynn. The prince looked deathly; his head was bleeding and so was his eye. He'd gone paler than usual, listlessly responding to whatever Ollie was saying to him. It was frightening. Godryk recalled, quite clearly, the detached, confused tone of Fynn's voice when the prince first regained consciousness that night, the insistence that he was fine despite how truly wretched he looked at the moment. Godryk frowned.

He drew in a deep breath. He, himself, wasn't in great condition. There was a nasty cut over the bridge of his nose, spanning from side to side. It had, thankfully, stopped bleeding a few hours ago. But it still stung, occasionally bringing tears to his eyes. He did his best to ignore it. It was more so his left wrist that was bothering him. It throbbed incessantly, swelling and darkening. He could move his fingers, and, for that he was glad. Certain it wasn't broken, Godryk chose to remain optimistic about the severity of the injury, assuring himself that there would be no long-term impact to his dexterity.

Godryk was jolted form his thoughts when something fell into his lap, something golden and shiny and perfectly key shaped. Beaming, he drew it up into his hand and admired it in the faint glow of the firelight. "Perfect."

Crawling on hands and knees, Godryk made his way toward the lock that clamped his cage shut and kept him prisoner. Reaching his arm through the bars, he fiddled with the key and the lock until he heard the tell-tale click of the lock springing open and the give of the cage door. With a push, he slipped out and stood, grateful to be able to stand up straight and stretch his back. He was sore all over. His legs felt weak and his arms and shoulders seemed limp and numb. His back ached terribly from having spent hours crumpled in the cage.

"I'll be back as soon as I can," he assured the first-and-second years confidently. "No matter what. I promise I'll be back."

The halls - if the winding tunnels composed of arching branches and piles of stones could be called halls - were long and impossibly dark. It was only the sound of Buttons swooping just above him that helped Godryk navigate through the maze. He didn't hear any voices, no sounds of life anywhere, save behind him in the small room he'd left - the small room or dungeon where the rest of the first-and-second years languished, anxiously awaiting his return. He bit his lip, chewing it between his teeth. It was curious, he thought, that the castle—their prison—would be so eerily quiet. Pushing the thought aside, the boy continued on.

A small opening in the trunk of the tree that stood as one of the walls was enough for Godryk to wiggle into; he clawed at the bark as he hauled his slender frame through, heedless of the splinters cutting his cheeks and forehead as he pressed onward. Emerging from the hole in the tree into the warm, night air, Godryk heaved a heavy sigh. He flopped down against the ground and panted. He hadn't been wandering through the maze-like structure for long, but the anxiety that accompanied him through his escape was enough to leave him feeling like he'd run for miles.

Pulling himself up, Godryk's good humor was expelled at once when he saw the steepness of the hills that encircled the structure, the stark incline that led back up to the jungle floor.

"Damn," he muttered with a shake of the head. There was nothing more he could do, other than force himself to continue onward, led by the steady beating of Buttons' wings and his inky, black body swirling up overhead. "Damn it," Godryk groaned as he stopped at the base of the incline. He stared up, studying the angle of the climb. "Damn…really, damn."

He struck the hill with his hands, hooking his fingers like claws into the dirt, letting his nails pierce into the earth as he tensed, hauling himself up. His toes bent against the incline, knees buckling as he ascended. He kept himself low, scared that if he tried to climb more upright, he'd reel backward and fall, breaking his neck undoubtedly. His shoulders were tense and ached, but he willed himself to keep slinging his arms forward, clawing and raking and snatching at the ground as he heaved upward. Godryk kept his eyes trained on the gliding bat dipping through the night air with poised ease. It was something to focus on, rather than thinking about the insurmountable task of trying to hunt down Fynn and the others in the dark, in a jungle full of all sorts of creatures.

There was a moment where the dirt shifted beneath his feet and hands and Godryk thought he would fall back. In that instant, his eyes screwed shut and he bit down so hard on his lip it began to bleed, the tangy metallic taste of blood prickling against his tongue as he clung to the ground, fearful of the fall that would await should he lose any more purchase beneath his grip. Godryk let out a deep breath when the ground settled, and he felt he could continue on without fear of falling to his death. A burning determination surged from the pit of his stomach and seared through his limbs, keeping him going despite the fatigue that was usurping his muscles one by one. Defiantly, he shook his head and blinked away the beads of sweat gathering at his lashes, blurring his vision.

Godryk had never known more gratitude than in the moment when his hand curled over the lip of the hill, the other joining it a moment later. As he pulled himself over the edge, flinging himself down over the grassy earth of the jungle floor like a fish flopping onto the deck of a ship, he floundered for a second as he caught his breath. But he couldn't help the delirious grin that sprung to his lips, curling and twisting his features as tears streamed down his cheeks. He sprawled out, stretching his arms and legs, grateful to be able to see the distinctive branches of the canopy converging like a lattice overhead.

"Made it." He heaved as he fought to calm his breathing.

"Took you a while." It was a sweet voice, a soft and gentle voice.

Startled, Godryk jumped to his feet. Whirling around, he saw a girl, looking about his age, standing just before him, staring back at him with curious, green eyes, tilting her head just to the side as she continued studying him with apparent fascination. She was a tiny thing, dressed in furs. Long, brown hair fell in frizzy braids all around her shoulders and down her back, stretching down to her hips. Her face was round, cheeks pink, tiny ears impossibly pointed. A delicate nose poked out at the center of her young face, framed by wide, doe-like eyes that watched Godryk squirm before her. Encircling her head was a crown of vines.

"You look tired," she commented.

Godryk nodded.

"Took you longer than I thought to make it up here," she added.

570

"*Who*…are you?" he asked, taking a tentative step away from her.

"Falena."

"*What* are you, Falena?"

"A fairy," she answered simply. "Couldn't you tell?"

"Right." Godryk cleared his throat. "Are you here to take me back, then?"

The little girl shook her head. "No."

"Then why *are* you here?" the boy asked.

"I couldn't let you wander into the wood alone." She smiled. "The fairies may not have killed you, but there are certainly other creatures here who would, given the chance."

"How do I know this isn't a trick?" Godryk questioned warily.

"If I wanted you dead, I would have just pushed you down the hill the moment you got up here." She smiled again, pleased with her explanation it seemed. "Ready?"

"For what?"

"You want to find your friends, right?"

He nodded.

"Ready?" she asked again.

"Alright," he said. He glanced up, spying Buttons amidst the dark. "Buttons, can you find Fynn?"

The bat swung in a wide gyre a few times, mulling over the request it seemed, before turning abruptly, wings beating, and soaring off into the distance, hanging beneath the canopy as he flew to keep Godryk in sight. The boy watched the bat's antics fondly before proceeding to follow, Falena joining him at his side as they headed into the tree-line.

They maintained an amiable sort of silence until the fairy asked, "What's it like…Estheria, I mean?"

"You've never been?"

She shook her head. "I've never left this island."

"Not even to go to the others in the archipelago?"

Again, Falena shook her head.

"Oh." Godryk sighed. "Well, uh, Estheria is certainly a lot different than here."

"How so?" she asked.

"It's not as hot, for one. Well, it is in the summer if you live in the south. But usually it's pretty comfortable."

"I don't think it's hot here," she argued.

"Well, you're used to it, I suppose," rationalized Godryk with a laugh. "You don't know anything else. Everything here is normal for you. It's not for me." Seeing her green eyes spark with piqued interest, Godryk continued, "We don't have jungles or anything like that back on the mainland. We have forests, but they're different. They're colder and foggier and there are only bears and boars and stags. There aren't fairies and mermaids. Well, at least not where I'm from." He combed his hand through his sweaty, red hair. "We have castles that are made of stone; they're grey and huge and have massive towers and battlements. The countryside is open and green and beautiful, really. There are towns, big and small, all around the main roadways. There are inns and taverns and all sorts of things, really. It's just *different*."

"The school...Morancy, what's it like? Every year they send new children through the islands, but you're the first one I've ever spoken to."

"Oh." Godryk laughed. "Well, it's a rough place sometimes. Lessons are hard, exhausting. I don't get to go many days without getting bruised or cut in some way, but it's not awful. It's nice to be around a bunch of people my age. I didn't have that much back home. I had my cousins. They attend Morancy as well, you see...but we didn't spend too much time together, really. So, it's nice to have friends."

"Are your friends the ones in the cages?"

Godryk nodded. "Many of them. But like you said, some of my friends are out there wandering around still. I've got to find them."

"You seem worried," she noted.

"I am. One of my friends...well, last I saw him he didn't look too good." Godryk frowned. "He'd hurt his head just before our camp was set upon. I'm scared for him."

"You seem like a good friend," Falena commented.

"Thank you."

"How did you train your bat?"

Godryk shook his head, "I didn't. And he's not mine."

"Your friend's? The one who's hurt?"

"Yes."

"Interesting," mused the girl.

"Trust me, you don't know the half of it," he scoffed.

Falena smirked. "I'm sure you're right."

Once more they lapsed into a comfortable, oddly companionable silence. It was only when Godryk reached up with his left hand to brush curling strands from his forehead, that Falena said, "Your wrist is swollen."

The boy shrugged. "Doesn't hurt too much."

Holding her small hand out, she motioned with a wave. "Give it here."

Quirking a brow, he asked, "Why?"

"I can fix it for you."

His curiosity outweighed his caution, so Godryk soon found himself holding his injured wrist out toward the fairy. He watched her carefully as she took his wrist between her hands. Her eyes fell shut, green eyes replaced by long-lashed lids fluttering, tickling the rise of her cheeks. She began to mutter under her breath in a language the boy had never heard before. He watched, amazed, as a pale, green glow emanated from her fingertips, lacing around the nasty bruise, disappearing as it sunk into his skin. At once, the purple bruise was gone, replaced by the freckled complexion that it had been obscuring. The swelling was gone too. Flexing his fingers, Godryk realized the pain that had previously accompanied that motion was no more.

"Wow," he gasped. He continued to stare down at his hand. "That's amazing." He turned hopeful, blue eyes to the fairy and asked, "Can you do that for my friends? I know Fynn's got a nasty cut to the head and I'm sure the others have a few bumps and bruises from our little encounter."

"I'll do what I can."

"Thank you." He smiled.

It was getting late. It was darker, cooler. The breeze barely reached them through the trees. Exhaustion found a home within Godryk as he continued on, winding his way through the trees as he followed Buttons, Falena just to his side, happily humming and entirely unbothered by the late hour. He yawned. He yawned again.

"Tired?" the fairy inquired.

Godryk nodded.

"We can stop for now," she offered pleasantly.

"No," he answered. "I'm not stopping until I find my friends."

Once again, it was peacefully quiet. Glancing up, Godryk just managed to catch sight of Buttons diving through the branches, disappearing from view entirely. The boy's eyes widened as he searched for the bat, yelling, "Buttons! Buttons!" Seeing no sign of the nocturnal creature returning, Godryk darted forward. He continued his frantic rush through the brush, batting away branches and sticks that jutted out at dangerous angles, flicking over him as he ran by. "Buttons!"

He was only faintly aware that Falena was just behind him. His attention was garnered by the sound of someone calling his name. Godryk recognized it instantly. It didn't matter that the voice was distant and strained and tired; he knew it was Penelope yelling for him. He figured she must have caught sight of Buttons and then heard him yelling. Hope sprang anew within him, urging him on. More twigs and branches and sticks and thorns cut at him as he hastened his pace, madly sprinting through the denseness until he broke through the brush and saw, to his supreme relief, his four teammates.

Penelope was at the front of the group, Buttons nestled in her arms. Her hair was matted, hanging limply at her shoulders, strands falling over her face. Her uniform was torn and bloodied and covered in all sorts of grime. Her eyes stood out amongst the clots of dirt clinging to her face, wide and fearful. She stared back at Godryk as if he were an apparition.

"Godryk?" she called weakly, nervously.

He nodded.

"Thank the gods," she whispered. Silvery tears poured down her cheeks. "You're back."

Albie shuffled forward. He looked no better than Penelope. His clothes were in tatters, nasty cuts littered his exposed knees. He was shaking. "Is it really you?"

Godryk smiled. "It is." He approached, slinging his arms around Albie and drawing him closer. "It is," he said again. His eyes stung as tears welled. He could feel Albie melting against him, quaking in his arms. Then, slender arms wrapped around Godryk's middle and clung to him. "It's going to be alright. Everyone's fine."

Albie pulled away. "They're not dead?"

Shaking his head, Godryk assured, "No. Hurt some, but not dead."

It was then that Godryk caught sight of Ollie and Fynn just behind Penelope and Albie. Ollie looked haggard, exhausted as he hauled Fynn along, propping the prince up at his side, arm curled around the prince's hips. Upon seeing Godryk, Ollie offered a pained smile. "You're alright," he rasped happily.

Without another word, Godryk rushed to the pair. He hardly registered that he practically shoved Ollie away from Fynn. He was blinded by the fear that gripped him when he saw the prince. Fynn looked deathly pale, his eyes peeking out through slits as he wavered between consciousness and a blissful, tired oblivion. Blood had dried over most his face, mingling in a sickly sort of fashion with the muck that covered him from head to toe. The putrid scent of vomit clung to his tunic. It nearly made Godryk heave with repulsion, but he couldn't bring himself to be sick in front of Fynn, not when the prince was in such a state.

Clasping Fynn by the shoulders, Godryk held him at arms' length and continued his scrutiny. "You look awful," he stated bluntly, sadness tinging every word.

A small, pained smirk appeared upon Fynn's face as he nodded numbly. "So, I've been told. Feeling like shit." He choked as he coughed. "Head hurts."

Godryk mumbled, "I can imagine." He tipped Fynn's chin up with a light touch, brows furrowing when he saw the other boy's left iris shining an abnormal, red color. "Your eye's the wrong color."

"Yes, I've been made aware…*several* times, in fact," Fynn wheezed, still smirking. "I'll be fine."

"Yes, you will," Godryk assured. "I've someone here who can help."

"Really?"

Godryk almost laughed. "Surprisingly, Fynneas, you're not the only one who can make useful friends."

"Oh?" Fynn chuckled breathily. "Find a mermaid to come fix up my head, did you?"

"Better than that."

Fynn desperately tried to focus on Godryk but failed miserably as the world around him kept spinning in a fast wash of colors. "Better than a mermaid?"

"I've brought you a fairy."

28

THE MORANCY MOTTO

Godryk's palm braced against Fynn's forehead, tipping the prince's head back as blue eyes studied the smaller boy. Frowning, he said, "Your left eye is still the wrong color." He glanced over to Falena who stood, towering over the seated Fynn, waving her hands by his head. She was humming to herself, the green glow pulsing from her fingertips and disappearing into the mess of black hair that hid the nasty cut on the prince's head. "Are you sure it's working?"

"Yes." She barely looked up at Godryk before returning her focus to Fynn, smiling as she watched the laceration knit itself back together. "All done."

"You sure?" asked Godryk.

Falena leveled the boy with a hard stare, nodding tersely. "Yes. He's fine."

Godryk pulled his hand back, motioning with a flourish of his wrist. "His eye's still red. It wasn't red before."

"Can you see out of it?" asked the fairy.

Fynn nodded.

Falena pressed on and asked, "Does your head still hurt?"

The prince shook his head.

The fairy once again regarded Godryk, smirking. "Seems like he's healed to me."

"But his *eye*," argued Godryk impetuously.

Fynn bounced to his feet, pleased that he could move around and not feel as though the world was melting into a rainbow swirl of confusion. Tilting his head side to side, he grinned. Yes, he could see and move again, no longer bogged down by nasty pain piercing through his head and eye.

"Godryk, I'm sure it's nothing," the prince said with a grin. He combed his hand through his matted hair, straightened himself up, and squared his shoulders. "Right." He turned to face the fairy, holding out his hand to her.

She eyed the motion warily before her green eyes flicked back up to the prince, scrutinizing his expression before quirking a brow.

He nodded to his outstretched hand. "You're supposed to shake it."

"Why?" asked Falena.

Fynn shrugged. "I don't know. You just are."

"No." She was smiling sweetly, eyes shining. "That's stupid."

Slowly retracting his hand, Fynn laughed. "Alright. Well, thank you. I feel much better."

"I'm sure you do," she chirped. "Your head was split in half. Now it's not. *Must* be an improvement."

"Right," Fynn said, nodding dumbly. "Much better."

As Falena began bustling around Ollie, Albie, and Penelope, Fynn turned to Godryk. The taller boy was still studying him with blatant concern coloring his expression. Sighing, Fynn assured, "*Really*, I'm fine."

"Your eye's still red," countered Godryk.

"Yes, so you've mentioned," chuckled Fynn with a careless shrug of his shoulders. "But at least I can see out of it again. You worry too much."

"You don't worry enough."

Fynn smirked. "*Some* would say that's a virtue."

Shaking his head, Godryk huffed, "*No one* would say that."

"*I* would."

"I don't know if you realize that doesn't exactly help your position here." Godryk laughed. "But I'm glad you're not blind anymore." He couldn't help the grin that tugged at the corners of his lips. "Your aim was bad enough before. Imagine if you could only see with one eye?"

"*My* aim's bad? Well, by that scale, *yours* is positively awful!"

"It's getting better," Godryk insisted as he seated himself upon the grassy ground.

Fynn sat at his side, nudging him with his elbow. "So, what's the plan?"

They sat at the edge of the tree-line, just ten or so feet before where the jungle floor gave way to the large pit that housed the wild castle. Godryk studied the area ahead of them intently, staring at the drop-off with narrowed eyes. "They know I'm gone."

"Probably," Fynn agreed.

"They don't know I've found the rest of our team," Godryk continued.

Fynn shrugged. "Well, I *would* say Falena may be a spy, *but* she's been with us since you found us all. There's no way she could've gotten a message back to the fairies and whatever else is down there."

"Right," said Godryk.

"What're you thinking?"

"A distraction." He craned his neck, turning to the side and watching Fynn. "For all they know, I never found you. You and Ollie and Penelope and Albie…you could all still be wandering around out there. I could stumble back, get captured…*re*-captured…and make a scene. While everyone's paying attention to me, you three can sneak in."

"Then what?" Fynn sighed, "We can't very well fight our way out. We're out matched in terms of brute strength. We don't have arrows, so that eliminates a long-range assault. We haven't any swords, so it wouldn't be smart to try and fight them again. We already know we'll lose."

"We don't need to fight them." Godryk continued, "You four can hide within the castle. Wait until they lock me back up and then come get us. We can wait until it's totally dark out, when they're less likely to see us sneak out."

"We can't treat this like we're fighting a mortal enemy," Fynn countered. "They have no problem seeing in the dark. They'll notice us. They'll be able to hunt us down before we ever make it out."

"Then what do you suggest?"

Fynn looked away from Godryk and began studying the empty place where the earth fell away into the pit. "Well, you said the castle was made of trees and vines and stuff?"

Godryk nodded.

"We could just burn it down as we make our escape. That would keep them occupied."

The red-haired boy's eyes became impossibly wide, mouth hanging open, gaping, as he stared at the prince. Shaking his head, he snorted, "That's *exactly* why you're not in charge of making the plans."

Ollie sauntered up, standing just beside Fynn. Like the other two, he chose to focus on the point before him where the world seemed to just fall away into shadows. He sighed, folding his arms over his chest. "So, what's the plan?"

"That's what we're working out," Godryk answered.

Smirking, Ollie looked between his two friends, then said, "I trust that we're not putting Fynn in charge of strategy?"

"Your lack of faith is a bit hurtful, Ollie," whined Fynn, smiling as he rose to his feet. He hadn't noticed before, but as he stood side by side with Ollie, he realized that they were now just about the same height. Spirits slightly raised, he said, "I have good ideas sometimes."

"No, *Hollyn* does and you agree with him," Ollie replied. "Hollyn's not here, though."

Godryk raked his hand through his hair as he exhaled deeply, "No, he's not. Would be nice if he was, but he's not."

"We can manage without him," Ollie assured them confidently. "What have we got so far?"

"Godryk's thinking distraction," Fynn explained. "It might work if we could figure out how to get everyone out without getting caught."

"What about a secondary distraction?" All three boys turned to face Albie. He joined the group easily, slipping into the conversation with practiced ease. "Might work," he suggested.

Godryk stood. They huddled together. "I'll be the first distraction. While they're taking care of me, three of you can slip in and break everyone out, then we can set off the secondary distraction." Flashing, blue eyes turned to Fynn, twinkling. "You'll be the secondary distraction."

"Me?" the prince repeated.

Albie nodded. "Makes the most sense."

"This *doesn't* mean you get to burn down their castle," Godryk added, doing his best to imitate Moriah's steady stare and failing spectacularly.

"Then what am I supposed to do?" Fynn inquired. "Smaller fire?"

"*Much* smaller fire," Godryk relented.

Penelope found her way to the small circle the boys had formed, nestling in between Fynn and Ollie. "I assume you've all come up with a plan to get everyone out?" she asked.

The boys nodded.

"Great, tell me everything." She smiled.

Having worked out the specifics of their retrieval and extrication plans, the children stood resolutely around one another in the huddle, confident looks shared amongst them before they broke apart and readied themselves.

Looking all around, Godryk asked, "Where's Falena?"

Fynn scurried around, scanning the waning darkness. There were only a few hours left before dawn would creep over the island, heralding the arrival of their third day out in the wild. "I don't see her." He had no trouble peering through the shadows, looking up and down and all around and finding nothing. He confirmed, "She's gone."

"Do you think she heard our plan?" asked Albie.

Penelope shook her head. "I don't think so. We were talking while she healed me. We couldn't hear much of what you all were saying…well, mumbles, but nothing really clear. And I didn't see her anywhere near us while we got the final details together."

"You're probably right." Ollie nodded. "Maybe she just got bored of us?"

"Let's hope you're right," Godryk grumbled uneasily, biting down on his lower lip.

"No matter what, we need to hurry," Fynn said firmly. "It'll be morning in a few hours. We'll be on day three and we haven't gotten a single flag. We'll have to make it to the beach in time for the land bridge if we want to get to the next island by tomorrow."

"He's right." Albie sighed. "We have to hurry."

"No time like the present," Godryk huffed. He tried to steel his nerves, readying himself for the seemingly impossible task before them. "Is everyone ready?"

Collectively, the other four nodded.

"Alright, then let's go."

As Godryk stood upon the precipice, staring down into the shadow-darkened pit, seeing only the dim illumination of the castle by way of the lazy firelight from barely burning torches, he felt his stomach knot. It was the hand that draped over his shoulder, the fingers that tightened into the fabric of his yellow tunic, that drew him back from the searching clutches of apprehension that threatened to steal him. He didn't need to look away from the darkness to know that it was Fynn who'd come up beside him, steadying him as he almost lost the battle with his mounting tension.

"We're all going to make it out," Fynn whispered.

"I know."

Fynn shuffled closer to Godryk until they stood, side by side, upon the brim of the pit. Both stared down into the obscurity of what was below, searching for something to keep their attention, something to distract them from their own nervousness.

"You'll be fine," Fynn said confidently. "They'll take you back to the cages and all you have to do is wait there. Ollie, Albie, and Penelope will sneak in and get you all out. It's going to be alright."

"And you?" asked Godryk quickly.

"I'll be fine."

"You're *never* fine. You attract trouble more than anyone I've ever met."

"I find it keeps life interesting." Fynn laughed. "Who'd want to live a dull life anyway?"

Shaking his head, Godryk chortled. "I don't think anyone would ever accuse you of being dull. But could you try...*just try*...to not get into *too* much trouble this time? Let's try and make this quick and maybe even efficient?"

"I'll do my best." Fynn smirked.

"Don't get hurt."

"I won't."

Godryk looked back down into the pit. "Are you sure you're ready?"

"Are you?"

"Let's do it."

As Godryk began carefully edging over the lip of the hill, Fynn's hand shot out and wrapped around his wrist, fixing him in place. When the red-haired boy peeked over his shoulder with a curious expression and quirked brow, Fynn smiled. "Please don't fall."

"I'll do my best."

When Fynn let go, Godryk began to ease himself down the steep decline. It took only a moment for him to realize that trying to walk down the hill wouldn't end well, nor would attempting to roll. So, he eased himself down and began slowly sliding, carefully controlling the speed of his descent with his palms flat to the earth, heels digging into the dirt. Under the cover of shadows, Godryk slid further and further. Soon, he was so far down he could no longer see the vague silhouette of Fynn leaning over the edge, watching him. But even then, he knew Fynn was still there; he could somehow feel the mismatched eyes watching him.

As he continued further down, Godryk heard the muffled chatter of Ollie, Albie, and Penelope about twenty feet to his left. They'd begun their slow slide down into the pit as well. He turned his head in the direction of their quiet commotion, but he couldn't see them through the darkness. They were too far down now, everything just seemed bleak and indistinguishable. The faint glow of the firelight at the bottom hardly reached them; it did little more than tinge the blackened earth a faint shade of red.

Settling his feet flat upon the ground, Godryk straightened to his full height and began heading toward the castle. It wasn't long before he caught sight of those same creatures standing like watchmen before the entrance. He froze when he saw green eyes glowing through the shadows, staring straight at him.

They saw him.

Godryk stopped where he stood, his right fingers flexed slightly as he thought about drawing up his knife. Everything was going according to plan; he'd been found out. It wouldn't do to get killed now.

So, in deciding to stick with the ruse, Godryk rushed forward, intent to make it to the entrance. He was caught; long-fingered hands with frightening, black claws closed around his arms and lifted him from the ground. He thrashed in their hold, kicking and flailing. He yelled, "No! Let me go!"

"Couldn't find your friends?" one of them mocked.

Godryk screwed his eyes shut and screamed. "They're dead! They're all dead! Let me go!"

He hadn't expected the thump that clattered over the back of his head. Everything went black in an instant. He hung from the clutches of his captors, seemingly weightless in their hold.

When Godryk blinked away the darkness, feeling the tickling sensation of his lashes ghosting over the crests of his cheeks, the whispering glow of torch light sparked. No longer was everything black, but it was still dark and dank. Groaning, he levered himself up only to find, to his abject dismay, that he was once more in a cage. Though, he wasn't alone. Glancing down to the body resting at his side, he saw the weary face of Penelope looking up at him. "What happened?" he wondered.

"They caught us," she supplied tiredly.

"They knocked you out before you could even try and make a scene," Ollie continued weakly.

Albie nodded. "They found us only a few minutes later."

Godryk, still trying to blink away the bleariness, asked, "Where's Fynn?"

From the green-team cage, Renwyn snorted. "Doing something stupid by now, I'm sure."

"They didn't find him?" Godryk inquired, choosing to ignore Renwyn entirely.

"No," Lux said. "Or if they have, he isn't here."

"What do we do now?" Ollie asked, letting his head loll to the side as he yawned. "We've got to come up with another plan and get out of here. We're running out of time to get to Nandulus."

Godryk let his head fall back against the wooden bars, closing his eyes. His hands were once more tied behind his back. He was tired, aching all over. Penelope, slumped at his side and hardly awake, didn't seem to be doing much better. Ollie looked as though he would fall asleep at any moment and Albie was remaining uncharacteristically quiet and still as he fidgeted in his corner of the cage.

Godryk sighed. "You're right."

Yelling sounded from beyond the room and they all snapped awake, sitting up a bit straighter in their cages, forcefully shaking the weariness from their frames as they stared, wide-eyed, toward the doorway, searching for any indication of what was going on. Despite their exhaustion, growing hunger, and lingering injuries, all of Morancy children were attentively watching, waiting.

A large creature, an ogre with dingy skin prickled with wiry, brown hair, loped into the room. He had a rather pronounced under-bite; large, yellow teeth curled over his upper lip. A wide, flat nose adorned a large, flat face. Bulging, green eyes leered through the darkness, sweeping over the cages with disinterest. One large hand held a club that was resting over a calloused shoulder. The other hand held a squirming boy who thrashed and lashed and yelped in the ogre's grip.

"Let me go!" Fynn yelled as he clawed at the great beast's hand, digging his nails in deep and raking them down the monster's meaty paw. "Let me go!"

The prince was thrown to the ground. The ogre stood, a monstrous tower of mass looming over the child sprawled out on the ground at the center of the room. The cages, positioned in a semi-circle, flanking the walls, rattled as the children clambered. They scrambled to take up position against the bars, watching in silent horror as the ogre stared down at Fynn with something akin to utter malice ablaze in its feral eyes.

Shakily, Fynn pushed himself up on hands and knees. He climbed to his feet, squared his shoulders, and turned defiant eyes up toward the monster. His narrow hands curled into fists. He scowled. "Now what? Are you going to throw me in a cage, then?"

There was no response. There was only a heated grunt as the ogre eyed the boy for a moment longer and then withdrew from the center of the room, stationing himself by the doorway. He levered his club downward, holding it between both hands, resting its head to the floor like a cane, leaning his immense weight against it as he continued his silent vigil over the boy.

"You're just going to stand there?" asked Fynn in a huff.

Fynn shook. He kept his hands balled tightly; his shoulders were stubbornly rigid. He wouldn't let his attention wander to his friends. He held his gaze, purposefully, coldly, to the ogre. His heart beat faster and faster, but he wouldn't let the monster see him panic. Instead, he narrowed his mismatched eyes and furrowed his brow, settling into a scowl as he continued his unwitting staring match with the beast.

However, their test of willful glaring was soon interrupted by a marching party of inhuman visitors flooding into the room. Fynn was surprised to see Falena leading the strange procession. She gave him a nod of acknowledgement as she took up residence across from the cages, watching coolly before letting her own attention settle over Godryk for a moment. It was a fleeting moment that gave way to her turning, watching Fynn remain rooted at the center of the room, seething. Falena was joined by the same creatures who'd abducted the children from the campfire. Their long, taut frames surrounding the tiny fairy.

"You told them?" Fynn asked, peeling his heated stare from the ogre and focusing it on Falena.

"I did."

"Why?" yelled Godryk.

"It's not much of a test of your military skills if you just sneak out and run away," she answered coyly.

"This was a trap, all along?" Albie asked. "You showing up, helping Godryk find us? Healing us up? It was all a trap?"

"Albie, you make it sound cold when you say it like that," Falena chided. Despite her youthful, fair appearance, she sounded as icy and detached as Odette often did during lessons. "This week is meant to be a test for all of you. So, here we are."

"Alright," said Fynn calmly.

Godryk bristled. His stomach twisted at the sound of Fynn's voice. It was too calm, too void of anything resembling the emotion the prince only just brimmed with. He swallowed back the remembrance of the time Fynn had completely withdrawn from them earlier in the year, when he'd all but closed off from everyone around him. Presently, Fynn's voice seemed to take on that same hollow, void timbre when he spoke. It unsettled Godryk greatly.

"What're your conditions?" Fynn questioned.

"What makes you think I *have* conditions?" countered the fairy.

Fynn's eyes seemed more iridescent than usual. The red of his left eye deepened into a frightening likeness of a ruby; so too did it have a beautiful, yet stony quality to it as it pierced through the dim lighting of the room. The silver of his right eye looked more ghostly than usual, almost entirely void of anything resembling color. Gone was the boyish expression Fynn easily adorned through the months and in its place was something far more vacant, chilly. He stood there, staring at Falena with barely contained disdain. When he spoke, his voice maintained that distant quality, bereft of warmth or life, "You said this is all meant to test our military skills, what we've learned. Right?"

"That's the gist."

"Well in war, if the opposition captures your soldiers, you have one of three options," Fynn began evenly. "Either you leave them to die and continue on, you find a way to break them out, or you parley."

"And you've decided to parley?" Falena asked, raising a single brow.

The prince nodded. "I have."

"By the way your comrades talked about you, I figured you'd be a bit denser," she commented idly. She glanced in the direction of the cages, smiling. "Godryk and the red-haired girl in the green cage, they seemed to be your loudest supporters. But there were a few others who seemed quite confident in your ability to get them out alive."

"I won't leave here without them," Fynn insisted.

"I'm aware."

"So, I'll ask again." He steadied himself, forcing the roiling anger back down. "What're your conditions?"

Falena languidly padded toward the cages. She walked by each one, glancing down at the caged Estherians therein, eyeing them curiously as she stalked by, hands clasped behind her back casually. She stopped before the yellow-team cage, fixing her stare upon Godryk. Though he sneered up at her, she still smiled. Spinning gracefully around on her heels, Falena once more steadied her attention upon Fynn. "There are five cages."

Fynn nodded, wryly hissing, "I can count."

"You will fight to free your friends." She set her hand down upon one of the cages, lazily trailing her fingers over the unevenness of the wood that confined the children. "For each fight you win, I will open one cage. Do you agree?"

"That's madness," protested Godryk. "You can't make him fight five fights in a row!"

"Those are the conditions of this parley, Prince Fynneas. Do you agree to the terms?" There was an almost playful brightness in Falena's green eyes as she stared back at the prince. Seeing the uneasiness tensing the boy's muscles, she continued, "I wouldn't offer it if I didn't think it was fair."

"How is it fair?" asked Fynn flatly.

Falena approached with all the quiet poise of a cat approaching a mouse. She wasn't much smaller than Fynn. When they stood toe to toe, she leaned up to him, hands braced over his slender shoulders, and whispered in his ear, "If it were anyone else who stood in your place, I'd offer them different terms. But I think you'll manage just fine."

"How would you know?" Fynn challenged.

One hand reached up slowly; her fingers curled through his mangy hair. "Because if any of them had been hit in the head as hard as you were, they'd be dead. You, despite having your head split open, were still walking around. It's interesting; I'll admit, I'm curious to see what else you'll be able to accomplish."

Fynn withdrew from the fairy's hold. He eyed her suspiciously, asking, "These are not the terms you normally provide for the Morancy class that comes through?"

She shook her head. "I amended them just for you. Honestly, I'd no intention of deviating from tradition until I met you. You've piqued my interest, Prince Fynneas."

"That doesn't normally bode well for me," he groused.

"I can imagine," she whispered. Taking a step back, holding her arms out and gesturing vaguely around the room, she asked, "Have we a deal?"

"We do."

"Are you *mad?*" Godryk screamed, throwing himself at the bars.

"Fynneas, no." Lux shook her head defiantly. "No."

Mismatched eyes stayed trained upon Falena for a moment more before Fynn turned and paced over to the cages. He stood between the green and yellow teams. His voice was low, hardly more than a whisper, as he said, "I promised that, *no matter what,* we'd all make it out of here."

"You're a loony, you know that, don't you?" scoffed Ceral from the black team cage.

Fynn shrugged. "If you say so."

"Fynneas, we'll get out another way," argued Penelope insistently. She was beside Godryk, a frantic look on her face, nervousness welling in her expression as she pled, *"Please."*

Fynn shook his head. "There isn't really an option now, is there?"

"Don't die." Godryk gripped the bars, knuckles white.

"Wasn't planning on it," joked Fynn irreverently.

Godryk was calmed by the sight of the lopsided grin gracing Fynn's features. The horrible coldness that had descended upon the prince had gone as quickly as it had arrived and, to Godryk's supreme delight, the energetic, arrogant prince he much preferred stood before him. He smiled toothily.

"Good. I don't want to be the one to tell Hollyn you got killed doing something stupid."

"He wouldn't take that too well, would he?" Fynn laughed.

"Don't think he would," agreed Godryk.

Fynn stood at the center of the room. Falena had ushered forward his first challenger. Thankfully, it wasn't an ogre like the one lounging by the doorway. Rather, it was another fairy. Before the prince stood a gaunt, tall creature with wiry arms that seemed far too long, clawed fingers twitching at the end, grasping at nothing as it awaited the commencement of the fight. From its forehead there arose antlers made of wood, like two small, spindly trees growing from its sickly, grey flesh. They reached to the sides before curling, tiny branches jutting out. There were minuscule green specks where tiny leaves seemed to be perched. The fairy bared his teeth—long, yellow, and jagged—at the prince as he eyed the boy.

The prince remained defiant in his stance. His shoulders were set, chin lowered, upper lip stiff. His eyes were narrowed, burning as if he could bore a hole right through the monster before him. Fynn's left hand twitched, eager to draw his dagger but refraining for the time being. Sinking lower, bending his knees, bracing himself on the balls of his feet, he waited for Falena to give the word. Fynn was ready. Every muscle in his body tensed, coiled, and waited for the moment when he could spring forward.

When Falena commanded it, the bout began. The monster lurched forward, but Fynn didn't really notice. It was times like these, when an opponent was close, within striking distance, that Fynn felt a surge of liveliness burst through him. He smiled. There was something quite sublime about the rush of a fight, about knowing that at any moment you could be hit and stricken down, that at any moment you could be faced with agonizing pain; yet, knowing that within that same span of time, you could emerge victorious, you could lord over your opponent and bask in the momentary bliss of your triumph. He supposed it was the duality of the moment, the possibility that you could either rise or fall, that ignited that primal eruption of life.

Fynn hadn't noticed that the monster's claws had struck him, torn away at his already tattered tunic and ripped at the flesh of his bicep. He didn't pay attention to the warm feeling of blood trickling down his right arm. He was entirely heedless of the ordeal, so fixed was his attention to the steady movement of his adversary. There was a lumbering weight to the way the fairy moved, the way he clawed at Fynn. It was a slow and steady, yet profoundly powerful, method of fighting. Fynn watched carefully, noting every muscle that twitched beneath the grey complexion of the monster. He saw the stretching and retracting of sinews there beneath the surface, almost as though the creature didn't have flesh at all.

The prince noticed more than that. Within moments of the fight beginning, he realized that everything seemed to move much slower. Normally when he fought during lessons, he experienced things slower, as if he was holding back time to see his opponent clearly. But now things seemed to be far more glacial. He felt as though he were more perceptive, more astute in his predatory appraisal of his enemy. In that moment, it was as though nothing else really existed but the steady shifting of weight, lunging, clawing, and flailing of the creature before him.

It was with leveled detachment that Fynn realized his leg had been hit, that he was crumpling to the ground. Though he could see everything clearly, slowly, and in impossible detail, he still wasn't able to quite move out of the way of every blow. So, Fynn toppled to the ground. His heart thudded harshly, beating violently in his chest. He heaved a breath and raised himself up once more, staring insolently up at the monster. His leggings were torn just above the knee; a fresh claw mark raked against the pale flesh. There was blood, yes, but it didn't draw Fynn's attention as it should have.

The prince smiled. He braced himself and then jumped forward. He didn't bother to draw his dagger. He didn't feel inclined to pull his weapon just yet. He would, he knew he would need it. But for now, the thrill of the fight swept him up in its manic fervor and he jumped, ignoring the size differential between himself and his adversary. Fynn drew his arm back, curled his fist, and then slung it forward. His knuckles struck hard into the monster's chest. His eyes widened in astounded glee as he watched the creature buckle beneath the pressure, staggering backward as it gasped. As it continued to reel from the force, the momentum carried Fynn along with it. Both prince and beast fell in a heap to the ground.

Fynn was the first to jump back to his feet, shifting his weight from foot to foot as he watched the injured monster huff and puff on the ground. When it made no move to get up, Fynn looked over his shoulder to Falena. She was smiling.

With a nod, she announced, "One down, one cage opened."

Fynn stared at Falena for a moment longer, watching the eager twist of her lips and curious flicker of her eyes. The defeated beast was of no consequence to him. There were yet fights to be fought and, if the intense gleam in Falena's eyes was any indicator, they would not be so easy.

As the black team's cage was unlocked and its occupants were ushered out, Fynn took a moment to catch his breath. In his periphery, he caught sight of Godryk nodding at him. He smiled back. His sweaty, black hair tumbled over his eyes. He was tired, but he shook off the weariness with relative ease. Brushing back the hair from his eyes, he saw the black team watching him intently. Ceral smiled at him, a confident sort of smile that, for some unknown reason, pleased the prince. Though their hands were still bound behind their backs, the black team seemed relatively more at ease as they huddled close together, edging away from the strange monsters all around the room, staying close to the other cages as they stared at Fynn.

Fynn's second opponent was a bit smaller than the first, but far bulkier. He was a stalwart fawn; furry goat legs curved backward, thick hooves planted firmly to the ground. His torso was wide, shoulders broad, arms quite substantial in their composition. His thick neck gave way to a square face whereupon beady, green eyes stared back, dark and dangerous beneath a heavy-set brow bone that sloped down from a balding head; sparse, brown hair poked out of sweaty, copper skin. Tiny horns jutted out just where eyebrows should be, stumpy things that looked ill formed. The fawn rolled its shoulders, snorting as it braced itself.

The boy drew in a deep breath. He felt his lungs expand with the air. His heartbeat calmed down, no longer banging into his chest violently. Still, Fynn didn't draw his dagger. As he turned to face the fawn, he once again bent at the knees and rolled to the balls of his feet, ready for the fight. At Falena's proclamation, they began.

Just as before, everything moved slowly. It was as though, with each swing of his arm, Fynn could feel the air moving away from him, parting from him as the sea had two days ago when he thought he might drown. The stagnant air in the room felt just as heavy, just as thick, as the water pressing down all around him. His body, too, felt just as it had that morning. The distinctive feeling of drowning in something oppressively weighty was a memory he would not soon forget, and so, as he swung his fist toward the fawn, he couldn't help but draw the comparison.

His fist slammed into the fawn's jaw. He felt the bone give way. There was a satisfying yelp of pain that emanated from his opponent. Watching as the creature pulled back, hands flying up to clasp over the offended jawbone, Fynn remained still with a gleam in his eye. As the fawn spluttered, it was then that Fynn realized he'd been struck again without his notice. Raising his hand up before his face, he saw a jagged cut lacing its way across his palm. It bled; the blood reached down his wrist as his hand shook before his eyes. He didn't register the pain; it simply wasn't there. Glancing down, he saw specks of red littering the floor.

Fynn stretched his arm out. For the first time, he took notice of the severity of the wound from his first fight. There, upon his right bicep, was a nasty claw mark. It seemed deep. The amount of blood that stained Fynn's yellow sleeve supported that assumption. There was certainly more red than Fynn had anticipated. He grimaced as he set his left hand over the wound. He felt the stickiness gathering against his palm, oozing between his fingers. Still, there was no pain.

The fawn collected himself and started to foray toward Fynn. Though the action seemed absurdly slow, the boy didn't have time to step aside. Instead, Fynn found himself falling backward after the fawn's own fist collided with the boy's jaw. Prone to the ground, Fynn gasped for air. The pain rushed upon him at once, a usurper to the numbness he'd bowed to earlier. Now, Fynn acutely felt the sting in his hand, his arm, his leg, and his jaw. Prickling tears found their way into his eyes. He wiped them away before they had the chance to fall.

Growling, the prince forced himself back to his feet. Fynn urged the pain away. In that moment, it was as though he had total control over his body, over everything he felt. He was, once more, a blissful ward of overwhelming numbness. Fynn smiled. The fawn never had the chance to see the prince fall away from the agony of his injuries back into the waiting arms of blankness, never had the chance to see the boy spring forward. As he had with his first opponent, Fynn opted for brute force. He curled his hand into a fist and punched as hard as he could, feeling the fawn's chest cave into the blow. He watched, almost stunned, as the creature fell before him unconscious.

"Another victory for the Morancy boy," Falena announced calmly. She eyed the fallen fawn apathetically before looking back to the prince. "Well done." She held out her arm, waving her hand. The white team was uncaged. "Let's see how you handle round three."

Fynn wasn't given a reprieve this time. Rather, he could only watch with muted horror as the ogre who'd been lingering by the doorway stepped forward. The boy's attention was riveted to the club the great, lumbering beast dragged along the ground. He choked back the lump his throat cradled. Fynn couldn't move. His body was wracked with a shuddering fear as he remained standing there, frozen, watching the ogre and his club approach.

"Let's see how you fair against Ludus." Falena smiled from her station.

Ludus reached out his free hand; heavy fingers wrapped around Fynn's wrist. Before Fynn could wrench himself free, the ogre threw him backward into a wall. Fynn yelped as the air was forcibly pushed from his lungs, leaving him choking as he collapsed to the ground on his hands and knees. He retched, feeling as though his stomach had jumped into his throat in one swift motion. Still shaking, Fynn hadn't noticed the ogre approach until he felt himself being lifted by the ankle.

Now upside down, Fynn began to panic. His eyes were wide, his whole body spasming as he kicked his free leg, flailed his arms, and yelled. He tried to twist free, tried to kick at the ogre's hand. Still, he remained dangling there. His eyes rested upon the club held in Ludus' other hand and then Fynn was once again choking down his horror.

Ludus swung.

Fynn saw it coming. He saw every painful second of it. He could do little more than raise his arms over his face and brace himself. He felt the wood of the club crash into his forearms. He felt the wood splinter. He felt his arms break. Then he was falling. Fynn saw the room around him spin. He rolled away from the ogre. He was on the ground, his cheek pressed to the warm dirt-floor.

The boy's vision was hazy, blurring with each passing second. But there was no pain. He reached his hand up; it was shaking. He pulled his pendant out from beneath the collar of his tunic. His thumb traced over the intricate details of the dragon. It felt cold against his touch. His fingers curled around it.

Then he was gone from the room and standing in a familiar blackness. Looking down, Fynn saw rippling beneath his feet, as though he stood upon shallow water. He forced himself to look back up, even though he knew he would see nothing more than a vast expanse of nothingness. He relaxed into it, closed his eyes. It was so very quiet. He hadn't realized he was still holding the pendant, not until he felt something burning in his hand. Opening his eyes, Fynn saw the ruby eyes of the dragon ablaze, searing his skin. He let go and the pendant fell against his chest. It didn't burn.

Fynn drew in a deep breath and closed his eyes once more. The air in the in-between place was neither hot nor cold. It simply was there. It wasn't fresh like the air of Dier Island and it wasn't stagnant like the air in the wooden castle. It simply was. And he liked it. He took another breath. When he opened his eyes, the darkness was still there.

He took a few steps forward. The blackness rippled beneath his feet, splashing with each step. Fynn continued further into it, journeying deeper into the void. Something was pulling him, calling him silently, summoning him onward. He didn't know what it was, what force was dragging him, but he obliged without a fight.

There was something in the distance—light. Two, pale moons were glowing through the blackness. Fynn continued onward. The light was calling him. And soon, he realized that they weren't moons, but eyes that were staring back at him through the abyss. Two, large, silver eyes with slatted pupils that looked, unblinking, back at Fynn. The boy swallowed heavily. He felt something warm ghost over him, like a summer breeze. He tensed for only a moment before stepping forward again. Fynn reached his hand out, holding it before him. He closed his eyes when the heated air wafted over him once more.

Then he felt it. His hand came to rest over something sharp and scaly, something cold and grim feeling. Tentatively, he sucked in a shallow breath and opened his eyes. Beneath Fynn's hand there were thick, jagged scales. Two, large, tilted nostrils blew out hot air that tore over him, tousling his hair. The silver eyes remained fixed to the prince, unblinking.

Again, the hot air blew and Fynn remained perfectly still. Slowly, he let his hand relax; his thumb traced tiny circles over a single scale. His mouth quirked into crooked grin. "Draekon?" he whispered.

He felt the snout of the scaly creature retreat from his touch. He marveled as a dragon unfolded from the darkness. Withdrawing from Fynn, it righted itself to its full height. Wings, like giant bat wings, unfurled from its back and stretched, disappearing into the blackness. The dragon stared down at Fynn, unmoving.

"You're Draekon, aren't you?"

The massive head lowered until it was once again even with Fynn. It stretched by the boy, pressing its cheek against the prince's shoulder. Its eye watched Fynn carefully as the boy raised his hand, settling his palm against its jutting cheek bone. It closed its eyes, as did Fynn.

The boy leaned closer to the dragon until he was flush against it. His cheek pressed against the scales, as if the dragon's coarse head was Fynn's personal pillow. The boy smiled. "I knew it was you." He pulled away. Draekon's head rose slightly, eyes opening once more. "Why're you here?"

"Beautiful, isn't he?"

Fynn turned around, not moving far from the dragon. He wasn't surprised to see Celestine, pristine in white, standing in the blackness. She admired Draekon with the same unbridled awe that Fynn had.

"Yes," answered Fynn.

"He's here because you called him," she explained. Celestine slid through the blackness with almost eerie grace. Within a second, she was beside her son. Her ghostly, white hand came to rest softly over one of Draekon's scales. "Are you scared?"

Fynn furrowed his brow and asked, "Of what?"

Celestine nodded to the pendant that hung around Fynn's neck. "Moriah gave that to you?"

Fynn nodded.

"Are you scared?" she repeated.

"I don't know if I'll be able to win," admitted Fynn. He felt himself give into the clawing emotions that were tearing away at him. "My friends...I made a deal. For each fight I win, another group will be set free. I'm scared that I can't win them all their freedom."

"You're stronger than you think," chided Celestine.

That was it.

Something inside Fynn snapped. He felt himself come undone. It was like a dam had ruptured and he was drowning in the aftermath, the calamity dragging him down. Gasping for air, he all but collapsed against the dragon's cheek. He set his forehead against Draekon's scaly face. His eyes fell closed hopelessly as he huffed; warm tears raced down his cheeks as his lower lip quivered. Fynn felt like he was choking, and he wasn't sure if he was willing to gasp for breath anymore. It all just seemed like too much.

"Why does everyone think I can do this?" He sounded broken, tired.

Celestine's hand moved from the dragon to cup Fynn's cheek. She brushed away a tear softly. "Because you *can*."

Fynn didn't pull away from Celestine's touch. He simply shook his head defiantly before nestling into her palm, deriving what little comfort he could from the contact. "I *can't*. It's too much."

"Fynneas."

The boy didn't feel like responding. There was something so strangely calming about standing there with his mother, letting her wipe away his tears. It was something he didn't know he'd longed for. But now that he had it, he didn't want it to end. He wished with everything he had that he could stay there with her forever, that she would remain for eternity holding him. She was the anchor in the blackness that he hadn't realized had been lowered. But now that she was there, tethering him in place, he didn't want to drift away.

"Fynneas."

He closed his eyes tighter.

"Fynneas, please look at me."

He didn't want to. It was so comfortable to stay as he was. Reluctantly, he opened his eyes. Celestine looked down at him, tears sliding down her white cheeks.

Fynn mumbled, "Please...don't make me go." He flung himself at his mother, his arms ensnaring her. He buried his face against Celestine's middle as she ran her fingers through his hair. "Please. I don't know what I'm supposed to do. I don't know why I'm supposed to do it. No one tells me anything! They just tell me I can do it and expect that's enough...and it's *not*. Please, don't make me go."

He was dissolving into hysteria as Celestine tried to comfort him. One hand came to rest atop Fynn's head, idly twisting black hair between her thumb and forefinger. Her voice was quiet when she said, "This isn't the place for you, darling." She held him closer. "You need to go back."

"I don't want to," Fynn protested through silent sobs.

"I know."

"Can you tell me...tell me *why*? Why me?"

"It's who you are," she whispered.

"What am I supposed to do?" Fynn asked searchingly.

Celestine stepped away from him. She saw him standing before her, hardly able to stop himself from shaking with unvoiced cries of confusion and silent anguish. "Right now, you're supposed to go back and show them all what you're capable of." Her slender hand reached out, taking her son by the chin. She tilted his head up until their eyes met. This time when she spoke, her voice was confident and even. "Don't ever back down, Fynneas. Don't ever surrender. Don't ever admit defeat. You're a dragon."

Fynn maintained unwavering eye contact with his mother, desperately searching her wintery gaze for some clue. He knew she wouldn't outright tell him anything. His experiences thus far dictated that such was the norm. He saw nothing but resolute determination and belief reflected in her pale eyes. He nodded. "Alright."

Celestine smiled. "Be strong."

"I will," he assured shyly. "I will."

She nodded toward Draekon. "Up you go."

594

"What?"

Celestine clamped her hands over Fynn's shoulders and marched him toward Draekon's upper back.

"Up you go," she said again. She gave her son a little shove.

Fynn reached out, grasping the scaly shoulder beneath his trembling hands. He hoisted himself up, climbing over the lowered shoulder until he sat upon the dragon's back, comfortably settled between its wings. From up upon his scaly saddle, Celestin seemed so far away, so much lower than before. Fynn looked down at her and smiled a soft, forlorn smile.

Draekon shifted beneath him. Fynn marveled openly as the dragon spread its wings once more, then beat them once—twice—thrice. Celestine was further away. Then she was nothing more than a white speck amongst the blackness far below them. Fynn held tightly to the dragon's back as they ascended. He didn't know how far up they were, or if, indeed, they were really going up. Everything around them was no more than endless nothingness, no points of reference to distinguish their movement at all—just the empty, solid blackness stretching on forever in every direction. Here, up was down and down was left and there was no sideways anymore, just confused nothingness.

But they kept going.

There was a rush of air as Draekon's wings rose and fell. Fynn felt the steady breathing of the dragon beneath him. Something grey and cloudy formed above them. It reminded him of the storm from the first day of the games. Fynn shuddered but pushed his dread down as far as he could. They were still climbing through the nothing, ascending toward the grey clouds that were lighting up with what Fynn thought to be lightning. It certainly looked like lightning.

Draekon roared a roar that sounded like thunder clapping. Fynn felt the rumble of the sound vibrate beneath his legs. Another burst of the dragon's thunder and they shot through the greyness, the clouds whipping around them in a cluster of curling, smoky tendrils. And then Fynn saw pale light.

The boy gasped for air. His eyes had flown open; he'd expected to see darkness, but all around he saw the low glow of firelight, the wooden walls of the castle in the pit, and the jagged shadows of the assembled creatures and his school mates. He heard the low, interested mutterings of the creatures and, distantly, familiar voices—worried voices—calling out to him.

"Get up!"

"Fynneas!"

"Is he going to die?"

"That's a lot of blood."

"This is bad."

"Fynn!"

"Get up!"

"Get up!"

"You *have* to get up!"

Everything came into focus at once. He was back in the wooden castle. Everything hurt. His arms felt broken. His leg was certainly injured to some extent. His head throbbed. His chest ached. He drew in a shaking breath. Gingerly, Fynn sat up. Looking around, his eyes focused on the ogre watching him amusedly.

The boy forced energy he didn't have into his muscles as he drew himself upright. He slumped forward, shoulders hunched inward; his head hung low. He huffed. His hair fell over his face, sweat and dirt and blood streaked down his temples and cheeks. He braced one hand over his knee as he tried to steady himself on wobbling legs.

"This isn't over," Fynn rasped. There was a tang that stung his tongue; red speckled the ground beneath his feet, blood and saliva mixed with the dirt by his booted toes. Undeterred, he stood to his full height, meager as it was, and stared back at the ogre. "It's *not* over."

Fynn coughed; more flecks of blood splattered over his split lip and oozed down his chin.

There was a moment of stunned silence where everyone in the small room seemed to collectively forget how to breathe and speak. They all watched, some in horror, some with great interest, as the small prince stood defiantly before the ogre.

Falena stepped forward slightly, pulling herself from the gathering of creatures and setting herself apart. "Are you sure? You're in pretty bad shape, Prince Fynneas."

"I'm fine," he barked.

"You're bleeding," the fairy commented flatly. "Quite badly."

"Doesn't matter." Fynn wheezed. He wiped the blood and sweat from his eyes, pushing his hair back from his face. "It's not over. I've only won twice. That means only ten of them are free. I'm not stopping until they're *all* out of those damn cages."

"How noble," Falena noted. "That's either very brave or very stupid of you."

"Probably stupid," Fynn snorted humorlessly.

Falena eyed the prince, quirking a brow. "You're probably right."

Ludus reeled his arm back, levering the club parallel with the ground. He swung. At the same time, Fynn raised his fisted hand and met the club with his knuckles. The wood, already splintered from its assault against Fynn's arms, shattered upon impact. Hundreds of splinters scattered across the floor.

Fynn screamed a most blood-curdling scream that left his throat raw. He cradled his now shattered hand in his other, ignoring the already broken bones of his arms. He fell to his knees in an instant, curling himself protectively around his hand as he pulled it to his chest. The pain was blinding, shooting from every nerve like a white-hot inferno scorching through him. He heard himself screaming. It didn't feel like it was coming from him, so consumed was he in trying to remain conscious as he held his hand shakily. By this point, tears fell unrestrained like a mass, salty exodus from his widened eyes.

A hand reached down and settled upon his head. Then everything was warm and soft and peaceful. Fynn closed his eyes, leaning into the touch. The pain in his hand dissipated until it was nothing. His arms, having been throbbing viciously from the broken bones, numbed at once. His leg no longer stung. His head was clearer. Opening his eyes, Fynn saw the distinctive pale, green glow of Falena's magic washing over him. She'd mended his bones.

Looking down at his palm, he no longer saw the nasty gash that had marred the pale flesh. "You healed me?" he questioned. He watched Falena standing over him, one hand still outstretched and set upon the top of his head. Her eyes were closed. He asked, "Why?"

When her eyes opened, they were the warm eyes he'd first associated with her back in the jungle. She grinned down at him sweetly, seeming to be the girl he'd first encountered and not the chilly, deceitful fairy who'd shown herself in the castle. "Truthfully, I would've stopped you after the first fight."

"*What?*" gasped the prince.

"I would have let them all go after your first victory, but you seemed so committed to our arrangement. I thought I'd see how far you could make it," she answered. Falena's hand fell from Fynn's head. It remained outstretched, waiting. When Fynn made no move, she said, "You're supposed to take it."

"Why?"

"It was interesting," she answered simply. "You lasted longer than I thought."

Fynn could do little more than stare dumbly at the fairy.

"Oh," the fairy chuckled softly, "you should know, your eyes match again."

Idly, Fynn traced his fingertips beneath his left eye as if trying to somehow assess if Falena were telling the truth.

She looked away, waving her hand as she beckoned, "Bring them their flags."

"*What?*" asked Godryk, stepping forward.

It was then that Fynn realized the remaining Estherians had been set free, their hands unbound. Godryk was the first to break away from their huddle. He positioned himself beside Fynn, wrapping his arm around the prince's shoulders to steady him.

"You have our flags here?" Godryk inquired.

Falena nodded.

Lux ran forward. She took up her position at Fynn's other side. She reached her hand down, taking his into hers, their fingers laced together. She squeezed reassuringly, glancing at him for a moment and then joining Godryk in staring at Falena with nothing short of sheer incredulousness. "We *all* get our flags? *All* five teams?"

Once more, the fairy nodded. "As far as I'm concerned, you *all* have passed."

Fynn shook his head. "I don't understand. Why?"

Lux elbowed him gently. "Don't question a good thing, just go with it and smile."

He obeyed dutifully, nodding his head. "Thank you...for the flags."

Godryk bent his head to the side, whispering in Fynn's ear, "It's probably a good thing we didn't go with your original plan of burning their castle down."

29

THE FLY

The children from Morancy sat huddled in a large circle upon the shore; the inky waters of the tide splashed over the white-sand beach of Green Isle. They'd rested and been fed. Falena tended to their wounds and ills before leading them from the pit and offering, in addition to their flags, gifts to applaud their triumph.

Four boats were angled upon the sand; the sea's lapping reach hardly traced over the merest inch of the hulls with every brush over the shore. They were of a simpler design than the sailed dinghies the teams had navigated from Dier Island, but that was all Falena had been able to offer them. The fifth boat, resting beside the four fairy-made crafts, was the blue team's boat that had, somehow, managed to survive the tempestuous sail from days prior. It was beaten and brittle, but it would serve its purpose.

They were waiting for dawn.

Every so often, one of the children would glance toward the beach and scan the fleeting darkness, searching for signs of the land bridge's arrival. None had been seen yet. And so, they waited in comfortable silence, occasionally broken by whispered conversations or gentle chuckles muffled by the sound of the lilting wind.

It was Ceral's deep sigh that interrupted the ease of the twilight companionship amongst the students. They all turned to the second-year, quizzical expressions puzzling their faces as they waited for him to say something. The boy ran his hand through his hair, shaking his head as he sighed yet again. "We've wasted a lot of time on this island."

"But we got the flags," argued Alice.

Ceral nodded tiredly. "But it cost us two whole days and here we are, *still* on this island, the morning of day three. We've still got to get across two more islands before we arrive at Nandulus."

Maeryk scowled. "You're right. But there isn't really anything we can do about it now. No use brooding over it."

"I'm *not* brooding!" snapped Ceral.

Fynn perked up, chirping, "I've an idea."

"This ought to be good," groused Renwyn with a sidelong glance toward the prince.

Godryk reached into the sand, curling his fingers around a hefty tuft of white flecks. He tossed them toward Renwyn with an exasperated huff. "Let's hear him out."

"Fine," Renwyn muttered, waving his hand in a beck of a motion. "Go on then, let's hear it."

Fynn's eyes shone through the darkness with the searching intelligence of an owl prowling through the night skies. With the same fierce sensibilities of the owl, the prince's eyes widened as he smiled at the rest of the students, fixing each of them with a twinkling gleam and sly smirk. He said, "Well, no one said we had to go in order."

"What's that supposed to mean?" questioned Renwyn.

The prince's smirk intensified. "Ceral was right. We wasted too much of our time on one island and we still have two to go. But, we're not all separated anymore. We're *all* here. And we won the first challenge, getting the first of the flags, by staying together. Maybe, that's it! Maybe we're supposed to figure out that we'll do best if we all work together."

"That's all very well and good and sweet of you, but what point are you trying to make?" Renwyn asked irritably.

"We know the land bridge only appears at dawn. That means, the best-case scenario is that we spend a day on Middle Isle to get the flags. We won't be able to get back to this island until dawn the next day. The vice lord expressly said we can't sail between Green and Middle because of the rocks, we would *need* to use the land bridge. But," Fynn turned his foxlike grin toward Renwyn, "he never said anything about sailing from Green to Little."

Ceral, realization dawning, burst into a smile of his own. "We can split into two teams."

Godryk clapped his hand over Fynn's shoulder, appraised the prince for a moment, and then offered a toothy grin of his own. "We'll be able to cover more ground and get all the flags *and* make it to Nandulus before time runs out!"

"What do you mean?" Wilder asked.

Fynn turned toward the boy, the burning brightness still blazing in his pale eyes. "One team will take the land bridge to Middle Isle. They'll collect all five team flags and return here. The other team will go to Little Isle and do the same. They'll sail back with their flags. We'll meet back up on *this* beach and sail to Nandulus. We'll have all our flags, but we won't *all* have to go to all three islands."

"That's *actually* not a bad plan," Renwyn relented.

"So, should we split into first-years and second-years?" asked Georgie. "I think we'd work best that way."

Ceral nodded. "Agreed. So, who wants to go to which island, then?"

Penelope leaned forward on her knees, brows furrowed in thought. "Middle Isle is dense with trees and surrounded by jagged rocks, but we don't know what else is there. All we know is that the only way to and from the island is by way of the land bridge."

Lux nodded. "Right."

"Then there's Little Isle," continued Penelope thoughtfully. "We know *that* one is essentially a floating mangrove forest."

"Either way," mused Albie, "we'll be working with a disadvantage. It'll be dense and wild, and we won't be able to see what's around us. There will be things watching us that we won't be able to see. There always *seems* to be, at least."

"Albie's right," agreed Ollie, with a curt nod of the head. "Both are going to be difficult in their own way. I don't think it matters much who takes what island. Does anyone have a preference?"

Tulip shuddered as she admitted, "I'd...well...I'd prefer to not have to sail more than I have to. Can the second-years take Middle Isle?"

Aldus turned to regard Tulip, studying her for a moment. He could see the fear shading her blue eyes, the slight grimace twisting her lips. He nodded affirmatively. "I don't see why not. Firsties, does that work for you?"

Firiel glanced around the circle of students, watching for any signs of disagreement amongst her year mates before nodding her agreement. "I think we can work with that." She smiled.

"Agreed," said Fynn heartily.

When dawn had made its grand arrival, bringing with it a pale, pink glow that swept over the horizon, bathing the beach in its fledgling light, the children began to stir. They rose to their feet in a collective wave of lanky limbs, stretching their arms and backs, yawning and blinking away the weary blur that slurred through their vision. The second-years amassed at the edge of the beach, keen eyes watching in silent awe as the water, ever so slowly, began to recede from the sand; the tide split apart, a path of slick sand and pebbles and shells emerged before them.

The first-years, gathering two of the boats and preparing to push them into the water, watched from a distance as the water continued to pull away from the sandbar and the emerging reef. Shallow columns of water split before the beach, allotting a five-foot wide path for the second-years to traverse. The fifteen began their careful shuffle onto the land bridge, wary of the precariousness of the situation, careful of their footing.

Aldus was the last of the group to part ways from the beach; he cast a cursory glance over his shoulder toward the first-years and smiled, nodding and flicking a short wave their way, before heading forward.

The yellow team jostled their rickety boat into the water, hopping aboard one by one. Godryk, perched upon the boat already, reached out to Fynn and smiled. "Ready?"

Fynn allowed himself to be hoisted from the shallows into the boat. He nodded, replying steadfastly, "Ready." He settled in between Godryk and Albie easily. He looked to the side, watching as Lux clambered into the green team's boat. He felt a familiar warmth rise in his cheeks as he watched her reach her hand out and pull Georgie aboard.

Firiel called to the yellow team, "Stay close!"

Ollie, at the bow of the tiny vessel, nodded. "You too!"

Godryk nudged Fynn, leaning down and whispering, "You're still staring at her."

The balmy feeling in the prince's cheeks erupted into an uncomfortable flame as he immediately tore his eyes away, choosing to focus intently on a vague point between his booted feet. Fidgeting between his friends and wrinkling his nose, Fynn muttered, "Am not."

They proceeded south from Green, making sure to plot a wide berth around Middle to avoid being inadvertently swept toward the rocky ring that encircled the tiny isle. The sun was above the horizon presently, the pink glow having melted away into an easy bronze that bore down over them; heat washed over their slight frames as they coasted through the relatively calm waters.

Fynn titled his head back, looking up and spotting Buttons beating his black wings through the morning light, gracefully flying up overhead and leading them toward shore. The prince smiled.

"Oddest bat I've ever seen." Albie laughed. "Never would've thought a bat would be out during the day like this."

"It's *Fynn's* bat, what did you expect?" jested Ollie, with a quick smile toward Fynn.

"You're not wrong there," agreed Albie.

Fynn shrugged, still watching the black bat cutting through the morning like a shadow flicking through the light. He could just barely see the crescent scar that marred Buttons' silken wing. Fynn's smile widened, pleased that the injury the animal sustained so early in his life was not impeding his natural grace, his intrinsic ability to glide with sublime poise.

"He's a good little bat," said Fynn wistfully. His pale eyes never wavered from Buttons. He imagined what it would be like to fly like that, to be able to hold your arms out and just glide, feeling the warm wind blowing by you as you soared over everything. He supposed it would be the greatest feeling one could experience, like tasting freedom as you went wherever you wanted. "A *very* good bat."

The waves were rather tepid and docile, swishing against the wood of the boats. Godryk leaned over the edge, watching the water go by. It was remarkably clear. He watched the fish swimming beneath them, dark shadows of all colors darting about in every direction with urgency. He settled himself upright once more. Tilting his head back, he joined Fynn in the apparently rather calming distraction of watching Buttons. He found himself marveling at the animal's ability to curl and distort into the most amazing and angled movements he'd ever beheld. "Why doesn't he just fly straight?" Godryk mused.

"Where's the fun in that?" asked Fynn.

It wasn't long before they saw the distant shape of Middle Isle passing far off from them, a fleck of deep green splattered over the crystalline horizon line, flanked on all sides by violently lapping waters beating against jutting rocks and smashing into a rather unfriendly looking shoreline. And so, they went on, grateful to be bypassing the dangers that seemed to lurk there, their boats gently rocking in the far calmer waters south of the island.

It was another two hours of slow sailing before Little Isle came into view. Truthfully, had Penelope not been scanning the surrounding waters so fixedly, they would've overshot their target. She jumped to her feet, pointing to the twisting grey shapes about three hundred feet away, "Just there!"

Fynn didn't bother following the trajectory of Penelope's insistent pointing. Instead, he watched as Buttons fluttered downward lazily, slipping from his course and redirecting toward the mass of curling trees twisting from the water. Once he'd watched Buttons disappear into the lattice of trees, Fynn climbed to his feet to join Penelope. While she stood, emphatically directing Ollie and Albie, Fynn turned to regard the green team just behind them. He called out, "The island's just there! We'll head in slowly. Be careful!"

The two boats drew in closer together, steadying through the waters as the soft waves became a bit more insistent. The water was darkened by something large and shadowy beneath the hulls as they came up toward the shore.

Fynn peeked over the edge, studying the shadow that lurked beneath the mangroves. He frowned. His stomach knotted uneasily. "The island goes deeper than I thought it would," he commented, still watching the shadow reaching beneath them.

Godryk appeared beside Fynn, leaning over and inspecting the darkened waters with a keen interest. "Looks like it." He straightened, catching Fynn by the collar and dragging him upright as well. When he was fixed with a curious glare, Godryk shrugged and smiled. He said, "Let's not worry about it until we know it's actually a problem. Until then, let's just focus on finding the flags and getting back to Green Isle, alright?"

"Fine," Fynn grumbled.

Wilder stood, bracing himself as best he could against the slow rocking of the boat, as he observed the island. He announced, "We may have a problem." Nodding toward the mingling trees, he continued, "There's nowhere to dock the boats. We'll have to tie them to the trees."

"What do you mean?" Penelope asked.

Hogan, standing at Wilder's side, scowled darkly. "There isn't a shore. There's just...*trees*."

"I hate this place already," huffed Renwyn. He pulled the short heap of twine into his hands, preparing to do just as Wilder had suggested.

Ollie mirrored the endeavor, pulling the yellow team's twine up and readying it in his hands. Thinking for a moment, he asserted, "At least one of us is going to need to be on shore...or whatever you want to call it...to tie the rope off."

"So, someone's going to have to swim for it." Firiel sighed. "Wonderful."

Fynn watched the water with unwavering focus. He thought, if he could, he might bore a hole through the ocean. He narrowed his eyes, curiously watching the ebbing of the shadow beneath the water. He caught a shift in the shadow, though it lasted only a moment, and he wasn't entirely sure he hadn't just imagined it. Fynn heard everyone talking around him, discussing something or other. He didn't care to listen. He let their voices drift away until the sound of their discussion-turned-argument was nothing more than a dull drumming sound. He continued watching until he saw the shadow shift once more.

"There!" he yelped, pointing to the murky shape below the surface.

The other ten first-years stopped their squabbling; expectant stares turned toward the prince. They watched as Fynn's shoulders went rigid, his body taut with roiling anxiety; his eyes narrowed further; his lips thinned into an impossibly straight line as he stared down into the water.

Firiel was the first to break the spell of bewildered silence, calling to the prince, "What is it?"

"There's something in the water," Fynn asserted.

"You probably just saw some fish," reasoned Renwyn.

Fynn rounded on the other boy, glaring at him from his own boat. "I know what *fish* look like. It wasn't fish."

"What was it, then?" Ollie asked. His hold on the rope tightened as he began nervously pawing at the twine slipping over his palms. His eyes were wide, watching Fynn nervously. "Something b-b-bad?" he stammered.

"I don't know," murmured Fynn, returning his attention to the water. "I saw something move. Something large."

"A shark?" asked Wilder.

The prince shook his head. "There aren't sharks by the archipelago."

"Another mermaid?" Georgie inquired hopefully. "The last one seemed nice."

"I don't think it's a mermaid," Fynn contended. "It was too big." He drew himself up, straightening his shoulders, willing the muscles and sinews to relax. He pulled in a deep, shaking breath. "I don't think we should go in the water."

"What do we do about the boats? We need to tie them up," Renwyn said.

"I know, I know." Fynn groaned. He looked to the mangroves, searching for a way to get to them safely. "We can just keep heading closer. We could just sail right up to them. The water seems deep enough. We shouldn't hit anything."

"That would work," Godryk agreed. "It's probably safer than one of us swimming over. I don't see a sandbar or reef beneath us. The boats should be fine. They won't break."

"I agree," Ollie nodded. "I think that's safer."

The yellow team edged closer to the mangroves. All the while, Fynn was hunched over the side, staring through the crystalline surface of the water to something deeper, darker. There was a flutter of movement. He saw the familiar curve of a shell and splayed green fins. The prince's lips curled upward as he announced, "Turtles."

Godryk knelt beside Fynn, leaning over the boat and looking down. He laughed. "A whole lot of them!"

Their boat sidled up beside the mangroves. Albie clambered from the boat and into the trees, clutching to the thin trunk of the nearest twisting mangrove. Ollie tossed him the rope and he tied it around the trunk, securing it and nodding back to his team. Albie remained in place as Wilder threw him the green team's rope. Slowly, the children began disembarking, stepping onto the mesh of twisting roots that entwined together to create something similar to steady ground.

Fynn found his way onto the roots, balancing over the curving tree limbs. He clung to the nearest tree, steadying himself, and stared into the depths of the island. It was larger than he'd expected. The ground sloped upward like a large hill toward the center. There were mangroves protruding from the water in every direction, sprouting close to one another, scarcely leaving room for any light to break through. Heavy, green leaves sprouted at the tops of the branches and trunks.

The children began wheedling their way through the mangrove-lattice, contorting themselves as best they could to slip through the narrow gaps between the trees. Their steps were tentative, precise, and well placed. They kept their eyes trained downward, watching for any pitfalls in the ground wherein they could slip and fall or twist their ankles. There were places where the roots beneath their booted feet felt old and worn and rotted; they could hear the splintering of the wood as they stepped over those most precarious places, wincing all the while with unspoken dread, hoping beyond hope they didn't fall through into the unknown beneath the trees.

"I can't see a thing!" yelled Firiel from the front of the pack. She hoisted herself atop a branch, kneeling as she leaned forward, peering through the seemingly never-ending maze of trees.

"How far in do you think we have to go to find the flags?" asked Wilder.

"Knowing Morancy, they've probably placed the flags at the top of the hill," speculated Renwyn, turning his attention slightly upward.

"Can Buttons find them?" asked Georgie. "If he can find them and then lead us there, that would certainly save us time."

Fynn, on his hands and knees in an effort to keep his balance, looked around in search of the bat. "Buttons!" he yelled out aimlessly. "Buttons!"

There was a brief silence just before the fluttering of wings was heard behind the group. Cocking his head to the side, Fynn remained silent, listening. The flapping came closer and closer until he felt the comforting sensation of the bat colliding with his back, wings curling around his shoulders as Buttons clung to him; a fuzzy snout nestled at the nape of the prince's neck. He reached back, feeling the brush of black fur against his fingertips.

"Hello there." Fynn smiled gently. He felt Buttons shift against him, clinging tighter to the yellow tunic beneath his wings. "Can you find the flags for us? We need all five."

The children watched as the bat once more took flight, lifting from Fynn's back and stealing away into the denseness of the mangroves.

Fynn rose to his feet, his legs shaking unsteadily as he began toeing over the roots and lower branches. "I think Renwyn's right," he began, reaching out his right hand and bracing his palm over the trunk of another twisting tree. "I think the flags will be at the center of the island, at the top of this hill. We should head that way. Staying here, waiting for Buttons, that's just wasting time."

"And if they're not there and we have to double back?" asked Wilder snidely.

"Then I was wrong, and you can tell me *all* about it on our way back." Fynn crawled under a thatch of low branches. "Fair?"

"Fine," Wilder huffed.

Climbing through the bark-netting was more work than anyone had imagined. The eleven first-years made slow, ever steady progress toward the center of the island. It was darker than it was before; the further toward the center they roamed, the less sunlight was able to break through the branches and leaves. Fynn realized that this was something that he was quite used to by now. They'd spent enough time in Nyle's survival classes and out in the wilds to know how to acclimate to low-light environments. He didn't quite mind. The darkness - the ever-present shadows - never really bothered Fynn. He didn't struggle to see what was around him; rather, everything was as clear as it would be in broad daylight. Frowning, he noticed the same was not true for his comrades, who now modeled various bruises and shallow cuts from the mangrove maze they were winding through.

As the island continued to curve upward, ascending through the thickness of the branches and the closeness of the trunks became more and more taxing. Fynn's arms began to ache from the unrelenting strain of having to pull himself up with the meager muscles of his spindly limbs, dragging himself over walls of branches. His back was sore. His feet ached. His palms were blistered and bleeding. As he reached out, gripping onto another branch and pulling himself forward, he bit back an annoyed groan of pain as another blister broke on his hand.

Fynn stole a peek over his shoulder and watched his year mates struggle through the branches. Lux was nearest to him, just at his heels, as she flung herself over the cresting of a particularly thick branch speckled with leaves. Her face was flush, cheeks a bright shade of red, as she breathed in deeply through her freckled nose. She struggled back to her knees, catching her breath as she eyed the unending twists and turns. Standing, she wavered for a moment, just shy of losing her balance.

The prince outstretched his blistered hand toward the girl, smiling softly as he watched her eye him for a moment - and only a moment - before taking his proffered hand in her own. Her fingers curled around his and he held tightly. Fynn was still smiling; his face nearly ached from the unyielding grin. His cheeks were warm again. Inwardly, he chastised himself for the reaction. They'd spent months together on Dier Island and yet, still, he found himself unreasonably flustered when she was nearby. Lux was still holding his hand as he levered her up toward himself. Fynn looked away, pouting indignantly at his own affect.

"Thanks," Lux said, as she righted herself at his side.

He nodded.

"I think we're almost there," she continued easily, comfortably.

Fynn looked forward, chin inclined slightly, as he gazed through the shadowed labyrinth toward what they all believed to be the center of the island. "I think you're right."

The flapping of wings caught the pair's attention. They turned in unison toward the source, pleased to see Buttons returning. The bat settled on a branch not far from them, hanging upside down and staring at them with his glowing, black eyes, wings wrapped around his fuzzy frame like a silken cloak.

Fynn snorted lightly. "I think he's waiting for us."

"I think you're right," Lux laughed. She pushed Fynn's back, giggling as the boy staggered for a moment before steadying once more. "Go on then, lead the way. I don't speak bat."

Shaking his head, Fynn sniggered under his breath. "Right, of course." He began his hesitant climb toward Buttons when a sudden darkness caught his attention. He lingered where he was, bracing his hand against a trunk. He looked down, marveling at the expanse of the blackness that seemed to have appeared from nowhere just beneath where he and Lux stood. "Do you see that?" he asked, nodding toward the empty hole threatening to swallow them to their deaths. "That wasn't there before."

Lux, her hands braced over Fynn's shoulders, peered around him and gaped. "That...no...that wasn't there before," she noted quietly. Her hold over Fynn's shoulders tightened until her knuckles went white. "What *is* that?"

"I don't know," Fynn admitted. He tensed. Fynn caught Lux's hand in his and held onto her with an iron grip. "Walk back *slowly*."

"Alright," she relented.

Lux took one step back; Fynn still clutched her hand. He began to retreat after her but the branch beneath his foot gave way. As he was falling, he felt Lux fist her hand into his tunic, her arm strained as she tried to keep him from plummeting downward.

It didn't work.

Instead, both children fell as the bark shattered beneath them. The darkness swallowed them greedily; the blue of the hardly visible sky and the green of the never-ending mangrove legion swirled overhead before fading away, totally gone from sight.

Fynn had expected the fall would kill them. Truly, from where they had stood, the hole seemed more like a gaping cavern that fell into oblivion itself. So, when he roused, feeling something soft and cool wrapped around his arms and legs, Fynn was surprised he was still breathing. His eyes fluttered open; his sight was instantly greeted by darkness. Forcing the fuzziness to retreat from the corners of his of sight, Fynn grimaced. He tried to draw up his arms, only to find them held firmly in place. Looking down, he saw thick, white webbing encircling his wrists. A quick assessment of his person revealed webbing laced around his ankles and thighs, belted around his waist, collaring his thin neck. The restrictive feeling came upon Fynn at once as he soon began struggling.

Eyes going wide with panic, Fynn searched his surroundings. The panic melted away into frantic hysteria when he found Lux, just five or so feet above him, suspended in the same fashion, caught in the thick webbing. The boy, despite knowing the results before he bothered exerting himself, tried to flex his arms and legs and break free of the webs. As he had expected, the endeavor was fruitless. He remained, suspended in a darkened cavern, trapped.

"Lux!" he yelled. When she didn't move, he cried out again, "Luxy! Luxy, wake up!" He saw her head loll to the side lifelessly. It felt as though his heart sank from his chest to the pit of his stomach, settling in the very bile that threatened to erupt into his throat at any moment. Warm tears swelled in his eyes. He choked out, "Lux!"

A sudden emergence of yellow eyes blazing through the darkness drew the boy's attention. There were two eyes and then four and then six and soon there were eight eyes all in a row, staring through the blackness straight at Fynn, glowing brilliantly like eight, tiny suns. Something snapped, then snapped again. Every nerve in Fynn's body seemed to coil at the sound; his body went rigid. The snap-snap-snap sounded again. Sweat rolled from his forehead, pooled beneath his tunic, then washed down his arms.

Desperate to look anywhere but those eight, fierce eyes, Fynn began assessing his immediate surroundings. There were great, big, spider webs crisscrossing in every direction; brilliant designs were woven into the intricate, silken threads. They reached far higher than Fynn thought the cavern rose. Webs etched through the bleakness as far as the boy's eyes could see.

Then, he found himself once more finding the eight eyes. They hadn't wavered since he'd looked away. There they were, intently watching him as he struggled to no avail. The snap-snap-snap thundered dangerously. Then again and again. Fynn thought, if he heard that awful sound once more, he may retch.

The webbing keeping him up seemed to bounce for a moment, then again. Fynn was jostled under the weight of something rather large approaching. To his profound horror, those awful, eight eyes were coming closer and closer, the snap-snap-snap grew louder and louder. The boy's stomach felt like it would rebel at any moment and, at the thought, Fynn couldn't help but snort with disdain at the realization that he hadn't eaten anything substantial since leaving Falena. The hollowness of his stomach was readily apparent when he did, in fact, retch when, again, the grisly snapping echoed through the void.

Eight, long, fuzzy legs stretched across the silvery threads, poised over the delicate webbing with elegant ease. Pincers, large and dangerous looking, snapped together. Eight, yellow eyes trained onto the boy. Scuttling closer, the eyes burned brighter.

Fynn wanted to scream in horror but found that he was simply too tense to manage a sound. There, lingering just beside him now, was a spider the size of a horse. The snap-snap-snap of its pincers didn't help ease the mounting terror that exploded in the boy's core.

"Hello there," the spider said. His voice was deep and calm, smooth and pleasant. Distantly, his voice reminded Fynn of Moriah's. "Glad to see you're awake."

Grey eyes impossibly wide, Fynn's jaw clamped shut as he tried to keep his heart from jumping out of his mouth. His stomach knotted and twisted. Every sinew and muscle in his body was strained and tensed as he tried to break free, wriggling within the clutches of the iridescent threads that restrained him. He thrashed his head back and forth, screwing his eyes shut.

"Now, don't do that," chided the spider almost amiably. "You'll knock yourself out doing that. Come now, stop it."

Heedless of the spider's instructions, Fynn continued his hopeless heroics, fighting with everything he could muster to break free and get away from the spider and get to Lux.

"Come on, lad, stop that. Let's open those eyes, yes, and calm down. You'll give yourself a fright, lad. Your heart's bound to just stop beating if you keep acting mad," the spider admonished.

Calming himself as best he could, Fynn went slack against the restrictive webbing. He turned his head toward the monstrous spider and slowly opened his eyes. Dismayed to find that he wasn't waking from a nightmare, Fynn let out a shuddering breath. "You can *talk*?" he whispered dazedly.

"Well, of course I can," insisted the spider.

"Oh." Fynn huffed. "Right, *of course*, silly me."

"You're in no position to be rude," said the spider. "You ought to remember your manners."

"Right, sorry." Fynn laughed humorlessly.

One large, spindly leg reached out and poked Fynn between the eyes with a bit more force than would have been necessary. The spider grumbled, "Stop that."

Fynn's mouth snapped shut instantly.

"Much better." The leg withdrew. "Right then, where are *my* manners? Introductions are, of course, due. You may call me Terry."

"Terry? Terry the spider?"

"Well," began the spider, "I don't go about introducing myself as *Terry the Spider*. But, as I am *Terry* and I am, as you've so cleverly pointed out, a *spider*...I suppose that, yes, I am, in fact, *Terry the Spider*." Terry's long leg reached out and thumped Fynn's forehead once more. "And you are?"

"Fynn," the prince supplied simply.

"Well then, *Fynn the Estherian*, ready to get out of these webs?" The leg once more tapped the boy's forehead. "You look a bit stuck."

"I am and yes...please," replied the boy.

Terry set to work releasing Fynn of the constraining webbing. The boy clung to the spider's leg, fearful of falling further into the seemingly endless hollow. The eight eyes watched Fynn as he maintained a frightful hold. "Go on, lad, climb up. Let's get your little friend, shall we?"

"Um...right...yes, thank you," the prince replied as he awkwardly scrambled atop the spider. "Thank you for helping us."

When Lux woke, the first thing she saw was eight, yellow, eyes, belonging to an absurdly large spider, staring at her. As she continued blinking, believing that she was simply dreaming something surreal, she noticed a boy straddling the shoulders of the spider, staring down at her. She recognized the messy, black hair and pale, grey eyes instantly. Groggily, she whispered, "Fynneas?"

"Before you panic, the giant spider won't hurt you," warned the prince, a touch of amusement in his boyish voice. "I promise."

"What?" she croaked, waking consciousness rearing itself slowly. "Spider?"

"Hello there," greeted Terry cheerfully. "Waking up, are we?"

At once, Lux felt something looped around her arms and legs, curling around her waist, tied like a sticky scarf at her collar. She blinked furiously, desperate for the fogginess to go away. Then she saw the eyes more clearly - the unnatural, eight, yellow eyes. She screamed. It was a deafening sort of scream that had both Terry and Fynn recoiling away from her until she could scream no more.

"Are we done?" asked the spider.

Dumbly, the girl nodded.

"Great." Terry reached out a leg and, as he'd done to Fynn, tapped Lux between the eyes. "Would you like me to help get you un-webbed?"

Too scared to attempt talking, Lux proceeded to nod again, silently.

Fynn leaned over Terry's head, coming into full view of the girl. He saw her blue eyes trained on him and smiled heartily. "I promise, Lux, it's going to be alright. Terry won't eat you."

Once freed, Lux instinctively reached out to Terry to steady herself upon the delicate webbing. She held tightly to one of his many legs. Fynn reached down, offering her his calloused and blistered hand once more. As she took it, the prince pulled her up onto the spider's back. Still fretting being in such proximity to a monstrous arachnid, Lux wound her arms around Fynn's middle and clung to him desperately.

"Are you alright?" Fynn asked.

Lux's voice was raspy when she answered, "Yes. I'm fine. Just…this is odd."

"What part?"

"Well, we're riding a talking spider for starters," Lux chuckled hoarsely.

Fynn shrugged. "To be fair, *we were* following a bat's directions earlier."

"Very true," conceded Lux with a small smile. She held Fynn tighter for a moment, calmed by feeling how relaxed and at ease the prince seemed to be. The girl withdrew, maintaining only a limp hold around Fynn's shoulders as she peeled away. She glanced down at the spider beneath them and said, "I'm very sorry. I've been rude. Thank you for rescuing us." She stroked the spider's furry side softly. "I'm Lux, by the way."

"It is a pleasure to make your acquaintance, *Lux the Estherian*," spoke Terry as he began scuttling over the webbing.

"Lux the Estherian?" asked the girl, turning a quizzical look toward the prince.

Fynn shook his head, pouting. "He thinks he's being funny." He held tightly to Terry as they sped along the intricate webs, jumping from one to another with effortless grace. "So, Terry, where are we going?"

"Right, right, now that you're both awake, I can explain," started the spider. "My master wishes to speak with you both. It's simply quicker, you see, if I take you to him. Otherwise, well, you'd still be stuck in the webs and I'd be bored."

"Bored?" asked Lux.

"Yes, yes, not many others to talk to around here," explained Terry. "It gets quite dull."

"And…where is *here*…exactly?" Fynn inquired.

The hollow was curved, that much was clear by the angles of the various webs. It was quite dark. There were, very distantly and far up above them, cracks that allowed in just a scant amount of light. However, those small vestiges of pale glow hardly reached down far enough to matter to the spider and his passengers. No, as far down as they were, it was still quite bleak. And, it seemed, they were headed lower into the supposed cavern.

"Well," started Terry, "you're in the shell right now."

"The shell?" repeated the prince.

"Yes. The *shell*," the spider snapped.

"What do you mean we're in the shell?" pressed Lux.

The spider grumbled, "I'm sure you've noticed the dome?"

The children nodded.

"And I'm sure you've noticed the island is rather round, just one large hill?"

"Yes," they chorused.

"Well, that's because it's a *shell*."

Fynn quirked a brow. "What…like a turtle shell?"

"Exactly!" cheered Terry. "Now you're getting it."

"Are we…Terry…is Little Isle a turtle shell?" Lux ventured curiously.

"No, no…of course not! Don't be absurd, Lux the Estherian," rebuked the spider haughtily. "It's not *just* a shell. That would be absurd. It's a whole turtle of course." Terry sighed. "Well, what's left of the turtle, I suppose. He's been dead a few hundred years now, poor thing. But you can spot his skeleton poking out at the sides, just under the water, if you look close enough. Big skeleton, it is."

30

ЄMPEROR ꝹARWYN

The depths of the turtle shell were deep and dark. Far below where Terry crept across the webbing, there was the distinctive light of fire. It burned dimly, flickering over the hollow walls of the shell's interior. They descended by what seemed to be a never-ending mesh of silvery webbing, crawling deeper and deeper, further down.

"Terry," began Fynn, as he peered over the spider's shoulder, watching the firelight grow stronger the further down they traveled, "who's down there?"

"My master, of course," the spider answered easily.

Lux, still holding onto Fynn, asked, "Who's your master?"

"Emperor Darwyn," Terry explained. "You'll like him, I suspect. Yes, I think you will, indeed."

"What's he like?" questioned Fynn. He sat up straighter, relaxed by the feeling of Lux braced against his back, holding onto him as she peeked over his slender shoulders

"You'll see for yourself, soon enough," assured Terry.

By the time they'd reached the bottom of the shell wherein the light grew far brighter, Lux's neck ached from her constant swiveling, as she awed and marveled at the great expanse beneath what she thought to be nothing more than a mangrove island.

Terry came to a halt, tapping the end of one long leg against the shell. Fynn jumped from the spider's back, holding his hand out to assist Lux as she dismounted. She didn't pay him any mind and, instead, slid off with far more grace than he'd managed, pushing by him as she continued to stare in every direction with wide-eyed wonder.

"Must've been a really big turtle," Lux commented. She tilted her chin upward, desperately trying to stare through the shadowy cavern of the hollow shell, eagerly searching for the hole through which they'd fallen.

"Oh yes, Promo-Toa was grand in his day, that he was," Terry informed. He shuffled forward. "He was the emperor, you see."

"Emperor of what?" asked Fynn.

Terry's pincers snap-snap-snapped before he clucked, "The turtles of course!"

"I didn't know turtles had an emperor," Lux admitted.

"How else do you think they're governed?" chided Terry as he sped along.

Fynn's brows raised, clearly puzzled. "I didn't know turtles *had* a government."

"Humans," muttered Terry irritably. "You think you're the only ones who have systems of organization. Honestly, how conceited. Of course, the turtles have a government! Now, the *dolphins*...well, they're constantly in a state of anarchy. Damn dolphins, can't stay still long enough to do a rollcall, let alone discuss matters of diplomacy. Always jumping about, they are! Ah, yes, well that's for another time."

The children remained side by side as they followed Terry through the darkness toward the firelight. Lux leaned closer to the prince, bowing her head toward his as she whispered, "What matters of diplomacy do you think dolphins *should* be discussing?"

Fynn shrugged. "Maybe they have border disputes with the sharks?"

Snorting down her laughter, Lux elbowed Fynn's ribs gently, shaking her head. "Be serious."

"How serious can I be when we've got a spider explaining ocean politics? Honestly, this is the strangest thing I think I've ever seen." He snorted quietly.

"Really?" Lux asked, quirking a brow. "I find that hard to believe."

"Well," grumbled Fynn, raking his hand through his hair, "maybe not the *absolute* strangest thing. But it is very well strange."

"That it is," she agreed with a sly smile in place. "You're not wrong there."

"Terry," called Fynn. "How did you come to live here?"

The spider didn't look back at the children as he replied, "I was born here, as far as I know. My master raised me, he did. He's a wise and ancient being, of course. Who better to raise you up?"

"There aren't any other spiders here?" Lux continued. "Just you?"

"Just me," Terry said solemnly. "I don't mind though. The master, well, he's plenty of company...for the most part."

They'd come upon the source of the fire. It was far larger than Fynn had anticipated. Terry scuttled ahead of them, gliding around the flame until the brightness obscured his very large form. When he returned, his eight, yellow eyes were aglow and he chirped rather merrily, "The master will see you now. Please, children, do remember to show the proper deference to the emperor, yes?"

Lux and Fynn nodded wordlessly, both far too engrossed in their own thoughts of what this ancient emperor could be like. Honestly, they thought, what sort of emperor lived inside a giant turtle shell with only a spider for company? Lux's hand found Fynn's just a moment later; her fingers interlaced with his.

Fynn straightened, looking insistently toward the fire, convincing himself that the warm swell in his cheeks came from the flurry of flames. He steeled himself and then, pulling Lux along with him, proceeded toward Terry. It was at that moment that Fynn found the answer to his question. There, just behind Terry, the emperor was seated. Fynn could do little more than stare with open confoundment.

Behind Terry there sat what appeared to be a boy no older than Fynn and Lux. He looked distinctively Estherian. His pale skin was practically porcelain in the light of the fire. What greatly alarmed Fynn were the barnacles that sprouted from the exposed flesh of his neck and chest, the starfish that clung where his right eye should be, and the seaweed that tumbled from his head where hair ought to. His left eye was a bright blue. Where there should be white surrounding the blue iris, there was nothing but a sickly yellow that seemed pale and dingy in comparison to the bright of his eye. His lips were thin and cracked, curled into a smile as his attention rounded on his newly arrived visitors. He stood on thin legs. Dressed in clothing that appeared vaguely similar to the uniforms Lux and Fynn adorned, he looked rather odd and dichotomous. This boy, the emperor, was a strange sort of mixture between the familiar and something utterly otherworldly and ghastly. When he moved toward them, it was with all the stuttering dyspraxia of a man ten times his age. He extended his hand to Fynn, revealing a barnacled palm and yellow-nailed fingers.

Dutifully, Fynn took the hand in his own and shook. The feeling of the hand in his was much akin to the feeling of touching a jellyfish, malleable and mushy, tender and strangely fragile. Fynn tried to hide his revulsion. After a firm shake, Fynn's hand recoiled and as inconspicuously as possible, he wiped his palm against his leggings to dispel the sticky feeling that still clung to his skin.

"Terry tells me you're Estherians," spoke the young emperor as he appraised the children before him, his eye lingering on Lux longer than Fynn would've liked.

The prince nodded. "We are."

"Ah, so it's time for the games again, then?"

Lux smiled. "We were just here on the island to retrieve our flags. We didn't mean to...intrude."

The emperor waved his hand dismissively. "No intrusion at all. Really, it's been quite lonely." He began to turn around and head toward his position by the fire once more but stopped abruptly and returned to face the newcomers. "I do apologize. Where are my manners? My name is Darwyn, by the way."

"It's a pleasure to meet you, Emperor Darwyn," Lux said, bowing her head respectfully.

"None of that emperor stuff, alright?" Darwyn offered them a pleasing smile. "Not from Estherians. It's embarrassing."

"Alright," Fynn agreed, casting a quick look back toward Terry before nodding his acknowledgement. "I'm Fynn." Looking down at their interlocked hands, Fynn grinned and then nodded toward the girl at his side. "This is Lux."

Darwyn smiled and then walked back to his station by the fire, ignoring the curious look Terry supplied. Settling down comfortably, Darwyn motioned for his guests to do the same. A wry smirk came upon his face when he watched Lux disentangle her fingers from Fynn's and approach. She seated herself at his side, looking expectantly toward Fynn.

With a huff, Fynn marched over and joined the pair around the fire.

Terry remained at a distance, eyeing them carefully.

"So, you're students at Morancy?" asked Darwyn casually.

"We are." Lux arched a brow. "Were...were you an Estherian? You look like one, I mean."

Darwyn cleared his throat. "I was."

"How'd you end up here?" Fynn wondered.

Darwyn watched the fire, as if he were expecting it to do something miraculous. It didn't, of course. It just flickered and leapt; embers sparked from the flames. He said, in a very measured voice, "I was here to collect my team's flag. The boat was rocking really bad. Everyone was arguing about what to do. I got into it with one of my teammates, you see. No one was paying attention; they were all yelling at each other about what they should

618

do…how to right the boat and all. That's when it happened. *He* pushed me. He knew I wasn't a good swimmer, and the sea was rough; it was storming that day. He pushed me in and watched as I went under. I drowned. My team thought I was dead, and they left me. They weren't wrong."

"What do you mean you drowned?" pressed Fynn curiously.

"Well," the emperor started, "I drowned. I died. I mean, not for long. But I died and, well, when I woke up, I was here." He gestured around, waving his wrist almost flippantly.

"Who brought you here?" Lux asked. "And how are you…well… how are you alive?"

Darwyn's voice maintained the detached indifference that Fynn had noted at the beginning of his exposition. "I suppose it must've been the turtles." He nodded tersely. "Yes, it was them. When I woke up, there were a bunch of them all huddled around me. It was scary, when I saw myself. There were these things…barnacles, I suppose…all over my skin. It was quite alarming. But the turtles kept me here and they kept me alive." Darwyn turned a warm smile toward Terry. "I found Terry not long after that. He was just a little thing then, all alone."

The spider shifted its weight, drawing up to its full height and ambling toward the little gathering. Lowering himself down on long, spindly legs, the spider's large body snuggled close to the barnacled boy-emperor, pincers just at his side, legs curled around Darwyn like a cocoon.

The emperor reached toward Terry absentmindedly as he continued on, "I've been here a long time now. But Terry's been great company! I do miss everyone else though, especially my mother. I suppose she's moved on, but I still think about her sometimes."

"She's an Estherian?" Fynn asked. "What house?"

"Pratchett. We're not a noble house or anything like that," Darwyn explained thoughtfully. "I only attended Morancy because my mother was close with some of the nobles, you see. They would come to her tavern and she got to know them. When she had me, well, I suppose she convinced them to let me attend, even though it went against the rules and tradition and all that."

Fynn narrowed his eyes, watching Darwyn quite carefully. A spark ignited in his thoughts and he couldn't keep himself from asking, "Your mother owned a tavern?"

Darwyn nodded.

"By chance, was it on Dier Island?"

"Yes, you know it?"

The prince sat upright, tension clamping his muscles at once. Uneasiness welled in the pit of his stomach, he felt almost sick. "Is it in More Town?"

Again, Darwyn nodded. His thoughtless patting of Terry ceased. The emperor leaned forward, curious. "Yes. The Wayward Turtle Tavern. Rather an ironic name, given my circumstances."

"Is your mother Nan?" Lux asked, realization dawning.

"Her name is Lizbet, but everyone always called her Nan," Darwyn answered shortly. "You know her? She's...doing well, then?"

Fynn nodded numbly. Tension completely overtook his body. His shoulders felt as though they were straining, ripping at the juncture of his neck. His back had gone rigid, taut with nerves firing every moment or so. His eyes remained narrow. Watching closely, he saw the darkening of Darwyn's eye, the eye now fixedly trained upon Fynn. Not realizing he was doing so, Fynn clutched his hands into fists. The blue eye turned toward Lux then, settling over her in a fashion that was easily definable—predatory.

Lux seemed to notice the look as she straightened, drawing herself taller as she leaned closer to Fynn. She squared her shoulders and set her jaw in a tense line as she watched the host watching her. Unnerved by his intense and unwavering scrutiny, she scooted ever closer to the prince. When their shoulders brushed, she felt Fynn lean toward her, angling himself between her and Darwyn ever so slightly.

"I've answered your questions," Darwyn began. His voice was heavier now, the apathetic chill gone, and the boyish smirk vanished. "I'd like for you to answer one of mine."

Refusing to recoil from the drastic change in persona, Lux steeled herself and nodded. "Alright."

"What houses are you from?"

The girl visibly shook at the question. Her blue eyes flitted to the side, watching Fynn in her periphery for a moment before returning to level Darwyn with a glance. "Astor."

"Fog," Fynn replied. There was a sort of challenging quality to his tone that clearly flustered Darwyn, for the emperor straightened instantly; his jaw set firmly as his teeth gnashed.

"You're the prince, then?" the emperor asked icily.

Fynn's pale eyes burned brightly in the firelight, piercing through the darkness of the turtle shell. "*One* of them. Yes."

"People will miss you then, should you not return from your little expedition," Darwyn ventured. The edge in his voice was unmistakable.

The prince stood abruptly. His quick motion startled Terry from his calm; a long, fuzzy leg curled tighter around Darwyn as eight, yellow eyes stared straight at Fynn.

Stepping just in front of Lux, Fynn towered over Darwyn. "Is that a *threat?*"

"Yes." Darwyn stood. Toe to toe, the two were just about the same height. There was no great advantage for Darwyn; that is, until Terry drew himself up and stood on those awfully long legs. Eight eyes glared down at the defiant prince.

"What do you want?" Fynn snapped.

Lux rose. Though Fynn tried to push her behind him, she shrugged off his attempt and stood at his side. Her blue eyes were dark in the shadows, but Fynn could easily see the embers of indignation burning within the azure irises; the sort that, had it been directed toward him, would have sent him cowering.

"We'd like to go now," she spoke flatly. "May we take our leave?"

"No." Darwyn's voice was deadly serious.

Flinching at the sound of the cold response, Fynn tried to remain undeterred. This time, when he pushed Lux back, he did it with the sort of force that asked for no argument from the girl. He knew well that she was capable, but the way Darwyn was staring at her made his skin crawl. Fynn felt a prick of something painful in his left eye. There was a pounding there in his temple that made him wince. And, though he tried to maintain a steady, frigid glare, he couldn't help but squint his left eye as the pain lanced through his pupil into the back of his head. It wasn't long after that, that he felt something warm streaking down his cheek.

Darwyn's eye went wide, fixed to Fynn's face. His once grinding teeth ceased and his jaw went slack. He watched the prince for another moment. Presently, he gathered his composure and resumed his glaring.

The barnacled-boy's reaction struck Fynn as odd. Tentatively, he reached to his face and touched trembling fingers to his cheek. Drawing his hand back, he saw blood staining his fingertips. "Damn," he muttered, as he began to quickly wipe the blood away.

Lux's hand fell over Fynn's shoulder quickly, drawing him back to her side. She reeled around him, gasping when she saw his left eye had changed colors. There, in place of the usual, icy grey, was the deep scarlet that she'd seen back on Green Isle. Her thumb ghosted over his cheek, brushing away the last traces of blood softly. "Your eye's gone red again," she whispered.

Darwyn advanced on them. His slimy hand curled around Lux's wrist, hauling her forcibly away from Fynn and tossing her to the ground. Astoundingly strong for someone so scrawny, Darwyn had no problem snatching Fynn's arm in his grasp and dragging him within a hair's breadth. "What *are* you?" growled the emperor darkly.

The prince wrenched himself from Darwyn's grasp awkwardly. He tripped backward and crumpled to the ground in a clatter of limbs. Gazing up at his attacker, he scowled. "I don't know what you mean."

"I think you do," said Darwyn. He knelt before the prince. His clammy hand caught Fynn's chin, discolored nails scraped against the alabaster flesh under his touch. "I think you know *exactly* what I mean." Craning his neck, Darwyn looked to the spider and said, "You can take him away now, Terry."

Darwyn stood, retreating from Fynn and retuning his attention toward Lux.

As Fynn tried to clamber back to his feet, he felt something impossibly sharp jab into his neck. There was a warm sensation that permeated from the point of contact, ebbing out from the wound like gentle waves rippling over a calm surface. The warmth grew into a most fuzzy sort of feeling, like a blanket being pulled snug around his shoulders. Bleary eyed, Fynn turned his head to see a large pincer buried into the juncture of his neck and shoulder. He thought, distantly, that he should be alarmed by such a sight. The blood that colored his yellow tunic was cause for concern. But, in that precise moment, Fynn found that the warm, fuzzy, comforting feeling that overwhelmed him in a matter of seconds was far more worth his attention than the clearly grotesque sight of his punctured neck.

The sharp pincer shifted against him. There was no pain, only the very vague feeling of pressure being applied to the point of entry. Fynn's vision, blurring with each passing second, caught the faintest glimpse of the spider disengaging from his neck. The warmth spread quickly, slipping down his arms, snaking down his spine. Soon, Fynn could hardly feel his legs. As he made an attempt to take stock of the situation, he noticed there was little more than tingling in his hands and feet.

Lux screamed Fynn's name. But, even in knowing she was little more than ten feet from him, she sounded as though she were calling his name from the other side of the world.

Then everything was spinning and tumbling all around. The darkness and the glow of fire and the deep red of the blood splattering to the ground, everything was a tangled mess of dulled hues that rushed all around Fynn's eyes. Where there had been a sharp pain permeating from his eye, there was presently little more than a tickling sensation that annoyed him. His limbs felt as though they were led, holding him down as he tumbled further into the mass of colors swirling around him.

Again, Fynn heard Lux calling out his name; or, at least, he thought it was his name that came bursting from her lips, but he couldn't quite be certain. Still, she seemed as though she were as far from him as east from west.

There was something cool and hard beneath his cheek all of a sudden. He blinked his eyes—once, twice, then five more times—trying to clear his vision. The world was tilted and off its axis and he could see little more than the blurry image of Lux screaming and thrashing, her wrist held tightly in Darwyn's grasp.

Fynn wanted to feel outraged at the sight. The very sound of Lux's voice normally galvanized some reaction out of him. But, as he watched the girl fight, slapping her palm over Darwyn's star-fish clad cheek, Fynn felt nothing more than a heavy numbness. He could just see the stepping of fuzzy legs around him before everything went black.

When the prince opened his eyes again, he found that he was restrained. He was set against the barely curving beginnings of the shell, near where the fire had been, he supposed, for he could faintly smell the scent of something burning. Glancing down, vision still quite muddled, he saw himself wrapped from ankle to neck in silvery webbing. Though he knew well he wouldn't be able to break free, Fynn feebly flexed his arms and legs and arched his back in a fruitless endeavor to do the impossible. Not surprised when he found himself arrested beyond all measure, the prince relaxed into the constraints and looked around. Everything was as it had been before. He could see the fire still burning. Staring through the shadowy cavern that was the shell, he saw Lux and Darwyn seated opposite one another. Upon closer inspection, he noticed that Lux had her hands bound behind her back, wrists tied with webbing.

He heard Darwyn's voice. Fynn couldn't tell what the boy was saying, but he noted the easy calmness and boyish manner of Darwyn's speech had returned. But, still, just beneath the surface lurked the chilling detachment that had originally made Fynn wary of the so-called emperor.

The warm sensation was still there, niggling at Fynn's neck. He wasn't sure if he should be feeling so calm, so content with his position restrained against the wall. Alas, there he was. He couldn't bring himself to be any more than relaxed, for that feeling of being safely swathed in something warm and soft and inviting still lingered. In the fleeting moment before he lost consciousness once more, Fynn thought the feeling was quite similar to when Fiona would wrap him up tightly after a nightmare, when she'd swaddled him in thick blankets and set him on his bed when he was little, reading to him or humming until he fell asleep. And so, with the thought of Fiona curled beside him, her arms wrapped around his blanket-cocooned figure, her voice warmly singing him to sleep, Fynn let his eyes slide closed once more.

Opening his eyes again, Fynn was dismayed to find that the warm sensation had gone. Now he was just cold and sore. It was, at that moment, that the reality of his situation truly came into focus. Fynn could feel where Terry had bitten him. The gentle numbness was now replaced by an awful stinging that singed the puncture wound, making the prince feel as though someone were stabbing at him with a hot poker. His head hurt. He could scarcely see out of his left eye anymore. Biting on his lip, he felt the panic rising within, the feeling of his chest constricting, the air supply seemingly inadequate all of a sudden.

At once, Fynn was distracted from the internal concerns that held his focus, the panic and hysteria completely forgotten. He hadn't before noticed the cool touch of something sliding against his chin. He glanced down, mismatched eyes alight by the soft touch of the distant fire. He saw it then, the curvy blade of the knife Hollyn had gifted him. Even more revolting was the hand that held the strange knife. There, holding the dagger beneath Fynn's chin, running the flat of the metal against the underside of the prince's jaw, was Darwyn. He could see the glean in the one, blue eye staring back at him. It was dark and malicious and made Fynn squirm.

"You're awake," Darwyn noted dully.

Fynn spat, "*Obviously*."

Darwyn continued his lazy motion of dragging the blade under Fynn's chin, delighting in the moment when the tip pressed too firmly into the pale column of the prince's throat, drawing meager red beads from his neck. "Ah," cooed the emperor, "sorry about that. Didn't mean to cut you just yet."

"What do you want?" asked Fynn. He was struggling against the webbing that bound him to the interior, shell wall. He knew he wouldn't be able to break free. Still, he did his best to struggle against his restraints.

"I want to make a deal with you."

Fynn ceased his fruitless efforts and relented into the clutches of the webbing. He eyed Darwyn curiously, quirking a single, black brow. "What sort of deal?"

"I'll let you go. But you leave the girl with me. You have everything. *You're* the *prince*. You don't need her. You can be on your way."

"Not a chance." Fynn started squirming again. He knew there was no point, but he felt like he had to be doing something—anything.

"That's too bad."

"And why's that?"

Darwyn pressed the dagger's tip more forcefully against Fynn's neck, drawing just a bit more blood. He pulled the blade back, admiring the fresh wash of red that colored the black steel. His free hand ran over the blade carefully; he marveled at the sticky touch of blood against his fingertips. "If you'd said yes, I would've let you live." He smiled fiendishly as he, once more, leveled the dagger's flat side just under Fynn's chin. "But you've gone and said no. So, I suppose that means you'll not be making it back to your friends. Pity, really."

Fynn could do little more than watch with horror-stricken eyes as the curved dagger strayed lower until it was poised over his chest. It plunged through the webbing and embedded just beneath his sternum. Again, he heard Lux screaming out his name. She didn't sound so far off this time; her voice echoed in his head thunderously, bouncing off the walls of his mind, ringing over and over again as she yelled for him. It took a few moments for Fynn to notice the pain that erupted in his chest. It was like nothing he'd felt before. It burned and stung and felt as though he'd been skewered because, as it were, he had been. Looking down, breathing frantically, he saw the dagger there, impaled into his lower chest.

The boy prince had never bled quite like this before. The amount of red that went pouring down from the knife's point was like a geyser of grotesque gore. He could recall only one other time where he'd seen something so objectively horrid. He remembered the blood that had gushed form his father's neck where the arrow had pierced through his jugular. Even then, Fynn thought, he didn't think there could have possibly been as much blood as there was now.

His breathing became quite labored. He'd felt pleasant numbness when Terry had bitten his neck, poisoning him with some mild venom he supposed. But now he felt nothing but vicious pain all over. It didn't matter what part of his body he chose to focus on, everywhere hurt. There was, simply put, no escape from the agony that assaulted him. Fynn looked away from the knife sticking out of his chest, doing his best not to concentrate on that, and found Darwyn still leering at him. There was a smug, self-satisfied look upon Darwyn's face.

Again, Fynn heard Lux calling to him. Her voice had dulled, it seemed. He wasn't sure if it was because he was finding it increasingly difficult to keep himself coherent or because she was running out of the energy needed to continue her hysterics, but she sounded faint and weak and, he noted with a pang of guilt, quite sad. Fynn bit back the scream that threatened to sound from his own throat. The pain was dreadful, but he would rather choke back his sobs than worry Lux further. And so, he remained there, silent cries warring in his throat and burning tears streaking down his face.

Something powerful, something entirely indescribable, was born within Fynn at that moment. His body regained its strength. It was a strength he wasn't sure was actually his own. He felt spurred to move. So, despite having failed before, he flexed his left arm experimentally. The webbing shifted at his movement. It felt weaker, like it may split apart if he moved a bit more. And so, Fynn did. With every bit of energy he had left, the prince willed his left arm to move forward.

The silver webbing tore asunder against the force of Fynn's reaching arm. His hand clamped over Darwyn's shoulder. The other boy tensed beneath his palm; Fynn felt the dilapidation of Darwyn's shirt, the sliminess of his skin, the distinct rise of small barnacles sprouting from his shoulder.

Fynn hadn't realized his eyes had fallen closed until he was once more opening them. He was no longer bound to the wall by the webbing. He was no longer within the turtle shell at all. No, he was in the place between places again. There was blackness all around. Looking down at his feet, he saw the familiar ripple of the inkiness under his step. His attention was riveted to a second set of feet there in the rippling waters of the void. Following the length of the legs upward, he saw Darwyn standing across from him.

"How are you here?" asked Fynn.

He reached to his chest, then. He didn't feel blood where he thought he should, didn't see a nasty wound where there should be one. Again, he looked to Darwyn. Fynn narrowed his eyes; that's when he noticed his left eye didn't sting as it had before. He could see quite clearly again, much to his relief.

Darwyn fixed his own gaze upon the prince, studying him silently for a long moment before replying, "I knew there was something weird about you."

"What do you mean?"

"If you were normal, if you were alive like everyone else, you wouldn't be able to be here," Darwyn answered.

"How do you know about *here*?"

The emperor gestured wildly with his arms, looking all about and then staring back to the prince. He answered easily, "Because I've been here many times before."

"How?"

Darwyn took a step closer. "The first time I was here, I was drowning, and I remember closing my eyes. I thought I'd died and when I opened my eyes, I was here." The smug smile slipped from his face. "I suppose it's the place you go when you're between life and death."

"I don't understand," admitted Fynn cautiously. "You were *here*?"

"I was *here* because I was going to *die*. I didn't get to go further because I was brought back," Darwyn answered genuinely. "I was brought back by some sort of magic. It was a blessing. I got to come back, and I didn't have to find out what, *or if*, there was anything more than this, anything after life. But sometimes when I dream or when I'm scared, I find myself here again."

Fynn saw the sadness creeping into Darwyn's eye, the familiar solemnness of someone both scared and embittered. He drew forward, approaching Darwyn warily. Slowly, Fynn reached out to the other boy until his hand came to rest softly on Darwyn's shoulder. This time, Fynn didn't find himself repulsed by the feel of the other boy's skin. His voice was soft and low, as he said, "I don't think it was a blessing what they did to you." Fynn smiled sadly, a touch of melancholy colored his words. "I think it was a curse. It wasn't fair, Darwyn. It wasn't fair to you, to keep you in a world you don't belong in."

Darwyn didn't pull away. He stared at the hand placed delicately on his shoulder. But still, he remained rooted in place. "What do you mean?"

"It must be lonely," Fynn began. "It must be really lonely there in that shell with no one but Terry to talk to."

"I have the turtles!" insisted Darwyn defiantly, jerking away from Fynn's touch. "I have them and Terry and that's all I need!"

Darwyn recoiled away from Fynn violently, drawing his shoulders up, hands fisting at his sides defensively. Something within Fynn softened at the sight of the other boy so flustered. He shook his head. "I don't think that's true." He took a step forward, closing the space between them. "I don't think *you* believe it's true either."

Darwyn shook his head. "You're wrong! You don't understand. You couldn't!"

Fynn's shoulders fell at that. The heaviness in his chest was back. It wasn't the heaviness that weighed his acute panic earlier, but rather an old friend he greeted with reluctant weariness. It was sadness. It was the most deep, profound sort of sadness. It was the sort that made you feel sick to your stomach because it felt like the world was set upon your chest and you couldn't breathe.

Fynn couldn't look at Darwyn when he spoke. He was hardly able to keep the utter defeat from his voice. "I do understand...*really*." He drew in a deep, quaking breath. "I think you wanted Lux to stay because you fancied her. I think you liked her and wanted her to stay because you've been lonely. Of course, you've got Terry and the turtles and all that, but it's not the same as being with other *people*. And, well...I think a part of you wanted her to stay because you wanted to hurt *me*. And, I don't know what I've done to make you feel that way. I really don't. But I'm sorry for it. Really, I am." Finally, Fynn forced himself to look up and stare at Darwyn, unabashedly trying to convey his understanding of the situation. He wasn't sure if it worked. "But you need to move on."

The emperor stomped his foot in the inky ripples like an enraged toddler. He pouted. "No, I don't. I don't *have* to do anything."

"Can I tell you something?"

Darwyn, having not expected that veer in the conversation's trajectory, nodded wordlessly.

"I think you'll be happier if you move on." Again, Fynn drew in a calming breath. "I know it may seem scary. It is. I know that. But I *know* there is something after death." He gestured about with his arms, looking around before looking back at Darwyn poignantly. "I know there's more than just this. My father died before I went to Morancy. And yet, even though he's gone, he still came to visit me not long ago. So, I know he had to have been *somewhere*. My mother, too. She died when I was a baby and she's come to see me a few times. They're somewhere that isn't...*here*. There's something more than *this* and I think you'll find that it's better to be there, among the people who love you, who miss you, rather than in that shell all alone."

When Darwyn at last spoke again, after a very long time of studying his feet in the waters, his voice was low and unsure. "Who are you?"

"I told you. My name's Fynn and I'm one of the princes. I'm a student at Morancy. I'm Estherian. There isn't much more to tell."

628

"Yes, there is." Darwyn's blue eye was steely and confident. His lips pulled into an impossibly flat line. "What more than that?"

Fynn shrugged. "I don't know. I suspect there's something more, but I don't know."

"How can you be alright with not knowing?" asked Darwyn incredulously.

Again, Fynn shrugged. "I don't think there's any point in trying to know everything. And when I *do* try to figure things out, no one ever gives me a straight answer."

"Doesn't…well…? Doesn't not knowing scare you?"

"Of course." Fynn laughed. "Everyone is scared of things they don't understand, things they don't know. That's part of being human. If you're never scared, you can never be brave."

"I don't want to be alone anymore," Darwyn whispered. A single tear trailed down his face. "It's been so long."

Fynn reached out, taking Darwyn's hand into his own. "I know."

"Will it hurt? Will it hurt to move on?"

Fynn shook his head. "I don't think so. I think…since you're already *here*…I think you just need to let go."

"I don't know how," Darwyn muttered.

Fynn held tighter to the other boy's hand. He glanced down and saw the water rippling beneath their feet as they both shifted their weight, uneasily standing still in the oppressive darkness.

"Just close your eyes and fall back," Fynn whispered.

"Will it work?"

"Something tells me it will." Fynn smiled

"Stay with me until…until it's over?"

"I won't leave you. I promise."

Darwyn's blue eye studied the prince's hand. He croaked, "Why are you doing this?"

"Doing what?"

"Why are you trying to help me?" The blue eye turned upward to observe Fynn's face. "I had Terry *poison* you. I tried to *kill* you."

"I'm not really thrilled about that part." Fynn snorted, amused. "But I suspect I'll be alright. Maybe a bit sore and with a nasty cut, but I'll live."

"What are you?" Darwyn asked again, shaking his head disbelievingly.

"I don't know," Fynn answered honestly. He looked away from their joined hands, tipping his head skyward or, what would be skyward if there was a sky to look at. All around them was the blackness, the void of the in between. "And I think that's alright. At least, it's alright for now."

"I'm sorry…for what I did."

"I forgive you," Fynn swore.

Darwyn said faintly, "You're not like *him*, you know? Not like the one who did this to me."

"The turtles? Who revived you?"

Darwyn shook his head. "No. The boy who murdered me."

"Who was it? Who pushed you into the water?" Fynn asked.

The boy emperor shook his head again. His voice was very weak, very tired. "It doesn't matter now." Darwyn's hand fell from Fynn's.

The prince watched as the other boy folded his arms over his chest. He cast one last, fateful look toward Fynn, before closing his eye and drawing in one final breath. His chest heaved with the effort, but never fell. Darwyn braced himself for a moment, his shoulders tensing, before all semblance of rigidity eased from him. He fell backward.

Fynn watched. It was like watching a feather drift in the wind. He felt as though he could see every waver of Darwyn's clothing, every shift of seaweed hair, every twitch of muscle beneath sickly-slick flesh. Then the blackness splashed around the boy's body, swallowing Darwyn down and down until Fynn could no longer see him.

He rushed to where Darwyn had stood in the blackness, only to find not a trace of the other boy left. He was gone. Fynn collapsed to his hands and knees. He felt the cool lick of the black waters beneath him. But, staring down into the depths of the abyss, he saw nothing more than utter nothingness.

Fynn's voice was soft as he whispered, "I think you'll be happier now."

At once, the prince's chest erupted into a flame of pain that burned up his throat. He retched at the sudden emergence of such agony, gripping his chest just beneath his sternum. He retched again, bringing up nothing but painful, rib-shaking coughs. He shuddered, laying himself down against the emptiness. Though he was in quiet agony, Fynn couldn't deny the peacefulness that came with being in the place between places.

Something broke the sound of silence, shattering it into a thousand, little pieces. It was familiar, but indistinct. Fynn closed his eyes, doing his best to block out the noise. He felt it then, the darkness reaching out from the depths, a million tendrils wrapping around him, dragging him down. The feeling of sinking slowly, further and further from the surface, was one he wasn't sure he would ever get used to. But he relaxed into it. For while, he sank down into the abyss.

There was no pain or fear or worry.

There was simply nothing.

There was nothingness all around. And that nothingness, strangely enough, bore with it the most unique sort of hope, the sort that made Fynn feel as though, if he gave into the embrace of the numbing darkness, there would never be pain again. He liked that thought.

But that indistinct sound flared again, and, for some inexplicable reason, he couldn't ignore it. He tried. He kept his eyes closed. He willed away the noise. But still, it reverberated through the endless blackness all around him, crashing over him like a tidal wave, the force of its call thunderously boisterous. His eyes opened of their own accord, entirely heedless of his command to remain closed.

"Fynn!"

He knew that voice. He knew it well. But it sounded far off and too distant for him to care.

"Fynn!"

Yes, he definitely knew that voice. He couldn't quite understand why it sounded worlds away.

"Fynneas!" Lux sounded as though she had completely given herself over to hysteria at this point. "Fynneas, you have to get up!"

The surface just above him broke, a freckled hand plunged downward, toward him. He knew that hand. Fynn reached out. He felt his fingertips graze those of the disembodied, splayed fingers reaching for him.

"Fynneas, please!"

The freckled fingers curled through the inky waters, but he was just out of reach. He was falling still, sinking deeper and deeper.

"Please! Don't leave me! Fynneas, wake up!"

The hand delved further. The speckled forearm dove into the water. He reached out as far as he could, straining his shoulder with his abrupt lurch forward. Her hand closed over his wrist, tightening once she'd made contact. Her arm began reeling back, pulling Fynn along with it. He smiled.

When he burst through the surface of the black water, feeling the numbing darkness fall away from him, rolling down the curvature of his features like droplets rushing down his skin, he didn't see the darkness he expected. Rather, Fynn saw a shadowy place, lit only by pale firelight. He was on his back, that much was for certain. Blinking his eyes, his vision righted itself. Red hair hung around him like curling curtains and blue eyes sparkled with tears.

Fynn coughed. He tasted something tangy and metallic in his mouth. He coughed again. Blood stained his lips. "What happened?" he wheezed. His chest felt terrible. He wasn't sure he could manage to stay conscious through the pain that weighed him down. He couldn't even bring himself to move a single finger.

"You'll be alright," Lux whispered.

Her hand clasped him just over the wrist. Fleetingly, Fynn looked down at her hand and realized that's where she'd taken hold of him in the place between places, that's where she'd grabbed him to pull him back out of the nothingness. He continued staring dazedly at her hand. He asked feebly, "Where's Darwyn?"

"I think he's dead," Lux answered shakily.

"What happened?" Fynn inquired for a second time.

"You…well…he stabbed you and you somehow managed to get out of Terry's web. All you did was touch him. And then you both just collapsed. I came over and Darwyn was…dead."

"I'm sorry," rasped Fynn. He coughed again. More blood pooled over his tongue.

"I don't know what happened with you two," Lux began. "I couldn't hear what you were both saying." A tear slid from her cheek and landed on Fynn's. "But Darwyn was smiling when he died."

"Are you alright?" Fynn asked. His head throbbed viciously. He struggled to think straight. Everything was muddled.

"I'm fine," she assured. She laughed a mirthless laugh, shaking her head. "You've got a hole in your chest and you're asking *me* if *I'm* alright."

"Well, I already knew *I* got stabbed. No use dwelling on it," he whispered weakly.

Lux's hand made the shaky journey from Fynn's wrist up to his chest. As gently as she could, she braced her palm over the wound. "It's not bleeding much anymore." She bit down on her lower lip, nervously chewing it. "It still looks bad though."

"If it looks as bad as it feels—"

Fynn's blood-soaked coughing fit interrupted him.

Lux held onto Fynn with more urgency. "It looks *bad*."

"Oh…well, it *feels* terrible," he quipped.

Despite the blood smeared all over, staining Fynn's shirt and her hand, Lux smiled. Tears slid down her freckled cheeks, smearing through blood and grime. "What now?" she asked as calmly as she could. She swiped her hand across her cheeks to clear away the tears, effectively smearing more filth across her face.

"We get out of here," Fynn murmured. "And get back. I'm sure they've found the damn flags by now."

"Do you think they're alright?"

Fynn closed his eyes, forcing himself not to think about the pain radiating from his chest. "They better be. I can't get stabbed to save *them* too." He tried to smile.

"Very funny." Lux chuckled. There was a long moment where neither of them spoke. She kept her hand pressed over Fynn's wound, doing her best to staunch what little blood still leaked from the hole in the prince's chest. "Do you think you'll be able to get up?"

"I'll need some help," he replied. "But I'll live." He opened his eyes again, pleased to see she was still staring down at him with the same hopelessly optimistic look. "Where's Terry?"

"With Darwyn's body."

"Angry?"

Lux shook her head. "I don't think so."

"Really?"

She nodded. "I think he knew. I think he knew that Darwyn needed to…I don't know. Maybe he knew that something was wrong with Darwyn. I don't think Terry seems angry. He's sad, of course. Darwyn raised him. But I think Terry understands that maybe this needed to happen."

"Good. Maybe Terry can get us out of here."

Not moving her hand from Fynn's chest, Lux snaked her other arm around the boy's waist and pulled him, slowly and gently, to his feet. She winced when she heard him hiss in pain. "Alright?"

A fresh splattering of vibrant red appeared over her splayed fingers upon Fynn's chest. She frowned.

"Let's just get out of here," he encouraged shakily. "I'm tired of this place."

"Me too."

"Lux?"

"Hmm?"

Fynn, despite the overwhelming exhaustion fighting to drag him back into unconsciousness, smiled. His voice was little more than a whisper. "I'm glad you're alright."

31

ALL TOGETHER NOW

Firiel watched, shaking her head and frowning, as Godryk and Renwyn went tumbling through the mangroves in a mess of whirling limbs. Penelope and Georgie flanked her on either side, peeking over Firiel's shoulders and watching with twin scowls as the boys continued their now hours-long spat.

Godryk had Renwyn pinned down, prone against the twisting roots. He beat a fist against Renwyn's jaw, snapping the boy's head to the side with a sickly thumping sound. He leaned nearer Renwyn, the heat of his breath washing over the other's face as he ground out, "Are we done?"

Renwyn gathered himself and shoved mightily against Godryk's chest, knocking the boy from his perch astride him and off to the side. Jumping to his feet far quicker than anyone had expected him to, Renwyn slung a forceful kick into Godryk's ribs, eliciting a pained gasp from the boy. "No, I don't think so!" he spat.

Hogan and Wilder stood side by side, eyes wide, as they watched the two go at it. Once more, Renwyn and Godryk had snatched hold of one another and went thrashing to the ground. Hogan whispered, never looking away from the scene, "This is really stupid."

Wilder nodded wordlessly.

Albie and Ollie were settled in amongst the small herd of spectators. Ollie winced when Renwyn kicked Godryk's ribs once again. "That's going to leave a nasty bruise," he commented.

"He'll be lucky if he has any ribs left that *aren't* bruised," mumbled Albie.

Georgie sighed. "We should try and stop them."

Penelope shrugged. "No. Let's let Godryk try and beat some sense into Renwyn."

Ollie nodded adamantly. "That's right. We're *not* leaving. We need to find Lux and Fynn."

634

Firiel lowered herself to the ground, crossing her legs. "We don't even know if they're still alive. They've been missing for hours."

"It's *Fynn*," scoffed Georgie. "He goes missing all the time and he always turns up. I'm sure Lux is with him."

"She's right," Albie agreed.

Renwyn had Godryk's back against the trunk of a particularly thick mangrove. He held him with one arm while the other reeled back before smashing forward; his knuckles crashed over Godryk's nose brutally. As Renwyn's hand fell away, uncoiling from the material of the other's yellow shirt, Godryk fell in a crumpled heap to the ground, clutching his bleeding face. "We need to get back to Green Isle. We can't just waste time here," Renwyn insisted. He shook his hand; his knuckles were smarting.

Godryk's hands were clamped over his nose, sticky blood seeped through his fingers and red rivers splayed over his lips and chin. He shook his head defiantly. Tears sprung into his eyes, poured over his cheeks. His shoulders shook, but he bit back the sobs. "No. We're *not* leaving them."

"This is ridiculous!" yelled Renwyn. He hauled Godryk to his feet unceremoniously, throwing his back once more into the tree.

Godryk remained hunched over, hands pressed to his face to staunch the bleeding, salty tears streaking his dirty cheeks. "I'm not leaving." His voice was muffled behind his hands, but the venom of his words was clear. "You're a *traitor* if you leave your comrades behind. I'm *not* leaving."

"We've got the flags," Renwyn argued, "and the rest of us are here. They're probably dead, killed by whatever sort of unnatural things live on this damn island. Do you want us to be next? You'd sacrifice the rest of us on the off-chance Lux and Fynneas are still alive?" Renwyn punched Godryk's stomach hard, effectively silencing any further protest from the other. With a self-satisfied smirk, he watched Godryk double over, folding at the hips, before pitching forward to the ground.

Raising himself on shaking arms, palms pressed against the twisted-root ground, Godryk wheezed, "I don't care. I'm *not* leaving."

A rustle amongst the mangroves caught the attention of the first-years. The fighting ceased. The spectator sport was entirely forgotten. They knew far too well from their time training at Morancy that when in the wilds, any unexpected sound was a sound worth investigating.

Without a thought given to his actions, Renwyn slipped his arm under Godryk's and levered the boy to his feet. They stood there, panting for air, bleeding, dirty, with eyes wide and watching. The rest of the first-years assembled themselves around their battered comrades, each of them scanning the surrounding area for the cause of the rustling.

It was then that they saw large, spindly legs ease around the curling trees. Yellow eyes - eight of them - stared back through the tangle of trunks. The legs, brown and fuzzy, eased further into sight, looking distinctly spider-like. Then the body appeared, massive and unnatural for an arachnid. Atop it, they noticed, were two slumped figures.

"Is that...a *spider*?" gasped Penelope, as she shuffled behind Albie, peering over his shoulder as she angled him before her like a human shield.

Albie nodded. "Looks like it."

"Oh, it's disgusting!" Georgie cringed. She wilted behind Ollie.

Godryk furrowed his brow, studying the approaching spider curiously. "That looks like Lux and Fynn! There! Look! On its back!"

Terry inched himself closer to the gawking gaggle of children. He came to a stop a cautious ten paces before them, yellow eyes intensely observing the group.

Lux, still holding Fynn against her, eased off Terry slowly. She held Fynn securely as they dismounted the spider, adjusting his meager weight against her side, curling his arm over her shoulder as he slumped listlessly beside her. Her voice was soft. "We found them."

Fynn nodded weakly. His sweaty hair clung to his forehead. His yellow shirt was stained beyond all recognition with dirt and blood, torn at the center of his chest. His leggings were ripped and battered, boots scuffed and stained. His normally alabaster skin had a worrisome grey tint to it. "Let's head back." He coughed. His chest rattled painfully. "I'm tired."

"I know," Lux replied, shifting him against her, tightening her hold. "Try and stay awake, alright?"

Godryk lunged forward toward the two. He was heedless of the horse-sized spider that kept to the pair's side. He bounded right up to them, staggering to a halt before Lux. His blue eyes swept over her, assessing the small cuts and bruises that muddled her freckled complexion before turning toward Fynn, tears already sliding down his cheeks. "Gods!" Godryk gasped. He reached to Fynn, encircling the prince's waist with his arm and taking his weight against his shoulder, easing Fynn from Lux's shaking hold. "What happened?" he asked, voice quaking uncontrollably.

Lux withered under Godryk's burning, blue eyes. She flung herself against his chest, heaviness overtaking her as she cried. "I'm sorry," she murmured, as she buried her face against his yellow tunic.

Godryk wound his arm around Lux's shoulders, holding her as best he could while still keeping Fynn upright. They both felt limp in his arms, like they'd given up what little energy they'd been clinging to once they saw the group of first-years. It didn't matter to Godryk. He held both of them like a lifeline, tethering them to reality while they both slipped away; their eyes fluttered closed and their breathing evened out into a soft rasp, denoting their lost war with consciousness.

Ollie and Albie were quick to run over. Albie clumsily peeled Lux off of Godryk. Ollie was more sluggish in his assistance, his eyes steadfastly turned toward the giant spider leering at them.

Still nervously watching Terry, Ollie asked, "How bad?"

"Bad." Albie struggled as he tried to shoulder Lux's taller frame.

"*Really* bad," Godryk added. He couldn't look away from the ashen color of Fynn's face and the nasty wound to his chest. "I wonder what happened."

"I may be of assistance," Terry said, his voice quite even and understanding.

The boys all rounded on the spider; jaws slackened. Ollie stammered, "It-it *spoke*. You heard it speak, right?"

Albie and Godryk nodded dumbly.

"Of course, I speak! Honestly, you're just as arrogant as these two," Terry scoffed, eight eyes training on the limp forms of Lux and Fynn. "The boy, Fynn, he was stabbed. Well, I'm sure you pieced that together yourselves by now. Or at least, I should hope so. It's rather obvious. The girl, Lux, well she wasn't stabbed. No, no, only tied up. Some bruises and scratches. Nothing terribly painful. I think it was the fright that got to her. She was quite upset by Fynn's little incident."

"Incident?" Godryk repeated flatly. "What happened *other* than being *stabbed*?"

Ollie interjected, "And *who* stabbed him?"

Fynn, limp against Godryk's side, knew little more about the situation than that of his current, rather dreadful, condition. He could faintly hear Terry explaining what had transpired in the hours since he and Lux had disappeared through the hole that seemed to come from nowhere. As best he could, Fynn listened through the fog in his head to Terry as he regaled the first-years with tales of Darwyn, the Turtle Emperor as he had been proclaimed, and all the strange, odd, magical details of his death and resurrection, his time on the island, his governing of the turtles around the archipelago, and, at last, his altercation and timely second-death at the hands of the prince. Throughout the retelling of all the unfortunate events that had led Fynn to be little more than a ragdoll clinging to Godryk with what little strength he had left, the prince was distantly aware that he was being moved. He felt himself jostled, levered this way and that, moved easily and gently from one spot to another. As time went on, as Fynn was sure it was, he tried multiple times to open his eyes. Unfortunately, his eyelids felt as heavy as the stones he and Hollyn had moved their first night of lessons at Morancy.

The thought of those rocks, that night out in the rain with Hollyn arguing over everything they could think of, brought a tinge of warmth to Fynn's muddled mind. He remembered the night so vividly, but so much seemed to have happened since then. His mind wandered to thoughts of Hollyn, curious to know if his cousin was on the mend as he said he was, if his shoulder would be ready for training in a few months, if he was brooding and scowling as he was wont to do on occasion.

The sound of muffled conversations persisted. He recognized the voices. Godryk was the most prevalent among them. Terry was doing his best to explain everything he could to the red-haired boy. He didn't need to be able to see, to know that Ollie was hovering nearby; the boy's familiar, soft voice floated through Fynn's head as he spoke quietly, urging the prince to wake up as kindly as he could. Fynn wished beyond everything else that he could oblige Ollie's request, but something was pulling him under, and it seemed he just couldn't bring himself to open his eyes.

With Fynn slumped against his back, Godryk carried the prince through the tangle of mangroves. He saw sunlight, darkening as evening approached, stretching through the lattice of branches and vines and trunks and roots. He heard the quiet sounds of water rushing over the roots at the edge of the island. Godryk smiled, absentmindedly readjusting Fynn's weight against his back as he pressed onward.

They were following Terry back to where they'd tied up their boats. In all the chaos that had accompanied Fynn and Lux's arrival, Godryk found that he didn't mind Terry all that much. Sure, he wasn't thrilled that the spider had gone along with Darwyn's utterly mad plan of kidnapping Lux and trying to murder Fynn, but Terry didn't seem like the type to do it out of any sort of genuine malice. Rather, Godryk supposed, he had done it at the behest of the person who'd raised him, the only company he'd had for his whole life. The boy couldn't fault Terry for that, for he knew, quite well in fact, that he would have done the same.

Wilder was carrying Lux on his back. He stayed near to Godryk, just behind Terry's eight heels as they crept closer to the water. He glanced in Godryk's direction, spying the dried blood that caked over the bridge of his freckled nose, the red stains that trailed over his lips and chin, the awful ruby splatter marring his yellow top. "Is your nose broken?" asked Wilder.

"I think so," Godryk answered with a sigh. "Doesn't hurt much now. I'll be alright."

"You took a nasty beating," Wilder commented. "I get why you did it though."

The red-haired boy turned in Dangerfield's direction with a sharp, blue stare. "If you agreed with my position on the matter, you could've jumped in to help."

"You seemed like you had it handled," Wilder muttered.

"Did I? Next time I *seem to have it handled*, maybe you still try and assist, alright?"

Embarrassed at his own inaction, Wilder shifted his weight awkwardly. "Will do."

The boats were still there, tied just where the first-years left them that morning. Terry watched with mild interest as the children embarked their vessels. Lux, waking finally from her exhaustion, lolled her head to the side to see the still-unconscious Fynn just there, limp as he had been for an hour now.

Godryk was the last to remain on the mangroves. He'd untied the green team's boat, watching tiredly as their small vessel rocked over the little waves passing a few feet from the edge of the island. The yellow team's boat remained tethered, waiting for Godryk to untie them. The boy faltered when he reached for the rope, looking back at Terry with the saddest eyes the spider had ever seen.

"Will you be alright here, now that you're alone?" the boy asked the spider.

"I haven't thought much about it," Terry replied earnestly. "Why do you ask?"

Godryk looked down, suddenly finding his feet quite interesting. His voice was low and careful, as he said, "I don't want to leave you here all alone, especially if you're not ready for it."

"You are a very kind boy," said the spider.

The boy shrugged his shoulders carelessly, sighing all the while. He forced himself to look up at Terry, to stare into the eight, yellow eyes pleadingly. Godryk offered, "You could come with us."

"Where would I go?"

"There are plenty of creatures living in the jungles on Dier Island," Godryk began. "I'm sure you could find a home there. And at least there, you wouldn't be alone."

"Why do you care so much?"

Blue eyes looked bluer as emotion flooded into them. "Because I don't want you to be lonely. It's no fun being lonely."

"You are not alone. You have your friends." Yellow eyes flicked from Godryk's lean person to the children huddled in the boats and back. "You've many friends it seems."

"I do *now*. But I didn't before. Fynn was the first real friend I ever made." Godryk combed his hand through his red hair, brushing the curls from his face. "Thank you, by the way, for bringing him and Lux back. I was worried...*really* worried." He laughed a humorless laugh. "I wouldn't have left the island until I found them. The games don't really matter. I just wanted to know they were alright and to see for *myself* that they were alive." He smirked. "But I should've known, you know? Fynn always goes off and gets lost and he always comes back, usually after some wild adventure. This time was no different. I would've preferred if he hadn't been stabbed, but, it's Fynn. He'll be alright."

Terry reached out his front leg and tapped it against Godryk's forehead. His voice was a low rumble. "You are a very kind boy. Don't change that about yourself, alright?"

"You're not coming with us, are you?" Godryk knowingly ventured.

"I am not."

"Please?"

"I can't."

"But why? Why choose to be all alone?" Godryk asked pitifully.

"I must stay and take up where my master left off," Terry answered. "The turtles will need someone to look after them. They're a right mess, you know. Can't handle a thing without someone there to supervise."

"Al-alright," stammered Godryk, unsure of what else he could say. Truthfully, the whole thing baffled him. He scratched at the nape of his neck thoughtlessly, still staring up at Terry. "You'll be alright?"

"I will."

"Then we'll be off," said the boy. He gathered himself and straightened up. Confidently, he nodded his head. "Be well, Terry."

"And you, Godryk."

The boy stepped into his boat gingerly, making sure not to rock it more than was unavoidable and risk rousing the prince. Catching sight of Fynn, Godryk's heart sunk. The prince's head rested upon Lux's shoulder. She looked bleary eyed and confused. Settling down, Godryk cast a final look to Terry. He waved. "Farewell!"

The spider clicked his pincers over the twine and let loose the boat, watching from the shore of the mangrove tangle as the small vessel coasted over the lapping waves, joining the green team as they crested over the watery hills, creeping further and further away at an impossibly slow pace. Terry called to them, "If you find you need help on your way to Nandulus, call for the dolphins!"

"Dolphins?" asked Ollie, quirking a brow.

Lux, with a rasping voice, grumbled, "Dolphins…*disorganized*…but helpful."

Penelope scooted closer to Lux; kneeling before the other girl, she was glad that they'd insisted she and Fynn remain together despite their disparate teams. Carefully, Penelope reached out and brushed an errant tangle of red hair from Lux's face. "Feeling better?"

Lux nodded.

"Must've been awful," Penelope continued.

"It was…*strange*," Lux answered sourly. "It was very strange." Wakefulness was upon her in full and she glanced down, seeing the red stained all over her green tunic. Her fingers brushed over the ruined fabric. She frowned. Tears sprung into her eyes, prickling and stinging. They fell hotly down her cheeks. Her hands shook as she held them out before her to study her red-stained palms. "It's *his* blood," she whispered. More tears fell down her cheeks as Lux lowered her head, biting back a sob. "There was so much of it."

A small hand draped over the girl's shoulder, forcibly pulling her out of her solemn reverie. Penelope stared back at Lux with earnest, warm eyes.

"He's *alive*," Penelope assured. She nodded to the limp prince toppled at Lux's side. "He's alive and well, knowing him, he'll be up and about in no time."

Lux's voice felt small and weak, reflecting the fragility that seemed to have beaten her down in the last few hours. Gone was all the strength she was accustomed to. The sight of all that blood—all of Fynn's blood—had sickened her to her very core, knocking her off her personal balance, coloring the world in a twisted sort of way she'd never considered before. She shook her head sadly. "I know." Another cry was warring in her throat. "I know…but it doesn't matter." She tried to swallow down her whine, but it made its way by gnashing teeth, tumbling out as little more than a pained whimper. "But you don't understand what it was like…what it was like to see all that blood all over him. It was…too much."

Penelope drew Lux into a hug, smoothing down the mangy, red hair, drawing circles between her shoulders, letting her hand trail up and down Lux's spine softly, comfortingly. "It's almost over. We have our flags. I'm sure the second-years have theirs. We'll meet back up with them and by late tomorrow morning, we'll all be sailing to Nandulus and this part, at least, will be over. We can rest for a while before everything else. It's fine. We're all fine."

Evening wore into night as the two boats, careful to stay within sight of each other, continued their slow crawl through the sea, inching ever closer back to the eastern shores of Green Isle. Grateful that the seas were fair and calm, the children allowed themselves to relax and stare up at the stars, watching as more and more seemed to appear from nowhere, blinking into the blackness and twinkling brilliantly. The night air was warm and soft and scented with the sour pinch of salt that lilted over the breeze. The sound of the waves delicately swiping by the hulls was like an eerie lullaby, rocking them off to sleep.

Ollie and Wilder remained tending to the barely-there sails that Falena and her people had strung up for them. The occupants of the green team's boat drowsed, far too tired by a day climbing through trees and hunting down the five flags to really care much about stargazing for too much longer. The yellow team's boat was much the same, save for the prince who was waking and the girl in the green shirt who couldn't look away from the starry sky.

Fynn opened his eyes slowly, adjusting to the dimness of the evening; the moon was now fully risen and shining like a king amongst a billion twinkling subjects. His hand, trembling, gently touched his chest where he remembered the lightning shock of pain from hours prior. Finding no knife embedded there, he let out a slow exhale of relief. His chest rattled with the breath, a painful sensation that caused his inhalation to hitch; inadvertently, he drew Lux's attention.

The girl, who now had Penelope tangled at her side in a mess of sprawled limbs and snoring softly, looked over to the prince with eyes still glimmering from tears long since shed. She smiled. It was a crooked, half smile that didn't quite reach her darkened eyes. "How're you feeling?"

Fynn felt the corners of his mouth curl upward. Despite the dull ache that pounded in his chest and the occasional twinge of horrendous pain that lanced through him just beneath his sternum, he couldn't help but smile. The grin, weak as it was, faded when his eyes trailed down and found the blood splattered on Lux's shirt. He frowned. "Are you alright?"

Lux choked on her own sadness, letting the feeling of utter defeat settle in her stomach like an anchor pulling her down. "It's not my blood."

"Oh," Fynn breathed. He looked away. He turned his attention skyward, counting the stars mindlessly, refusing to look back to Lux.

"The stars are bright tonight," Lux commented. She found herself trailing Fynn's gaze, letting her attention wander to whatever had caught his focus.

"I like the stars," Fynn said meekly. He knew quite well that the statement, in light of what had happened, was wholly out of place. But he couldn't bring himself to look at the sight of the red splashed over Lux's green tunic or the nastiness of it congealed under her nails. And the stars, they shone with something brilliant and unknown and alluring, starkly contrasting the final vestiges of horror and pain that marred Lux's person.

Fynn supposed it was far more hopeful and calming to look up at the stars, to try, in perfectly well-informed vain, to count them from one to infinity. He smiled at the thought. There was a warmth that touched him, smoothed over him, swaddled him in unseen comfort and protection, like arms wrapping around him. For the faintest of moments, he thought he heard his mother's voice whisper in his ear. The prince couldn't tell what it was she said, but it didn't matter. Her voice, alone, was enough to set every coiling muscle in his body at ease.

"You can't count them all. But I like to try," Fynn explained.

"How many have you managed to count…on your best night?"

He shrugged, wincing at the slight sting of pain. His hand, palm still braced over the healing wound, held to his chest just a bit tighter. "I don't know. I suppose I lose count." Fynn smiled thoughtfully. It was the sort of smile that brought light to his pale eyes. "I like to try and make shapes too." He pointed up to a cluster of stars, saying, "You connect the stars like the points of a picture." He waited until Lux's analytical gaze followed the trajectory of his index finger and then said, "See there? That cluster looks like a cat's head. You can see its ears and some whiskers."

Lux looked up at the cat outlined in the stars. There, just as Fynn had said, were the ears and the whiskers, the pointed cheeks, and two, very bright stars shining for eyes. She smiled. "Can I ask you something?"

"Anything."

"You won't laugh?"

"*Probably* not," he joked.

She remained staring up at the stars. They flickered and shone and blinked in and out of brightness, fading and then coming back more luminous than before. Lux's voice was hardly more than a whisper. "Do you think that the stars get old?"

"What do you mean?"

"Like people. We grow old. We get wrinkles and we get weaker and we die. Do you think—well, do you suppose the stars do too? Do you suppose that they get old and fade away and then one day they're gone?" Her smile faded. "Do you think that when they stop shining, anyone even remembers they were there?"

Fynn's thumb lazily stroked back and forth over the blood-stained fabric of his tunic, whisking over the torn bits where his skin lay exposed to the warm breeze. He could feel the knitting of his shirt, stiffened by the dried blood, crackling under his touch. Just under his palm, he felt the torn skin, the nasty mark where the blade had dug away at his chest. Beneath his fingertips, crusty blood dried over his pale skin.

There was only a beating pain there now, the sharpness all but faded away for the time being. But he knew that there would be pain if he moved. There would be absolute agony if he tried to stand right now. Fynn kept his eyes trained upward, refusing to look back at Lux. Despite knowing movement would almost certainly be excruciating, he wanted nothing more than to jump out of the boat and swim away as far as he could. He watched the stars winking overhead; their brightness cut through the dull black of the night. There was something mysteriously beautiful about the stars, like they were diamonds suspended in an endless tapestry of black. They were some place people couldn't reach, a far-off place that people couldn't ruin. They were immune to the awfulness of the world. It didn't matter what happened amongst men, the stars would keep shining. The very thought that they would age, that one day they would fade away and be gone forever, that the sky would be just a little bit darker, was all too much for Fynn.

It didn't really matter that he didn't want to think about it. The thought had been planted in his head. It had been sowed and, like a seed, it was sprouting roots like tendrils that crept through his mind as the idea bloomed into full-fledged dread. He soured at the nagging thought.

But there, as he stared up at the bespangled night sky, he couldn't help but see blue eyes staring back at him. He knew them instantly; he could see the fear and pain and sadness welling within the blue depths. He knew that it was the darkness the eyes were scared of, frightened by the very concept that there may not be anything more than the life one lives. Or, that there may be something terrible waiting on the other side. The uncertainty of what lies beyond death, that was certainly worth fretting over for some.

The more Fynn studied the stars, the more he saw his father's eyes reflected in them. And the more he thought of those blue eyes staring back at him, the more he dreaded the idea that the stars would blink out of existence, that their light would flicker away forever and leave behind nothing but a void where they once shone.

He didn't want to think about it. He shifted where he sat, fidgeting slightly. Fynn knew Lux had turned her attention toward him, but he kept on looking at the stars. He wasn't entirely sure if he was simply watching them or if he was doing all he could to will them to keep shining. When, at last, he chose to answer, his voice was hoarse and pained and far heavier than usual. He lowered his eyes from the sky and fixed them to a point between his feet, studying the splintered wood of the small boat. "I hope they don't. I hope they're better than people and they go on shining forever." His black hair tumbled over his eyes, but he didn't bother to brush it away. He let the strands obscure his field of vision, bringing a bit of darkness to his line of sight. "But if they do get old like people and if they do fade away over time, I hope that there are people who remember where they once were."

"Me too," whispered Lux.

Fynn's hand fell away from his chest. Ever so slowly, he reached out and draped his hand over Lux's. He let his thumb rove over the peaks and valleys of her knuckles. He kept his eyes trained to the floor of the boat. He knew she was still staring at him, but he wasn't sure he could bring himself to look at her just yet. Beneath the pad of his thumb, he felt where her skin had been torn from the sharp twigs of the mangroves, leaving behind thin cuts here and there. He softened his touch, fearful of hurting her. His pale eyes wandered up until they settled over his chest. His head bowed; he could plainly see the awful red splattered all over his front. It was strange, he mused, that he felt so utterly disconnected from such a grievous injury. He saw it there, looking awful and festering beneath his attention, but it didn't really bother him. It hurt, but the pain was something he could ignore.

They reached Green Isle only an hour later. The tide and the wind had been against them, making their already slow journey far slower. Both boats lurched over the shore. The jerking of the vessels coming to a halt shook the sleeping children awake. Ollie and Wilder, exhausted from having maintained watchful vigil and for keeping their respective boats on course, jumped from their crafts and fell to the beach wearily. They crawled from the sandy shores up to where the grass began. They nestled against the emerald field tiredly.

The other children clambered out of the boats. Godryk and Renwyn hauled them far enough from the shore that they wouldn't accidentally be pulled out by the tides. Groggily, the first-years made their way from the beach up to the grass to join the now-sleeping Dangerfields.

Lux, her eyes drooping, padded ahead of Fynn. She stopped for a moment and glanced over her shoulder. "I hope you're right...about the stars." She turned around and joined the others in the grass, gingerly laying herself down.

With weariness beating him down savagely, Fynn plodded through the sand. Godryk appeared at his flank, looping an arm around his waist. Fynn, too weak to protest being treated like an invalid, slid his arm around the other boy's shoulders and allowed himself to be led up to the grass. The movement caused the pain in his chest to spark and he winced, choking back an anguished yelp.

"Even for you, that may take a while to heal up completely," Godryk said quietly.

Fynn nodded. His teeth crashed down over his lip so hard he drew blood. "You're probably right," he grumbled painfully.

Seeing Fynn visibly paling beside him, Godryk pulled the other boy closer. He kept their pace slow and steady, watching the prince's gait for any sign of staggering or pitching forward. He held the other boy tightly, refusing to let him fall. "Do you want to talk about it?"

"I think...I think that I did the right thing," Fynn said sadly. "But I'm not sure I did it for the right reason." Each word stung as he said it. His chest burned. "I don't want to talk about it. Not yet."

"Alright," Godryk consented.

He helped angle Fynn, as comfortably as he could, down to the grass. Seating himself at the prince's side, he watched as Fynn carefully eased himself backward. Fynn's pale eyes glowed eerily in the moonlight.

"You're not going to sleep?" Godryk inquired with a quirk of a brow.

"Not yet," whispered Fynn. "I'm not tired yet."

Godryk fell down unceremoniously against the earth. He let the grass pillow his cheek as he rolled onto his side. He failed to stifle the dramatic yawn that contorted his features. "Good night, Fynn."

The prince smiled. "Good night, Godryk."

It was the sound of splashing and footsteps that caught Fynn's attention. He didn't remember falling asleep. He couldn't say it was a restful sleep that he'd unwittingly found, but it had been a welcomed reprieve from the horrendous events on the turtle shell island. The footsteps stopped. They were nearby; he could tell that much without opening his eyes.

"What happened to you?" Ceral asked, gently poking at Fynn's hip with his booted toe. "That's a lot of blood. You alright?"

Groaning as he forced himself awake, Fynn yawned. He smoothed his hand over his face, trying to wipe the sleepiness away. "I'm fine." He coughed as he hauled himself to his feet. He ran his fingers through his matted hair, scowling when he found it was nearly beyond all hope of being tamed. "Just a nasty cut. It'll be fine in few days."

"Looks to be a bit more than a cut," argued Ceral, arching a brow. "Looks like someone *stabbed* you."

"That's because someone did." Godryk yawned. He climbed to his feet, blinking away the fuzziness at the corners of his sight. "Long story. But we got the flags and Fynn should be alright."

"You sure?" a rather skeptical Ceral asked, doing his best to assess the extent of Fynn's injury in the scant light of dawn.

Godryk clapped his hand over Fynn's shoulder softly, smiling a crooked smile. "I'm sure it hurts something awful! But, it's Fynn. He's got a way about him. He'll be alright in a few days."

The prince tiredly smirked back at Ceral with a boyish gleam in his pale eyes. "Nothing to worry about." He peered around the older boy, looking between the second-years trotting up the beach. "Did you get your flags?"

Ceral looked back at his year mates and smiled. "Maeryk's got them. Give us a few hours to rest and we can head out."

"Sounds like a plan," agreed Godryk. He laughed. "So, where were yours?"

"Up in a tree," Ceral answered.

"That's all?" Godryk sighed, cocking his head to the side. "That's dull."

"No monsters to fight?" asked Fynn curiously.

Ceral shrugged. "No monsters to fight. Had to answer a few riddles posed by island trolls, but no fighting was had." A lop-sided grin graced

Ceral's handsome features as he studied the two first-years before him. "What about you?"

"Ours were at five different points around the island. Nothing too terrible, just tedious, really," Godryk explained. "A lot of walking in the wrong direction before we realized it."

"That sounds remarkably uneventful." Ceral snorted. "That's *genuinely* surprising."

Playfully, Godryk elbowed Fynn's side, mindful of jostling the other boy too much. "Don't worry. Fynn made friends with a talking spider while the rest of us were actually looking for the flags."

"That sounds more like it." Ceral chuckled.

32

SNAKES ON THE ISLAND

The villas were situated along the eastern shore of Nandulus Island; they were a small village of opulent, white marble abodes colored by crawling vines, adorned by a veritable rainbow of tropical blooms, winding around their grand pillars. They were the temporary homes of the nobility who'd come to watch the games. The smallest of the villas were situated at the base of the three hills that rose at the shoreline. Those at the top of the hills, the ones whose balconies overlooked the small valleys and the amphitheater in the distance, played host to the three families in the highest choir of nobility, as well as the royal house itself.

The afternoon was balmy. But to the relief of all the Estherians who'd come south for the event, it wasn't oppressively hot. Moriah leaned over the bannister of the balcony, watching the clouds limp by overhead. He straightened, lazily stretching his back, as he continued his distracted appraisal of his surroundings. He hadn't bothered to change out of his formal attire from the morning, where he'd spent his time doing his leveled best to maintain a semblance of control so as not to start angrily screaming at Ridley—again. He didn't mind the constraining garbs much; the long, black sleeves kept the sun from burning his snowy-pale arms.

"Hiding?"

Moriah returned to leaning over the bannister, idly watching the commotion going on below at the Becketts' villa.

Odette found her way to Moriah's side and joined her brother in quiet voyeurism. She ran her fingers through her blonde hair, brushing it back behind her ears. "You know, Father's going to start getting mad if you keep hiding from him."

"I'm not *hiding*." Moriah hadn't meant to sound as petulant as he did, but he supposed he didn't really care. "And what are *you* doing here, if not *hiding*?"

"I never said *I* wasn't hiding." Odette laughed slyly. There was a wry twinkle in her green eyes that easily blinked into appearance at her words. She arched a brow and pouted dramatically. "Don't go telling on me, alright?"

"Wouldn't dream of it." Moriah smirked. "If I did, I'd have to incriminate myself. That wouldn't do."

"Not at all," agreed Odette.

Much like her brother, Odette hadn't bothered to change her clothes since morning, though not for lack of desire. The long, black sleeves clung to her lean arms; the tight-fitted torso of her dress was perfectly cinched, not a seam out of place. The golden snakes embroidered over her shoulders and chest, though she felt them a bit overdone, certainly looked striking in the tropical sunlight. She sighed, finding the dress constricting. It was certainly something she wasn't accustomed to anymore. "I don't see why he *insists* I wear this thing."

"You're his *daughter*. He wants you looking like a lady." Moriah chuckled. "He can't have you going around dressed like your brothers, can he?"

"Do you remember when I used to steal your clothes when we were little?"

"How could I forget?" Moriah snorted wryly. "I never seemed to have any trousers in my wardrobe. It was really *quite* the inconvenience."

"You survived," mocked Odette. "And anyway, it kept me from having to wear these awful things!" She fidgeted with the material of the dress' skirt some more.

Moriah laughed.

"You wouldn't be laughing if he put *you* in a damn dress," muttered Odette bitterly.

Still fidgeting with the skirt of her dress, adjusting it for the most comfort she could possibly obtain, Odette asked, "Where's Noel? I haven't seen him since morning."

"Hiding."

"Where?"

Moriah turned his lop-sided grin toward his sister; his green eyes beamed in the midday sun. "If I knew, that would certainly defeat the point of hiding, now wouldn't it?"

"Is he hiding from *you*?"

"From *all of us*, I suppose," Moriah answered flatly.

In another of the grand villas at the top of the hill, Vance Mordray sat around a marble table opposite Novian Godsbane and Warwyk Redmayne.

Vance, a rather tall and lanky man, leaned back into his chair, maintaining perfect posture while making a show of relaxing. His once black hair was greying at his temples; small patches of white now colored his barely-there beard intermittently. His eyes were an icy blue that seemed to burn with some unspoken, unrelenting fire that made people squirm uneasily under the intensity of his stare. When he did speak, his voice was a gravely timbre that was well-suited to his rigid exterior. "The children should be arriving in the next few days," Vance said easily. His attention wasn't really paid to those around him; instead, he found himself absentmindedly admiring the mosaic decorating the western wall. It depicted, much to his interest, a school of mermaids gathered around a rocky shore, scores of colorful tiles arranged just so all about the edges, as if a myriad of southern fish had gathered in stagnant schools.

"I suspect by tomorrow at the earliest," agreed Novian. Lord Godsbane, being from the northern peninsula of Estheria, had all the characteristics one would expect of such a man. His white mane was slicked back, falling in straight lengths of hair down to his shoulders. White eyebrows arched over pale, nearly colorless, blue eyes. His long nose was perfectly straight; his cheek bones were strung high upon his pale face, carving sharply toward a thin mouth. Fleetingly, he glanced to the mosaic that had conquered the attention of Lord Mordray, and found himself, much the same way, admiring the intricacies of the tile placements. "Any favorites for who might win?" asked Novian distantly. He didn't bother to look away from the tiled image.

Warwyk, finely dressed in various shades of scarlet, with his deep, red hair kempt as best as it could be, cleared his throat. He frowned at the way the older men seemed to be bored by his company, both of them examining the mosaic as if it may actually come to life. He scoffed, forcing down a feeling of growing disdain. "I hear there are many talented children this year," he said amicably.

"Your son is competing, right?" asked Novian. His attention slowly returned to Warwyk; a burst of curiosity sparked in his pale eyes. "One of your nephews as well?"

"Both," Warwyk agreed. "Maeryk, my nephew, is a second-year. My boy, Godryk, is a first-year."

Novian nodded, bored. "I see." He rounded toward Vance with a quirked, white brow. "Speaking of sons, I haven't seen any of yours around, Mordray. Where are they off to?"

With the same sort of tepid reluctance that had punctuated Novian's return to the conversation, Vance's head swiveled back toward the table. He turned his frightening, blue eyes toward the two lords who kept his company. "My best guess?" he started, a frown tugging the corners of his lips down, only slightly. "They're off hiding somewhere. The girls too."

"Surely, they're not *hiding*," chided Warwyk with a nasty grin.

Vance huffed. "You'd be surprised what they can come up with when they don't want me to find them."

It came as no surprise to Vance, as he let his focus once again wander, that in his periphery he saw Ridley creeping around a marble pillar, skulking quietly as he headed for the door. Shaking his head, Vance sighed. "They really do *think* they're clever."

Ridley hadn't heard his father's last remark. He'd only cast a quick glance over his shoulder, comfortably certain he hadn't been spotted, before creeping out the door as quietly as he could. In his estimation, it was a lovely day. It would be evening soon, and with the approaching night steadily getting closer and closer, the weather had become quite pleasant. Sprightly, Ridley traipsed down the stone trail leading from the villa over the hills, intent on making his way to the Fog's villa before finding something else to occupy both his time and attentions.

There were large palms that skirted the walkway that interwove each of the grand estates on the hillside. The shadow provided was comfortable, the summery breeze quite effortlessly calming. Ridley continued winding his way along the path until he came upon the largest of the villas on Nandulus Island.

Draped from a balcony overhanging the front entry was the black banner of House Fog, the red bat splendid in its crown, sprawled over the infinitely dark field. The banner wrinkled softly in the wind, making the bat look almost as though its wings were fluttering, like it may just leap off the banner and take to the sky.

Without another thought, Ridley headed inside. He'd made it three steps before one of the servants stopped him, assessing him with a cocked head and raised brow, a mild frown cooling their expression.

Ridley smiled a toothy smile, tawny eyes aglow as he nodded politely. "I'd like to request an audience with Princess Fiona. You may tell her Ridley Mordray has come to speak with her."

"Yes, m'lord." The servant nodded rather cautiously. Sweeping his attention over Ridley once more, the man crept off through the villa in search of the princess.

There was an intricate mosaic laid out on the floor, surrounded by pristine, white marble as far as Ridley could see. Upon the walls, portraits of all manner of important, stately men kept a silent, sullen vigil over the space. Stepping further inside, the smell of fresh flowers caught the man's attention. There were large, red vases in every corner of the space, filled to capacity with exotic plants and blooms. They were captivating; so much so, that Ridley made his way toward one vase. He gently caught a bright pink pedal between his fingers. The scent was rich and sweet and enticing.

"M'lord."

At the sound of the servant's voice, Ridley quickly turned around. He straightened, squaring his shoulders, and nodded. "Yes?"

"The queen requests your presence," answered the servant.

Thinking it odd that Ursalyn would call for him, and yet, at the same time now infinitely curious as to why he was being summoned, Ridley smiled a most charming, calculated smile. With a wave of his hand, he said, "Lead the way."

Walking through the rest of the royal villa was an astoundingly long affair. There were tapestries, silken and exquisitely expensive looking, hanging over large, arching windows and doorways. More paintings littered the walls; their brushed-oil eyes seemed to follow Ridley as he moved gracefully along, just at the heels of the servant. More vases occupied each corner of the villa. The same sweet scent he'd smelt before permeated every speck of air within the confines of the marble walls. Emerald vines wormed their way over some of the pillars, crawling out from the confines of the red vases and tracing over the marble. There were cages hanging from the ceiling wherein tropical birds stood upon little perches, their beady, black eyes following Ridley as they ruffled rainbow feathers and chattered amongst themselves. The entirety of the villa had a wild, exotic feel to it that Ridley found intriguing.

The servant came to a decisive halt and held his arm aloft toward an arching doorway obscured by a thick, red curtain. He nodded his head, averting his eyes from Ridley. "Just through there, m'lord."

Pushing the curtain aside, Ridley stepped into a large room. It was garish if nothing else. The walls were painted a deep red. Golden tapestries hung from the raftered ceiling. Gold filigree was expertly painted along the juncture of the high walls and the ceiling. Red sofas and lounges and plush red chairs were scattered all around the room. The queen lazed on one such sofa, sipping at a goblet of wine, blue eyes blazing over the brim as she drank, intently watching Ridley as he drew nearer.

"You wished to see me, Your Grace," Ridley said, bowing half-heartedly before taking a seat opposite the woman.

"I must say, I was surprised when my servant told me you'd come calling," Ursalyn began.

A fox-like smirk blossomed over Ridley's handsome features. "Not the Mordray you were expecting? Or rather, not the one you *wanted* to come calling?"

Ursalyn, unamused by the insinuation, let her steely gaze linger over the younger man. She took another sip of her wine with all the enthusiasm one would exude if drinking from a goblet of snake venom. She scowled, setting the goblet aside. "You've come calling, as you say, for my niece?"

Ridley shrugged. "I figured she may be a little bored here with nothing to do but wait. I've nothing sinister planned for her, if that's what you're getting at... *Your Grace.*"

"Fiona's busy," Ursalyn said simply. She tossed her head back against the raised backing of the lounge. Her expression was that of a woman utterly disinterested, but her voice was icy as she continued, "And Ridley?"

"Hmm?"

"Be a bit more careful about what you say and to whom," she warned darkly. "Other people may not take so *kindly* to your...gossip."

Rising ever so slowly, Ridley pulled himself from his seat. And, just as slowly, he took a step forward and knelt down on one knee at the edge of the lounge. He leaned over until his lips nearly touched Ursalyn's ear and he whispered, "You and I both know it's more than idle gossip." He stood, a smug smirk firmly in place. "Your Grace."

The quiet rumble of a voice from the doorway sounded. "Am I interrupting something?"

Ridley stood, looming dangerously over the queen. With a vibrant smile, he turned toward the newest arrival and nodded with feigned deference. "Not at all."

"Ridley was just leaving," Ursalyn hissed. Her stormy stare flicked up toward the man towering at her lounge-side with a sort of chilly menace that withered most men in an instant. It did little to wipe the smug look from Ridley's face. "Isn't that right?"

"Of course, Your Grace," intoned the youngest Mordray brother. "It was a pleasure, as always." He took the queen's hand in his and pressed a soft kiss to her knuckles. His golden eyes never wavered from her face. His voice dropped to a deep whisper. "Until next time, eh?"

Moriah, swathed from head to toe in black, stood like the embodiment of darkness in the doorway, flashing eyes brooding with barely contained disdain as he watched his brother stalk by. He tensed for a moment when Ridley halted just at his side. "I thought you were on your way out," Moriah said.

"I am." Ridley grinned. His hand shot out, clamping over his brother's arm and pulling him nearer. He leaned up to whisper into the older man's ear, "I do hope Father didn't see you coming this way."

And, with that, before Moriah could even think of responding, Ridley slipped by the curtain and was gone from them.

Sweeping through the villa, back the way he came, Ridley grumbled to himself, irritated, until he saw movement at the other end of the grand foyer. Curious, he proceeded by the front entrance and headed in the direction of whatever it was that had caught his eye. His inquisitiveness was rewarded. His eyes narrowed like a fox who'd spied a rabbit when he saw Fiona pass by. He stole away after her, prowling through the villa, quietly going unnoticed by the servants buzzing by.

Ridley rounded another corner, surprised when he found he'd lost sight of his target. A slender hand reached out and curled over his wrist, pulling him back behind a pillar and out of sight. Turning, he found the princess staring back at him with a rather pleased expression warming her features. "You caught me," he chuckled.

"You're not nearly as good at sneaking around as you *think* you are." She laughed, batting his arm. "What're you doing here?"

"I came to see *you*, actually," Ridley answered calmly. His amber eyes burned with the same eerie iridescence of a cat's.

At the sight, Fiona couldn't help but draw similarities between Moriah and Ridley. Souring at the thought, Fiona huffed. "Is that so?"

Ridley nodded. A boyish glint sprang to his countenance, softening the harsh angles. "It is."

As quickly as the brotherly resemblance had appeared, it faded. Fiona smiled. "Bored, were you?"

"Maybe." Ridley shrugged carelessly.

"Or is it that you're hiding from your family?" mocked the princess.

"Not doing a very good job of it then. I just saw Moriah a moment ago."

"I don't think he's the one you're hiding from," Fiona contended.

"No, I suppose you're right." Looking around with practiced dramatics, Ridley paused before continuing. Turning his attention back to Fiona, his voice dropped to a faint whisper. "Must be getting better at hiding, then. I don't see my father anywhere."

"Nor do I." She smiled. Her hand took his and she gave it a light squeeze. "Want to go for a walk?"

"I don't think you grasp the concept of *hiding*, princess." Ridley laughed.

Fiona pulled Ridley along regardless and he followed without a fuss. Hand in hand, they swept through the villa, avoiding any curious eyes, and left through one of the side entrances. They were hopping down the stairway outside, surrounded on nearly all sides by large, potted plants and towering palms with fronds the length of one's arm, when Fiona caught sight of someone coming toward them. In a panic, she all but shoved Ridley away from her side. She smoothed the wrinkles from her dress and straightened up, tilting her chin just slightly as she regarded Ridley with the cool indifference that was rather reminiscent of the queen.

Without missing a beat, Ridley had spied the latest arrival to villa and assumed the role of courtly advisor. Stepping away from Fiona, he casually began inspecting the greenery around them. When Noel was within sight, Ridley rounded on him, cooing, "Noel! What a fine day, isn't it? What're you doing out here?"

Noel stopped only a few paces from the pair. He stood silently, watching them. The look of annoyed indignation on Fiona's face was nearly comical, but he did well not to outright laugh at her. Ridley's practiced charm was nauseating, but Noel, after so many years of dealing with his younger brother, knew how to temper his overwhelming urge to roll his eyes. "I was just looking for Moriah."

"And you came *here*?" Fiona asked, arching a black brow.

"Yes. Was I wrong to?" asked Noel with a faint smile touching his lips.

Fiona laughed to herself, privately entertained by the flash of humor that touched Noel's summer eyes. As she began to head along the path she'd been following, prior to the interruption, she said amusedly, "Not at all."

And so, Noel remained quite still as the princess and his brother trotted along, both careful to keep themselves at a distance the nobility and Crown would find acceptable. Once they'd gone from view, Noel continued plodding toward the villa, only to stop once more at the sight of Odette heading his way. He sighed.

Odette stopped when she saw her brother and asked, "What're *you* doing here?"

"Looking for Moriah. You?"

Odette seemed to consider the question for a moment, turning it over in her head as her eyes narrowed, surveying the surrounding proximity for any uninvited listeners and gossips. "Same."

"Bored?" asked Noel knowingly.

"Ben's gone," she answered. "He and Drake are at the piers waiting for the children. They're on watch duty."

"Must be more interesting than this," Noel sighed tiredly.

"I think we're the only ones *not* enjoying our time on the island," Odette grumbled.

Looking back over his shoulder down the path Fiona and Ridley had disappeared down, Noel smirked. "So, it would seem."

"Why're you looking for Moriah?" questioned Odette.

The sound of his sister's voice caught his attention. Noel fidgeted under her all-too green stare. "I don't really know, actually. I was just getting lonely, I think, spending all day avoiding our villa."

Odette softened slightly at the sight of Noel looking quite dejected. His blue eyes, having only a moment ago seemed bright and vibrant, dulled somewhat as he looked away from her, forlorn. She lightly punched his shoulder, eliciting a surprised look from him. She grinned. "Why don't you go down to the harbor and wait with Ben and Drake? It'll give you something to do."

"What about you?"

"I have something to discuss with Moriah," she answered. There was a tenseness to her voice that hardened her words. "I'll tell you about it later."

"You're sure?"

She nodded.

"Alright."

As Noel began to turn away, Odette added, "Tell Benadykt I say…hello. Won't you?"

"I will."

With that, Noel was off and headed down the hill and away from the valley, set on a course in the harbor's direction. He smiled, chuckling under his breath as he recalled the laughable cover Ridley and Fiona had constructed. He shook his head; brown hair tumbled in front of his eyes.

At the harbor, far removed from the comings and goings of nobles up in the high villas, Benadykt's legs hung over the edge of the pier, kicking idly as he watched the horizon for any signs of movement. Still, there was nothing. The late afternoon was waning into evening as the sun began to slip away from its perch; its golden glow gave way to a pale pink that stretched over the sky.

Drake was prone against the worn wood of the pier, staring up at the clouds as they inched by, seemingly slower than usual. They didn't speak a word between them, both drowned in the tedious boredom that had taken root after being assigned to wait for the children's arrival. Drake yawned; he stretched his arms over his head and arched his back, feeling a delightful pop at the movement.

The sound of wood creaking beneath heavy footsteps caught Benadykt's attention. He looked over his shoulder and watched as Noel's wiry frame ambled closer and closer. Noel flopped down beside Benadykt, flinging his legs over the edge of the pier and letting them dangle limply as he rolled his shoulders. He craned his neck from side to side before yawning.

Benadykt quirked a brow, asking, "What're you doing here?"

"What do you mean?" Noel mumbled, combing back his messy hair.

Drake sat up, scooting over to join the other two at the edge of the structure. He settled in at Noel's other side. He elbowed the younger man in the side with a sly smile. "Trying to get away from your family?"

Noel grinned a lop-sided grin, blue eyes shining all the while. "Something like that."

"Why?" Benadykt intoned curiously. "You don't get to see your father much. I thought you'd like the chance to spend a little time with him."

"I would." Noel's smile became toothy and boyish. "If it were *just* he and I. But *all* of them...well, *most* of them together like that...no."

"I'll ask again. Why?" Benadykt's head angled to the side; an expectant expression claimed features.

"You've been out here since day one," Noel began. "You haven't seen what it's been like. And it's not just my father being here. It's *all* of them. Warwyk's been awful and Cedryk's little better. Novian's downright uninterested. And Ursalyn? Well, she's become the ice queen."

"I see." Benadykt nodded. "And...Dot?"

"Spoke to her for a moment earlier before heading here." Noel shrugged. "She and Moriah have stayed close. I think they're doing their best to avoid my father and Ridley at all costs. Honestly, I haven't seen either of them around much." He chuckled under his breath for a moment before adding, "Oh, and she wanted me to tell you hello...from her."

"Did she say anything else?" pressed Benadykt.

"You should know," Noel began with a laugh, "she's a woman of few words."

Drake sprung to his feet, leaning at the edge of the pier as far as he could without toppling over into the water. He pointed, "There! Look...I see something."

Noel and Benadykt gathered themselves to their full heights. Both stared through the evening-onset and found, to their surprise, the muddled shadows of five shapes coming toward the shore.

Benadykt smiled. "That was quicker than I expected."

"Much quicker," agreed Noel evenly. "Wonder how they managed…and how they managed to all arrive at the same time."

"They figured it out." Drake laughed. "They worked together and got it done quicker that way. Clever children."

"Impressive." Benadykt nodded happily. "*Quite* impressive."

"That's the fastest any year has completed the first stage of the games in…well…*years*," Noel commented thoughtfully. "Well done indeed."

Drake's eyes narrowed as he continued staring out toward the sea. The boats came into view more clearly. He could see that aside from the blue team's boat, they weren't the vessels originally bequeathed to the teams. He thought that quite curious, though another detail about the approaching crafts struck him as a bit more noteworthy. "Are those…*dolphins?*"

Intrigued, Noel shuffled forward until he was physically leaning over Drake' shoulder, keeping a steady hold on the other man so as not to fall. "I think you're right. Those *are* dolphins."

"*Dolphins?*" repeated a skeptical Benadykt. "This close to shore? That's odd."

Drake snorted. "What's odd is that they seem to be pulling the boats."

"Well, that's certainly different," marveled Benadykt.

"I suppose if your sails are ripped to shreds, a dolphin-drawn water chariot isn't such a bad back-up plan," mused Noel.

"I wonder how they managed that," Drake pondered.

"Oh." Noel grinned broadly. "I don't *have* to guess."

The five boats skittered through the waves, bouncing and rocking as they drew nearer the shores. They were cruising through the tropical waters far more quickly than they had previously on their journey. No longer relying on the wind to carry them along, the children were able to amass themselves around the edges of their crafts and stare with wide-eyed fascination down into the waters sweeping by, watching with rapt interest at the various colors washing away beneath their vessels - the fish darting back and forth, the large fins splashing here and there. When they'd found themselves idling in the water after leaving Green Isle mid-morning, they'd despaired at what would certainly be a long trip. That was until Godryk, Lux, and Fynn decided to splash their hands in the waters and call out, yelling for the assistance of dolphins. Sure enough, within moments the porpoises arrived, happily springing from the waters and rolling around, flippers flapping, tails wagging and splashing. Despite Terry's continued assertion to the contrary, they were quite easily organized into action. And so, the five boats were presently pulled along by a pod of rather enthusiastic dolphins, the sort that preferred odd curves and strange turns to that of taking the straightforward route to Nandulus. Nevertheless, the children glanced up from the waters rushing by and saw the island within view - the pier jutting out from the shoreline, the harbor structures shadowed along the beach.

"We made it." Ceral bounded to his feet. "I see the island!"

Lux leaned over the bow of the boat, laughing as the sea spray sprinkled over her face. "It's just there!"

Once the pier was within ten or so feet, the dolphins released the twine they'd held between their teeth to pull their sea-bound chariots along. As the ropes fell away and slid into the waves, the dolphins submerged and began their incessant darting, looping this way and that beneath the bellies of the boats, springing up at the sides and playfully splashing the children. As the last of the dolphins began to retire from the children's company, it stopped and turned, eyeing the first-and-second years before giving a final flick of the tale and splashing every last one of them. The dolphin chattered and clacked as it dove back under water.

The boats coasted toward the pier easily enough. As they came upon the long walkways of the docks, the children slung their ropes over the edge. Drake and Benadykt caught them with practiced nonchalance and tied the boats off, assisting the children as they clambered out of the vessels.

Stepping back and taking a good look at the twenty-six students, the three adults were quite concerned to see the poor condition they were in. Yes, all five teams had collected all three of their flags, but no one commented on that. Rather, their eyes went wide when they saw the dirt and filth scraped over the children's cheeks, the cuts raking over their faces, the bruises blooming around their eyes and jaws. Their uniforms were torn, mud stained, and sprinkled with blood. Noel's concern transmuted into alarm when he saw the frightening tear through the chest of Fynn's yellow shirt and the blood that pooled around the destroyed fabric, staining the majority of his front.

"Dear gods, what happened to all of you?" Drake sighed gently. "You look a mess."

Noel didn't wait for any sort of response. Instead, he launched himself toward Godryk and Fynn. Kneeling before the two boys, he first found himself reaching out, flattening his palm over Fynn's chest. He felt the wound scabbing over under his touch, but when he pulled his hand back, there was still a tinge of red sprinkled over his palm. "How badly does it hurt?" he asked.

Fynn shook his head. "Doesn't hurt much anymore. I'll be alright." The prince offered the man a crooked, yet easy smile. His eyes seemed alert, bright. "Really."

Frowning at the still-healing chest wound, Noel reluctantly nodded. He turned his attention to Godryk, cupping the boy's face in his hand. He carefully brushed his thumb across the boy's jaw. "That's a nasty bruise," he said factually. His blue eyes turned from the purple jaw to the cut reaching over the bridge of Godryk's nose, the healing split lip, the bruising beneath his eyes. "Broken nose?"

"It's fine," assured Godryk easily. There was no trace of pain weighing down his words. He let Noel prod at his face gently for another moment, before adding, "Really, sir, I'm alright."

Noel shook his head, relenting to the boy's assurance hesitantly. He stood, reaching out absentmindedly and brushing Fynn's hair back. "Is everyone else alright?"

The herd of children chorused their response. "Yes."

Benadykt led the procession of children down the docks toward the harbor. Drake lingered at the middle of the herd, eyeing each of the passing first-and-second years for any signs of serious injury. He remained quiet as they went by. Noel stayed at the rear of the flock; watchful, blue eyes flitted over each of the twenty-six bodies that slowly trudged over the worn, wooden boards.

As they proceeded, Noel's hand fell over Fynn's shoulder softly, pulling the prince back slightly, slowing him down.

Fynn looked up at Noel curiously. He kept his voice low. "Is everything alright, sir?"

"I was about to ask you the same thing," Noel answered simply.

Fynn shrugged. "Really. I'm fine."

"What happened?"

"Had a bit of trouble on Little Isle," Fynn replied.

Noel arched a fine brow disbelievingly. His gaze lowered from the boy's face to his chest once more. "Looks like more than a *bit of trouble*."

"I got stabbed," Fynn admitted dully. "But really, I'm fine now. It doesn't hurt much. Just feels like a little cut, is all."

Noel's hold on Fynn tightened until he halted the boy in his tracks. He rounded on him, kneeling before the prince yet again. The whole of his attention now fixed to the wound puncturing the pale flesh of the boy's narrow chest. Carefully, Noel traced his fingertips along the edge of the injury, worried when Fynn sharply inhaled at the gesture. At the edges of the wound, Noel could plainly see a red tinge that seemed unnatural, certainly not good. "What were you stabbed with?"

Fynn withdrew the dagger from his belt, still sheathed, and handed it to Noel. "It was my grandfather's knife. Hollyn gave it to me. He said it would do more damage because of the curved blade. Guess he was right."

Taking the dagger from the boy, Noel withdrew it from its sheath and froze. His breath was caught in his chest. He felt sick at the sight of it. Replacing the dagger within its sheath once more, he handed it back to Fynn. "Moriah's going to want to have a look at that."

"What's the matter?" Fynn asked. Noel's hand was still ever so slightly resting on his chest. The barest touch of the man's hand was sending shooting pain through Fynn's whole body. The boy did his best to keep the pain from showing on his face, to keep the tears from welling in his eyes, to keep his voice flat and calm. "It'll heal like everything else always does. It's nothing bad, really, Noel."

Fynn's head felt fuzzy and stuffed, like clouds had built up in his mind. He struggled to think clearly, to keep himself focused on the conversation. Noel was saying something, he was sure of it. But it just sounded like a jumble of mumbles. Fynn's eyesight was beginning to fail. Blackness encroached at his periphery. Blinking rapidly, he tried to clear his sight but couldn't. There was too much darkness now. He could scarcely see Noel. He heard the familiar timbre of the man's voice; he knew Noel was still talking, but he couldn't understand a word of it.

The prince clutched at his chest all of a sudden, pitching forward with a startled cry. He felt Noel's arms wrap around him, keeping him from falling flat on his face. Fynn's shoulders shook terribly as he coughed. The tangy taste of blood infiltrated his mouth. He let himself fall against Noel's chest, breathing in gasping breaths. Closing his eyes, tears slickened his lashes before falling down his face. Noel's arms encircled him tighter. "I'm fine," rasped Fynn weakly.

Noel's hand traced soft circles over Fynn's back. His voice was low and gentle, but Fynn didn't know what he was saying. He supposed Noel was probably muttering words of reassurance, careful platitudes meant to keep him calm. Still, Fynn couldn't stop shaking. He wanted to desperately; he hated - absolutely detested - how weak he must look. But he couldn't bring himself to peel away from the secure embrace of the man, the familiar scent that was so much like Moriah's, the voice so similar that when Fynn began slipping away into unconsciousness, he was almost certain it really was Moriah there.

Fynn went completely limp against Noel's chest.

"Fynn." Noel shook the boy as gently as he could. "Fynn, wake up." Still, there was no sign of acknowledgement from the prince. "Fynneas. Open your eyes, Fynn."

The dull sound of Noel's voice tore through the fogginess and Fynn blinked blearily; his head felt like a boulder as he pulled his cheek away from Noel's chest, staring dazedly into the man's brilliant, blue eyes. But it was a shifting shape in Fynn's periphery that caught his attention. He turned his head slowly, doing his best to adjust his eyes to the evening din, clearing away the shadows. He saw it again, the flittering of a figure in the distance, standing at the harbor. Fynn, still intently staring at the figure, leaned weakly against Noel, far too scared that he might collapse if he didn't use the man as a crutch to keep upright. "Noel, do you see that?"

"See what?"

Tiredly, Fynn nodded toward the harbor. "I saw someone there."

"Might have been Ben or Drake," Noel explained. "Don't worry about it."

"Wasn't them," insisted Fynn.

The pain in his chest ebbed away slowly. He felt his strength returning. It was as though each muscle in his body spasmed at once and, all of a sudden, he felt infinitely better. Drawing himself upright and squaring his shoulders evenly, Fynn pulled away from Noel. "I feel better now," he assured. Seeing the unconvinced look on Noel's face, Fynn smiled. "Really. I feel better. It was just a quick flash of pain. It's nothing."

"It's not *nothing*," Noel argued. "You lost consciousness for a minute. That's not exactly a good thing."

Fynn cradled his hand over his chest gently, careful not to put too much pressure over the wound. "It's only a dull ache. It's a lot better than it was. Please." He looked back at the end of the pier where, sure enough, the rest of the students were milling about, evidently waiting for him and Noel to rejoin their party. "Let's just go."

Slowly, Noel drew himself upright. He kept his hand fixed to Fynn's shoulder, carefully steering the boy along, holding just tight enough to be able to prevent the child from stumbling forward and falling. Beneath his hand, Noel felt Fynn's muscles alternating between smooth and calm, to taut and clearly distressed. Mindful of Fynn's constant leering toward his year mates, Noel remained silent on the matter. He didn't let go of the boy, however. He directed him along the walkway until they joined the other children and two instructors at the harbor. When Benadykt steadied an inquisitive glance in their direction, Noel discreetly shook his head and sighed.

As Fynn melded back into the fold of children, Godryk tactfully positioned himself at the prince's side. He kept his voice quiet, asking, "Are you alright? You were doing better for a while. What happened?"

"I'm fine," grumbled Fynn, head hanging low.

"You sure?"

"I'm sure."

"Will you tell me if something's wrong?" asked Godryk.

Fynn turned a sly smile toward his friend, eyes alight. "Probably not."

"At least you're honest," groused Godryk, with a good-natured punch to Fynn's upper arm. "Try not to get hurt again, alright?"

"I'll see what I can do." Fynn chuckled.

33

WAKING

A soft touch fluttered over Fynn's cheek affectionately. A tender voice whispered, "It's time to get up now, darling." Deft fingers combed through his black hair. "It's morning, Fynneas. Time to get up."

Wakefulness dawned upon the prince and he opened his eyes slowly. His cheek was pressed against something soft. He was lying in bed. He saw the familiar blue of the pillow tucked beneath his head, the grey fur of his blankets, the intricate stitching upon his bed linens in an all-so familiar pattern of grey needle work over blue silk. He felt warm and comfortable. He wanted to burry himself back into the welcoming fluff of his blanket, but the hand that stroked over his cheek kept its ministrations rhythmic.

"It's time to wake up now, darling." The voice was so soft and warm and rich.

He knew it at once.

Rolling onto his back, Fynn wasn't surprised to see his mother there. Celestine was seated on the edge of his bed, dressed in a blue nightgown; wide sleeves enveloped her slender arms. Long, white fingers roved over his cheek softly. Fynn sat upright, leaning against his headboard. He watched as a smile crept over his mother's face; her pale eyes seemed infinitely sunny and inviting.

His voice was little more than a tired rasp. "Mother?"

"Of course."

Fynn watched as Celestine slid from her perch and stood at his bedside, looking down at him. Reaching out, her hand once more brushed through his hair. There was a soft fondness, an ease that he hadn't seen in her before.

"What're you doing here?" he asked.

"Where else would I be?" She turned toward the door. Before leaving, she said, "Get dressed. Your father's waiting for you. He wanted to take you out today."

"Oh." Fynn nodded. "Alright."

He rose from his bed and padded over to his wardrobe. He threw his shirt over his head and laced up the collar quickly enough. He'd apparently fallen asleep in his trousers he realized, as he glanced down. He pulled stockings over his feet and then his worn, leather boots rimmed by thick fur. He grabbed the warmest cloak he owned. It was a heavy grey fabric with thick, black fur lining the shoulders. Fynn smiled.

He stepped into the corridor and found Fiona there, a strange smile upon her face. "Fi?" Fynn asked, quirking a brow.

The princess' blue eyes seemed bluer today. She smiled, the sincerity of it touching her eyes. "Good morning," Fiona bid, as she looped her arm around her brother's, beginning to drag him through the hall. "Father's been waiting for you all morning. He wanted to let you sleep in a bit, but enough's enough, Fynny. You can't sleep the day away."

Puzzled, Fynn furrowed his brow. "What're you talking about?"

"Honestly, you'd forget your own name if you were left to yourself," chided Fiona with a huff.

The pair continued through the corridors; passing servants nodded their heads and averted their eyes as the royal siblings wound through the halls. When Fiona and Fynn stepped outside, it was as cold and grey as it always was in the north. The snow fell lazily.

Wistfulness colored Fynn's icy eyes. He hadn't seen snow in almost a year. He wasn't sure if he missed it, but the realization that he'd been away from home for so long was one that nearly brought a longing tear to his eye. Instead, he forced the emotion down until he forgot about.

He looked back to his sister and kept his voice steady when he asked, "What're we doing here?"

He couldn't shake the strange feeling that niggled at the back of his mind, the feeling that there was something off.

"What're you talking about?" she asked. She made a strange sort of face as she studied him.

Fynn gestured with his arms in no particular direction, vaguely indicating their surroundings. "*Here*. What're we doing *here*? Why are we back home?"

"Back home?" she repeated.

He nodded.

"Where else would you be?" Fiona pressed. Concern weighted her words.

Fynn took a step back from her, withdrawing himself from her worried attentions. He kept his voice flat and calm, but the annoyance was nearly overpowering him. "I was at Morancy all year, Fi. Don't you remember? You came to visit me just before summer."

She shook her head. "You must've dreamed it."

"I didn't dream ten months of my life!" snapped Fynn, stomping his foot indignantly. "I was there and so were you. Don't you remember? We went to the capital during the summer. Uncle Lachlan called for Father and Father wanted us to spend a little time there at Batsbeckon with the family. Then I went to Morancy and you stayed with Emrys and Ridley. You must remember *that*, right?"

Fiona's blue eyes went wide. She knelt in front of Fynn before he had time to realize she'd even made a move to approach. She placed her hand over his forehead. "You don't have a fever," she mumbled. "Are you sure you're feeling well?"

Fynn shoved his sister away. He took another step back. "I feel fine, Fi. You're the one who's acting odd." Then something struck Fynn, a thought that he had overlooked before. He turned his head back toward the castle, craning his neck as he looked up toward one of the towers. "Mother's here."

"*Of course,* she is, Fynneas. Where else would she be?"

"Dead," answered the boy matter-of-factly.

He didn't see Fiona's arm move, but all at once Fynn felt the force of her hand slapping him across the face. Stunned, his jaw went slack as he stared back at his sister. Gingerly, he raised his hand to cup his stinging cheek.

"Why would you say something like that?" demanded Fiona. She balled her fists into his cloak, hauling him toward her forcefully. She shook him. "Why would you say something like that, Fynneas?" Hysterics swarmed over Fiona like locusts to the fields. Tears freely ran from her bright eyes as she continued viciously shaking him. "Why? *Why?* Tell me why you said that?"

Fynn's stomach felt as though it was twisting itself into knot after knot. He'd never seen Fiona so emotional. He didn't think she had the composition of character to swing so wildly into extreme emotion, as she'd just done. But still, she shook him harshly, all the while frantically demanding why he would say their mother was dead. The more he stared into her vibrant eyes, so much brighter than he recalled them ever being, the more he felt like his heart may in fact rip apart. There was something quite unsettling about watching his sister unravel right before his eyes, watching her easily give into tidal waves of emotion. And, all the while, the niggling in the back of his mind persisted.

Fiona kept her chant going. "Tell me! Tell me why you said that? That's cruel, Fynneas! Tell me!" She was unrelenting in her hysteria. It was alarmingly uncharacteristic.

The prince felt limp in his sister's hold, so much weaker than he recalled feeling not long ago. She kept shaking him. She seemed to have no intention of stopping. It was only when large hands pried Fiona away from him that she finally ceased. Fynn heard her sobs growing faint until the shrill reminder of her righteous sadness faded altogether.

Those same large hands suddenly clapped over his shoulders. Fynn focused on what—or rather, who—was before him. He wished he hadn't.

Blue eyes stared back at him with unabashed concern; black brows furrowed deeply. A voice, one Fynn hadn't heard in a while, sounded. "Fynneas, what happened?"

The boy couldn't help himself. Fynn reached out a shaking hand and touched his fingers to his father's neck softly. Convinced, only now that he had touched the older prince's throat for himself, that there was no gaping wound, Fynn shrugged.

"I don't know," he answered almost meekly.

Felix pulled back from his boy, studying the child in his grasp. He ran his hand over Fynn's unruly hair. "Your sister seems quite upset."

Fynn lied, "I don't know what I did to upset her."

Much as Fiona had done, Felix pressed the back of his hand to his son's forehead. He frowned. "Are you sure you're feeling well? You're acting a little…strange."

Fynn nodded.

"Never mind that," Felix said, shaking his head. "I wanted to go out on a hunt with you this morning. But maybe we should stay in today. Is that alright with you?"

"Yes," mumbled Fynn weakly. He hung his head, hair falling before his eyes, purposely obscuring his visible disappointment from his father.

Fynn allowed himself to be led back into the castle. A firm hand was set between his shoulders, ushering him through the stony corridors. They walked along in silence for a long while. It was a companionable silence, the sort that the two had shared ever since Fynn could remember. He felt quite at ease in his father's presence - safe and protected and happy. The thought faded instantly when he looked up. His pale eyes were riveted to the man's neck. A red spot had appeared there upon the pale column of flesh.

"Father," said Fynn.

"Hmm?" the prince mumbled, glancing down to the boy at his side.

"Your...neck," stammered Fynn. He felt his chest tightening, constricting around his rapidly beating heart. "Your neck...it's bleeding...it's bleeding!" His heart's pounding went from erratic to vicious, smashing into his chest painfully with every beat. Fynn heard his own voice, terrified and broken, as he cried, "Your neck's bleeding!"

Felix moved with astounding swiftness. He knelt before his son and wrapped his arms around the shaking child. But Fynn couldn't let himself relax into the warm envelopment. There was thick redness seeping from a puncture wound in Felix's throat; wide streams seeped over the fair flesh, reached over the furry shoulders of his cloak, stained the white material of his shirt until it was a deep red.

Fynn wrenched himself from his father's arms. His eyes went wider as he reeled backward, tripping over his own feet as he fell to the ground. There, beneath his hands, he felt it. There was something warm and sticky congealing beneath his palms. Shakily, he looked down to find himself sprawled in a pool of gore. Splotches of blood tracked from where Fynn remained fixed to the ground, to where his father stood. There was red everywhere. When Fynn's horror-stricken gaze made its way up to Felix's face, he had to fight with everything he had not to vomit.

The man's face was gaunt, his cheeks hollow. His skin had lost all color, looking as white as the snow falling outside. His lips were a blue sort of hue, cracked and dried and wrinkled. His eyes looked as though they'd sunken into his skull. The blue of his irises was little more than a shadowy puddle of unseeing nothingness, settled between bruised-black sockets. Those eyes, the dead eyes that seemed entirely void of life, watched Fynn intently.

"Fynn, what's the matter?" Felix's voice sounded as it always did.

Desperate to get away, Fynn scooted backward on the floor. The feeling of the blood slickening his hands as he pushed by the stony ground was revolting. The very thought that he was covered in Felix's blood was heart-wrenching. The memory of the morning of the funeral was still quite fresh, burned for all eternity into his memory. It felt much the same now as it did then—the blood against his skin, that warm feeling as it crept between his fingers. He despised it.

Fynn - spurred on by the traumatizing memory of watching Felix lie there before him, life literally spilling out of him with each passing moment - jumped to his feet. He staggered, slipping in the alarming amount of blood spilled all over the floor. Ignoring it as best he could, the boy sprinted away from his father. He headed back toward the castle's entrance. Red footprints glimmered in Fynn's wake.

"Fynn! Fynn!"

He heard his father's voice clearly. He heard the worried tinge to Felix's cries. But Fynn didn't care. He careened around the corner and bolted for the door. The front entrance of the castle - two large, wooden doors that stretched three men high - swung open of their own accord. The blistering wind gusted inside. Fynn jolted through the doorway, flinging himself forward. He stumbled not far from the entryway, falling into the snow.

It was cold, biting at his fingers. Pushing himself up on hands and knees, Fynn gasped as the white of the snow slowly turned pink; the blood from his palms seeped into each flake beneath his touch. His chest heaved, rising and falling with alarming rapidity. His heart crushed against his ribs, smashed forcefully in his chest cavity with every labored breath. His head swam in fogginess. He felt heavy all over.

"Fynneas, darling…are you alright?"

Looking up, he saw his mother. He hadn't heard her approach. He hadn't seen her when he rushed outside. She just appeared, as if carried by the snowy winds. Fynn knew, he could feel it. The niggling had burst from the back of his mind to the forefront, bringing with it justified fear.

Trembling, unsure if it was from the chill of the air or the utter terror laying siege to his person, Fynn crawled over to her. When she held her arms out for him, he rose to his feet shakily and curled against her, letting her arms drape around him like a shield. He wasn't cold anymore. He wasn't scared. Peeking back down to his feet, he saw the snow was white again. There were no more traces of the horror and gore. Just pure, white, untouched snow. It was as though everything had been a nightmare, one that had receded the moment his mother appeared.

Celestine gently stroked Fynn's hair as she whispered, "Tell me what's wrong."

He didn't want to. He wanted to stay where he was, secure in his mother's arms, comfortable in her embrace, safe from all the grotesque redness that had spluttered from his father's neck, the sickly redness that had clung to his hands, wormed between his fingers. He just wanted to stay there, nestled against his mother's middle, eyes screwed shut. When he felt the familiar prick of tears stinging his eyes and the tell-tale streaking of something heated striking over his cheeks, Fynn couldn't bring himself to feel annoyed or ashamed by his emotional display. He simply burrowed his face more firmly against Celestine, clinging to her with all the strength in his arms, fingers clawing at the silken night-gown she still wore. He wondered, fleetingly, if she may be cold out in the snow with little more than a silk slip on.

"Tell me what's wrong," she said again.

Fynn heaved a reluctant sigh and disentangled himself from her. His eyes went wide when he saw the red speckled over her front.

"You're bleeding," he whispered shakily. "You're bleeding."

She shook her head. There was a somber look in her eyes. Silvery tears trailed over her fair face. "It's not my blood." She lifted a quivering hand and pointed toward Fynn.

All of a sudden, he couldn't breathe. Everything felt hot and tense and strained. He reached a wavering hand to his chest. Sure enough, his chest was warm to the touch. He knew what blood felt like. He was all too well acquainted with the feeling to mistake it for anything else.

"I'm bleeding," Fynn whispered. His voice was flat and dull. "It's *me*. *I'm* bleeding." He looked down. His white shirt was a deep scarlet. Rivers of red coursed down his trousers. He stood in speckled snow. "I'm bleeding," he repeated absently.

It was snowing harder. Fynn heard the wind howling strangely. The snow fell in gusting sheets of impossible white. He looked up, searching for his mother. But Celestine had disappeared in the sudden onset of the snowstorm.

"Mother," Fynn called tentatively. Confusion began to muddle his thoughts, mingling disastrously with his mounting disconcertion.

He heard nothing more than the screaming of the wind as the storm picked up.

"Mother!"

It was snowing more and more, harder and harder.

"Mother!"

Everything had gone white.

"No!" he screamed.

Fynn's body jerked upward. He looked around, breathing heavily; sweat pooled at his hairline and slowly crept down his temples. He was in bed. It wasn't the one he'd woken in before. The bedding was a dark red, woven

lightly to accommodate the warm climate. Distantly, Fynn heard the squawk-
ing of birds. He blinked his eyes, trying to clear the lingering cloudiness that
persisted at the edges of his sight. He pressed the heels of his hands over
his eyes, swiping at them in an effort to see clearly.

A palm came to rest on his back. Fynn withdrew his hands from his
eyes. Everything was blurry, but it wasn't a muddled cloud of whiteness
anymore. Slowly, he calmed his breathing. With a sigh, he followed the line
of black denoting a long, lean arm that soon met with wide shoulders and a
long neck. He saw the pair of green eyes he'd know anywhere, the eyes that
shone through even the darkest shadows. They were, as they always were,
alight with some unknown knowledge.

"Moriah?" rasped Fynn weakly. He felt something, a light weight, settle
by his ankles. Looking away from the man, he saw Hollyn seated in a chair
at his bedside, doubled over with his head resting in his arms at the foot of
Fynn's bed. "Hollyn?" he mumbled, confused.

Moriah's hand inched upward; long fingers stretched from the nape
of the boy's neck into the sweaty mess of hair soothingly. He cocked his
head to the side with the sort of curiosity of a cat staring at a wounded
mouse. His eyes were narrowed as he appraised the prince, his expression apathetic and bored. "You were having a nightmare," Moriah surmised quietly. "Hollyn's been waiting for you to wake up." Withdrawing
his hand, he sank back into his own chair. He cast a quick look to the
red-haired prince, who still drowsed soundly just to his side. Idly, he
reached his hand over to Hollyn, combing his fingers through the well-
kept mane. Light touched his eyes softly; a tiny smile curled the corner
of his lips. "Don't wake him just yet. He must be exhausted. He hasn't
slept in almost two days."

"Two days?"

"The tournament starts in the morning."

Fynn wrinkled his nose in thought. "Two days?"

"Noel was concerned. Rightly so, it seems. Your wound, the one on
your chest, didn't heal all too quickly. You've been out for almost two days,"
explained Moriah. He reached to his belt and withdrew a familiar dagger.
"When Hollyn gave this to you, it wasn't so someone could stab *you* with it.
That wasn't really the point."

The prince snorted. "It wasn't exactly my intention either."

Carefully, Moriah set the dagger down on the bed beside Fynn. "Be that
as it may, it happened. Emrys tended to your wound. It's looking better. It's

healed, actually. You'll have a scar. You may have some pain there for a while or forever. I don't know. But you'll live."

Ever so carefully, Fynn reached down to the hem of his shirt and pulled up. Tossing the garment aside, he took a minute to relish the feeling of the warm air brushing over him. Just by his sternum, there was a long and jagged, red scar. It seemed far bigger than it should be. Darwyn had only stabbed into his chest; he hadn't dragged the blade down. Fynn turned to look at Moriah, nervousness flooding through him once more.

Before he could begin hyperventilating, Moriah clapped his hands over Fynn's shoulders and held him tightly.

"Don't panic," the man in black instructed. He gently pushed Fynn backward, letting the boy's head settle over the pillows. He pulled the blanket, thin as it was, over the boy's chest, hiding the scar away behind the red linen. "You'll be fine."

"Why's the scar so big?" the prince asked weakly.

Moriah nodded to the dagger at Fynn's side. "That blade there, that wasn't meant to be used like a regular knife. It was designed to kill certain... *things.*"

"Monsters?" supplied the boy.

"Yes...monsters. Had it hit your heart, you'd be dead, of course. Even *you*, Fynn, wouldn't have survived that. There'd be no way to nurse you back to health, even for someone like Emrys doing the healing. *Thankfully*, it didn't hit your heart. *Unfortunately*, by the time you got to Nandulus, the... let's call it an *infection*...the infection had taken hold and was eating away at you from the inside out. Emrys fixed it. Don't worry. But that's why it's such a large scar. That's also why it's such a dark, red color." As carefully as he could, Moriah set his hand over Fynn's chest. He felt the steady beating of the prince's heart beneath his palm. "Does it still hurt?"

"No." When Moriah's touch grew firmer, Fynn winced. "Alright, it's a bit sore."

The man nodded. His hand moved away, once more reaching toward Fynn's head, brushing hair from his face, smoothing it over the pillow. "You shouldn't compete tomorrow," Moriah asserted calmly.

Fynn wanted to bolt upright in protest, but Moriah had obviously anticipated the move before the prince could flinch and, thus, held him in place softly. Fynn begged, "Please...*please*, Moriah, you have to let me compete."

"Emrys doesn't think you should," said Moriah. "Neither does Imogen."

"And Blythe? You could get a third opinion," suggested Fynn hopefully.

Moriah shook his head. "The less people who know about...*this*...the better."

"I feel alright," assured Fynn. "Really."

"That's what you told Noel. An hour later, you'd lost consciousness and were in bed, dead to the world, for almost two whole days," debated Moriah drearily. "That's not *fine*."

"I've come this far," whispered Fynn. He wouldn't let the defeated feeling that welled in his chest color his voice any more than it already had. He curled his fingers into fists, knuckles going paler. "I've come this far. I've made it all the way here. Let me finish. Please."

"Fynn—"

The prince interrupted, snatching Moriah's hand in his two smaller ones. He held tightly, as tight as he could. "Please!"

Moriah frowned, relenting, "Fine. But if you notice something's off, you tell me or Noel or Emrys right away. *Immediately*. Understood?"

"Yes."

"The *moment* you feel anything weird," Moriah persisted.

Fynn smiled sheepishly. "I understand."

Moriah huffed as he rose to his feet. "Get some sleep."

He left the boys there as he stole away from the room as quietly as he could.

The black-haired prince settled against his pillows. With a smile tilting his lips, he gave into exhaustion and fell into a far more restful sleep. When he next woke, he found a pair of dark, blue eyes intently staring at him through the relative darkness of the small room. Rolling onto his back, he asked, "What time is it?"

"Night," Hollyn answered easily. He was seated on the edge of Fynn's bed, leaning to the side, hovering over Fynn's chest as he eyed his cousin with a frown. He quirked a black brow; an arrogant expression fell into place. "You got stabbed."

"Well spotted," mumbled Fynn, still not entirely sure he wanted to be awake just yet.

"*Idiot*, how do you get stabbed with your own knife?"

"Surprisingly, you're not the first one to mention that little fact," grumbled Fynn. He sat upright, shoving Hollyn back. He yawned. "How's your shoulder?"

"Better than your chest, I suspect." Hollyn smirked.

Fynn shrugged. "I don't know. My chest doesn't really hurt. You, on the other hand, are favoring your left side. It still hurts, then?"

The amusement slipped from Hollyn's eyes as quickly as it had appeared. "When'd you become so clever?"

"Maybe you're just getting dumber," quipped Fynn.

Choosing to ignore Fynn's snide jab, Hollyn asked, "Moriah's letting you compete tomorrow?"

The smaller boy nodded. He fidgeted under the blankets, letting them slip away from his shoulders, exposing the abnormally dark scar. "Yes."

Hollyn shifted forward, eyes intently roving over Fynn's newly healed stab wound. He nodded to the scar. "That doesn't look good."

"It's not as bad as it looks," assured Fynn. His hand quickly flew up to cover the unsightly mark. "Really."

Knowing better than to press his cousin just yet, Hollyn readjusted, returning to his original position, staring at Fynn thoughtfully. "You still think you can win, even with that nasty thing?" he asked, vaguely gesturing to Fynn's chest.

"I do."

"Don't think it'll slow you down?"

Fynn smirked. "It might. But that doesn't mean I won't win."

Hollyn's voice dropped to a barely-there whisper. There was something about his face, his lop-sided grin, his burning, blue eyes, that Fynn found very familiar and, oddly, comforting. "Between you and me," Hollyn started, "I think you'll win, too."

34

FIRST BLOOD

The amphitheater was made of pale stone. At its base, there were grand statues depicting Estheria's most storied heroes, from kings and princes, to knights and champions, to gods and monsters. Some of the statues were falling apart, their noses having come loose, an arm or ear missing. There were some with cracks and some with vines creeping over their stony ankles, entangling around artistically rendered waists. The statue of King Kiernan, the newest of the lot, was in pristine condition. His squared jaw and thin nose were strikingly lifelike; his broad set shoulders and wide torso couldn't have been more realistic; it was more indicative of what the man had looked like in his youth than his appearance while actually king. He stood nearest the arching entryway, his stone gaze fixed to a horizon that was lost behind an emerald cropping of fronds pinching out from palm trees that covered the island.

Just through the entryway, beyond the still unlit torches, there were rows upon rows of seating. A pulpit was raised up above all other seats, covered by a black cloth canopy. From the sides of the pulpit, hanging from the marbled columns that decorated its corners, were the banners of House Fog. The brilliant red bat, with its wings spanned out, was braced there at each side for all to see. At the foot of the pulpit, hanging down, nearly brushing over the sand floor of the arena, were three more banners. To the left was the banner of House Redmayne, the white field pure, but emblazoned brilliantly by the red lion rearing at its center, mane flared, and claws raised. To the right was the banner of House Godsbane, the blue banner sharp and brilliant, almost matching the warm, nearly-summer sky. The white owl at its center with two, large, blue eyes remained vigilant, staring out over the crowds. The banner at the center, as black as House Fog's, bore the curling figure of a golden snake, the embodiment of House Mordray.

Despite the early morning hours, the members of those most storied of Estheria's houses sat in the pulpit's plump chairs. Ursalyn sat at the center, her crown delicately poised upon her head, red hair elegantly drawn back with black ribbon. Her gown, a deep, rich red matched the tint of her lips. To her right sat Novian Godsbane, garbed in white with his pale hair slicked back, glint-ing eyes narrowed as he looked out upon those in attendance. His thin lips were drawn into a solemn line. At the queen's left was Warwyk Redmayne, finely dressed in red, a lion embroidered on his right sleeve, rearing just as upon his family's banner.

In a row of chairs behind the three were the other pivotal members of the assembled great houses. Cedryk Redmayne and his wife sat, dutifully looking dour and austere and with no hint of anything resembling interest upon either of their faces. Assorted members of the Godsbane family were seated about, intermingling with other Redmaynes present.

Fiona lounged, worn out by the oppressive heat of the island, expectantly waiting for the tournament to commence. She chanced quick looks back to Ridley before hastily averting her eyes forward once more. A small smile twisted her lips.

The Mordrays stood at the back of the pulpit, looking most grim. Each of them was swathed in black, with various adornments of gold twisted and melded in a serpentine fashion. They stood with their backs uncomfortably straight, chins raised, and eyes sharp and alert. Ridley was at his father's side, idly toeing at the ground, frowning subtly as he sighed. Emrys enjoyed a hushed, careful conversation with Noel. Odette busied herself with counting the cracks in the pulpit's ceiling.

The rest of the amphitheater was filled by a host of Estheria's nobility and many of the people from More Town. There were members from all the great houses, from the middle nobility, and from Estherian Erza. They stayed together, clumped in cliques populated by their kinsmen, whispering amongst themselves. On either side of the pulpit, the students of Morancy gathered. They were assembled by division, each of them garbed in their formal uniforms, their divisions denoted by the arm bands fitted on their left. They, by far, were the most outwardly interested in the day's proceedings.

Beyond the arena, just through a grated archway, there was a small staircase that led ten or so feet down, just below the structure. Therein was a chamber, dark and lit only by torchlight, that played host to the first-and-second years. The twenty-six competitors, dressed finely in uniforms of all black, waited patiently to be called. Their injuries had been tended, cleaned, stitched, patched, and wrapped. Though they looked far from their best condition, the children appeared infinitely better and healthier than when they'd arrived on Nandulus' shores. They stood in an oblong sort of shape, shuffling about, keeping their voices low. The anticipation permeating the small chamber was nearly palpable, both oppressive and inspirational. The energy teeming within each student was infectious. Anxious jitters jerked their shoulders, shook their hands.

Hollyn appeared from a side corridor that linked the chamber to the other underground rooms beneath the building. Dressed in his Morancy uniform, right arm free of the sling that had bound it for far too many weeks, he seemed in great spirits. With absolute ease, he assimilated into the group of children, garnering nods of approval, smiles of warm welcome, and a few amiable claps on the back.

He stood, fixed in place between Fynn and Ollie. He elbowed Ollie and, when the other boy raised a puzzled brow, Hollyn offered him a meager smile. "Ready?"

"As I'll ever be." Ollie looked from Hollyn's face, his dark eyes unusually bright for once, and then to his arm. "Is your shoulder better?"

As if to prove himself, Hollyn raised his arm and, ever so slowly, rotated it. "It's getting there." He grinned an arrogant sort of grin, the cockiness burning into his eyes as he stared back at Ollie. "You know, I've been out of practice for months, Ollie. Do you think you've had time to catch up?" he joked.

Chuckling, Ollie answered, "I've gotten better. Still not sure I'd be able to beat *you* though."

Fynn chirped, "Ollie, don't let him get in your head like that." He grinned a toothy smile that swept over his tired features. His voice was warm. "I bet you'd knock Hollyn clear on his backside if you two fought right now."

"That so?" mocked Hollyn easily.

"It is."

"Rather bold claim to make," the taller prince commented.

"I've become rather bold in your absence." Fynn laughed.

Hollyn eyed his cousin carefully, smirking as he said, "I'm not surprised. It's not like any of them could rein you in."

Godryk edged closer to the three, slinging an arm around Fynn's shoulders and making a show of hauling him back a few paces. "We did our best,

Hollyn." His blue eyes were calm, alight, as he smiled down at Fynn. "But he isn't the best at listening."

"I've noticed," drawled Hollyn.

Moriah's approach caught their attention. The children turned at the sound of his footsteps, straightening up and quieting down the moment they saw Moriah join them. His black hair was elegantly slicked back, his green eyes downcast and tired looking. He wore a high, black collared garb that stretched to his jaw; it made his neck look longer, thinner. His shoulders were draped in a black cloak; golden snakes were stitched along the hem. He looked to be both the specter of death and the personification of dismal poise as he swept toward them, standing just behind Fynn and Hollyn. His iridescent eyes shone keenly in the relative darkness, occasionally flashing even brighter when the glow from the torchlight angled over his face just right. Finally, he addressed them after a long while of standing and observing silently, smirking as they began to uneasily fidget under the weight of his pressing, green gaze. "Good morning."

"Good morning, sir," the children chorused.

"This is your final test. At the end of the tournament, one of you will emerge victorious. That person will be named champion." As ever, his voice was leveled and dull, entirely detached from the situation. "You will be called in pairs. You and your opponent will proceed up those stairs." He nodded to his right. "You will step into the arena. You will answer to your queen. Then, you will fight. For your bouts, you will be using practice swords. There will be no lopping off limbs today. You'll be given a shield, as well. That's all you will have. The match will continue until either the lord paramount or vice lord paramount calls for you to stop. Is this understood?"

The twenty-six answered evenly. "Yes, sir."

"You will all fight. There will be no division between first-and-second years. If this seems unfair to you, get over it. War isn't fair. You and your adversaries will not always have received the same level of training. Adapt and overcome. That is all you can do. Should you fail to do so, you will surely lose. Now, are there any questions?"

A stark silence infiltrated the chamber. All eyes were trained on Moriah. No voices sounded.

"Alright. Stay here and stay quiet until I return." With that, he swept from the room and stole up the stairs.

The grate partitioning the archway and the arena raised slowly. Moriah stepped into the center of the arena, undaunted by the hundreds of eyes now trained solely upon him. He stood, resolutely fixed at the center, staring up at the pulpit. His focus did not waver, rather it tightened, eyes narrowing, as Ursalyn slowly rose from her seat.

The queen drew herself to the edge of the pulpit, bracing her hands over the bannister. "Good morning, to all of you," she began. She, far more than Lachlan, had the sort of voice that demanded attention, deference. It was silken and feminine without losing the commanding edge the Crown demanded. "On this day, we gather to name a champion for this year's class at Morancy. The children have all worked hard, trained hard, studied hard. Their instructors have said nothing but the best of each of them. They braved the first leg of the games and made their way here to Nandulus Island, quicker than any group has in seventeen years. They braved the dangers of each isle, retrieved their flags, and more importantly, learned the value of camaraderie, of unwavering loyalty. They are commanders in the making. And, on this morning, we honor them and applaud their efforts."

A deafening roar overtook the nobles in the arena. They cheered and hollered, clapped their hands almost feverishly. As quickly as the wave of raucous lauds had crested over the silence, it broke and tapered off with little more than a wave of Ursalyn's hand.

She looked down, seeing nothing more than Moriah standing there at the arena's center, unmoved by the enthusiasm of the crowd. "State your name, my lord."

"I am Moriah Thomas Mordray, Lord Commander of the Night Corps."

"And why do you stand before us all on this day, lord commander?"

Moriah bowed deeply. His baritone voice was louder than most had ever heard it before. "I, Moriah Mordray, Lord Commander of the Night Corps, have come to Nandulus Island on this day to present you, Queen Ursalyn Ormand Fog, the students of this year's first-and-second-year classes from the Morancy Academy of Military Arts, for the purpose of determining a champion."

"And have you anything to say for them?"

Moriah straightened. "I, as both Lord Commander of the Night Corps and instructor of close combat at the Morancy Academy of Military Arts, do hereby attest to the readiness and willingness of each student to be presented before you here today. I do so attest to their right to bear arms in the name of Crown, king, and country."

The children were just at the foot of the stairs, looking up the short distance to where they stopped and gave way to blinding light. They could hear Moriah and Ursalyn talking.

680

Albie scoffed at the monotonous sound of both voices. "Seems rather practiced," he commented.

Fynn shrugged. "It probably is."

"Who do you think will be the first of us to fight?" Albie asked. He looked between Godryk, Hollyn, and Fynn, who all stood shoulder to shoulder, intently listening to the muffled tedium that continued. "Do you think it's at random or do you suppose they devised some way of matching us against our opponents?"

"Probably random," Lux asserted.

Her presence startled both Godryk and Fynn, who managed to both lurch forward with such a profound lack of spatial awareness as to run into one another, clattering their foreheads together.

Groaning, Fynn rubbed at his bruised head. "Watch where you're going," he mumbled.

Godryk shoved Fynn to the side, laughing, "I could say the same to you and your impossibly hard head."

Lux eyed the boys for a moment, shaking her head reproachfully. "Now isn't the time to be silly. You do realize this is important, right? *Everyone's* out there."

"*Almost* everyone." Hollyn added, "But she's right. Could you both *try* and be serious?"

Fynn shrugged, turning a lopsided grin toward Godryk. "They're no fun today, are they?"

"Not at all," agreed Godryk with a wry smile. "But they're probably right." He drew a deep, steadying breath. "But we'll be fine. We'll *all* be fine."

"Not a doubt in my mind about that." Fynn smiled confidently.

Lux cast a quick look over her shoulder before huddling closer to the boys. She whispered, "Besides, we need to come out on top. We can't let one of the second-years win this."

Albie laughed. "She's right, you know."

Their huddle was broken by Moriah striding down the stairs. He caught them with their heads bowed together, whispering amongst themselves. The man in black waved them off, ushering them toward the rest of the children.

Once the children were again collected in a jumbled group, Moriah began, "The bouts will begin in just a moment. The first match will be between Godryk and Maeryk. Are you both ready?"

Maeryk sauntered forward, his sword fastened to his side, shield over one arm. He nodded, stopping to stand at the base of the stairs. "Ready."

Godryk inhaled sharply, setting his shoulders evenly. He let his hand drape over the sword he'd affixed to his belt earlier. He said tensely, "Yes."

Fynn braced his hand over Godryk's shoulder, pulling his attention back. "Godryk," he whispered. When the other boy slowly turned toward him, Fynn continued, "You'll do great." His voice dropped to a whisper as he leaned closer, softly saying, "You've *got* to win. You can't be eliminated from the tournament before I have a chance to fight you. Got it?"

"Got it." Godryk nodded sharply.

The Redmaynes were shown up the stairs and soon found themselves stepping through the threshold, emerging from the shadowy stairway into the morning light. They made their way to the center of the arena, backs straight as they stood, heads tilted upward toward the pulpit. Godryk was stunned by how imposing Ursalyn looked; she was a tower of red leaning over the bannister, piercing eyes staring his way. He choked back his hesitance.

"Your names," she commanded gently.

As the older of the two, Maeryk spoke first. He drew his sword and held it at his side with a careful grip. "My name is Maeryk Robert Balder of House Redmayne, Your Grace." He looked to his cousin, waiting for the younger boy to speak.

Godryk wasn't entirely sure if he could keep himself as collected and calm as Maeryk seemed to be. He took a moment, willing himself to relax. He said, "My name is Godryk Warren Edgar of House Redmayne, Your Grace."

The queen favored the boys with a chilling smile before continuing with her intonement. "Maeryk and Godryk of House Redmayne, are you ready and willing to bear arms for Crown, king, and country?"

"Yes, Your Grace," they answered.

"And are you ready and willing to spill blood, both your own and that of your enemies, those who would oppose your Crown, king, and country?"

"Yes, Your Grace." They nodded dutifully.

"Then," her voice darkened considerably, "let us see what you can do."

The cousins turned toward one another. Their swords were drawn; their shields were raised. They poised their weapons toward the other; the dulled edges of their swords glinted dangerously in the sunlight. And at the command of the lord paramount, their bout began.

Maeryk, ever the aggressor, lunged toward Godryk with frightening speed. But when his blade smashed against his cousin's, he was found to be lacking in sheer brute force. Struggling against Godryk's sword, Maeryk withdrew and took a step back. Collecting himself, he lunged forward once more. This time, his attack broke through Godryk's defenses and sliced at the boy's shoulder, knocking Godryk backward a few paces.

Skidding in the dirt, Godryk stumbled for a moment. He righted himself quickly enough, before taking it upon himself to man the offensive, drawing his sword upward and slinging it down. With a fierce clash, his weapon banged into Maeryk's shield. As the older Redmayne struggled against the pressing assault, Godryk took a bold step forward. His eyes narrowed when he saw Maeryk faltering. He'd caught the other off-guard, disrupted his footing. Godryk smiled before swinging again and again, angling his sword at Maeryk's head and next his shoulder and then his middle. The barrage of assaults was unrelenting; each swing punctuated Godryk's foray forward.

Maeryk grappled to keep himself unscathed; the flurry of Godryk's movements and the power propelling each strike was not what he'd expected when the match began. He forced his shield forward, eager to push Godryk back as far as he could. His attempt, however, was of little consequence. The moment his shield moved away from his body by just a fraction, Godryk saw the opening and pressed forward. The tip of his sword caught Maeryk in the ribs, effectively forcing the air from his lungs. Gasping, the older Redmayne stumbled backward, uneasy on his feet.

Seeing Maeryk weakened and disregarding his shield, Godryk swung heartily. The dulled edge of his sword beat bodily into Maeryk's ribs. And as Maeryk fell to the ground, prostrate, with a rasping shudder for air, he dropped his shield entirely. Godryk didn't waste a second of his time. He was upon his cousin faster than anyone could have thought possible. Astride the other's chest, Godryk buried his knee at Maeryk's ribs, pinning him in place. He levered the edge of his sword over Maeryk's neck, holding it there without allowing the dullness to brush over his cousin's flesh.

The lord paramount sprung to his feet, pronouncing Godryk the victor. A rush of applause swept over the arena, heralding the end of the tournament's first match. As the praise was heaped upon him, Godryk rose to his feet. He offered his hand to his cousin and pulled the other to his feet. He smiled and said, "I thought you had me there, for just a moment."

Maeryk wound his arm across his middle, holding his bruised ribs. His voice was breathy and pained as he winced. "I did too."

"Maybe next time." Godryk grinned. He held his hand out to Maeryk.

Taking the proffered hand in his, Maeryk shook it. "Well done."

Before heading back to the archway to depart the arena, which still rang with residual cheers and lingering hollers, Godryk looked up to the pulpit. His blue eyes met those of his father's, still seated with a straight back and perfectly squared shoulders. When Warwyk gave the most imperceptible of nods with the tiniest of grins tugging at the corners of his lips, Godryk took his leave of the arena and headed down the stairs.

Godryk's arrival amongst his year mates was met with joyous cheering once they'd heard the outcome of the bout.

Fynn clapped him over the back and whispered, "One down, a lot to go."

Godryk laughed, "Don't worry, you'll get your turn with me."

"You better believe it." The prince grinned affably.

Firiel and Lux were the next pair called for their bout. As they ascended the stairs, the rest of the children hung around one another, occasionally glancing back up to where the girls had disappeared into the sunlight.

Renwyn sauntered toward Fynn, a self-satisfied grin etched over his smug features. "Who do you think will win?"

Fynn tensed at the sound of Renwyn's voice. Something in him darkened and he felt the concerning urge to pounce on the boy and beat his face into the ground. He didn't. He wasn't entirely sure if it was because he had, in recent months, begun obtaining a modicum of self-control, or if it was because Hollyn's hand had clasped over his wrist and deftly begun tugging him back, away from Renwyn. It didn't matter. Fynn gnashed his teeth. His blood roiled in his veins the longer he watched Renwyn. The taller boy had crossed his arms over his chest, cocking his head to the side with the sort of haughty condescension Fynn had associated with him since day one.

"I think it'll be Firiel," continued Renwyn with a glower in the princes' direction. He looked between Hollyn and Fynn before adding, "What do you think?"

Ollie waded through the throng of students, sliding between Renwyn and the princes, placing himself in the middle of what would surely result in a fight if no one stepped in. He offered Renwyn a placating grin and curt nod. "She's definitely one of the best in our year," he said amiably. "But Lux is good too. It'll be a close match, I'm sure."

The sound of a garbled argument flitted through the air, barely reaching the two girls who stood at the center of the arena. Their swords were drawn, lazily resting in their hands as the queen addressed them.

"Your names," Ursalyn commanded.

Lux spoke first, blue eyes flicking from Firiel up to the pulpit, settling on the startlingly irritated looking Ursalyn. "My name is Lux Diane of House Astor, Your Grace."

Firiel leveled her shoulders. Her hold on her sword's hilt tightened a fraction. "My name is Firiel Amelda Rosalind of House Blackthorn, Your Grace."

Ursalyn straightened; her shadow stretched over the girls. She proceeded with the same inquiries she'd asked of the Redmaynes, her voice remaining even and frightfully chilled.

The girls answered with their assent keenly, fire burning in their voices with their crisp replies.

When the lord paramount sounded his instruction, commanding the bout to begin, there was a lull where silence reigned as king, starkly contrasting the speed with which the boys had sprung into action. Rather, both girls held their swords before them and raised their shields. It was a quiet moment shared between combatants, where both knew that the other was willing to do nearly anything to win. That understanding - that simple revelation - was both a comfort and terror to each of them.

Lux's fingers squeezed around her sword's hilt; her arm flexed beneath the weight of the shield. Her muscles tensed, each and every one coiling, awaiting the moment she would spring forward. Firiel seemed to be of a like mind, for her clutch around her hilt strengthened and her shield raised just a hair more; her eyes narrowed ferally as she watched Lux. Then, as if able to read the other's minds, they burst forward.

The sound of steel slashing into steel was shrill and screeching. Neither recoiled from the ear-splitting noise. They pressed onward, both determined to out muscle the other, only to find themselves evenly matched.

Lux curled her shoulders forward, doing her best to force all her weight over her sword, beating down upon Firiel's blade more and more until she saw it quaver under the force. At the slight tremble of steel, Lux brightened. She threw herself forward, catching Firiel by surprise. But before she could swing again, Firiel had recovered her footing and sidestepped.

Awkwardly stumbling forward, Lux did her best to regroup quickly and round on the other girl. She swung with the sort of force one would use when they were intending to lop a head clean from a neck. The dull edge of Lux's sword smacked into the blunt face of Firiel's shield, splintering the wood under the momentum of the blow.

The ferocity with which the two girls fought caught Ursalyn by surprise. She cocked her head to the side; a small smirk snaked over her lips. "Well, I didn't expect that," she whispered.

Odette found her way to the queen's side. She peered over the bannister and watched the two girls below with rapt interest. She saw the intensity with which Firiel swung, the strength behind each raised shield, each deft parry. But it was the precision with which Lux aimed and slashed, the force that propelled each movement, that she found intriguing. "They've come a long way."

"I haven't seen girls do this well at the games in a long time," Ursalyn remarked. Her lips continued quirking at the corners until a genuine smile blossomed, brightening her expression as she watched the bout progress. "It's quite impressive."

"It's an impressive lot of students we have this year," Odette admitted. "You'll be surprised by them, I'm sure."

"I already am," the queen assured. "And I look forward to what the rest of the day has to offer."

Lux's sword once more beat into the splintering wood of Firiel's shield.

Firiel gasped as the force reverberated through her arm - shaking her core, rocking her foundation - as she took a staggering step backward. Their bout had been going far longer than Maeryk and Godryk's. Both girls swung, parried, and side-stepped with practiced ease and frightening strength. They snapped at one another, hurled biting comments between gasping breaths. Sweat trickled down their brows; their hair was slick against their necks.

Again, Lux swung. The impact was bruising.

Firiel shuddered at the force.

When Firiel's shield looked as though it couldn't withstand the force of another strike, the girl didn't hesitate to cast it aside, garnering confused looks from many in the crowd. She pounced forward without defense, simply reeling her sword back and swinging. She caught Lux's hip with a particularly stinging strike. And as Lux stepped back, determined to keep her footing, Firiel swung again. She loomed over her opponent.

Lux was on one knee. She'd tossed her own shield aside. Her now-free hand clamped over her hip, pressing down on the swelling bruise. She forced back the whimper of pain that threatened to peel from her lips. She tasted the sweat as it streaked down her face; it traversed the cut of her jaw and slipped down the column of her neck. Red hair, tangled and sweaty, fell over her face as she looked up at Firiel. The hand over her hip clamped down harder, pushing back the throbbing pain. Lux tensed; her teeth gnashed as she watched Firiel lazily circling her like a bored vulture waiting for the last bit of life to leave whatever almost-carcass it had found.

"Ready to give in?" asked Firiel.

"Not a chance." Lux winced as she climbed back to her feet.

Firiel arched a brow curiously. "I'm getting bored."

"I'll make it more interesting for you, then," Lux said, before running toward the girl.

Before Firiel knew how to react, Lux had tackled her to the ground. Both girls dropped their swords, letting them fall to the dirt entirely forgotten. Firiel was prone to the ground as Lux pinned her. Lux pulled a fist back before her knuckles collided with Firiel's cheek.

"I certainly didn't expect that," Ursalyn said, amused. "Interesting tactic."

Odette smiled. "From what I've heard from Noel, throwing your sword away in favor of a fist fight has become a regular occurrence with this lot."

Ursalyn shook her head. "Not the most advisable strategy but certainly unique."

"You've no idea just *how* unique this bunch is." Odette laughed quietly.

Lux punched Firiel once more. Her fist hit the girl's lip. Blood poured from Firiel's mouth; a grotesque mixture of blood and saliva washed over her chin, stained her shirt, colored the dirt beneath her a sickening hue. Firiel spluttered, heaving her chest as she coughed; more bloody sputum splattered into the dirt. Before Lux had the chance to strike once more, Firiel bucked upward and threw the girl from her perch. As Lux tumbled away, landing awkwardly on her side, Firiel was on her feet once more.

Gasping for air and cringing at the throbbing feeling radiating from her side, Lux blearily blinked up in time to watch, helpless, as Firiel threw herself down over her. Pinned beneath the other girl's weight, Lux could do little more than raise her arms to cover her face and head as Firiel swung a fist down. The bruising force of the blow was painful, but not enough to bring down Lux's defense.

The fourth time Firiel swung, Lux had managed to gather her composure enough to roll. And as she did so, she brought Firiel down in an unbalanced heap just to her side. Both girls, sprawled in the dirt and panting for air, trembled for a moment longer before forcing themselves up on hands and knees. But it was Lux who was faster, whose intense desire to win outweighed Firiel's. And so, it was Lux who once more pinned Firiel down.

Her fist collided with the other girl's face forcefully, snapping her head to the side.

Her chest heaved, her breathing was labored, but Lux wouldn't allow herself to stop. She could feel Firiel fighting beneath her, her hands reaching up and clawing desperately. But Lux was heedless of the other's resistance. She hit her once more. And then, as her arm pulled back for another assault, she heard the voice of the lord paramount calling an end to their bout. As her name was spoken, declaring her the victor, Lux just stared into the middle distance almost disbelievingly.

Firiel didn't move much. Her eyes were open but glazed, her expression slack and empty. Lux rose slightly, kneeling before Firiel, and held her hand out. As the other girl weakly raised her hand, acknowledging her defeat, Lux took hold and pulled her to her feet. When Firiel stumbled, Lux steadied her with a gentle hand.

"Didn't think you could hit so hard." Firiel wiped the blood from her mouth. Her eyes were still dulled and foggy, but her expression was more alert, more keenly aware of her defeat and of the awful pain throbbing in her face where fresh, purple bruises bloomed. "Damn."

As they made their way back down the stairs, the sounds of shouting caught their attention. They paused, looking at one another.

"What do you think they're fighting about?" Firiel asked.

"Something stupid, I'm sure." Lux sighed and rolled her eyes. "Shall we?" she asked, throwing her arm forward, nodding toward the bottom of the stairs.

"Oh, this should be interesting," muttered Firiel as she proceeded.

When they reached the bottom and found themselves once more in the chilly embrace of the shadowy chamber, they saw the second-years pressed against the walls, arms crossed over the chests; quiet murmurs flitted between them as they watched the riotous scene unfold. Ollie was stamping his foot petulantly, like an enraged toddler; he yelled and demanded that the altercation, presently raging in the center of the room, cease. Albie was doing his best to pry Fynn off a struggling Renwyn, making little progress.

Fynn's hands were fisted in Renwyn's shirt, holding him firmly as he yelled. Renwyn jerked free of the prince, lunging forward and tackling him to the ground. Albie went crashing down under the weight of both boys. He tried to throw them off, but again, was unsuccessful. Godryk and Wilder waded into the fray, each of them choosing a combatant to try and wrangle. As Wilder managed to snatch Renwyn's wrists and wrench them behind his back, Godryk made quick work of pushing Fynn away, whispering something in his ear and calming him down.

"You know, we weren't gone that long," Firiel began. "Certainly not long enough for everything to turn into chaos like this. What happened?"

It was as if, at the sound of her voice, the boys realized that they had new spectators amongst their audience. They each turned with guilty expressions toward Firiel and Lux. At the sight of the girls' cool appraisals, they wilted backward and looked away, unwilling to explain what had transpired in their absence.

"Well," pressed Lux, "what happened?"

Renwyn, his nose bloodied and lip split, stepped forward and offered little more than a noncommittal shrug. He looked back to Fynn, who himself bore fresh bruising under his right eye and a nasty bloody nose.

The prince pouted. "Nothing."

"Nothing?" repeated Firiel.

"Nothing," said Renwyn.

Lux shook her head and snapped out, "Funny…I don't believe you."

Moriah appeared on the stairs, paying no attention to the bruised boys who toed at the ground sheepishly. "Ollie, Rory, it's your turn," he announced.

The boys padded by him, ascending the stairs. Still, Moriah made no move to leave.

Green eyes flitted across the room until they landed on Hollyn and Fynn. The boys stood side by side, both attentively watching Moriah. The man slowly made his way toward the princes. His hands fell over their shoulders, leading them deeper into the chamber, away from the others. When they were at a distance, Moriah let his eyes hardened. His voice was deathly deep and cold, as he asked, "Do either of you want to tell me what just happened?"

Looking quickly to Fynn and then back to Moriah, Hollyn stepped before his cousin, angling himself between the man and the other prince. He looked up squarely, eyes confidently shining in the pale glow of the torches. "Renwyn was being an ass. Fynn hit him. Renwyn hit back."

"Is that so?" Moriah asked lamely.

Fynn couldn't quite bring himself to look at the green eyes he felt trained on him. "Yes," he grumbled.

"What did he do that got you so riled up?" queried Moriah. He reached out, stretching by Hollyn toward Fynn. His forefinger and thumb curled over the small prince's chin, pulling the boy's face back toward him, tilting his head up. Their eyes met at last. "Look at me when I'm talking to you, Fynneas."

The black-haired boy made no move to escape Moriah's hold. He relented in the man's grasp, unwilling or unable—he wasn't sure which—to pull away. "He said Lux was weak. So, I hit him."

"That seemed like the right thing to do?" Moriah asked, arching a brow almost comically.

Hollyn snorted at the indignant look on Fynn's face.

Fynn answered tersely, "Yes."

The man in black pressed, "So, you think you did the right thing?"

The bruised prince nodded.

"If you could do it over, would you?"

"Yes." Fynn's voice was resolute.

Moriah continued, "You wouldn't change a thing?"

"I didn't say that," mumbled Fynn.

"What would you change?" Moriah wondered, a touch of curiosity lightening his tone.

A sly smile graced Fynn's bruised features as he answered with a chuckle, "I'd hit him harder."

Moriah shook his head and rolled his eyes but couldn't help laughing under his breath at the boy's brazen response. His hand lifted from Fynn's chin; long fingers traced over the purple bloom around the boy's eye and cheek. "Save it for the arena, alright?"

Fynn murmured, "Alright."

The man turned, intent on leaving, but stopped. "Fynneas?"

"Hmm?"

"You managed a few good punches, judging by Renwyn's face," Moriah commented flatly. Fynn brightened for a moment, but Moriah continued quickly, "But if you want to win against him out there, you're going to need to hit him a *lot* harder."

35

THE QUEEN'S MAN

The morning wore into afternoon. Matches had been declared, fought, and concluded. As time went on, the relentless heat of the southern archipelago became more and more oppressive.

Fynn held his hand out to Ollie when the boy's name was called alongside Renwyn's. Ollie took it, shaking it firmly. A smile splayed over his rounded features.

"You'll do great," Fynn assured.

"If you say so," Ollie jested, despite the creeping sensation of dread settling in his stomach.

The prince whispered in Ollie's ear, "Make sure to give him a good crack to the head, alright?"

Smirking, Ollie laughed, "I make no promises."

Side by side, Ollie and Renwyn ascended the stairs, crossing the border from the shadows into the light of the afternoon. They stood at the center of the arena; their necks craned as they looked up to the pulpit. The lithe, red figure of the queen leaned over the banister; long fingers curled around its edge. The sun cast a golden glow over her features, defining the sharp angles of her face quite dramatically. She looked more like an artistic rendering of the queen, rather than the woman herself. Her shoulders were set firmly, defiantly. And when she inclined her chin, the shadows made her cheeks seem nearly hollow. Her voice was thick and commanding as she asked, "Your names?"

Renwyn puffed his chest arrogantly, grinning as he answered, "My name is Renwyn Peter Herbert of House Strangelove, Your Grace."

With far more deference and humility, Ollie bowed his head and spoke evenly, "My name is Oliver Linus of House Dangerfield, Your Grace."

The queen's head tipped forward; shadows stretched beneath her burning,blue eyes. She swept her gaze over the boys with feral appraisal. "Renwyn of House Strangelove, Oliver of House Dangerfield, are you ready and willing to bear arms for Crown, king, and country?"

Renwyn nodded enthusiastically, assuring, "Yes, Your Grace."

But Ollie remained quiet for a moment, truly taking in the words. He hesitated and then answered, "Yes, Your Grace."

Ursalyn continued with her customary queries, all the while watching the two boys below with the interest of an owl watching mice fidget over the forest floor. Her lips quirked upward at the readiness of their voices. She drummed her fingers over the stony banister, idly waiting for the lord paramount to call for the match's start. When Maekon Malcourt's voice boomed, ushering the boys into action, Ursalyn relaxed into the ease of watching the bout.

Ollie wasn't quite prepared for the viciousness with which Renwyn pro-ceeded. As such, he could do little more than raise his shield as firmly as he could, as the blunted edge of Renwyn's sword smashed against the shield's wooden face.

Renwyn swung with the same mindless brute force that Noel warned him about time and time again. Noel's dissuasion from this method was apparently lost on Renwyn, or consciously discarded in the heat of the mo-ment, for he went on clobbering Ollie's shield with bone-breaking force. He swung, the dull edge striking over and over and over again. The wood was beginning to splinter where he kept clattering his sword.

There was a wild look in Renwyn's eyes.
Ollie kept his shield raised, bracing himself for each swing. The shock of every blow lanced up his arm, shaking his shoulder. He knew Renwyn was stronger and faster than he could hope to be. But Ollie took comfort in the understanding that his opponent was arrogant and brash, as well. And though he knew well that he was outclassed in terms of strength, he also knew he was more stalwart in build. Armed with that knowledge, he hunkered down; he drove his heels into the dirt and allowed Renwyn to keep smashing away at his defense.

Gradually, Renwyn's swings began to slow down. They remained as strong as before, but they struck with the rhythmic pattern of a drum, beat-ing along steadily rather than the erratic lightning-like strikes he'd managed earlier in the bout.

Ollie smirked. He saw sweat trickling down Renwyn's face; his hair was dampened, and shirt soaked through. The heat and effort and constant bar-rage of attacks were wearing him down, whittling away at him. Slowly, but ever so obviously, Renwyn was growing tired.

When a heavy strike smashed into Ollie's shield, he pressed forward. Having not expected Ollie to move the shield, Renwyn was taken off guard and stumbled back a step, reeling his sword back with him. And Ollie struck. The dull edge came from the side and caught Renwyn under his right arm, slicing bodily against his ribs.

Renwyn hissed at the sudden slash of pain that bruised his flank. He lowered his arm protectively to shield himself from further assault. He doubled over, gasping for breath. His eyes went wide, attention averting from his target and falling to the ground as he caught his breath.

Ollie saw the opportunity and swung again. Renwyn's was shield down, his sword's tip braced against the dirt. Ollie slung down his sword and caught Renwyn hard in the shoulder. Stunned by his own success, the stalwart boy watched as Renwyn toppled to his side.

Ollie took a step back, cautiously watching as the other boy struggled to catch his breath. Renwyn was now sprawled in the dirt, his shield cast to the side, forgotten. The crowd cheered, applauding Ollie's tactic of letting your overzealous opponent wear himself out.

Renwyn, amidst the wild cheering of the crowd, pushed himself up unsteadily, still coughing. He turned raging eyes toward Ollie, narrowing them predatorily. It didn't matter to him that he no longer held his shield. By his summation of the situation, he wouldn't need it. He tightened his hold around his sword's hilt, and with one final, shuddering breath, bolted forward toward Ollie. He knew he'd caught the other by surprised when Ollie's eyes went wide as saucers. Ollie was too slow in raising his shield. Renwyn was upon him, pushing the shield aside, throwing Ollie to the ground.

Astride his now-unarmed opponent's chest, Renwyn punched his left fist across Ollie's cheek. The boy's round head snapped to the side. Tears instantly sprung into his eyes. Salty trails slid over his curved features and splattered to the dirt ground pillowing his face. Renwyn raised his sword slowly, ever so maliciously setting the edge against Ollie's exposed throat. His left hand curled in Ollie's shirt, holding him tightly, pressing him harder against the ground.

Renwyn's voice was dark as he whispered, "You didn't really think you would win, did you?"

The lord paramount called for an end to the match, declaring Renwyn the victor.

As Renwyn rose from atop Ollie's chest, he cast down one last, heated glare before stalking off. Ollie watched, tears still pooling in his eyes. He brushed them away and stood.

By the time he'd made his way down the stairs, he'd managed to wipe away all traces of the tears that had streaked his cheeks only moments before. And when Fynn rushed over, worry in his eyes as he assessed his friend, Ollie did his best to smile. "I didn't manage to get him in his big head," he said quietly. He shrugged, smiling all of a sudden. "I did get him in the ribs, though."

"Did you really?" asked Fynn, grinning from ear to ear.

Ollie nodded. "He toppled right over."

The prince clapped Ollie on the back. "That a boy, Ollie. Well done."

The boy couldn't help but well with pride at the prince's acknowledgement. There was something about Fynn's easy nature and calming presence that made Ollie want to please him, want to be acknowledged by him. He beamed under Fynn's attention and, after a moment's consideration, said, "Your match should be coming up. You're one of the last to fight in the first round."

The prince wore a lopsided grin as he laughed, absentmindedly tracing his hand over his chest. "I suppose that's a good thing. Gave me some extra time to recover all the way."

Ollie shook his head. "It's weird, you know. You got stabbed in the chest and a few days later…? Well, look at you. You're fine."

"A little sore," Fynn amended. "But yes, I'm fine."

The clopping of footsteps down the stairs stole away Fynn's attention, though he knew for certain, simply by the sound, that it wasn't Moriah returning to their chilly chamber. He turned to see Benadykt stepping into the room. The man seemed tired, scowling as he waded through the throng of children.

"Right," Benadykt began, "the next match will be Ransom and Fynn. Come on, then. Let's not keep *Her Grace* waiting."

As Ransom headed toward the stairs, Ollie caught Fynn's wrist, offering the prince the warmest of smiles. "Try not to kill him," beseeched Ollie with a light smile that broke through the myriad of bruises blemishing his face.

Fynn couldn't help but laugh as he answered with a sly wink, slinking away from Ollie off toward the stairs. He called back, "I make no promises."

And, so it was, that Fynn and Ransom ascended from the shadowy chamber up into the light of the afternoon. As the pair of combatants approached the center of the arena, Ransom leered down at Fynn. He whispered, "You won't last ten minutes."

Carelessly, Fynn shrugged, not bothering to look up at Ransom. He kept his voice leveled and flat, managing to lace his words with the same dripping boredom that often accompanied Moriah's speech. "I won't *need* ten minutes."

Ursalyn was perched at the edge of the pulpit, elbows braced over the banister as she regarded the boys below. She arched a brow upon seeing her nephew. He'd grown. That much was for certain. Alas, he was still much smaller than his opponent. Ursalyn smirked as she watched the black-haired prince. He looked tired and worn, his skin paler than usual; dark circles ringed his ghostly eyes. But he stood with his shoulders squared, back straight, and head tilted just to the side with an almost familiar feline listlessness. When his icy eyes flicked in her direction - the sunlight bursting in the near colorless depths of his irises - Ursalyn couldn't help but grin.

The queen drew herself to her full height. The tilt of her chin and slant of her eyes, as she looked down upon them from on high, caught the sun over her brow, casting long, talon-like shadows from her eyes down her cheeks. She spoke, "Your names."

Ransom lifted his chin, an arrogant smile crept over his expression. "My name is Ransom George of House Blackthorn, Your Grace."

The prince shrugged off the conceit of his opponent, maintaining an even, albeit amused sounding, tone as he answered his aunt. "My name is Fynneas Draekon of House Fog, Your Grace."

Odette was once more at the queen's side, a spark of interest igniting in her emerald eyes. She whispered, "This should be interesting to watch."

"I didn't doubt that for a moment." Ursalyn nodded. Her voice rose as she once more addressed the competitors. "Ransom of House Blackthorn, Fynneas of House Fog, are you ready and willing to bear arms for Crown, king, and country?"

"Yes, Your Grace," the pair replied.

"And are you ready and willing to spill blood, both your own and that of your enemies, those who would oppose your Crown, king, and country?" There was no hesitation from Fynn. "Yes, Your Grace." He smiled; an easiness befell him. As Ransom replied the same, Fynn couldn't help but ignore the other boy. There was no simpler question for him. He knew. He knew with everything he had, that he would bleed for his people, for his friends, for his family. And so, his smile broadened. He'd already bled for them and he would gladly do it again.

The lord paramount called for the match to begin.

Ransom turned toward Fynn, a haughty look of excitement about his person as he drew up his sword, levering it in the prince's direction; the dull-sharp of the tip glittered in the sunlight. He held up his shield, drawing it across his body. Peeking over the brim, he spied the prince drawing his own sword. He scowled. "I thought you were left-handed?"

Fynn, sword in his right hand, laughed. "Oh, I am." He looked down at the sword and shrugged. "I figured it wouldn't be much of a fight if I used my left."

"Arrogant ass," grumbled Ransom.

Ransom lunged forward, brandishing his sword. He was faster and more precise than Fynn would have thought him. His sword clanged over Fynn's shield once, twice, and then a third time before the prince knew what had hit him. Smirking, Ransom proceeded with his relentless assault. He beat his sword into Fynn's shield over and over, bearing down his weight upon the smaller boy with every swing, every thudding blow. He swung again, feigning another foray into Fynn's shield, and then angled his sword so as to catch the prince's unprotected flank.

Had Fynn been slower, he would have found himself toppled over on the ground, gasping for air. Alas, the familiar slowness of battle kept Fynn calm for the time being. Thus, he easily saw Ransom's maneuver, side stepping and parrying the blow with little difficulty. Watching as his own blade caught Ransom's, Fynn chuckled under his breath at the wide-eyed confusion displayed upon the other's countenance - the sort of surprised indignation that abounds when one is so thoroughly thwarted.

However, Fynn was reminded quickly of his own struggle when his sword was forced to the side, leaving his chest open. He'd practiced a great deal with his right hand during the time Hollyn was forced to use his left, but he'd never quite mastered swordsmanship with his weaker arm. His co-ordination, though better than most, was not as refined when he used his right, his grip not as strong, his aim not as strikingly precise.

Ransom was able to easily push Fynn's defense to the side and, in doing so, seized the opportunity to drive his blade forward. The blunted end beat into Fynn's right shoulder, just under the collar bone, with bruising force.

Grimacing, Fynn took a quick step back to steady himself. He'd all but forgotten about his shield. It hadn't quite occurred to him to draw it up and prevent the painful blow. So, without a second thought, Fynn tossed it aside. He heard the alarmed and rightfully confused whispers fluttering through the crowded stands. Disregarding them, he rolled his left shoulder, happy to be free of the shield's weight.

"Is this some sort of trick?" asked Ransom.

"No."

It was Fynn's turn to foray with unbridled enthusiasm. Free of the cumbersome shield, the prince was more at home in the arena, more at ease in the fray. He swung, playfully smashing his sword into Ransom's shield over and over, delighting in the frustrated harrumphs coming from the other boy with every strike, with every deafening bang of dull steel against wood. Much lighter on his feet now, Fynn spun around in that graceless sort of way that was so quintessentially him; he stunned Ransom into a stand-still. The prince's sword careened into the other boy's shoulder, sending him howling as he fell to his knees.

Fynn made no move to attack again. Rather, he lazily circled Ransom as the other boy growled, standing painfully to his feet, his left arm clearly paining him. The prince arched a black brow, mocking cheerily, "If you're going to bother with using your shield, you may want to actually *use* it."

Ransom rolled his eyes, grinding his teeth as he stood and turned to face Fynn. "Funny," he spat.

They were at it once more. Fynn ran toward Ransom with inhuman speed, advancing on the boy in a flash. Their swords struck through the afternoon air, tearing the warm breeze asunder with a violent clash; steel screamed as it slid over rival steel. Withdrawing slightly, allowing Ransom to stumble forward off balance, Fynn reeled back and swung into Ransom's shield again. He heard the faint sounds of the wood splintering under the pressure, the shield weakening. He grinned. Pulling his sword back, he once more drove the dull edge against the wood. Over and over again, he swung. Ransom did his best to keep his guard up, wincing as the shield began pressing into his arm uncomfortably under the blinding force of each blow.

Fynn swung again. Ransom's sword rose to meet the flurry, catching the edge against his own, halting the prince's attack before it could truly begin. Raising himself to his full height, Ransom leaned over his sword arm, forcing his superior weight against the blade, pushing Fynn back inch by inch.

"Not so strong now, are you?" he taunted. He continued edging the prince backward.

Unable to physically overpower Ransom, Fynn scowled. Ransom kept his shield pressed close to his body, protecting his flank and chest as he pressed forward. Fynn's eyes narrowed as a cunning smirk tugged at his lips. He allowed Ransom to lever his weight and when it seemed as though the boy would force Fynn's sword aside, Fynn pulled back. He drew his left arm back, fingers coiling into a white-knuckled fist, and he swung. His fist collided with the other's shield, ripping through it. The wood splintered into a thousand, little pieces.

Ransom's eyes went impossibly wide when Fynn's arm impaled through the shield. The prince's fist slammed into Ransom's chest with unprecedented force, knocking him back and to the ground. He laid, prostrate against the sand of the arena, shield long forgotten, gasping for air. His chest stung wickedly at the point of impact. Ransom forced himself to sit up, holding his weight upon his forearms. Sweat slipped down his temples. He shook when he saw it, the sight of Fynn looming over him, left arm bloodied from the splinters protruding from his skin. Looking to the side, Ransom was both astounded and frightened to his very core to see his shield lying discarded in smithereens.

"What…how?" stammered Ransom, too fearful of the boy standing over him to bring himself to move. "*How?*"

Fynn stalked closer until he stood at Ransom's feet, his shadow reaching over the fallen boy. He glanced down to his left hand; an annoyed frown tilted his lips when he saw the red rivulets tracking along the ridges of his knuckles and the tears in his black shirt. His ghostly eyes turned back to Ransom, blazing as a strange cacophony of colors swirled within the grey pools, like two rainbows caught in the ice. Fynn shrugged and said, "Told you I wouldn't need ten minutes."

In an instant, Ransom watched as all traces of arrogance fell away from his opponent, leaving in its wake nothing more than a genuine grin and amused expression. As the prince reached down, offering his hand, Ransom sighed. He didn't need to hear the lord paramount call out the victor; he already knew. He took the proffered hand and was helped to his feet.

"I don't know how you did it," Ransom began, "but that was impressive."

From up in the pulpit, Ridley smirked. He stared down at the golden sands of the arena, intently focusing on the speckles of red that littered the ground. "Well, that was *interesting*."

As the crowds leapt to their feet, clapping furiously and yelling their excitement, Fynn and Ransom stepped down the stairwell, descending into the chamber beneath the amphitheater. The sounds of cheering and clapping faded away as they folded back into the waiting embrace of their school

698

mates. The throng of Morancy students huddled around the two, instantly focusing on the strange pattern of cuts lacing their way up from Fynn's knuckles to his elbow.

Hollyn waded through the group of children and came up to stand before Fynn. Gingerly, he took his cousin's hand in his and examined the splinters that still stuck out from the alabaster skin. Shaking his head, he suggested, "You may want to pull those out."

"Right." Fynn didn't pull his hand away. He relented, easily enough, to Hollyn's careful examination. "Looks worse than it feels."

"You always say that," muttered Hollyn, as he oh-so-carefully plucked a small piece of wood from Fynn's knuckles.

"It's true," grumbled Fynn, wincing as Hollyn pulled another splinter from his skin.

Rolling his blue eyes, Hollyn groused, "*Right*, I'm sure."

Ceral clapped Ransom over the back, placating the boy as he bemoaned his defeat. The second-years enveloped their bested year mate with words of condolences, some of them light-heartedly disparaging Ransom for his losing performance. They made their way deeper into the chamber, leaving the first-years to clamber around the princes.

Hollyn was still gently plucking the protruding wood from Fynn's arm when Lux found her way to Fynn's side. She furrowed her brow as she looked at the assortment of bruises and scrapes muddling his pale limb. The black material of his shirt was stripped away in places. Softly, her hand curled around his shoulder, steadying his arm as Hollyn continued his careful tending. "Ransom said something about you punching *through* his shield?" she mentioned.

"Is that how you got these splinters?" Hollyn gaped.

Fynn nodded.

"You just went and *punched* through it?" Godryk snorted amusedly. "Why am I even asking? *Of course*, you did."

"Worked, didn't it?" Fynn huffed.

Lux laughed quietly. "Well, you won, if that's what you mean." She reached out, ghosting her fingertips over one of the bruises blooming over his wrist. "But maybe, next time, try winning in a less self-destructive manner?"

"I'll see what I can do." Fynn smirked.

A smudge of black in the rafters and the familiar sound of wings fluttering drew Fynn's attention upward. He saw there, hanging upside down and cloaked in silken wings, the fuzzy form of a particular bat. Inky black eyes stared back at Fynn, a charming light to them.

"Buttons." Fynn smiled as the bat fell from the rafters, lifted up on fragile wings, and swooped over to him. He perched upon Fynn's back, wings coming around the prince's shoulders like a strange, fluttering scarf. Ignoring the slight sting of pain as Hollyn proceeded wiggling the wood from the gauges in his knuckles, Fynn reached up with his free hand and stroked Buttons' nose, trailing between his ears, scratching gently at his shoulders. "What're you doing here?"

Buttons chattered; hot breath tickled the nape of Fynn's neck.

"Well, I'm glad you're here," Fynn chortled cheerily. "Stay for a while, won't you?"

The bat held tighter to Fynn's shoulders, nose pressed against his neck. Fynn smiled.

Tulip and Georgie were the next to be called for their bout. Shoulder to slender shoulder, the two girls made their way into the arena.

Ursalyn was nearly draped over the pulpit's bannister, physically wilting in the tropical heat. Slick sweat rolled down her face, glistening just over her lips. The heat darkened her eyes. She regarded the two girls with mild interest, amused by the slight tremble in Georgie's gait. Her voice was tired and heavy when she commanded, "Your names."

The second-year spoke first. "My name is Tulip Fairheart of House Malcourt, Your Grace."

The younger girl said, "My name is Georgina Marina of House Belclaire, Your Grace."

Before Ursalyn could find her next words, she turned around at the feeling of someone approaching. She didn't need to look to know who it was, but when her eyes fell over Moriah's person as he came nearer, she couldn't arrest the knowing smile that curled her deep, red lips. She whispered, "Moriah."

Moriah neared Ursalyn, ignoring the stagnating malice permeating his father's watchful, blue eyes. He didn't bother to cast a glance toward Vance, knowing well that his father's attention was firmly fixed upon them. At Ursalyn's side, Moriah's head dipped lower, his breath brushed by her ear as he stated, "Something isn't right here."

Ursalyn inquired, "What's wrong?"

Darkness lurked in Moriah's eyes as he looked at Ursalyn. His voice was low when he said, "I don't know. But I don't trust whatever it is."

"Is that why you disappeared?" Ursalyn asked. "Is something *bad* going to happen?"

Moriah nodded slowly. "Yes, I believe so. Be ready."

"And you?"

"I'll be close by." A humorless smirk curled his lips as he continued, "Like I always am."

For just a moment, Ursalyn's fingertips swept over Moriah's arm. She felt the tension that pulled at him. "Promise?"

Moriah's voice was like a purr as he whispered, "I'll always come for you when you need me, you *and* the boys…and yes, even Fiona. Nothing will happen to *any* of you as long as I'm here, as long as I yet breathe."

"Dramatic as always," Ursalyn softly jested.

"Would you have me any other way?"

"Never."

Moriah turned to take his leave but stopped at the feeling of fingers curling around his wrist. He glanced down to the pale hand that held tightly to him, the familiar touch not unwelcome in such a troubling moment. "Do you require anything more, Your Grace?"

"Whatever is going on, don't get yourself killed," Ursalyn commanded with all the force of a pained plea.

"What? And leave you?" Moriah's cat-like eyes were alight. "You can't get rid of me so easily."

36

RAISE THE DRAGON

The afternoon waned into evening. The golden glow of the day died steadily into a pale reflection of what it had been hours before, petering away into a dull and heavy blue. The second round had started and, presently, Fynn bounded across the arena, kicking up dirt beneath graceless footsteps as he launched toward Renwyn. He'd gotten his wish. He was definitely sure that Moriah had found a way to pair the two of them together. He swung his sword harshly, smashing it with reckless abandon against the wood of Renwyn's shield, delighting in the distinct sound of splintering wood caving beneath the force of his strike.

Renwyn shuddered under the pressure; his shield visibly trembled just beneath the smarting strength of the blade's dull edge. It groaned under the weight, dipping inward, allowing Fynn more purchase to bury the blade deeper, piercing through the wood.

Renwyn could do nothing to stop Fynn from reeling his arm back and smashing his sword pointedly into the cracking shield. His eyes went wide as he watched Fynn bust through the shield with frightening ease. It was a sort of fright he was unaccustomed to and it jolted through him as a thousand splinters burst around his arm, shattering apart, leaving him vulnerable.

Not one to hesitate, Fynn surged by the battered, broken shield and jammed his sword over Renwyn's shoulder, sending the other boy falling to the ground with a pained yelp. Before Renwyn had time to gather himself back up, Fynn pounced; his sword and shield discarded, he flung himself down over Renwyn's bruised body. His fist unceremoniously collided with Renwyn's jaw, snapping the fallen boy's head to the side. As Fynn pulled his fist back, ready to strike what he hoped to be the final blow of the bout, Renwyn jerked suddenly from beneath him, sending him sailing to the side in a twist of lanky limbs.

"Like I'd make it that easy." Renwyn scowled, swiping at the blood trickling from the corner of his mouth. He clambered back to his feet, intent on pinning Fynn while the prince was still down. But as he lurched forward, his own sword thrown heedlessly to the ground, Fynn jumped back to his feet in a flurry of motion. "Damn," Renwyn muttered.

And so, bereft of their swords and shields, the boys grappled with one another in a fierce deadlock, teeth bared as they locked arms, each struggling to gain the upper hand. Renwyn leaned over Fynn, looming imposingly as he pushed his superior weight forward against the prince.

From his position, Fynn shouldered the weight, leveraging it as he rolled his shoulders; he hunched forward and pulled to the side, sending Renwyn hurling over him and back to the ground with a satisfying groan.

With that, Fynn once more threw himself down over the other boy. Disregarding anything akin to strategy, Fynn settled for mindlessly swinging his fists down upon his opponent, launching a storm of bloodied knuckles over Renwyn's already swollen face. He felt the boy gasping for breath beneath him; the rattling of his chest shook Fynn's legs. The sound of wheezing and the scent of blood mingling with spit, as they both cascaded freely from Renwyn's mouth, overtook Fynn with such intemperance that he felt his thoughts swimming in a sea of sensation, completely overwhelmed by it all.

There'd been moments before, Fynn recognized, where he felt a strange sense of displacement stemming from the unnatural glee overtaking him at the prospect of physically wounding his opponent. But, presently, it was something he wasn't sure he'd be able to temper back down. The prince's blood had reached a violent simmer as it bubbled just beneath his snowy skin. He fleetingly thought that his blood actually may boil and melt away the alabaster sheath that kept it from spilling over.

Fynn's fist smashed against Renwyn's face once more, breaking his nose.

Renwyn saw colors - all sorts of colors - as his vision began to blur. Spying Fynn reeling back for another strike, Renwyn forced himself to buck upward. He snapped his head forward; his forehead collided with Fynn's with enough force to throw the prince off his perch. As Fynn laid sprawled against the dirt, Renwyn seized the moment to draw in frantic, shaking breaths; he coughed up blood over his own shirt and the sand of the arena.

The dull thudding that sounded in Fynn's head didn't calm the roiling feeling that clawed at him from the inside, tore at him from just beneath the skin - shaking his bones, coiling his muscles. It was a distraction, however, and he chose to utilize it. As best he could, Fynn focused on the dull ache that emanated from the bruise that now blossomed between his eyebrows. It was faint and paled in comparison to injuries he'd sustained before, but it was there, and it kept him from focusing on the concerning desire to beat Renwyn senseless.

He steadied himself, forcing the erratic jumping of his thoughts to cease, furling them back together, pushing down the feral bloodlust that scratched at the gates of his consciousness. Fynn's breathing calmed and evened out; no longer were his shoulders quaking and chest heaving with the effort of inhalation. He watched with a sort of detached interest, the kind a fox would project when watching a wounded rabbit trying to limp to safety, as Renwyn drew himself back up to his feet.

Fynn stood easily enough, unencumbered by any debilitating injuries. The same could not be said for his opponent, whose face was swollen nearly beyond recognition. Renwyn's left eye closed under the throbbing bubble of a bruise that had arisen just at the crest of his cheek.

"You want to take a break? Maybe sit down, get your bearings back?" asked Fynn with a smirk twisting his lips. "I don't mind, really."

"Not on your life," Renwyn snapped.

He snatched Fynn by the collar of his shirt quicker than either of them had thought possible. He threw the prince down hard, smiling when the smaller boy gasped, the air knocked straight out of his lungs. Without hesitation, Renwyn kicked his booted toe into Fynn's ribs, eliciting a surprised whimper as the prince curled in on himself, arms reaching around his middle to protect his injured side. Frightening grey eyes turned upward, catching Renwyn's. Undeterred, Renwyn swung another kick into Fynn's ribs. Then, for the briefest of moments, he thought he saw the prince's eyes flash a most menacing shade of red.

Looming over the boy prince haughtily, Renwyn asked, "You sure you don't want to take a break, Fynneas? Looks like you may need one."

Fynn rolled onto his back, catching his breath. His side stung. That was certain enough. But it wasn't the sort of pain that would keep him down. With labored breaths, Fynn drew himself back up to his feet. Two steps into his charge, he stopped suddenly at the sight of something catching the light of the sun unnaturally, a shine emanating from above. His head snapped upward in search of the strange glinting. He arched a brow and cocked his head, eyes narrowed in their search.

"Did you see something just then?" he asked shakily.

"I'm not playing this game with you," Renwyn barked, proceeding forward. He caught hold of the prince and threw him to the ground.

Fynn didn't fight back. He fell against the sand and remained there as he turned, searching for the light that had distracted him. Again, there was a glare that he thought oddly displaced. "There! You didn't see it?"

Noticing that Fynn was making no attempt to fight back or put up any sort of defense, Renwyn considered the boy's strategy for a moment. Then, reluctantly, he angled his head to the side. He searched for anything out of place. "No." He shrugged. "I don't see anything odd."

"Something's wrong," Fynn muttered under his breath. "*Very* wrong. I can feel it in my bones."

A metallic glimmer broke through the pale gold of the arena. An archer stood atop the pulpit. He wore a mask and chainmail and a cloak of deep red. Time stopped for Fynn. Everything slowed until nothing was left. The man drew up his bow and strung his arrow. Fynn's breathing hitched in his chest. He shook his head back and forth emphatically. "This can't be happening," he rasped.

The sound of the arrow as it burst from the string was like a thousand wolves howling. Yet the sound it made as it broke skin, buried in the white column of Fynn's throat, was nothing more than the sound of a plucked harp, a gentle wisp of a noise that was drowned out by the ensuing screams of horror and the rush of madness that descended upon the amphitheater.

As Fynn's body went limp, time slowed to a blur. The colors of his surroundings rushed by him at all angles until his head struck the ground and his eyes went wide, desperate to focus but finding nothing but smudges; a cacophony of noisy colors bled together into a muddled mess that didn't make sense, one that he couldn't recognize as anything more than a puddle of shades splashing by his eyes.

Fynn heard Ursalyn's scream; it rang out louder than anyone else's. Maybe it didn't, he supposed. Maybe it was just the only one he recognized. But it sounded like a steady ringing that chimed over the maelstrom. Heels thudded against stone as people rushed to flee the stadium, pushing by one another, women wailing and men yelling.

He felt warm. He heard the all-too-familiar sound of fire crackling. Then the explosion that ensued - all consuming - drowned out all other noises, all other distractions. Stone shattered and rained down from the rows of seats, showering over the arena floor, falling all around Fynn. Dirt spewed into the air and danced with the smoke that welled from the flames as they tore through the many winding corridors of the ancient amphitheater. Embers blinked into existence, lilting on the heated winds like fireflies in the fields, sparking here and there before burning out of existence, out of sight. And then, once again, Fynn was left with a sea of distorted colors and shapes and nothing more.

The tangy taste of blood pooled in Fynn's mouth. He coughed, feeling the sprinkle of something warm spray over his lips and chin; it dribbled down onto his chest. The same sickly warmth spread from his neck, dripping over his shoulder, dampening the dirt beneath him. He reached a shaking hand toward his neck, pressing down where the arrow still protruded in some vain attempt to staunch the bleeding. He was failing—not to his surprise.

Someone was running toward him, yelling his name. The voice was joined by another. They drifted in and out, twisting together, merging so elegantly that Fynn wasn't sure if there were actually two voices at all. It didn't matter much. The sound of his name was little more than further fodder for the chaos abounding, joining the terror-stricken screams and the persistent sizzling of the fire. Fynn gurgled the blood welling in his throat, coughing; it spilled over his lips. Everything was slipping away. He thought that this must've been what it was like for his father, what those final moments lying on the cobblestoned street were like. He was draining away moment by moment, second by second, until there was nothing left but the cold and the numbness.

And then the blackness.

Fynn was drowning in the blackness again and he took to it with the welcomed ease of a child nestling in his mother's arms, safe and secure in the knowledge that no harm would come while tucked away there. He sank deeper and deeper. It was so dark that there was no surface to the sea of nothing that rushed around him. Fynn laughed humorlessly, figuring that there never was a surface. No, a surface would denote the partition between the sea of blackness that led into the belly of the abyss and the brink whereupon he walked so many times before this past year. But now there was nothing like that, no division between walking upon the precipice of oblivion and oblivion itself; the endless void was all-consuming and all-ensnaring as it pulled him deeper and deeper into the depths, into the pit of blackness itself where there was nothing.

But Fynn didn't mind. He thought back to what he'd said to Darwyn. A light came to his tired, grey eyes at the thought. He found himself imagining what the place beyond the blackness might be like, a place where everyone you'd loved and lost waited for you, where time meant nothing and you could just spend every moment of your own personal eternity in the company of those who adored you, who loved you without inhibition, ceaselessly and unfathomably. He thought that sounded nice. And as he sank away further and further down, nearing what he expected would be the point where he'd find his way to paradise, he hoped that Darwyn had found such a peace.

Fynn's eyes closed serenely.

There was no pain. There was no sadness. There was simply that unrelenting realness of existing in a place beyond and between places where nothing could touch you, harm you, make you bleed. There was simply the sublime realness of existing in a moment displaced from all other things. He sank further and further down with little care to the matter, little bitterness about his life not yet fully lived.

The silence was tranquil and rocked him like a child. He was lulled into the calm. He tried to recall what he'd heard before he'd slipped away, what the voices yelling his named had sounded like, who they belonged to. But he couldn't place them. It was as if his memory was fading away like sand swept from the shore by an unyielding tide, constantly ebbing over the beach, heedless to the grains it pulled away with every brush of its sprawling, tidal snatch.

When he opened his eyes, he saw not the vast blackness he'd expected, but an unending expanse of snow. Something cold was beneath his palms. A winter wind bit at his nose. Blinking, eyes adjusting to the light, he sat up. The clouds seemed close enough to touch. Straining his neck, he peered to the side and realized, in a moment, he was laid across the battlements of a castle made of pale stone.

He rose to his feet, mindful not to slip on the ice that sheathed the cracking-stone surface. The clouds were heavy and grey. Winter frost snapped at the wind as it blew by; flurries of white were in every direction, disappearing into the snow that stretched across the land. The storm melded with the horizon to create a tableau that seemed eternal.

Fynn looked outward, stretching his sights through the snowstorm. His booted feet nearly hung over the edge of the battlements. He didn't mind heights; the thought of falling was never really one of his fears. As he looked out across the landscape, the snow ceased falling and the wind relented in its frozen scratching. The grey clouds huddled together and darkened until there was nothing left of the sky but a vast expanse of blackness, much like, he thought, the place from which he'd awoken.

His head was turned skyward, watching the darkness overthrow the tempest, leaving nothing but a terrifying void overhead. He hadn't heard the footsteps of someone approaching. But when he turned back to look out from the battlements, he saw Celestine standing up upon the same tower, staring thoughtfully out toward the horizon. Without a word to his mother, Fynn turned his attention toward the land stretched out before him.

With the snow no longer falling, he could see all of the great castles of Estheria looming in the distance. He saw them frozen over with frost that clung to their ancient stone, spires of glimmering ice blocks stretched taller than the tallest tower. Everything shone with a sort of splendid brilliance Fynn couldn't bring to words. The light that came from nowhere, born from the nothingness all around, reflected off the ice until a million rainbows burst all around them. But it was a brilliance sired by impermanence, tainted by the knowledge that the ice, and the cruel winter from which it was born, brought with it naught but death and pain and desolation.

The more Fynn looked out upon the desolate landscape, the more he watched the castles of Estheria crumble beneath the weight of the ice, the more despondent he found himself becoming. Far off, amidst the castles of House Astor and House Belclaire, he could see Morancy rising from the snow. It seemed so incongruous to what he knew it to be; the dark stone was overwrought by creeping tendrils of ice that slipped through every crack, burrowed deep into the castle's bowels. The frost brought it down from the inside like a frozen infection.

The sight of Morancy toppling into the snow, lost to the winter, wounded him in a way he wasn't quite sure he understood. The pain permeated from deep within. So much so, that a silver tear fell from Fynn's cheek and landed as a flurry of snow upon the battlement that served as his altar. In that moment, he knew he could not bear to watch anything else fall apart.

He recalled what Minnie said about feeling fire as though it were your blood rushing in your veins. He leaned forward on his tiptoes and drew in a deep breath. He felt the air in his lungs and the blood pumping through his heart, circulating through each limb and then back again. And he imagined the fire.

Fynn let loose a breath and inwardly marveled as the air expelled from his lungs erupted from his lips and burned into fire as it streamed out, crackling madly in the air as it eased through the chill, melting away the ice. The blackness seeped away from the sky and the clouds returned; the snow turned to grass, and the spires of ice were replaced by trees and vines and lush greenness as far as he could see. Triumphantly, Fynn leaned back, appraising his work, grinning.

Celestine turned to him then, as if seeing him there for the first time. She regarded him with pale eyes alive with wonderment. She stepped down from the battlement and drew closer to Fynn until she stood before him, looking up at him with marvel in her expression. Her hand reached out tentatively, fingers shaking.

Fynn lowered his head, hunching forward.

Celestine's hand cupped his cheek. Her thumb traced over the curve of his face. She smiled up at him.

Another tear fell down his face and, this time, she was there to wipe it away.

"So beautiful," she whispered.

Shadows fell upon them, stretching from side to side, covering them in a pale greyness. Curiously, Fynn withdrew from his mother's touch and straightened. Still towering over her, standing upon the battlements, he looked down confusedly. He watched the shadows stretch further and further. He craned his neck to the side and there spied the source; large wings, looking quite similar to Buttons' in a way, stretched from his shoulders. Ever so carefully, Fynn raised his hand and let his fingertips trace over the scaled skin he felt protruding from his back. Intently, he studied the wings that seemed to be his own. They were black as a starless night.

"I've got wings?" he muttered, still letting his hand rove the surface of the new addition to his shoulder-span.

Celestine didn't seem bothered in the least by this new revelation. Rather, her own icy eyes traveled from wing to wing, admiring the sharp angles and blackness of the scales, before returning to look into eyes that were so like her own. "I've never seen a dragon before," she whispered. She edged just a little closer, her hand still outstretched to Fynn.

Once more, Fynn lowered his head to his mother's hand, letting her trace over his features with awed reverence. But when he focused upon her eyes, he saw therein reflected not his own face, but the long nose of a dragon he'd seen before. He saw in her eyes, as clearly as if he were looking into twin mirrors, Draekon staring back at him.

The revelation didn't startle him; he didn't pull away from her touch. Rather, he leaned in further, letting his face rest in the curve of her palm. He breathed gently through his mouth and saw embers spring from his parted lips; they were stolen into the wind and then blinked out of sight.

"Do you have a name?"

Without a moment's thought, Fynn whispered, "Draekon."

"Draekon," repeated Celestine thoughtfully. She seemed to consider him for a moment longer before continuing, "I think you've come to me for a reason." Her left hand curled over her stomach, eyes lowering to stare down upon the hand that draped across her middle. "Rather, I think you've come to *him* for a reason."

Fynn felt her touch soften against his cheek and he smiled.

Celestine continued. "Protect him, won't you? I won't be around to protect him myself," she admitted tearfully. "I won't be around for much longer at all. But please…when he's here…when things become too much for him, when he's not strong enough on his own…protect him."

"I will," Fynn whispered.

"Thank you."

Her alabaster hand slipped from his cheek and he watched on sadly as his mother fell away into a cloud of smoke, vanishing right before his eyes. And then he stood alone at the top of a tower, staring out at a renewed Estheria, where the ancient castles of legends still stood proudly, unbroken by a malicious winter. Looking up, he no longer saw the vastness of wings stretched out from his shoulders. The shadows were gone. He stood, now, in the light of a warm day.

Fynn drew in a deep, steady breath. He inched forward. His toes hung over the edge. Fynn held his arms aloft and with one last, deep breath, he stepped over the edge and began to fall. He had always thought that jumping off a tower would be quick, that you'd be at the top one moment and then splattered across the ground in a mess of blood and gore the next. He never suspected that falling would be such a drawn-out affair, that you'd feel each fragment of air like sand, abrasively scraping by. He never thought you'd have the time to admire the blueness of the sky overhead, to inspect the cracks of the tower's stones as they slinked by. He never thought you'd have time to smell each individual flower that sprouted in the garden, or to recognize the scent of bread being pulled from the ovens in the kitchens. But there he was, falling ever so slowly, plummeting like a feather gliding on a breeze.

When the impact came, when his back struck the hard earth with the sort of force that should shatter his spine, his eyes went wide, and he gasped. He could taste something tangy wash over his tongue, something warm splatter over his lips, something ghastly dribble from his chin. The colors all around fell away like paint melting from a mural, blurring together until the brilliant hues of the summer he'd found there atop the battlements gave way to the bursting reds and vibrant golds of sand and fire and he knew he'd woken up.

Blood still spilled from his lips all over his chin, his chest. Red oozed from his neck. He couldn't breathe. But his heart beat in his chest, hammering away with desperate intentions. He knew he was alive. He wasn't sure what had happened, but in that very moment, he could feel the life pour back into him. The warmth of the burning amphitheater lapped at him, the flames tickling him with the promise to burn as they encroached upon him more so.

Hands were upon his shoulders, holding him steady. Another set of hands were braced over his neck, staunching the blood flow. Blearily, he looked through the heated hues and blinked away the stinging sensation born from the towers of billowing smoke, and he saw two familiar and quite welcomed faces looking down at him.

Tears freely poured over Lux's freckled and bruised cheeks. She was saying something, but he couldn't hear her. Hollyn had his hands over Fynn's neck, determination burning in his dark, blue eyes as he focused on keeping his cousin from bleeding to death.

Fynn coughed. The small action pained his chest, stung his throat. He coughed again and wheezed, "What happened?"

Lux's arms curled around his shoulders, tightly holding him in place against her chest. She leaned forward and smiled at him with the sort of sad smile that found its way through misery when the smallest sliver of hope was presented. She hugged the prince to her gently, letting her forehead rest against his shoulder as she shook. "You're alive," she whispered. "Gods, you're *alive*."

Hollyn pulled his shirt over his head, bundled it up, and placed it against the wound. Blood still rushed everywhere, but the shirt performed adequately in soaking it away. "Stop talking," he insisted. He didn't sound calm.

"Where's Renwyn?" Fynn asked. He coughed again. More red flecks jumped from his lips. "Where's everyone else?"

"Some lunatic shot you from up over the pulpit," Hollyn explained, doing his best to keep pressure over the wound. He shook his head, adjusting his hold over his shirt. "He shot…and *killed* Renwyn. We thought you were dead but…it being *you*…we had to come check. We couldn't leave you out here."

"I knew you cared," rasped Fynn with a tilted grin, ignoring the foul taste that clung to his mouth.

711

"Idiot," grumbled Hollyn with a sorrowful smile.

"*Your* idiot," Fynn corrected weakly.

It was the first time Fynn had ever seen such pained tears trickle down Hollyn's face.

Raw emotion darkened Hollyn's eyes as he watched Fynn. Then he nodded affirmatively, confidently. "Exactly. *My* idiot, who I couldn't leave here to bleed to death." He laughed a dark laugh and added, "Now stop talking."

Fynn softly pushed Hollyn away. He drew himself up away from Lux. Before either could protest his actions, Fynn was up and to his feet. He looked around, utterly astonished to see the amphitheater collapsing. Large cracks snaked across the stone; fire warped the beams that held the structure until they bowed beneath the heat and shattered, falling away and leaving more stone to topple.

Through the thickness of the smoke, he could see the silhouette of someone face down in the arena's sand, unmoving. Fynn knew who it was, but it didn't keep him from staggering toward the still form of Renwyn. He collapsed to his knees at the boy's side. Arrows stuck out from Renwyn's back - five of them. Blood darkened the sand beneath his prone body.

Fynn reached out and gently rolled Renwyn onto his side. The boy's eyes were open, vacant and unseeing. They were like looking at the dense, unfeelingness of glass. Shakily, Fynn ran his hand over Renwyn's face, closing the boy's eyes. His hand kept sliding downward until it came to a stop over Renwyn's heart. He didn't feel it beating under his palm. Fynn closed his own eyes, willing the pulse to start again. But nothing happened. All he could feel beneath his touch was the radiating chill of death coming to claim Renwyn's body.

"It's alright," said Renwyn.

The prince's eyes flew open and, for the second time that evening, he found himself in the blackness. But when he stood, he saw the ripples of the darkness beneath his feet and he knew he was not sinking, but instead standing upon the surface of the nothingness. And there, just before him, was Renwyn. He was dressed in his tattered uniform, blood and bruises still spangled over his face. But he smiled easily when Fynn looked at him.

"You're dead," said Fynn flatly.

Renwyn nodded. "About to be."

"I'm...so sorry," Fynn whispered. His eyes stung from the tears prickling in their corners. "I'm *so* sorry."

The taller boy's hand draped over Fynn's shoulder, urging the prince to look back up at him. When he did, Renwyn shook his head. "This wasn't your fault."

"But you're *dead*," Fynn argued. "Why aren't you mad at me? You're *always* mad at me. Now would be one of the few times it would actually be *justifiable* and yet…well…you're not."

"I'm not," Renwyn agreed easily. He squeezed Fynn's shoulder. "You're a real dense idiot, Fynneas. But I don't *hate* you. I don't think I ever really did."

Fynn wrenched himself away from Renwyn's hand. He yelled, "Liar! Why? Why now? Is this to get back at me?"

"You and Hollyn…you had it so easy. Everyone liked you from the start. Him too. You were so easy going; everyone just flocked to you. And Hollyn…? Everyone thought he was so smart and so talented. It was disgusting. They saw the two of you as their leaders…like, without trying, you both just jumped to the top of the pecking order." Renwyn shrugged. "It was annoying. I…maybe I was jealous." He sighed. "I just wanted everyone to know I was good enough too."

"But you were," Fynn admitted earnestly. "You always were. If you hadn't been such an ass all the time, everyone would've followed your lead like they did with Hollyn."

"I'm sorry," Renwyn said quietly.

"*You're* sorry? *You're* the one who's *dying* and *you're* sorry?"

Renwyn nodded.

"I don't understand," Fynn relented.

"I was awful to you," Renwyn explained. "I was awful to you and you didn't deserve it. I'm sorry. I just wanted to be good enough." His voice cracked as he said, "For once…I just wanted to be good enough."

Fynn extended his hand toward Renwyn. And when the other boy took it, Fynn said, "I'm sorry too. For everything."

"Apology accepted."

"Yours too." Fynn nodded sadly.

Pulling his hand away, Renwyn looked down to his feet, watching the ripples ebb from his toes. "What do you think it's going to be like?"

"Peaceful and warm," Fynn answered.

"Peaceful and warm? I think I'd like that," the taller boy whispered.

"I think you will too."

"Fynn! Renwyn!"

Both boys turned at the sound of Penelope's voice echoing through the blackness.

Renwyn furrowed his brow. "Penelope?" he asked incredulously.

Penelope bound toward them, emerging from the eerie, unending darkness, splashing away the inky black at her heels. She threw her arms out, one slung around each boy, and pulled them close. She cried softly. "I'm so glad we found you."

As his hand settled over Penelope's back, Fynn asked, "We?"

"I'm not alone." She withdrew from Fynn and Renwyn and nodded into the blackness. "We all ended up here."

Hogan, Wilder, and the Shoregore twins joined the trio. They were in varying states of disarray. Blood was stained down one side of Penelope's face; her uniform was torn apart at the collar and over her left leg. Through the shredded, black material, Fynn could see more blood. The twins bore similar injuries; red was splattered over their faces, staining their uniforms. Hogan's right cheek was badly burned; the flesh bubbled in some places and was completely seared off in others. Wilder's black shirt was torn over his ribs; there was a horrific hole there. His cracked bones showed through the fleshy bits still clinging to his torso.

Fynn choked back the bile that rose in his throat at the sight of them.

"Where are we?" asked Crane.

"What *is* this place?" Sparrow added.

Fynn prepared himself to speak, squaring his shoulders and rooting his heels against the blackness. He fixed them all with an even stare. "This is the place between places. It's where you go before you…die."

"How do you know?" Penelope questioned hopefully, wishing beyond all reason that Fynn may be wrong about his summation. "How *could* you know?"

"Because I've been here before," Fynn replied simply. "Many times."

"So…we're dead?" Wilder asked, defeat darkening his words.

Fynn nodded guiltily. "About to be."

"Oh," murmured Penelope, looking away.

"This is it, then?" Crane asked. He looked as though he were pleading with Fynn. "This is *it?*"

"No," the prince retorted. "This isn't it." He looked down at his feet. The mirror-like blackness ebbed away from where he stood, reflecting a distorted version of himself in its rippled surface. "You're not on the other side yet."

"How do we cross over?" Sparrow asked.

Penelope looked back at Fynn, sadness taking hold of her fair features. "Is it scary there? On the other side, I mean."

"I don't think so." Fynn smiled weakly. "I think you may like it there." He took a step, once more watching the blackness wave around his feet. "You just need to let go and fall back."

Renwyn was the first to nod. He drew in one last breath and, before falling into the blackness, said, "Fynneas, I'm sorry again for everything I did. You'll be great. *Probably.*"

"Probably?" Fynn asked.

Renwyn shrugged. "Yes. *Probably.* As long as you don't do anything *exceedingly* stupid."

"I don't know if I can manage that," Fynn joked, though there was little levity in his voice.

"That's what you have Hollyn and Godryk for," Renwyn answered easily.

Fynn watched as Renwyn fell into the inky waters of the abyss, vanishing from sight as the tendrils of the deep furled around him. He was gone.

"Thanks, Renwyn," Fynn whispered. Melancholy wormed through his heart.

One by one Fynn watched the other students fall away into the blackness until only Penelope remained. She trembled, having watched the boys all seep away into the nothingness. When Fynn's hand took hers, his fingers laced with her own. She looked up at him with a start, teary eyed.

"I'm scared," Penelope whispered.

Fynn nodded. "I know."

"Stay with me...until the end?"

"I will." He smiled softly.

"Can I tell you something?"

"Of course," Fynn agreed. He felt a heaviness in his chest. He choked back a sob that threatened to sound.

Penelope smiled sheepishly. "It's going to sound a bit silly." She giggled mirthlessly. "I really liked Hollyn. I don't know if you knew that already or not."

"Oh," Fynn said awkwardly. "Alright?"

"I really liked him and I'm sad that...well, that I'm here." She shrugged her shoulders listlessly. "Here I am, about to die, and he never even noticed me...at all. I was just another one of the group."

Fynn elbowed her playfully, a certain softness reaching his eyes. "I think he *did* notice you. Trust me. And he'll miss you."

"Could you tell him something for me?"

The prince agreed readily.

"Could you tell him that I'm sorry I won't be there to see all the great things he'll do? All the amazing things you two will do *together*."

Fynn squeezed her hand. "I'll tell him." He smiled sadly; the brief easiness he'd felt disappeared in a flash. "You won't be gone totally, you know. We'll all remember you."

Tears fell down Penelope's cheeks. "Thank you, Fynn." She drew in a deep breath, still shaking. "So, just fall back?"

"Just fall back."

"You won't leave me?"

"Never," whispered the prince. "I'll be here until it's over."

Penelope held his hand tightly. She closed her eyes and smiled to herself, and then fell back.

As she descended into the darkness, Fynn knelt down upon the surface and let his arm fall away with her. She was swallowed up by the tidal blackness, as was his arm. He could still feel her hand in his own as she was pulled under. And then, ever so slowly, her hand slipped away from his and she was gone.

"Goodbye," Fynn whispered solemnly as he stood.

He opened his eyes and found himself staring down at Renwyn's lifeless corpse, the eyes closed as if he were just sleeping. The fire still burned all around them. Hollyn and Lux had run over to him, looped their arms under his, and hauled him up to his feet.

"I'm sorry," Fynn muttered.

Hollyn pulled him away, urging him toward the stairwell. "We have to go!"

The blood from Fynn's neck wound ceased pouring, leaving in its wake a most horrific red stain that stretched the length of his body from neck to ankle, spilling over his uniform, marring his fair complexion. Ash clung to his already bruised and filthy face, sweat-slicked hair stuck to his forehead and the nape of his neck. They'd expected Fynn to look such a state, but when he turned to regard Lux and Hollyn, both gasped and withdrew from him. His eyes - both eyes - burned brilliantly, like twin fires had been set off in his irises. Their icy color had melted away. Instead, violent crimson stared back at them with ethereal iridescence, glinting in the firelight.

Lux didn't falter for long. She righted herself beside Hollyn and said plainly, "Your eyes... *both* of them are red."

The fire intensified. It stretched into the newly darkened evening sky. The black clouds of smoke distorted the fresh sprinkling of stars beginning to smatter the sky, leaving little light left for the children ensconced in the inferno. Fynn reached out quickly, grabbing Lux's wrist tightly. Despite the thickness of the smoke and the darkness of the destroyed arena, his eyes glowed brightly, the vibrant red astoundingly clear despite the utter chaos unfurling around them.

"Listen to me," Fynn implored. "Don't worry about it."

Lux nodded wordlessly.

Fynn dragged Lux along behind him as he waded into the flames, spying the shadow of the stairwell archway just beyond a sheet of fire. Hollyn kept close to Lux's other side, one hand braced over the small of her back, keeping her from stumbling on the debris that littered the arena. The heat of the fire began to lash toward them threateningly. Both Hollyn and Lux leveled dubious looks toward the towering flames just ahead, recoiling from the heat as it flared dangerously. Fynn, keeping his right hand tightly clasped around Lux's wrist, flicked his left hand dismissively, banishing the fire from their path.

As the three of them stole away into the stairwell, making quick work of the descent into the lower chambers of the amphitheater, Hollyn asked, "What was that? Just then, with the fire?"

"I don't know," Fynn answered absentmindedly.

They came upon waves of smoke that crashed around them and stung their lungs. As Lux raised her arm, burying her nose in the crook of her elbow, Hollyn and Fynn pressed onward. Lux coughed shakily. She grew unsteady on her feet as the scent of the smoke, the thickness of its constitution, began taking its toll on her lungs.

As she wavered, Hollyn looped his arm around her waist and kept her on her feet. His stormy eyes gleamed in the firelight as he looked down at the nearly unconscious girl at his side. He shifted her weight more evenly against his flank and said worriedly, "Fynn, this isn't good. We've got to get out of here."

Fynn nodded. "I know. I know." His blazing eyes sought out refuge through the fire, searching for a way out. Beams from the rafters overhead shifted, some cracked; sand from the arena up above slipped through and rained down on them. A few of the large, wooden beams had fallen completely. One of the beams had collapsed before the northern corridor that led from the chamber, but the southern exit was clear of debris and obstacles.

"There!" yelled Fynn through the thickness of the smoke.

Fynn curled his arm around Lux's waist and, together with Hollyn, they staggered toward the exit. They hurried into the corridor. The embers and sparks that brushed through the antechamber bristled, until yet another beam collapsed. As it fell, booming, a large cloud of smoke and dirt blew into the corridor, swallowing the trio.

They fell to their knees, unsteadied by the collapse. Fynn braced himself easily, keeping Lux from landing painfully upon the ground.

As Hollyn made his way back to his feet, Fynn eased Lux to a standing position. Her eyes were closed. Soot and ash and dirt collected over her freckled cheeks, congealing with the blood and bruises. She didn't look herself. Red hair tumbled over her face in sweaty curls, errant strands clung to paling skin. Her head lolled against Hollyn's shoulder as the red-haired prince settled her weight against his chest.

"Hollyn," started Fynn.

"No."

Fynn arched a brow. "You don't even know what I was about to say."

Hollyn snapped, "Whatever it is, I'm sure it's *stupid*. This isn't the time for your heroics. We need to get out of here." He glanced down to the girl in his arms. "Lux isn't going to last much longer in this smoke."

"Take her."

"You're coming with us," ordered Hollyn indignantly. "I'm not leaving you here."

Fynn shook his head somberly, his red eyes radiant in the darkness. "Whoever it was who shot me and who *killed* Renwyn, whoever it was who set the arena on fire...they were there the day my father died. They shot *him* too. I know it. It was the same mask, Hollyn. I saw it. I saw *him*." His eyes narrowed. Fresh anger swelled in his chest. "I know it's the same person. I can feel it in my bones, Hollyn."

"So, you're going to leave Lux and I?" Hollyn ground out. "How *noble* of you."

"No." Fynn stepped closer to them, looking at the unconscious girl who swayed on her feet. His eyes turned upward to look into Hollyn's, beseeching him to understand. "You made it out of Batsbeckon with James without a problem. He was suffering from the smoke, just like Lux. But you, *you* were fine."

"What're you saying?"

Fynn's black lashes beat over his red eyes as he continued looking at Hollyn with a searching stare. "Whatever *this* is," he said, as he threw his hand out, vaguely gesturing around while the smoke continued to weigh over them. "I just have a feeling you'll make it out. But you *need* to hurry."

A moment stretched between the two where they stood, staring at one another, each intently searching for something they, themselves, couldn't quite understand. Finally, Hollyn nodded. "I'll see you out there?"

"I promise."

"You're such an idiot." Hollyn smiled.

Fynn shrugged, smirking all the while. "I know. But I'm *your* idiot, don't you remember?"

"You're only *my* idiot so long as you're alive," Hollyn reminded him.

"I'll see you out there," Fynn swore.

Hollyn answered thickly, "You better."

Fynn watched as Hollyn, Lux limp at his side, waded into the corridor until the heaviness of the smoke overcame their silhouettes and he could scarcely see them. But he knew, though he wasn't sure how, that Hollyn would be alright. He knew that Hollyn would get Lux out of the fire. He trusted the other prince with every fiber of his being, with every shred of his composition. When Hollyn and Lux were gone from his sight, Fynn rounded and headed back into the subterranean antechamber. Heedless of the flames that violently struck out in all directions, ignoring the thick, black smoke that had choked Lux into unconsciousness, Fynn bounded through the room and back up the stairs.

He bolted through the archway and was once more standing in the arena. He looked through the pillars of swirling flames, searching the stands for any sight of the archer. He saw a flicker, a shadow passing by beyond the curtains of fire. Lunging forward, Fynn made quick work of leaping over the rubble, hurtling by the debris and the scorched stones that once stood tall and proud. The arena was crumbling; the rows of seating caved inward, concave as the fire began pooling more and more so. Fynn wound through the cracked stands and marble pillars and found his way up the arena, bypassing the pulpit and stealing upwards, chasing after the shadow.

"Stop!" Fynn yelled.

But still, the figure weaved along the tangled mess of rock and flame.

Fynn urged his tired legs forward, catching up quickly to the man. The prince jumped, tackling the archer to the heated ground. Astride the man's stomach, Fynn stared down at the masked face of his would-be-murderer.

"Why?" asked the boy.

There was silence.

Fynn ripped the mask from the man's face. His voice was deathly dark as he demanded, "Tell me *why*."

"Don't ask questions you know the answers to," the man replied.

Fynn curled his arm back and then, with all the force he could manage, brought his knuckles cracking down against the man's cheek. Spit flew from the prince's lips as he screamed into the chaos, "Why? You could've killed *everyone*!"

"Not *everyone*," croaked the man.

"What do you mean?" Tears shone brightly over Fynn's cheeks as the fire burned around them. "Who commands you?"

With a shaking hand the man reached to his neck and pulled from beneath his chainmail a pendant. "I've lived my life to serve."

The prince stared down at the trinket held there within the felled man's grasp. He couldn't bring himself to look away from the crown etched into the gold of the pedant. "My uncle told you to do this…commanded you to?"

"We are all victims to duty, Prince Fynneas," whispered the man. "You are no safer than I."

Pain erupted from Fynn's stomach. He hadn't thought the man had the energy to fight back, much less to move so quickly. Scarlet eyes flicked down and beheld the dagger that pierced through his tattered uniform. Deep red, nearly black in the light of the embers, spilled down Fynn's front; some of it splashed over the man below. A second wave of agony crashed over the prince as the dagger was withdrawn. Fynn tasted the blood once again swilling in his mouth; he despised the nasty tang of it as it slipped by his lips and raced down his chin.

"Why…has he done this?" Fynn's hands, paler than he'd ever seen them, trembled as he reached to press his wound.

The man did not stir beneath the prince, unmoved was he by the sight of the boy choking on his own blood. He drew the dagger back and, for a moment, simply stared at the shimmer of the blood coating the blade. "No one is safe anymore," the man said. "No one has *ever* been safe. But we do as the Crown bids, for that is our duty. A duty, Prince Fynneas, we both share. A duty for which we shall both die." He cut the blade over his own throat; as the blood gushed from the wound, the man's head lolled to the side lifelessly. Dull eyes stared into the fire.

Fynn reached a red-stained hand towards the man and snatched the necklace from his neck. He held to the pendant with crushing force. His shoulders felt heavy as they curled forward. The energy he'd felt before quickly left him. Red eyes roved from the man dead beneath him out toward the pandemonium stretching all around him. "You're wrong," Fynn mumbled.

The boy rose on shaking legs, half doubled over, still pressing one hand to his stomach. He staggered forward, only just barely catching himself before pitching face first into the stands. With a will he didn't believe he possessed, Fynn pressed on through the curtains of smoke, brushing aside the embers that still blinked in the wind.

He'd not made it far before his knees gave way and he collapsed. The scratch of the stone scraped his face and arms. He felt impossibly heavy and tired. The smoke stung his eyes. Still, Fynn refused to let go of the pendant.

A black figure emerged from the blur of colors that tangled in Fynn's line of sight. The lithe form took shape and soon familiar eyes, greener than summer grasses, stared down at him. Fynn felt long arms snake around him and then the stone gave way to something softer, more comforting. The prince heard the beating of Moriah's heart against his cheek as his head came to rest over the man's chest; the constant thrumming kept him focused, kept him awake.

With effort incongruous to the task, Fynn managed to raise his hand. "Take it," he insisted. "Take this. It's proof."

The chain was still clutched in Fynn's hand; the pendant slipped from his palm. It glittered there, just before Moriah, plain as could be.

"That medal," Moriah said, nearly disbelieving, "is worn only by the King's Guard."

"*He* did this," Fynn muttered. He allowed himself to relax in Moriah's arms.

"You're going to be alright," the man in black assured as he made his way through the crumbling ruins of the amphitheater.

"Moriah," the prince protested, "I'm too old to be carried."

37

THE FAMILY SECRET

Fynn stood on what seemed to be the edge of the world; the blackness fell away in cascades from the tips of his toes. He stared out toward the nothingness that had become oddly familiar and yet was still disconcerting. He took a step forward, half expecting to fall downward into the grim abyss, but instead carried on through the shadowed tides; ripples emanated from the soles of his feet. Fynn tilted his head back, staring at the infinite expanse of darkness and wished that there were stars there to count. Instead, he forced himself to look back out toward the grand stretch of black in search of something or someone.

He took another step.

The prince's legs buckled beneath his weight and he fell to his knees, palms catching his weight and smashing into the pool of blackness. Slowly he started to sink, slipping further and further down. Weightlessness overtook him as he fell beneath the surface and into the inky grasp of the black depths. What pain he could remember feeling in his stomach, where the dagger had struck, was gone and forgotten; he felt nothing but the feathery numbness that ghosted over his whole body.

Reason gave way to wistfulness and, as he sank, he wished that the feeling would never end, that there would never be fear or pain to be felt. He'd hoped to hold onto the numbness for a while longer, but a pale hand plunged through the dark waters and reached for him, fingers splayed with strain. Idly, Fynn remained and did nothing more than stare at the hand, admiring the snowy complexion and the elegant palm that gave way to an impossibly slender wrist.

Familiarity struck Fynn through the heart with a pang and the prince was moved into action. He reached his arm outward, stretching to meet the hand that beckoned him back. When at last he caught the hand, those familiar fingers wound around his wrist and pulled him upward. He breached the surface, gasping for air as though he'd been drowning for ages. Life once more swelled up within him and his heart beat powerfully, smashing into his chest with wild abandon.

Fynn blinked away the deathly calm that had slowly wormed into him. Alert once more, he stared up at the ethereal face that awaited him. There, shrouded almost entirely by the blackness, Celestine knelt; there was a soft smile upon her face, but her eyes were sad, their icy glow dimmed some.

"You're tired," she said.

The prince nodded, though he felt more awake than he had when he'd first come back to the place between places.

"You can't sleep just yet. It's not your time," Celestine continued.

Fynn answered sheepishly, "I know. I wasn't trying to run away. It was just nice to not feel anything for a moment. But it never lasts."

Celestine cupped Fynn's cheek. "I know." She swept her hand through his mess of hair. Her fingers gently raked over his scalp. "There are people waiting for you, dearest boy. You have to go back to them. They need you."

"Can't I stay here with you for just a while longer?"

In a blur of movement, Celestine pulled Fynn to her chest and encircled her arms around him, holding him tightly. She buried her face against his shoulder as she said, "I wish you could stay, or I could go back. But for now, we can do neither. You need to go."

"I saw you," Fynn started, "when I was hurt. You were standing atop Gods-reach, up by the battlements on the tower, and you asked if I had a name."

"And you were a great, black dragon and you answered that you were called Draekon," whispered Celestine. She pulled back, staring at Fynn. Her eyes brightened. "And you breathed life back into the frozen kingdom."

"It was just like the dream you said you'd had before I was born," mused Fynn. "It was exactly how you'd said it was, but this time *I* was there…but I wasn't quite *me*."

Celestine pushed a stray, black hair from Fynn's forehead. "Oh, but you were."

"How could I have seen your dream like that?" he asked.

"You've seen many things, haven't you? Things past and present?"

Fynn nodded. "I saw your dream and I saw the day Father died. I saw *that* day too many times."

"Time is funny, isn't it? We all just exist at one point or another, fixed in place, tied to the present," Celestine said. "But if you go beyond that world, things don't work quite the same. When you're here, time doesn't mean quite as much."

"I don't understand," admitted Fynn with a frown. "Biel talked to me about time before."

"Biel talks about a great many things, most of which are rarely important," chuckled Celestine.

"You know him?"

She laughed. "I know too many people, Fynneas. Not all of whom you've met just yet."

"Can I trust Biel?"

"Darling boy," she lamented, "there are a precious few that you can trust. Biel, I fear, is not one of them."

"Is anything he says true?"

"*Regrettably*, yes."

Fynn steeled himself, dismayed by the turn in their conversation. He righted himself at his full height, meager though it still was. He leveled his voice, forcing the uncertainty from it, as he inquired, "Can I ask you something before I go back?"

Celestine nodded.

"There's a book that Biel gave me, *The Mortanomicon*. There are names in it, the Mordrays, and mine, and Hollyn's amongst them. They're there because of whatever it is the Crown was doing, whatever dark things they were up to that you mentioned before. Right?"

"Yes."

"Did they know about the book? The Crown, I mean."

Solemnness befell Celestine's pale eyes. "They did."

"What's it for?" queried Fynn, fledgling fright sparking in his gut. "What's the book for? Tell me!" he demanded.

"I never wanted to be the one who told you," whispered Celestine.

"Well now you've no choice," Fynn snapped. "I'm here now and so are you. I deserve to know, don't I? Biel's been taunting me with this book, this big secret you've all kept from me my entire life. I want to know why my name is in it."

"It's a long story," Celestine evaded.

Fynn shrugged unenthusiastically. "I'm *not* going anywhere."

"People are waiting for you, Fynneas."

"They can wait a little longer. Tell me, Mother. Because I think I've got an idea of what it is, but I'm hoping, *more than I've hoped for anything before*, that I'm wrong."

"It's not of your world, the *living* world," she murmured weakly. "It keeps track of anything—*anyone*—else who isn't *quite* of that world."

"What do you mean?" begged Fynn imploringly.

"Generations back, hundreds of years ago, when Estherians first landed in Erza, they didn't go to conquer. Well, they didn't *just* go to conquer. They'd heard stories of men who conjured up magic, who could commune with the world around them the same way creatures could, like the mermaids and the Iba-Jii and the fairies and fawns. They went looking for these men called Mancers, conjurers of things beyond the realm of men." Great sadness drowned Celestine's expression as she continued, "They found them and they found the book, *The Mortanomicon*. The Mancers we didn't kill, we took back to Estheria to teach us what they knew. That's when the Crown got the idea, the *terrible* idea, to summon up creatures who didn't belong in our world."

"Like demons?" Fynn asked.

Celestine shook her head. "Not always. Demons, yes, but other things too. Nightlings and specters as well. Ghouls and golems and all manners of unnatural things."

"What did the Crown do with them?"

"Things from the world beyond ours, the Otherworld, they can't survive in the land of the living indefinitely. They're not suited for it. But they were strong, and close with the natural world —with animals and water and fire, with the earth and living things. Odd as it is, they had a sort of bond with the world that men don't share, the sort of bond that mermaids and fairies have with it." A lone tear streaked over Celestine's pale cheek. "More than that, these creatures they called to our world were stronger than any man; they were faster, their senses heightened, their endurance unyielding."

"But what would *that* matter? It would've been no use to try and enslave them for any purpose if they were unsuited to living in our world," reasoned Fynn. "The moment you convince one to side with you, they'd probably up and die. Right?"

Celestine nodded. "That was the problem."

"And what was the solution?" pressed Fynn.

"Breed them."

Fynn choked back the bile that rose in his gullet as he rasped, "You can't mean with people, with *human* people?"

Numbly, the white-haired woman nodded. "The idea was to retain the otherworldly attributes but have them housed in a body more suited for the land of the living. The Crown sought to create soldiers as strong as ten men, soldiers who could fight for days without sleep or food or water. Men and women who could be stabbed without flinching in pain, who could be burned without even wincing."

"They succeeded, didn't they?" ventured Fynn, uncomfortable memories of the Mordrays' seeming indifference toward injury and their casual irreverence when it came to summoning fire from nothing.

"It took years, decades for them to get it right," Celestine continued, sickened. "Most of the children died after a day or two. Those who didn't were often cast into the dungeons to rot for looking too abnormal. But there were a few who survived infancy, who were nurtured and grew to adulthood. I think you know a few."

"The Mordrays?"

"Them," Celestine answered, "and more. Not many more, but a few."

"That's why their names are in the book; they're not entirely human," Fynn realized. "Who writes the names down? Could there be any mistake?"

Celestine shook her head. "No one writes the names down. The book's enchanted."

Fynn grumbled, "*Of course,* it is."

"If a child born from something not of the living survives a year, their name will appear in *The Mortanomicon.*"

"Are these...*experiments*...still going on? Is Uncle Lachlan still practicing this dark, *I don't know what to call it,* magic?"

"No. Your grandfather, your father's father, put a stop to it when he could."

"He didn't approve?"

Celestine explained, "He didn't think we should be playing with things so far beyond our control. He didn't like the idea of it at all. He wanted it ended, all of it. He went looking for the book, wanting to find exactly who it was who should be *cleansed,* so to speak."

"I'm guessing he didn't find it."

"Queen Elsinora hid it," Celestine replied. "She wasn't nearly as opposed to the practice as he was."

"Gran did seem close with Moriah," mused Fynn.

Celestine nodded. "She was. She wouldn't have let the king kill him or any of the Mordrays."

"How could *he* have killed them? He was just a man, but they're more than that," argued Fynn.

"The Mancers were not so arrogant as to summon up creatures from beyond without having a way to protect themselves."

Fynn couldn't rid himself of the mounting dread that welled in the pit of his stomach, churning like a sea during a storm. "Grandfather gave Hollyn a dagger. Noel said it was special, meant to kill monsters." Fynn couldn't look his mother in the eyes as he continued, so he looked down at his feet and watched the ripples ebb by his toes. "Monsters like those who have their names in the book. He didn't know, did he? Grandfather didn't know Hollyn's name was in that book." Icy eyes burned as they looked up to Celestine once more. "Grandfather was trying to protect Hollyn from the Mordrays and whoever else is in that book because he didn't know that *Hollyn* was one of them too. Hollyn's Moriah's *son*, isn't he?"

Startled by that revelation, Celestine's eyes went wide.

The prince continued undeterred, "I've seen the way Aunt Ursalyn looks at Moriah. I've heard the whispered comments about it." He steadied himself as he added, "When Batsbeckon caught fire, Hollyn was fine. James struggled to breathe, but Hollyn was *fine*. I *knew* there was something strange about that. And when the arena caught fire, Hollyn didn't seemed bothered by it then either. It's because he's Moriah's son; he's not entirely human, is he?"

"Fynneas—"

But Fynn interrupted his mother quickly, hissing, "And *what* am I? *Whose* son am I?" Suddenly taken aback, Fynn stammered, "I-I-I-It's not…Moriah is it?"

"No. It's not Moriah."

"Then who?" demanded the boy. "*Who* is he? Tell me! Who's my father?"

Bells sounded like thunder, chiming once, then twice, and thrice. Celestine, her retort caught in her throat, looked around, wide-eyed and dismayed. Swallowing back her answer, she instead said, "I have to be going. And so do you."

Fynn shook his head, anger flaring further. "No! You'll tell me and you'll tell me now."

Again, the bells sounded, louder this time. Celestine's eyes filled with tears unshed. Her voice was hardly more than a rasp, "I can't. Not just yet."

"Those bells," Fynn noted, "have never sounded before. I've never heard a sound like it in this place. Someone's calling for you, aren't they?"

Celestine nodded.

"It's *him*, isn't it? My real father, I mean," ventured the prince. "Whoever he is, he doesn't want you telling me. Is that it?"

The late princess reached out her hand to her son and combed her fingers through his midnight hair. "Don't let anyone *ever* tell you that you're not clever."

"Why can't I know?" pleaded Fynn. "I've a right to know." Tears ran down his cheeks.

"You do have the right to know," whispered Celestine. "And what we've done to you, what we've consigned you to, is terribly unfair. I know this now. And I'm sorry. *Truly*, Fynneas, I had not wished such a fate upon you."

Fynn asked softly, "What fate is that, Mother?"

"A dark one," she answered.

Celestine's hand fell away from Fynn. All at once, the boy found himself missing the feel of his mother's hand against him, of the reminder that she was with him, even if seemingly beyond his grasp most of the time. He watched her, his pale eyes like moons in the darkness. She righted herself to her full height, her gaze dark and sad as she looked down at him. Fynn's stomach felt heavy and rebellious, his heart a beating drum that banged along with an erratic beat.

"We both need to be going," the woman reminded the prince, a touch of wistful longing clinging to her words. "Open your eyes, Fynneas. People are waiting for you."

"And you?"

"There is but one who calls me," Celestine answered. "And I fear I shouldn't keep him waiting much longer."

"Don't go," Fynn choked out; his words tasted heavy in his mouth, strangling him.

"I'm never gone from you." Celestine smiled. "You're never *truly* alone."

Fynn answered, "That's not how it feels sometimes."

"I know," began Celestine solemnly. "I'm sorry for that."

The bells chimed, even louder this time. Fynn watched the darkness ripple beneath his feet as the sound yelled through the abyss, ringing madly. "Bye," whispered Fynn, still staring at the ripples.

"It's never really goodbye with us, Fynneas," Celestine assured almost grimly.

She was gone before he'd realized it.

His eyes closed without him noticing they'd fallen shut.

He felt the flutter of his lashes brushing the swell of his cheeks and then there was light, pale and yellow and flickering. Fynn blinked, the blackness retreated from the corners of his vision until he saw nothing but the room wherein he lay, the crimson blankets that swaddled him, and the torches fixed to the wall and their dim firelight.

As his sight cleared further, Fynn saw Fiona sitting beside his bed. She was hunched over his bedside, her head cradled atop her folded arms. Her black curls tumbled over her back, thick locks twisted over her shoulders and were splayed out over his bedding. For a moment, he watched her back rise and fall subtly with every breath she took, every assurance that she was—indeed—alive.

There was a light throbbing in Fynn's stomach, one which reminded him of the wound he'd been dealt by the King's Guard knight who'd driven a dagger into him. Feeling as though he would retch at the memory of the man who'd been laid out beneath him, the man who'd betrayed the Crown upon the king's orders, Fynn looked to the ceiling to find comfort in the familiar habit of counting cracks in the stone. He remained unmoving for some time, desperately willing the sickening knot that twisted in his stomach to unwind itself.

At last, mostly free of the unsettling feeling of recollection, Fynn dragged himself to sit upright. Each movement pained him, and the stiffness of his limbs made extricating himself from his blankets and sliding from the bed - without disturbing Fiona - a tricky task. Successful though he was after a tedious bout of fighting with his bedding, Fynn stood just to the side of his sister's chair, exhaustion rooting in his chest. His heart was beating slower, he noticed; it no longer hammered with the riled anger that welled when his mother decided to mention he was not really Felix Fog's son.

The sting of that betrayal hadn't lessened but had been shoved to the side in favor of Fynn's more expedient quest. Quietly stealing from the room into the hall of the villa, Fynn went in search of his sister's room. He heard mumbled voices echoing from all around; he supposed, after the disaster that had occurred, everyone had gone to ground in their villas to regroup, to make sense of the chaos, and to tend to their wounded. The voices continued; hushed names were whispered between them.

Fynn continued to silently creep through the halls, distantly wondering what had become of his friends. He'd seen some die. That much was for certain and that hurt him in a manner to which he was not quite accustomed. But he hadn't seen Godryk in the maelstrom, hadn't seen Him in the place between places. Fynn worried, but much like the anger he'd thrown to the side, he pushed away his concern in favor of his single-minded pursuit.

As he'd expected, Fiona's room was tidy. Fynn found her trunk at the foot of her bed. He riffled through her things, tossing aside papers in search of the book. He found a deck of tarot cards much like the ones she'd sent him for his birthday. Not knowing entirely why he did it, Fynn reached for the deck and pulled the top card. He stared at the familiar image looking back at him, the same scrawled writing inked onto the card's face. He scowled as whispered the name, "Nine of Swords." He continued to hold the card before him. A pang of pain lanced through his chest. "Same card as before," he idly noted as he replaced it atop the deck and carefully set the cards aside.

Fynn continued shuffling through Fiona's things. He moved to the wardrobe that stood in the corner and then to a small writing desk by the far wall. Frustration spilling over the brim of Fynn's threshold for tolerance, the prince kicked the feeble wooden chair from the desk and watched, detached, as it clattered to the floor. He beat his fist against the wall, not caring when his knuckles squealed their protest. He punched his fist into the wall again and again, heedless to the torn flesh that now began to bleed over the paleness of the stone and furnishings.

"Damn it." Fynn smashed his knuckles against the wall again. "Damn it!"

"Up already?"

Fynn whirled around at the dulcet sound of Moriah's voice.

Moriah stared back; his cat-like eyes glowed in the murkiness of the torchlight. Gloom and weariness clung to Moriah with sickening claws that seemed to rake into the man deeply, peeling away any sense of invincibility he'd had before. There, before Fynn, stood a man with worry etched into every feature of his face. Tiredness haunted his emerald eyes. "I didn't think you'd wake up so soon."

"I didn't want to," countered Fynn. "But I didn't really have a choice in the matter. A common theme with me, I'm beginning to notice."

"Had a talk with your mother, I'm assuming," said Moriah.

The dullness of his voice was a comfort to Fynn, who found himself leaning forward ever so slightly, as if wishing he could feel the touch of Moriah's words the way he'd felt the touch of his mother's hand against his cheek, combing through his hair. Fynn replied, "We had a long talk, she and I." Once more, the anger ignited within Fynn and burned him, searing him from inside. His voice was harsher as he continued, "Was anyone going to *tell* me? Tell *Hollyn*, perhaps?"

"Tell you what?" prodded Moriah innocently enough.

Fynn felt the fire touch his eyes. Something warm slid down his cheek, inching slower than any tear he'd ever experienced. Touching his fingers gently to his face, Fynn withdrew his hand only to find his fingertips colored a deep red. A humorless smirk contorted Fynn's mouth. The icy grey of his eyes bled away and there, in its place, a bright red shone in the gloom of the room.

The prince's voice was hushed and jagged as he said, "That we aren't who we think we are. That we've been lied to our whole lives. *Deceived.* Led to believe we were one thing when we weren't. That we're *monsters.*"

"She told you," Moriah surmised. Seeing the glowing, red eyes staring back at him and the viciousness that marred Fynn's fair features, the man in black sighed. He pinched the bridge of his nose, a meager attempt to stave off the headache he felt encroaching on his temples. "*Great.* Not really the best time for her to mention this sort of thing."

"I *made* her tell me," Fynn ground out between gnashing teeth. There was a feral quality to the way his shoulders curled forward slightly. "I've seen the book, seen our names in it! Mine, Hollyn's, yours…all your siblings… *Minnie's.* I asked her about it, made her tell me." Defeat suddenly usurped anger and resentment and soon Fynn was left standing before Moriah, shivering under the chill of his own emotions. "She didn't tell me much. She wouldn't tell me who he is, my father that is. She wouldn't say."

"You *know* who."

Fynn shook his head. "I don't!"

"Felix."

"That's a lie," whimpered Fynn. "He's no more my father than Lachlan is Hollyn's."

"Felix loved you with all his heart," insisted Moriah, a rare color of passionate insistence brightening his words. "He loved you as much as he loved Fiona. He raised you, taught you how to walk and talk and hold a sword. He watched over you, Fynneas, protected you from all of this for as long as he could. He *loved* you. You were his son. *Are* his son."

"Not really though," Fynn insisted weakly.

Moriah was across the room and kneeling in front of Fynn before the prince had even registered movement from the man. Two, large hands clasped Fynn's shoulders and squeezed them tightly. "Yes. *Really.*" He held the boy before him fixedly, refusing to let Fynn wriggle free.

Fynn forced himself to meet Moriah's unwavering gaze and whispered, "I once told someone that I knew I was different. I told him I didn't know what I was but that I didn't think it mattered." The boy choked back the lump in his throat and continued, "I was happy not knowing, not thinking about it. But, with everything that's happened, I don't think I've got a choice. I can't keep ignoring it, Moriah. I want to know. I've a *right* to know. But I'm scared of it too." Fynn's voice cracked under the pressure of the sob that threatened to escape. "I don't want to be a *monster.*"

The man in black encircled the prince in his arms and drew him close. Fynn buried his face against Moriah's shoulder. The cries he'd been keeping at bay finally broke free and wracked his whole frame.

Moriah held Fynn in place, letting him break down there in his arms. When the prince finally calmed, the man in black said softly, "No matter who your father really is, no matter what you are as a living creature, *none of it matters*, Fynneas. None of it matters because, no matter what, you're no *monster*. You never could be."

Fynn's voice was muffled by the shoulder that remained solidly pillowed beneath his cheek as he protested, "But my name's in the book."

"As is mine. As are Noel's and Dot's and all my brothers and sisters and even little Minnie's," Moriah argued. "Do you think we're monsters? I grant you that Ridley and Mortyma aren't the most shining examples of humanity one could find." He cracked a teasing smile. "Tell me, Prince Fynneas, do you think *I'm* a monster."

Slowly, Fynn pulled out of Moriah's hold and once more stared into the impossibly green eyes. He shook his head slowly. "No."

"Then neither are you. We are who we choose to be," Moriah corrected. "So, tell me, Fynneas Fog, who do *you* want to be?"

"I don't know," admitted the boy. "Someone good."

Moriah's lips curled at the corners ever so slightly. "I've news for you, Prince Fynneas. You're *already* good."

"I didn't kill him...the knight from the King's Guard," Fynn said meekly.

"He killed himself. Slit his throat," Moriah said.

"He did."

"Did you *want* to kill him?"

"Yes," Fynn whispered.

"If he hadn't slit his throat," began Moriah, "would you have killed him? Would you have gotten the revenge you so wanted?"

Fynn stared unflinchingly back at Moriah. "No." He continued more confidently, "I wanted to. I hated him. I *wanted* him dead. But no. I wouldn't have done it. There's a time for killing…war, self-defense, to protect those you love. You said it yourself, revenge isn't the path to take. Revenge wouldn't have brought anyone back. Killing him for revenge…I think it would've made things worse." He admitted darkly, "*That*, I think, would've really made me a monster." The reds of his eyes were grey once more.

"I don't know if I would call you a monster, even then," Moriah said dourly. "But you're right. It would've solved nothing." He smiled slightly. "And, anyway, that's just not who you are."

"Will you tell him?" Fynn asked suddenly. "Hollyn, I mean. Will you tell him the truth?"

"I've a feeling he's worked it out for himself already," drawled Moriah. "He's annoyingly clever like that sometimes."

"You should still tell him," Fynn insisted. "He deserves to hear it from you."

"You're right."

"You knew I'd come here to Fiona's room, looking for the book," Fynn speculated.

Moriah nodded.

"Where is it?"

"I took it," answered Moriah.

"Where to?"

"It's someplace safe," promised Moriah. "No one else needs to see it, needs to know about it. It's dangerous."

"Because of what it means?"

"Yes. Because of what it means for you and Hollyn especially," explained Moriah. "I won't have the two of you in more danger than you already are."

"You promise you'll tell him?"

"Yes."

Fynn added, "About everything? You and Aunt Ursalyn, the book, and why his name is in it?"

Moriah did nothing more than nod.

Surprised that Moriah relented so quickly, Fynn chewed his lip for a moment. There were questions swimming around in his head, but he chose to forgo them in favor a simpler inquiry. "Can I ask you something else?"

"Yes."

"Did Godryk make it out of the fire and everything alright? I…didn't see him. I was only with Lux and Hollyn."

Moriah nodded. "You'd be proud of your friend's thoughtless heroics, I suspect. He helped get the children out after the first explosion. You've clearly been, well I'm not sure if it's a good or bad influence, but certainly an *influence* of some sort. He received some burns, mostly to his chest and shoulder. He'll live. Emrys tended to him upon Hollyn's insistence."

"And Hollyn? He's alright, I know fire doesn't seem to get to him."

"No, it certainly doesn't," agreed Moriah. "He's been sitting with Godryk. Once he was convinced you weren't going to die and that Fiona would stay with you, Hollyn insisted on sitting with Godryk. He hasn't left his bedside in the days since the incident."

"Can I go see them?"

Moriah nodded. A mischievous glint sparked in his eyes as he stood. "I do believe Lux is with them as well."

Fynn jolted to full attention. Any weariness that had lingered within him was immediately dispelled. "She's alright, right? I mean, Hollyn got her out safely? She isn't hurt or anything?"

"She's fine, Fynneas."

A comfortable warmth blossomed in Fynn's chest as he followed Moriah through the halls of the Fog villa. They stepped into the night; a warm breeze brushed by them as they continued toward the Redmayne lodgings. The stars were unobscured by clouds, twinkling overhead. Fynn smiled as he stared up at them. He hoped that for as long as the stars still shone, there was something right left in the world.

Walking into the Redmayne villa, Fynn immediately took note of the differences. Red banners swung from the high ceilings and white vases lined the halls; for as far as he could see, there were images of lions everywhere. Even beneath his feet, he noted with a slight smirk, there was an intricate, tile mosaic depicting the images of several lions tangled amongst jungle foliage and vines.

Fynn kept quiet as he and Moriah walked on. A sloping shadow cut across his line of sight for a moment, before the torchlight spilled over enough to illuminate the worn looking face of Warwyk Redmayne. The lord stood before the two, quirking a brow as he asked, "Breaking in, are you, Moriah?"

The lord commander smiled a frighteningly dull smile as he purred, "Of course not, *my lord*. The prince just wanted to come see his friends. I didn't feel the need to bother you for something so trivial, so I let myself in."

"Of course, you did," grumbled Warwyk. He looked down to Fynn, eyeing the bedraggled looking prince. "I'm surprised to see you up and out of bed, Prince Fynneas. I was told your injuries were quite grave."

"I'm fine, my lord," Fynn said evenly. "Is it alright if I see Godryk?" He cast a quick glance to Moriah before looking up to Warwyk once more. "We didn't mean to intrude, of course."

"Think nothing of it," Lord Redmayne insisted sourly. He swept his arm out, beckoning the two onward. "Last door on the left. If you'll both excuse me, I was on my way to speak with the queen."

Neither bothered to look back as Warwyk stalked down the hall.

Fynn took off quickly, pushing open the indicated door and poking his head in. The room was comfortably decorated with banners of red and matching bedding that swaddled Godryk, making him look small. The boy's pale, freckled complexion starkly contrasted with the ruby coloring of his blankets. Fynn couldn't help the touch of a grin that found its way to his face upon seeing Godryk looking awake and well, save for the bandages around his chest and shoulders.

All heads turned Fynn's way. Disbelieving eyes assessed the prince as he entered.

Hollyn, who'd been seated at Godryk's bedside, dutifully rose. "You're up," he stated. "I suppose I shouldn't be surprised."

"What?" Fynn laughed lightly. "Not happy to see me?"

"Of course, he is," Lux huffed as she stood, shoving Hollyn gently. "Aren't you?"

Hollyn eyed the girl for a moment before snorting and looking back to his cousin, an incredulous gleam in his stormy eyes. "Right, of course I am." He stared at Fynn a moment more before saying plainly, "You'd lost a lot of blood this time, what with being shot and then stabbed and all. I just didn't think you'd be up so soon. But...I'm happy to see you are."

Fynn shifted his weight from foot to foot, uneasy under the weight of Hollyn's stare. "You're all alright?" he asked quietly.

"We'll be fine," promised Godryk from his plush, blanket cocoon. He moved uncomfortably in his bed, angling his back more against the cushion of the pillows behind him. "You look awful."

"I'm just tired," Fynn lied. He crossed the room to Godryk's bedside. "I'm glad to see you're alright. I'd heard you'd been burned and...I don't know, I supposed you'd look worse."

"Sorry to disappoint." Godryk grinned amiably.

Fynn shrugged. "I'm glad you have." His grey eyes looked to the linen bandages crisscrossing Godryk's bare chest and shoulders. "Doesn't look too bad."

"Hurt like you wouldn't believe," Godryk said. "Well," he added, "you, of all people, might believe it."

"And what's this I hear about your heroics?" taunted Fynn.

"Yes," snorted Godryk with a toothy grin spreading over his face, "I've apparently spent too much time around you! Though, unlike you and Hollyn, it seems I'm not fireproof."

Moriah loomed in the doorway, watching the children for a while. Finally, he requested, "Hollyn, can I talk to you for a moment? Alone?"

Hollyn looked from Moriah to Fynn and back to the lord commander. He straightened his back and squared his shoulders. His nod was curt. "Alright."

Lux watched the prince follow the lord commander out of the room. Falling back into her chair tiredly, she asked, "What do you think that's about?"

Fynn, taking Hollyn's seat at Godryk's bedside, hunched forward slightly. A nagging chill clamped around his heart and squeezed mercilessly. "It's between them."

"Fynneas," Godryk started, "do you know what happened at the arena? No one's saying anything about it."

The prince remained quietly reflective for a moment, recalling the flames and the chaos; he could almost feel the embers as they brushed by, could almost smell the burning flesh and the blood as it boiled in the dirt. Fynn swallowed back the bile rising in his throat, unwilling to let Godryk and Lux see the toll the catastrophe had taken on him.

He knew what he had to do, knew it well, but still despised what was asked of him. His own words tasted like poison as they slid from his lips. "It was an anti-monarchist. You remember the funeral, how there were rioters who wanted the king dead. Who *did* kill my father. Same sort, it looks like, was responsible for this disaster."

"Do you think there'll be rebellion?" Lux inquired, leaning closer to the prince. "Civil war?"

The grip around his heart was so unbearably tight that Fynn was surprised to still feel it beating in his chest. He forced himself to answer. "I don't know. He's dead, the archer. Died in the fire. They're pretty sure he was involved last time, back at the capital...involved in shooting the arrows into the crowds…causing all that panic. We don't know if he was working alone or if there were others."

"This is madness," Godryk declared. He leaned even further into the soft fluff of his pillows.

Fynn nodded. "That it is."

"What do you think's going to happen?" Lux asked shakily.

Fynn replied thickly, "There will be more blood spilled. I don't know whose. But there's no doubt in my mind that it's going to get bloody."

38

STARS ARE FOREVER

The sun climbed over the horizon; pale shades of pink and yellow stretched skyward and chased away the last vestiges of night. Fynn sat with his knees drawn up to his chest, arms wrapped around his legs, shoulders curled forward. It had been six days since the disaster. He stared out from the hilltops down to the valley, listening as the new morning brought with it a rush of sounds; he heard horses clopping over streets and the distinct bustle of shopkeepers and taverns readying for the day.

Fynn's arms fell away from his knees; his legs stretched out as he fell back, prone against the emerald waves of the hillside. The grass was cool, and dew slickened. It tickled his cheeks and palms as he laid there, looking up at the clouds.

"That one looks like a dog."

Fynn smiled at the sound of Godryk's voice. His mood further lightened when the young Redmayne laid down beside him, joining him in his cloud-watching game. Fynn amended, "A *fat* dog."

"Maybe it's more like a rabbit then," Godryk offered by means of compromise.

"How're your burns?"

"Sore. But I'll live. How're your neck and stomach?"

"Same." Fynn reached an arm skyward and pointed. "That one there, you see it? It looks like a horse with wings."

"I was thinking more like a squid."

"A squid?" Fynn repeated doubtfully. "*Darling* Godryk, you must've hit your head. It's a horse with wings!"

The pair remained settled in the grass, content to talk about nothing important and just watch the clouds go by, arguing over what shapes they resembled. Both boys wore identical, pleasant smiles as the morning progressed.

Footsteps plodding across the grass and dirt caught their attention. Mindful that Godryk was still injured, Fynn rolled to his side and propped himself up on his elbow; contorting slightly, he spied the remaining first-years, save for Hollyn, coming their way. He announced softly, "Looks like we've got company."

Georgie and Firiel sat with their legs crossed and stared out beyond the valley toward the sea. Ollie joined them, sadness clinging to every inch of him. Albie settled at Fynn's side, a similar melancholy claiming hold of him as well. Lux curled into the grass beside Godryk and smiled up at the clouds, watching them as they inched by.

"What've you two been doing out here this morning?" Albie wondered.

Fynn laid himself back down in the grass, comfortable in the knowledge that everyone— scathed by the events though they were—seemed more or less alright, for the time being. "Watching the clouds," he answered. He pointed. "That one looks like a cat with one ear."

"I would've said starfish," Lux argued with a laugh.

Ollie looked up, squinting as he tried to discern the exact shape of the cloud they were debating. "More like a big, fat toad." He eased himself back into the grass, joining his friends as they admired the sky.

Soon, Georgie and Firiel had ceased their sea-gazing and joined the others. The seven children were sprawled out in the grass, occasionally pointing up with something close to enthusiasm when they spotted a particularly interesting shape.

When the morning began to wind into early afternoon, Fynn sat up. For a moment, he took the time to look down at each of his friends - his year mates. He watched their faces, studied their eyes. Finally, he looked around, black hair tumbling in the warm breeze, and asked, "Has anyone seen Hollyn today?"

Godryk shook his head. "No. Haven't seen him since he left with Moriah the other day."

"Not at all?" Fynn pressed. "That was *days* ago."

"No," Lux replied. "*You* haven't seen him either, Fynn?"

"No. I was giving him some space, but I think enough's enough." Fynn rose to his feet.

Before he could leave, Georgie said, "Don't go wandering around for too long. The memorial's tonight."

"Graduation for the older years and division appointment for us and the second-years is tonight too, right after," Firiel added.

Georgie nodded tightly. "Exactly. You can't go wandering around and get lost or caught up doing whatever you're going to go and do. You *can't* be late, Fynn."

The prince assured them, "Trust me, I won't be."

"Do you want me to come with you?" questioned Godryk.

"No. I'll be fine. I'll be back in time for the memorial, I promise," Fynn repeated. "Don't worry."

"It'd be easier not to worry if you hadn't been stabbed twice in a week," grumbled Lux. She forced herself to remain watching the clouds. "That's not even *mentioning* being shot in the throat."

It didn't take Fynn long to hunt Hollyn down. He took a step into the room, eyeing the disarray of everything; the chair at the small vanity was turned over, the bedding was knotted and tossed to the floor, pillows were scattered in every direction. But it was the still form of Hollyn standing by the window that Fynn found most disconcerting. Looking back to the mess once more, Fynn sighed as he righted the chair and tossed the blankets back onto the bed. Slowly, he sidled up beside Hollyn and joined the other prince in staring out toward the valley.

"I take it you know, given the state of your room," Fynn commented quietly. He chanced a sidelong glance to Hollyn's eyes before quickly looking away, fixing his attention to the stream of sunlight that rippled down the hillside.

"What about? Moriah being my *real* father or my *fake* father staging some anti-monarchist coup as a cover for murdering us all?"

"Both." Fynn shrugged. "How're you doing?"

Hollyn pulled his attention from the valley's tableau and stared at Fynn, startled to notice the other prince was so close; he hadn't quite realized Fynn had been standing quite literally shoulder to shoulder with him. "How do you think?" he answered flatly. "How'd you find out?"

"Me?"

The taller boy nodded. "When you came to Godryk's room with Moriah, you didn't seem surprised when he called me away for our little *chat*. I take it, then, that you know. So, I'll ask again. How?"

"Which part?"

"*All* of it."

Fynn's voice ached as he replied, "About the king sending the would-be assassin? I was the one who pulled the King's Guard pendant off him. Before he died, he told me that it was Uncle Lachlan who'd sent him. That he and I would both be victims of duty, destined to die because the king willed it so. Honestly, in hindsight, his little speech was a *tad* dramatic." Fynn continued, "I didn't put it all together myself, you know."

"I wouldn't expect you to." Hollyn snorted.

Fynn elbowed his cousin's side, a smirk quirking his lips as he did so. "I'm smarter than I look."

"Smarter? No. Full of surprises? Well, I'll grant you that, Fynneas."

The smaller prince continued, "I gave Moriah the pendant before I lost consciousness. I wanted him to have proof of what the king had done."

Hollyn nodded thoughtfully. "My fath—Lachlan, I mean… must've found out about Moriah and my mother. I think, looking back, he most certainly always knew. He must've wanted us out of the way." He shrugged. "Wanted us *dead*, more like it. I don't think he gave it as much thought as he should've. Ciaran could've died in the disaster too. He always loved Ciaran. I don't think he intended for that to happen. But, whatever his reasons, I don't pretend to know fully what he's thinking. He's a mad man, you know. He wanted us gone."

"It wasn't just you and the queen," Fynn contended.

"What do you mean?"

"The day of the funeral, I saw something. I told Moriah about it, but I wasn't quite sure what I really saw. But I've seen it more since then, had time to think about it. Lachlan set it up. *All* of it. It wasn't some anti-monarchist peasant who shot my father dead. It was the same King's Guard knight as at the arena. He's been planning this, the king, for some time."

"Why? Not that I don't believe you," Hollyn began. "The king's certainly mad enough to do something like that."

"I saw the king and queen and my father all walking close together after the funeral, down the road. And then, the king and queen were retreating just as everything started to happen and my father, he was standing all alone when he was shot. It was like Lachlan knew what was going to happen."

"Then why'd he pull my mother out of the way along with him? Why not let her get killed that day as well?"

Fynn's shoulders sagged. "Don't know."

"And about Moriah? How'd you find out I'm…well, *his*?"

The smaller prince smiled as he looked at Hollyn, bewildered by how he hadn't realized it far sooner. There, standing right next to him, may be a face that looked so much like Ursalyn, but the behaviors were all Moriah. Fynn chuckled, "It's *obvious*, once you know what you're looking for. But that's not how I found out."

"What do you mean?"

"Did Moriah tell you about the book?"

"*The Mortanomicon?*"

Fynn nodded. "Did he tell you what's in it?"

"Names. *Our* names. Mine, his, yours…the other Mordrays'…Minnie's… some other people I don't know." Hollyn's eyes darkened as he said, "Our names are in that book because we're not human, *not really*. We're something more. Something darker. Moriah said he found the book in Fiona's trunk and hid it away where no one would find it, so no one would find out about us, so no one would know we're not really princes…not really Fogs."

"I'm sorry," whispered Fynn.

Pale tears rounded Hollyn's fair cheeks and his voice was heavy as he said, "Did it hurt? When you found out, I mean. Did you feel sick about it all?"

"I thought it meant I was a monster," admitted Fynn.

"*Thought?* So, what do you think of it now?"

"I don't know. I was upset when I first found out. *Really* upset. But now that I've had some time to think about it, I don't think it changes much. I mean, I've always been this way, been who and what I am. Just like you have. Us knowing now that we are *whatever it is* we *are*, that doesn't change *who* we are." He offered Hollyn the best smile he could, small and damaged as it was. "You're still Prince Hollyn, total ass that you've always been and pompous as ever."

"And *you?*" Hollyn asked, arching a brow. "Still Prince Fynneas, thick-headed idiot you've always been?"

"That's me," snickered Fynn.

"We're *more* than that, you know." Hollyn turned all the way around until he stood nearly toe to toe with Fynn. "We're more than just illegitimate princes of Estheria and maybe possible monsters in the flesh."

"What *are* we then?"

"Brothers, you and me. We may not be bound by blood—"

Fynn interrupted knowingly, "But by a shared secret? Or by the awful fate we seem condemned to?"

"Both, I think."

"Brothers, then?" asked Fynn with a hopeful light in his eyes, one that hadn't been there for some time.

"Brothers," Hollyn agreed firmly.

Fynn said with a sly smile, "I know something that may help to cheer you up."

"Go on."

"Hold out your hands," instructed Fynn.

Doing as he was told, Hollyn held his hands out before Fynn. He stared down confusedly as Fynn braced his own hands against his. "What're you doing?"

"Think about fire," Fynn instructed.

"Fire?"

"Right." Fynn nodded. "Think about the blood in your veins becoming hot embers and then fire. Concentrate on the feel of your fiery blood pumping from your heart down your arms and into your hands. And then think of a fire burning in your palms, like a spark."

"Why?"

Rolling his eyes, Fynn huffed. "Just do it."

Fynn expected that it would take Hollyn a while to muster a flicker of flame; he was, instead, surprised to see a flash of fire and then a steadily burning flame held in the curvature of Hollyn's cupped palms. His brows raised almost to his hairline. Fynn exclaimed, "You did that so quickly!"

Hollyn, eyes gone wide with astonishment, stared at the tiny, dancing flame he held. "How'd I do that? How'd you *know* I could do that?"

Fynn shook his head in disbelief, slightly annoyed that Hollyn had taken to conjuring fire much quicker than he, himself, had. "Nice little trick, isn't it?"

Realization struck Hollyn suddenly and he asked, "You can do it too, can't you? That's how you've been lighting fires in class and torches out in the jungle. And that thing you did, in the arena…waving the fire away. When did you plan on telling me?"

"Oh." Fynn laughed. "I didn't think about that. Guess I should've mentioned it before. I just, I don't know, didn't want you to think *I* was a monster or a freak or something."

"I already knew you were weird, Fynn," Hollyn joked. "You talk to *bats*."

The door to Hollyn's bedchambers swung open. His hands parted; the fire extinguished upon his movement. Both princes whirled around on their heels, facing the doorway wherein stood Ciaran. The eldest of the princes looked frazzled; the whites of his eyes had gone pink with lack of sleep and his hair looked decidedly untidy.

"Mother wants to talk to us," announced Ciaran, eyeing the two boys suspiciously. "What were you two doing?"

"Nothing," Hollyn said hastily.

"Right," drawled Ciaran, disbelief evident in his expression. "Whatever it is, do it later. Fiona's already with Mother. They're just waiting on us."

Ciaran turned to leave. The younger princes caught up to him quickly and fell into step just a pace behind. The villa was grimly quiet, whistling with only the sound of the breeze as it blew through open windows and doors. Their footfalls sounded as beats against a drum, thrumming through the expanse of the halls until they found their way to Ursalyn's room.

The queen was sat at the windowsill, staring out absently as Hollyn had done. Fiona was primly sitting at the foot of the bed, her black hair, for once, elegantly tied back without a single curl errant. Both women wore gowns of the deepest black with lace gloves shrouding their pale hands. When the door closed behind the boys, Ursalyn looked from the valley view toward the assembled royal children. There was a darkness to her sharp, blue eyes.

Without a word, the queen stood and withdrew from her gown's pocket the same pendant Fynn had taken from the arena's assailant; dried blood crusted over the medal. She held it aloft for the four of them to see, letting it dangle from the chain clasped in her fingers. The afternoon light set it nearly aglow. When she spoke, Ursalyn's voice was grave. "Do you all know what this is?"

One by one the children of the Crown nodded.

"Good. And do you all know what it means?"

"That it wasn't a rebel commoner or disgruntled lower noble who attacked the arena, but a member of the King's Guard," Ciaran replied.

"And what does that mean to you, Ciaran?" pressed Ursalyn.

The eldest prince choked back the unease that welled within him and answered with a rasping voice, saying, "That they were acting on Father's orders. That everything they did was at the behest of the king."

"Right," clipped Ursalyn. She flung the necklace to Ciaran who caught it with ease. The queen's shark-like eyes roved from one child to the next before settling on Hollyn. "And tell me, my boy, what does all of this mean?"

"He wanted us dead," Hollyn said. "He wanted us *all* dead for whatever reasons he may have had."

"It's a *betrayal*," Ursalyn asserted. "The worst and most vile sort of betrayal one can perpetrate—the betrayal committed against family." Again, her penetrating eyes swept from royal to royal, searching out any perceivable weakness or wavering. She found none; a smile curled her lips. "Look around you. Look at the people assembled in this room. This is your family." The queen found her way to Fiona's side. Her hand reached for the princess'; their fingers entangled. "Each of you is bound to the other, bound by title and duty and the bonds of family. You *don't ever* betray your family. Without each other, you are nothing; you are alone and weak. Without each other, you are vulnerable. And vulnerability is *not* something the Crown can afford." Ursalyn persisted, "You will stand by each other, fight for each other, defend each other, bleed for each other, and—if need be—die for each other. This *betrayal* by our king cannot stand. If anyone finds out what he's done, how he's transgressed against his *family*, we are all in danger. There is blood in the water and think not that you are safe."

"What do we do?" asked Hollyn.

Fiona looked down to her hand, joined with the queen's, and then up to Ursalyn's eyes. There, in their depths, she saw the tempest on the verge of breaking. Fiona answered, "We're only strong when we're together, when we're united. What Uncle Lachlan did was *vile*. He tried to break us. We can't let this stand."

Ursalyn gave Fiona's hand a quick squeeze. "Good girl." She looked to the boys and inquired, "Have any of you any thoughts on the matter?"

"He'll try it again, a different way," Ciaran contended. "Poisoning or something, or maybe he'll incite the commoners more; he could fashion a convenient excuse to send us all somewhere and then set the hordes upon us, get us all out of the way—*his* way."

Hollyn decided gravely, "He has to die. It's him or all of us."

Fynn shifted his weight from foot to foot; his hands squirmed at his sides. Hollyn's words hung in the air as the embers had during the fire, the same sparking intensity shared by both. "We can't be the ones to do it," Fynn insisted softly. "It'll be treason if we kill the king." Distantly, he thought of the conversation he'd had with Moriah.

"An accident, then?" Fiona suggested.

Ursalyn shook her head. "Darlings," she began, "none of you need worry yourselves over the specifics." She waved her free hand toward the three princes. "Come here, come closer."

They did.

The five royals stood together in a nearly perfect circle, each looking at the others with the same expressively grave stare.

"No matter what," promised the queen, "you will be taken care of. You've each other, as I'm sure I've made very clear, but you've me as well. I won't let *anything* happen to *any* of you. Do you all understand?"

Slowly, the four children nodded their heads.

"No matter what, you will be taken care of. You will be safe so long as I draw breath," the queen assured. "There are few you can trust in this world. People will see you, hear your names, and want to befriend you, get close to you. They will use you, abuse your power, pervert it to suit their own aims. In the end, darlings, you can trust so very few. I swear to you this; you can trust those in this room, and you can trust Moriah, Dottie, and Noel. I give you my word; they will not turn from you, not betray you, not abuse you."

"What about our friends?" Fynn asked.

"You may have your friends," Ursalyn retorted kindly. "But always remember that they are beneath you, that once you're grown and leave the academy, they will serve you. Though you all may be on equal footing now, one day they will look up to you. And there may come a day, I'm sorry to say, that they might resent you for it. That is the day that you have to remind them of their place, or they will come for you, and they will come for blood."

Fynn argued innocently, "They wouldn't."

"Don't be so blind, Fynneas, as to think the angered commoners are your only enemies. There are dangers that lurk from behind all corners, dangers you should not let slip by. The events here on this island should have taught you, by now, that there are traitors from within, as well." The queen looked from the princes to Fiona and back, making sure she had their full attention. "Be kind to one another, protect each other, and, above all, don't let anyone tear you apart. Together, you're stronger than *all* of them."

Ursalyn straightened her back and set her shoulders, inclining her chin just slightly. Her tone was tighter; the severity of her words lessened as an odd glibness overtook her voice. "Right. We have to be getting to the memorial and ceremonies down on the beach soon. Get changed and make yourselves look proper and decent. I'll call for you when it's time to leave."

By the time evening came upon Nandulus Island, the princes were dressed in their Morancy uniforms, the queen and princess garbed in the same dramatic gowns they'd worn during their family meeting. Sheer, black veils were drawn over the women's faces. Ursalyn's red hair was the only touch of color to be seen between the two as they made their way from the villa, like specters of death strolling down the path. Ciaran marched along just behind his mother, head slightly bowed, red hair tousled by the forthcoming-night's breeze.

Hollyn and Fynn remained in step, side by side, as they followed the black-garbed procession down to the water's edge.

Fynn eyed Hollyn for a moment, disconcerted by the other prince's quiet demeanor. He asked, "Are you doing alright?"

"Fine as can be expected," Hollyn replied dully. He glanced to Fynn and then back out before him, watching the gentle sway of his mother's hair against the back of her black dress. "Can I ask you something?"

"Of course."

"How long does it take for it to stop hurting? For you to get over someone being gone?"

At Hollyn's words, something needled through Fynn's heart. It was the same sort of sharp pain he felt any time he thought about his father dying in front of him, about his blood-gurgled words as he lived his final moments. It was a pain that never failed to steal Fynn's breath away every time it struck.

"After my father died, it took a while for me to accept he wasn't going to be here anymore, that I'd never see him around the castle or spar with him ever again. Once I got to Morancy, I guess I was distracted from it all by everything that was going on, all the lessons and new people. But there were times when I thought about him, about what happened. And that's when it hurt again. I miss him every day and I don't think I'll ever stop missing him. But it starts to hurt a little less every day." He quirked a brow oddly and inquired, "Why do you ask?"

Hollyn shrugged and looked down, watching the path pass beneath his feet. "I know it's not the same. But the king was my father still. He raised me all my life. And all my life I'm pretty sure he hated me; I don't know if he hated me because he knew about my mother and Moriah. If he did, I don't know if he hated me because I was Moriah's son or because of Mother's affair. I don't know if he hated me because I look like *her* or because I act like *him*. Maybe he hated me for *me*." A sad laugh tripped from Hollyn's lips. "Maybe I'm trying to place the blame on them and, all along, it's just been that he really hates me for *me*. I don't know. He's always loved Ciaran, fawned over him for as long as I can remember. All these years, Ciaran has always tried to tell me that Father...*the king*...really loved me, cared about me just the same. But I always knew it wasn't true. I'm not blind. But I never thought he wanted me *dead*."

Fynn caught Hollyn's hand in his own and held on as tight as he could. His shoulders shook with sadness or anger; he wasn't quite sure which. The defeated sound of Hollyn's normally confident voice broke Fynn in a way he wasn't quite used to. He held to Hollyn even tighter, unwilling to let the prince go without a fight.

"It doesn't matter if you hated him," Fynn said. "He was still your father all this time. That's how you knew him, at least. And what he's done is terrible. It's like, in a way, he died. Well, at least he's dead to you now, I suppose." Pain swelled in Fynn's chest and his throat felt as though it would clamp shut at any moment. "You can grieve him nevertheless, Hollyn. You can be sad for that loss. No one will think you weak for it."

"I'm not going to cry for the man who wanted to kill me," Hollyn argued coldly.

The taller prince tried to yank his hand away, but Fynn just clamped down on it harder. "You don't have to cry for him. But you can still be sad about it. You can still let it hurt, even if only for a moment."

"Do you believe what my mother said?" Hollyn clarified, "That we only have each other."

"Yes and no," Fynn answered. "We have our friends. I don't think Godryk or Lux or Ollie or Albie would turn on us…even when we're older. I *trust* them. They wouldn't want to hurt us." Fynn drew in a deep breath and then continued, "But I think they're a step apart from us. In the end, we'll always be separated from them. We'll always be pulled in a different direction, asked to do things they will never have to do. In that sense, I suppose, we *do* only have each other."

"They can't know," Hollyn whispered. "They can't know about us, about the book, or any of it."

Fynn nodded his agreement.

"Brothers?"

"*Forever*," Fynn promised. "You won't get rid of me easily."

"Good." Hollyn huffed, looking back down at his arrested hand. "Can I have my hand back, then?"

"Sorry." Fynn chuckled before releasing Hollyn's hand.

As they continued down the path toward the beach, any hint of ease that blossomed during the boys' interaction wilted by the time they'd reached the bottom of the hill. Solemnness and despair clawed at both princes; ugly claws fashioned from contempt and betrayal raked over them, seeming to peel their flesh away until they were left raw.

Fynn felt even more exposed than when he'd spoken with his mother, even more hurt and confused. Venturing a sneaky look over toward Hollyn, he surmised that the other boy felt much the same way.

It was early evening. The sun had set. The first draping curtains of darkness overtook the light of day; stars began to spangle the sky. A breeze ghosted over the island. The sea-spray scented the air.

Upon the white-sand beach of Nandulus Island stood the assembled nobility of Estheria who'd come to witness the year's games. The banners of each house were raised, their poles buried into the depths of the sand, colors unfurled and curled in the breeze. All along the shore there stood lords and ladies with small candles in their hands; hundreds of little flames flickered in the wind. The mood was oppressively sad and despondent as the aristocracy of the kingdom looked skyward, remembering those they'd lost to the flames and to the crumbling stone.

The royal procession made their way over the alabaster sands and took their place before the crowd; members of the big three rallied around them like pillars supporting a toppling castle. Fynn found himself standing between Moriah and Hollyn.

Hushed murmurs rippled over the shores as the masses continued to talk amongst themselves. Fynn looked skyward, studying the stars up overhead. At the sight of them, burning brighter and brighter against the increasingly dark sky, he found himself feeling slightly more at ease. He began his favorite pastime of counting the stars. He'd managed to get to thirty-three before Moriah's hand settled on his shoulder, pulling him from his mind-numbing task. Fynn's pale eyes flicked up, studying the man at his side.

Moriah wasn't paying him any attention; the only indication that he even recognized Fynn's presence was the hand that held firmly to the prince. The intense, green eyes were leveled upon the queen, watching her every movement. It didn't matter that Moriah wasn't looking at him. Fynn knew, and he would bet his life on the fact, that Moriah was quite aware of his existence. The hand that held to him was his tether, anchoring him firmly in the moment, fixing him to the grim reality of the night. He shifted, ever so slightly, toward the man in black.

"Do you ever try and count the stars?" Fynn asked, his voice hardly more than a breathy whisper.

Hollyn shook his head. "No."

"You should," Fynn said. "It might help you forget everything…at least for a while."

"There are too many to count," Hollyn asserted.

Fynn smiled. "That's why it's a good distraction when you've got a lot on your mind. You'll never be able to count them all, so you can spend as much time as you want just trying."

"Do you count the stars?"

"I try to."

Hollyn paused, unsure of how to proceed. His words were labored and dark, his voice a muffled, pale attempt at his usual, dull approach. "Does it ever just seem like too much?"

"The stars?" Fynn asked, puzzled.

"No…just…*everything.*"

"I suppose."

"Penelope's dead," Hollyn said without preamble. He scowled. "She died in the fire." His brows furrowed. "Just another person *he* took away for no reason, no *sensible* reason."

"She didn't burn," Fynn said simply.

"How could you know that?"

"I saw her…in *that* place."

Hollyn turned toward Fynn, imploring eyes pleading with the other prince for answers. He did his best to not let the pained desperation seep into his inflection, but he failed miserably. "You *saw* her?"

Fynn looked away from the sky. His grey eyes shone with the same, strange brilliance as the stars overhead, piercing through the encroaching night-born darkness and regarding Hollyn thoughtfully. He nodded. "She said she was sorry." Salty tears stung his eyes. "She asked me to tell you that…to tell you she knew you'd grow up to do great things and that she was sorry she wouldn't be here to see it. She…well…really liked you, Hollyn. She'll miss you."

Never before had Fynn seen Hollyn cry as he was presently. He'd never seen such sheer, raw, intense anguish cloud over the tempestuous eyes he knew so well. When Hollyn's hand reached out suddenly, interlocking with his, holding on with a sort of strength born of tragic desperation, Fynn was left without words. He watched silently as Hollyn's shoulders buckled forward, as his head dropped; red hair tumbled over his eyes. Fynn could only faintly hear the sound of suppressed sobbing over the hum of whispered conversations going on all around.

But as quickly as emotion had stolen Hollyn away, the prince returned to sense. He wiped away his tears, sniffed back a choked whimper, and righted himself. It was almost unnerving, thought Fynn, the way Hollyn could compose himself so quickly, the way he could swing from distraught mournfulness to carefully crafted indifference within seconds.

"Are you alright?" Fynn asked cautiously.

Hollyn's eyes hardened. "Fine." He recoiled his hand from Fynn's without hesitation.

"If you say so," muttered Fynn. His uneasiness at Hollyn's drastic mood swing intensified as he continued to watch the other boy school his expression into a mask of utter blankness.

Moriah's hand lowered down Fynn's back and ushered him forward. The lord commander whispered, "Go join the other children. They're about to start the graduation and then they'll appoint you to your divisions. Take Hollyn with you."

Fynn nodded dutifully and withdrew from the throng of the royal court, Hollyn at his side, and joined the amassed students of Morancy. The two princes waited for the announcements with tepid eagerness.

Ursalyn stepped away from Novian and Vance and the rest of the rallied royal court and came to stand before the masses on the beach. The instructors of Morancy fell into place around her, the lord paramount and the vice lord taking up at her flanks like weary watchmen. She cut a sorrowful figure in black, rising over the pale sand and seeming to meld seamlessly with the nocturnal shade.

Her voice was loud, naturally commanding, as she said, "Thank you all for coming here tonight, for gathering to memorialize those lost in the fire. It was a tragedy the likes of which Estheria has not known for generations and it is one that will not be forgotten. It will not go unpunished either. Rest assured in the knowledge that steps have been taken to bring the perpetrators of such an act of treason to justice." She paused, collecting herself for a moment. "Tonight, we gather to remember those we lost to the fire, and the chaos that came with it."

The lord paramount stepped forward, a scroll in hand. As Ursalyn withdrew, standing between Moriah and Odette, head bowed, Maekon Malcourt began to read from his list. He called the name of each house and, at the call, they drew forward and raised their banners and candles. The victims from each house were read off one by one, their names quickly accompanied by mournful wails and solemn remembrances of their life's achievements, their deeds, their fame, their glory. One by one, during the most painstaking hour Fynn thought he'd ever endured, the names were read. He noticed at the mention of Penelope's name, Hollyn stiffened for a brief moment before shaking away the tension and composing himself once more into the embodiment of compartmentalization.

As Maekon stepped back, his task now complete, Indigo stepped forward. In his hands, he held his own scroll. He cleared his throat, forcing back the torrent of emotions that teemed within him. Drawing his parchment level with his eyes, he began, "We'd normally hold a large ceremony back on Dier Island for the graduating year...*years* in this case. But it seems more appropriate for us all to remain here, to remain together, to marry the sadness for those we've lost with the pride we feel for those who've made it this far, for those who will graduate from the Morancy Academy. Such is life, it seems, that such tragedy should go hand in hand with moments of triumph and joy."

The fourth, fifth, and sixth year students from each of the divisions dutifully took their turns, upon their names being called, bowing before the lord and vice lord paramount. Each of them, in time, recited the words they'd worked hard to memorize, the commitment they'd spent years devoting their training to.

When Ciaran knelt before Maekon, his attention wandered from the lord paramount to his mother, who stood resolutely at Moriah's side, just behind Malcourt. Their eyes met then and something wordless was promised, something unbreakable was vowed.

Upon the graduation ceremony's completion, Indigo drew up a second scroll. He began, "Traditionally, we would've placed the children in their divisions following the conclusion of the tournament and the naming of a champion. Alas, this year, we do not have the good fortune to do just that. But, nevertheless, it is my great honor to place this year's competitors into the division in which they will serve. May you serve your divisions well and justly. May you not only strive for the best you can offer for the sake and glory of your own name and the name of your house, but in remembrance of your fallen comrades who will never have the chance to serve Crown, king, and country."

That particular sentiment stung Fynn more viciously than he would have thought possible. Yet again, his hand reached out for Hollyn's. And though the other boy glanced down at their entwined fingers with a studious stare, he said nothing about it and, for that, Fynn was grateful.

"We'll start with the Medical Corps," Indigo began. "Those students selected for the Medical Corps, please step forward: Tulip Malcourt and Alice Hillwater."

The two girls, teary eyed and red-cheeked, withdrew themselves from the collection of nobility on the beach and stepped toward the Morancy instructors. Imogen met them and placed the purple armbands, emblazoned with the Medical Corps insignia, upon their left arms. The three retreated into the ranks of Morancy's instructors and graduates, quietly awaiting the next division to be called.

Indigo said, "Those students selected for the Archer Brigade, please step forward: Bram Magdolyn, Aldus Singer, Oren Bridger, and Georgina Belclaire."

Once Odette placed the armbands around their arms, they retreated back behind the vice lord. And, as the Medical Corps procession had done, began the patient wait for the other divisions to have their turn.

The vice lord called out next, "Those students selected for the Cavalry, please step forward: Ox Stonecraft, Rory Blackthorn, Draven Malcourt, Ransom Blackthorn, Godryk Redmayne." He paused, smiling. "And lastly, Firiel Blackthorn and Lux Astor."

As the students began to assemble before Benadykt, eagerly awaiting the placement of their bands, an astounded whisper erupted through everyone on the beach. Benadykt found his ways to the girls last, beaming down at them proudly. Slipping the armband over Firiel's arm, he said quietly between the three of them, "There hasn't been a girl appointed to our division in forty years. Last time, it was the queen mother who made Cavalry. You two have really accomplished something of note tonight." He slipped Lux's band over her thin arm before patting her head affectionately as she stared up at him, smile affixed to her face.

The newly appointed Cavalry members trotted behind the vice lord, mingling with the rest of the Morancy gathering. Lux turned back, searching the crowd, seeking out a certain dark-haired prince. When she saw him, her cheeks burned under the magnificence of the smile he bore. His eyes shone brightly through the candle-lit night, staring straight at her. He nodded, a lopsided grin in place. Her cheeks burned more as she shuffled back, melding in with the Cavalry Division.

Indigo continued, "Those students selected for the Armada, come forward: Ceral Belclaire, Wallace Hillwater, Albatross Shoregore, and Oliver Dangerfield."

Ollie, his eyes wide with shock, lurched forward to join the other students who'd been called. He coasted through the crowd of lords and ladies, still reeling with the impossibility that he'd been chosen for the Armada.

But as he drew closer to Indigo and the Morancy crowd, he saw the proud look in Drake's eyes. Peering back over his shoulder, he saw the silent lauds exuded in the princes' expressions. Ollie swelled with well-deserved pride. His back straightened and shoulders squared. At last, when his armband was placed upon his left arm, he looked up and found a reverent smile creeping over Drake's countenance.

The instructor clapped his hand over Ollie's head and ruffled his hair. Drake whispered, "Well done, lad. Very, *very* well done, indeed. I knew you had it in you."

The vice lord paramount stood proudly, stately, before them all. He cleared his throat, preparing to call out the final division's recruits. "Lastly, will those students chosen for Paladin, step forward: Hollyn and Fynneas Fog."

The two princes disentangled their hands, not having realized they still clutched to one another like a lifeline. But as they withdrew, the loss of contact felt disturbingly profound, almost painful. They stayed close, shoulder to shoulder, as they headed forward. Moriah met them, and though his face remained impassive, his eyes were blindingly bright with pride and conviction. The boys stopped before him, each looking up at him, smiling. His hands draped over their shoulders, keeping them firmly rooted.

Moriah whispered, "You've both done well. I'm proud of you."

Hollyn brightened under the weight of the praise while Fynn felt as though he might float away. Moriah reached down and affixed the Paladin armband to Hollyn's arm. Fynn's attention sought out Lux. He nearly melted right where he stood when she looked at him, red-faced and delighted at his appointment. He nodded. She smiled. And all was well in that one, fleeting moment.

They remained where they stood, their bands in place, denoting their division in splendid, golden stitching. The other students, newly appointed to their own divisions, were ushered forward to join the princes. And so, they stood facing the vice lord expectantly. When the lord paramount and Ursalyn came forward, addressing them, the students dutifully fell to one knee, heads bowed.

Ursalyn, with all the austere sincerity of a queen fighting back dejection, regarded them coolly for a moment before speaking. The heaviness hadn't left her voice, but there was now a deep sense of something more, something stronger, more hopeful intertwining with it. "Let me be the first to say how proud we are of all of you. You've done so well, been through so much. And, at last, you've been placed where you each belong. Each division has its own merits, its own strengths, its own virtues that should be admired.

"The Medical Corps is invaluable. Your knowledge and dedication to the medicinal arts ensures Estheria's soldiers are all well maintained, that our wounded are tended and ready to fight another day. You are calm, yet brave. You are quiet, but strong. Don't let anyone ever downplay your vitality, your role in keeping our kingdom prosperous, powerful, and ready for anything.

"Archer Brigade, you are the most precise bowmen the world knows. You're dedicated to accuracy, to detail, and to precision. You play to win, but you play to win in the long run. You're patient; you're calm; you're exact. Your presence on the field of battle is integral to our victory.

"To the Cavalry, we salute you. You are the fiercest, the bravest, those who will command the most troops, the first to defend your Crown, your king, and your country. You are bold and you go fearlessly where others will not tread willingly. Your courage and gallantry are the envy of all of Estheria.

"Armada, you are Estheria's power extended to the sea. You are the most far-reaching of the divisions. You are the first to sail across horizons others don't even know exist. You're patient; you're tactical; you're calm, even when the tides change in your enemies' favor. Your willingness to take on the sea, to conquer the unknown, is commendable. We salute you.

"Lastly," Ursalyn said, a sly smile upon her face. She shed the weighty despondency that had taken root since the tragedy of the fire. The queen continued, "Paladin Division, you are the best of the best. You're brave; you're resourceful; you're ambitions; you're relentless and, it is that relentlessness that keeps pulling you back to your feet when you're knocked down. It is that unwillingness to lose that keeps you fighting, despite the odds. Your division is truly the embodiment of Morancy's words." She looked upon Hollyn and Fynn with tender eyes, nodding firmly, resolutely. "By any means necessary. Remember that. You don't give up, no matter the odds. You don't surrender, no matter your fears. You don't retreat, for your pride would never allow it. You are the terror that strikes the hearts of those who dare oppose your Crown, your king, and your country. We commend your excellence.

"To all of Morancy's newly appointed, on behalf of *Crown, king, and country*, I hereby salute you and your service, and I ask you to say the words, to solidify your placement, your commitment." She nodded toward Maekon before stepping back and joining Indigo.

Maekon took up his place before the students. He said, "I, Maekon Malcourt, Lord Paramount of the Morancy Academy of Military Arts, ask you to rise."

And so, the students stood. They held their heads high, their shoulders set in firm lines, their hands clasped behind their backs.

"Repeat after me. I do hereby swear to uphold the standards, practices, and traditions of the Morancy Academy of Military Arts readily, willingly, and with every piece of my being."

The students chorused their words, all eyes focused solely on their lord paramount.

"I do hereby pledge my body, my mind, and my soul to the protection of my homeland, to uphold our values, our traditions, and our way of life, no matter the cost."

The children sounded as one, their voices a tidal wave that crashed over the silent beach.

"I do hereby readily and willingly commit my undying loyalty to Crown, to king, and to country, to serve and protect at the risk of my life."

As Fynn spoke the final words of his oath, he felt his conviction wrap around him like armor and he wore it proudly. All the months of pain, of awful bruises and nasty cuts, of sleepless nights, of going into the wild and getting attacked by all manners of beasts, had finally culminated into this very moment on the beach. It was then that Fynn felt truly, utterly, wholly committed to his purpose. He wanted to succeed for his father, for his sister, for his house, and for those friends he'd lost in the fire. His breath hitched in his throat. A mournful cry knotted in his chest; he forced it back down. Fynn let the words just spoken hang in the air, let them echo for just a little longer.

It was late into the night. Almost everyone had gone from the beach, leaving behind their small candles tucked into the sand, looking for all the world like earth-bound stars glittering in the moonlight. The inky, black waves stroked over the beach. The only sound in the night was that of the tide steadily carrying on, even as all the world seemed to be sleeping.

Fiona and Ciaran approached the throng of newly appointed first and second years. Spying them headed nearer, Fynn edged closer. Hollyn was just at his side. The four royals gathered in a small huddle amongst only themselves.

The princess combed her hand through her brother's hair. She smiled down at him fondly. "Paladin? Well done, Fynneas. Father would be very proud of you." A single tear slid down her cheek. She wiped it away quickly. "*I'm* very proud of you. Grandfather is too. He asked me to pass along his congratulations before he left with Aunt Ursalyn and Lord Redmayne." She swiveled her attention to the red-haired prince at Fynn's side. "And you, Hollyn," Fiona started with an easy smile. "From what I hear, my little brother wouldn't have made it this far without you. Thank you for all you've done for him."

"Keep watching out for each other," Ciaran added seriously. "Things are only going to get harder from here on out. Not just at Morancy, but *everywhere*. Stay strong and stay *together*." He clapped a hand over Hollyn's back heartily, still mindful not to accidentally reinjure his brother's tender shoulder. "And, so you know - so you *both* know - I'm also very proud of you. I know it's been hard. I've seen first-hand how awful the two of you have looked sometimes, how badly you've been hurt, how scared you've been. I don't think I could be prouder of you two. Paladin? You've made it, really, you have. You've been deemed the best of your year."

"It's late," Fiona noted. "Let's get back to the villa. I think we're all still tired, not quite recovered from everything that's happened. We could do with some proper rest."

The princess and the eldest prince turned and took a few weary steps before stopping, curiously looking back at their younger brothers.

Ciaran asked, "Aren't you coming?"

Hollyn glanced to Fynn and then back to the pair some feet in front of them. "Not just yet."

"We'll be back soon. Promise." Fynn smiled a genuine smile, one unencumbered by lingering sadness. "I think we just need a minute with everyone...with our friends."

"Don't stay out here too long," Fiona instructed, a motherly sharpness to her voice. "You both look half dead on your feet as it is."

"We won't," assured Hollyn.

The night was deep and sublime and wondrously tranquil, completely unbothered by the destruction of the amphitheater some nights prior. Only the first-years remained then. They settled down into the sand and stared out at the sea. It was like being perched on the edge of the world; blackness stretched out as far as they could see; the dark waters melded with the pitch of the sky and formed a strange, seemingly endless expanse.

"You made Paladin," Hollyn finally said.

"Told you I would." Fynn beamed.

"I never doubted you for a minute," Hollyn promised.

Godryk laughed. "Liar."

"Alright, *maybe* in the beginning," Hollyn relented easily. "But you always had it in you."

"*Of course,* he did," Lux insisted.

Ollie stared at the waters lapping over the shore. "I thought I'd be happier about this year being over and finally getting my appointment."

"What's the matter?" Albie asked. "We know you wanted Archer Brigade, but Armada's a real honor, don't you think?"

"It's not that." Ollie sighed.

"It's that we'll all be separated next year," Georgie surmised. "Is that it?"

Sinking deeper into the sand, Ollie nodded. "That's it."

"Just because we'll be in different divisions…well, it doesn't mean we'll suddenly stop being friends," Albie argued heatedly.

"It'll be different," Hollyn said evenly.

"We'll share some lessons." Fynn smiled. "And if we don't see each other during the days, we can still find time to go to More Town and relax every now and then."

"Wishful thinking," Firiel mocked.

"Don't say that," Ollie despondently pled. His chest heaved as he breathed in. He admitted, "It's just…you'll all do so well in your divisions, I know it."

"And you think you won't?" Lux inquired. "You're great at sailing and like learning about it. Gods know why, but you do."

"I just don't want to feel left behind in all this," Ollie lamented uneasily. His tears shone in the moonlight as they tracked down his rounded cheeks.

"Ollie," Fynn said sharply, sitting upright at once, "have we ever left you behind?"

"No," whispered Ollie.

"And we *never* will," Lux added insistently. "Promise."

Ollie ventured, "You mean it?"

Georgie swore, "Yes, of course we mean it, Ollie. You're our friend. We'll all get through next year together, even if we *are* apart most days."

"She's right." Albie grinned.

"You shouldn't even have to ask something so stupid." Godryk laughed. "That's Fynn's job."

Firiel slumped against the sand and relented, "Right, right. *Friendship* and all that. We won't leave you behind, Ollie. You can stop worrying over it."

Fynn felt the uncomfortably familiar sensation of his stomach doing flips and his lungs becoming heavy. He threw himself back into the sand, prone at Hollyn's side. He could tell the other prince was thinking along the same lines he was. The queen's words rang in his ears like a thousand bells smashing into one another. But, looking at the other newly appointed first-years gathered around him, all laying in the sand when everyone else had gone, he felt he couldn't quite bring himself to look at them any differently.

Godryk, spying the princes both lost in quiet reverie, their eyes angled toward the sky, asked, "What're you two doing?"

"Counting the stars," Hollyn answered.

"How many are you up to?" asked Godryk.

"Just got to eleven before you decided to interrupt me," scoffed Hollyn.

Godryk shook his head, a genuine grin spread over his face. "Sorry, didn't mean to interrupt."

"You're *still* interrupting," Hollyn chided. "Now either lie down and be quiet or go away." He cast a sidelong glance to his year mates. "That goes for all of you."

"Yes, Your Highness," giggled Lux. She pillowed the back of her head against her folded arms and looked up to join the princes in their stargazing. "There's so many up there."

At the sound of Lux's voice, Fynn recalled the conversation they'd had on their little boat after he'd been stabbed by Darwyn. He thought of how her red hair contrasted with the darkness of the night; he remembered the tableau of red against black and the halo of stars as she counted them at his side. He turned his head slightly, silently observing as Lux tried to count all the twinkling lights spangled above. Fynn smiled and looked back up to the night sky himself, joining the others in their mad quest to count as many stars as they could.

The only sounds that could be heard were the waves rushing over the shore, stealing the sands away. Fynn wasn't sure how long they'd all been laying there, sprawled in the sand with their eyes fixed upward. He broke the quiet when he asked, "Do you think that stars get old and die?"

"Like fade away?" Hollyn questioned.

Fynn nodded. "Exactly."

Hollyn's dark eyes remained skyward bound. He studied the endless array of shining lights that seemed to hang in the blackness, looking down on them like a thousand eyes, unblinking. And as he looked up, as he studied them more closely, as he gave up on ever trying to count them all, Hollyn smiled. In that moment, he found such a deep sense of being accepted, of being watched by a million sets of eyes, of being held in the protective gaze of something far greater than he could understand. He couldn't help the warmth that burst in his chest. It was nice, Hollyn figured, to feel as though there was someone—or something—watching you, worrying for you. He replied in a careful whisper, "I hope not."

"Why do you say that?" asked Godryk.

"Because if they do…they're no better than us." Hollyn laughed a very dark and sad laugh. "And I'd like to think that there's something out there that *is* better than us."

"Me too," Fynn agreed.

"I think they must be better," Lux mused. She stood; sand tumbled from her hair. She walked to the very edge of the shore until the tide brushed over her booted toes. She stared out at the sea. The water was black as pitch; the silvery reflections of a million stars blinked atop its surface. She smiled. "I don't think they fade away at all."

Fynn was at her side before he realized he'd even moved. The water sloshed at his feet; the shine of the stars rippled against his boots. "You're right." His cheeks erupted with heat when he felt Lux's hand find his. The prince looked at her and smiled, an easy and sincere smile that set his icy eyes alight with wonderment and awe. He whispered, his voice only scarcely heard over the wash of waves, "Stars are forever."

CPSIA information can be obtained
at www.ICGtesting.com
Printed in the USA
BVHW032046110621
609375BV00010B/122